THE BEST
SCIENCE FICTION AND
FANTASY OF THE YEAR
Volume Eight

Also Edited by Jonathan Strahan

Best Short Novels
(2004 through 2007)
Fantasy: The Very Best of 2005
Science Fiction: The Very Best of
2005
The Best Science Fiction and
Fantasy of the Year: Volumes 1 - 8
Eclipse: New Science Fiction and
Fantasy (Vols 1 - 4)
The Starry Rift: Tales of New
Tomorrows
Life on Mars: Tales of New
Frontiers
Under My Hat: Tales from the
Cauldron (forthcoming)
Godlike Machines
Engineering Infinity
Edge of Infinity
Fearsome Journeys
Reach for Infinity (forthcoming)

With Lou Anders
Swords and Dark Magic: The New
Sword and Sorcery

With Charles N. Brown
The Locus Awards: Thirty Years
of the Best in Fantasy and Science
Fiction

With Jeremy G. Byrne
The Year's Best Australian Science
Fiction and Fantasy: Volume 1
The Year's Best Australian Science
Fiction and Fantasy: Volume 2
Eidolon 1

With Jack Dann
Legends of Australian Fantasy

With Gardner Dozois
The New Space Opera
The New Space Opera 2

With Karen Haber
Science Fiction: Best of 2003
Science Fiction: Best of 2004
Fantasy: Best of 2004

With Marianne S. Jablon
Wings of Fire

EDITED BY **JONATHAN STRAHAN**

THE BEST SCIENCE
FICTION & FANTASY
OF THE YEAR
VOLUME EIGHT

First published 2014 by Solaris
an imprint of Rebellion Publishing Ltd,
Riverside House, Osney Mead,
Oxford, OX2 0ES, UK

www.solarisbooks.com

US ISBN 978 1 78108 216 4
UK ISBN 978 1 78108 215 7

Cover by Dominic Harman

Selection and "Introduction" by Jonathan Strahan.
Copyright © 2014 by Jonathan Strahan.

Pages 615-618 represent an extension of this copyright page

10 9 8 7 6 5 4 3 2 1

A CIP catalogue record for this book is available from the
British Library.

Designed & typeset by Rebellion Publishing

Printed in the US

For Bill Schafer, friend and maker of wonderful books...

ACKNOWLEDGEMENTS

EDITING THIS YEAR'S book has been a special pleasure and I would like to thank everyone who has been involved in compiling it, from the publishers and writers who have sent me their work, to the authors who generously allow their stories to appear here. Some people deserve special thanks, though. I feel very fortunate that the *Best Science Fiction and Fantasy of the Year* has found a new home at Solaris, and I'd like to thank my new editor, Jonathan Oliver, for bringing his editorial skill to the book: he has been consistently terrific to deal with, especially when issues arose. I'd also like to thank Ben Smith, Michael Molcher, David Moore and the entire Solaris team. Special thanks, too, to my brilliant agent, Howard Morhaim, who stood with me through a long and difficult year. And finally, as always, my sincere thanks to my loving wife Marianne, and daughters Jessica and Sophie. Every moment working on this book was stolen from them, and I am grateful to them for their kindness and understanding.

CONTENTS

INTRODUCTION

Jonathan Strahan

WELCOME TO THE *Best Science Fiction and Fantasy of the Year*. Sixty-five years ago two readers, Everett Bleiler and Ted Dikty, assembled the first science fiction 'best of the year' annual. It collected a dozen stories from *Astounding Science Fiction*, *Planet Stories* and other magazines of the time, a number of which, like Ray Bradbury's "Mars is Heaven!", went on to become classics and are now part of the SF canon.

That book, *The Best Science Fiction Stories: 1949*, was the first annual snapshot of the SF field, and it appeared at an interesting time. Up until 1950 SF had been published almost exclusively in pulp magazines. Pulp magazines were published on cheap paper in enormous numbers, often with huge print runs. They were low-cost productions with bright, garish covers and lurid sensationalistic contents. The first SF pulp, Hugo Gernsback's *Amazing Stories*, appeared in 1926 and was followed by magazines with titles like *Startling Stories*, *Thrilling Wonder Stories*, *Fantastic Adventures*, and, most notably, *Astounding Science Fiction*.

Campbell took on the editorship of *Astounding* in 1937 and under his guidance it became the flagship publication of the first 'Golden Age of Science Fiction'. Campbell preferred and promoted a particular sort of writing: hard SF stories with linear narratives where protagonists, almost exclusively white males, solved problems or countered threats often using technological or engineering solutions. It was a period that established many of the most enduring tropes of the field, and it was almost exclusively told in short stories in pulp magazines.

By the time Bleiler & Dikty assembled their book, though, that era was almost over. World War 2 paper shortages had a devastating effect on pulp magazine production, and there seemed to be a push for SF to grow up and move on. Robert Silverberg argued in a recent essay for the Library of America that the true Golden Age of SF was the 1950s, saying that, "Until the decade of the fifties there was essentially no market for SF books at all" and that the 1950s saw "a spectacular outpouring of stories and novels that quickly surpassed both in quantity and quality the considerable achievement of the Campbellian golden age."

Bleiler & Dikty's annual, the first of six they'd produce covering the first half of the 1950s, was an important part of that second Golden Age. Their books, and books like them that began to appear through the decade, provided the useful service to readers of presenting a selection of the 'best' and hopefully most enjoyable new stories, while also making an argument for what good SF was and what it might be. I also suspect that they were a symptom of a new self-awareness in SF, as it began to look back critically on its short history and forward to what it might become.

Bleiler & Dikty were followed by Judith Merril, who between 1956 and 1967 edited a series of annuals that deliberately pushed the boundaries of what was considered to be SF, reading widely and presenting stories that promoted higher literary standards in a series that actively worked to break down the barriers between SF and the mainstream. Edmund Crispin performed an equally vital role at a similar time in the UK. They, in turn, were followed in the mid-1960s by Donald A. Wollheim and Terry Carr, Lester Del Rey, Arthur Saha, Harry Harrison, Brian Aldiss, and others.

These books, these annual reports from one reader to the SF world, became a feature of the field, entertaining and rewarding readers and both arguing for a particular kind of SF (or fantasy) and reflecting the SF of the day. The most significant best of the year annuals of the modern era, the enormous books edited by Gardner Dozois, define the period from the mid-1980s through to the end of the 1990s, and continue to the present day. Dozois, a fine and literary writer and editor, assembled a series of books that were definitive and all-encompassing, but very much aimed at what he considered 'core SF'. David G. Hartwell, editor of the other major SF annual anthology series of the time, often discussed in his annuals how he was deliberately attempting to shape the SF field by presenting a selection of stories that clearly belonged within the bounds of genre.

When I began this series in 2007 I hoped to steer a path between Judith Merril and David G. Hartwell, to assemble a book that was broad and wide-ranging, but didn't lose sight of science fiction's history or its core. It's an awareness that I hope you will find reflected in this latest volume of *The Best Science Fiction and Fantasy of the Year* where stories like Geoff Ryman's "Rosary and Goldenstar", an alternate history that sits on the boundaries of SF sits alongside a space opera like Yoon Ha Lee's "Effigy Nights" and the networked future of Ramez Naam's "Water", and where a slipstream fantasy like M. John Harrison's "Cave and Julia" is in the same volume as a Neil Gaiman fairy tale retelling in "The Sleeper and the Spindle" or Priya Sharma's powerful "Rag and Bone". I have restricted this book to stories that I believe are definitely SF or fantasy in some way. That's the contract I have with you, the reader, so some stories that I loved this year aren't here because I couldn't convince myself they belonged (the best example of this is Karen Joy Fowler's wonderful "The Science of Herself" which has a science fictional worldview, but isn't really SF at all), while the stories you're about to encounter will hopefully delight and entertain while providing a view of what SF was about in 2013.

I'm often asked, was this a good year? The stories in this book come from a 365 day period during which thousands of stories appeared in magazines, in anthologies and collections, shoehorned into the back of novels and downloaded as giveaways, featured on websites and sent as email. So many stories were published, and often on such short turnarounds, that I was still being sent new ones as I sat down to write this introduction. Was it a good year? Well, it depended what you stumbled upon. I think you could have had a great reading year, or a pretty ordinary one, based on nothing more than luck. It was certainly an interesting one. I was encouraged by the way SF stories in books like *Twelve Tomorrows*, *An Aura of Familiarity*, and *We See a Different Tomorrow* engaged with the world in a way SF sometimes manages to avoid, while I felt the fantasy in books like *Rags and Bones* and *Once*

Upon a Time helped to push the boundaries of fantasy. It was a good year for me, and I think you'll see that as you read through this book.

Were there stories I'd like to have included that aren't here? Certainly. A handful of stories eluded me for contractual and other reasons, and practical limitations meant that I avoided really long stories. If I could encourage you to seek out one story that's not in this book (if I could sneak one more in) it would be Caitlín R. Kiernan's extraordinary and hallucinatory SF novella "Black Helicopters", which deserves to be here and to be seen as one of the best stories of the year.

There is one final thing I should mention here. This year sees *The Best Science Fiction and Fantasy of the Year* moving to a new home. After seven years in sunny California, the book now comes to you from Solaris Books in what sounds like an almost perpetually rainy part of England. I'd like to thank Jonathan Oliver (a talented anthologist in his own right and, very happily for me, my editor), Ben Smith and the Solaris crew for making me and the series feel so welcome and for doing such an incredible job on it. I'd also like to thank you for picking up this book. If you're a long-time reader: welcome back. If you're new to the series: pull up a chair, I think you're going to enjoy yourself.

Jonathan Strahan
Perth, Western Australia
January 2014

SOME DESPERADO
Joe Abercrombie

Joe Abercrombie (www.joeabercrombie.com) attended Lancaster Royal Grammar School and Manchester University, where he studied psychology. He moved into television production before taking up a career as a freelance film editor. His first novel, *The Blade Itself*, was published in 2004, and was followed by sequels *Before They Are Hanged*, *Last Argument of Kings*, and stand-alone novels *Best Served Cold*, *The Heroes*, and *Red Country*. His next book is young adult fantasy novel *Half a King*. Joe lives in Bath with his wife, Lou, and his daughters, Grace and Eve, and his son Teddy. He still occasionally edits concerts and music festivals for TV, but spends most of his time writing edgy yet humorous fantasy novels.

SHY GAVE THE horse her heels, its forelegs buckled and, before she had a notion what was happening, she and her saddle had bid each other a sad farewell.

She was given a flailing instant aloft to consider the situation. Not a good one at a brief assay, and the impending earth gave her no time for a longer. She did her best to roll with the fall – as she tried to do with most of her many misfortunes – but the ground soon uncurled her, gave her a fair roughing up and tossed her flopping into a patch of sun-shrivelled scrub.

Dust settled.

She stole a moment just to get some breath in. Then one to groan while the world stopped rolling. Then another to shift gingerly an arm and a leg, waiting for that sick jolt of pain that meant something was broke and her miserable shadow of a life would soon be lost in the dusk. She would've welcomed it, if it meant she could stretch out and not have to run no more. But the pain didn't come. Not outside of the usual compass, leastways. As far as her miserable shadow of a life went, she was still awaiting judgement.

Shy dragged herself up, scratched and scuffed, caked in dust and spitting out grit. She'd taken too many mouthfuls of sand the last few months but she'd a dismal premonition there'd be more. Her horse lay a few strides distant, one foamed-up flank heaving, forelegs black with blood. Neary's arrow had snagged it in the shoulder, not deep enough to kill or even slow it right off, but deep enough to make it bleed at a good pace. With her hard riding that had killed it just as dead as a shaft in the heart.

There'd been a time Shy had got attached to horses. A time – despite reckoning herself hard with people and being mostly right – she'd been uncommon soft about animals. But that time was a long time gone. There wasn't much soft on Shy these days, body or mind. So she left her mount to its final red-frothed breaths without the solace of her calming hand and ran for the town, tottering some at first but quickly warming to the exercise. At running she'd a heap of practice.

Town was perhaps an overstatement. It was six buildings and calling them buildings was being generous to two or three. All rough lumber and an entire stranger to straight angles, sun-baked, rain-peeled and dust-blasted, huddled about a dirt square and a crumbling well.

The biggest building had the look of tavern or brothel or trading post or more likely all three amalgamated. A rickety sign still clung to the boards above the doorway but the name had been rubbed by the wind to just a few pale streaks in the grain. *Nothing, nowhere,* was all its proclamation now. Up the steps two by two, bare feet making the old boards wheeze, thoughts boiling away at how she'd play it when she got inside, what truths she'd season with what lies for the most likely recipe.

There's men chasing me! Gulping breath in the doorway and doing her best to look beyond desperate – no mighty effort of acting at that moment, or any occupying the last twelve months, indeed.

Three of the bastards! Then – provided no one recognised her from all the bills for her arrest – *They tried to rob me!* A fact. No need to add she'd good and robbed the money herself from the new bank in Hommenaw in the company of those three worthies plus another since caught and hung by the authorities.

They killed my brother! They're drunk on blood! Her brother was safe at home where she wished she was and if her pursuers were drunk it would likely be on cheap spirits as usual, but she'd shriek it with that little warble in her throat. Shy could do quite a warble when she needed one, she'd practiced it 'til it was something to hear. She pictured the patrons springing to their feet in their eagerness to aid a woman in distress. *They shot my horse!* She had to admit it didn't seem overpowering likely that anyone hard-bitten enough to live out here would be getting into a sweat of chivalry but maybe fate would deal her a winning hand for once.

It had been known.

She blundered through the tavern's door, opening her mouth to serve up the tale, and stopped cold.

The place was empty.

Not just no one there but nothing, and for damn sure no winning hand. Not a twig of furniture in the bare common room. A narrow stairway and a balcony running across the left hand wall, doorways yawning empty upstairs. Chinks of light scattered where the rising sun was seeking out the many gaps in the splitting carpentry. Maybe just a lizard skittering away into the shadows – of which there was no shortage – and a bumper harvest of dust, greying every surface, drifted into every corner. Shy stood there a moment, just blinking, then dashed back out, along the rickety stoop and to the next building. When she shoved the door it dropped right off its rusted hinges.

This one hadn't even a roof. Hadn't even a floor. Just bare rafters with the careless, pinking sky above, and bare joists with a stretch of dirt below every bit as desolate as the miles of dirt outside.

She saw it now, as she stepped back into the street with vision unhindered by hope. No glass in the windows, or wax-paper even. No rope by the crumbling well. No animals to be seen – aside from her own dead horse, that was, which only served to prove the point.

It was a dried-out corpse of a town, long since dead.

Shy stood in that forsaken place, up on the balls of her bare feet as though she was about to sprint off somewhere but lacked the destination, hugging herself with one arm while the fingers of the other hand fluttered and twitched at nothing, biting on her lip and sucking air fast and rasping through the little gap between her front teeth.

Even by recent standards, it was a low moment. But if she'd learned anything the last few months it was that things can always get lower. Looking back the way she'd come Shy saw the dust rising. Three little grey trails in the shimmer off the grey land.

"Oh, hell," she whispered, and bit her lip harder. She pulled her eating knife from her belt and wiped the little splinter of metal on her dirty shirt, as though cleaning it might somehow settle the odds. Shy had been told she had a fertile imagination, but even so it was hard to picture a more feeble weapon. She'd have laughed if she hadn't been on the verge of weeping. She'd spent way too much time on the verge of weeping the last few months, now she thought about it.

How had it come to this?

A question for some jilted girl rather than an outlaw with four thousand marks offered, but still a question she was never done asking. Some desperado. She'd grown expert on the desperate part but the rest remained a mystery. The sorry truth was she knew full well how it came to this – the same way as always. One disaster following so hard on another she just bounced between 'em, pinging about like a moth in a lantern. The second usual question followed hard on the first.

What the fuck now?

She sucked in her stomach – not that there was much to suck in these days – and dragged the bag out by the drawstrings, coins inside clicking together with that special sound only money makes. Two thousand marks in silver, give or take. You'd think a bank would hold a lot more – they told depositors they always had fifty thousand on hand – but it turns out you can't trust banks any more than bandits.

She dug her hand in, dragged free a fistful of coins and tossed money across the street, leaving it gleaming in the dust. She did it like she did most things these days – hardly knowing why. Maybe she valued her life a lot higher'n two thousand marks, even if no one else did. Maybe she hoped they'd just take the silver and leave her be, though what she'd do once she was left be in this corpse town – no horse, no food, no weapon – she hadn't thought out. Clearly she hadn't fixed up a whole plan, or not one that would hold too much water, leastways. Leaky planning had always been a problem of hers.

She sprinkled silver as if she was tossing seed on her mother's farm, miles and years and a dozen violent deaths away. Whoever would've thought she'd miss the place? Miss the bone-poor house and the broke-down barn and the fences that always needed mending. The stubborn cow that never gave milk and the stubborn well that never gave water and the stubborn soil that only weeds would thrive in. Her stubborn little sister and brother too. Even big, scarred, soft-headed Lamb. What Shy would've given now to hear her mother's shrill voice curse her out again. She sniffed hard, her nose hurting, her eyes stinging, and wiped 'em on the back of her frayed cuff. No time for tearful reminiscences. She could see three dark spots of riders now beneath those three inevitable dust trails. She flung the empty bag away, ran back to the tavern and –

"Ah!" She hopped over the threshold, bare sole of her foot torn on a loose nail head. The world's nothing but a mean bully, that's a fact. Even when you've big misfortunes threatening to drop on your head, small ones still take every chance to prick your toes. How she wished she'd got the chance to grab her boots. Just to keep a shred of dignity. But she had what she had, and neither boots nor dignity were on the list, and a hundred big wishes weren't worth one little fact – as Lamb used boringly to drone at her whenever she cursed him and her mother and her lot in life and swore she'd be gone in the morning.

Shy remembered how she'd been, then, and wished she had the chance now to punch her earlier self in the face. But she could punch herself in the face when she got out of this.

She'd a procession of other willing fists to weather first.

She hurried up the stairs, limping a little and cursing a lot. When she reached the top she saw she'd left bloody toe prints on every other one. She was working up to feeling pretty damn low about that glistening trail leading right to the end of her leg, when something like an idea came trickling through the panic.

She paced down the balcony, making sure to press her bloody foot firm to the boards, and turned into an abandoned room at the end. Then she held her foot up, gripping it hard with one hand to stop the bleeding, and hopped back the way she'd come and through the first doorway, near the top of the steps, pressing herself into the shadows inside.

A pitiful effort, doubtless. As pitiful as her bare feet and her eating knife and her two thousand mark haul and her big dream of making it back home to the shit-hole she'd had the big dream of leaving. Small chance those three bastards would fall for that, even stupid as they were. But what else could she do?

When you're down to small stakes you have to play long odds.

Her own breath was her only company, echoing in the emptiness, hard on the out, ragged on the in, almost painful down her throat. The breath of someone scared near the point of an involuntary shitting and all out of ideas. She just couldn't see her way to the other side of this. She ever made it back to that farm she'd jump out of bed every morning she woke alive and do a little dance, and give her mother a kiss for every cuss, and never snap at her sister or mock Lamb again for being a coward. She promised it, then wished she was the sort who kept promises.

She heard horses outside, crept to the one window with half a view of the street, and peered down as gingerly as if she was peering into a bucket of scorpions.

They were here.

Neary wore that dirty old blanket cinched in at the waist with twine, his greasy hair sticking up at all angles, reins in one hand and the bow he'd shot Shy's horse with in the other, blade of the heavy axe hanging at his belt as carefully cleaned as the rest of his repugnant person was beyond neglect. Dodd had his battered hat pulled low, sitting his saddle with that round-shouldered cringe he always had around his brother, like a puppy expecting a slap. Shy would have liked to give the faithless fool a slap right then. A slap for starters. Then there was Jeg, sitting up tall as a lord in that long red coat of his, dirt-fringed tails spread out over his big horse's rump, hungry sneer on his face as he scanned the buildings, that tall hat which he thought made him look quite the personage poking off his head slightly crooked, like the chimney from a burned-out farmstead.

Dodd pointed to the coins scattered across the dirt around the well, a couple of 'em winking with the sun. "She left the money."

"Seems so," said Jeg, voice hard as his brother's was soft.

She watched them get down and hitch their mounts. No hurry to it. Like they were dusting themselves off after a jaunt of a ride and looking forward to a nice little evening among cultured company. They'd no need to hurry. They knew she was here, and they knew she was going nowhere, and they knew she was getting no help, and so did she.

"Bastards," Shy whispered, cursing the day she ever took up with them. But you have to take up with someone, don't you? And you can only pick from what's on offer.

Jeg stretched his back, took a long sniff and a comfortable spit, then drew his sword. That curved cavalry sword he was so proud of with the clever-arsed basketwork, which he said he'd won in a duel with a Union officer but Shy knew he'd stolen, along with the best part of everything else he'd ever owned. How she'd mocked him about that stupid sword. She wouldn't have minded having it to hand now, though, and him with only her eating knife.

"Smoke!" bellowed Jeg, and Shy winced. She'd no idea who'd thought that name up for her. Some wag had lettered it on the bills for her arrest and now everyone used it. On account of her tendency to vanish like smoke, maybe. Though it could also have been on account of her tendencies to stink like it, stick in folks' throats, and drift with the wind.

"Get out here, Smoke!" Jeg's voice clapped off the dead fronts of the buildings and Shy shrank a little further into the darkness. "Get out here, and we won't hurt you too bad when we find you!"

So much for taking the money and going. They wanted the price on her too. She pressed her tongue into the gap between her teeth and mouthed, "cocksuckers." There's a certain kind of man, the more you give him, the more he'll take.

"We'll have to go and get her," she heard Neary say in the stillness.

"Aye."

"I told you we'd have to go and get her."

"You must be pissing your pants with joy over the outcome, then, eh?"

"Said we'd have to get her."

"So stop pointing it out and get it done."

Dodd's wheedling voice. "Look, the money's here, we could just scrape this up and get off, there ain't no need to –"

"Did you and I really spring from between the same set o' legs?" sneered Jeg at his brother. "You are the stupidest bastard."

"Stupidest," said Neary.

"You think I'm leaving four thousand marks for the crows?" said Jeg. "You scrape that up, Dodd, we'll break the mare."

"Where do you reckon she is?" asked Neary.

"I thought you was the big tracker?"

"Out in the wild, but we ain't in the wild."

Jeg cocked an eyebrow at the empty shacks. "You'd call this the highest extent of civilisation, would you?"

They looked at each other a moment, dust blowing up around their legs, then settling again.

"She's here somewhere," said Neary.

"You think? Good thing I got the self-described sharpest eyes west of the mountains with me, so I don't miss her dead horse ten fucking strides away. Yes, she's here somewhere."

"Where do you reckon?" asked Neary.

"Where would you be?"

Neary looked about the buildings and Shy jerked out of the way as his narrowed eyes darted over the tavern.

"In that one, I reckon, but I ain't her."

"Course you ain't fucking her. You know how I can tell? You got bigger tits and less sense. If you was her I wouldn't have to fucking look for her now, would I?"

Another silence, another dusty gust. "Guess not," said Neary.

Jeg took his tall hat off, scrubbed at his sweaty hair with his fingernails, and jammed it back on at an angle. "You look in there, I'll try the one next to it, but don't kill the bitch, eh? That'll half the reward."

Shy eased back into the shadows, feeling the sweat tickling under her shirt. To be caught in this worthless arsehole of a place. By these worthless bastards. In bare feet. She didn't deserve this. All she'd wanted was to be somebody worth speaking of. To not be nothing, forgotten the day of her death. Now she saw that there's a sharp balance between too little excitement and a huge helping too much. But like most of her lame-legged epiphanies, it had dawned a year too late.

She sucked air through the little gap between her teeth as she heard Neary creaking across the boards in the common room, maybe just the metal rattle of that big axe. She was shivering all over. Felt so weak of a sudden she could hardly hold the knife up, let alone imagine swinging it. Maybe it was time to give up. Toss the knife out the door and say, "I'm coming out! I'll be no trouble! You win!" Smile and nod and thank 'em for their betrayal and their kind consideration when they kicked the shit out of her or horsewhipped her or broke her legs and whatever else amused them on the way to her hanging.

She'd seen her share of those and never relished the spectacle. Standing there tied while they read your name and your crime, hoping for some last reprieve that wouldn't come while the noose was drawn tight, sobbing for mercy or hurling your curses and neither making the slightest hair of difference. Kicking at nothing, tongue stuck out while you shat yourself for the amusement of scum no better'n you. She pictured Jeg and Neary, up front in the grinning crowd as they watched her do the thief's dance at rope's end. Probably arrayed in even more ridiculous clothes secured with the reward money.

"*Fuck* them," she mouthed at the darkness, lips curling back in a snarl as she heard Neary's foot on the bottom step.

She had a hell of a contrary streak, did Shy. From when she was a tot, when someone told her how things would be, she started thinking on how she'd make 'em otherwise. Her mother had always called her mule stubborn, and blamed it on her Ghost blood. "That's your damn Ghost blood," as though being quarter savage had been Shy's own choice rather than on account of her mother picking out a half-Ghost wanderer to lie with who turned out – no crashing surprise – to be a no-good drunk.

Shy would be fighting. No doubt she'd be losing, but she'd be fighting. She'd make those bastards kill her, and at least rob 'em of half the reward. Might not expect such thoughts as those to steady your hand, but they did hers. The little knife still shook, but now from how hard she was gripping it.

For a man who proclaimed himself the great tracker, Neary had some trouble keeping quiet. She heard the breath in his nose as he paused at the top of the steps, close enough to touch if it hadn't been for the plank wall between them.

A board groaned as he shifted his weight and Shy's whole body tensed, every hair twitching up. Then she saw him – not darting through the doorway at her, axe in his fist and murder in his eyes – but creeping off down the balcony after the bait of bloody footsteps, drawn bow pointed exactly the wrong way.

When she was given a gift, Shy had always believed in grabbing it with both hands rather than thinking on how to say thank you. She dashed at Neary's back, teeth bared and a low growl ripping at her throat. His head whipped around, whites of his eyes showing and the bow following after, head of the arrow glinting with such light as found that abandoned place.

She ducked low and caught him around the legs, shoulder driving hard into his thigh and making him grunt, her hand finding her wrist and clamping tight under Neary's arse, her nose suddenly full of the horse and sour sweat stink of him. The bowstring went but Shy was already straightening, snarling, screaming, bursting up and – big man though he was – she hoisted Neary right over the rail as neat as she used to hoist a sack of grain on her mother's farm.

He hung in the air a moment, mouth and eyes wide with shock, then he plummeted with a breathy whoop and crashed through the boards down below.

Shy blinked, hardly able to believe it. Her scalp was burning and she touched a finger to it, half-expecting to feel the arrow stuck right in her brains, but she turned and saw it was in the wall behind her, a considerably happier outcome from her standpoint. Blood though, sticky in her hair, tickling at her forehead. Maybe the lath of the bow scratched her. Get that bow, she'd have a chance. She made a step towards the stairs, then stopped dead. Jeg was in the doorway, his sword a long, black curve against the sun-glare street.

"Smoke!" he roared, and she was off down the balcony like a rabbit, following her own trail of bloody footprints to nowhere, hearing Jeg's heavy boots clomping towards the stairs. She hit the door at the end full tilt with her shoulder and burst into the light, out onto another balcony behind the building. Up onto the low rail with one bare foot – better to just go with her contrary streak and hope it somehow carried her through than to pause for thought – and she jumped. Flung herself writhing at a ramshackle balcony on the building across the narrow lane, as if flapping her hands and feet like she was having a fit might carry her further.

She caught the rail, wood smashing her in the ribs, slipped down, groaning, clawing for a grip, fought desperately to drag herself up and over, felt something give –

And with a groan of tortured wood the whole weather-blasted thing tore from the side of the building.

Again, Shy was given a flailing instant aloft to consider the situation. Again not good, at a brief assay. She was just starting to wail when her old enemy the ground caught up with her – as the ground always will – folded up her left leg, span her over then smashed her in the side and drove her wind right out.

Shy coughed, then moaned, then spat more grit. That she had been right about her earlier sandy mouth not being her last was scant comfort. She saw Jeg standing on the balcony where she'd jumped. He pushed his hat back and gave a chuckle, then ducked back inside.

She still had a piece of the rail in her fist, well rotted through. A little like her hopes. She tossed it away as she rolled over, waiting again for that sick pain that told her she was done. Again it didn't come. She could move. She worked her feet around and guessed she could stand. But she thought she might leave that for now. Chances were she'd only get to do it one more time.

She floundered clear of the tangle of broken wood against the wall, her shadow stretching out towards the doorway, groaning with pain as she heard Jeg's heavy footsteps inside. She started wriggling back on her arse and her elbows, dragging one leg after, the little knife blade hidden up behind her wrist, her other fist clutching at the dirt.

"Where are you off to?" Jeg ducked under the low lintel and into the lane. He was a big man, but he looked a giant right then. Half a head taller than Shy, even if she'd been standing, and probably not much short of twice her weight, even if she'd eaten that day. He strutted over, tongue wedged into his lower lip so it bulged out, heavy sword loose in his hand, relishing his big moment.

"Pulled a neat trick on Neary, eh?" He pushed the brim of his hat up a little to show the tan mark across his forehead. "You're stronger'n you look. That boy's so dumb he could've fallen without the help, though. You'll be pulling no tricks on me."

They'd see about that, but she'd let her knife say it for her. Even a little knife can be a damned eloquent piece of metal if you stick it in the right place. She scrambled back, kicking up dust, making it look like she was trying to push herself up then sagging back with a whimper as her left leg took her weight. Looking badly hurt was taking no great effort of acting. She could feel blood creeping from her hair and tickling her forehead. Jeg stepped out of the shadow and the low sun shone in his face, making him squint. Just the way she wanted it.

"Still remember the day I first put eyes on you," he went on, loving the sound of his own bleating. "Dodd come to me, all excited, and said he met Smoke, her whose killer's face is on all them bills up near Rostod, four thousand marks offered for her capture. The tales they tell on you!" He gave a whoop and she scrambled back again, working that left leg underneath her, making sure it would work when she needed it. "You'd think you was a demon with two swords to a hand the way they breathe your name. Picture my fucking *disappointment* when I find you ain't naught but a scared girl with gappy teeth and a powerful smell o' piss about her." As if Jeg smelled of summer meadows. He took another step forward, reaching out for her with one big hand. "Now don't scratch, you're worth more to me alive. I don't want to –"

She flung the dirt with her left hand as she shoved up hard with her right, coming onto her feet. He twisted his head away, snarling as the dust showered across his face. He swung blind as she darted at him low and the sword whipped over her head, wind of it snatching at her hair, weight of it turning him sideways. She caught his flapping coat tail in her left hand and sank her eating knife into his sword-shoulder with the other.

He gave a strangled grunt as she pulled the knife clear and stabbed at him again, blade ripping open the arm of his coat and the arm inside it too, almost cutting into her own leg. She was bringing up the knife again when his fist crunched into the side of her mouth and sent her reeling, bare feet wrestling with the dirt. She caught hold of the corner of the building and hung there for a moment, trying to shake the light from her skull. She saw Jeg a pace or two off, bared teeth frothy with spit as he tried to fumble the sword from his dangling right hand into his left, fingers tangled with the fancy brass basketwork.

When things were moving fast Shy had a knack for just doing, without thoughts of mercy, or thoughts of outcomes, or thoughts of much at all. That was what had kept her alive through all this shit. And what had landed her in it in the first place, for that matter. Ain't many blessings aren't mixed blessings, once you got to live with them, and she'd a curse for thinking too much after the action, but that was another story. If Jeg got a good grip on that sword she was dead, simple as that, so before she'd quite stopped the street spinning she charged at him again. He tried to free an arm but she managed to catch it with her clawing left hand, pressing up against him, holding herself steady by his coat as she punched wildly with the knife – in his gut, in his ribs, in his ribs again, her snarling at him and him grunting at her with every thump of the blade, the grip slippery in her aching hand.

He got hold of her shirt, stitches tearing as the arm half-ripped off, tried to shove her away as she stabbed him again but there was no strength in it, only sent her back a step. Her head was clearing now and she kept her balance but Jeg stumbled and dropped on one knee. She lifted the knife up high in both hands and drove it right down on that stupid hat, squashing it flat, leaving the blade buried to the handle in the top of Jeg's head.

She staggered back, expecting him just to pitch on his face. Instead he lurched up suddenly like a camel she'd once seen at a fair, brim of his hat jammed down over his eyes to the bridge of his nose and the knife handle jutting straight up.

"Where you gone?" The words all mangled as if his mouth was full of gravel. "Smoke?" He lurched one way then the other. "Smoke?" He shuffled at her, kicking up dust, sword dangling from his bloody right hand, point scratching grooves in the dust around his feet. He reached up with his left, fingers all stretched out stiff but the wrist all floppy, started prodding at his hat like he had something in his eye and wanted to wipe it clear.

"Shmoke?" One side of his face was twitching, shuddering, fluttering in a most unnatural way. Or maybe it was natural enough for a man with a knife lodged through his brains. "Thmoke?" There was blood dripping from the bent brim of his hat, leaving red streaks down his cheek, shirt half way soaked with it, but he kept coming on, bloody right arm jerking, hilt of his sword rattling against his leg. "Thmoe?" She backed away, staring, her own hands limp and all her skin prickling, until her back hit the wall behind her. "Thoe?"

"Shut your mouth!" And she dived at him with both palms, shoving him over backwards, sword bouncing from his hand, bloody hat still pinned to his head with her knife. He slowly rolled over, onto his face, right arm flopping. He slid his other hand underneath his shoulder as though he'd push himself up.

"Oh," he muttered into the dust. Then he was still.

Shy slowly turned her head and spat blood. Too many mouthfuls of blood the last few months. Her eyes were wet and she wiped them on the back of her trembling hand. Couldn't believe what had happened. Hardly seemed she'd had any part in it. A nightmare she was due to wake from. She pressed her eyes shut, and opened them, and there he still lay.

She snatched in a breath and blew it out hard, dashed spit from her lip, blood from her forehead, caught another breath and forced it free. Then she gathered up Jeg's sword, gritting her teeth against the urge to spew, rising in waves along with the thumping pain in the side of her face. Shit but she wanted to sit down. Just stop. But she made herself turn away. Forced herself up to the back door of the tavern. The one Jeg had come through, still alive, a few moments before. Takes a lifetime of hard work to make a man. Only takes a few moments to end one.

Neary had dragged himself out of the hole his fall had put through the floorboards, clutching at his bloody trouser leg and looking quite put out about it. "Did you catch that fucking bitch?" he asked, squinting towards the doorway.

"Oh, no doubt."

His eyes went wide and he tried to drag himself towards his bow, not far out of reach, whimpering all the way. She hefted Jeg's big sword as she got close and Neary turned over, eyes wide with terror, holding up one desperate arm. She hit it full-blooded with the flat of the sword and he moaned, clutching it to his chest. Then she hit him across the side of the head and rolled him over, blubbering into the boards. Then she padded past him, sliding the sword through her belt, picked up the bow and dragged some arrows from his quiver. She made for the door, stringing one as she went, and peered out into the street.

Dodd was still scraping coins from the dust and into the bag, working his way towards the well. Insensible to the fates of his two companions. Not as surprising as you might suppose. If one word summed up Dodd, it was insensible.

She padded down the steps of the tavern, near to their edges where they were less likely to give a warning creak, drawing the bow halfway and taking a good aim on Dodd, bent over in the dust with his back to her, dark sweat patch down the middle of his shirt. She gave some long, hard consideration to making that sweat patch the bull's eye and shooting him in the back right there. But killing a man isn't easy, especially after hard consideration. She watched him pick up the last coin and drop it in the bag, then stand, pulling the drawstrings, then turn, smiling. "I got the –"

They stayed there a while. He crouched in the dusty street, bag of silver in one hand, uncertain smile lit up in the sun, but his eyes looking decidedly scared in the shadow of his cheap hat. She on the bottom step of the tavern – bloody bare feet, bloody split mouth, bloody hair plastered across her bloody forehead – but the bow good and steady.

He licked his lips, swallowed, then licked them again. "Where's Neary?"

"In a bad way." She was surprised by the iron in her voice. Sounded like someone she didn't even know. Smoke's voice, maybe.

"Where's my brother?"

"In a worse."

Dodd swallowed, sweaty neck shifting, starting to ease gently backwards. "You kill him?"

"Forget about them two and stop still."

"Look, Shy, you ain't going to shoot me, are you? Not after all we been through. You ain't going to shoot. Not me. Are you?" His voice was rising higher and higher, but still he edged back towards the well. "I didn't want this. It weren't my idea!"

"Course not. You need to think to have an idea and you ain't up to it. You just went along. Even if it happened to mean me getting hung."

"Now look, Shy –"

"Stop still I said." She drew the bow all the way, string cutting tight into her bloody fingers. "You fucking deaf, boy?"

"Look, Shy, let's just talk this out, eh? Just talk." He held his trembly palm up like that might stop an arrow, his pale blue eyes were fixed on her, and suddenly she got a memory rise up of the first time she met him, leaning back against the livery, smiling free and easy, none too clever but plenty of fun. She'd had a profound lack of fun in her life since she'd left home. You'd never have thought she left home to find it.

"I know I done wrong, but... I'm an idiot." And he tried out a smile, no steadier than his palm. He'd been worth a smile or two, Dodd, at least to begin with, and though no artist of a lover had kept the bed warm, which was something, and made her feel as if she weren't on her own on one side with the whole rest of the world on the other, which was something more.

"Stop still," she said, but more softly now.

"You ain't going to shoot me." Still he was edging back towards the well. "It's me, right? Me. Dodd. Just don't shoot me, now." Still going. "What I'm going to do is –"

She shot him.

It's a strange thing about a bow. Stringing it, and drawing it, and nocking the arrow, and taking your aim – all that takes effort, and skill, and a decision. Letting go the string is nothing. You just stop holding it. In fact, once you've got it drawn and aimed it's easier to let fly than not to.

Dodd was less than a dozen strides distant, and the shaft flitted across the space between them, missed his hand by a whisker and stuck silently into his chest. Surprised her, the lack of a sound. But then flesh is soft. Specially in comparison to an arrow-head. Dodd took one more wobbly pace, like he hadn't quite caught up with being arrow-stuck yet, his eyes going very wide. Then he blinked down at the shaft.

"You shot me," he whispered, and he sank to his knees, blood already spreading out into his shirt in a dark oval.

"Didn't I bloody warn you!" She flung the bow down, suddenly furious with him and with the bow too.

He stared at her. "But I didn't think you'd do it."

She stared back. "Neither did I." A silent moment, and the wind blew up one more time and stirred the dust around them. "Sorry."

"Sorry?" he croaked.

Might've been the stupidest thing she'd ever said, and that with some fierce competition, but what else could she say? No words were going to take that arrow out. She gave half a shrug. "I guess."

Dodd winced, hefting the silver in one hand, turning towards the well. Shy's mouth dropped open, and she took off running as he toppled sideways, hauling the bag into the air. It turned over and over, curving up and starting to fall, drawstrings flapping, Shy's clutching hand straining for it as she sprinted, lunged, fell...

She grunted as her sore ribs slammed into the wall around the well, right arm darting down into the darkness. For a moment she thought she was going in after the bag – which would probably have been a fitting conclusion – then her knees came back down on the dirt outside.

She had it by one of the bottom corners, loose canvas clutched by broken nails, drawstrings dangling as dirt and bits of loose stone filtered down around it.

Shy smiled. For the first time that day. That month, maybe.

Then the bag came open.

Coins tumbled into the darkness in a twinkling shower, silver pinging and rattling from the earthy walls, disappearing into the inky nothingness, and silence.

She straightened up, numb.

She backed away slowly from the well, hugging herself with one hand while the empty bag hung from the other.

She looked over at Dodd, lying on his back with the arrow sticking straight up from his chest, his wet eyes fixed on her, his ribs going fast. She heard his shallow breaths slow, then stop.

Shy stood there a moment, then doubled over and blew puke onto the ground. Not much of it, since she'd eaten nothing that day, but her guts clenched up hard, and made sure she retched up what there was. She shook so bad she thought she was going to fall, hands on her knees, sniffing bile from her nose and spluttering it out.

Damn but her ribs hurt. Her arm. Her leg. Her face. So many scrapes, twists and bruises she could hardly tell one from another, her whole body was one overpowering fucking throb.

Her eyes crawled over to Dodd's corpse, she felt another wave of sickness and forced them away, over to the horizon, fixing them on that shimmering line of nothing.

Not nothing.

There was dust rising there. She wiped her face on her ripped sleeve one more time, so filthy now that it was as like to make her dirtier as cleaner. She straightened, squinting into the distance, hardly able to believe it. Riders. No doubt. A good way off, but as many as a dozen.

"Oh, hell," she whispered, and bit her lip. Things kept going this way she'd soon have chewed right through the bloody thing. "Oh, hell!" And Shy put her hands over her eyes and squeezed them shut and hid in self-inflicted darkness in the desperate hope she might have somehow been mistaken. Would hardly have been her first mistake, would it?

But when she took her hands away the dust was still there. The world's a mean bully, alright, and the lower down you are the more it delights in kicking you. Shy put her hands on her hips, arched her back and screamed up at the sky, the word drawn out as long as her sore lungs would allow.

"Fuck!"

The echoes clapped from the buildings and died a quick death. No answer came. Perhaps the faint droning of a fly already showing some interest in Dodd. Neary's horse eyed her for a moment then looked away, profoundly unimpressed. Now Shy had a sore throat to add to her woes. She was obliged to ask herself the usual questions.

What the fuck now?

She clenched her teeth as she hauled Dodd's boots off and sat in the dust beside him to pull them on. Not the first time they'd stretched out together in the dirt, him and her. First time with him dead, though. His boots were way too loose on her, but a long stride better than no boots at all. She clomped back into the tavern in them.

Neary was making some pitiable groans as he struggled to get up. Shy kicked him in the face and down onto his back, plucked the rest of the arrows from his quiver and took his heavy belt-knife too. Back out into the sun and she picked up the bow, jammed Dodd's hat onto her head, also somewhat on the roomy side but at least offering some shade as the sun got up. Then she dragged the three horses together and roped them into a string – quite a ticklish operation since Jeg's big stallion was a mean bastard and seemed determined to kick her brains out.

When she'd got it done she frowned off towards those dust trails. They were headed for the town alright, and fast. With a better look she reckoned on about nine or ten, which was two or three better than twelve but still an almighty inconvenience.

Bank agents after the stolen money. Bounty hunters looking to collect her price. Other outlaws got wind of a score. A score that was currently in the bottom of a well, as it went. Could be anyone. Shy had an uncanny knack for making enemies. She found she'd looked over at Dodd, face down in the dust with his bare feet limp behind him. The only thing she had worse luck with was friends.

How had it come to this?

She shook her head, spat through the little gap between her front teeth and hauled herself up into the saddle of Dodd's horse. She faced it away from those impending dust clouds, toward which quarter of the compass she knew not.

Shy gave the horse her heels.

ZERO FOR CONDUCT
Greg Egan

Greg Egan (www.gregegan.net) published his first story in 1983, and followed it with twelve novels, six short story collections, and more than fifty short stories. During the early 1990s Egan published a body of short fiction – mostly hard science fiction focused on mathematical and quantum ontological themes – that established him as one of the most important writers working in the field. His work has won the Hugo, John W Campbell Memorial, Locus, Aurealis, Ditmar, and Seiun awards. His latest book is the novel *The Arrows of Time*, which concludes the "Orthogonal" trilogy.

1

LATIFA STARTED THE web page loading, then went to make tea. The proxy she used convinced her internet provider that every page she accessed belonged to a compendium of pious aphorisms from uncontroversial octogenarians in Qom, while to the sites themselves she appeared to be a peripatetic American, logging on from Pittsburgh one day and Kansas City the next. Between the sanctions against her true host country and that host's paranoia over the most innocent interactions with the West, these precautions were essential. But they slowed down her already sluggish connection so effectively that she might as well have been rehearsing for a flight to Mars.

The sound of boiling water offered a brief respite from the televised football match blaring down from the apartment above. "Two nil in favour of the Black Pearls, with fifteen minutes left to play! It's looking like victory for the home team here in Samen Stadium!" When the tea had brewed, she served it in a small glass for her grandfather to sip through a piece of hard sugar clenched between his teeth. Latifa sat with him for a while, but he was listening to the shortwave radio, straining to hear Kabul through the hum of interference and the breathless commentary coming through the ceiling, and he barely noticed when she left.

Back in her room after fifteen minutes, she found the scratched screen of the laptop glistening with a dozen shiny ball-and-stick models of organic molecules. Reading the colour coding of the atoms was second nature to her by now: white for hydrogen, black for carbon, cherry red for oxygen, azure for nitrogen. Here and there a yellow sulfur atom or a green chlorine stood out, like a chickpea in a barrel of candy.

All the molecules that the ChemFactor page had assigned to her were nameless – unless you counted the formal structural descriptions full of cis-1,3-dimethyl-this and 2,5-di-tert-butyl-that – and Latifa had no idea which, if any, of them, had actually been synthesised in a lab somewhere. Perhaps a few of them were impossible beasts, chimeras cranked out by the software's mindless permutations, destined to be completely unstable in reality. If she made an effort, she could probably weed some of them out. But that could wait until she'd narrowed down the list of candidates, eliminating the molecules with no real chance of binding strongly to the target.

The target this time was an oligosaccharide, a carbohydrate with nine rings arranged in pleasingly asymmetric tiers, like a small child's attempt to build a shoe rack. Helpfully, the ChemFactor page kept it fixed on the screen as Latifa scrolled up and down through the long catalogue of its potential suitors.

She trusted the software to have made some sensible choices already, on geometric grounds: all of these molecules ought to be able to nestle reasonably snugly against the target. In principle she could rotate the ball-and-stick models any way she liked, and slide the target into the same view to assess the prospective fit, but in practice that made the laptop's graphics card choke. So she'd learnt to manipulate the structures in her head, to picture the encounter without fretting too much about precise angles and distances. Molecules weren't rigid, and if the interaction with the target liberated enough energy the participants could stretch or flex a little to accommodate each other. There were rigorous calculations that could predict the upshot of all that give and take, but the equations could not be solved quickly or easily. So ChemFactor invited people to offer their hunches. Newcomers guessed no better than random, and many players' hit rates failed to rise above statistical noise. But some people acquired a feel for the task, learning from their victories and mistakes – even if they couldn't put their private algorithms into words.

Latifa didn't over-think the puzzle, and in twenty minutes she'd made her choice. She clicked the button beside her selection and confirmed it, satisfied that she'd done her best. After three years in the game she'd proved to be a born chemical match-maker, but she didn't want it going to her head. Whatever lay behind her well-judged guesses, it could only be a matter of time before the software itself learnt to codify all the same rules. The truth was, the more successful she became, the faster she'd be heading for obsolescence. She needed to make the most of her talent while it still counted.

LATIFA SPENT TWO hours on her homework, then a call came from her cousin Fashard in Kandahar. She went out onto the balcony where the phone could get a better signal.

"How is your grandfather?" he asked.

"He's fine. I'll ask him to call you back tomorrow." Her grandfather had given up on the shortwave and gone to bed. "How are things there?"

"The kids have all come down with something," Fashard reported. "And the power's been off for the last two days."

"*Two days?*" Latifa felt for her young cousins, sweltering and feverish without even a fan. "You should get a generator."

"Ha! I could get ten; people are practically giving them away."

"Why?"

"The price of diesel's gone through the roof," Fashard explained. "Blackouts or not, no one can afford to run them."

Latifa looked out at the lights of Mashhad. There was nothing glamorous about the concrete tower blocks around her, but the one thing Iran didn't lack was electricity. Kandahar should have been well-supplied by the Kajaki Dam, but two of the three turbines in the hydroelectric plant had been out of service for more than a year, and the drought had made it even harder for the remaining turbine to meet demand.

"What about the shop?" she asked.

"Pedalling the sewing machine keeps me fit," Fashard joked.

"I wish I could do something."

"Things are hard for everyone," Fashard said stoically. "But we'll be all right; people always need clothes. You just concentrate on your studies."

Latifa tried to think of some news to cheer him up. "Amir said he's planning to come home this Eid." Her brother had made no firm promises, but she couldn't believe he'd spend the holidays away from his family for a second year in a row.

"Inshallah," Fashard replied. "He should book the ticket early though, or he'll never get a seat."

"I'll remind him."

There was no response; the connection had cut out. Latifa tried calling back but all she got was a sequence of strange beeps, as if the phone tower was too flustered to offer up its usual recorded apologies.

She tidied the kitchen then lay in bed. It was hard to fall asleep when her thoughts cycled endlessly through the same inventory of troubles, but sometime after midnight she managed to break the loop and tumble into blackness.

"AFGHANI SLUT," GHAMZEH whispered, leaning against Latifa and pinching her arm through the fabric of her manteau.

"Let go of me," Latifa pleaded. She was pressed against her locker, she couldn't pull away. Ghamzeh turned her face towards her, smiling, as if they were friends exchanging gossip. Other students walked past, averting their eyes.

"I'm getting tired of the smell of you," Ghamzeh complained. "You're stinking up the whole city. You should go back home to your little mud hut."

Latifa's skin tingled between the girl's blunt talons, warmed by broken blood vessels, numbed by clamped nerves. It would be satisfying to lash out with her fists and free herself, but she knew that could only end badly.

"Did they have soap in your village?" Ghamzeh wondered. "Did they have underwear? All these things must have been so strange to you, when you arrived in civilisation."

Latifa waited in silence. Arguing only prolonged the torment.

"Too stuck up to have a conversation?" Ghamzeh released her arm and began to move away, but then she stopped to give Latifa a parting smile. "You think you're impressing the teachers when you give them all the answers they want? Don't fool yourself, slut. They know you're just an animal doing circus tricks."

WHEN LATIFA HAD cleared away the dinner plates, her grandfather asked her about school.

"You're working hard?" he pressed her, cross-legged on the floor with a cushion at his back. "Earning their respect?"

"Yes."

"And your heart is still set on engineering?" He sounded doubtful, as if for him the word could only conjure up images of rough men covered in machine oil.

"Chemical engineering," she corrected him gently. "I'm getting good grades in chemistry, and there'd be plenty of jobs in it."

"After five more years. After university."

"Yes." Latifa looked away. Half the money Amir sent back from Dubai was already going on her school fees. Her brother was twenty-two; no one could expect him to spend another five years without marrying.

"You should get on with your studies then." Her grandfather waved her away amiably, then reached over for the radio.

In her room, Latifa switched on the laptop before opening her history book, but she kept her eyes off the screen until she'd read half the chapter on the Sassanid kings. When she finally gave herself a break the ChemFactor site had loaded, and she'd been logged in automatically, by cookie.

A yellow icon of a stylised envelope was flashing at the top of the page. A fellow player she'd never heard of called "jesse409" had left her a message, congratulating "PhaseChangeGirl" on a cumulative score that had just crossed twenty thousand. Latifa's true score was far higher than that, but she'd changed her identity and rejoined the game from scratch five times so far, lest she come to the notice of someone with the means to find out who she really was.

The guess she'd made the previous night had paid off: a rigorous model of the two molecules showed that the binding between them was stable. She had saved one of ChemFactor's clients the time and expense of doing the same calculations for dozens of alternatives, and her reward was a modest fraction of the resources she'd effectively freed. ChemFactor would model any collection of atoms and molecules she liked, free of charge – up to a preset quota in computing time.

Latifa closed her history book and moved the laptop to the centre of her desk. If the binding problems were easy for her now, when it came to the much larger challenge she'd set herself the instincts she'd honed on the site could only take her so far. The raw computing power that she acquired from these sporadic prizes let her test her hunches and see where they fell short.

She dug out the notebook from her backpack and reviewed her sketches and calculations. She understood the symmetries of crystals, the shifts and rotations that brought any regular array of atoms back into perfect agreement with itself. She understood the thrillingly strange origins of the different varieties of magnetism, where electrons' spins became aligned or opposed – sometimes through their response to each other's magnetic fields, but more often through the Exclusion Principle, which linked the alignment of spin to the average distance between the particles, and hence the energy they needed in order to overcome electrostatic repulsion. And after studying hundreds of examples, she believed she had a sense for the kind of crystal that lay in a transition zone where one type of magnetism was on the verge of shifting to another.

She'd sketched her ideal crystal in the notebook more than a year before, but she had no proof yet that it was anything more than a fantasy. Her last modelling run had predicted something achingly close, but it had still not produced what she needed. She had to go back one step and try something different.

Latifa retrieved the saved data from that last attempt and set the parameters for the new simulation. She resisted the urge to stab the CONFIRM button twice; the response was just taking its time weaving its way back to her through the maze of obfuscation.

Estimated time for run: approximately seven hours.

She sat gazing at the screen for a while, though she knew that if she waited for the prediction to be updated she'd probably find that the new estimate was even longer.

Reluctantly, she moved the laptop to the floor and returned to the faded glory of the Sassanids. She had to be patient; she'd have her answer by morning.

"WHORE," GHAMZEH MUTTERED as Latifa hurried past her to her desk.

"You're ten minutes late, Latifa," Ms Keshavarz declared irritably.

"I'm very sorry." Latifa stood in place, her eyes cast down.

"So what's your excuse?"

Latifa remained silent.

"If you overslept," Ms Keshavarz suggested, "you should at least have the honesty to say so."

Latifa had woken at five, but she managed a flush of humiliation that she hoped would pass for a kind of tacit admission.

"Two hours of detention, then," Ms Keshavarz ruled. "It might have been half that if you'd been more forthcoming. Take your seat, please."

The day passed at a glacial speed. Latifa did her best to distract herself with the lessons, but it was like trying to chew water. The subject made no difference: history, literature, mathematics, physics – as soon as one sentence was written on the blackboard she knew exactly what would follow.

In detention with four other girls, she sat copying pages of long-winded homilies. From her seat she could see a driveway that led out from the staff car park, and one by one the vehicles she most needed to depart passed before her eyes. The waiting grew harder than ever, but she knew it would be foolish to act too soon.

Eighty minutes into her punishment, she started holding her breath for ever longer intervals. By the time she raised her hand there was nothing feigned in her tone of discomfort. The supervising teacher, Ms Shirazi, raised no objections and played no sadistic games with her. Latifa fled the room with plausible haste.

The rest of the school appeared deserted; the extra time had been worth it. Latifa opened the door to the toilets and let it swing shut, leaving the sound echoing back down the corridor, then hurried towards the chemistry lab.

The students' entrance was locked, but Latifa steeled herself and turned into the warren of store rooms and cubicles that filled the north side of the science wing. Her chemistry teacher, Ms Daneshvar, had taken her to her desk once to consult an old university textbook, to settle a point on which they'd both been unsure.

Latifa found her way back to that desk. The keys were hanging exactly where she remembered them, on labelled pegs. She took the one for the chemistry lab and headed for the teachers' entrance.

As she turned the key in the lock her stomach convulsed. To be expelled would be disastrous enough, but if the school pressed criminal charges she could be imprisoned and deported. She closed her eyes for a moment, summoning up an image of the beautiful lattice that the ChemFactor simulation had shown her. For a week she'd thought of nothing else. The software had reached its conclusion, but in the end the only test that mattered was whether the substance could be made in real life.

Late afternoon sunlight slanted across the room, glinting off the tubular legs of the stools standing upside-down on the black-painted benches. All the ingredients Latifa needed – salts of copper, barium and calcium – sat on the alphabetised shelves that ran along the eastern wall; none were of sufficient value or toxicity to be kept locked away, and she wouldn't need much of any of them for a proof of principle.

She took down the jars and weighed out a few grams of each, quantities too small to be missed. She'd written down the masses that would yield the right stoichiometry, the right proportions of atoms in the final product, but having spent the whole day repeating the calculations in her head she didn't waste time now consulting the slip of paper.

Latifa mixed the brightly coloured granules in a ceramic crucible and crushed them with a pestle. Then she placed the crucible in the electric furnace. The heating profile she'd need was complicated, but though she'd only ever seen the furnace operated manually in class, she'd looked up the model number on the net and found the precise requirements for scripting it. When she pushed the memory stick into the USB port, the green light above flickered for a moment, then the first temperature of the sequence appeared on the display.

The whole thing would take nine hours. Latifa quickly re-shelved the jars, binned the filter paper she'd used on the scales, then retreated, locking the door behind her.

On her way past the toilets she remembered to stage a creaking exit. She slowed her pace as she approached the detention room, and felt cold beads of sweat on her face. Ms Shirazi offered her a sympathetic frown before turning back to the magazine she'd been reading.

Latifa dreamt that the school was on fire. The blaze was visible from the balcony of her apartment, and her grandfather stood and watched, wheezing alarmingly from the toxic fumes that were billowing out across Mashhad. When he switched on the radio, a newsreader reported that the police had found a memory stick beside the point of ignition and were checking all the students for a fingerprint match.

Latifa woke before dawn and ate breakfast, then prepared lunch for the two of them. She'd thought she'd been moving silently, but her grandfather surprised her as she was opening the front door.

"Why are you leaving so early?" he demanded.

"There's a study group."

"What do you mean?"

"A few of us get together before classes start and go over the lessons from the day before," she said.

"So you're running your own classes now? Do the teachers know about this?"

"The teachers approve," Latifa assured him. "It's their lessons that we're revising; we're not just making things up."

"You're not talking politics?" he asked sternly.

Latifa understood: he was thinking of the discussion group her mother had joined at Kabul University, its agenda excitedly recounted in one of the letters she'd sent him. He'd allowed Latifa to read the whole trove of letters when she'd turned fourteen – the age her mother had been when he'd gone into exile.

"You know me," Latifa said. "Politics is over my head."

"All right." He was mollified now. "Enjoy your study." He kissed her goodbye.

As Latifa dismounted from her bicycle she could see that the staff car park was empty except for the cleaners' van. If she could bluff her way through this final stage she might be out of danger in a matter of minutes.

The cleaners had unlocked the science wing, and a woman was mopping the floor by the main entrance. Latifa nodded to her, then walked in as if she owned the place.

"Hey! You shouldn't be here!" The woman straightened up and glared at her, worried for her job should anything be stolen.

"Ms Daneshvar asked me to prepare something for the class. She gave me the key yesterday." Latifa held it up for inspection.

The woman squinted at the key then waved her on, muttering unhappily.

In the chemistry lab everything was as Latifa had left it. She plucked the memory stick from the port on the furnace, then switched off the power. She touched the door, and felt no residual heat.

When she opened the furnace the air that escaped smelt like sulfur and bleach. Gingerly, she lifted out the crucible and peered inside. A solid grey mass covered the bottom, its surface as smooth as porcelain.

The instruments she needed to gauge success or failure were all in the physics lab, and trying to talk her way into another room right now would attract too much suspicion. She could wait for her next physics class and see what opportunities arose. Students messed around with the digital multimeters all the time, and if she was caught sticking the probes into her pocket her teacher would see nothing but a silly girl trying to measure the electrical resistance of a small paving stone she'd picked up off the street. Ms Hashemi wouldn't be curious enough to check the properties of the stone for herself.

Latifa fetched a piece of filter paper and tried to empty the crucible onto it, but the grey material clung stubbornly to the bottom where it had formed. She tapped it gently, then more forcefully, to no avail.

She was going to have to steal the crucible. It was not an expensive piece of equipment, but there were only four, neatly lined up in a row in the cupboard below the furnace, and its absence would eventually be missed. Ms Daneshvar might – just might – ask the cleaners if they'd seen it. There was a chance that all her trespasses would be discovered.

But what choice did she have?

She could leave the crucible behind and hunt for a replacement in the city. At the risk that, in the meantime, someone would take the vessel out to use it, find it soiled, and discard it. At the risk that she'd be caught trying to make the swap. And all of this for a grey lump that might easily be as worthless as it looked.

Latifa had bought a simple instrument of her own in the bazaar six months before, and she'd brought it with her almost as a joke – something she could try once she was out of danger, with no expectations at all. If the result it gave her was negative that wouldn't really prove anything. But she didn't know what else she could use to guide her.

She fished the magnet out of the pocket of her manteau. It was a slender disk the size of her thumbnail, probably weighing a gram or so. She held it in the mouth of the crucible and lowered it towards the bottom.

If there was any force coming into play as the magnet approached the grey material, it was too weak for her to sense. With a couple of millimetres still separating the two, Latifa spread her fingers and let the magnet drop. She didn't hear it strike the bottom – but from such a height how loud would it have been? She took her fingers out of the crucible and looked down.

It was impossible to tell if it was touching or not; the view was too narrow, the angle too high.

Latifa could hear the woman with the mop approaching, getting ready to clean the chemistry lab. Within a minute or less, everything she did here would take place in front of a witness.

A patch of morning sunlight from the eastern window fell upon the blackboard behind her. Latifa grabbed an empty Erlenmeyer flask and held it in the beam, tilting it until she managed to refract some light down into the crucible.

As she turned the flask back and forth, shifting the angle of the light, she could see a dark circle moving behind the magnet. Lit from above, an object barely a millimetre high couldn't cast a shadow like that.

The magnet was floating on air.

The door began to open. Latifa pocketed the crucible. She put the Erlenmeyer flask back on its shelf, then turned to see the cleaner eyeing her suspiciously.

"I'm all done now, thanks," Latifa announced cheerfully. She motioned towards the staff entrance. "I'll put the key back on my way out."

Minutes later, Latifa strode out of the science wing. She reached into her pocket and wrapped her hand around the crucible. She still had some money Amir had given her last Eid; she could buy a replacement that afternoon. For now, all she had to do was get through the day's lessons with a straight face, while walking around carrying the world's first room-temperature superconductor.

2

EZATULLAH WAS SAID to be the richest Afghani in Mashhad, and from the look of his three-storey marble-clad house he had no wish to live down that reputation. Latifa had heard that he'd made his money in Saudi Arabia, where he'd represented the mujahedin at the time of the Soviet occupation. Wealthy Saudi women with guilty consciences had filed through his office day after day, handing him bags full of gold bullion to help fund the jihad – buying, they believed, the same promise of paradise that went to the martyrs themselves. Ezatullah, being less concerned with the afterlife, had passed on their donations to the war chest but retained a sizeable commission.

At the mansion's gate, Latifa's grandfather paused. "I promised your mother I'd keep you out of trouble."

Latifa didn't know how to answer that; his caution came from love and grief, but this was a risk they needed to take. "Fashard's already started things rolling on his side," she reminded him. "It will be hard on him if we pull out now."

"That's true."

In the sitting room Ezatullah's youngest daughter, Yasmin, served tea, then stayed with Latifa while the two men withdrew to talk business. Latifa passed the time thinking up compliments for each rug and item of furniture in sight, and Yasmin replied in such a soft, shy voice that Latifa had no trouble eavesdropping on the conversation from the adjoining room.

"My nephew owns a clothing business in Kandahar," her grandfather began. "Some tailoring, some imports and exports. But recently he came across a new opportunity: a chance to buy electrical cable at a very fair price."

"A prudent man will have diverse interests," Ezatullah declared approvingly.

"We're hoping to on-sell the wire in Mashhad," her grandfather explained. "We could avoid a lot of paperwork at the border if we packed the trucks with cartons labelled as clothing – with some at the rear bearing out that claim. My granddaughter could run a small shop to receive these shipments."

"And you're seeking a partner, to help fund this venture?"

Latifa heard the rustle of paper, the figures she'd prepared changing hands.

"What's driven you to this, haji?" Ezatullah asked pointedly. "You don't have a reputation as a businessman."

"I'm seventy years old," her grandfather replied. "I need to see my daughter's children looked after before I die."

Ezatullah thought for a while. "Let me talk to my associates in Kandahar."

"Of course."

On the bus back to the apartment, Latifa imagined the phone calls that would already be bouncing back and forth across the border. Ezatullah would soon know all about the new electrification project in Kandahar, which aimed to wire up a dozen more neighbourhoods to the already-struggling grid – apparently in the hope that even a meagre ration of cheap power would turn more people against the insurgents who bombed every convoy that tried to carry replacement parts to the hydroelectric plant.

International donors had agreed to fund the project, and with overhead cables strung from pole to pole along winding roads, some discrepancy between the surveyed length and the cable used was only to be expected. But while Fashard really had come to an agreement with the contractor to take the excess wire off his hands, with no family ties or prior connection to the man he had only managed to secure the deal by offering a price well above the going rate.

Latifa didn't expect any of these details to elude their partner, but the hope was that his advisers in Kandahar would conclude that Fashard, lacking experience as a smuggler, had simply underestimated his own costs. That alone wouldn't make the collaboration a bad investment: she'd structured the proposal in such a way that Ezatullah would still make a tidy return even if the rest of them barely broke even.

They left the bus and made their way home. "If we told him the truth –" her grandfather began as they started up the stairs.

"If we told him the truth, he'd snatch it from our hands!" Latifa retorted. Her words echoed in the concrete stairwell; she lowered her voice. "One way or another he'd get hold of the recipe, then sell it to some company with a thousand lawyers who could claim they'd invented it themselves. We need to be in a stronger position before we take this to anyone, or they'll eat us alive." A patent attorney could do a lot to protect them before they approached a commercial backer, but that protection would cost several thousand euros. Raising that much themselves – without trading away any share in the invention – wasn't going to be easy, but it would make all the difference to how much power they retained.

Her grandfather stopped on a landing to catch his breath. "And if Ezatullah finds out that we've lied to him –"

His phone buzzed once, with a text message.

"You need to go to the house again," he said. "Tomorrow, after school."

Latifa's skin prickled with fear. "*Me?* What for?" Did Ezatullah want to quiz her about her knowledge of retail fashion for the modern Iranian woman – or had his digging already exposed her other interests?

"Most of the money's going straight to Fashard, but we'll need some cash at our end too," her grandfather explained. "He doesn't want me coming and going from the house, but no one will be suspicious if you've struck up a friendship with his daughter."

LATIFA HAD ASKED the electricians to come at seven to switch on the power to the kilns, but when they hadn't shown up by eight she gave up any hope of making it to her history class.

For the first hour she'd killed time by sweeping; now she paced the bare wooden floor, optimistically surveying her new fiefdom. Finding the factory had been a huge stroke of luck; it had originally produced ceramic tableware, and when the tenants went out of business the owner of the premises had taken possession of the kilns. He'd been on the verge of selling them for scrap, and had parted with them for a ridiculously low price just to get her grandfather to sign the lease. The location wasn't perfect, but perhaps it was for the best that it wasn't too close to the shop. The separation would make it less likely that anyone would see her in both places.

When the electricians finally arrived they ignored Latifa completely, and she resisted the urge to pester them with odd questions. *What would you do if you cut into an overhead power line and found that its appearance, in cross-section, wasn't quite what you were used to?*

"Delivery for Bose Ceramics?" a man called from the entrance.

Latifa went to see what it was. The courier was already loading one box, as tall as she was, onto his trolley. She guided him across the factory floor. "Can you put it here? Thank you."

"There are another two in the truck."

She waited until the electricians had left before finding a knife and slicing away the cardboard and styrofoam – afraid that they might recognise the equipment and start asking questions of their own. She plugged in one of the cable winders and put it through a test sequence, watching the nimble motorised arms blur as they rehearsed on thin air.

One machine would unpick, while the other two wove – and for every kilometre of cable that came into the factory, two kilometres would emerge. With half as many strands as the original, the new version would need to be bulked out from within to retain the same diameter. The pellets of ceramic wound in among the steel and aluminium wouldn't form a contiguous electrical path, but these superconducting inclusions would still lower the overall resistance of the cable, sharing the current for a large enough portion of its length to compensate for the missing metal.

So long as the cable was fit for use, the Iranian contractors who bought it would have no reason to complain. They'd pocket the difference in price, and the power grid would be none the worse for it. Everyone would get paid, everyone would be happy.

Latifa checked her watch; she'd missed another two classes. All she could do now was write the whole day off and claim to have been sick. She needed to chase down the heat-resistant moulds that would give the ceramic pellets their shape, and try again to get a promise from the chemical suppliers that they could deliver the quantities she was going to need to keep the kilns going day after day, week after week.

"Do you have this in size sixteen?" the woman asked, emerging from the changing room. Latifa looked up from her homework. The woman was still wearing the oversized sunglasses that she hadn't deigned to remove as she entered the shop, as if she were a famous singer afraid of being mobbed by fans.

"I'm sorry, we don't."

"Can you check your storeroom? I love the colours, but this one is a bit too tight."

Latifa hesitated; she was certain that they didn't stock the blouse in that size, but it would be impolite to refuse. "Of course. One moment."

She spent half a minute rummaging through the shelves, to ensure that her search didn't seem too perfunctory. It was almost six o'clock; she should close the shop and relieve her grandfather at the factory.

When she returned to the counter, the customer had left. The woman had taken the blouse, along with two pairs of trousers from the rack near the door. Latifa felt a curious warmth rising in her face; most of all she was annoyed that she'd been so gullible, but the resentment she felt at the brazen theft collided unpleasantly with other thoughts.

There was nothing to be done but to put the incident out of her mind. She looked over her unfinished essay on the Iran-Iraq war; it was due in the morning, but she'd have to complete it in the factory.

"Are these goods from your shop?"

A policeman was standing in the doorway. The thief was beside him, and he was holding up the stolen clothes.

Latifa could hardly deny it; the trousers were identical to the others hanging right beside him.

"They are, sir," she replied. He must have seen the woman emerging, hastily stuffing everything into her bag. Why couldn't she have done that out of sight?

"This lady says she must have dropped the receipt. Should I look for it, or will I be wasting my time?"

Latifa struggled to choose the right answer. "It's my fault, sir. She must have thought I'd given her the receipt along with the change – but she was in a hurry, she didn't even want one of our bags..."

"So you still have the receipt?"

Latifa pointed helplessly at the waste-paper basket beside the counter, full to the brim with discarded drafts of her essay. "I couldn't leave the shop and chase after her, so I threw it in there. Please forgive me, sir, I'm just starting out in this job. If the boss learns what I've done, he'll fire me straight away." It was lucky that the thief was still wearing her ridiculous glasses; Latifa wasn't sure how she would have coped if they'd had to make eye contact.

The policeman appeared sceptical: he knew what he'd seen. Latifa put the back of her hand to her eyes and sniffed.

"All right," he said. "Everyone makes mistakes." He turned to the woman. "I'm sorry for the misunderstanding."

"It's nothing." She nodded to Latifa. "Good evening."

The policeman lingered in the doorway, thinking things over. Then he approached the counter.

"Let me see your storeroom."

Latifa gestured to the entrance, but stayed beside the cash register. She listened to the man moving about, rustling through discarded packaging, tapping the walls. What did he imagine he'd find – a secret compartment?

He emerged from the room, stony faced, as if the lack of anything incriminating only compounded his resentment.

"ID card."

Latifa produced it. She'd rid herself of her accent long ago, and she had just enough of her father's Tajik features that she could often pass as an Iranian to the eye, but here it was: the proof of her real status.

"Ha," he grunted. "All right." He handed back the ID. "Just behave yourself, and we'll get along fine."

As he walked out of the shop, Latifa began shaking with relief. He'd found an innocent explanation for her reticence to press charges: the card entitled her to remain in the country at the pleasure of the government, but she wasn't a citizen, and she would have been crazy to risk the consequences if the woman had called her a liar.

Latifa wheeled her bicycle out of the storeroom and closed the shop. The factory was six kilometres away, and the traffic tonight looked merciless.

"I HAD A call from Ezatullah," Latifa's grandfather said. "He wants to take over the transport."

Latifa continued brushing down the slides from the superconductor hopper. "What does that mean?"

"He has another partner who's been bringing goods across the border. This man has a warehouse in Herat."

Herat was just a hundred kilometres from the border, on the route from Kandahar to Mashhad. "So he wants us to make room for this other man's merchandise in our trucks?" Latifa put the brush down. It was an unsettling prospect, but it didn't have to be a disaster.

"No," her grandfather replied. "He wants us to bring the wire across in this other man's trucks."

"*Why?*"

"The customs inspectors have people coming from Tehran to look over their shoulders," her grandfather explained. "There's no fixing that with bribes, and the clothes make too flimsy a cover for the real cargo. This other man's bringing over a couple of loads of scrap metal every week; hiding the wire won't be a problem for him."

Latifa sat down on the bench beside the winders. "But we can't risk that! We can't let him know how many spools we're bringing in!" Ezatullah had kept his distance from their day-to-day operations, but the black market contacts to whom they passed the altered wire had long-standing connections to him, and Latifa had no doubt that he was being kept apprised of every transaction. Under-reporting their sales to hide the fact that they were selling twice as much wire as they imported would be suicidal.

"Can we shift this work to Kandahar?" her grandfather asked.

"Maybe the last part, the winding," Latifa replied. So long as they could double the wire before it reached Herat, there'd be no discrepancies in the numbers Ezatullah received from his informants.

"What about the kilns?"

"No, the power's too erratic. If there's a blackout halfway through a batch that would ruin it – and we need at least two batches a day to keep up."

"Couldn't we use a generator?"

Latifa didn't have the numbers she needed to answer that, but she knew Fashard had looked into the economics of using one himself. She texted him some questions, and he replied a few minutes later.

"It's hopeless," she concluded. "Each kiln runs at about twenty kilowatts. Getting that from diesel, we'd be lucky to break even."

Her grandfather managed a curt laugh. "Maybe we'd be better off selling the rest of the wire as it is?"

Latifa did a few more calculations. "That won't work either. Fashard is paying too much for it; we'd be making a loss on every spool." After sinking money into the factory's lease and other inputs to the doubling process, any attempt to get by without the benefits of that doubling would leave them owing Ezatullah more cash than the remaining sales would bring in.

"Then what choice is left to us?"

"We could keep making the superconductor here," Latifa suggested.

"And get it to Kandahar how?" her grandfather protested. "Do you think we can do business with anyone working that route and expect Ezatullah not to hear about it? Once or twice, maybe, but not if we set up a regular shipment."

Latifa had no answer to that. "We should talk about this in the morning," she said. "You've been working all day; you should get some sleep now."

At her insistence he retired to the factory's office, where they'd put in a mattress and blankets. Latifa stood by the hopper; the last batch of superconductor should have cooled by now, but she was too dejected to attend to it. If they moved the whole operation to Kandahar, the best they could hope for was scraping through without ending up in debt. She didn't doubt that Fashard and her other cousins would do whatever needed to be done – working unpaid, purely for the sake of keeping her grandfather out of trouble – but the prospect of forcing that burden onto them filled her with shame.

Her own dawdling wasn't helping anyone. She put on the heat-proof gloves, took the moulds from the kiln and began filling the hopper. She'd once calculated that if Iran's entire grid were to be replaced with a superconducting version, the power no longer being lost in transmission would be enough to light up all of Afghanistan. But if that was just a fantasy, all her other plans were heading for the same fate.

Latifa switched on the winders and watched the strands of wire shuttling from spool to spool, wrapping the stream of pellets from the hopper. Of all the wondrous things the superconductor made possible, this had seemed the simplest – and the safest way to exploit it without attracting too much attention.

But these dull grey beads were all she had. If she wanted to rescue the whole misbegotten venture, she needed to find another way to turn them to her advantage.

*   *   *

LATIFA'S GRANDFATHER RAN from the office, barefoot, eyes wide with fear. "What happened? Are you hurt?"

Latifa could see dents in the ceiling where the pellets had struck. "I'm all right," she assured him. "I'm sorry, I didn't mean to wake you." She looked around; the kilns and the winders were untouched, and there was no damage to the building that a plasterer couldn't fix.

"*What did you do?* I thought something exploded – or those machines went crazy." He glared at the winders, as if they might have rebelled and started pelting their owners with shrapnel.

Latifa switched off the power from the outlet and approached what remained of her test rig. She'd surrounded it with workbenches turned on their sides, as safety shields. "I'm going to need better reinforcement," she said. "I didn't realise the field would get so strong, so quickly."

Her grandfather stared at the shattered assembly that she'd improvised from a helix of copper pipe. The previous tenants had left all kinds of junk behind, and Latifa had been loath to discard anything that might have turned out to be useful.

"It's a storage device," she explained. "For electricity. The current just sits there going round and round; when you want some of it back you can draw it out. It's not all that different from a battery."

"I'd say it's not all that different from a bomb."

Latifa was chastened. "I was careless; I'm sorry. I was impatient to see if I could make it work at all. The current generates a strong magnetic field, and that puts the whole thing under pressure – but when it's built properly, it will be a solid coil of superconductor, not a lot of pellets stuffed inside a pipe. And we can bury it in the ground, so if it does shatter no one will get hurt."

"How is this meant to help us?" her grandfather asked irritably. He lifted his right foot to examine the sole; a splinter of superconductor was poking through the skin.

Latifa said, "The mains power in Kandahar is unreliable, but it's still far cheaper than using a generator. A few of these storage coils should be enough to guarantee that we can run the kilns through a blackout."

"You're serious?"

Latifa hesitated. "Give me a few days to do some more experiments, then we'll know for sure."

"How many days of school have you missed already?"

"That's not important."

Her grandfather sat on the ground and covered his eyes with one hand. "School is not important now? They *murdered your mother* because she was teaching girls, and your father because he'd defended her. When she grew so afraid that she sent you to me, I promised her you'd get an education. This country is no paradise, but at least you were safe in that school, you were doing well. Now we're juggling money we don't have, living in fear of Ezatullah, blowing things up, planning some new madness every day."

Latifa approached him and put a hand on his shoulder. "After this, there'll be nothing to distract me. We'll close the factory, we'll close the shop. My whole life will be school and homework, school and homework all the way to Eid."

Her grandfather looked up at her. "How long will it take?"

"Maybe a couple of weeks." The coils themselves didn't have to be complicated, but it would take some research and trial and error to get the charging and discharging circuitry right.

"And then what?" he asked. "If we send these things to Kandahar – with the kilns and everything else – do you think Fashard can put it all together and just take over where we left off?"

"Maybe not," Latifa conceded. Fashard had wired his own house, and he could repair a sewing machine blindfold. But this would be tricky, and she couldn't talk him through the whole setup on the phone.

She said, "It looks like Eid's coming early for me this year."

In Herat, in the bus station's restroom, Latifa went through the ritual of replacing her headscarf and manteau with the burqa and niqab that she'd need to be wearing when she arrived in Kandahar.

She stared through the blue gauze at the anonymous figure reflected in the restroom's stained mirror. When she'd lived in Kabul with her parents, she'd still been young enough to visit Kandahar without covering her hair, let alone her face. But if anything, she felt insufficiently disguised now. On top of her anxiety over all her new secrets, this would be her first trip home without Amir travelling beside her – or at least, ten metres ahead of her, in the men's section of the bus. Fashard had offered to come and meet her in Herat, but she'd persuaded him to stay in Kandahar. She couldn't help being nervous, but that didn't mean she had to be cowed.

It was still early as the bus set out. Latifa chatted with the woman beside her, who was returning to Kandahar after visiting Herat for medical treatment. "I used to go to Quetta," the woman explained, "but it's too dangerous there now."

"What about Kabul?" Latifa asked.

"Kabul? These days you'll wait six months for an appointment."

The specialists in Herat were mostly Iranian; in Kabul, mostly European. In Kandahar, you'd be lucky to find anyone at all with a genuine medical degree, though there was a wide choice of charlatans who'd take your money in exchange for pharmaceuticals with expiry dates forged in ballpoint.

"Someone should build a medical school in Kandahar," Latifa suggested. "With ninety percent of the intake women, until things are evened out."

Her companion laughed nervously.

"I'm serious!" Latifa protested. "Aren't you sick of travelling to every point of the compass just to get what other people have at home?"

"Sister," the woman said quietly, "it's time to shut your mouth."

Latifa took her advice, and peered past her out the scratched window. They were crossing a barren, rock-strewn desert now, a region infamous for bandits. The bus had an armed guard, for what that was worth, but the first time Latifa had made the journey Amir had told her stories of travellers ambushed on this road at night. One man on a motorbike, carrying no cash, had been tortured until he phoned his family to deposit money into his assailant's account.

"Wouldn't that help the police catch the bandits?" Latifa had asked him, logical as ever but still naive.

Amir had laughed his head off.

"When it comes to the police," he'd finally explained, "*money in the bank* tends to have the opposite effect."

FASHARD WAS WAITING for Latifa in the bus station. He spotted her before she saw him – or rather, he spotted the bright scarf, chosen from the range she sold in the shop, that she'd told him she'd be tying to the handle of her suitcase.

He called out, then approached her, beaming. "Welcome, cousin! How was your trip?" He grabbed the suitcase and hefted it onto his shoulders; it did have wheels, but in the crowded station any baggage at foot level would just be an impediment.

"It was fine," she said. "You're looking well." Actually, Fashard looked exhausted, but he'd put so much enthusiasm into his greeting that it would have been rude to mention anything of the kind.

Latifa followed him to the car, bumping into people along the way; she still hadn't adjusted to having her peripheral vision excised.

The sun was setting as they drove through the city; Latifa fought to keep her eyes open, but she took in an impression of peeling advertising posters, shabby white-washed buildings, crowds of men in all manner of clothing and a smattering of women in near-identical garb. Traffic police stood at the busiest intersections, blowing their whistles. Nothing had changed.

Inside the house, she gratefully shed her burqa as Fashard's five youngest children swarmed towards her. She dropped to her knees to exchange kisses and dispense sweets. Fashard's wife, Soraya, his mother, Zohra, eldest daughter, sister, brother-in-law and two nephews were next to greet her. Latifa's weariness lifted; used as she was to comparative solitude, the sense of belonging was overpowering.

"How is my brother?" Zohra pressed her.

"He's fine. He sends his love to you especially."

Zohra started weeping; Fashard put an arm around her. Latifa looked away. Her grandfather still had too many enemies here to be able to return.

When Latifa had washed and changed her clothes, she rejoined the family just as the first dizzying aromas began escaping from the kitchen.

She had fasted all day and the night before, knowing that on her arrival she was going to be fed until she burst. Soraya shooed her away from the kitchen, but Latifa was pleasantly surprised: Fashard had finally improved the chimney to the point where the wood-fired stove no longer filled the room with blinding smoke.

As they ate by the light of kerosene lamps, everyone had questions for her about life in Mashhad. What did things cost now, with the new sanctions in place? What were her neighbours like? How were the Iranians treating Afghanis these days? Latifa was happy to answer them, but as she looked around at the curious faces she kept thinking of eight-year-old Fatema tugging on her sleeve, accepting a sweet but demanding something more: *What was school like? What did you learn?*

In the morning, Fashard showed Latifa the room he'd set aside for their work. She'd sent the kilns, the winders, and the current buckets to him by three different carriers. Fashard had found a source for the superconductor precursors himself: a company that brought a variety of common industrial chemicals in through Pakistan. It was possible that news of some of these shipments had reached Ezatullah, but Latifa was hoping that it wouldn't be enough to attract suspicion. If Fashard had decided to diversify into pottery, that hardly constituted a form of betrayal.

The room opened onto the courtyard, and Fashard had already taken up the paving stones to expose a patch of bare ground. "This is perfect," Latifa said. "We can run some cable out along the wall and bury the current buckets right here."

Fashard examined one of the halved diving cylinders she'd adapted to the purpose. "This really might burst?" he asked, more bemused than alarmed.

"I hope not," Latifa replied. "There's a cut-off switch that should stop the charger if the magnetic field grows too strong. I can't imagine that switch getting jammed – a bit of grit or friction isn't going to hold the contacts together against a force that's threatening to tear the whole thing apart. But so long as you keep track of the charging time there shouldn't be a problem anyway."

It took a couple of hours to dig the holes and wire up the storage system. Late in the morning the power came on, giving them a chance to test everything before they covered the buckets with half a metre of soil.

Latifa switched on the charger and waited ten minutes, then she plugged a lamp into the new supply. The light it produced was steadier and brighter than that it had emitted when connected to the mains: the voltage from the buckets was better regulated than the incoming supply.

Fashard smiled, not quite believing it. The largest of the components inside the cylinders looked like nothing so much as the element of an electric water heater; that was how Latifa had described the ceramic helices in the customs documents.

"If everyone had these..." he began enthusiastically, but then he stopped and thought it through. "If everyone had them, every household would be drawing more power, charging up their buckets to use through the blackouts. The power company would only be able to meet the demand from an even smaller portion of its customers, so they'd have to make the rationing periods even shorter."

"That's true," Latifa agreed. "Which is why it will be better if the buckets are sold with solar panels."

"What about in winter?" Fashard protested.

Latifa snorted. "What do you want from me? Magic? The government needs to fix the hydro plant."

Fashard shook his head sadly. "The people who keep bombing it aren't going to stop. Not unless they're given everything they want."

Latifa felt tired, but she had to finish what she'd started. She said, "I should show you how to work the kilns and the winders."

It took three days for Latifa and Fashard to settle on a procedure for the new factory. If they waited for the current buckets to be fully charged before starting the kilns, that guaranteed they could finish the batch without spoiling it – but they could make better use of the time if they took a risk and started earlier, given that the power, erratic though it was, usually did stay on for a few hours every day.

Fashard brought in his oldest nephew, Naqib, who'd be working half the shifts. Latifa stayed out of these training sessions; Naqib was always perfectly polite to her, but she knew he wasn't prepared to be shown anything by a woman three years younger than himself.

Sidelined, Latifa passed the time with Fatema. Though it was too dangerous for Fatema to go to school, Fashard had taught her to read and write and he was trying to find someone to come and tutor her. Latifa sat beside her as she proudly sounded out the words in a compendium of Pashtun folk tales, and practised her script in the back of Latifa's notebook.

"What are these?" Fatema asked, flicking through the pages of calculations.

"Al-jabr," Latifa replied. "You'll understand when you're older."

One day they were in the courtyard, racing the remote-control cars that Latifa had brought from Mashhad for all the kids to share. The power went off, and as the television the other cousins had been watching fell silent, Fatema turned towards the factory, surprised. She could hear the winders still spinning.

"How is that working?" she asked Latifa.

"Our cars are still working, aren't they?" Latifa revved her engine.

Fatema refused to be distracted. "They use batteries. You can't run anything big with batteries."

"Maybe I brought some bigger batteries from Iran."

"Show me," Fatema pleaded.

Latifa opened her mouth to start explaining, her mind already groping for some simple metaphors she could use to convey how the current buckets worked. But... *our cousin came from Iran and buried giant batteries in the ground?* Did she really want that story spreading out across the neighbourhood?

"I was joking," Latifa said.

Fatema frowned. "But then *how...?*"

Latifa shrugged. Fatema's brothers, robbed of their cartoons, were heading towards them, demanding to join in the game.

*   *   *

THE BUS STATION was stifling. Latifa would have been happy to dispense a few parting hugs and then take her seat, but her cousins didn't do quiet farewells.

"I'll be back at Eid," she promised. "With Amir."

"That's months away!" Soraya sobbed.

"I'll phone every week."

"You say that now," Zohra replied, more resigned than accusing.

"I'm not leaving forever! I'll see you all again!" Latifa was growing tearful herself. She squatted down and tried to kiss Fatema, but the girl turned her face away.

"What should I bring you from Mashhad next time?" Latifa asked her. Fatema considered this. "The truth."

Latifa said, "I'll try."

3

"I DID MY best to argue your case," Ms Daneshvar told Latifa. "I told the principal you had too much promise to waste. But your attendance records, your missed assignments..." She spread her hands unhappily. "I couldn't sway them."

"I'll be all right," Latifa assured her. She glanced up at the peg that held the key to the chemistry lab. "And I appreciate everything you did for me."

"But what will you do now?"

Latifa reached into her backpack and took out one of the small ceramic pots Fashard had sent her. Not long after the last spools of wire had left Kandahar, two men had come snooping on Ezatullah's behalf – perhaps a little puzzled that Fashard didn't seem quite as crushed as the terms of the deal should have left him. He had managed to hide the winders from them, but he'd had to think up an alibi for the kilns at short notice.

"I'm going to sell a few knickknacks in the bazaar," Latifa said. "Like this." She placed the pot on the desk and made as if to open it. When she'd twisted the lid through a quarter-turn it sprang into the air – only kept from escaping by three cotton threads that remained comically taut, restraining it against the push of some mysterious repulsive force.

Ms Daneshvar gazed in horror at this piece of useless kitsch.

"Just for a while!" Latifa added. "Until my other plans come to fruition."

"Oh, Latifa."

"You should take a closer look at it when you have the time," Latifa urged her. "There's a puzzle to it that I think you might enjoy."

"There are a couple of magnets," Ms Daneshvar replied. "Like pole aimed at like. You were my brightest student...and now you're impressed by *this*?" She turned the pot over. "Made in Afghanistan. Patent pending." She gave a curt laugh, but then thought better of mocking the idea.

Latifa said, "You helped me a lot. It wasn't wasted." She stood and shook her former teacher's hand. "I hope things go well for you."

Ms Daneshvar rose and kissed Latifa's cheek. "I know you're resourceful; I know you'll find something. It just should have been so much more."

Latifa started to leave, but then she stopped and turned back. The claims had all been lodged, the details disclosed. She didn't have to keep the secret any more.

"Cut one thread, so you can turn the lid upside-down," she suggested.

Ms Daneshvar was perplexed. "Why?"

Latifa smiled. "It's a very quick experiment, but I promise you it will be worth it."

EFFIGY NIGHTS
Yoon Ha Lee

Yoon Ha Lee's works have appeared in *Clarkesworld*, *Lightspeed*, *Beneath Ceaseless Skies*, and the *Magazine of Fantasy and Science Fiction*. Her short story collection *Conservation of Shadows* came out in 2013 from Prime Books. Currently she lives in Louisiana with her family and has not yet been eaten by gators.

THEY ARE CONNOISSEURS of writing in Imulai Mokarengen, the city whose name means *inkblot of the gods*.

The city lies at the galaxy's dust-stranded edge, enfolding a moon that used to be a world, or a world that used to be a moon; no one is certain anymore. In the mornings its skies are radiant with clouds like the plumage of a bird ever-rising, and in the evenings the stars scatter light across skies stitched and unstitched by the comings and goings of fire-winged starships. Its walls are made of metal the color of undyed silk, and its streets bloom with aleatory lights, small solemn symphonies, the occasional duel.

Imulai Mokarengen has been unmolested for over a hundred years. People come to listen to the minstrels and drink tea-of-moments-unraveling, to admire the statues of shapeshifting tigers and their pliant lovers, to look for small maps to great fortunes at the intersections of curving roads. Even the duelists confront each other in fights knotted by ceremony and the exchange of poetry.

But now the starships that hunt each other in the night of nights have set their dragon eyes upon Imulai Mokarengen, desiring to possess its arts, and the city is unmolested no more.

*   *   *

THE SOLDIERS CAME from the sky in a glory of thunder, a cascade of fire. Blood like roses, bullets like thorns, everything to ashes. Imulai Mokarengen's defenses were few, and easily overwhelmed. Most of them would have been museum pieces anywhere else.

The city's wardens gathered to offer the invading general payment in any coin she might desire, so long as she left the city in peace. Accustomed to their decadent visitors, they offered these: wine pressed from rare books of stratagems and aged in barrels set in orbit around a certain red star. Crystals extracted from the nervous systems of philosopher-beasts that live in colonies upon hollow asteroids. Perfume symphonies infused into exquisite fractal tapestries.

The general was Jaian of the Burning Orb, and she scorned all these things. She was a tall woman clad in armor the color of dead metal. For each world she had scoured, she wore a jewel of black-red facets upon the breastplate. She said to the councilors: what use did she have for wine except to drink to her enemies' defeat? What use was metal except to build engines of war? And as for the perfume, she didn't dignify that with a response.

But, she said, smiling, there was one thing they could offer her, and then she would leave with her soldiers and guns and ships. They could give her all the writings they treasured so much: all the binary crystals gleaming bright-dark, all the books with the bookmarks still in them, all the tilted street signs, all the graffiti chewed by drunken nanomachines into the shining walls, all the tattoos obscene and tender, all the ancestral tablets left at the shrines with their walls of gold and chitin.

The wardens knew then that she was mocking them, and that as long as any of the general's soldiers breathed, they would know no peace. One warden, however, considered Jaian's words of scorn, and thought that, unwitting, Jaian herself had given them the key to her defeat.

SERAN DID NOT remember a time when his othersight of the city did not show it burning, no matter what his ordinary senses told him, or what the dry pages of his history said. In his dreams the smoke made the sky a funeral shroud. In waking, the wind smelled of ash, the buildings of angry flames. Everything in the othersight was wreathed in orange and amber, flickering, shadows cinder-edged.

He carried that pall of phantom flame with him even now, into the warden's secret library, and it made him nervous although the books had nothing to fear from the phantoms. The warden, a woman in dust-colored robes, was escorting him through the maze-of-mists and down the stairs to the library's lowest level. The air was cool and dry, and to either side he could see the candle-sprites watching him hungrily.

"Here we are," the warden said as they reached the bottom of the stairs.

Seran looked around at the parchment and papers and scrolls of silk, then stepped into the room. The tools he carried, bonesaws and forceps and fine curved needles, scalpels that sharpened themselves if fed the oil of certain olives, did not belong in this place. But the warden had insisted that she required a surgeon's expertise.

He risked being tortured or killed by the general's occupation force for cooperating with a warden. In fact, he could have earned himself a tidy sum for turning her in. But Imulai Mokarengen was his home, for all that he had not been born here. He owed it a certain loyalty.

"Why did you bring me here, madam warden?" Seran said.

The warden gestured around the room, then unrolled one of the great charts across the table at the center of the room. It was a stardrive schematic, all angles and curves and careful coils.

Then Seran saw the shape flickering across the schematic, darkening some of the precise lines while others flowed or dimmed. The warden said nothing, leaving him to observe as though she felt he was making a difficult diagnosis. After a while he identified the elusive shape as that of a girl, slight of figure or perhaps merely young, if such a creature counted years in human terms. The shape twisted this way and that, but there were no adjacent maps or diagrams for her to jump to. She left a disordered trail of numbers like bullets in her wake.

"I see her," Seran said dryly. "What do you need me to do about her?"

"Free her," the warden said. "I'm pretty sure this is all of her, although she left a trail while we were perfecting the procedure –"

She unrolled another chart, careful to keep it from touching the first. It appeared to be a treatise on musicology, except parts of it had been replaced by a detritus of clefs and twisted staves and demiquavers coalescing into a diagram of a pistol.

"Is this your plan for resistance against the invaders?" Seran said. "Awakening soldiers from scraps of text, then cutting them out? You should have a lot more surgeons. Or perhaps children with scissors."

The warden shrugged. "Imulai Mokarengen is a city of stories. It's not hard to persuade one to come to life in her defense, even though I wouldn't call her *tame*. She is the Saint of Guns summoned from a book of legends. Now you see why I need a surgeon. I am given to believe that your skills are not entirely natural."

This was true enough. He had once been a surgeon-priest of the Order of the Chalice. "If you know that much about me," he said, "then you know that I was cast out of the order. Why haven't you scared up the real thing?"

"Your order is a small one," she said. "I looked, but with the blockade, there's no way to get someone else. It has to be you." When he didn't speak, she went on, "We are outnumbered. The general can send for more soldiers from the worlds of her realm, and they are armed with the latest weaponry. We are a single city known for artistic endeavors, not martial ones. Something has to be done."

Seran said, "You're going to lose your schematic."

"I'm not concerned about its fate."

"All right," he said. "But if you know anything about me, you know that your paper soldiers won't last. I stick to ordinary surgery because the prayers of healing don't work for me anymore; they're cursed by fire." And, because he knew she was thinking it: "The curse touches anyone I teach."

"I'm aware of the limitations," the warden said. "It will have to do. Now, do you require additional tools?"

He considered it. Ordinary scissors might be better suited to paper than the curved ones he carried, but he trusted his own instruments. A scalpel would have to do. But the difficult part would be getting the girl-shape to hold still. "I need water," he said. He had brought a sedative, but he was going to have to sponge the entire schematic, since an injection was unlikely to do the trick.

The warden didn't blink. "Wait here."

As though he had somewhere else to wait. He spent the time attempting to map the girl's oddly flattened anatomy. Fortunately, he wouldn't have to intrude on her internal structures. Her joints showed the normal range of articulation. If he hadn't known better, he would have said she was dancing in the disarrayed ink, or perhaps looking for a fight.

Footsteps sounded in the stairwell. The woman set a large pitcher of water down on the table. "Will this be enough?" she asked.

Seran nodded and took out a vial from his satchel. The dose was pure guesswork, unfortunately. He dumped half the vial's contents into the pitcher, then stirred the water with a glass rod. After putting on gloves, he soaked one of his sponges, then wrung it out.

Working with steady strokes, he soaked the schematic. The paper absorbed the water readily. The warden winced in spite of herself. The girl didn't seem capable of facial expressions, but she dashed to one side of the schematic, then the other, seeking escape. Finally she slumped, her long hair trailing off in disordered tangles of artillery tables.

The warden's silence pricked at Seran's awareness. *She's studying how I do this,* he thought. He selected his most delicate scalpel and began cutting the girl-shape out of the paper. The medium felt alien, without the resistances characteristic of flesh, although water oozed away from the cuts.

He hesitated over the final incision, then completed it, hand absolutely steady.

Amid all the maps and books and scrolls, they heard a girl's slow, drowsy breathing. In place of the paper cutout, the girl curled on the table, clad in black velvet and gunmetal lace. She had paper-pale skin and inkstain hair, and a gun made of shadows rested in her hand.

It was impossible to escape the problem: smoke curled from the girl's other hand, and her nails were blackened.

"I warned you of this," Seran said. Cursed by fire. "She'll burn up, slowly at first, and then all at once. I suspect she'll last a week at most."

"You listen to the news, surely," the warden said. "Do you know how many of our people the invaders shot the first week of the occupation?"

He knew the number. It was not small. "Anything else?" he said.

"I may have need of you later," the warden said. "If I summon you, will you come? I will pay you the same fee."

"Yes, of course," Seran said. He had noticed her deft hands, however; he imagined she would make use of them soon.

NOT LONG AFTER Seran's task for the warden, the effigy nights began.

He was out after curfew when he saw the Saint of Guns. Imulai Mokarengen's people were bad at curfews. People still broke the general's curfew regularly, although many of them were also caught at it. At every intersection, along every street, you could see people hung up as corpse-lanterns, burning with plague-colored light, as warnings to the populace. Still, the city's people were accustomed to their parties and trysts and sly confrontations. For his part, he was on his way home after an emergency call, and looking forward to a quiet bath.

It didn't surprise him that he should encounter the Saint of Guns, although he wished he hadn't. After all, he had freed her from the boundary of paper and legend to walk in the world. The connection was real, for all that she hadn't been conscious for its forging. Still, the sight of her made him freeze up.

Jaian's soldiers were rounding up a group of merry-goers and poets whose rebellious recitations had been loud enough to be heard from outside. The poets, in particular, were not becoming any less loud, especially when one of them was shot in the head.

The night became the color of gunsmoke little by little, darkness unfolding to make way for the lithe girl-figure. She had a straight-hipped stride, and her eyes were spark-bright, her mouth furiously unsmiling. Her hair was braided and pinned this time. Seran had half-expected her to have a pistol in each hand, but no, there was only the one. He wondered if that had to do with the charred hand.

Most of the poets didn't recognize her, and none of the soldiers. But one of the poets, a chubby woman, tore off her necklace with its glory's worth of void-pearls. They scattered in all directions, purple-iridescent, fragile. "The Saint of Guns," the poet cried. "In the city where words are bullets, in the book where verses are trajectories, who is safe from her?"

Seran couldn't tell whether this was a quotation or something the poet had made up on the spot. He should have ducked around the corner and toward safety, but he found it impossible to look away, even when one of the soldiers knocked the pearl-poet to the street and two others started kicking her in the stomach.

The other soldiers shouted at the Saint of Guns to stand down, to cast away her weapon. She narrowed her eyes at them, not a little contemptuous. She pointed her gun into the air and pulled the trigger. For a second there was no sound.

Then all the soldiers' guns exploded. Seran had a blurry impression of red and star-shaped shrapnel and chalk-white and falling bodies, fire and smoke and screaming. There was a sudden sharp pain across his left cheek where a passing splinter cut it: the Saint's mark.

None of the soldiers had survived. Seran was no stranger to corpses. They didn't horrify him, despite the charred reek and the cooked eyes, the truncated finger that had landed near his foot. But none of the poets had survived, either.

The Saint of Guns lowered her weapon, then saluted him with her other hand. Her fingers were blackened to their bases.

Seran stared at her, wondering what she wanted from him. Her lips moved, but he couldn't hear a thing.

She only shrugged and walked away. The night gradually grew darker as she did.

Only later did Seran learn that the gun of every soldier in that district had exploded at the same time.

IMULAI MOKARENGEN HAS four great archives, one for each compass point. The greatest of them is the South Archive, with its windows the color of regret and walls where vines trace out spirals like those of particles in cloud chambers. In the South Archive the historians of the city store their chronicles. Each book is written with nightbird quills and ink-of-dedication, and bound with a peculiar thread spun from spent artillery shells. Before it is shelved, one of the city's wardens seals each book shut with a black kiss. The books are not for reading. It is widely held that the historians' objectivity will be compromised if they concern themselves with an audience.

When Jaian of the Burning Orb conquered Imulai Mokarengen, she sent a detachment to secure the South Archive. Although she could have destroyed it in a conflagration of ice and fire and funeral dust, she knew it would serve her purpose better to take the histories hostage.

It didn't take long for the vines to wither, and for the dead brown tendrils to spell out her name in a syllabary of curses, but Jaian, unsuperstitious, only laughed when she heard.

THE WARDEN CALLED Seran back, as he had expected she would.

Seran hadn't expected the city to be an easy place to live in during an occupation, but he also hadn't made adequate preparations for the sheer aggravation of sharing it with legends and historical figures.

"Aggravation" was what he called it when he was able to lie to himself about it. It was easy to be clinical about his involvement when he was working with curling sheets, and less so when he saw what the effigies achieved.

The Saint of Guns burned up within a week, as Seran had predicted. The official reports were confused, and the rumors not much better, but he spent an entire night holed up in his study afterward estimating the number of people she had killed, bystanders included. He had bottles of very bad wine for occasions like this. By the time morning came around, he was comprehensively drunk.

Six-and-six years ago, on a faraway station, he had violated his oaths as a surgeon-priest by using his prayers to kill a man. It had not been self-defense, precisely. The man had shot a child. Seran had been too late to save the child, but not too late to damn himself.

It seemed that his punishment hadn't taught him anything. He explained to himself that what he was doing was necessary; that he was helping to free the city of Jaian.

The warden next had him cut out one of the city's founders, Alarra Coldly-Smiling. She left footsteps of frost, and where she walked, people cracked into pieces, frozen all the way through, needles of ice piercing their intestines. As might be expected, she burned up faster than the Saint of Guns. A pity; she was outside Jaian's increasingly well-defended headquarters when she sublimated.

The third was the Mechanical Soldier, who manifested as a suit of armor inside which lights blinked on-off, on-off, in digital splendor. Seran was buying more wine – you could usually get your hands on some, even during the occupation, if your standards were low – when he heard the clink-clank thunder outside the dim room where the transaction was taking place. The Mechanical Soldier carried a black sword, which proved capable of cutting through metal and crystal and stone. With great precision it carved a window in the wall. The blinking lights brightened as it regarded Seran.

The wine-seller shrieked and dropped one of the bottles, to Seran's dismay. The air was pungent with the wine's sour smell. Seran looked unflinchingly at the helmet, although a certain amount of flinching was undoubtedly called for, and after a while the Mechanical Soldier went away in search of its real target.

It turned out that the Mechanical Soldier liked to carve cartouches into walls, or perhaps its coat-of-arms. Whenever it struck down Jaian's soldiers, lights sparked in the carvings, like sourceless eyes. People began leaving offerings by the carvings: oil-of-massacres, bouquets of crystals with fissures in their shining hearts, cardamom bread. (Why cardamom, Seran wasn't sure. At least the aroma was pleasing.) Jaian's soldiers executed people they caught at these makeshift shrines, but the offerings kept coming.

Seran had laid in a good supply of wine, but after the Mechanical Soldier shuddered apart into pixels and blackened reticulations, there was a maddening period of calm. He waited for the warden's summons.

No summons came.

Jaian's soldiers swaggered through the streets again, convinced that there would be no more apparitions. The city's people whispered to each other that they must have faith. The offerings increased in number.

Finding wine became too difficult, so Seran gave it up. He was beginning to think that he had dreamed up the whole endeavor when the effigy nights started again.

Imulai Mokarengen suddenly became so crowded with effigies that Seran's othersight of fire and smoke was not much different from reality. He had not known that the city contained so many stories: women with deadly hands and men who sang atrocity-hymns. Colonial intelligences that wove webs across the pitted buildings and flung disease-sparks at the invaders. A cannon that rose up out of the city's central plaza and roared forth red storms.

But Jaian of the Burning Orb wasn't a fool. She knew that the effigies, for all their destructiveness, burned out eventually. She and her soldiers retreated beneath their force-domes and waited.

Seran resolved to do some research. How did the warden mean to win her war, if she hadn't yet managed it?

By now he had figured out that the effigies would not harm him, although he still had the scar the Saint of Guns had given him. It would have been easy to remove the scar, but he was seized by the belief that the scar was his protection.

He went first to a bookstore in which candles burned and cogs whirred. Each candle had the face of a child. A man with pale eyes sat in an unassuming metal chair, shuffling cards. "I thought you were coming today," he said.

Seran's doubts about fortune-telling clearly showed on his face. The man laughed and fanned out the cards face-up. Every one of them was blank. "I'm sorry to disappoint you," he said, "but they only tell you what you already know."

"I need a book about the Saint of Guns," Seran said. She had been the first. No reason not to start at the beginning.

"That's not a story I know," the man said. His eyes were bemused. "I have a lot of books, if you want to call them that, but they're really empty old journals. People like them for the papers, the bindings. There's nothing written in them."

"I think I have what I came for," Seran said, hiding his alarm. "I'm sorry to trouble you."

He visited every bookstore in the district, and some outside of it, and his eyes ached abominably by the end. It was the same story at all of them. But he knew where he had to go next.

GETTING INTO THE South Archive meant hiring a thief-errant, whose name was Izeut. Izeut had blinded Seran for the journey, and it was only now, inside one of the reading rooms, that Seran recovered his vision. He suspected he was happier not knowing how they had gotten in. His stomach still felt as though he'd tied it up in knots.

Seran had had no idea what the Archive would look like inside. He had especially not expected the room they had landed in to be welcoming, the kind of place where you could curl up and read a few novels while sipping citron tea. There were couches with pillows, and padded chairs, and the paintings on the walls showed lizards at play.

"All right," Izeut said. His voice was disapproving, but Seran had almost beggared himself paying him, so the disapproval was very faint. "What now?"

"All the books look like they're in place here," Seran said. "I want to make sure there's nothing obviously missing."

"That will take a while," Izeut said. "We'd better get started."

Not all the rooms were welcoming. Seran's least favorite was the one in which sickles hung from the ceiling, their tips gleaming viscously. But all the bookcases were full.

Seran still wasn't satisfied. "I want to look inside a few of the books," he said.

Izeut shot him a startled glance. "The city's traditions –"

"The city's traditions are already dying," Seran said.

"The occupation is temporary," Izeut said stoutly. "We just have to do more to drive out the warlord's people."

Izeut had no idea. "Humor me," Seran said. "Haven't you always wanted to see what's in those books?" Maybe an appeal to curiosity would work better.

Whether it did or not, Izeut stood silently while Seran pulled one of the books off the shelves. He hesitated, then broke the book's seal and felt the warden's black kiss, cold, unsentimental, against his lips. *I'm already cursed,* he thought, and opened the covers.

The first few pages were fine, written in a neat hand with graceful swells. Seran flipped to the middle, however, and his breath caught. The pages were empty except for a faint dust-trace of distorted graphemes and pixellated stick figures.

He could have opened up more books to check, but he had already found his answer.

"Stop," Izeut said sharply. "Let me reshelve that." He took the book from Seran, very tenderly.

"It's no use," Seran said.

Izeut didn't turn around; he was slipping the book into its place. "We can go now."

It was too late. The general's soldiers had caught them.

SERAN WAS SEPARATED from Izeut and brought before Jaian of the Burning Orb. She regarded him with cool exasperation. "There were two of you," she said, "but something tells me that you're the one I should worry about."

She kicked the table next to her. All of Seran's surgical tools, which the soldiers had confiscated and laid out in disarray, clattered.

"I have nothing to say to you," Seran said through his teeth.

"Really," Jaian said. "You fancy yourself a patriot, then. We may disagree about the petty legal question of who the owner of this city is, but if you are any kind of healer, you ought to agree with me that these constant spasms of destruction are good for no one."

"You could always leave," Seran said.

She picked up one of his sets of tweezers and clicked it once, twice. "You will not understand this," she said, "and it is even right that you will not understand this, but I will try to explain. This is what I do. Worlds are made to be pressed for their wine, cities taste of fruit when I bite them open. Do you think I am ignorant of the source of the apparitions that leave their smoking shadows in the streets? You're running out of writings. All I need do is wait, and this city will yield in truth."

"You're right," Seran said. "I don't understand you at all."

Jaian's smile was like knives and nightfall. "I'll write this in a language you do understand, then. You know something about how this is happening, who's doing it. Take me to them or I will start killing your people in earnest. Every hour you make me wait, I'll drop a bomb, or send out tanks, or soldiers with guns. If I get bored I'll get creative."

Seran closed his eyes and made himself breathe evenly. He didn't think she was bluffing. Besides, there was a chance – if only a small chance – that the warden could come up with a defense against the general; that the effigies would come to her aid once the general came within reach.

"All right," he said. "I'll take you where it began."

SERAN WAS BOUND with chains-of-suffocation, and he thought it likely that there were more soldiers watching him than he could actually spot. He led Jaian to the secret library, to the maze-of-mists.

"A warden," Jaian said. "I knew some of them had escaped."

They went to the staircase and descended slowly, slowly. The candle-sprites flinched from the general. Their light was almost violet, like dusk.

All the way down the stairs they heard the snick-snick of many scissors.

The downstairs room, when they reached it, was filled with paper. Curling scraps and triangles crowded the floor. It was impossible to step anywhere without crushing some. The crumpling sound put Seran in mind of burnt skin.

Come to that, there was something of that smell in the room, too.

All through the room there were scissors snapping at empty space, wielded by no hand but the hands of the air, shining and precise.

At the far end of the room, behind a table piled high with more paper scraps, was the warden. She was standing sideways, leaning heavily against the table, and her face was averted so that her shoulder-length hair fell around it.

"It's over," Jaian called out. "You may as well surrender. It's folly to let you live, but your death doesn't have to be one of the ugly ones."

Seran frowned. Something was wrong with the way the warden was moving, more like paper fluttering than someone breathing. But he kept silent. *A trap,* he thought, *let it be a trap.*

Jaian's soldiers attempted to clear a path through the scissors, but the scissors flew to either side, avoiding the force-bolts with uncanny grace.

Jaian's long strides took her across the room and around the table. She tipped the warden's face up, forced eye contact. If there had been eyes.

Seran started, felt the chains-of-suffocation clot the breath in his throat. At first he took the marks all over the warden's skin to be tattoos. Then he saw that they were holes cut into the skin, charred black at the edges. Some of the marks were logographs, and alphabet letters, and punctuation stretched wide.

"Stars and fire ascending," Jaian breathed, "what is this?"

Too late she backed away. There was a rustling sound, and the warden unfurled, splitting down the middle with a jagged tearing sound, a great irregular sheet punched full of word-holes, completely hollowed out. Her robe crumpled into fine sediment, revealing the cutout in her back in the shape of a serpent-headed youth.

Jaian made a terrible crackling sound, like paper being ripped out of a book. She took one step back toward Seran, then halted. Holes were forming on her face and hands. The scissors closed in on her.

I did this, Seran thought, *I should have refused the warden.* She must have learned how to call forth effigies on her own, ripping them out of Imulai Mokarengen's histories and sagas and legends, animating the scissors to make her work easier. But when the scissors ran out of paper, they turned on the warden. Having denuded the city of its past, of its weight of stories, they began cutting effigies from the living stories of its people.

Seran left Jaian to her fate and began up the stairs. But some of the scissors had already escaped, and they had left the doors to the library open. They were undoubtedly in the streets right now. Soon the city would be full of holes, and people made of paper slowly burning up, and the hungry sound of scissors.

ROSARY AND GOLDENSTAR
Geoff Ryman

Geoff Ryman is the author of *The Warrior Who Carried Life*, "The Unconquered Country", *The Child Garden*, *Was*, *Lust*, and *Air*. His work **253, or** *Tube Theatre* was published as hypertext fiction and won the Philip K. Dick Memorial Award. He has also won the World Fantasy, Campbell Memorial, Arthur C Clarke, British Science Fiction Association, Sunburst, James Tiptree, and Gaylactic Spectrum awards. His most recent novel, *The King's Last Song,* is set in Cambodia. Ryman currently lectures in Creative Writing at the University of Manchester in the United Kingdom.

THE ROOM WAS wood – floor, walls, ceiling.

The doorbell clanged a second time. The servant girl Bessie finally answered it; she had been lost in the kitchen amid all the pans. She slid across the floor on slippers, not lifting her feet; she had a notion that she polished as she walked. The front door opened directly onto the night: snow. The only light was from the embers in the fireplace.

Three huge men jammed her doorway. "This be the house of Squire Digges?" the smallest of them asked; and Bessie, melting in shyness, said something like, "Cmn gud zurs."

They crowded in, stomping snow off their boots, and Bessie knelt immediately to try to mop it up with her apron. "Shoo! Shoo!" said the smaller guest, waving her away.

The Master roared; the other door creaked like boots and in streamed Squire Digges, both arms held high. "Welcome! Good Count Vesuvius! Guests! Hah!" Unintroduced, he began to pump their hands.

Vesuvius, the smaller man, announced in Danish that this was Squire Digges, son of Leonard and author of the lenses, then turned back and said in English that these two fine fellows were Frederik Rosenkrantz and Knud Gyldenstierne.

"We have corresponded!" said Squire Digges, still smiling and pumping. To him, the two Danes looked huge and golden-red with bronze beards and bobbed noses, and he'd already lost control of who was who. He looked sideways in pain at the Count. "You must pardon me, sirs?"

"For what?"

The Squire looked harassed and turned on the servant. "Bessie! Bessie, their coats! The door. Leave off the floor, girl!"

Vesuvius said in Danish, *"The gentleman has asked you to remove your coats at long last. For this he is sorry."*

One of the Danes smiled, his face crinkling up like a piecrust, and he unburdened himself of what must have been a whole seal hide. He dumped it on Bessie, who could not have been more than sixteen and was small for her years. Shaking his head, Digges slammed shut the front door. Bessie, buried under furs, began to slip across the gleaming floor as if on ice.

"Bessie," said Digges in despair then looked over his shoulder. "Be careful of the floors, Messires, she polishes them so. Good girl, not very bright." He touched Bessie's elbow and guided her toward the right door.

"He warns us that floors are dangerous."

Rosenkrantz and Gyldenstierne eyed each other. *"Perhaps we fall through?"* They began to tiptoe.

Digges guided Bessie through the door, and closed it behind her. He smiled and then unsmiled when there was a loud whoop and a falling crash within.

"All's well, Bessie?"

"Aye, zur."

"We'll wait here for a moment. Uh, before we go in. The gentlemen will excuse me but I did not hear your names."

"He's forgotten your names. These English cannot speak." Vesuvius smiled. "Is so easy to remember in English. This be noble Rosary and Goldenstar."

"Sirs, we are honored. Honored beyond measure!"

Mr. Goldenstar sniffed. *"The whole place sags and creaks. Haven't the English heard of bricks?"*

Mr. Rosary beamed and gestured at the panelling and the turd-brown floor. "House. Beautiful. Beautiful!"

Squire Digges began to talk to them as if they were children. "In. Warm!" He beat his own arms. "Warrrrrrrrrrm."

Goldenstar was a military man, and when he saw the room beyond, he gave a cry and leapt back in alarm.

It was not a dining hall but a dungeon. It had rough blocks, chains, and ankle irons that hung from the wall. *"It's a trap!"* he yelped, and clasped young Rosary to pull him back.

From behind the table a tall, lean man rose up, all in black with a skull cap and lace around his neck. *Inquisitor.*

"Oh!" laughed the Squire and touched his forehead. "No, no, no, no alarms, I beg. Hah! The house once belonged to Philip Henslowe; he owns the theater out back; this is like a set from a play."

Vesuvius blinked in fury. *"This is his idea of a joke."*

"You should see the upstairs; it is full of naked Venuses!"

"I think he just said upstairs is a brothel."

Goldenstar ran his fingers over the walls. The rough stones, the iron rings and the chains had all been frescoed onto plaster. He blurted out a laugh. *"They're all mad."*

"They are all strolling players. They do nothing but go to the theater. They pose and declaim and roar."

Digges flung out a hand toward the man in black. "Now to the business at hand. Sirs! May... I... introduce... Doctor John DEE!"

For the Doctor, Vesuvius had a glittery smile; but he said through his teeth, *"They mime everything."*

"Ah!" Mr. Rosary sprang forward to shake the old man's hand. He was in love, eyes alight. "Queen Elisabetta. Magus!"

Dr. John Dee rumbled, "I am called Mage, yes, but I am in fact the Advisor Philosophical to her Majesty."

Digges beamed. "His *Parallaticae commentationis* and my own *Alae seu scalae mathematicae* were printed as a pair."

Someone else attended, pale skinned, pink cheeked, and glossy from nose to balding scalp, with black eyes like currants in a bun and an expression like a barber welcoming you to his shop.

"And this example," growled Digges, putting his hand on the young man's shoulder, "will not be known to you, but we hold him in high esteem, a family friend. This is Guillermus Shakespere."

The young man presented himself. "A Rosary and a Goldenstar. These are names for poetry. Especially should one wish to contrast Religion and Philosophy."

Vesuvius's lip curled. "You mock names?"

"No no, of course not. I beg! Not that construction. It is but poetic... convenience. My own poor name summons up dragooned peasants shaking weapons. Or, or, an actor whose only roles are those of soldiers." The young man looked back and forth between the men, expecting laughter. They blinked and stood with their hands folded not quite into fists.

"My young friend is a reformed Papist and so thinks much on issues of religion and philosophy. As do we." Digges paused, also waiting. "Please sit, gentlemen."

Cushions, food, and wine all beckoned. Digges busied himself pouring far too much wine into tankards. Mr. Rosary hunkered down with pleasure next to Dr. Dee, and even took his hand. He then began to speak, sometimes closing his eyes. "My dear Squire Digges and honorable Doctor Dee. My relative Tycho Brahe sends his greatest respects and has entrusted us to give you this, his latest work."

He sighed and chuckled, relieved to be rid of both a small gray printed pamphlet, and his speech. Digges howled his gratitude, and read a passage aloud from the pamphlet and passed it to Dr. Dee, and pressed Rosary to pass on his thanks.

Rosary began to recite again. "I am asked by Tycho Brahe to say how impress-ed with your work. Sir. To describe the universe as infinite with mathematical argument!" His English sputtered and died. "Is a big thing. We are all so amuzed."

"Forgive me," said the young man. "Is it the universe or the argument that is infinite?"

"Guy," warned Digges in a sing-song voice. He pronounced it with a hard "G" and a long eeee.

"And is it the universe or the numbers that are amusing?"

Mr. Rosary paused, understood, and grinned. "The two. Both."

"We disagree on matters of orbitals," said Squire Digges.

Vesuvius leaned back, steepling his fingers; his nails were clean and filed. "A sun that is the circumference of Terra." He sketched with his finger a huge circle and shook his head.

Almost under his breath the young man said, "A sonne can be larger than his father."

Digges explained. "My young friend is a poet."

Vesuvius smiled. "I look forward to him entertaining us later." Then he ventriloquized in Danish, "*And until then, he might eat with the servants.*"

Mr. Rosary looked too pleased to care and beamed at Digges. "You... have... lens."

Digges boomed. "Yes! Yes! On roof." He pointed. "*Stierne. Stierne.*"

Rosary laughed and nodded. "Yes! *Stierne!* Star."

"Roof. We go to roof." Squire Digges mimed walking with his two fingers. Blank looks, so he wiped out his gesture with a wave.

Vesuvius translated with confidence. "*No stars tonight, too cloudy.*"

"No stars," said Mr. Rosary, as if someone's cat had died.

"Yes." Digges looked confused. "*Stierne.* On roof."

Everything stalled: words, hands, mouths and feet. Nobody understood.

Young Guy made a sound like bells, many of them, as if bluebells rang. His fingers tinkled across an arch that was meant to be the Firmament. Then his two flat hands became lenses and his arms mechanical supports that squeedled as they lined up his palms.

Goldenstar gave his head an almost imperceptible shake. "*What the hell is he doing?*"

Vesuvius: "*I told you they have to mime everything.*"

"*No wonder that they are good with numbers. They can't use words!*"

"*It's why there will never be a great poet in English.*"

Rosary suddenly rocked in recognition. He too mimed the mechanical device with its lenses. He twinkled at young Guy. Young Guy twinkled back.

"Act-or," explained Digges. "Tra-la! Stage. But poet. Oh! Such good poet. New poem. *Venus and Adonis!*" He kissed the tips of his fingers. Vesuvius's eyes, heavy and unmoved, rested on his host.

"Poet. Awww," Rosary said in sympathy. "No numbers."

John Dee, back erect, sipped his wine.

Bessie entered, rattling plates and knives in terror. Goldenstar growled, and his hands rounded in the air the curvature of her buttocks. She noticed and fled, soles flapping, polishing no more.

The Squire poured more wine. "Now. I want to hear more of your great relation, Lord Tycho. I yearn to visit him. He lives on an island? Devoted to philosophy!" He pronounced the name as "Tie-koh."

Vesuvius corrected him. "Teej-hhho."

"Yes, Tycho."

"The island is called *Hven*. You should be able to remember it as it is the same word as 'haven.' It is called in Greek Uraniborg. Urania means study of stars. Perhaps you know that?"

Digges's face stiffened. "I do read Greek."

Rosary beamed at Guy. "Your name Gee. In Greek is Earth."

Guy laughed. "Is it? Heaven and Earth. And I was born Taurus." He waited for a response. "Earth sign?" He looked at them all in turn. "You are all astrologers?"

Dr. Dee said, "No."

"And your name," said Guy, turning suddenly on the translator as if pulling a blade. "You are called Vesuvius?"

"A pseudonym, Guy," said Digges. "Something to hide. *A nom de plume.*"

"What's that?"

"French," growled Vesuvius. "A language."

Rosary thought that was a signal to change languages, and certainly the subject. "*Mon cousin a un nez d'or.*"

Squire Digges jumped in to translate ahead of Vesuvius. "Your cousin has a…" He faltered. "A golden nose."

Rosary pointed to his own nose. "*Oui. Il l'a perdu ça par se battre en duel.*"

"In… a… duel."

Goldenstar thumped the table. "Over *matematica!*"

Squire Digges leaned back. "Now that is a good reason to lose your nose."

"*Ja! Ja!*" Goldenstar laughed. "*Principiis mathematicis.*"

"I trust we will not come to swords," said Digges, half-laughing.

Rosary continued. "*De temps en temp il port un nez de cuivre.*"

Vesuvius translated. "Sometimes the nose is made of copper."

Guy's mouth crept sideways. "He changes noses for special occasions?"

Vesuvius glared; Goldenstar prickled. "Tycho Brahe great man!"

"Evidently. To be able to afford such a handsome array of noses."

Squire Digges hummed "no" twice.

Rosary pressed on. "*Mon cousin maintain comme un animal de familier un élan.*"

Vesuvius snapped back, "He also has a pet moose."

Digges coughed. "I think you'll find he means elk."

"*L'élan peut danser!*" Rosary looked so pleased.

Digges rattled off a translation. "The elk can dance." He paused. "I might have that wrong."

Goldenstar thought German might work better. "*Der elch ist tot.*"

Digges. "The elk is dead."

"Did it die in the duel as well?" Guy's face was bland. "To lose at a stroke both your nose and your moose."

Rosary rocked with laughter. "*Ja-ha-ha. Ja! Der elch gesoffenwar von die treppen gefallen hat.*"

Sweat tricked down Digges's forehead. "The elk drank too much and fell down stairs."

Guy nodded slightly to himself. "And you good men believe that the Earth goes around the sun." His smile was a grimace of incredulity and embarrassment.

Dr. Dee tapped the table. "No. Your friend Squire Digges believes the Earth goes around the sun. Our guests believe that the sun goes around the Earth, but that all the other planets revolve around those two central objects. They believe this on the evidence of measurements and numbers. This evening is a conference on numbers and their application to the ancient study of stars. Astronomy. But the term is muddled."

Guy's face folded in on itself.

"Language fails you. Thomas Digges is described as a designer of arms and an almanacker. Our Danish friends are called astrologers, I am called a mage. I call us philosophers, but our language is numbers. Numbers describe, sirrah, with more precision than all your poetry."

Shakespere bowed.

"The Queen herself believes this and thus so should you." Dee turned away from him.

"But the numbers disagree," said Shakespere.

BESSIE LABORED INTO the room backwards, bearing on a trencher a whole roast lamb. It was burnt black and smelled of soot. The company applauded nonetheless. The parsnips and turnips about it were cinders shining with fat.

Digges continued explaining. "Now, this great Tycho saw suddenly appear in the heavens...."

Goldenstar punched the air and shouted over the last few words, "By eye! By eye!"

"Yes, by eye. He saw a new light in the heavens, a comet he thought, only it could not be one."

"Numbers by eye!"

"Yes, he calculated the parallax and proved it was not a comet. It was beyond the moon. A new star, he thought."

"Nova!" exclaimed Goldenstar.

"More likely to be a dying one, actually. But it was a change to the immutable sphere of the stars!"

"Oh. Interesting," said Shakespere. "Should... someone carve?"

"You're as slow as gravy! Guy! The sphere of the stars is supposed to be unchanging and perfect."

"Spheres, you mean the music of the spheres?"

Goldenstar bellowed. "*Ja*. It move!"

"I rather like the idea of the stars singing."

Digges's hand moved as if to music. "It means Ptolemy is wrong. It means the Church is wrong, though why Ptolemy matters to the Church I don't know. But there it was. A new light in the heavens!"

Guy's voice rose in panic. "When did this happen?"

John Dee answered him. "1572."

Shakespere began to count the years on his fingers.

John Dee's mouth twitched and he squeezed shut Shakespere's hand. "Twenty. Years. And evidently the world did not end, so it was not a portent." As he spoke, Vesuvius translated in an undertone.

Squire Digges grinned like a wolf. "There are no spheres. The planets revolve around the sun, and we are just another planet."

"Nooooooooooo ho-ho!" wailed Rosary and Goldenstar.

Digges bounced up and down in his chair, still smiling. "The stars are so far away we cannot conceive the distance. All of them are bigger than the sun. The universe is infinitely large. It never ends."

The Danes laughed and waved him away. Goldenstar said, "Terra heavy. Sit in center. Fire light. Sun go around Terra!"

"Could we begin eating?" suggested Guy.

"Terra like table. Table fly like bird? No!" One of Goldenstar's fists was matter, the other fire and spirit.

"I'll carve. Shall I carve?" No one noticed Shakespere. He stood up and sharpened the knife while the philosophers teased and bellowed. He sawed the blackened hide. "I like a nice bit of crackling." He leaned down hard on the knife and pushed; the scab broke open and a gout of blood spun out of it like a tennis ball and down Guy's doublet. The meat was raw. He regained his poise. "Shall we fall upon it with lupine grace?"

Vesuvius interpreted. "*He says you have the manners of wolves.*"

Rosary said, "Hungry like wolves."

The knife wouldn't cut. Guy began to wrestle the knuckle out of its socket. Like a thing alive, the lamb leapt free onto the floor.

"Dear, dear boy." Digges rose to his feet and scooped up the meat, and put it back on the board. "Give me the knife." He took it and began with some grace to carve. "He really is a very good poet."

"Let us hope he is that at least," said Vesuvius.

Digges paused, about to serve. "He's interested in everything. History. Ovid. Sex. And then spins it into gold."

He put a tranche onto Goldenstar's plate. Knud did not wait for the others and began to press down with his knife. The meat didn't cut.

He speared it up whole and began to chaw one end of it. The fat was uncooked and tasted of human genitals; the flesh had the strength of good hemp rope. He turned the turnip over in his fingers. It looked like a lump of coal and he let it fall onto his plate. "*I suggest we sail past this food and go and see the lenses.*"

Rosary tried to take a bite of the meat. "*Yes. Lenses.*"

THOMAS DIGGES'S HOUSE stood three stories high, dead on Bankside opposite the spires of All Hallows the Great and All Hallows the Lesser. Just behind his house, beyond a commons, stood Henslowe's theater, The Rose, which was why Guy was such a frequent houseguest. Digges got free tickets in the stalls as a way of apologizing for the groundlings' noise and litter and the inconvenience of Guy sleeping on his floor. Guy didn't snore but he did make noises all night as if he were caressing a woman or jumping down from trees.

No noise in February at night. The wind had dropped, and a few boats still plied across the river, lanterns glowing like planets. The low-tide mud was luminous with snow. The sky looked as if it had been scoured free of cloud.

Over his slated roof, Digges had built a platform. Its scaffolding supports had splintered; it groaned underfoot, shifting like a boat. The moon was full-faced and the stars seemed to have been flung up into the heavens, held by nets.

The cold had loosened Guy's tongue. "S-s-s-size of lenses, you look with both eyes. No squinting. C-c-can you imagine f-f-f-folk wearing them as a collar, they lift up the arms and have another set of eyes to see distant things. W-w-w-would that make them philosophers?"

"The gentlemen are acquainted with the principle, Guy." Digges was ratcheting a series of mechanical arms that supported facemask-sized rounds of glass.

"But not the wonder of it. D-do you sense wonder, Mr. Rosary?"

Rosary's red cheeks swelled. "I do not know."

"Many things I'm sure, Rosie, are comprehended by you. Are you married, perchance?"

"Geee-eee – heee," warned Digges. He bent his knees to look through the corridor of lenses and made an old-man noise.

Goldenstar answered. "Married."

"As am I. That signifies, b-b–but not much." Guy arched back around to Rosary. "Come by day the morrow and walk alongside the river with me. The churches and the boats, moorhens, the yards of stone and timber."

Vesuvius shook his head. "We have heard about you actors."

Goldenstar said, "We leave tomorrow." Rosary shrugged.

Digges stood up and presented his lenses to them. "Sirs." Vesuvius and Rosary did a little dance, holding out hands for each other, until the Count put a collegial hand on Rosary's back and pushed. Rosary crouched and stared, blinking.

Squire Digges sounded almost sad. "You see. The moon is solid too. Massy with heft."

Rosary was still. Finally he stood up, shaking his head. "That is…" He tried to speak with his hands, but that also failed. "Like being a sea." He looked sombre. "The stars are made of stone."

Goldenstar adopted a lunging posture as if grounding a spear against an advancing horde. "*This could get us all burnt at the stake.*"

John Dee answered in Danish. Vesuvius looked up in alarm. "*Yes, but not here, not while my Queen lives.*"

Shakespere understood the tone. "Everything is exploding, exploding all at once. When I was in Rome – it's so important to g-g-get things right, don't you think? Research is the best part of the j-job. Rome. Verona. Carthage. I was in a room with a man who was born the same year I was and his first name was the same as his last, G-G-Galileo Galilei. I told him about Thomas and he told me that he too has lenses. He told me that Jupiter has four moons and Saturn wears a rainbow hat. He is my pen pal, Galileo, I send him little things of my own, small pieces you understand –"

Vesuvius exploded. "Please you will stop prattle!" He ran a hand across his forehead. "We are meeting of great astrological minds in Europe, not prattle Italian!"

Digges placed an arm around Guy as if to warm him. Rosary phalanxed next to them as though shielding him from the wind. "Please," Rosary said to Vesuvius.

John Dee thought: People protect this man.

*   *   *

GUILLERMUS SHAKESPERE THOUGHT:

I can be in silence. My source is in silence. Words come from silence.

How different they be, these Danes, one all stern and leaden, forceful with facts, the other leavening dough. Their great cousin. All by eye? Compromise by eye, just keep the sun going around the Earth, to pacify the Pope and save your necks. Respect him more if he declared for the Pope forthrightly and kept to the heavens and Earth as we knew them. Digges digs holes in heaven, excavating stars as if they were bones. Building boats of bone. He could build boxes, boxes with mirrors to look down into the heart of the sea, show us a world of narwhales, sharks, and selkies.

All chastened by Mr. Volcano. All silent now. Stare now – by eye – you who think you see through numbers, stare at what his lenses show. New eyes to see new things.

How do rocks hang in the sky?

How will I tell my groundlings: the moon is a mountain that doesn't fall? The man with gap in his teeth; the maid with bruised cheek, the oarsman with rounded back? What can I say to them? These wonders are too high for speaking, for scrofulous London, its muddy river. Here the moon has suddenly descended onto our little eye-land. Here where the future is hidden in lenses and astrolabes. The numbers and Thomas's clanking armatures.

"Guy," says old Thomas, full of kindness. "Your turn."

I bow before the future, into the face of a new monarch of glass who overturns. I look through his eyes; see as he sees, wide and long. I blink as when I opened my eyes in a basin of milk. Dust and shadow, light and mist cross and swim and I look onto another world.

I can see so clearly that it's a ball, a globe. Its belly swells out toward me, a hint of shadow on its crescent edge.

It is as stone as any granite tor. Beige and hot in sunlight. The moon must see us laced in cloud but no clouds there, no rain, no green expanse. Nothing to shield from the shriveling sun. No angels, nymphs, orisons, bowers, streams, butterflies, lutes. Desiccated corpses. No dogs to devour. A circle of stone. Avesbury. A graveyard. Breadcrumbs and mold.

Not man in the moon, but a skull.

Nothing for my groundlings. Or poetry.

I look on Digges's face. He stares as wide as I do; no comfort there. He touches my sleeve. "Dear Guy. Look at the stars."

He hoists the thing on some hidden bearing, and then takes each arm and gears into a new niche. The lenses rise and intersect at some new angle, and I look again, and see the stars.

Rosie was right, it is an ocean. What ship could sail there? Bejewelled fish. That swallow Earth. Carry it to God. I can see. I can see they are suns, not tiny torches, and if suns then about those too other Earths could hang. Infinite suns, infinite worlds, deeper and deeper into bosom of God, distances vast, they make us more precious because so rare and small, defenseless before all that fire.

Here is proof of church's teaching. God must love us to make any note of us when the very Earth is a mote of soot borne high on smoky gas.

My poor groundlings.

JOHN DEE WATCHED.

The boy pulled back from the glass, this actor-poet-playwright. Someone else for whom there is no word. In the still and icy air, tears had frozen to his cheeks. Digges gathered him in; Rosary stepped forward; Goldenstar stared astounded. Only the spy stood apart, scorn on his face.

"You are right, Squire Digges," said the boy. "It is without end. Only that would be big enough for God." He looked fallen, pale and distracted. "The cold bests me. I must away, gentlemen."

"The morrow?" Rosary asked. "We meet before we go?"

The wordsmith nodded, clasped Rosary's hand briefly and then turned and trundled down the steps. The platform shook and shuddered. Dee stood still and dark for a moment, decided, and then with a swirl, followed.

Winding down the stairwell past people-smelling bedrooms, through the dungeon of a dining room. The future that awaited them? Out into the paneled room, flickering orange.

"Young Sir! Stay!"

The boy looked embarrassed. "Nowhere else to go."

Such a poor, thin cloak. Was that the dust of Rome on it? Or only Rome wished for so hard that mind-dust fell upon it? But his eyes: full of hope, when I thought to see despair. "Young master. Have you heard of the Brotherhood of Night?"

Hope suspended like dust, only dust that could see.

"I see you have not, for which I am thankful. We are a brotherhood devoted to these new studies late from Germany and Denmark, now Austria and Italia. None of us can move, let alone publish, without suspicion. That man Vesuvius is as much spy as guide, the Pope's factotum. How, young Guillermus, would you like to see Brahe's island of philosophy, in sight of great Elsinore? Uraniborg, city of the heavens, though in fact given over to the muse of a study that has late been revived. And all this by a man with a golden nose. Would you like to see again your starry twin Galileo? See Rome, Verona, Athens? Not Carthage, not possible, don't say that in good company again. But Spain, possible now. The courtship of Great Elizabeth by Philip makes travel even there approved and safe."

"My... I'm an actor. I used to play women."

"You still do." Dee's grim smile lengthened. "Men like Vesuvius dismiss you. Bah! Religion is destroying itself. The Protestants prevent the old Passion Plays, and in their stead grow you and Marlowe. You write the history of tragic kings. That has not happened since the Greeks."

Guy shook his head. "Ask Kit to do this."

He is, thought Dee, a good, faithful, fragile boy. And something in his thin shoulders tells me that he's contemplating going into Orders. That must be stopped.

Dee said aloud, "Kit draws enemies." The boy's eyes stared into his. "Men who want to kill him. They love you."

Out of cold policy, Dee took the boy into his arms and kissed him full on the lips, held him, and then pushed him back, to survey the results in the creature's eyes: yes: something soft, something steel.

Guy said, "You taste of gunpowder."

"You would still be able to wright your poetry. Send it to Kit in packets to furnish out the plays. In any case he will be undone, caught up in these Watchmen unless we hide him. As you might well be undone if you stay here and miss your chance to see the world blossom. Move for us and write it down. And learn, boy, learn! See where Caesar walked; breathe the scents of Athens's forest. Go to high Elsinore."

Shakespere stood with his eyes closed. The old house crackled and turned about them. The world was breaking. "Are there tales in Denmark of tragic kings?"

Dr. Dee nodded. "And things as yet undreamt of." He took up his long staff and the black cloak that was taller than himself. He put his arm around the slender shoulders and said, "Riverwalk with me."

THE DOOR SHUT tight behind them, and only then did Bessie come to open it.

Outside, white carpeted everything, and Bessie stepped into the hush. Somehow it was snowing again, though the sky overhead was clear. She kicked snow off the stone step and sat down, safe and invisible. It looked as if the stars themselves were falling in flakes. The idea made her giggle. She saw thistledown: stars were made of dandelion stuff.

As so often once it starts to snow, the air felt warmer. The blanket of white would be melted by morning; if she were abed now she'd have missed it. So she warmed the stone step by sitting on it, and let the snow tingle her fingertips. She scooped up a ridge of it and tasted: cold and fresh, sweeter than well water.

She looked up, and snow streaked past her face like stars. Her stomach turned over and it felt as if she were falling upward, flying into heaven where there would be angels. She could see the angels clearly; they'd be tall and thin with white hair because they were so old, but no wrinkles, with the bodies of men and the faces of women. The thought made her giggle, for it was a bit naughty trying to picture angels. She lifted up her feet, which made her feel even more like she was flying.

*   *   *

AN HOUR LATER and Guy came back to find her still seated on the step.

"Hello, Bessie." He dropped down next to her and held up his own pink-fingered ridge of snow. "It's like eating starlight."

She gurgled with the fun of it and grabbed her knees and grinned at him. She was missing a tooth. "Did you see the old gent'man home?"

"Aye. He wants me to go to Denmark. He'll pay."

"Oooh! You'll be off then!"

He hugged his knees too and rested his head on them, saying nothing. She nudged him. "Oh. You should go. Chance won't come again."

"I said I would think on it. He wants me to spy. Like Kit. I'd have to carry a knife."

"You should and all. Round here." She nudged him again. "Wouldn't want you hurt."

"You're a good lass, Bessie."

"Aye," wistfully, as if being good had done her no good in return. He followed her eyeline up into the heavens, that had been so dreary and cold. The light of stars sparkled in her eyes and she had a sweet face: long nosed, with a tiny mouth like a little girl, stray hair escaping her kerchief, a smudge of ash on her face. He leaned forward and kissed her.

"Hmm," she said happily and snuggled in. These were the people he wanted to make happy; give them songs, dances, young blades, fine ladies in all their brocade, and kings halfway up the stairs to God.

"What do you see when you look at stars, Bessie?"

She made a gurgling laugh from deep within. "You know when the sun shines on snow and there's bits on it? Other times it's like I've got something in my eye, like I'm crying. But right now, I'm flying through 'em. Shooting past!"

"Are you on a ship?" He glimpsed it, like the royal barge all red and gold, bearing Queen Elizabeth through the Milky Way, which wound with a silver current. Bessie sat on the figurehead, kicking her heels.

"Oh, I don't know!"

"Like Sir Walter Raleigh with a great wind filling the sails."

"That'll be it," she said and kicked her heels. She leaned forward for another kiss, and he gave it to her, and the rising of her breath felt like sails.

"Wind so strong we're lifted up from the seas, and we hang like the moon in the air." He could see the sails fill, and a storm wave that tossed them free of the sea, up into the sky, away from whatever it was held them to the Earth. "We'll land on the moon first, beaching in sand. It's always sunny there, no clouds. We'll have taken salt pork and hardtack."

"Oh no, we'll take lovely food with us. We'll have beer and cold roast beef."

"And we'll make colonies like in the Caribbean now, on Mars, and then Jupiter. They'll make rum there out of a new kind of metal. We'll go beyond to the stars."

Bessie said, "There'll be Moors on Mars."

Shakespere blinked. She was a marvel. They all were, that's why he wrote for them. He loved them.

That old man: *like the Greeks had done*, he said. Their great new thing that he and Kit were doing. And the others, even miserable old Greene; their *Edwards* and their *Henrys*. Mad old John Dee had made them sound old-fashioned, moldy from the grave. Bessie didn't care about the past. She was traveling to Araby on Mars.

So why write those old things from the grammar school? Write something that was part of the explosion in the world.

I need to bestir myself. I need to learn; I can turn their numbers into worlds, such as Bessie sees, where stars are not crystals, where the moon is a beach of gravel and ice.

Dee would be gone by dawn. He and the Danes were sailing. Were the Danes still in the house? If they were he could leave with them.

As if jabbed, Guy sat up. "Bessie, I'm going to go."

"I knew you would," she said, her face dim with pleasure for him.

Go to that island of philosophy, be there with Rosary; he liked Rosie, wanted to kiss him too – and Rosie could explain the numbers. Guy jittered up to his feet, slipping on the slush. He saw Fortune: a salmon shooting away under the water. He nipped forward, gave Bessie a kiss on the cheek, and ran into the house, shouting, "Squire. My good sirs!"

From inside the house came thumps and racketing and shouts, the Squire bellowing "Take this coat!" and the Danes howling with laughter. Outside, it started to snow again, drifting past Bessie's face.

Well, thought Bessie, *I never had him really.*

She was falling between stars again on a silver ship shaped like a swan with wings that whistled. They docked on a comet that was made not of fire, but ice; and they danced a jig on it and set it spinning with the lightness of their feet; and they went on until clouds of angels flew about them with voices like starlings and the voyagers wouldn't have to die because they already were in Heaven, and on the prow stood Good Queen Bess in silver armor and long red hair, but Good Queen Bess was her.

Shakespere's next play was called *A Midwinter's Nonesuch on Mars.*

THE SLEEPER AND THE SPINDLE
Neil Gaiman

Neil Gaiman (www.neilgaiman.com) was born in England and worked as a freelance journalist before co-editing *Ghastly Beyond Belief* (with Kim Newman) and writing *Don't Panic: The Official Hitchhiker's Guide to the Galaxy Companion*. He started writing comics with *Violent Cases*, and established himself as one of the most important comics writers of his generation with award-winning series *The Sandman*. His first novel, *Good Omens* (with Terry Pratchett), appeared in 1991, and was followed by *Neverwhere*, *Stardust*, *American Gods*, *Coraline*, *Anansi Boys*, and *The Graveyard Book*. His most recent book is major novel *The Ocean at the End of the Lane*. Gaiman's work has won the Caldecott, Newbery, Hugo, World Fantasy, Bram Stoker, Locus, Geffen, International Horror Guild, Mythopoeic and Will Eisner Comic Industry awards.

IT WAS THE closest kingdom to the queen's, as the crow flies, but not even the crows flew it. The high mountain range that served as the border between the two kingdoms discouraged crows as much as it discouraged people, and it was considered unpassable.

More than one enterprising merchant, on each side of the mountains, had commissioned folk to hunt for the mountain pass that would, if it were there, have made a rich man or woman of anyone who controlled it. The silks of Dorimar could have been in Kanselaire in weeks, in months, not years. But there was no such pass to be found and so, although the two kingdoms shared a common border, no travelers crossed from one kingdom to the next.

Even the dwarfs, who were tough, and hardy, and composed of magic as much as of flesh and blood, could not go over the mountain range.

This was not a problem for the dwarfs. They did not go over the mountain range. They went under it.

THREE DWARFS WERE traveling as swiftly as one through the dark paths beneath the mountains.

"Hurry! Hurry!" said the dwarf in the rear. "We have to buy her the finest silken cloth in Dorimar. If we do not hurry, perhaps it will be sold, and we will be forced to buy her the second-finest cloth."

"We know! We know!" said the dwarf in the front. "And we shall buy her a case to carry the cloth back in, so it will remain perfectly clean and untouched by dust."

The dwarf in the middle said nothing. He was holding his stone tightly, not dropping it or losing it, and was concentrating on nothing else but this. The stone was a ruby, rough-hewn from the rock and the size of a hen's egg. It would be worth a kingdom when cut and set, and would be easily exchanged for the finest silks of Dorimar.

It had not occurred to the dwarfs to give the young queen anything they had dug themselves from beneath the earth. That would have been too easy, too routine. It's the distance that makes a gift magical, so the dwarfs believed.

THE QUEEN WOKE early that morning.

"A week from today," she said aloud. "A week from today, I shall be married."

She wondered how she would feel to be a married woman.

It seemed both unlikely and extremely final. It would be the end of her life, she decided, if life was a time of choices. In a week from now she would have no choices. She would reign over her people. She would have children. Perhaps she would die in childbirth, perhaps she would die as an old woman, or in battle. But the path to her death, heartbeat by heartbeat, would be inevitable.

She could hear the carpenters in the meadows beneath the castle, building the seats that would allow her people to watch her marry. Each hammer blow sounded like a dull pounding of a huge heart.

THE THREE DWARFS scrambled out of a hole in the side of the riverbank, and clambered up into the meadow, one, two, three. They climbed to the top of a granite outcrop, stretched, kicked, jumped, and stretched themselves once more. Then they sprinted north, toward the cluster of low buildings that made the village of Giff, and in particular to the village inn.

The innkeeper was their friend: they had brought him a bottle of Kanselaire wine – deep red, sweet and rich, and nothing like the sharp, pale wines of those parts – as they always did. He would feed them, and send them on their way, and advise them.

The innkeeper, chest as huge as his barrels, with a beard as bushy and as orange as a fox's brush, was in the taproom. It was early in the morning, and on the dwarfs' previous visits at that time of day the room had been empty, but now there must have been thirty people in that place, and not a one of them looked happy.

The dwarfs, who had expected to sidle in to an empty taproom, found all eyes upon them.

"Goodmaster Foxen," said the tallest dwarf to the innkeeper.

"Lads," said the innkeeper, who thought that the dwarfs were boys, for all that they were four, perhaps five times his age, "I know you travel the mountain passes. We need to get out of here."

"What's happening?" said the smallest of the dwarfs.

"Sleep!" said the sot by the window.

"Plague!" said a finely dressed woman.

"Doom!" exclaimed a tinker, his saucepans rattling as he spoke. "Doom is coming!"

"We travel to the capital," said the tallest dwarf, who was no bigger than a child, and had no beard. "Is there plague in the capital?"

"It is not plague," said the sot by the window, whose beard was long and gray, and stained yellow with beer and wine. "It is sleep, I tell you."

"How can sleep be a plague?" asked the smallest dwarf, who was also beardless.

"A witch!" said the sot.

"A bad fairy," corrected a fat-faced man.

"She was an enchantress, as I heard it," interposed the pot girl.

"Whatever she was," said the sot, "she was not invited to a birthing celebration."

"That's all tosh," said the tinker. "She would have cursed the princess whether she'd been invited to the naming-day party or not. She was one of those forest witches, driven to the margins a thousand years ago, and a bad lot. She cursed the babe at birth, such that when the girl was eighteen she would prick her finger and sleep forever."

The fat-faced man wiped his forehead. He was sweating, although it was not warm. "As I heard it, she was going to die, but another fairy, a good one this time, commuted her magical death sentence to one of sleep. Magical sleep," he added.

"So," said the sot. "She pricked her finger on something-or-other. And she fell asleep. And the other people in the castle – the lord and the lady, the butcher, baker, milkmaid, lady-in-waiting – all of them slept, as she slept. None of them have aged a day since they closed their eyes."

"There were roses," said the pot girl. "Roses that grew up around the castle. And the forest grew thicker, until it became impassible. This was, what, a hundred years ago?"

"Sixty. Perhaps eighty," said a woman who had not spoken until now. "I know, because my aunt Letitia remembered it happening, when she was a girl, and she was no more than seventy when she died of the bloody flux, and that was only five years ago come Summer's End."

"...and brave men," continued the pot girl, "aye, and brave women too, they say, have attempted to travel to the Forest of Acaire, to the castle at its heart, to wake the princess, and, in waking her, to wake all the sleepers, but each and every one of those heroes ended their lives lost in the forest, murdered by bandits, or impaled upon the thorns of the rose bushes that encircle the castle –"

"Wake her how?" asked the middle-sized dwarf, hand still clutching his rock, for he thought in essentials.

"The usual method," said the pot girl, and she blushed. "Or so the tales have it."

"Right," said the tallest dwarf, who was also beardless. "So, bowl of cold water poured on the face and a cry of 'Wakey! Wakey!'?"

"A kiss," said the sot. "But nobody has ever got that close. They've been trying for sixty years or more. They say the witch –"

"Fairy," said the fat man.

"Enchantress," corrected the pot girl.

"Whatever she is," said the sot. "She's still there. That's what they say. If you get that close. If you make it through the roses, she'll be waiting for you. She's old as the hills, evil as a snake, all malevolence and magic and death."

The smallest dwarf tipped his head on one side. "So, there's a sleeping woman in a castle, and perhaps a witch or fairy there with her. Why is there also a plague?"

"Over the last year," said the fat-faced man. "It started a year ago, in the north, beyond the capital. I heard about it first from travelers coming from Stede, which is near the Forest of Acaire."

"People fell asleep in the towns," said the pot girl.

"Lots of people fall asleep," said the tallest dwarf. Dwarfs sleep rarely: twice a year at most, for several weeks at a time, but he had slept enough in his long lifetime that he did not regard sleep as anything special or unusual.

"They fall asleep whatever they are doing, and they do not wake up," said the sot. "Look at us. We fled the towns to come here. We have brothers and sisters, wives and children, sleeping now in their houses or cowsheds, at their workbenches. All of us."

"It is moving faster and faster," said a thin, red-haired woman who had not spoken previously. "Now it covers a mile, perhaps two miles, each day."

"It will be here tomorrow," said the sot, and he drained his flagon, then gestured to the innkeeper to fill it once more. "There is nowhere for us to go to escape it. Tomorrow, everything here will be asleep. Some of us have resolved to escape into drunkenness before the sleep takes us."

"What is there to be afraid of in sleep?" asked the smallest dwarf. "It's just sleep. We all do it."

"Go and look," said the sot. He threw back his head, and drank as much as he could from his flagon. Then he looked back at them, with eyes unfocused, as if he were surprised to still see them there. "Well, go on. Go and look for yourselves." He swallowed the remaining drink, then he lay his head upon the table.

They went and looked.

"Asleep?" asked the queen. "Explain yourselves. How so, asleep?"

The dwarf stood upon the table so he could look her in the eye. "Asleep," he repeated. "Sometimes crumpled upon the ground. Sometimes standing. They sleep in their smithies, at their awls, on milking stools. The animals sleep in the fields. Birds, too, slept, and we saw them in trees or dead and broken in fields where they had fallen from the sky."

The queen wore a wedding gown, blindingly white, whiter than the snow, as white as her skin. Around her, attendants, maids of honor, dressmakers, and milliners clustered and fussed.

"And why did you three also not fall asleep?"

The dwarf shrugged. He had a russet-brown beard that had always made the queen think of an angry hedgehog attached to the lower portion of his face. "Dwarfs are magical things. This sleep is a magical thing also. I felt sleepy, mind."

"And then?"

She was the queen, and she was questioning him as if they were alone. Her attendants began removing her gown, taking it away, folding and wrapping it, so the final laces and ribbons could be attached to it, so it would be perfect.

Tomorrow was the queen's wedding day. Everything needed to be perfect.

"By the time we returned to Foxen's inn they were all asleep, every man jack and jill of them. It is expanding, the zone of the spell, a few miles every day. We think it is expanding faster with each day that passes."

The mountains that separated the two lands were impossibly high, but not wide. The queen could count the miles. She pushed one pale hand through her raven-black hair, and she looked most serious.

"What do you think, then?" she asked the dwarf. "If I went there. Would I sleep, as they did?"

He scratched his arse, unselfconsciously. "You slept for a year," he said. "And then you woke again, none the worse for it. If any of the bigguns can stay awake there, it's you."

Outside, the townsfolk were hanging bunting in the streets and decorating their doors and windows with white flowers. Silverware had been polished and protesting children had been forced into tubs of lukewarm water (the oldest child always got the first dunk and the hottest, cleanest water) and then scrubbed with rough flannels until their faces were raw and red; they were then ducked under the water, and the backs of their ears were washed as well.

"I am afraid," said the queen, "that there will be no wedding tomorrow."

She called for a map of the kingdom, identified the villages closest to the mountains, and sent messengers to tell the inhabitants to evacuate to the coast or risk royal displeasure.

She called for her first minister and informed him that he would be responsible for the kingdom in her absence, and that he should do his best neither to lose it nor to break it.

She called for her fiancé and told him not to take on so, and that they would still soon be married, even if he was but a prince and she already a queen, and she chucked him beneath his pretty chin and kissed him until he smiled.

She called for her mail shirt.

She called for her sword.

She called for provisions, and for her horse, and then she rode out of the palace, toward the east.

It was a full day's ride before she saw, ghostly and distant, like clouds against the sky, the shape of the mountains that bordered the edge of her kingdom.

The dwarfs were waiting for her, at the last inn in the foothills of the mountains, and they led her down deep into the tunnels, the way that the dwarfs travel. She had lived with them, when she was little more than a child, and she was not afraid.

The dwarfs did not speak to her as they walked the deep paths, except, on more than one occasion, to say, "Mind your head."

"HAVE YOU NOTICED," asked the shortest of the dwarfs, "something unusual?" They had names, the dwarfs, but human beings were not permitted to know what they were, such things being sacred.

The queen had once a name, but nowadays people only ever called her Your Majesty. Names are in short supply in this telling.

"I have noticed many unusual things," said the tallest of the dwarfs.

They were in Goodmaster Foxen's inn.

"Have you noticed, that even among all the sleepers, there is something that does not sleep?"

"I have not," said the second tallest, scratching his beard. "For each of them is just as we left him or her. Head down, drowsing, scarcely breathing enough to disturb the cobwebs that now festoon them…"

"The cobweb spinners do not sleep," said the tallest dwarf.

It was the truth. Industrious spiders had threaded their webs from finger to face, from beard to table. There was a modest web between the deep cleavage of the pot girl's breasts. There was a thick cobweb that stained the sot's beard gray. The webs shook and swayed in the draft of air from the open door.

"I wonder," said one of the dwarfs, "whether they will starve and die, or whether there is some magical source of energy that gives them the ability to sleep for a long time."

"I would presume the latter," said the queen. "If, as you say, the original spell was cast by a witch, seventy years ago, and those who were there sleep even now, like Red-beard beneath his hill, then obviously they have not starved or aged or died."

The dwarfs nodded. "You are very wise," said a dwarf. "You always were wise."

The queen made a sound of horror and of surprise.

"That man," she said, pointing. "He looked at me."

It was the fat-faced man. He had moved slowly, tearing the webbing and moving his face so that he was facing her. He had turned toward her, yes, but he had not opened his eyes.

"People move in their sleep," said the smallest dwarf.

"Yes," said the queen. "They do. But not like that. That was too slow, too stretched, too meant."

"Or perhaps you imagined it," said a dwarf.

The rest of the sleeping heads in that place moved slowly, in a stretched way, as if they meant to move. Now each of the sleeping faces was facing the queen.

"You did not imagine it," said the same dwarf. He was the one with the red-brown beard. "But they are only looking at you with their eyes closed. That is not a bad thing."

The lips of the sleepers moved in unison. No voices, only the whisper of breath through sleeping lips.

"Did they just say what I thought they said?" asked the shortest dwarf.

"They said, 'Mama. It is my birthday,'" said the queen, and she shivered.

THEY RODE NO horses. The horses they passed all slept, standing in fields, and could not be woken.

The queen walked fast. The dwarfs walked twice as fast as she did, in order to keep up.

The queen found herself yawning.

"Bend over, toward me," said the tallest dwarf. She did so. The dwarf slapped her around the face. "Best to stay awake," he said, cheerfully.

"I only yawned," said the queen.

"How long, do you think, to the castle?" asked the smallest dwarf.

"If I remember my tales and my maps correctly," said the queen, "the Forest of Acaire is about seventy miles from here. Three days' march." And then she said, "I will need to sleep tonight. I cannot walk for another three days."

"Sleep, then," said the dwarfs. "We will wake you at sunrise."

She went to sleep that night in a hayrick, in a meadow, with the dwarfs around her, wondering if she would ever wake to see another morning.

*　*　*

THE CASTLE IN the Forest of Acaire was a gray, blocky thing, all grown over with climbing roses. They tumbled down into the moat and grew almost as high as the tallest tower. Each year the roses grew out farther: close to the stone of the castle there were only dead, brown stems and creepers, with old thorns sharp as knives. Fifteen feet away the plants were green and the blossoming roses grew thickly. The climbing roses, living and dead, were a brown skeleton, splashed with color, that rendered the gray fastness less precise.

The trees in the Forest of Acaire were pressed thickly together, and the forest floor was dark. A century before, it had been a forest only in name: it had been hunting lands, a royal park, home to deer and wild boar and birds beyond counting. Now the forest was a dense tangle, and the old paths through the forest were overgrown and forgotten.

The fair-haired girl in the high tower slept.

All the people in the castle slept. Each of them was fast asleep, excepting only one.

The old woman's hair was gray, streaked with white, and was so sparse her scalp showed. She hobbled, angrily, through the castle, leaning on her stick, as if she were driven only by hatred, slamming doors, talking to herself as she walked. "Up the blooming stairs and past the blinking cook and what are you cooking now, eh, great lard-arse, nothing in your pots and pans but dust and more dust, and all you ever ruddy do is snore."

Into the kitchen garden, neatly tended. The old woman picked rampion and rocket, and she pulled a large turnip from the ground.

Eighty years before, the palace had held five hundred chickens; the pigeon coop had been home to hundreds of fat white doves; rabbits had run, white-tailed, across the greenery of the grass square inside the castle walls, and fish had swum in the moat and the pond: carp and trout and perch. There remained now only three chickens. All the sleeping fish had been netted and carried out of the water. There were no more rabbits, no more doves.

She had killed her first horse sixty years back, and eaten as much of it as she could before the flesh went rainbow-colored and the carcass began to stink and crawl with blueflies and maggots. Now she butchered the larger mammals only in midwinter, when nothing rotted and she could hack and sear frozen chunks of the animal's corpse until the spring thaw.

The old woman passed a mother, asleep, with a baby dozing at her breast. She dusted them, absently, as she passed and made certain that the baby's sleepy mouth remained on the nipple.

She ate her meal of turnips and greens in silence.

IT WAS THE first great grand city they had come to. The city gates were high and impregnably thick, but they were open wide.

The three dwarfs were all for going around it, for they were uncomfortable in cities, distrusted houses and streets as unnatural things, but they followed their queen.

Once in the city, the sheer numbers of people made them uncomfortable. There were sleeping riders on sleeping horses, sleeping cabmen up on still carriages that held sleeping passengers, sleeping children clutching their toys and hoops and the whips for their spinning tops; sleeping flower women at their stalls of brown, rotten, dried flowers; even sleeping fishmongers beside their marble slabs. The slabs were covered with the remains of stinking fish, and they were crawling with maggots. The rustle and movement of the maggots was the only movement and noise the queen and the dwarfs encountered.

"We should not be here," grumbled the dwarf with the angry brown beard.

"This road is more direct than any other road we could follow," said the queen. "Also it leads to the bridge. The other roads would force us to ford the river."

The queen's temper was equable. She went to sleep at night, and she woke in the morning, and the sleeping sickness had not touched her.

The maggots' rustlings, and, from time to time, the gentle snores and shifts of the sleepers, were all that they heard as they made their way through the city. And then a small child, asleep on a step, said, loudly and clearly, "Are you spinning? Can I see?"

"Did you hear that?" asked the queen.

The tallest dwarf said only, "Look! The sleepers are waking!"

He was wrong. They were not waking.

The sleepers were standing, however. They were pushing themselves slowly to their feet, and taking hesitant, awkward, sleeping steps. They were sleepwalkers, trailing gauze cobwebs behind them. Always, there were cobwebs being spun.

"How many people, human people I mean, live in a city?" asked the smallest dwarf.

"It varies," said the Queen. "In our kingdom, no more than twenty, perhaps thirty thousand people. This seems bigger than our cities. I would think fifty thousand people. Or more. Why?"

"Because," said the dwarf, "they appear to all be coming after us."

Sleeping people are not fast. They stumble; they stagger; they move like children wading through rivers of treacle, like old people whose feet are weighed down by thick, wet mud.

The sleepers moved toward the dwarfs and the queen. They were easy for the dwarfs to outrun, easy for the queen to outwalk. And yet, and yet, there were so many of them. Each street they came to was filled with sleepers, cobweb-shrouded, eyes tightly closed or eyes open and rolled back in their heads showing only the whites, all of them shuffling sleepily forward.

The queen turned and ran down an alleyway and the dwarfs ran with her.

"This is not honorable," said a dwarf. "We should stay and fight."

"There is no honor," gasped the queen, "in fighting an opponent who has no idea that you are even there. No honor in fighting someone who is dreaming of fishing or of gardens or of long-dead lovers."

"What would they do if they caught us?" asked the dwarf beside her.

"Do you wish to find out?" asked the queen.

"No," admitted the dwarf.

They ran, and they ran, and they did not stop from running until they had left the city by the far gates, and had crossed the bridge that spanned the river.

*   *   *

A WOODCUTTER, ASLEEP by the bole of a tree half-felled half a century before, and now grown into an arch, opened his mouth as the queen and the dwarfs passed and said, "So I hold the spindle in one hand, and the yarn in the other? My, the tip of the spindle looks so very sharp!"

Three bandits, asleep in the middle of what remained of the trail, their limbs crooked as if they had fallen asleep while hiding in a tree above and had tumbled, without waking, to the ground below, said, in unison, without waking, "My mother has forbidden me to spin."

One of them, a huge man, fat as a bear in autumn, seized the queen's ankle as she came close to him. The smallest dwarf did not hesitate: he lopped the hand off with his ax, and the queen pulled the man's fingers away, one by one, until the hand fell on the leaf mold.

"Let me just spin a little thread," said the three bandits as they slept, with one voice, while the blood oozed indolently onto the ground from the stump of the fat man's arm. "I would be so happy if only you would let me spin a little thread."

THE OLD WOMAN had not climbed the tallest tower in a dozen years, and even she could not have told you why she felt impelled to make the attempt on this day. It was a laborious climb, and each step took its toll on her knees and on her hips. She walked up the curving stone stairwell, each small shuffling step she took an agony. There were no railings there, nothing to make the steep steps easier. She leaned on her stick, sometimes, to catch her breath, and then she kept climbing.

She used the stick on the webs, too: thick cobwebs hung and covered the stairs, and the old woman shook her stick at them, pulling the webs apart, leaving spiders scurrying for the walls.

The climb was long, and arduous, but eventually she reached the tower room.

There was nothing in the room but a spindle and a stool, beside one slitted window, and a bed in the center of the round room. The bed was opulent: unfaded crimson and gold cloth was visible beneath the dusty netting that covered it and protected its sleeping occupant from the world.

The spindle sat on the ground, beside the stool, where it had fallen seventy years before.

The old woman pushed at the netting with her stick, and dust filled the air. She stared at the sleeper on the bed.

The girl's hair was the golden yellow of meadow flowers. Her lips were the pink of the roses that climbed the palace walls. She had not seen daylight in a long time, but her skin was creamy, neither pallid nor unhealthy.

Her chest rose and fell, almost imperceptibly, in the semidarkness.

The old woman reached down and picked up the spindle. She said, aloud, "If I drove this spindle through your blooming heart, then you'd not be so pretty-pretty, would you? Eh? Would you?"

She walked toward the sleeping girl in the dusty white dress. Then she lowered her hand. "No. I can't. I wish to all the gods I could."

All of her senses were fading with age, but she thought she heard voices from the forest. Long ago she had seen them come, the princes and the heroes, and watched them perish, impaled upon the thorns of the roses, but it had been a long time since anyone, hero or otherwise, had reached as far as the castle.

"Eh," she said aloud, as she said so much aloud, for who was to hear her? "Even if they come, they'll die screaming on the blinking thorns. There's nothing they can do – that anyone can do. Nothing at all."

THEY FELT THE castle long before they saw it: felt it as a wave of sleep that pushed them away. If they walked toward it their heads fogged, their minds frayed, their spirits fell, their thoughts clouded. The moment they turned away they woke up into the world, felt brighter, saner, wiser.

The queen and the dwarfs pushed deeper into the mental fog.

Sometimes a dwarf would yawn and stumble. Each time the other dwarfs would take him by the arms and march him forward, struggling and muttering, until his mind returned.

The queen stayed awake, although the forest was filled with people she knew could not be there. They walked beside her on the path. Sometimes they spoke to her.

"Let us now discuss how diplomacy is affected by matters of natural philosophy," said her father.

"My sisters ruled the world," said her stepmother, dragging her iron shoes along the forest path. They glowed a dull orange, yet none of the dry leaves burned where the shoes touched them. "The mortal folk rose up against us, they cast us down. And so we waited, in crevices, in places they do not see us. And now, they adore me. Even you, my stepdaughter. Even you adore me."

"You are so beautiful," said her mother, who had died so very long ago. "Like a crimson rose fallen in the snow."

Sometimes wolves ran beside them, pounding dust and leaves up from the forest floor, although the passage of the wolves did not disturb the huge cobwebs that hung like veils across the path. Also, sometimes the wolves ran through the trunks of trees and off into the darkness.

The queen liked the wolves, and was sad when one of the dwarfs began shouting, saying that the spiders were bigger than pigs, and the wolves vanished from her head and from the world. (It was not so. They were only spiders, of a regular size, used to spinning their webs undisturbed by time and by travelers.)

THE DRAWBRIDGE ACROSS the moat was down, and they crossed it, although everything seemed to be pushing them away. They could not enter the castle, however: thick thorns filled the gateway, and fresh growth was covered with roses.

The queen saw the remains of men in the thorns: skeletons in armor and skeletons unarmored. Some of the skeletons were high on the sides of the castle, and the queen wondered if they had climbed up, seeking an entry, and died there, or if they had died on the ground and been carried upward as the roses grew.

She came to no conclusions. Either way was possible.

And then her world was warm and comfortable, and she became certain that closing her eyes for only a handful of moments would not be harmful. Who would mind?

"Help me," croaked the queen.

The dwarf with the brown beard pulled a thorn from the rosebush nearest to him, jabbed it hard into the queen's thumb, and pulled it out again. A drop of deep blood dripped onto the flagstones of the gateway.

"Ow!" said the queen. And then, "Thank you!"

They stared at the thick barrier of thorns, the dwarfs and the queen. She reached out and picked a rose from the thorn-creeper nearest her and bound it into her hair.

"We could tunnel our way in," said the dwarfs. "Go under the moat and into the foundations and up. Only take us a couple of days."

The queen pondered. Her thumb hurt, and she was pleased her thumb hurt. She said, "This began here eighty or so years ago. It began slowly. It spread only recently. It is spreading faster and faster. We do not know if the sleepers can ever wake. We do not know anything, save that we may not actually have another two days."

She eyed the dense tangle of thorns, living and dead, decades of dried, dead plants, their thorns as sharp in death as ever they were when alive. She walked along the wall until she reached a skeleton, and she pulled the rotted cloth from its shoulders, and felt it as she did so. It was dry, yes. It would make good kindling.

"Who has the tinder box?" she asked.

THE OLD THORNS burned so hot and so fast. In fifteen minutes orange flames snaked upward: they seemed, for a moment, to engulf the building, and then they were gone, leaving just blackened stone. The remaining thorns, those strong enough to have withstood the heat, were easily cut through by the queen's sword, and were hauled away and tossed into the moat.

The four travelers went into the castle.

THE OLD WOMAN peered out of the slitted window at the flames below her. Smoke drifted in through the window, but neither the flames nor the roses reached the highest tower. She knew that the castle was being attacked, and she would have hidden in the tower room had there been anywhere to hide, had the sleeper not been on the bed.

She swore, and began, laboriously, to walk down the steps, one at a time. She intended to make it down as far as the castle's battlements, where she could make it to the far side of the building, to the cellars. She could hide there. She knew the building better than anybody. She was slow, but she was cunning, and she could wait. Oh, she could wait.

She heard their calls rising up the stairwell. "This way!" "Up here!" "It feels worse this way. Come on! Quickly!" She turned around, then did her best to hurry upward, but her legs moved no faster than they had when she was climbing earlier that day. They caught her just as she reached the top of the steps, three men, no higher than her hips, closely followed by a young woman in travel-stained clothes, with the blackest hair the old woman had ever seen.

The young woman said, "Seize her," in a tone of casual command.

The little men took her stick. "She's stronger than she looks," said one of them, his head still ringing from the blow she had got in with the stick before he had taken it. They walked her back into the round tower room.

"The fire?" said the old woman, who had not talked to anyone who could answer her for seven decades. "Was anyone killed in the fire? Did you see the king or the queen?"

The young woman shrugged. "I don't think so. The sleepers we passed were all inside, and the walls are thick. Who are you?"

Names. Names. The old woman squinted, then she shook her head. She was herself, and the name she had been born with had been eaten by time and lack of use.

"Where is the princess?"

The old woman just stared at her.

"And why are you awake?"

She said nothing. They spoke urgently to one another then, the little men and the queen. "Is she a witch? There's a magic about her, but I do not think it's of her making."

"Guard her," said the queen. "If she is a witch, that stick might be important. Keep it from her."

"Eh? It's my blooming stick," said the old woman. "I think it was my father's. But he had no more use for it."

The queen ignored her. She walked to the bed, pulled down the silk netting. The sleeper's face stared blindly up at them.

"So this is where it began," said one of the little men.

"On her birthday," said another.

"Well," said the third. "Somebody's got to do the honors."

"I shall," said the queen, gently. She lowered her face to the sleeping woman's. She touched the pink lips to her own carmine lips and she kissed the sleeping girl long and hard.

"Did it work?" asked a dwarf.

"I do not know," said the queen. "But I feel for her, poor thing. Sleeping her life away."

"You slept for a year in the same witch-sleep," said the dwarf. "You did not starve. You did not rot."

The figure on the bed stirred, as if she were having a bad dream from which she was fighting to wake herself.

The queen ignored her. She had noticed something on the floor beside the bed. She reached down and picked it up. "Now this," she said. "This smells of magic."

"There's magic all through this," said the smallest dwarf.

"No, this," said the queen. She showed him the wooden spindle, the base half wound around with yarn. "This smells of magic."

"It was here, in this ruddy room," said the old woman, suddenly. "And I was little more than a girl. I had never gone so far before, but I climbed all the steps, and I went up and up and round and round until I came to the topmost room. I saw that bed, the one you see, although there was nobody in it. There was only an old woman I didn't know, sitting on the stool, spinning wool into yarn with her spindle. I had never seen a spindle before. She asked if I would like a go. She took the wool in her hand and gave me the spindle to hold. And then she held my thumb and pressed it against the point of the spindle until blood flowed, and she touched the blooming blood to the thread. And then she said..."

A voice interrupted her.

A young voice it was, a girl's voice, but still sleep-thickened. "I said, now I take your sleep from you, girl, just as I take from you your ability to harm me in my sleep, for someone needs to be awake while I sleep.

Your family, your friends, your world will sleep too. And then I lay down on the bed, and I slept, and they slept, and as each of them slept I stole a little of their life, a little of their dreams, and as I slept I took back my youth and my beauty and my power. I slept and I grew strong. I undid the ravages of time and I built myself a world of sleeping slaves."

She was sitting up in the bed. She looked so beautiful, and so very young.

The queen looked at the girl and saw what she was searching for: the same look that she had seen, long ago, in her stepmother's eyes, and she knew what manner of creature this girl was.

"We had been led to believe," said the tallest dwarf, "that when you woke, the rest of the world would wake with you."

"Why ever would you think that?" asked the golden-haired girl, all childlike and innocent (ah, but her eyes! Her eyes were so old). "I like them asleep. They are more... biddable." She stopped for a moment. Then she smiled. "Even now they come for you. I have called them here."

"It's a high tower," said the queen. "And sleeping people do not move fast. We still have a little time to talk, your darkness."

"Who are you? Why would we talk? Why do you know to address me that way?" The girl climbed off the bed and stretched deliciously, pushing each fingertip out before running each fingertip through her golden hair. She smiled, and it was as if the sun shone into that dim room. "The little people will stop where they are, now. I do not like them. And you, girl. You will sleep too."

"No," said the queen.

She hefted the spindle. The yarn wrapped around it was black with age and with time.

The dwarfs stopped where they stood, and they swayed, and closed their eyes.

The queen said, "It's always the same with your kind. You need youth and you need beauty. You used your own up so long ago, and now you find ever-more-complex ways of obtaining them. And you always want power."

They were almost nose to nose now, and the fair-haired girl seemed so much younger than the queen.

"Why don't you just go to sleep?" asked the girl, and she smiled guilelessly, just as the queen's stepmother had smiled when she wanted something. There was a noise on the stairs, far below them.

"I slept for a year in a glass coffin," said the queen. "And the woman who put me there was much more powerful and dangerous than you will ever be."

"More powerful than I am?" The girl seemed amused. "I have a million sleepers under my control. With every moment that I slept I grew in power, and the circle of dreams grows faster and faster with every passing day. I have my youth – so much youth! I have my beauty. No weapon can harm me. Nobody alive is more powerful than I am."

She stopped and stared at the queen.

"You are not of our blood," she said. "But you have some of the skill." She smiled, the smile of an innocent girl who has woken on a spring morning. "Ruling the world will not be easy. Nor will maintaining order among those of the Sisterhood who have survived into this degenerate age. I will need someone to be my eyes and ears, to administer justice, to attend to things when I am otherwise engaged. I will stay at the center of the web. You will not rule with me, but beneath me, but you will still rule, and rule continents, not just a tiny kingdom." She reached out a hand and stroked the queen's pale skin, which, in the dim light of that room, seemed almost as white as snow.

The queen said nothing.

"Love me," said the girl. "All will love me, and you, who woke me, you must love me most of all."

The queen felt something stirring in her heart. She remembered her stepmother, then. Her stepmother had liked to be adored. Learning how to be strong, to feel her own emotions and not another's, had been hard; but once you learned the trick of it, you did not forget. And she did not wish to rule continents.

The girl smiled at her with eyes the color of the morning sky.

The queen did not smile. She reached out her hand. "Here," she said. "This is not mine."

She passed the spindle to the old woman beside her. The old woman hefted it, thoughtfully. She began to unwrap the yarn from the spindle with arthritic fingers. "This was my blooming, bollocking life," she said. "This thread was my life..."

"It was your life. You gave it to me," said the sleeper, irritably. "And it has gone on much too long."

The tip of the spindle was still sharp after so many decades.

The old woman, who had once, long, long ago, been a princess, held the yarn tightly in her left hand, and she thrust the point of the spindle at the golden-haired girl's breast.

The girl looked down as a trickle of red blood ran down her breast and stained her white dress crimson.

"No weapon can harm me," she said, and her girlish voice was petulant. "Not anymore. Look. It's only a scratch."

"It's not a weapon," said the queen, who understood what had happened. "It's your own magic. And a scratch is all that was needed."

The girl's blood soaked into the thread that had once been wrapped about the spindle, the thread that ran from the spindle to the raw wool in the old woman's left hand.

The girl looked down at the blood staining her dress, and at the blood on the thread, and she said only, "It was just a prick of the skin, nothing more." She seemed confused.

The noise on the stairs was getting louder. A slow, irregular shuffling, as if a hundred sleepwalkers were coming up a stone spiral staircase with their eyes closed.

The room was small, and there was nowhere to hide, and the room's windows were two narrow slits in the stones.

The old woman, who had not slept in so many decades, she who had once been a princess, said, "You took my blinking dreams. You took my sleep. Now, that's enough of all that." She was a very old woman: her fingers were gnarled, like the roots of a hawthorn bush. Her nose was long, and her eyelids drooped, but there was a look in her eyes in that moment that was the look of someone young.

The old woman swayed, and then she staggered, and she would have fallen to the floor if the queen had not caught her first.

The queen carried the old woman to the bed, marveling at how little she weighed, and placed her on the crimson counterpane. The old woman's chest rose and fell.

The noise on the stairs was louder now. Then a silence, followed, suddenly, by a hubbub, as if a hundred people were talking at once, all surprised and angry and confused.

The beautiful girl said, "But –" and now there was nothing girlish or beautiful about her. Her face fell and became less shapely. She reached down to the smallest dwarf, pulled his hand ax from his belt. She fumbled with the ax, held it up threateningly, with hands all wrinkled and worn.

The queen drew her sword (the blade's edge was notched and damaged from the thorns) but instead of striking, she took a step backward.

"Listen! They are waking up," she said. "They are all waking up. Tell me again about the youth you stole from them. Tell me again about your beauty and your power. Tell me again how clever you were, your darkness."

When the people reached the tower room, they saw an old woman asleep on a bed, and they saw the queen, standing tall, and beside her, the dwarfs, who were shaking their heads, or scratching them.

They saw something else on the floor also: a tumble of bones, a hank of hair as fine and as white as fresh-spun cobwebs, a tracery of gray rags across it, and over all of it, an oily dust.

"Take care of her," said the queen, pointing with the dark wooden spindle at the old woman on the bed. "She saved your lives."

She left, then, with the dwarfs. None of the people in that room or on the steps dared to stop them or would ever understand what had happened.

A MILE OR so from the castle, in a clearing in the Forest of Acaire, the queen and the dwarfs lit a fire of dry twigs, and in it they burned the thread and the fiber. The smallest dwarf chopped the spindle into fragments of black wood with his ax, and they burned them too. The wood chips gave off a noxious smoke as they burned, which made the queen cough, and the smell of old magic was heavy in the air.

Afterward, they buried the charred wooden fragments beneath a rowan tree.

By evening they were on the outskirts of the forest, and had reached a cleared track. They could see a village across the hill, and smoke rising from the village chimneys.

"So," said the dwarf with the beard. "If we head due west, we can be at the mountains by the end of the week, and we'll have you back in your palace in Kanselaire within ten days."

"Yes," said the queen.

"And your wedding will be late, but it will happen soon after your return, and the people will celebrate, and there will be joy unbounded through the kingdom."

"Yes," said the queen. She said nothing, but sat on the moss beneath an oak tree and tasted the stillness, heartbeat by heartbeat.

There are choices, she thought, when she had sat long enough. There are always choices.

She made her choice.

The queen began to walk, and the dwarfs followed her.

"You do know we're heading east, don't you?" said one of the dwarfs.

"Oh yes," said the queen.

"Well, that's all right then," said the dwarf.

They walked to the east, all four of them, away from the sunset and the lands they knew, and into the night.

CAVE AND JULIA
M. John Harrison

M. John Harrison (ambientehotel.wordpress.com) joined *New Worlds* in 1968 as editor and reviewer. His first novel, *The Committed Men*, appeared in 1971, as did *The Pastel City*, first in the "Viriconium" fantasy series that continued with *A Storm of Wings*, *In Viriconium*, and collections *Viriconium Nights* and *Viriconium*. His other novels include *The Centauri Device*, *Signs of Life*, *Climbers*, and Kefahuchi Tract trilogy *Light*, *Nova Swing*, and *Empty Space*. Harrison has also written four contemporary cat fantasies as Gabriel King (collaborating with Jane Johnson), beginning with *The Wild Road*, and several short story collections, including *Things That Never Happen*. He continues to review fiction and non-fiction for the *Guardian*.

WHEN CAVE MET Julia Vicente, she was living quietly in one of the four storey houses on the hill which overlooks the harbour.

People still gave her space. They knew her founding narrative – the loss of her brother and the subsequent prosecution for manslaughter. They knew more about those two events than the life that had followed – the long struggle to adjust to self-imposed exile on our side of things, the bouts of post-traumatic stress which made her work difficult, the disastrous marriages to bankers and minor celebrities, the failed film career, the eventual return to Autotelia to live quietly in a post-industrial port which, though it reminded her daily of her tragedy, seemed at a safe remove from some other concept that frightened her more. She was a gaunt woman by then, tallish, full of an energy that rarely showed. A heavy smoker. She liked to walk in the gentrified dockyards, where art galleries were replacing ships, and restaurants the old dock furniture. She had written two or three volumes of theatre criticism, a successful novel. She had a daughter, three or four years old, from her third marriage.

Cave, a cultural journalist with a broad remit, took her to restaurants she claimed she was no longer able to afford. In return she showed him the town's prized possessions: a collection of early Doul Kiminic watercolours of eviscerated horses and grieving women; and the municipal crematorium, the curious truncated cylinder of which was decorated on the outside with a wrap-around mural like a 1920s woodcut, showing the dead silhouetted by the invisible sun of the afterlife.

"This is awful," Cave said.

"Isn't it?"

They got on well together. Then one morning she telephoned him and said: "You don't ask me about my life."

She was known to be difficult, and Cave had come to Autotelia to write a piece about someone else. He didn't want complications; he wanted his relationship with Julia to remain personal. More importantly, perhaps, he felt emotionally disqualified by the central event of her history. He felt he had nothing to offer. All of this made him wary, so he replied:

"No one likes to pry."

"Are you dishonest, or only naive?" she asked, and hung up.

Perhaps an hour later he called her back. "I'm sorry," he said. He thought she would put the phone down again but instead she said:

"I don't see my brother anymore."

"That's a curious way to put it."

"I mean literally. For years afterwards I saw him almost every day. He wasn't here, obviously: he was dead. But I saw him." She still dreamed of the event itself – if, she said, that word could be used to describe what she remembered. "But I don't see him anymore. He's invisible now. I don't even miss him. He's just one of the fictions that lives here."

She was silent for a moment. Then she said:

"I'm sorry, my daughter has woken up. Will you wait a moment while I see to her? Do you mind?"

Cave said he didn't mind, and for some time all he heard was the child's voice, thin and distant at the other end of the connection. He began to think Julia Vicente had forgotten him. "Hello?" he said. If the child had turned out to be ill, he should ring off and try later. Instead he hung on, listening to that long, unassuageable, archaic complaint. "She's always disoriented when she wakes up," Julia said when she returned to the phone. "Always at a loss." For a moment she seemed both impatient and puzzled. Then she laughed. "I'm her mother," she said, as if this wasn't just a new discovery but a new kind of fact

WHEN AUTOTELIANS SAY "those who came before us", it's clear they aren't talking about genetic precursors. There is archeological evidence all over the continent, but the Autotelians resist connection to it.

Age fourteen, Julia Vicente had taken her brother up to one of the mysterious sites on the karst plateau above the town and there, she claimed, "lost him". Since this was clearly unlikely, it was assumed by the court that they had approached one of the flimsily fenced sink-holes which penetrate the limestone foundations of the site, and that he had fallen in. Subsequently the girl had wandered distractedly about in the ruins, being found asleep near a dry fountain after a week-long search by police and local quarry workers. Some months later, on her fifteenth birthday, she was still unable to provide a coherent account of what had happened. No one, the court concluded, could mistake such a tragic incident for "manslaughter"; the child – eight years old and dark-eyed, skinny, lively, beloved by everyone – had been as difficult to control as his sister. But by then, as far as Julia Vicente was concerned, the damage was done.

The Autotelian karst drains itself, through a complex of vast underground caverns – many of which have never been entered – directly into the sea. That whole year, and to a lesser extent the year after, bodies were washed up all along that part of the coast, some whole, some in pieces. A proportion were claimed; many – like the mysterious "Mr English", delivered by a high tide one summer afternoon on what the European news services referred to as "Autotelia's Riviera" – were not. The sexes tended to be evenly represented. The oldest item was the lower left leg of a woman of at least sixty years; the youngest a complete male toddler wearing a wristband with the name Ellis, never identified. There were pairs of hands in an expensive suitcase, and heads wrapped carefully in clingfilm or hastily tied up, bunny-ears, in plastic bags. In the south of Autotelia, especially, it was a bad year for bodies; but the body of the vanished brother didn't show up among them. Passive and silent, full of some incommunicable anger, the sister attempted suicide, spent time in institutions; then, her work suddenly becoming popular, left the country for a new life on our side of things.

All of this, Julia rehearsed for Cave over supper in the maze of old docks not far from his hotel, adding nothing to the popular account.

They had spent the afternoon in the port's only cinema, lit by a dull greenish light from above while the sound system produced faint tango music and they waited for a film that never played. Cave had been as delighted by the cinema – the mossy folds of the curtain, the faintly glowing exit sign, the rows of grubby empty seats – as by the incompetence of the projectionist. Now the lamp swung above their table, moving the shadows of the wineglasses regularly but uncomfortably across the tablecloth, like the umbrae and penumbrae of planets. They were the only customers there. The cook came out of his kitchen to look at them. The woman talked, the man bent towards her. Their voices were quiet. The shadows of their hands touched, flickered, then lay flat. The cook watched them with a kind of suppressed amusement.

"So now you know," Julia Vicente said.

"I'm not sure I know any more than I did."

She shrugged. "We'll go there then," she said, "and I'll show you things I told no-one at the time."

The restaurant's pink napery and white wrought-iron partitions reminded Cave of a hairdresser's in 1968. Unsure of what he was being offered, but certain that this bald proposition could only move things in a direction he didn't trust, he explained that his visa only had two days left to run. "There wouldn't be time." She pretended not to understand this. "You should come," she said. "If you had any courage you'd come." It was one thirty in the morning: a waiter dragged a chair around. By then only the casino across the square remained open, drawing people in, fixing them like insects under a jam jar, where they buzzed about energetically without much sign of getting anywhere. A wind came up off the sea, blew sand across the neat cobbles, died away.

"All right," Cave said.

HE WAITED FOR her early next morning at the tourist beach, a deserted, artificial curve of white sand. The day was already sullen and humid, with hidden light penetrating the cloud and heat resonating from the limestone buttresses above the town. Faint residual smells clung in the corners of the sea wall: the previous day's fish, salt, perfume, fried food. For a moment it seemed to Cave like a language, but when he listened it had nothing to say. While he was considering this, Julia came down between the houses towards him, wearing a white sleeveless frock with a picture hat and gloves, waving happily like a much younger woman. "Isn't this awful?" she called. "I bet you hate it!" And when she got close enough to stir the sand with her toe: "Every grain imported from the other side of the country."

Round the point at the south end, she showed him, lay a different kind of beach: brisk inshore winds drove the sea up over the jumbled rocks, the water was a detergent of grey and green, and huge banks of black weed had formed on the tideline. A few yards inland, a path wound its way into the hinterland between undercut slabs of shale. Julia set off along this so quickly Cave was hard put to keep up. His mouth soon became dry, the glare made his eyes sore. The path climbed and climbed. Away from the sea, the air smelled of leafless, thorny vegetation, and behind that its own dry heat. Thirsty and irritable, dazzled by Julia Vicente's bone white frock, he called: "How much further?" She didn't answer. Perhaps she hadn't heard him. A hot breeze rose among the vegetation; her hand went up in a graceful gesture to secure her picture hat. When, a moment later, she stopped and said, "There," in a curiously flat voice, Cave saw the plateau stepping away from him in every direction, a series of shallow, imbricated terraces linked by the remains of broad white avenues. Each terrace supported a clutter of patterned mounds, platforms and ramps – some more sophisticated than others – beneath which, he knew, an elaborate system of tunnels opened into the karst below.

"My god," he said.

"But hardly a new story."

"I don't know what you mean when you say that."

Cave had got to Autotelia by credit card and asking, "Do you speak English?" The day he arrived he had emailed a friend: "Travel is no longer measured by change, only by the time it takes to go the distance. It's tedious, but it's not a journey." Now he wasn't so sure.

In recent centuries, some attempt had been made to reoccupy the ruins. It was hard to see why. There was no water above ground. Shade trees were few and far between. Successive waves of colonialists had fought each other over water rights, relics and ideological interpretation of the remains, and were as long gone now, you felt, as their enigmatic predecessors. Their buildings, assembled from the rubble and set down at the junctions of avenues where they could command the longest view, resembled fortified abbeys or monasteries, the cloisters of which often guarded the only well for miles around. It was to the courtyard of one of these structures that Julia Vicente now led him, via dark shiny passageways, the old laundry, the household gardens choked with a plant that reminded Cave of amarynth, its seedheads like accretions of oily dust at a city corner.

"This is much later than the rest."

Pale rhyolite columns. The sense of an unending afternoon. Light slanted in from the right. Each side of the cloister was six arches long. The courtyard was cobbled with smooth oval stones tipped up on their thin edges. In its centre an octagonal pavement at four corners of which were placed two fluted pillars. From each point of the pavement radiated star-shapes in cobbles of a darker colour, between which a short, parched vegetation grew – not grass but some herb. In the centre stood the fountain, a shallow basin supported by a plinth of caryatids. There was a thin, intermittent central jet of water. A veil of droplets hung down from the edges of the basin.

"Isn't it wonderful?"

"It's very striking," Cave said.

"Why don't you have a closer look?" she invited him.

After three or four paces into the sunlight, Cave was disoriented. He could see the fountain in front of him, but it appeared to be further away than when he had started. From above, the structure was four-lobed, like a clover. The sun baked down on it but it was as if all the heat were generated there between the eight pillars and the pistil of the fountain, then projected upward and outward. Heat ripple affected Cave's vision in some way he didn't understand: everything remained sharp, but he was experiencing a mild vertigo, a stretching-out of things. His lips felt numb and he could no longer feel the cobbles under his feet. "This was a culture of engines," Julia Vicente said. "Some architectural, some sacrificial, some both." Her voice seemed close and intimate. The woman herself leaned out of the cloister, shading her eyes as if Cave had become difficult to see. "What fourteen year old could understand that?"

"I don't care why it was constructed," Cave said, retreating hastily to the cloister. "I don't want to know."

She laughed at him from the shadows.

"If you had any courage you would go all the way," she said.

Cave, who still couldn't see well, took a moment to locate her. She had turned away and was trying to light a cigarette like someone in a strong wind. He made her look at him. "*This* is where the boy disappeared," he said. "This is where you lost him." She shrugged. "Jesus," he said. "When they found you, you'd been here all along." He stared at her for a moment, then pushed her against the back wall of the cloister.

"You weren't lost. You were never lost."

She pulled away from him, took his hand and led him out of the cloister as if he were blind. "Listen," she said, and after a moment or two he thought he heard water rushing through the limestone somewhere deep beneath his feet. By the time they got down from the plateau, it was afternoon and rain was falling on the sea.

"Do you want to swim?"

"In this?"

They sat in the empty cinema again. Cave found he couldn't stop talking. She in turn seemed preoccupied. Eventually she said:

"There are sites like that one all over Autotelia. It's a heritage, but not our own. We've failed to colonise or commodify it. The local town is always named after a flower. The women make fabrics. The men drive around in pick-up trucks trying to sell one another liquid propane. After two or three days it's the most boring place you've ever been. Those old priests convinced each other that the world wouldn't work without intervention. But they're long dead. The gods don't come forth and the approaching thundercloud stays on top of the hill. After a few grand but silent flashes of light, nothing happens. And do you know what?" she said. "That's a good thing, because they were all quite clearly mad anyway."

"Astonishing," Cave said, but only because he felt he had to say something.

His dreams that night were full of mirages.

THE NEXT MORNING he had to leave. He had closed out his other project a little early, but in the end he thought he'd probably done enough. He left his hotel and went down to the tourist beach, where he found the sea calm. Two men were running about on the tideline, throwing something between them. It didn't look like a ball. Heat already blurred the air, resonated from the steep cliffs of the plateau. Cave sat on the sand, and around him everything was suspended in light; everything like a film, wrapped in cameraman sublime, documentary sublime. Light, silhouettes, warmth like a perfect saturated colour, all at once. Distant objects seemed too large. In the end, he told himself for the hundredth time in his life, you are the only description of what there is. All that counts is to be there. A little later, wandering up into the town through the maze of net shops and fish stalls, he read the words "locally sourced" as "locally soured". He knocked on Julia Vicente's door, and she let him in.

"I feel scared this morning," she said. "I don't know what you feel."

"Neither do I," Cave said.

He sat reluctantly watching her prepare the little girl's breakfast, perhaps deliberately allowing a silence to grow.

"Don't you see," she said suddenly, "I can't talk now?"

She studied the base of an enamel milk pan. "The life I'm living," she said, "the life I've been living – I wasn't like this but now I am." And then, suddenly: "I wasn't like this but now I am. Can you see that?" Cave, though he couldn't, said he could. "My brother, all those years ago!" He had no idea what she was trying to say. She put the pan down, then picked it up again. "If nothing happened in the cloister I can't explain the life I've had." She stared at him. "Everything that happened in the cloister was already there. It was already present in some way," she said. "My brother knew that. At the end it tired him out."

"At the end?"

She shrugged but didn't reply.

"I think you've been defending for a long time now," Cave offered.

Julia Vicente considered this. "I have," she said. "I've been defending *so heavily*, but I don't know why. It was all those years ago." She sniffed back a tear. Her daughter looked up instantly from the floor.

Later, unable to make himself leave, Cave tried to work. The sun shone across his eyes. It was impossible to concentrate. Julia had finished the ironing. She was upstairs dressing. She was putting on her make up. Her little girl followed her from room to room, talking softly in the local language and making kissing noises; later, came downstairs and rode a scooter shyly round the tiled floor of the lounge, stopping every often to make sure Cave was paying attention. The phone rang; rang again. The shutters banged in the wind under an eggshell sky. Eventually he got up and took a taxi to the airport.

If it's difficult to understand Autotelia as a place which is both here and not here, a place congruent with what we used to know as the North Sea, the idea that it was once inhabited by something neither human nor pre-human is almost impossible to grasp. In other circumstances, Cave would have described the site on the plateau as a kind of cultural chewing gum, something irritating stuck to the sole of everyone's shoe. He would have dismissed its history, and described his morning among the ruins by describing the landscape – the footprint planed off the top of the hill thousands of years ago for reasons he could never hope to understand; the white cloud bouffant above the mountains to the south; the black smoke on an adjacent hilltop. A single shade tree in the high, dry heat.

TWO MONTHS LATER he was back. He wasn't sure why. He pushed a note under the door of her empty house, discovered the next morning that she was halfway through a tour of provincial theatres and scheduled to return the exact day he left. He spent his mornings visiting by bus the official archeological sites on the plateau, and in the evenings recovered his expenses by writing lacklustre reviews of the beach cafés. He photographed the crematorium murals. He bought a small, not-very-well-known Doul Kiminic – *The Ruined Harvest*, oil on canvas with some water damage in one corner – intending to have it reframed and shipped back to our side of things where he could profit from its mildew tones and desperate body language. He drank. "When the menu offers 'tiny fishes'," he warned his readers, "be cautious. For me, whitebait are tiny fishes. These fishes are three inches long. On the whole, they eat like whitebait; but tiny is a misnomer. 'Quite small' would be better."

Back in London he barely thought of her, yet soon found himself outbound again on a 787 Dreamliner from Heathrow. "Before you ask," he told her when she found him on her doorstep five hours later, "I have no memory of buying the ticket, let alone making the decision." He'd brought the clothes he stood up in, he said; a credit card and his passport.

She laughed. "I've got someone here," she said. "But I can get rid of him tomorrow."

"I don't mind," Cave said.

She shut the door. "Yes you do," she called from inside.

After that, he made the crossing two or three times a year; visits between which the rest of his life suspended itself like a bridge. He drifted across London from employer to employer, assignment to assignment. His career, never spectacular, scaled down to a sort of lucrative pastime. He travelled the Americas, photographing the monastic architecture of the Spanish and Portuguese colonial eras; he bought a garden flat in Barnsbury, Islington. Moving into his forties and perhaps a little fearful, he drank determinedly; as a consequence broke his hip cycling along the bank of the Regents Canal to an interview with two narcissistic conceptual artists in Hackney. Otherwise things remained quiet. He felt his age. He felt his surfaces change and soften, but detected beneath them a concreted layer of debris, an identity he could date very accurately to his struggle across the cloister, a condition of anxiety which founded not just his memories of Autotelia but of himself.

"The fact is," he emailed Julia Vicente, "I can recover so little of that time. The shoreline cliffs crumble into side-streets of tall pastel-coloured apartments. The old dockyard, with its rusty machinery revisioned as art, is an endlessly fragmenting dream, endlessly reconstructing itself. As for you and me, we seem like characters in a film. You never stopped smoking cigarettes; I bought a yellow notebook which I never wrote in. For years I've kept these fragments floating around one another – it's such an effort – attracted into patterns less by the order in which they occurred or by any 'story' I can make about them than by gravity or animal magnetism. But I have no memory at all of the experience as it fell out. Perhaps if I could see you more often, I'd remember more."

It was hard to know what she made of that.

"I've grown used to you being here just the once or twice a year," she replied. "Don't come again too soon, I wouldn't know what to think." In an effort to lessen the impact of this, he saw, she had struck through the word "think" and replaced it with "cook".

He was grateful for the joke. But that night he dreamed he was back in the cloister. This dream was to recur for the rest of his life, presenting as many outcomes as iterations; from it, he would always wake to an emotion he couldn't account: not quite anxiety, not quite despair. He dreamed the white blur of Julia Vicente's face watching from the shadows, immobile and fascinated until the procession of search-and-rescue teams found her and bore her triumphantly home on a stretcher in the bald light and shimmering air of the plateau. The fountain seemed to roar silently. The cloister cobbles softened and parted in the heat, encouraging Cave to slip easily between them into the vast system of varnished-looking natural tubes and slots which, he now saw, underlay everything. It was cold down there; damp, but not fully dark. He could not describe himself as lost, because he had never known where he was. He heard water gushing over faults and lips in tunnels a hundred miles away. Full of terror, he began counting his arms and legs; before he could finish, woke alone. A feeling of bleakness and approaching disaster came out of the dream with him. His room was full of cold grey light. 5am, and traffic was already grinding along Caledonian Road into Kings Cross. He made some coffee, took it back to bed, opened his laptop. Although he knew it would mean nothing, he emailed her:

"What can any of us do but move on? How?" And then: "Did I ever have the slightest idea of your motives?", to which she could only reply puzzledly:

"Of course you did. Of course you did."

Work remained central in Julia's life. She continued to write and publish, though none of her books had the same impact on our side of things as her first. Still pursued, though now by cultural historians rather than cultural journalists, she made hasty public statements about herself which she came to regret. She and Cave exchanged emails, argued, fell out, made friends again. In her fifties she entered a fourth marriage, which lasted as long as any of the others. (At around that time, Cave wrote in his journal, "She arrives at the airport either an hour early or an hour late but in any case attractively deranged. She has no money and her car won't start. She greets you by saying in a loud voice, 'Oh god, things have been horrible,' and doesn't stop talking for some hours. She will insist on driving you somewhere and then forget how to get there and phone husband #4 – who is at that time in another town – for directions.") She dyed the grey out of her hair but rejected all forms of cosmetic surgery; experienced some symptoms of mild arthritis in the fingers of her right hand.

"It's sad to think," she wrote, "that people long ago stopped making full use of you as a human being. You feel as if you have let them down by somehow not being persuasive enough."

The daughter, meanwhile, grew up, evolving from a curious olive-skinned scrap with very black hair into a tall, graceful adolescent obsessed with dogs. This surprised Julia as much as it did Cave. "One moment she was five, the next she was fifteen. I was a little upset at first, but now I'm delighted. Luckily she's very self-absorbed." And then, out of nowhere, a year or two later: "She wants to be an archeologist. I think I might come to London now. There's nothing to keep me here." Cave looked forward to a new beginning, but it was more as if something had ended. The closer they came geographically, the further they drew apart. Sometimes it was as if they had simply changed places: Cave buried himself in his Autotelian journals and memories, revisiting a relationship that had changed so much it was to all intents and purposes over; while Julia Vicente, camped less than two miles away from him in a rather nice house on the banks of the Regents Canal, waited impatiently for his return.

THEY WERE DRINKING red wine in Islington one afternoon when part of the sky went dark. Eddies of wind bullied the street trees around. A single feather floated into view, made its way across Cave's lawn and out over the garden wall, its weird calm transit defining a layer of privileged air at about twice the height of a person. "People don't give in to age now the way they used to," said Julia. The windows behind her blurred with rain, rattled a little in their frames. A summer squall always made her excited. "Age has to find its expression in new ways." It was her topic of the moment. "I don't know anyone, for instance – not anyone who really accepts and understands what age means to them – who hasn't experienced the urge to act out the coming journey."

"Which journey is that?" he teased her.

"You know exactly what I mean!" And then: "Some kind of walkabout: as soon as you get the idea, you feel relief. Here's a way of recognising and accepting that urge to leave everything behind. A way of being thrown by it." Cave considered these rationalisations with as much dignity as he could, then poured her another half glass of red and wondered out loud what would happen to the feather. The rain stopped. "Seriously," she said: "What kind of a map would you use for a journey like that? A final journey?"

Then she laughed and added: "You don't have to answer."

When he first met her, Cave had sometimes glimpsed for an instant the older, tireder woman she would become; now that she was tired all the time, there were brief instants in which the younger woman showed through. Seeing what he thought might be his last chance, he offered:

"I'll answer if you answer."

She stared at him intently. "Answer what?" she said.

"Tell me what you expected to happen in the cloister."

She seemed to relax, as if she had been afraid he might ask something else. "To you? The same as him, perhaps. To me?" She shrugged. "Who knows? Something new."

A child, playing in a garden several houses away, began shouting, "I said I can't do it! I said I can't do it! I said I *can't do it*!" over and over again. At first it was part of a game with friends or siblings, with a pause for laughter between each iteration. Then the other children dropped out and the chant took on values and momentum of its own, on and on, real meaning, real confusion, real rage. After two or three minutes Cave realised it wasn't even the child's own rage, any more than the sentence itself was the child's sentence. It was the rage of some significant adult, overheard in god knew what circumstances.

THE HERONS OF MER DE L'OUEST
M. Bennardo

M. Bennardo (www.mbennardo.com) is the author of more than 40 short stories. His first story appeared in 1999, but the majority of his work has been published in the last two years. He has had stories in *Lightspeed Magazine*, *Asimov's Science Fiction*, *Beneath Ceaseless Skies*, and others. Bennardo is also co-editor of the *Machine of Death* series of anthologies. He lives in Cleveland, Ohio.

NOVEMBER 1761

A LOON CALLED this morning, loud and clear in the cold hours before dawn, but it was not that which woke me from my sleep.

As I opened my eyes, the bay and the beach were wrapped in heavy blackness, invisible clouds shutting out any hint of starlight above. For a moment, I lay in my lean-to, breathing heavily under the shaggy bison skin blanket.

The back of my neck still tingled with the touch that had woken me – light and soft, like the caress of my wife when she wanted me to put more logs on the grate. But she has been gone these two years, and in that time there has been no other. I am alone here, and have been for months.

Out on the water, the loon called again – her high, mournful keening sounding like the weary howl of a lost wolf. I had thought the loons had all flown already, south to warmer climes. For here it grows colder every day, and soon winter will pin me to this chilly beach.

I do not know the exact date today, for I have not kept careful count, but it must be November by now. Neither do I know precisely where I am, save that I am far beyond any claims of Nouvelle-France, over the stabbing peaks of the Montagnes de Pierres Brilliantes in the watershed of some west-flowing Missouri of Nueva California, which I take to be the Rio Santa Buenaventura that the Spaniards have long sought.

I call this wide expanse of water Bais des Cedres, but it may yet prove an interior sea. If I do find an outlet, it will not be until spring. And then I will know at last that I have charted the rumored Mer de l'Ouest – that great bulbous basin of the sea which Nolin marked on the map he stole from De l'Isle, and which must be the last leg of my two years' wanderings, the terminus of what will prove to be a Northwest Passage, which will lead me finally out, to die, on the Océan Pacifique.

MOMENTS LATER, THE loon called several times more, rapidly and angrily, her voice sounding strange in the shifting curtains of mist – first near, then far, then near again. I have never heard a loon cry with such alarm, save once when my canoe chanced to separate a mother from her young, so I peered from my lean-to out into the biting air of the night, watching for intruders.

There was nothing save the dim white tops of the low waves as they rolled in from darkness and obscurity. Wave after wave, lapping in regular beats, just as it has always done, in all the months I have stopped on this beach.

But then there was something else.

On the tip of a prominence to the west of my camp, something moved. At first, it was barely visible through the screen of trees that crowded the spit. But soon, it had rounded the point into open view, and was sliding down the near side toward me, following the contour of the beach where it met the waves.

I could see it clearly enough now, but still it had no form or shape. It was simply a glow – simply the glitter of the sand and the mist where some light or energy passed, bright and eerie enough to raise the hairs on my neck as I watched. On and on, the patch of light crept along, cold and quiet, rapidly spilling across the flat beach and up toward the treeline above, until even the sand at the opening of my lean-to began to glitter, a mere arm's length away.

Then, with swift suddenness, a sharp ray of light pierced my eyes from the inky bosom of the bay, dazzling and half-blinding me.

Dark again, the sharp ray gone – but its echoes still blotting out everything in the darkness. I could not be sure of what I saw, could not be sure of the long black shape that seemed to pass in the water below my lean-to, trailing close after the light. But my ears were not dazzled, and plainly I heard the faint dribble of water as a paddle broke the surface of the water – then the creak of a bowstring, and the soft low hiss of a hunter who spies his prey.

The light had moved some distance down the beach, and had caught the yellow-green glow of a deer's eyes. There it hung as the animal stood transfixed to the spot, a silhouette in black shadows and red fur above the still-glittering sand.

Then something dark and thin shot through the light, and the animal staggered suddenly as if struck by a blow. Foundering to its knees, it disintegrated into thrashing hooves and arching neck. Splashes followed and something dragged the dying deer out of the lantern glow toward the bay. For I understood everything now – the light was a lantern on a canoe, shined by hunters to dazzle deer and wapiti that strayed close to the shore.

For an instant only, I saw the hunter himself as he bent over the stiffening legs of the deer – a black shadow, hunched and distorted in the dim yellow glow, but the shape plainly, incongruously visible all the same.

And as I watched, I knew – whatever it was, it was not a man.

Instead, my eye followed the lines of the shape, and clearly I saw the head and neck and wings of an enormous prowling heron, seven feet tall at least, towering over the carcass of the deer amidst the flickering lamplight, and glaring down the beach – head and eyes leveled coolly in my direction.

Then the deer was pulled away into the water, and the lantern blinked out, and all was dark again.

*　　*　　*

IN THE FIRST light of morning, I followed the waterline and saw none of the splay-toed marks of heron's feet I expected. But instead, cut sharply into the frosty sand, I found a single smooth oval – unmistakable for what it was, the fresh and clear print of a man's leather moccasin.

DECEMBER 1761

IF MY RECKONING is true and December has now come, then it is now the second winter since I shook the wretched dust of Lac Supérieur, the canting voyageurs, and the Compagnie de la Baie d'Hudson all from the soles of my feet.

For had I not come back from laying the company's traplines to find my wife, a Salteaux Chippewa, fled into the forest with my infant son? Did I not follow her along the trail that led to her father's village among the Anishinaabeg until I found her bones strewn among underbrush, where wolves and worse had thrown them?

But enough. That memory does not bring her back. And here, though I have fled far enough from the lying tongues of men, I fear I may have found things even more damned instead.

I made the discovery as I entered a wide clearing, at least two hundred yards across, empty of all trees except a sparse collection of ancient thick-trunked oaks. A carpet of dead, brown ferns as high as my knees covered the ground below, dried leaves bowed under the light falling of snow that dusted them.

The place was charming in its way, or at least different from the endless woods of wrinkled red cedars and lichen-spotted hemlocks that otherwise ringed the bay. Rattling my snares loosely in my hand, I crossed – eyes alert for the million little disturbances that mark the trails of hares, of foxes, of mink.

But only ten yards across, my foot kicked something under the ferns, and it rolled end over end to stop among the roots of an oak. Bending to pick it up, I found myself holding the ribcage of a small deer. Smooth white ribs showed through the accumulated dirt and patches of still-clinging fur. Carelessly, I threw it aside.

The woods are full of such things, and more than once I have squatted on a trail, only to slowly realize that the last remains of some animal are splayed horrifically about me. It all eventually blends with the earth itself – dirty bones, patches of fur, hooves, antlers, teeth.

But there, in that oak clearing, I was not squatting on the remains of one deer. Instead, looking about, I saw there must have been a hundred animals slain there – a thousand – more! I had only to put my foot into any clump of ferns to turn up some grisly remnant of the slaughter.

I kicked up beaver skulls and shattered turtle shells, far from any water. Then disintegrating rabbit skins, the fur falling out in great tufts. The parts of small deer were everywhere – the usual leftovers after the crows and the ants have done their work. And then there was what, with a sudden flash of horror, I realized must be the still-articulated bones of a human child's arm.

I dropped that with a cry, waves of shock suddenly transforming the place around me. Then I looked up to the sky.

My eyes followed the trunk of one of the oaks up to the bare branches that spread against the white winter sky like cracks in the firmament. And there, silhouetted in black, I could see the loose ovoid webs of nests balanced precariously – herons' nests, in tree after tree, everywhere surrounding me, two dozen of them in the clearing or more.

But the nests were wrong. They were large – much too large by an inconceivable factor. Where there should have been four or five in each tree, only one or two seemed to fit.

By now, all charm had drained from the clearing. It felt instead like some ceremonial place, with the litter of sacrifices strewn about my ankles. No living bird could have built those nests – they must be the handiwork of depraved men.

I loosened my rifle and unscrewed my powder horn, but nothing stirred in the woods around me. There was no sign of men. Then I saw, at the base of an oak, a huge contorted shape. It was a feathered neck, as thick as my own upper arm, curving up from a crushed riot of feathers and then back down to earth again, where lay the terrible head – the long slashing beak, the hollowed and rotten eye sockets, the obscene bulge of its gullet.

Shivering, I stepped closer, but the bubble of the nightmare refused to burst. With trembling hand, I plucked a feather from the wreckage. It extended the length of my forearm and longer – and this was a baby, some fledgling that had fallen from its nest above before it was able to fly. I stepped back and looked again from tree to tree, then at the remains of the dead animals around me.

Instinctively, I crossed myself – but the evil-feeling chill only deepened.

FEBRUARY 1762

THOUGH I HAD hoped never to see them again, the hunters of last November have returned. Indeed, I would rather never have thought of them at all – or of that terrible oak clearing. I had hoped to spend the winter minding my traplines in quiet solitude, and then to depart alone again in the spring.

It is February now, I think – not yet spring. And in the past months, even I could not escape noticing what I know is wrong about these woods. It is nothing definitive, and all easily ignored by a pigheaded man who wants to be blind. But there is the profound emptiness and quietness, the absence of so many smaller game animals, and the strange scratchings on stumps that I know are not the work of bears or cougars.

Having seen all that, it should have been no surprise to me that the hunters would return.

They came by canoe, and my first sight of them was out amid the mist of the bay – that same great heron shape, head cocked in hunting stance, standing terribly in the prow of the canoe as it silently glided past the tip of the prominence in the golden glow of sunset. And the unnatural size again – man-sized or more.

My heart turned to ice but still I looked, and I saw the canoe was paddled by four other figures – apparently herons themselves. It was in looking at those four, who moved so much like men, that finally the illusion was broken and I saw that the heron was not any real heron at all, but rather a man in monstrous bird dress, worn for God knew what reason.

*   *   *

How long had it been, before today, since I had seen another man? Six months, at least – but for two full years now I have avoided all as much as possible. That I knew now I had to deal with humans and not some monstrous birds was not, to me, much of an assurance or improvement.

If my rifle had been at my hand and charged, I would have shot over their heads at once. But it was in my lean-to, and I sat on a stony hillock above my camp. All I could do was watch as the canoe come to rest against my beach and the man in the bow leaped nimbly out.

The intruder called up to me, his voice sounding strange after so many months of hearing no talk. He spoke some jargon unknown to me, very different from the Indian languages of Haute-Louisiane. Grudgingly, I called back in Spanish, French, and Chippewa. I tried fragments of other languages I had learned, but by the time we stood face to face at the foot of the hillock, it was clear we could not understand each other.

My relief at this remains immeasurable.

Night has fallen and the canoe has departed, but the man is with me still. Despite all my signs of indifference and even unfriendliness, he insisted on teaching me his name, which is seemingly Ololkolt, and then in interrogating me by signs.

At first, I merely ignored him, and instead stole glances at his strange costume. I am no longer surprised that I was deceived by the night hunters into thinking they were not men, for even in daylight the illusion is very convincing. These men wear gray tunics and cover their arms and faces with streaks of silver mud. They carry heavy capes that they can throw into a remarkable semblance of wings, and affix long wooden carved herons' heads to their own shaved skulls.

But more than all this, these heron-men also have a curious way of standing that causes them to disappear almost entirely into their costumes. As soon as they strike the correct pose, the human melts away and the monstrous avian appears.

With this evidence before my eyes, I wonder now if the creature I thought I saw in the oak clearing was not really some such fabrication as well. Tomorrow it seems I will have a chance to find out – for Ololkolt insists on my accompanying him to that cursed place. Or so, at least, have I gathered from his signs.

I regret to say that I made the mistake of recognizing a sign he showed me – a circular collection of overlapping sticks that I knew at once must be a heron nest. But no sooner had he noticed my understanding, then he began making sign after sign. He had guessed what I had seen, and he inquired about their size, number, distance, and location. Now he will not leave me, staying even after sending the canoe away, and it is clear he means me to take him to see the nests tomorrow.

GOD PRESERVE ME. That dead creature in the clearing is real, and more horrible even than I had thought.

MARCH 1762

I GAVE MY wife all the money I had when I left to lay the company's lines with the voyageurs. This was two years ago at Lac Supérieur. I want to write this in case I do not have another chance.

As I said, I left her my money, and it should have been enough. But while I was gone, the wild rice turned spotted and feeble, and the knockers could harvest no berries, no matter how they brushed the grass. Then, one of her lying neighbors swindled her out of half the money. Another pressed collection of an old debt. A third refused her credit, even against my salary. A fourth promised to help, then left the village without doing anything. A fifth demanded offensive terms.

I learned that she fled into the forest on the trail back to her father's village – hungry and friendless as she found herself at the trading post, it had seemed the only course. As soon as I heard, I followed. But all I found were half of her bones, and none of my son's.

It is a mysterious fact that in any village or settlement there is always one going hungry, one shivering cold, one dying alone, one rotting in prison. Yet, despite all of this, there is never anyone found to be responsible for any of it.

And so I left and came west, looking for this Northwest Passage and death. Coureur de bois, the woodland runner, no longer having to do with any other man.

IT WAS MY wife's touch that awoke me again this morning. But there was no loon and no night hunters – only the ceaseless lapping of the waves upon the beach. Still, I could not shake the dark premonition that called me from my sleep, and by mid-morning I saw the canoes round the tip of the western prominence.

Ololkolt has brought a dozen canoes with sixty hunters – all dressed in full costumes. Impassively, I watched them land from my hillock, filling up my beach with false heron-men. They could not want me or need me. I had already shown Ololkolt the way to the nests. It was their affair now.

But two hunters dashed up the hillside to me and dragged me down – not roughly, but not allowing any resistance. Ololkolt threw a tunic and a wooden heron head on the ground before me, and insisted by sign that I dress. He is young – or so he seems – but he is not a man to be defied. A moment later, I shivered as two hunters pressed cool silver mud to the exposed skin of my arms and face.

THE ANCIENT OAK grove is as dark and baleful as I remember. Later in the year, the branches will fill with leaves, hiding the cursed nests from view. But for now they hang heavily above, large and thick enough almost to cast shadows on the clearing floor in the cold spring afternoon.

The march has taken almost half the day, but Ololkolt gives little time to rest – just enough to scribble these few words. And already he is striding actively about, dispatching his men in parties of two or three among the trees. Just as quickly, they begin to climb, ascending the thick trunks with dizzying speed. He has assigned me a tree as well – the same apparently as Ololkolt himself intends to climb.

I have no choice – I will be forced up. The oaks on every side of me are already full of warriors armed to the teeth with bows, axes, spears, and cudgels. If I were to resist or flee, it would be the work of a moment to cut me down, a thicket of arrows sprouting from my back.

All around me, squirrels fling themselves wildly out of branches, fleeing from the climbing warriors, but otherwise the woods are eerily calm. Even the breeze has died in the air, and the ceremonial feeling has returned to the place.

I cannot help but feel that something awful is about to follow.

THE CLIMBING WAS quicker than I expected, but still I found it difficult and was soon outpaced by Ololkolt. Long before, the other warriors had found perches high in the swaying branches near the massive nests, their legs wrapped around slim, springy limbs as they fussed with the weapons they had brought and traded low words with each other. Even so, I felt no special need to hurry myself, and I lingered several yards below the top.

Above, Ololkolt gestured impatiently from near the top. As I looked up for my next hand-hold, my foot suddenly slipped. Instinctively, I clung to the tree, the bark smell thick in my face as I scrabbled over the abyss, feet fighting for purchase. But no sooner had I fixed my place securely again than I felt a shift in the air. Looking around, I saw that the others had all braced their positions and were fitting arrows to their bowstrings.

My heart sank. Was this to be it? Here, helpless in a tree, was I to be shot down – never even to learn what it all meant? Even as I had climbed, I had suspected the whole horror of those woods – the clearing, the dead animals, the nests – must be some human evil, and I felt like a fool that I had not fought them at once, even if it had meant death.

But I was wrong. Ololkolt called low and pointed to the south, and then I saw. The fading afternoon sky was dotted by great terrible shapes, skimming the tops of the distant cedars, but gaining altitude with every second. I knew at once what they were, although they were still little more than spots above the canopy.

They were herons, and they were huge. And they were real.

AS THE BIRDS closed the distance, they began to take form – their folded necks, long bills, triangular wings, and elegant trailing legs. I tried to count them as they approached, flying in a loose formation, a huge specimen leading the way. Twenty, twenty-five, at least thirty great birds bore down, over the tops of the trees toward the nests where we now clung.

At some silent signal, every bow in those treetops bent and released, and a cloud of arrows rose into the sky. Few found their marks, and the ones that did only caused the birds to falter – not to fall.

It was in watching the arrows descend upon the advancing flock that I at last saw the birds' true size. They were unbelievable creatures, wings eighteen feet across or more. It was all I could do to keep from trembling.

Meanwhile, the bows bent and released again and again, volley after volley raining upon the oncoming birds with hardly any effect. And at last, the herons were practically upon the trees themselves, the final volley discharged at point blank range.

Until now, everything had happened in complete silence, broken only by whistling of wind through fletching and feather, and the occasional squawks of wounded birds. But now the sickening creaking and pinioning of wings was in the air all around me, and the warriors let out an angry, noisome squawking of their own.

Striking their practiced avian poses, they assumed the shapes of herons themselves, acting as though the nests had already been occupied by a rival colony. At last I understood the purpose of the elaborate costumes – they were neither ceremonial nor decorative. They were simply practical, meant to frighten or confuse these monsters if the hunters should encounter them outside their village.

But there was no time for further thought. They were upon us.

* * *

THE HERONS BROKE and wheeled away at the last sting of the arrows, angrily swerving in and out of the trees and past each other in a confusion of feathers and legs. Stiff feathers bristled against my shoulder as one of the birds dived in its maneuvers – that careless touch almost enough to knock me off my perch.

For a moment, I thought of reversing my climb and dropping out of the tree. After all, I had never invited these hunters to my beach, and had not asked to share their troubles. Simply by virtue of being their neighbor, they had pressed me into their fight. It could hardly be cowardice to go my own way.

But somehow, the sight of Ololkolt stayed me. He clung bravely alone by only his legs five yards above me. We had never – indeed could not – exchange a single intelligible word between us, but I felt that I had somehow given him my promise. Even now I can barely explain why I should have felt any obligation, but I did – and even when dealing with the worst of men, I had never been the one to break faith first.

The herons now made a tight turn, and dropped almost immediately back among us. With no arrows ready to oppose them, the birds grabbed clumsily onto branches near the occupied nests. I ducked my head as a shower of twigs and acorns dropped on my head, then looked up again in time to see the warriors now jousting with spears.

In horror, I watched as one bird impaled a man through his chest with its bill. The sharp point slipped in and out cleanly and easily, like a surgeon's lance piercing a boil. Then the man's grip loosened on the tree as the life drained from his body, and soon he was falling heavily through space.

Meanwhile, Ololkolt was engaged with two of the birds. They had landed one on either side of him, and lunged at him from both sides. With deft handling, Ololkolt managed to dodge the attacks, and struck back with the sharp bill affixed to his own head. Whipping around quickly, he brought the point of the bill down like the ball of a hammer, slicing a deep incision into the neck of the heron. But no sooner did one back off a step than I saw the other advancing.

* * *

IT WAS THEN that I found my limbs moving automatically, unslinging the rifle from my back as I straddled a branch above the abyss. I had no thought for myself, though the whole tree now swayed at the push and pull of the two huge herons above. I was like a voyageur again, dumbly paddling with my comrades – my movements a part of the greater machine, hardly controlled by my conscious mind, but necessary enough for all that.

I charged my rifle with powder, then drove the ball home. Pointing skyward, I aimed between the shearing branches and squeezed the trigger.

The explosion almost knocked me from my seat, and for a moment my heart hung in the air as it seemed that either I or my rifle must take the plunge. But grasping the tree in one hand and the gun in the other, I at last came to rest safely prone along the limb, and slowly pushed myself upright again.

Around me, all was confusion. The shot had drawn the startled stare of every man and bird within earshot. And the men, quicker to recover from their surprise, had pressed home what advantage they could on the bewildered herons. Several were forced back into the air, and one or two dropped to the earth below, spiraling down at dangerous speeds on broken wings.

As to Ololkolt, I could at first see nothing of what had happened to him. I peered upward, sick at heart if I should have been too late. But then the gunsmoke parted, and Ololkolt's face appeared in the gap, eagerly urging me to repeat the shot. One of the herons above now showed a bright red circle oozing blood from its breast, but both were still very much alive.

Tipping my powder horn, I charged and loaded the rifle a second time. Raising the gun again, I braced myself as best I could and aimed straight at the heart of the injured heron.

Again, the deafening report – again, the wild confusion.

From behind the smoke, I watched as the twice-shot bird leapt heavily out, its wings stretched in gliding formation, branches gyrating wildly as its weight was suddenly lifted. It flapped futilely once and twice, and then sank rapidly through the branches below, snapping limbs and plunging with a terrible screech to the clearing floor.

Only then did the smoke blow away from the treetop, and I saw Ololkolt gasping and straining, one entire side of his body covered in blood and gore. I leapt up, a mad man now, covering the last several yards to the top of the tree in a careless scramble, where I discovered Ololkolt with a knife plunged elbow deep into the neck of the remaining heron, smiling in vicious satisfaction as gallons of the bird's blood washed over him.

APRIL 1762

I TOLD NO one I was leaving, and no one saw me go.

Not knowing how far it would be to the outlet of the bay, I took enough food from the storehouses of Ololkolt's village to last for a month or more – camas bulbs, acorns, roots, and a pot of oolichan oil. Fish I can catch as I go, and there are always clams for the digging. But meat I must forgo, for I have left my rifle, powder, and balls behind at the village.

Though the herons were driven off this spring, no one can say how far they went or when they will return. Ololkolt's village will sleep more soundly this year, but in the future the rifle will do more good for them than it would for me.

From here, I will follow the coastline west, and scout the outlet to the Océan Pacifique. After that – what more is there to do?

FOR THE THIRD time, I woke at what seemed to be the touch of my wife. It was dawn, the stars fading fast from the steel-blue sky. It was my first morning alone – the first since that battle with the herons that I had not risen to the sound of children laughing and women singing, or the smell of roasting vegetables in the fires.

I sighed softly, but then the feather touch came again. I rolled over and swatted my neck, and found Ololkolt squatting next to me, laughing as he brushed my cheek with the fletching of the arrow he held.

"Armistead," he said, calling me by name.

"Ololkolt," I replied, grinning in spite of myself.

He had seen the rifle I had left in the storehouse, and he had seen that my canoe was gone. All night, he had tracked me alone by lantern light, only to find my canoe overturned on this beach as the sun began to rise.

Even if we spoke the same language, I am not sure how I could have told him that I did not belong in the village – his or any other. Much as I had grown to accept the company of the people there, I could not remain among the cooking pots, the hearth fires, the raising of children, the talk of politics, the annoyances, the bickering, the reconciliations, the thefts, the gossip – in short, among the daily struggle and strife and joy of men and women living close to one another.

So I gave no explanation, and Ololkolt asked for none.

Instead, he placed a fine bow and twenty long arrows into my canoe, clasped my hand warmly in his for the last time, and left me alone to finish my journey.

JUNE 1762

WHEN I FOUND the outlet at last, after following hundreds of miles of westing coastline, I was surprised to see that I hesitated. To be sure, it was no easy road to the Pacific – it was in fact a tumultuous, rock-strewn channel, too narrow for the torrent of water that dropped through it on the way to the ocean.

Mountains towered on either side of the opening, and the water rushed through in a terrible roaring frenzy, twisted and corded into streams of white foam, and framed by dancing jets and sprays that leapt up toward the sky.

A more exhilarating ending I could not have asked for, but I paused a long while on the brink of the maelstrom. The channel was certain death, but it was the only way to finish the Northwest Passage I had begun. I knew that if I paddled but a little ways further, I would find myself pulled inexorably and finally down into the rapids until, some hours later, my body would wash out in the surf of the Pacific along with the fragments of my canoe.

All that was true. But then – why did I still hesitate?

*   *   *

LATER THAT EVENING, as I sat in my camp still within earshot of the torrent, I took up Ololkolt's bow and inspected it closely for the first time. I had never used such a thing, and had preferred to live on fish and clams for the past months. But as I turned the bow in my hands, a deer wandered dumbly across the beach, not fifty feet from me. Almost without thinking, I drew an arrow from the quiver.

The deer turned to look at me – a young buck, brazen and strong. He barely flinched as I rose and slotted the arrow's nock against the string. The bow's grip was warm, the arrow fletching light against my face.

And the arrow, when it flew, was true.

WATER

Ramez Naam

Ramez Naam (rameznaam.com) is a computer scientist and the H.G. Wells Award-winning author of four books: the near future science-fiction brain-hacking thrillers *Nexus* and *Crux* and the non-fiction books *More Than Human* and *The Infinite Resource: The Power of Ideas on a Finite Planet*. He's a fellow of the Institute for Ethics and Emerging Technologies and serves as Adjunct Faculty at Singularity University, where he lectures on energy, environment, and innovation. He lives in Seattle.

THE WATER WHISPERED to Simon's brain as it passed his lips. It told him of its purity, of mineral levels, of the place it was bottled. The bottle was cool in his hand, chilled perfectly to the temperature his neural implants told it he preferred. Simon closed his eyes and took a long, luxurious swallow, savoring the feel of the liquid passing down his throat, the drops of condensation on his fingers.

Perfection.

"Are you drinking that?" the woman across from him asked. "Or making love to it?"

Simon opened his eyes, smiled, and put the bottle back down on the table. "You should try some," he told her.

Stephanie shook her head, her auburn curls swaying as she did. "I try not to drink anything with an IQ over 200."

Simon laughed at that.

They were at a table at a little outdoor café at Washington Square Park. A dozen yards away, children splashed noisily in the fountain, shouting and jumping in the cold spray in the hot mid-day sun. Simon hadn't seen Stephanie since their last college reunion. She looked as good as ever.

"Besides," Stephanie went on. "I'm not rich like you. My implants are ad-supported." She tapped a tanned finger against the side of head. "It's hard enough just looking at that bottle, at all of this…" She gestured with her hands at the table, the menu, the café around them. "Without getting terminally distracted. One drink out of that bottle and I'd be hooked!"

Simon smiled, spread his hands expansively. "Oh, it's not as bad as all that." In his peripheral senses he could feel the bottle's advertech working, reaching out to Stephanie's brain, monitoring her pupillary dilation, the pulse evident in her throat, adapting its pitch in real-time, searching for some hook that would get her to drink, to order a bottle for herself. Around them he could feel the menus, the table, the chairs, the café – all chattering, all swapping and bartering and auctioning data, looking for some advantage that might maximize their profits, expand their market shares.

Stephanie raised an eyebrow. "Really? Every time I glance at that bottle I get little flashes of how good it would feel to take a drink, little whole body shivers." She wrapped her arms around herself now, rubbing her hands over the skin of her tanned shoulders, as if cold in this heat. "And if I did drink it, what then?" Her eyes drilled into Simon's. "Direct neural pleasure stimulation? A little jolt of dopamine? A little micro-addiction to Pura Vita bottled water?"

Simon tilted his head slightly, put on the smile he used for the cameras, for the reporters. "We only use pathways you accepted as part of your implant's licensing agreement. And we're well within the FDA's safe limits for…"

Stephanie laughed at him then. "Simon, it's *me*! I know you're a big marketing exec now, but don't give me your corporate line, okay?"

Simon smiled ruefully. "Okay. So, sure, of course, we make it absolutely as enticing as the law lets us. That's what advertising's for! If your neural implant is ad-supported, we use every function you have enabled. But so what? It's *water*. It's not like it's going to hurt you any."

Stephanie was nodding now. "Mmm-hmmm. And your other products? VitaBars? Pure-E-Ohs? McVita Burgers?"

Simon spread his hands, palms open. "Hey look, *everybody* does it. If someone doesn't buy our Pura Vita line, they're gonna just go buy something from NutriYum or OhSoSweet or OrganiTaste or somebody else. We at least do our best to put some nutrition in there."

Stephanie shook her head. "Simon, don't you think there's something wrong with this? That people let you put ads in their *brains* in order to afford their implants?"

"You don't have to," Simon replied.

"I know, I know," Stephanie answered. "If I paid enough, I could skip the ads, like you do. You don't even have to experience your own work! But you know most people can't afford that. And you've got to have an implant these days to be competitive. Like they say, wired or fired."

Simon frowned inwardly. He'd come to lunch hoping for foreplay, not debate club. Nothing had changed since college. Time to redirect this.

"Look," he said. "I just do my job the best I can, okay? Come on, let's order something. I'm starving."

Simon pulled up his menu to cut off this line of conversation. He moved just fast enough that for a split second he saw the listed entrees still morphing, optimizing their order and presentation to maximize the profit potential afforded by the mood his posture and tone of voice indicated.

Then his kill files caught up, and filtered every item that wasn't on his diet out of his senses.

Simon grimaced. "Looks like I'm having the salad again. Oh joy."

He looked over at Stephanie, and she was still engrossed in the menu, her mind being tugged at by a dozen entrees, each caressing her thoughts with sensations and emotions to entice, each trying to earn that extra dollar.

Simon saw his chance. He activated the ad-buyer interface on his own implant, took out some extremely targeted ads, paid top dollar to be sure he came out on top of the instant auction, and then authorized them against his line of credit. A running tab for the new ad campaign appeared in the corner of his vision, accumulating even as he watched. Simon ignored it.

Stephanie looked up at him a moment later, her lunch chosen. Then he felt his own ads go into effect. Sweet enticements. Subtle reminders of good times had. Sultry undertones. Subtle, just below normal human perception. And all emanating from Simon, beamed straight into Stephanie's mind.

And he saw her expression change just a tiny bit.

HALF AN HOUR later the check came. Simon paid, over Stephanie's objection, then stood. He leaned in close as she stood as well. The advertech monitors told him she was receptive, excited.

"My place, tonight?" he asked.

Stephanie shook her head, clearly struggling with herself.

Simon mentally cranked up the intensity of his ads another notch further.

"I can make you forget all these distractions," he whispered to her. "I can even turn off your ads, for a night." His own advertech whispered sweeter things to her brain, more personal, more sensual.

Simon saw Stephanie hesitate, torn. He moved to wrap his arms around her, moved his face towards hers for a kiss.

Stephanie turned her face away abruptly, and his lips brushed her cheek instead. She squeezed him in a sudden, brisk hug, her hands pressing almost roughly into his back.

"Never," she said. Then she pushed away from him and was gone.

SIMON STOOD THERE, shaking his head, watching as Stephanie walked past the fountain and out of his view.

In the corner of his sight, an impressive tally of what he'd just spent on highly targeted advertising loomed. He blinked it away in annoyance. It was just a number. His line of credit against his Pura Vita stock options would pay for it.

He'd been too subtle, he decided. He should have cranked the ads higher from the very beginning. Well, there were plenty more fish in the sea. Time to get back to the office, anyway.

*   *   *

STEPH WALKED NORTH, past layers of virtual billboards and interactive fashion ads, past a barrage of interactive emotional landscape ads trying to suck her into buying perfume she didn't need, and farther, until she was sure she was out of Simon's senses.

Then she reached into her mind, and flicked off the advertising interfaces in her own implant.

She leaned against a building, let her brain unclench, let the struggle of fighting the advertech he'd employed against her pass.

That bastard, she thought, fuming. She couldn't believe he'd tried that crap on her. If she'd had any shred of doubt remaining, he'd eliminated it. No. He deserved what was coming.

Steph straightened herself, put out a mental bid for a taxi, rode it to Brooklyn, and stepped up to the door of the rented one-room flat. She knocked – short, short, long, long, short. She heard motion inside the room, then saw an eye press itself to the other side of the ancient peephole.

They knew too well that electronic systems could be compromised.

The door opened a fraction, the chain still on it, and Lisa's face appeared. The short-haired brunette nodded, then unlatched the chain, opened the door fully.

Steph walked into the room, closed the door behind her, saw Lisa tucking the home-printed pistol back into her pocket. She hated that thing. They both did. But they'd agreed it was necessary.

"It's done?" Lisa asked.

Steph nodded.

"It's done."

SIMON WALKED SOUTH along Broadway. It was a gorgeous day for a stroll. The sun felt warm on his brow. He was overdressed for the heat in an expensive grey silk jacket and slacks, but the smart lining kept him cool nonetheless. The city was alive with people, alive with data. He watched as throngs moved up and down the street, shopping, chatting, smiling on this lovely day. He partially lowered his neural firewalls and let his implants feed him the whisper of electronic conversations all around him.

Civic systems chattered away. The sidewalk slabs beneath his feet fed a steady stream of counts of passers-by, estimates of weight and height and gender, plots of probabilistic walking paths, data collected for the city planners. Embedded bio-sensors monitored the trees lining the street, the hydration of their soils, the condition of their limbs. Health monitors watched for runny noses, sneezing, coughing, any signs of an outbreak of disease. New York City's nervous system kept constant vigil, keeping the city healthy, looking for ways to improve it.

The commercial dataflow interested Simon more than the civic. His pricey, top-of-the-line implants let him monitor that traffic as only a few could.

In Tribeca he watched as a woman walked by a store front. He saw a mannequin size her up, then felt the traffic as it caressed her mind with a mental image of herself, clothed in a new summer dress, looking ten years younger and twenty pounds lighter. Beneath the physical the mannequin layered an emotional tone in the advert: feelings of vigor, joy, carefree delight. Simon nodded to himself. A nice piece of work, that. He took note of the brand for later study. The woman turned and entered the shop.

He felt other advertech reaching out, all around him, to the networked brains of the crowd. Full sensory teasers for beach vacations from a travel shop, a hint of the taste of chocolate from a candy store, the sight and feel of a taut, rippling body from a sports nutrition store. He passed by a bodega, its façade open to the warm air, and came close enough that the individual bottles of soda and juice and beer and water reached out to him, each trying a pitch tailored to his height and weight and age and ethnicity and style of dress.

Simon felt the familiar ping of one of the many Pura Vita water pitches and smiled. Not bad. But he had a few ideas for improvements. None of it really touched him, in any case. His implants weren't ad-sponsored. He felt this ad chatter only because he chose to, and even now it was buffered, filtered, just a pale echo of what most of the implanted were subjected to. No. Simon tuned into this ambient froth of neural data as research. He sampled it, observed it from afar, because he must. His success in marketing depended on it.

He was almost to his own building when he passed the headquarters of Nexus Corp, the makers of the neural implant in his brain and millions more. Stephanie didn't understand. This was the real behemoth. So long as Nexus Corp maintained their patents on the neural implant technology, they held a monopoly. The ad-based model, all that most people could afford, was their invention. Simon was just one of thousands of marketers to make use of it to boost demand for their products.

And hell, if people didn't like it, they didn't have to get an implant! It was just the way the world worked. Want to be smarter? Want a photographic memory? Want to learn a new language or a new instrument or how to code overnight? Want all those immersive entertainment options? Want that direct connection with your loved ones? But don't have the cash?

Then accept the ads, boyo. And once you do, stop complaining.

Not that Simon wanted the ads himself, mind you. No, it was worth the high price to keep the top-of-the-line, ad-free version running in his brain, to get all the advantages of direct neural enhancement without the distraction of pervasive multi-sensory advertising. And, of course, to be able to monitor the traffic around him, to better understand how to optimize his own pitches.

Simon reached his building at last. The lobby doors sensed him coming and whisked themselves open. Walking by the snack bar in the lobby, he felt the drinks and packaged junk food reaching out to him. His own Pura Vita water, of course. And NutriYum water. Simon gave their top competitor's products the evil eye. Someday Pura Vita would own this whole building, and then he'd personally see to it that not a single bottle of NutriYum remained.

The lobby floor tiles whispered ahead to the inner security doors, which in turn alerted the elevators. Simon strode forward confidently, layers of doors opening for him of their own accord, one by one, perfectly in time with his stride. He stepped into the waiting elevator and it began to ascend immediately, bound for his level. The lift opened again moments later and he strode to his window office. Smart routing kept subordinates out of his path. The glass door to his magnificent office swung open for him. A bottle of cold Pura Vita was on his desk, just how he liked it.

Simon settled into his ready-and-waiting chair, kicked his feet up on the table, and reached through his implant to the embedded computing systems of his office. Data streamed into his mind. Market reports. Sales figures. Ad performance metrics. He closed his eyes and lost himself in it. This was the way to work.

On the back of his jacket, a tiny device, smaller than a grain of sand, woke up and got to work as well.

LISA STARTED INTENTLY at Steph. "He didn't notice?"

Steph shook her head. "Not a clue."

"And you still want to go through with it?" Lisa asked.

"More than ever."

Lisa looked at her. "The ones who're paying us – they're just as bad as he is, you know. And they're going to profit."

Steph nodded. "For now they will," she replied. "In the long run – they're just paying us to take the whole damn system down."

Lisa nodded. "Okay, then."

She strode over to the ancient terminal on the single desk in the flat and entered a series of keypresses.

Phase 1 began.

AROUND THE WORLD, three dozen different accounts stuffed with crypto-currency logged on to anonymous, cryptographically secured stock market exchanges. One by one, they began selling short on Pura Vita stock, selling shares they did not own, on the bet that they could snap those same shares up at a far lower price in the very near future.

In data centers around the world, AI traders took note of the short-sales within micro-seconds. They turned their analytical prowess to news and financial reports on Pura Vita, on its competitors, on the packaged snack and beverage industries in general. The computational equivalent of whole human lifetimes was burned in milliseconds analyzing all available information. Finding nothing, the AI traders flagged Pura Vita stock for closer tracking.

"Now we're committed," Lisa said.

Steph nodded. "Now let's get out of here, before Phase 2 starts."

Lisa nodded and closed the terminal. Five minutes later they were checked out of their hotel, and on their way to the airport.

In a window office above the financial heart of Manhattan, a tiny AI woke and took stock of its surroundings.

Location – check.

Encrypted network traffic – check.

Human present – check.

Key...

Deep within itself, the AI found the key. Something stolen from this corporation, perhaps. An access key that would open its cryptographic security. But one with additional safeguards attached. A key that could only be used from within the secure headquarters of the corporation. And only by one of the humans approved to possess such a key. Triply redundant security. Quite wise.

Except that now the infiltration AI was here, in this secure headquarters, carried in by one of those approved humans.

Slowly, carefully, the infiltration AI crawled its tiny body up the back of the silk suit it was on, towards its collar, as close as it could come to the human's brain without touching skin and potentially revealing itself. When it could go no farther, it reached out, fit its key into the cryptographic locks of the corporation around it, and inserted itself into the inner systems of Pura Vita enterprises, and through them, to the onboard processors of nearly a billion Pura Vita products on shelves around the world.

*   *   *

IN A WAREHOUSE outside Tulsa a bottle of Pura Vita water suddenly labels itself as RECALLED. Its onboard processor broadcasts the state to all nearby. Within milliseconds, the other bottles in the same case, then the rest of the pallet, then all the pallets of Pura Vita water in the warehouse register as RECALLED. The warehouse inventory management AI issues a notice of return to Pura Vita, Inc.

In a restaurant Palo Alto, Marie Evans soaks up the sun, then reaches out to touch her bottle of Pura Vita. She likes to savor this moment, to force herself to wait, to make the pleasure of that first swallow all the more intense. Then, abruptly, the bottle loses its magic. It feels dull and drab, inert in her hand. An instant later the bottle's label flashes red – RECALL. The woman frowns. "Waiter!"

In a convenience store in Naperville, the bottles of Pura Vita on the store shelves suddenly announce that they are in RECALL, setting off a flurry of electronic activity. The store inventory management AI notices the change and thinks to replace the bottles with more recently arrived stock in the store room. Searching, it finds that the stock in the back room has been recalled as well. It places an order for resupply to the local distribution center, only to receive a nearly instant reply that Pura Vita water is currently out of stock, with no resupply date specified. Confused, the inventory management AI passes along this information to the convenience store's business management AI, requesting instructions.

Meanwhile, on the shelves immediately surrounding the recalled bottles of Pura Vita, other bottled products take note. Bottles of NutriYum, OhSoSweet, OrganiTaste, and BetterYou, constantly monitoring their peers and rivals, observe the sudden recall of all Pura Vita water. They virtually salivate at the new opportunity created by the temporary hole in the local market landscape. Within a few millionths of a second, they are adapting their marketing pitches, simulating tens of thousands of scenarios in which buyers encounter the unavailable Pura Vita, angling for ways to appeal to this newly available market. Labels on bottles morph, new sub-brands appear on the shelves as experiments, new neural ads ready themselves for testing on the next wave of shoppers.

In parallel the rival bottles of water reach out to their parent corporate AIs with maximal urgency. Pura Vita bottles temporarily removed from battleground! Taking tactical initiative to seize local market opportunity! Send further instructions/best practices to maximize profit-making potential!

For there is nothing a modern bottle of water wants more than to maximize its profit-making potential.

At the headquarters of OhSoSweet and OrganiTaste and BetterYou, AIs receive the flood of data from bottles across the globe. The breadth of the calamity to befall Pura Vita becomes clear within milliseconds. Questions remain: What has caused the recall? A product problem? A contaminant? A terrorist attack? A glitch in the software?

What is the risk to their own business?

Possible scenarios are modeled, run, evaluated for optimal courses of action robust against the unknowns in the situation.

In parallel, the corporate AIs model the responses of their competitors. They simulate each others' responses. What will NutriYum do? OhSoSweet? OrganiTaste? BetterYou? Each tries to outthink the rest in a game of market chess.

One by one, their recursive models converge on their various courses of action, and come to that final, most dreaded set of questions, which every good corporate AI must ask itself a billion times a day. How much of this must be approved by the humans? How can the AI get the human-reserved decisions made quickly, and in favor of the mathematically optimal course for the corporation that its machine intelligence has already decided upon?

Nothing vexes an AI so much as needing approval for its plans from slow, clumsy, irrational bags of meat.

JOHNNY RAY WALKED down the refrigerated aisle, still sweaty from his run. Something cold sounded good right now. He came upon the cooler with the drinks, reached for a Pura Vita, and saw that the label was pulsing red. Huh? Recalled?

Then the advertech hit him.

"If you liked Pura Vita, you'll love Nutra Vita, from NutriYum!"

"OrganiVita is the one for you!"

"Pura Sweet, from OhSoSweet!"

Images and sensations bombarded him. A cold refreshing mountain stream crashed onto the rocks to his left, splashing him with its cool spray. A gaggle of bronzed girls in bikinis frolicked on a beach to his right, beckoning him with crooked fingers and enticing smiles. A rugged, shirtless, six-packed version of himself nodded approvingly from the bottom shelf, promising the body that Johnny Ray could have. An overwhelmingly delicious citrus taste drew him to the top.

Johnny Ray's mouth opened in a daze. His eyes grew glassy. His hands slid the door to the drinks fridge open, reached inside, came out with some bottle, the rest of him not even aware the decision had been made.

Johnny Ray looked down at the bottle in his hand. Nutri Vita. He'd never even heard of this stuff before. His mouth felt dry, hungry for the cold drink. The sweat beaded on his brow. Wow. He couldn't wait to try this.

WHILE THE CORPORATE AIs of the other brands dithered, wasting whole precious seconds, debating how to persuade the inefficient bottleneck of humans above them, the controlling intelligence of NutriYum launched itself into a long prepared course of action.

NutriYumAI logged on to an anonymous investor intelligence auction site, offering a piece of exclusive, unreleased data to the highest bidder.

30 SECOND ADVANTAGE AVAILABLE – MARKET OPPORTUNITY TO SELL FORTUNE 1000 STOCK IN ADVANCE OF CRASH. GREATER THAN 10% RETURN GUARANTEED BY BOND. AUCTION CLOSES IN 250 MILLISECONDS. RESERVE BID $100 MILLION. CRYPTO CURRENCY ONLY.

Within a quarter of a second it had 438 bids. It accepted the highest, at $187 million, with an attached cryptographically sealed and anonymized contract that promised full refund of the purchase price should the investment data fail to provide at least an equivalent profit.

In parallel NutriYumAI sent out a flurry of offer-contracts to retailers throughout North America and select markets in Europe, Asia, and Latin America.

ADDITIONAL NUTRI-YUM WATER STOCK AVAILABLE IN YOUR AREA. 10 CASES FREE, DELIVERY WITHIN 1 HOUR, PLUS 40% DISCOUNT ON NEXT 1000 CASES – EXCHANGE FOR 75% ALLOCATION OF PURA VITA SHELF SPACE AND NEURAL BANDWIDTH ALLOCATION. *REPLY* WITH CRYPTOGRAPHIC SIGNATURE TO ACCEPT.

Within seconds, the first acceptances began to arrive. Retailers signed over the shelf space and neural bandwidth that Pura Vita had once occupied in their stores to NutriYum, in exchange for a discount on the coming cases.

By the end of the day, NutriYum would see its market share nearly double. A coup. A rout. The sort of market battlefield victory that songs are sung of in the executive suites.

THE AI TRADED fund called Vanguard Algo 5093 opened the data package it had bought for $187 million. It took nanoseconds to process the data. This was indeed an interesting market opportunity. Being the cautious sort, Vanguard Algo 5093 sought validation. At a random sample of a few thousand locations, it hired access to wearable lenses, to the anonymized data streams coming out of the eyes and brains of Nexus Corp customers, to tiny, insect-sized airborne drones. Only a small minority of the locations it tried had a set of eyes available within the 1 second threshold it set, but those were sufficient. In every single location, the Pura Vita labels in view were red. Red for recall.

Vanguard Algo 5093 leapt into action. SELL SHORT! SELL SHORT!

It alerted its sibling Vanguard algorithms to the opportunity, earning a commission on their profits. It sent the required notifications to the few remaining human traders at the company as well, though it knew that they would respond far too slowly to make a difference

Within milliseconds, Pura Vita Stock was plunging, as tens of billions in Vanguard Algo assets bet against it. In the next few milliseconds, other AI traders around the world took note of the movement of the stock. Many of them, primed by the day's earlier short sale, joined in now, pushing Pura Vita stock even lower.

Thirty two seconds after it had purchased this advance data, Vanguard Algo 5093 saw the first reports on Pura Vita's inventory problem hit the wire. By then, $187 million in market intelligence had already netted it more than a billion in profits, with more on the way as Pura Vita dipped even lower.

SIMON'S FIRST WARNING was the stock ticker. Like so many other millionaires made of not-yet-vested stock options, he kept a ticker of his company's stock permanently in view in his mind. On any given day it might flicker a bit, up or down by a few tenths of a percent. More up than down for the last year to be sure. Still, on a volatile day, one could see a swing in either direction of as much as two percent. Nothing to be too worried about.

He was immersing himself in data from a Tribeca clothing store – the one he'd seen with the lovely advertech today - when he noticed that the ticker in the corner of his mind's eye was red. Bright red. Pulsating red.

His attention flicked to it.

-11.4%

What?

It plunged even as he watched.

-12.6%

-13.3%

-15.1%

What the hell? He mentally zoomed in on the ticker to get the news. The headline struck him like a blow.

PURA VITA BOTTLES EXPIRING IN MILLIONS OF LOCATIONS.

No. This didn't make any sense. He called up the sales and marketing AI on his terminal.

Nothing.

Huh?

He tried again.

Nothing.

The AI was down.

He tried the inventory management AI next.

Nothing.

Again.

Nothing.

Simon was sweating now. He could feel the hum as the smart lining of his suit started running its compressors, struggling to cool him off. But it wasn't fast enough. Sweat beaded on his brow, on his upper lip. There was a knot in his stomach.

He pulled up voice, clicked to connect to IT. Oh thank god.

Then routed to voicemail.

Oh no. Oh please no.

-28.7%.

-30.2%

-31.1%

-33.9%

IT WAS EVENING before IT called back. They'd managed to reboot the AIs. A worm had taken them out somehow, had spread new code to all the Pura Vita bottles through the market intelligence update channel. And then it had disabled the remote update feature on the bottles. To fix those units, they needed to reach each one, *physically*. Almost *a billion* bottles. That would take whole *days*!

It was a disaster. And there was worse.

NutriYum had sealed up the market, had closed 6 month deals with tens of thousands of retailers. Their channel was gone, eviscerated.

And with it Simon's life.

The credit notice came soon after. His options were worthless now. His most important asset was gone. And with it so was the line of credit he'd been using to finance his life.

[NOTICE OF CREDIT DOWNGRADE]

The message flashed across his mind. Not just any downgrade. Down to zero. Down into the red. Junk status.

The other calls came within seconds of his credit downgrade. Everything he had – his mid-town penthouse apartment, his vacation place in the Bahamas, his fractional jet share – they were all backed by that line of credit. He'd been living well beyond his means. And now the cards came tumbling down.

[NexusCorp Alert: Hello valued customer! We have detected a problem with your account. We are temporarily downgrading your neural implant service to the free, ad-sponsored version. You can correct this at any time by submitting payment *here*.]

Simon clutched his head in horror. This couldn't be happening. It couldn't.

Numbly, he stumbled out of his office and down the corridor. Lurid product adverts swam at him from the open door to the break room. He pushed past them. He had to get home somehow, get to his apartment, do...something.

He half collapsed into the elevator, fought to keep himself from hyperventilating as it dropped to the lobby floor. Adverts from the lobby restaurants flashed at him from the wall panel as they dropped, inundating him with juicy steak flavor, glorious red wine aroma, the laughter and bonhomie of friends he didn't have. The ads he habitually blocked out reached him raw and unfiltered now, with an intensity he wasn't accustomed to in his exclusive, ad-free life. He crawled back as far as he could into the corner of the lift, whimpering, struggling to escape the barrage. The doors opened, and he bolted forward, into the lobby and the crowd, heading out, out into the city.

The snack bar caught him first. It reached right into him, with its scents and flavors and the incredible joy a bite of a YumDog would bring him. He stumbled towards the snack bar, unthinkingly. His mouth was dry, parched, a desert. He was so hot in this suit, sweating, burning up, even as the suit's pumps ran faster and faster to cool him down.

Water. He needed water.

He blinked to clear his vision, searching, searching for a refreshing Pura Vita.

All he saw was NutriYum. He stared at the bottles, the shelves upon shelves of them. And the NutriYum stared back into him. It saw his thirst. It saw the desert of his mouth, the parched landscape of his throat, and it whispered to him of sweet relief, of an endless cool stream to quench that thirst.

Simon stumbled forward another step. His fingers closed around a bottle of cold, perfect, NutriYum. Beads of condensation broke refreshingly against his fingers.

Drink me, the bottle whispered to him. *And I'll make all your cares go away.*

The dry earth of his throat threatened to crack. His sinuses were a ruin of flame. He shouldn't do this. He couldn't do this.

Simon brought his other hand to the bottle, twisted off the cap, and tipped it back, letting the sweet cold water quench the horrid cracking heat within him.

Pure bliss washed through him, bliss like he'd never known. This was nectar. This was perfection.

Some small part of Simon's brain told him that it was all a trick. Direct neural stimulation. Dopamine release. Pleasure center activation. Reinforcement conditioning.

And he knew this. But the rest of him didn't care.

Simon was a NutriYum man now. And always would be.

THE TRUTH OF FACT,
THE TRUTH OF FEELING

Ted Chiang

Ted Chiang is the author of *Stories of Your Life and Others* and *The Lifecycle of Software Objects*. He was born and raised in Port Jefferson, New York, and attended Brown University, where he received a degree in computer science. His work has received four Nebula Awards, four Hugo Awards, four Locus Awards, a Sturgeon Award, a Sidewise Award, and a British Science Fiction Association Award. He lives outside of Seattle, Washington.

WHEN MY DAUGHTER Nicole was an infant, I read an essay suggesting that it might no longer be necessary to teach children how to read or write, because speech recognition and synthesis would soon render those abilities superfluous. My wife and I were horrified by the idea, and we resolved that, no matter how sophisticated technology became, our daughter's skills would always rest on the bedrock of traditional literacy.

It turned out that we and the essayist were both half correct: now that she's an adult, Nicole can read as well as I can. But there is a sense in which she has lost the ability to write. She doesn't dictate her messages and ask a virtual secretary to read back to her what she last said, the way that essayist predicted; Nicole subvocalizes, her retinal projector displays the words in her field of vision, and she makes revisions using a combination of gestures and eye movements. For all practical purposes, she can write. But take away the assistive software and give her nothing but a keyboard like the one I remain faithful to, and she'd have difficulty spelling out many of the words in this very sentence. Under those specific circumstances, English becomes a bit like a second language to her, one that she can speak fluently but can only barely write.

It may sound like I'm disappointed in Nicole's intellectual achievements, but that's absolutely not the case. She's smart and dedicated to her job at an art museum when she could be earning more money elsewhere, and I've always been proud of her accomplishments. But there is still the past me who would have been appalled to see his daughter lose her ability to spell, and I can't deny that I am continuous with him.

It's been more than twenty years since I read that essay, and in that period our lives have undergone countless changes that I couldn't have predicted. The most catastrophic one was when Nicole's mother Angela declared that she deserved a more interesting life than the one we were giving her, and spent the next decade criss-crossing the globe. But the changes leading to Nicole's current form of literacy were more ordinary and gradual: a succession of software gadgets that not only promised but in fact delivered utility and convenience, and I didn't object to any of them at the times of their introduction.

So it hasn't been my habit to engage in doomsaying whenever a new product is announced; I've welcomed new technology as much as anyone. But when Whetstone released its new search tool Remem, it raised concerns for me in a way none of its predecessors did.

Millions of people, some my age but most younger, have been keeping lifelogs for years, wearing personal cams that capture continuous video of their entire lives. People consult their lifelogs for a variety of reasons – everything from reliving favorite moments to tracking down the cause of allergic reactions – but only intermittently; no one wants to spend all their time formulating queries and sifting through the results. Lifelogs are the most complete photo album imaginable, but like most photo albums, they lie dormant except on special occasions. Now Whetstone aims to change all of that; they claim Remem's algorithms can search the entire haystack by the time you've finished saying "needle."

Remem monitors your conversation for references to past events, and then displays video of that event in the lower left corner of your field of vision. If you say "remember dancing the conga at that wedding?",

Remem will bring up the video. If the person you're talking to says "the last time we were at the beach," Remem will bring up the video. And it's not only for use when speaking with someone else; Remem also monitors your subvocalizations. If you read the words "the first Szechuan restaurant you ate at," your vocal cords will move as if you're reading aloud, and Remem will bring up the relevant video.

There's no denying the usefulness of software that can actually answer the question "where did I put my keys?" But Whetstone is positioning Remem as more than a handy virtual assistant: they want it to take the place of your natural memory.

IT WAS THE summer of Jijingi's thirteenth year when a European came to live in the village. The dusty harmattan winds had just begun blowing from the north when Sabe, the elder who was regarded as chief by all the local families, made the announcement.

Everyone's initial reaction was alarm, of course. "What have we done wrong?" Jijingi's father asked Sabe.

Europeans had first come to Tivland many years ago, and while some elders said one day they'd leave and life would return to the ways of the past, until that day arrived it was necessary for the Tiv to get along with them. This had meant many changes in the way the Tiv did things, but it had never meant Europeans living among them before. The usual reason for Europeans to come to the village was to collect taxes for the roads they had built; they visited some clans more often because the people refused to pay taxes, but that hadn't happened in the Shangev clan. Sabe and the other clan elders had agreed that paying the taxes was the best strategy.

Sabe told everyone not to worry. "This European is a missionary; that means all he does is pray. He has no authority to punish us, but our making him welcome will please the men in the administration."

He ordered two huts built for the missionary, a sleeping hut and a reception hut. Over the course of the next several days everyone took time off from harvesting the guinea-corn to help lay bricks, sink posts into the ground, weave grass into thatch for the roof. It was during the final step, pounding the floor, that the missionary arrived. His porters appeared first, the boxes they carried visible from a distance as they threaded their way between the cassava fields; the missionary himself was the last to appear, apparently exhausted even though he carried nothing. His name was Moseby, and he thanked everyone who had worked on the huts. He tried to help, but it quickly became clear that he didn't know how to do anything, so eventually he just sat in the shade of a locust bean tree and wiped his head with a piece of cloth.

Jijingi watched the missionary with curiosity. The man opened one of his boxes and took out what at first looked like a block of wood, but then he split it open and Jijingi realized it was a tightly bound sheaf of papers. Jijingi had seen paper before; when the Europeans collected taxes, they gave paper in return so that the village had proof of what they'd paid. But the paper that the missionary was looking at was obviously of a different sort, and must have had some other purpose.

The man noticed Jijingi looking at him, and invited him to come closer. "My name is Moseby," he said. "What is your name?"

"I am Jijingi, and my father is Orga of the Shangev clan."

Moseby spread open the sheaf of paper and gestured toward it. "Have you heard the story of Adam?" he asked. "Adam was the first man. We are all children of Adam."

"Here we are descendants of Shangev," said Jijingi. "And everyone in Tivland is a descendant of Tiv."

"Yes, but your ancestor Tiv was descended from Adam, just as my ancestors were. We are all brothers. Do you understand?"

The missionary spoke as if his tongue were too large for his mouth, but Jijingi could tell what he was saying. "Yes, I understand."

Moseby smiled, and pointed at the paper. "This paper tells the story of Adam."

"How can paper tell a story?"

"It is an art that we Europeans know. When a man speaks, we make marks on the paper. When another man looks at the paper later, he sees the marks and knows what sounds the first man made. In that way the second man can hear what the first man said."

Jijingi remembered something his father had told him about old Gbegba, who was the most skilled in bushcraft. "Where you or I would see nothing but some disturbed grass, he can see that a leopard had killed a cane rat at that spot and carried it off," his father said. Gbegba was able to look at the ground and know what had happened even though he had not been present. This art of the Europeans must be similar: those who were skilled in interpreting the marks could hear a story even if they hadn't been there when it was told.

"Tell me the story that the paper tells," he said.

Moseby told him a story about Adam and his wife being tricked by a snake. Then he asked Jijingi, "How do you like it?"

"You're a poor storyteller, but the story was interesting enough."

Moseby laughed. "You are right, I am not good at the Tiv language. But this is a good story. It is the oldest story we have. It was first told long before your ancestor Tiv was born."

Jijingi was dubious. "That paper can't be so old."

"No, this paper is not. But the marks on it were copied from older paper. And those marks were copied from older paper. And so forth many times."

That would be impressive, if true. Jijingi liked stories, and older stories were often the best. "How many stories do you have there?"

"Very many." Moseby flipped through the sheaf of papers, and Jijingi could see each sheet was covered with marks from edge to edge; there must be many, many stories there.

"This art you spoke of, interpreting marks on paper; is it only for Europeans?"

"No, I can teach it to you. Would you like that?"

Cautiously, Jijingi nodded.

As a journalist, I have long appreciated the usefulness of lifelogging for determining the facts of the matter. There is scarcely a legal proceeding, criminal or civil, that doesn't make use of someone's lifelog, and rightly so. When the public interest is involved, finding out what actually happened is important; justice is an essential part of the social contract, and you can't have justice until you know the truth.

However, I've been much more skeptical about the use of lifelogging in purely personal situations. When lifelogging first became popular, there were couples who thought they could use it to settle arguments over who had actually said what, using the video record to prove they were right. But finding the right clip of video often wasn't easy, and all but the most determined gave up on doing so. The inconvenience acted as a barrier, limiting the searching of lifelogs to those situations in which effort was warranted, namely situations in which justice was the motivating factor.

Now with Remem, finding the exact moment has become easy, and lifelogs that previously lay all but ignored are now being scrutinized as if they were crime scenes, thickly strewn with evidence for use in domestic squabbles.

I typically write for the news section, but I've written feature stories as well, and so when I pitched an article about the potential downsides of Remem to my managing editor, he gave me the go-ahead. My first interview was with a married couple whom I'll call Joel and Deirdre, an architect and a painter, respectively. It wasn't hard to get them talking about Remem.

"Joel is always saying that he knew it all along," said Deirdre, "even when he didn't. It used to drive me crazy, because I couldn't get him to admit he used to believe something else. Now I can. For example, recently we were talking about the McKittridge kidnapping case."

She sent me the video of one argument she had with Joel. My retinal projector displayed footage of a cocktail party; it's from Deirdre's point of view, and Joel is telling a number of people, *"It was pretty clear that he was guilty from the day he was arrested."*

Deirdre's voice: *"You didn't always think that. For months you argued that he was innocent."*

Joel shakes his head. *"No, you're misremembering. I said that even people who are obviously guilty deserve a fair trial."*

"That's not what you said. You said he was being railroaded."

"You're thinking of someone else; that wasn't me."

"No, it was you. Look." A separate video window opened up, an excerpt of her lifelog that she looked up and broadcast to the people they've been talking with. Within the nested video, Joel and Deirdre are

sitting in a café, and Joel is saying, *"He's a scapegoat. The police needed to reassure the public, so they arrested a convenient suspect. Now he's done for."* Deidre replies, *"You don't think there's any chance of him being acquitted?"* and Joel answers, *"Not unless he can afford a high-powered defense team, and I'll bet you he can't. People in his position will never get a fair trial."*

I closed both windows, and Deirdre said, "Without Remem, I'd never be able to convince him that he changed his position. Now I have proof."

"Fine, you were right that time," said Joel. "But you didn't have to do that in front of our friends."

"You correct me in front of our friends all the time. You're telling me I can't do the same?"

Here was the line at which the pursuit of truth ceased to be an intrinsic good. When the only persons affected have a personal relationship with each other, other priorities are often more important, and a forensic pursuit of the truth could be harmful. Did it really matter whose idea it was to take the vacation that turned out so disastrously? Did you need to know which partner was more forgetful about completing errands the other person asked of them? I was no expert on marriage, but I knew what marriage counselors said: pinpointing blame wasn't the answer. Instead, couples needed to acknowledge each other's feelings and address their problems as a team.

Next I spoke with a spokesperson from Whetstone, Erica Meyers. For a while she gave me a typically corporate spiel about the benefits of Remem. "Making information more accessible is an intrinsic good," she says. "Ubiquitous video has revolutionized law enforcement. Businesses become more effective when they adopt good record-keeping practices. The same thing happens to us as individuals when our memories become more accurate: we get better, not just at doing our jobs, but at living our lives."

When I asked her about couples like Joel and Deirdre, she said, "If your marriage is solid, Remem isn't going to hurt it. But if you're the type of person who's constantly trying to prove that you're right and your spouse is wrong, then your marriage is going to be in trouble whether you use Remem or not."

I conceded that she may have had a point in this particular case. But, I asked her, didn't she think Remem created greater opportunities for those types of arguments to arise, even in solid marriages, by making it easier for people to keep score?

"Not at all," she said. "Remem didn't give them a scorekeeping mentality; they developed that on their own. Another couple could just as easily use Remem to realize that they've both misremembered things, and become more forgiving when that sort of mistake happens. I predict the latter scenario will be the more common one with our customers as a whole."

I wished I could share Erica Meyers' optimism, but I knew that new technology didn't always bring out the best in people. Who hasn't wished they could prove that their version of events was the correct one? I could easily see myself using Remem the way Deirdre did, and I wasn't at all certain that doing so would be good for me. Anyone who has wasted hours surfing the internet knows that technology can encourage bad habits.

MOSEBY GAVE A sermon every seven days, on the day devoted to resting and brewing and drinking beer. He seemed to disapprove of the beer drinking, but he didn't want to speak on one of the days of work, so the day of beer brewing was the only one left. He talked about the European god, and told people that following his rules would improve their lives, but his explanations of how that would do so weren't particularly persuasive.

But Moseby also had some skill at dispensing medicine, and he was willing to learn how to work in the fields, so gradually people grew more accepting of him, and Jijingi's father let him visit Moseby occasionally to learn the art of writing. Moseby offered to teach the other children as well, and for a time Jijingi's age-mates came along, mostly to prove to each other that they weren't afraid of being near a European. Before long the other boys grew bored and left, but because Jijingi remained interested in writing and his father thought it would keep the Europeans happy, he was eventually permitted to go every day.

Moseby explained to Jijingi how each sound a person spoke could be indicated with different mark on the paper. The marks were arranged in rows like plants in a field; you looked at the marks as if you were walking down a row, made the sound each mark indicated, and you would find yourself speaking what the original person had said. Moseby showed him how to make each of the different marks on a sheet of paper, using a tiny wooden rod that had a core of soot.

In a typical lesson, Moseby would speak, and then write what he had said: "When night comes I shall sleep." *Tugh mba a ile yo me yav.* "There are two persons." *Ioruv mban mba uhar.* Jijingi carefully copied the writing on his sheet of paper, and when he was done, Moseby would look at his paper.

"Very good. But you need to leave spaces when you write."

"I have." Jijingi pointed at the gap between each row.

"No, that is not what I mean. Do you see the spaces within each line?" He pointed at his own paper.

Jijingi understood. "Your marks are clumped together, while mine are arranged evenly."

"These are not just clumps of marks. They are. . . I do not know what you call them." He picked up a thin sheaf of paper from his table and flipped through it. "I do not see it here. Where I come from, we call them 'words.' When we write, we leave spaces between the words."

"But what are words?"

"How can I explain it?" He thought a moment. "If you speak slowly, you pause very briefly after each word. That's why we leave a space in those places when we write. Like this: How. Many. Years. Old. Are. You?" He wrote on his paper as he spoke, leaving a space every time he paused: *Anyom a ou kuma a me?*

"But you speak slowly because you're a foreigner. I'm Tiv, so I don't pause when I speak. Shouldn't my writing be the same?"

"It does not matter how fast you speak. Words are the same whether you speak quickly or slowly."

"Then why did you say you pause after each word?"

"That is the easiest way to find them. Try saying this very slowly." He pointed at what he'd just written.

Jijingi spoke very slowly, the way a man might when trying to hide his drunkenness. "Why is there no space in between *an* and *yom*?"

"*Anyom* is one word. You do not pause in the middle of it."

"But I wouldn't pause after *anyom* either."

Moseby sighed. "I will think more about how to explain what I mean. For now, just leave spaces in the places where I leave spaces."

What a strange art writing was. When sowing a field, it was best to have the seed yams spaced evenly; Jijingi's father would have beaten him if he'd clumped the yams the way the Moseby clumped his marks on paper. But he had resolved to learn this art as best he could, and if that meant clumping his marks, he would do so.

It was only many lessons later that Jijingi finally understood where he should leave spaces, and what Moseby meant when he said "word." You could not find the places where words began and ended by listening. The sounds a person made while speaking were as smooth and unbroken as the hide of a goat's leg, but the words were like the bones underneath the meat, and the space between them was the joint where you'd cut if you wanted to separate it into pieces. By leaving spaces when he wrote, Moseby was making visible the bones in what he said.

Jijingi realized that, if he thought hard about it, he was now able to identify the words when people spoke in an ordinary conversation. The sounds that came from a person's mouth hadn't changed, but he understood them differently; he was aware of the pieces from which the whole was made. He himself had been speaking in words all along. He just hadn't known it until now.

THE EASE OF searching that Remem provides is impressive enough, but that merely scratches the surface of what Whetstone sees as the product's potential. When Deirdre fact-checked her husband's previous statements, she was posing explicit queries to Remem. But Whetstone expects that, as people become accustomed to their product, queries will take the place of ordinary acts of recall, and Remem will be integrated into their very thought processes. Once that happens, we will become cognitive cyborgs, effectively incapable of misremembering anything; digital video stored on error-corrected silicon will take over the role once filled by our fallible temporal lobes.

What might it be like to have a perfect memory? Arguably the individual with the best memory ever documented was Solomon Shereshevskii, who lived in Russia during the first half of the twentieth century. The psychologists who tested him found that he could hear a series of words or numbers once and remember it months or even years later. With no knowledge of Italian, Shereshevskii was able to quote stanzas of *The Divine Comedy* that had been read to him fifteen years earlier.

But having a perfect memory wasn't the blessing one might imagine it to be. Reading a passage of text evoked so many images in Shereshevskii's mind that he often couldn't focus on what it actually said, and his awareness of innumerable specific examples made it difficult for him to understand abstract concepts. At times, he tried to deliberately forget things. He wrote down numbers he no longer wanted to remember on slips of paper and then burnt them, a kind of slash-and-burn approach to clearing out the undergrowth of his mind, but to no avail.

When I raised the possibility that a perfect memory might be a handicap to Whetstone's spokesperson, Erica Meyers, she had a ready reply. "This is no different from the concerns people used to have about retinal projectors," she said. "They worried that seeing updates constantly would be distracting or overwhelming, but we've all adapted to them."

I didn't mention that not everyone considered that a positive development.

"And Remem is entirely customizable," she continued. "If at any time you find it's doing too many searches for your needs, you can decrease its level of responsiveness. But according to our customer analytics, our users haven't been doing that. As they become more comfortable with it, they're finding that Remem becomes more helpful the more responsive it is."

But even if Remem wasn't constantly crowding your field of vision with unwanted imagery of the past, I wondered if there weren't issues raised simply by having that imagery be perfect.

"Forgive and forget" goes the expression, and for our idealized magnanimous selves, that was all you needed. But for our actual selves the relationship between those two actions wasn't so straightforward. In most cases we had to forget a little bit before we could forgive; when we no longer experienced the pain as fresh, the insult was easier to forgive, which in turn made it less memorable, and so on. It was this psychological feedback loop that made initially infuriating offences seem pardonable in the mirror of hindsight.

What I feared was that Remem would make it impossible for this feedback loop to get rolling. By fixing every detail of an insult in indelible video, it could prevent the softening that's needed for forgiveness to begin. I thought back to what Erica Meyers said about Remem's inability to hurt solid marriages. Implicit in that assertion was a claim about what qualified as a solid marriage. If someone's marriage was built on – as ironic as it might sound – a cornerstone of forgetfulness, what right did Whetstone have to shatter that?

The issue wasn't confined to marriages; all sorts of relationships rely on forgiving and forgetting. My daughter Nicole has always been strong-willed; rambunctious when she was a child, openly defiant as an adolescent. She and I had many furious arguments during her teen years, arguments that we have mostly been able to put behind us, and now our relationship is pretty good. If we'd had Remem, would we still be speaking to each other?

I don't mean to say that forgetting is the only way to mend relationships. While I can no longer recall most of the arguments Nicole and I had – and I'm grateful that I can't – one of the arguments I remember clearly is one that spurred me to be a better father.

It was when Nicole was sixteen, a junior in high school. It had been two years since her mother Angela had left, probably the two hardest years of both our lives. I don't remember what started the argument – something trivial, no doubt – but it escalated and before long Nicole was taking her anger at Angela out on me.

"You're the reason she left! You drove her away! You can leave too, for all I care. I sure as hell would be better off without you." And to demonstrate her point, she stormed out of the house.

I knew it wasn't premeditated malice on her part – I don't think she engaged in much premeditation in anything during that phase of her life

– but she couldn't have come up with a more hurtful accusation if she'd tried. I'd been devastated by Angela's departure, and I was constantly wondering what I could have done differently to keep her.

Nicole didn't come back until the next day, and that night was one of soul searching for me. While I didn't believe I was responsible for her mother leaving us, Nicole's accusation still served as a wake-up call. I hadn't been conscious of it, but I realized that I had been thinking of myself as the greatest victim of Angela's departure, wallowing in self-pity over just how unreasonable my situation was. It hadn't even been my idea to have children; it was Angela who'd wanted to be a parent, and now she had left me holding the bag. What sane world would leave me with sole responsibility for raising an adolescent girl? How could a job that was so difficult be entrusted to someone with no experience whatsoever?

Nicole's accusation made me realize her predicament was worse than mine. At least I had volunteered for this duty, albeit long ago and without full appreciation for what I was getting into. Nicole had been drafted into her role, with no say whatsoever. If there was anyone who had a right to be resentful, it was her. And while I thought I'd been doing a good job of being a father, obviously I needed to do better.

I turned myself around. Our relationship didn't improve overnight, but over the years I was able to work myself back into Nicole's good graces. I remember the way she hugged me at her college graduation, and I realized my years of effort had paid off.

Would those years of repair have been possible with Remem? Even if each of us could have refrained from throwing the other's bad behavior in their faces, the opportunity to privately rewatch video of our arguments seems like it could be pernicious. Vivid reminders of the way she and I yelled at each other in the past might have kept our anger fresh, and prevented us from rebuilding our relationship.

JIJINGI WANTED TO write down some of the stories of where the Tiv people came from, but the storytellers spoke rapidly, and he wasn't able to write fast enough to keep up with them. Moseby said he would get better with practice, but Jijingi despaired that he'd ever become fast enough.

Then, one summer a European woman named Reiss came to visit the village. Moseby said she was "a person who learns about other people" but could not explain what that meant, only that she wanted to learn about Tivland. She asked questions of everyone, not just the elders but young men, too, even women and children, and she wrote down everything they told her. She didn't try to get anyone to adopt European practices; where Moseby had insisted that there were no such thing as curses and that everything was God's will, Reiss asked about how curses worked, and listened attentively to explanations of how your kin on your father's side could curse you while your kin on your mother's side could protect you from curses.

One evening Kokwa, the best storyteller in the village, told the story of how the Tiv people split into different lineages, and Reiss had written it down exactly as he told it. Later she had recopied the story using a machine she poked at noisily with her fingers, so that she had a copy that was clean and easy to read. When Jijingi asked if she would make another copy for him, she agreed, much to his excitement.

The paper version of the story was curiously disappointing. Jijingi remembered that when he had first learned about writing, he'd imagined it would enable him to see a storytelling performance as vividly as if he were there. But writing didn't do that. When Kokwa told the story, he didn't merely use words; he used the sound of his voice, the movement of his hands, the light in his eyes. He told you the story with his whole body, and you understood it the same way. None of that was captured on paper; only the bare words could be written down. And reading just the words gave you only a hint of the experience of listening to Kokwa himself, as if one were licking the pot in which okra had been cooked instead of eating the okra itself.

Jijingi was still glad to have the paper version, and would read it from time to time. It was a good story, worthy of being recorded on paper. Not everything written on paper was so worthy. During his sermons Moseby would read aloud stories from his book, and they were often good stories, but he also read aloud words he had written down just a few days before, and those were often not stories at all, merely claims that learning more about the European god would improve the lives of the Tiv people.

One day, when Moseby had been eloquent, Jijingi complimented him. "I know you think highly of all your sermons, but today's sermon was a good one."

"Thank you," said Moseby, smiling. After a moment, he asked, "Why do you say I think highly of all my sermons?"

"Because you expect that people will want to read them many years from now."

"I don't expect that. What makes you think that?"

"You write them all down before you even deliver them. Before even one person has heard a sermon, you have written it down for future generations."

Moseby laughed. "No, that is not why I write them down."

"Why, then?" He knew it wasn't for people far away to read them, because sometimes messengers came to the village to deliver paper to Moseby, and he never sent his sermons back with them.

"I write the words down so I do not forget what I want to say when I give the sermon."

"How could you forget what you want to say? You and I are speaking right now, and neither of us need paper to do so."

"A sermon is different from conversation." Moseby paused to consider. "I want to be sure I give my sermons as well as possible. I won't forget what I want to say, but I might forget the best way to say it. If I write it down, I don't have to worry. But writing the words down does more than help me remember. It helps me think."

"How does writing help you think?"

"That is a good question," he said. "It is strange, isn't it? I do not know how to explain it, but writing helps me decide what I want to say. Where I come from, there's a very old proverb: *verba volant, scripta manent*. In Tiv you would say, 'spoken words fly away, written words remain.' Does that make sense?"

"Yes," Jijingi said, just to be polite; it made no sense at all. The missionary wasn't old enough to be senile, but his memory must be terrible and he didn't want to admit it. Jijingi told his age-mates about this, and they joked about it amongst themselves for days. Whenever they exchanged gossip, they would add, "Will you remember that? This will help you," and mimic Moseby writing at his table.

On an evening the following year, Kokwa announced he would tell the story of how the Tiv split into different lineages. Jijingi brought out the paper version he had, so he could read the story at the same time Kokwa told it. Sometimes he could follow along, but it was often confusing because Kokwa's words didn't match what was written on the paper. After Kokwa was finished, Jijingi said to him, "You didn't tell the story the same way you told it last year."

"Nonsense," said Kokwa. "When I tell a story it doesn't change, no matter how much time passes. Ask me to tell it twenty years from today, and I will tell it exactly the same."

Jijingi pointed at the paper he held. "This paper is the story you told last year, and there were many differences." He picked one he remembered. "Last time you said, 'the Uyengi captured the women and children and carried them off as slaves.' This time you said, 'they made slaves of the women, but they did not stop there: they even made slaves of the children.'"

"That's the same."

"It is the same story, but you've changed the way you tell it."

"No," said Kokwa, "I told it just as I told it before."

Jijingi didn't want to try to explain what words were. Instead he said, "If you told it as you did before, you would say 'the Uyengi captured the women and children and carried them off as slaves' every time."

For a moment Kokwa stared at him, and then he laughed. "Is this what you think is important, now that you've learned the art of writing?"

Sabe, who had been listening to them, chided Kokwa. "It's not your place to judge Jijingi. The hare favors one food, the hippo favors another. Let each spend his time as he pleases."

"Of course, Sabe, of course," said Kokwa, but he threw a derisive glance at Jijingi.

Afterwards, Jijingi remembered the proverb Moseby had mentioned. Even though Kokwa was telling the same story, he might arrange the words differently each time he told it; he was skilled enough as a storyteller that the arrangement of words didn't matter. It was different for Moseby, who never acted anything out when he gave his sermons; for him, the words were what was important. Jijingi realized that Moseby wrote down his sermons not because his memory was terrible, but because he was looking for a specific arrangement of words. Once he found the one he wanted, he could hold on to it for as long as he needed.

Out of curiosity, Jijingi tried imagining he had to deliver a sermon, and began writing down what he would say. Seated on the root of a mango tree with the notebook Moseby had given him, he composed a sermon on *tsav*, the quality that enabled some men to have power over others, and a subject which Moseby hadn't understood and had dismissed as foolishness. He read his first attempt to one of his age-mates, who pronounced it terrible, leading them to have a brief shoving match, but afterwards Jijingi had to admit his age-mate was right. He tried writing out his sermon a second time and then a third before he became tired of it and moved on to other topics.

As he practiced his writing, Jijingi came to understand what Moseby had meant; writing was not just a way to record what someone said; it could help you decide what you would say before you said it. And words were not just the pieces of speaking; they were the pieces of thinking. When you wrote them down, you could grasp your thoughts like bricks in your hands and push them into different arrangements. Writing let you look at your thoughts in a way you couldn't if you were just talking, and having seen them, you could improve them, make them stronger and more elaborate.

PSYCHOLOGISTS MAKE A distinction between semantic memory – knowledge of general facts – and episodic memory – recollection of personal experiences. We've been using technological supplements for semantic memory ever since the invention of writing: first books, then search engines. By contrast, we've historically resisted such aids when it comes to episodic memory; few people have ever kept as many diaries or photo albums as they did ordinary books. The obvious reason is convenience; if we wanted a book on the birds of North America, we could consult one that an ornithologist has written, but if we wanted a daily diary, we had to write it for ourselves. But I also wonder if another reason is that, subconsciously, we regarded our episodic memories as such an integral part of our identities that we were reluctant to externalize them, to relegate them to books on a shelf or files on a computer.

That may be about to change. For years parents have been recording their children's every moment, so even if children weren't wearing personal cams, their lifelogs were effectively already being compiled. Now parents are having their children wear retinal projectors at younger and younger ages so they can reap the benefits of assistive software agents sooner. Imagine what will happen if children begin using Remem to access those lifelogs: their mode of cognition will diverge from ours because the act of recall will be different. Rather than thinking of an event from her past and seeing it with her mind's eye, a child will subvocalize a reference to it and watch video footage with her physical eyes. Episodic memory will become entirely technologically mediated.

An obvious drawback to such reliance is the possibility that people might become virtual amnesiacs whenever the software crashes. But just as worrying to me as the prospect of technological failure was that of technological success: how will it change a person's conception of herself when she's only seen her past through the unblinking eye of a video camera? Just as there's a feedback loop in softening harsh memories, there's also one at work in the romanticization of childhood memories, and disrupting that process will have consequences.

The earliest birthday I remember is my fourth; I remember blowing out the candles on my cake, the thrill of tearing the wrapping paper off the presents. There's no video of the event, but there are snapshots in the family album, and they are consistent with what I remember. In fact, I suspect I no longer remember the day itself. It's more likely that I manufactured the memory when I was first shown the snapshots and over time, I've imbued it with the emotion I imagine I felt that day. Little by little, over repeated instances of recall, I've created a happy memory for myself.

Another of my earliest memories is of playing on the living room rug, pushing toy cars around, while my grandmother worked at her sewing machine; she would occasionally turn and smile warmly at me. There are no photos of that moment, so I know the recollection is mine and mine alone. It is a lovely, idyllic memory. Would I want to be presented with actual footage of that afternoon? No; absolutely not.

Regarding the role of truth in autobiography, the critic Roy Pascal wrote, "On the one side are the truths of fact, on the other the truth of the writer's feeling, and where the two coincide cannot be decided by any outside authority in advance." Our memories are private autobiographies, and that afternoon with my grandmother features prominently in mine because of the feelings associated with it. What if video footage revealed that my grandmother's smile was in fact perfunctory, that she was actually frustrated because her sewing wasn't going well? What's important to me about that memory is the happiness I associated with it, and I wouldn't want that jeopardized.

It seemed to me that continuous video of my entire childhood would be full of facts but devoid of feeling, simply because cameras couldn't capture the emotional dimension of events. As far as the camera was concerned, that afternoon with my grandmother would be indistinguishable from a hundred others. And if I'd grown up with access to all the video footage, there'd have been no way for me to assign more emotional weight to any particular day, no nucleus around which nostalgia could accrete.

And what will the consequences be when people can claim to remember their infancy? I could readily imagine a situation where, if you ask a young person what her earliest memory is, she will simply look baffled; after all, she has video dating back to the day of her birth. The inability to remember the first few years of one's life – what psychologists call childhood amnesia – might soon be a thing of the past. No more would parents tell their children anecdotes beginning with the words "You don't remember this because you were just a toddler when it happened." It'll be as if childhood amnesia is a characteristic of humanity's childhood, and in ouroboric fashion, our youth will vanish from our memories.

Part of me wanted to stop this, to protect children's ability to see the beginning of their lives filtered through gauze, to keep those origin stories from being replaced by cold, desaturated video. But maybe they will feel just as warmly about their lossless digital memories as I do of my imperfect, organic memories.

People are made of stories. Our memories are not the impartial accumulation of every second we've lived; they're the narrative that we assembled out of selected moments. Which is why, even when we've experienced the same events as other individuals, we never constructed identical narratives: the criteria used for selecting moments were different for each of us, and a reflection of our personalities. Each of us noticed the details that caught our attention and remembered what was important to us, and the narratives we built shaped our personalities in turn.

But, I wondered, if everyone remembered everything, would our differences get shaved away? What would happen to our sense of selves? It seemed to me that a perfect memory couldn't be a narrative any more than unedited security-cam footage could be a feature film.

WHEN JIJINGI WAS twenty, an officer from the administration came to the village to speak with Sabe. He had brought with him a young Tiv man who had attended the mission school in Katsina-Ala. The administration wanted to have a written record of all the disputes brought before the tribal courts, so they were assigning each chief one of these youths to act as a scribe. Sabe had Jijingi come forward, and to the officer he said, "I know you don't have enough scribes for all of Tivland. Jijingi here has learned to write; he can act as our scribe, and you can send your boy to another village." The officer tested Jijingi's ability to write, but Moseby had taught him well, and eventually the officer agreed to have him be Sabe's scribe.

After the officer had left, Jijingi asked Sabe why he hadn't wanted the boy from Katsina-Ala to be his scribe.

"No one who comes from the mission school can be trusted," said Sabe.

"Why not? Did the Europeans make them liars?"

"They're partly to blame, but so are we. When the Europeans collected boys for the mission school years ago, most elders gave them the ones they wanted to get rid of, the layabouts and malcontents. Now those boys have returned, and they feel no kinship with anyone. They wield their knowledge of writing like a long gun; they demand their chiefs find them wives, or else they'll write lies about them and have the Europeans depose them."

Jijingi knew a boy who was always complaining and looking for ways to avoid work; it would be a disaster if someone like him had power over Sabe. "Can't you tell the Europeans about this?"

"Many have," Sabe answered. "It was Maisho of the Kwande clan who warned me about the scribes; they were installed in Kwande villages first. Maisho was fortunate that the Europeans believed him instead of his scribe's lies, but he knows of other chiefs who were not so lucky; the Europeans often believe paper over people. I don't wish to take the chance." He looked at Jijingi seriously. "You are my kin, Jijingi, and kin to everyone in this village. I trust you to write down what I say."

"Yes, Sabe."

Tribal court was held every month, from morning until late afternoon for three days in a row, and it always attracted an audience, sometimes one so large that Sabe had to demand everyone sit to allow the breeze to reach the center of the circle. Jijingi sat next to Sabe and recorded the details of each dispute in a book the officer had left. It was a good job; he was paid out of the fees collected from the disputants, and he was given not just a chair but a small table too, which he could use for writing even when court wasn't in session. The complaints Sabe heard were varied – one might be about a stolen bicycle, another might be about whether a man was responsible for his neighbor's crops failing – but most had to do with wives. For one such dispute, Jijingi wrote down the following:

> Umem's wife Girgi has run away from home and gone back to her kin. Her kinsman Anongo has tried to convince her to stay with her husband, but Girgi refuses, and there is no more Anongo can do. Umem demands the return of the £11 he paid as bridewealth. Anongo says he has no money at the moment, and moreover that he was only paid £6.
>
> Sabe requested witnesses for both sides. Anongo says he has witnesses, but they have gone on a trip. Umem produces a witness, who is sworn in. He testifies that he himself counted the £11 that Umem paid to Anongo.

Sabe asks Girgi to return to her husband and be a good wife, but she says she has had all that she can stand of him. Sabe instructs Anongo to repay Umem £11, the first payment to be in three months when his crops are saleable. Anongo agrees.

It was the final dispute of the day, by which time Sabe was clearly tired. "Selling vegetables to pay back bridewealth," he said afterwards, shaking his head. "This wouldn't have happened when I was a boy."

Jijingi knew what he meant. In the past, the elders said, you conducted exchanges with similar items: if you wanted a goat, you could trade chickens for it; if you wanted to marry a woman, you promised one of your kinswomen to her family. Then the Europeans said they would no longer accept vegetables as payment for taxes, insisting that it be paid in coin. Before long, everything could be exchanged for money; you could use it to buy everything from a calabash to a wife. The elders considered it absurd.

"The old ways are vanishing," agreed Jijingi. He didn't say that young people preferred things this way, because the Europeans had also decreed that bridewealth could only be paid if the woman consented to the marriage. In the past, a young woman might be promised to an old man with leprous hands and rotting teeth, and have no choice but to marry him. Now a woman could marry the man she favored, as long as he could afford to pay the bridewealth. Jijingi himself was saving money to marry.

Moseby came to watch sometimes, but he found the proceedings confusing, and often asked Jijingi questions afterwards.

"For example, there was the dispute between Umem and Anongo over how much bridewealth was owed. Why was only the witness sworn in?" asked Moseby.

"To ensure that he said precisely what happened."

"But if Umem and Anongo were sworn in, that would have ensured they said precisely what happened too. Anongo was able to lie because he was not sworn in."

"Anongo didn't lie," said Jijingi. "He said what he considered right, just as Umem did."

"But what Anongo said wasn't the same as what the witness said."

"But that doesn't mean he was lying." Then Jijingi remembered something about the European language, and understood Moseby's confusion. "Our language has two words for what in your language is called 'true.' There is what's right, *mimi*, and what's precise, *vough*. In a dispute the principals say what they consider right; they speak *mimi*. The witnesses, however, are sworn to say precisely what happened; they speak *vough*. When Sabe has heard what happened he can decide what action is *mimi* for everyone. But it's not lying if the principals don't speak *vough*, as long as they speak *mimi*."

Moseby clearly disapproved. "In the land I come from, everyone who testifies in court must swear to speak *vough*, even the principals."

Jijingi didn't see the point of that, but all he said was, "Every tribe has its own customs."

"Yes, customs may vary, but the truth is the truth; it doesn't change from one person to another. And remember what the Bible says: the truth shall set you free."

"I remember," said Jijingi. Moseby had said that it was knowing God's truth that had made the Europeans so successful. There was no denying their wealth or power, but who knew what was the cause?

IN ORDER TO write about Remem, it was only fair that I try it out myself. The problem was that I didn't have a lifelog for it to index; typically I only activated my personal cam when I was conducting an interview or covering an event. But I've certainly spent time in the presence of people who kept lifelogs, and I could make use of what they'd recorded. While all lifelogging software has privacy controls in place, most people also grant basic sharing rights: if your actions were recorded in their lifelog, you have access to the footage in which you're present. So I launched an agent to assemble a partial lifelog from the footage others had recorded, using my GPS history as the basis for the query. Over the course of a week, my request propagated through social networks and public video archives, and I was rewarded with snippets of video ranging from a few seconds in length to a few hours: not just security-cam footage but excerpts from the lifelogs of friends, acquaintances, and even complete strangers.

The resulting lifelog was of course highly fragmentary compared to what I would have had if I'd been recording video myself, and the footage was all from a third-person perspective rather than the first-person that most lifelogs have, but Remem was able to work with that. I expected that coverage would be thickest in the later years, simply due to the increasing popularity of lifelogs. It was somewhat to my surprise, then, that when I looked at a graph of the coverage, I found a bump in the coverage over a decade ago. Nicole had been keeping a lifelog since she was a teenager, so an unexpectedly large segment of my domestic life was present.

I was initially a bit uncertain of how to test Remem, since I obviously couldn't ask it to bring up video of an event I didn't remember. I figured I'd start out with something I did remember. I subvocalized, "The time Vince told me about his trip to Palau."

My retinal projector displayed a window in the lower left corner of my field of vision: I'm having lunch with my friends Vincent and Jeremy. Vincent didn't maintain a lifelog either, so the footage was from Jeremy's point of view. I listened to Vincent rave about scuba diving for a minute.

Next I tried something that I only vaguely remembered. "The dinner banquet when I sat between Deborah and Lyle." I didn't remember who else was sitting at the table, and wondered if Remem could help me identify them.

Sure enough, Deborah had been recording that evening, and with her video I was able to use a recognition agent to identify everyone sitting across from us.

After those initial successes, I had a run of failures; not surprising, considering the gaps in the lifelog. But over the course of an hour-long survey of past events, Remem's performance was generally impressive.

Finally it seemed time for me to try Remem on some memories that were more emotionally freighted. My relationship with Nicole felt strong enough now for me to safely revisit the fights we'd had when she was young. I figured I'd start with the argument I remembered clearly, and work backwards from there.

I subvocalized, "The time Nicole yelled at me 'you're the reason she left.'"

The window displays the kitchen of the house we lived in when Nicole was growing up. The footage is from Nicole's point of view, and I'm standing in front of the stove. It's obvious we're fighting.

"You're the reason she left. You can leave too, for all I care. I sure as hell would be better off without you."

The words were just as I remembered them, but it wasn't Nicole saying them.

It was me.

My first thought was that it must be a fake, that Nicole had edited the video to put her words into my mouth. She must have noticed my request for access to her lifelog footage, and concocted this to teach me a lesson. Or perhaps it was a film she had created to show her friends, to reinforce the stories she told about me. But why was she still so angry at me, that she would do such a thing? Hadn't we gotten past this?

I started skimming through the video, looking for inconsistencies that would indicate where the edited footage had been spliced in. The subsequent footage showed Nicole running out of the house, just as I remembered, so there wouldn't be signs of inconsistency there. I rewound the video and started watching the preceding argument.

Initially I was angry as I watched, angry at Nicole for going to such lengths to create this lie, because the preceding footage was all consistent with me being the one who yelled at her. Then some of what I was saying in the video began to sound queasily familiar: complaining about being called to her school again because she'd gotten into trouble, accusing her of spending time with the wrong crowd. But this wasn't the context in which I'd said those things, was it? I had been voicing my concern, not berating her. Nicole must have adapted things I'd said elsewhere to make her slanderous video more plausible. That was the only explanation, right?

I asked Remem to examine the video's watermark, and it reported the video was unmodified. I saw that Remem had suggested a correction in my search terms: where I had said "the time Nicole yelled at me," it offered "the time I yelled at Nicole." The correction must have been displayed at the same time as the initial search result, but I hadn't noticed. I shut down Remem in disgust, furious at the product. I was about to search for information on forging a digital watermark to prove this video was faked, but I stopped myself, recognizing it as an act of desperation.

I would have testified, hand on a stack of Bibles or using any oath required of me, that it was Nicole who'd accused me of being the reason her mother left us. My recollection of that argument was as clear as any memory I had, but that wasn't the only reason I found the video hard to believe; it was also my knowledge that – whatever my faults or imperfections – I was never the kind of father who could say such a thing to his child.

Yet here was digital video proving that I had been exactly that kind of father. And while I wasn't that man anymore, I couldn't deny that I was continuous with him.

Even more telling was the fact that for many years I had successfully hidden the truth from myself. Earlier I said that the details we choose to remember are a reflection of our personalities. What did it say about me that I put those words in Nicole's mouth instead of mine?

I remembered that argument as being a turning point for me. I had imagined a narrative of redemption and self-improvement in which I was the heroic single father, rising to meet the challenge. But the reality was... what? How much of what had happened since then could I take credit for?

I restarted Remem and began looking at video of Nicole's graduation from college. That was an event I had recorded myself, so I had footage of Nicole's face, and she seemed genuinely happy in my presence. Was she hiding her true feelings so well that I couldn't detect them? Or, if our relationship had actually improved, how had that happened? I had obviously been a much worse father fourteen years ago than I'd thought; it would be tempting to conclude I had come farther to reach where I currently was, but I couldn't trust my perceptions anymore. Did Nicole even have positive feelings about me now?

I wasn't going to try using Remem to answer this question; I needed to go to the source. I called Nicole and left a message saying I wanted to talk to her, and asking if I could come over to her apartment that evening.

*　　*　　*

IT WAS A few years later that Sabe began attending a series of meetings of all the chiefs in the Shangev clan. He explained to Jijingi that the Europeans no longer wished to deal with so many chiefs, and were demanding that all of Tivland be divided into eight groups they called 'septs.' As a result, Sabe and the other chiefs had to discuss who the Shangev clan would join with. Although there was no need for a scribe, Jijingi was curious to hear the deliberations and asked Sabe if he might accompany him, and Sabe agreed.

Jijingi had never seen so many elders in one place before; some were even-tempered and dignified like Sabe, while others were loud and full of bluster. They argued for hours on end.

In the evening after Jijingi had returned, Moseby asked him what it had been like. Jijingi sighed. "Even if they're not yelling, they're fighting like wildcats."

"Who does Sabe think you should join?"

"We should join with the clans that we're most closely related to; that's the Tiv way. And since Shangev was the son of Kwande, our clan should join with the Kwande clan, who live to the south."

"That makes sense," said Moseby. "So why is there disagreement?"

"The members of the Shangev clan don't all live next to each other. Some live on the farmland in the west, near the Jechira clan, and the elders there are friendly with the Jechira elders. They'd like the Shangev clan to join the Jechira clan, because then they'd have more influence in the resulting sept."

"I see." Moseby thought for a moment. "Could the western Shangev join a different sept from the southern Shangev?"

Jijingi shook his head. "We Shangev all have one father, so we should all remain together. All the elders agree on that."

"But if lineage is so important, how can the elders from the west argue that the Shangev clan ought to join with the Jechira clan?"

"That's what the disagreement was about. The elders from the west are claiming Shangev was the son of Jechira."

"Wait, you don't know who Shangev's parents were?"

"Of course we know! Sabe can recite his ancestors all the way back to Tiv himself. The elders from the west are merely pretending that Shangev was Jechira's son because they'd benefit from joining with the Jechira clan."

"But if the Shangev clan joined with the Kwande clan, wouldn't your elders benefit?"

"Yes, but Shangev was Kwande's son." Then Jijingi realized what Moseby was implying. "You think our elders are the ones pretending!"

"No, not at all. It just sounds like both sides have equally good claims, and there's no way to tell who's right."

"Sabe's right."

"Of course," said Moseby. "But how can you get the others to admit that? In the land I come from, many people write down their lineage on paper. That way we can trace our ancestry precisely, even many generations in the past."

"Yes, I've seen the lineages in your Bible, tracing Abraham back to Adam."

"Of course. But even apart from the Bible, people have recorded their lineages. When people want to find out who they're descended from, they can consult paper. If you had paper, the other elders would have to admit that Sabe was right."

That was a good point, Jijingi admitted. If only the Shangev clan had been using paper long ago. Then something occurred to him. "How long ago did the Europeans first come to Tivland?"

"I'm not sure. At least forty years ago, I think."

"Do you think they might have written down anything about the Shangev clan's lineage when they first arrived?"

Moseby looked thoughtful. "Perhaps. The administration definitely keeps a lot of records. If there are any, they'd be stored at the government station in Katsina-Ala."

A truck carried goods along the motor road into Katsina-Ala every fifth day, when the market was being held, and the next market would be the day after tomorrow. If he left tomorrow morning, he could reach the motor road in time to get a ride. "Do you think they would let me see them?"

"It might be easier if you have a European with you," said Moseby, smiling. "Shall we take a trip?"

NICOLE OPENED THE door to her apartment and invited me in. She was obviously curious about why I'd come. "So what did you want to talk about?"

I wasn't sure how to begin. "This is going to sound strange."

"Okay," she said.

I told her about viewing my partial lifelog using Remem, and seeing the argument we'd had when she was sixteen that ended with me yelling at her and her leaving the house. "Do you remember that day?"

"Of course I do." She looked uncomfortable, uncertain of where I was going with this.

"I remembered it too, or at least I thought I did. But I remembered it differently. The way I remembered it, it was you who said it to me."

"Me who said what?"

"I remembered you telling me that I could leave for all you cared, and that you'd be better off without me."

Nicole stared at me for a long time. "All these years, that's how you've remembered that day?"

"Yes, until today."

"That'd almost be funny if it weren't so sad."

I felt sick to my stomach. "I'm so sorry. I can't tell you how sorry I am."

"Sorry you said it, or sorry that you imagined me saying it?"

"Both."

"Well you should be! You know how that made me feel?"

"I can't imagine. I know I felt terrible when I thought you had said it to me."

"Except that was just something you made up. It actually *happened* to me." She shook her head in disbelief. "Fucking typical."

That hurt to hear. "Is it? Really?"

"Sure," she said. "You're always acting like you're the victim, like you're the good guy who deserves to be treated better than you are."

"You make me sound like I'm delusional."

"Not delusional. Just blind and self-absorbed."

I bristled a little. "I'm trying to apologize here."

"Right, right. This is about you."

"No, you're right, I'm sorry." I waited until Nicole gestured for me to go on. "I guess I am... blind and self-absorbed. The reason it's hard for me to admit that is that I thought I had opened my eyes and gotten over that."

She frowned. "What?"

I told her how I felt like I had turned around as a father and rebuilt our relationship, culminating in a moment of bonding at her college graduation. Nicole wasn't openly derisive, but her expression caused me to stop talking; it was obvious I was embarrassing myself.

"Did you still hate me at graduation?" I asked. "Was I completely making it up that you and I got along then?"

"No, we did get along at graduation. But it wasn't because you had magically become a good father."

"What was it, then?"

She paused, took a deep breath, and then said, "I started seeing a therapist when I went to college." She paused again. "She pretty much saved my life."

My first thought was, *why would Nicole need a therapist?* I pushed that down and said, "I didn't know you were in therapy."

"Of course you didn't; you were the last person I would have told. Anyway, by the time I was a senior, she had convinced me that I was better off not staying angry at you. That's why you and I got along so well at graduation."

So I had indeed fabricated a narrative that bore little resemblance to reality. Nicole had done all the work, and I had done none.

"I guess I don't really know you."

She shrugged. "You know me as well as you need to."

That hurt, too, but I could hardly complain. "You deserve better," I said.

Nicole gave a brief, rueful laugh. "You know, when I was younger, I used to daydream about you saying that. But now... well, it's not as if it fixes everything, is it?"

I realized that I'd been hoping she would forgive me then and there, and then everything would be good. But it would take more than my saying sorry to repair our relationship.

Something occurred to me. "I can't change the things I did, but at least I can stop pretending I didn't do them. I'm going to use Remem to get an honest picture of myself, take a kind of personal inventory."

Nicole looked at me, gauging my sincerity. "Fine," she said. "But let's be clear: you don't come running to me every time you feel guilty over treating me like crap. I worked hard to put that behind me, and I'm not going to relive it just so you can feel better about yourself."

"Of course." I saw that she was tearing up. "And I've upset you again by bringing all this up. I'm sorry."

"It's all right, Dad. I appreciate what you're trying to do. Just... let's not do it again for a while, okay?"

"Right." I moved toward the door to leave, and then stopped. "I just wanted to ask... if it's possible, if there's anything I can do to make amends..."

"Make amends?" She looked incredulous. "I don't know. Just be more considerate, will you?"

And that what I'm trying to do.

AT THE GOVERNMENT station there was indeed paper from forty years ago, what the Europeans called "assessment reports," and Moseby's presence was sufficient to grant them access. They were written in the European language, which Jijingi couldn't read, but they included diagrams of the ancestry of the various clans, and he could identify the Tiv names in those diagrams easily enough, and Moseby had confirmed that his interpretation was correct. The elders in the western farms were right, and Sabe was wrong: Shangev was not Kwande's son, he was Jechira's.

One of the men at the government station had agreed to type up a copy of the relevant page so Jijingi could take it with him. Moseby decided to stay in Katsina-Ala to visit with the missionaries there, but Jijingi came home right away. He felt like an impatient child on the return trip, wishing he could ride the truck all the way back instead of having to walk from the motor road. As soon as he had arrived at the village, Jijingi looked for Sabe.

He found him on the path leading to a neighboring farm; some neighbors had stopped Sabe to have him settle a dispute over how a nanny goat's kids should be distributed. Finally, they were satisfied, and Sabe resumed his walk. Jijingi walked beside him.

"Welcome back," said Sabe.

"Sabe, I've been to Katsina-Ala."

"Ah. Why did you go there?"

Jijingi showed him the paper. "This was written long ago, when the Europeans first came here. They spoke to the elders of the Shangev clan then, and when the elders told them the history of the Shangev clan, they said that Shangev was the son of Jechira."

Sabe's reaction was mild. "Whom did the Europeans ask?"

Jijingi looked at the paper. "Batur and Iorkyaha."

"I remember them," he said, nodding. "They were wise men. They would not have said such a thing."

Jijingi pointed at the words on the page. "But they did!"

"Perhaps you are reading it wrong."

"I am not! I know how to read."

Sabe shrugged. "Why did you bring this paper back here?"

"What it says is important. It means we should rightfully be joined with the Jechira clan."

"You think the clan should trust your decision on this matter?"

"I'm not asking the clan to trust me. I'm asking them to trust the men who were elders when you were young."

"And so they should. But those men aren't here. All you have is paper."

"The paper tells us what they would say if they were here."

"Does it? A man doesn't speak only one thing. If Batur and Iorkyaha were here, they would agree with me that we should join with the Kwande clan."

"How could they, when Shangev was the son of Jechira?" He pointed at the sheet of paper. "The Jechira are our closer kin."

Sabe stopped walking and turned to face Jijingi. "Questions of kinship cannot be resolved by paper. You're a scribe because Maisho of the Kwande clan warned me about the boys from the mission school. Maisho wouldn't have looked out for us if we didn't share the same father. Your position is proof of how close our clans are, but you forget that. You look to paper to tell you what you should already know, here." Sabe tapped him on his chest. "Have you studied paper so much that you've forgotten what it is to be Tiv?"

Jijingi opened his mouth to protest when he realized that Sabe was right. All the time he'd spent studying writing had made him think like a European. He had come to trust what was written on paper over what was said by people, and that wasn't the Tiv way.

The assessment report of the Europeans was *vough*; it was exact and precise, but that wasn't enough to settle the question. The choice of which clan to join with had to be right for the community; it had to be *mimi*. Only the elders could determine what was *mimi*; it was their responsibility to decide what was best for the Shangev clan. Asking Sabe to defer to the paper was asking him to act against what he considered right.

"You're right, Sabe," he said. "Forgive me. You're my elder, and it was wrong of me to suggest that paper could know more than you."

Sabe nodded and resumed walking. "You are free to do as you wish, but I believe it will do more harm than good to show that paper to others."

Jijingi considered it. The elders from the western farms would undoubtedly argue that the assessment report supported their position, prolonging a debate that had already gone on too long. But more than that, it would move the Tiv down the path of regarding paper as the source of truth; it would be another stream in which the old ways were washing away, and he could see no benefit in it.

"I agree," said Jijingi. "I won't show this to anyone else."

Sabe nodded.

Jijingi walked back to his hut, reflecting on what had happened. Even without attending a mission school, he had begun thinking like a European; his practice of writing in his notebooks had led him to disrespect his elders without him even being aware of it. Writing helped him think more clearly, he couldn't deny that; but that wasn't good enough reason to trust paper over people.

As a scribe, he had to keep the book of Sabe's decisions in tribal court. But he didn't need to keep the other notebooks, the ones in which he'd written down his thoughts. He would use them as tinder for the cooking fire.

WE DON'T NORMALLY think of it as such, but writing is a technology, which means that a literate person is someone whose thought processes are technologically mediated. We became cognitive cyborgs as soon as we became fluent readers, and the consequences of that were profound.

Before a culture adopts the use of writing, when its knowledge is transmitted exclusively through oral means, it can very easily revise its history. It's not intentional, but it is inevitable; throughout the world, bards and griots have adapted their material to their audiences, and thus gradually adjusted the past to suit the needs of the present. The idea that accounts of the past shouldn't change is a product of literate cultures' reverence for the written word. Anthropologists will tell you that oral cultures understand the past differently; for them, their histories don't need to be accurate so much as they need to validate the community's understanding of itself. So it wouldn't be correct to say that their histories are unreliable; their histories do what they need to do.

Right now each of us is a private oral culture. We rewrite our pasts to suit our needs and support the story we tell about ourselves. With our memories we are all guilty of a Whig interpretation of our personal histories, seeing our former selves as steps toward our glorious present selves.

But that era is coming to an end. Remem is merely the first of a new generation of memory prostheses, and as these products gain widespread adoption, we will be replacing our malleable organic memories with perfect digital archives. We will have a record of what we actually did instead of stories that evolve over repeated tellings. Within our minds, each of us will be transformed from an oral culture into a literate one.

It would be easy for me to assert that literate cultures are better off than oral ones, but my bias should be obvious, since I'm writing these words rather than speaking them to you. Instead I will say that it's easier for me to appreciate the benefits of literacy and harder to recognize everything it has cost us. Literacy encourages a culture to place more value on documentation and less on subjective experience, and overall I think the positives outweigh the negatives. Written records are subject to every kind of error and their interpretation is subject to change, but at least the words on the page remain fixed, and there is real merit in that.

When it comes to our individual memories, I live on the opposite side of the divide. As someone whose identity was built on organic memory, I'm threatened by the prospect of removing subjectivity from our recall of events. I used to think it could be valuable for individuals to tell stories about themselves, valuable in a way that it couldn't be for cultures, but I'm a product of my time, and times change. We can't prevent the adoption of digital memory any more than oral cultures could stop the arrival of literacy, so the best I can do is look for something positive in it.

And I think I've found the real benefit of digital memory. The point is not to prove you were right; the point is to admit you were wrong.

Because all of us have been wrong on various occasions, engaged in cruelty and hypocrisy, and we've forgotten most of those occasions. And that means we don't really know ourselves. How much personal insight can I claim if I can't trust my memory? How much can you? You're probably thinking that, while your memory isn't perfect, you've never engaged in revisionism of the magnitude I'm guilty of. But I was just as certain as you, and I was wrong. You may say, "I know I'm not perfect. I've made mistakes." I am here to tell you that you have made more than you think, that some of the core assumptions on which your self-image is built are actually lies. Spend some time using Remem, and you'll find out.

But the reason I now recommend Remem is not for the shameful reminders it provides of your past; it's to avoid the need for those in the future. Organic memory was what enabled me to construct a whitewashed narrative of my parenting skills, but by using digital memory from now on, I hope to keep that from happening. The truth about my behavior won't be presented to me by someone else, making me defensive; it won't even be something I'll discover as a private shock, prompting a re-evaluation. With Remem providing only the unvarnished facts, my image of myself will never stray too far from the truth in the first place.

Digital memory will not stop us from telling stories about ourselves. As I said earlier, we are made of stories, and nothing can change that. What digital memory will do is change those stories from fabulations that emphasize our best acts and elide our worst, into ones that – I hope – acknowledge our fallibility and make us less judgmental about the fallibility of others.

Nicole has begun using Remem as well, and discovered that her recollection of events isn't perfect either. This hasn't made her forgive me for the way I treated her – nor should it, because her misdeeds were minor compared to mine – but it has softened her anger at my misremembering my actions, because she realizes it's something we all do. And I'm embarrassed to admit that this is precisely the scenario Erica Meyers predicted when she talked about Remem's effects on relationships.

This doesn't mean I've changed my mind about the downsides of digital memory; there are many, and people need to be aware of them. I just don't think I can argue the case with any sort of objectivity anymore. I abandoned the article I was planning to write about memory prostheses; I handed off the research I'd done to a colleague, and she wrote a fine piece about the pros and cons of the software, a dispassionate article free from all the soul-searching and angst that would have saturated anything I submitted. Instead, I've written this.

The account I've given of the Tiv is based in fact, but isn't precisely accurate. There was indeed a dispute among the Tiv in 1941 over whom the Shangev clan should join with, based on differing claims about the parentage of the clan's founder, and administrative records did show that the clan elders' account of their genealogy had changed over time. But many of the specific details I've described are invented. The actual events were more complicated and less dramatic, as actual events always are, so I have taken liberties to make a better narrative. I've told a story in order to make a case for the truth. I recognize the contradiction here.

As for my account of my argument with Nicole, I've tried to make it as accurate as I possibly could. I've been recording everything since I started working on this project, and I've consulted the recordings repeatedly when writing this. But in my choice of which details to include and which to omit, perhaps I have just constructed another story. In spite of my efforts to be unflinching, have I flattered myself with this portrayal? Have I distorted events so they more closely follow the arc expected of a confessional narrative? The only way you can judge is by comparing my account against the recordings themselves, so I'm doing something I never thought I'd do: with Nicole's permission, I am granting public access to my lifelog, such as it is. Take a look at the video, and decide for yourself.

And if you think I've been less than honest, tell me. I want to know.

THE INK READERS OF DOI SAKET

Thomas Olde Heuvelt

Dutch novelist and short fiction writer Thomas Olde Heuvelt (en. oldeheuvelt.com) is the author of five novels, *De Onvoorziene*, *PhantasAmnesia*, *Leerling Tovenaar Vader & Zoon*, *Harten Sara*, and *HEX*. His work has been awarded the Paul Harland Prize (for best Dutch work of the fantastic) on three occasions, received an honourable mention in the Science Fiction & Fantasy Translation Awards and was nominated for the Hugo Award for Best Novelette in 2013. His short fiction has appeared in English from *Tor.com*, Oxygen Books, *Lightspeed*, and PS Publishing. His novel *HEX* will be published in English in 2015.

IT WAS DURING a night in the twelfth lunar month of this year when two strong hands pushed young Tangmoo down into the bed of the Mae Ping River, and by doing so, ironically, fulfilled his only wish. Tangmoo flailed his arms wildly, churning up the swirling water. The whites of his eyes reflected flashes from the fireworks as his smothered cries rose in bubbles to the surface, where they burst in silence: *help, help, help, help!*

These filtered cries of alarm were mistaken by a pair of dragonflies, fused in flight, their only wish to remain larvaless and so prolong their love dance endlessly, for the dripping of morning dew. So unsettled was the pair that their breaths caught, and for a second, just when the male ejaculated, they separated. Force of habit subsequently incited them to repeat this in all their future climaxes, making their fondest wish actually come true.

But this was a chance circumstance. The point here is that young Tangmoo screamed, and his lungs filled with water, and please, he did not want to die this way.

In order to fully grasp the tragedy of this drama, we'll have to flash back a few days and take a peek at the village of Doi Saket, situated on the exact same river shore. Late one afternoon, about an hour before it was time for his third bowl of rice of the day, the well-bellied weed exterminator Uan[1] came running into the temple square. Winded as a consequence of the oversized behind that had given him his name, he stopped to catch his breath, leaning against the enormous stone phallus outside the temple (though not on the temple grounds themselves, since Buddha doesn't approve of that kind of non-Buddhist folly), before wheezing, "Come see, come see! The first wish has arrived!"

"Watch out!" cried the malodorous lampshade maker Tao[2], whose nickname did not spring from his shell-head or his tortoise appearance, but from his extreme robustness, and he nodded toward the phallus.

In his frenzy, Uan had forgotten all about the general consensus around the ancient fertility symbol. The adulterous rice peeler Somchai[3] had once cheated on her husband with three neighbors and a shopkeeper from a nearby village after she had been spotted on the phallic altar, touching herself and wrapped in nothing but silk ribbons. As a penalty, Somchai was buried waist-deep in the rice field so that her excess fertility could seep into the crops, and it was decided that the bewitched phallus was never to be touched again, and was only to be greeted by passers-by with a brief nod of the head, something that was ardently copied by the villagers and which consequently led to an abundance of oral sex. (There were rumors that the stone was not in fact bewitched at all, but that lustful Somchai suffered from some type of obsessive exhibitionism. Nonsense, of course.)

Quick as lightning, Uan let go of the stone (but he was too late: in the following year his wife would give birth to triplets) and yelled, "Come

---

[1] Uan means "hugely fat" in Thai – not necessarily an insult.

[2] "Turtle"

[3] "Real woman"

to the river, all of you! The first wish is arriving – I've seen it with my own eyes!"

"So soon?" said the well-mannered crab gatherer Kulap, just returning from the rice field with her basket. "I don't believe it. It's way too early."

Inside his house the generally respected Puu Yaybaan, chief of the village, heard the commotion and came running out the door. "What's going on?" he shouted, scattering chickens in his wild dash. "What's all this racket?"

"Uan says the first wish is here," Kulap said, crinkling her nose in a way that was all in contrast to her gentle nature. "But I don't believe it."

"Is this true?" the Puu Yaybaan asked.

"It's as true as me standing here," Uan insisted, and indeed: there he stood.

"Well... So did you retrieve it?" Tao asked, placing his lampshade at his feet.

"Certainly not," Uan responded. "I can't swim, I'm too heavy to stay afloat. Come on, everybody! To the river!"

The hubbub caused many a window shutter to open, many a cell phone to ring, and many a banana leaf to furl bashfully back into its tree, as curiosity was the one thing that could mobilize all the villagers in unison. And sure enough, when they arrived at the riverside, they all saw it. A trace of brilliance on the tranquil stream. A floating lily made of plastic and crepe paper. A pearl inside a lotus blossom. The first wish of Loi Krathong.

The philosophical irrigator Daeng[4], named after the blood that covered him when he was born, waded through the shallows saying, "Is it a wish for happiness? A love wish? A last wish? Wishful thinking?"

The short-spoken restaurant owner Sorn[5], named after some curious agricultural mishap that no one remembered, pointed his stone pestle toward the brilliance on the water and said, "If we don't do something, it's going to float right past."

---

[4] "Red"

[5] "Wild goat"

"Someone needs to go get it!" the Puu Yaybaan cried, shushing the onlookers. Men hesitated on the shore, children waded into the river until their mothers whistled them back, and the scrawny frog catcher Yai[6] took off his clothes and dove into the deep green water.[7]

"What is it? What's the first wish?" the people shouted when Yai finally resurfaced and reached the little boat. "Does it have a note inside?"

Treading water, Yai unfolded the lotus leaves and produced a moist piece of paper. "Wait. I'm having trouble reading it. The words are smudged. But it says..." – dramatic pause as the river held its breath in anticipation – "'I wish for my dying water buffalo to get well – Bovorn S. from San Phak Wan.'"

"LOI KRATHONG HAS STARTED!" the Puu Yaybaan declared over the PA-system, used for announcing all important and unimportant news in the village, and his tinny words were greeted by cheers from the crowds on the riverbank. The cunning monk Sûa[8] broke into the traditional Loi Krathong song, soon joined by the village elders clapping their hands and the children splashing each other with water, while miles upstream, in the city of Chiang Mai, thousands upon thousands of wishes were being launched onto the river:

November full moon shines
Loi Krathong, Loi Krathong
And the water's high in local river and the klong
♪♫ Loi, Loi Krathong, Loi, Loi Krathong ♪♫
Loi Krathong is here and everybody's full of cheer

---

[6] "Beanpole"

[7] The Thai custom of addressing one another by nicknames is meant to remember oneself better and to fool the spirits into forgetting people's real names. As do the Thai themselves, for that matter. Irrespective of how unflattering the nickname may be, it is freely used in everyday life and no longer necessarily has a traditional origin. The wayward harvester driver Sungkaew, for instance, named his daughter Loli, after Marlboro Lights, and the unemployed mushroom picker Pakpao named her son Ham, after David Beckham. (Until his classmates discovered that in the mountain dialect "Ham" means "sack full of testicles', causing his well-meaning mother, unable to resist his ceaseless badgering, to rename him Porn.)

[8] "Tiger"

We're together at the klong
Each one with his krathong
As we push away we pray
We can see a better day

Young Tangmoo[9] heard the noise from where he was perched in the crown of the slender teng-rang tree, slinging a piece of plaited cotton around a broken and dreadfully sagging branch. The tree had been struck by lightning the previous summer. No matter how Tangmoo propped, nailed, tethered or jiggled the dead wood, every day around noontime it produced a loud *CRACK* and the infernal thing sank down a little closer toward his father's house. Every day Tangmoo climbed the tree with new boards or ropes, and every day the proportion of natural versus artificial outgrowths in the teng-rang tree shifted a little more in favor of the shoring material. His mother kept her tip money in an old wok, saving up so she could one day afford to call in a landscaper to eliminate the danger. But Tangmoo did not mind his daily chore. It somehow reminded him of a sacred ritual. The crown and leaves of the tree triggered a subconscious memory of the hollowed-out watermelon after which he had been named; a crib that had afforded him many sheltered days and nights when he was a baby.

"EVERYBODY DOWN TO THE RIVER!" the Puu Yaybaan's voice rang across the fields. "THERE ARE WISHES TO BE GRANTED! OH, AND REMEMBER TO PIN PLENTY A PENNY TO THE MONEY TREE OUTSIDE THE TEMPLE. WE WILL SEE A BETTER DAY!"

Tangmoo climbed down. He stopped to leave an offering of fresh oranges and cigarettes in the little spirit house and say a prayer, to thank the tree spirit for blessing them with a still-uncrushed house beneath the dead branch. (While Tangmoo naturally believed in Buddha and his lessons and rebirth and all, it didn't mean he had no room for spirits. And in fact the branch's benevolence had nothing to do with the tree spirit – so traumatized by the lightning strike that it had long since gone

---

[9] "Watermelon"

to live in another tree – but was closely related to young Tangmoo's own exceptional karma.)

Arriving at the riverside, Tangmoo spotted his little brother Nataphun vacantly digging holes in the sand.

"Hey, Tangmoo," Nataphun said.

"Aren't you going to watch?" Tangmoo asked. "The wishes are here."

"Nah, don't wanna. I'm hungry. I wish time would go faster so I could have supper."

"M'okay," Tangmoo said, shrugging.

A bit further down, where the tranquil Mae Ping River was now the scene of a splashing and churning bustle, Tangmoo picked a butterfly orchid, merely on impulse. As he did so, the orchid's calyx shook, causing minute grains of pollen, invisible to the naked eye, to drift up into the air and be carried upstream by a sudden gust of wind. A tremor went through the village. Those who peeled rice looked up from their work. Lovers fell silent. And the pollen? It landed on one of bored little Nataphun's nostrils. As soon as the boy took a breath, a rare allergy made him fall asleep instantly, only to be woken by the chirping of crickets about an hour later. Surprised by the swift fulfillment of his wish, Nataphun ran home to fill his growling stomach.

But this, the same as with the dragonflies, was purely coincidental, and nothing should be read into it.

By now the surface of the river was teeming with *krathongs*. Like any other boy in Doi Saket, Tangmoo had been told the tragicomic story of Loi Krathong's origins countless times, and so he was aware of the invaluable influence of the village he called home. Seven hundred years ago Neng Tanapong, daughter of a Brahman priest in the kingdom of Sukhothai, had been playing on the riverbank. The wench was so startled by the appearance of river goddess Phra Mae Khongkha (who by coincidence had picked the exact same spot to take a bath) that she made an unfortunate tumble into the water and drowned. Everyone knew that, in death, she read the wishes in the lotus boats passing above her dead eyes and made them all come true. And everyone knew that this event in honor of the river goddess was reenacted in Doi Saket every year, and it was *they* who granted the wishes with their ceremony.

Oh, the festival! All over Thailand people drank themselves into a stupor on cheap whiskey, sang their throats sore at moonlit karaoke parties, and made love, night after night, beneath fireworks and lantern lights. Everyone, everyone launched *krathongs* on the water and floated *khom loi*[10] into the air. Everyone made wishes.

But while the people in Chiang Mai partied, the villagers of Doi Saket set to work. Under guidance of the wayward harvester driver Sungkaew, they strung nets across the river and caught the *krathongs*. Men rowed to and fro in tiny boats while women waited on the bank to unburden them. Burnt incense sticks were tossed onto a pile of smoldering embers, spreading a fabulous aroma that the sultry breeze carried across the rice fields like a whispered message. Candle stubs were melted down, the wax used as fuel for the *khom loi*. Money, jewelry and other valuables sacrificed to the river goddess were collected by the Puu Yaybaan and pinned to the timber tree frame standing beside the stone phallus outside the temple, so that all could follow the example of the generous ones. Woe to the mortal who tried to steal: a night of dangling upside down from the holy daeng tree would await him, and a next life as the larva of a dengue mosquito.

"Filthy thieves," the Puu Yaybaan would fume.

But the wish notes were what mattered most. If they were still legible they were collected in a pile: *a life filled with love and happiness* here, *a new hip joint for my mother* there, and sometimes entire wish lists: *1) A fair amount of luck; 2) 20,000 Baht*[11] *(that ain't too much, is it?); 3) A bit more headway with my neighbor girl Phailin, though rumor has it that just recently she spread her legs for chicken farmer Kai, and if that's true then never mind; 4) A new screen door, which I would have bought ages ago if my boss Kemkhaeng wasn't too bloody stingy to give me a leg up from time to time; 5) A broken leg for Kemkhaeng; 6)...*

In other wish notes the ink had run so much from the journey on the water that special Ink Readers, initiated for the occasion, were sent into the river. Three monks, Sûa, Mongkut, and Sungkaew, were given the

---

[10] Wish lanterns made of rice paper with a burning firelighter underneath

[11] About 650 dollars

task of interpreting the running tendrils of ink beneath the water surface. For three days they swam back and forth, dragging themselves watery-eyed ashore to reel off their messages to the scribes on the riverbank, before they submerged again. If no note was found at all, the *krathong* was taken to the Exalted Abbot Chanarong[12], who would metaphysically distill the intended wish from its little boat.

Everyone in the village would tell you that they had once seen the Exalted Abbot floating a meditative little bit over his prayer rug, a *krathong* in his hands and mountains upon mountains of them beneath his exalted bare feet. All of them had been told the story so often in their formative years that they firmly believed it to be true. Yet no one had seen it with their own eyes. In fact, the Abbot was a senile old man who had trouble reading the verses and more importantly, who drooled a lot. If at some point he had been able to levitate, he had forgotten how ever since his first walker. Still, after much heated debate, voting, counting, and recounting, the village council had decided that clairvoyance was more sacred than dementia and therefore should always be given the benefit of the doubt. And so they unscrambled the Exalted Abbot's inarticulate prattle, and every single wish from northern Thailand was read in anticipation of the ceremony to be performed on the final night.

And the wishes?

They came true. At least, some of them.

Because in the dead of night the Puu Yaybaan, accompanied by his monks Sûa and Mongkut, drove his rickety pick-up truck to the village of San Phak Wan. On the way over, they spotted a water buffalo in radiant health and coaxed it from its rice paddy. While Mongkut kept watch outside the hut of sleeping Bovorn S., the other two swapped his terminally ill buffalo, more dead than alive where it lay tied to a rope, for the perfectly fit animal. Downstream, they tossed the weakened ox off a bridge. It resurfaced only once, mooing, and after that nothing more was heard besides the cicadas.

"SUCH GOOD FORTUNE!" the Puu Yaybaan declared when the new day dawned. "BOVORN S. FROM SAN PHAK WAN FILLED HIS *KRATHONG* WITH 100 BAHT AND HIS WIFE'S GOLDEN

---

[12] "Mighty warrior"; the Abbot is the head monk of the temple

RING, AND HIS WISH CAME TRUE! HIS BUFFALO IS SPRY AS A JUMPING MOUSE! DO AS HE DID, DONATE GENEROUSLY, AND YOUR WISHES SHALL BE HEARD! OH, AND PLEASE SPECIFY YOUR NAME CLEARLY ON YOUR WISH NOTE – BUDDHA IS NOT A MINDREADER, YOU KNOW."

The rumor spread like wildfire through the PA-systems of the surrounding villages and the villages beyond, and it was not long before the miracle was confirmed by a rapturous Bovorn S., who wept tears of joy on the hide of his bewildered buffalo.

"Huh?" some people in Doi Saket thought. "But the ceremony isn't until tomorrow night. We haven't even granted his wish yet."

Sûa, however, stated that the ritual in itself was purely symbolical and that granting wishes is about karma (of the wish granters, of course, shrewdly leaving aside whether he was referring to the gullible villagers or the flaccid monks) and that was the end of it.

More riches than ever before were piled onto the *krathongs*. From far and wide, people flocked to the temple to donate money, which looked very handsome on the money tree (making it increasingly healthy) and then looked very handsome in the Puu Yaybaan's bank account (making him increasingly wealthy). The temple didn't see a penny. A shamefully puny amount was budgeted for granting a wish here and there, just to keep the legend alive. The Exalted Abbot invariably mumbled a thank you and would have no part of the deception, for if there was anyone who would not take the old geezer seriously, it was the Puu Yaybaan.

Of course, the villagers themselves had their wishes too. Countless wishes. Widely varying wishes that would be floated into the air on wish balloons during the ceremony. And even though they were adept at granting wishes and so, at least in theory, should be able to reshape their own lives, every man needs wishes to be able to believe in something.

The well-bellied weed exterminator Uan wished for love, and if that wasn't in the books, the *idea* of love, and if that wasn't in the books, a cursory embrace.

The mournful neighbor Isra had been wishing for a letter from her grandson Om for six years, as he had gone to study "computer" in Singapore and never wrote.

The well-mannered crab huntress Kulap wished for a gong, just because she loved the sound.

Tangmoo's benevolent father Gaew wished for a good life for his children, Singha, Nataphun, and Noi, and of course for Tangmoo himself.

The philosophical irrigator Daeng wished he were dead.

The adulterous rice peeler Somchai begged for potency in her husband's ever-failing manhood so that she could finally, after all these years, take his virginity.

Even the corrupt monk Sûa had a wish. He wished that, just for once, he could set eyes on river goddess Phra Mae Khongkha, even though he did not believe in her.

Only young Tangmoo wished for nothing. He had never wished for anything. *Wouldn't it be wonderful if I had something to wish for?* he often thought. Tangmoo approached the world in all sincerity, always searching for something worth wishing for, but he never found anything that moved him sufficiently to engender a desire. All the things that occupied the other villagers, their disputes and worries, their questions and futilities, their dramas and embraces... nothing felt like it was more than what it seemed to be. And so Tangmoo's life became a string of pure experiences that he endured, and in which he performed no appreciable miracles.

But on that first night of Loi Krathong he could not sleep. Silently, he padded outside. Further down, by the river, the night shift and the Ink Readers continued their work, but here in the village only the chichaks[13] were awake.

Tangmoo looked up. Thousands upon thousands of *khom loi* floated like swarms of fluorescent jellyfish against the nocturnal canopy. The sky was laden with wishes. The closest ones seemed to be moving more quickly, drifting southward. When they reached higher altitudes they veered west, toward the mountains. *Where are they going?* Tangmoo wondered. They all drifted past steadily, purposely, aiming for an unknown destination. They flew toward the edge of the universe and then beyond.

---

[13] Small lizards intelligent enough to articulate their own name

Next morning, Tangmoo set out at dawn. He walked all day, for miles and miles, and when evening fell he reached the golden temple of Doi Suthep, situated on a hilltop with a view of Chiang Mai. The Gentle Abbot gave him a small bowl of rice to eat and sat beside him on the steps.

"Why have you come here, my son?" the wise man asked.

Tangmoo nodded at the purple sky above the city and said, "The wishes. I want to know where they're going."

The Gentle Abbot had an exceptional talent for invoking Buddha's teachings on all relevant and irrelevant matters people came to him for advice on. Even when a dilemma seemed nigh on impossible to solve, he would astound his audience with the only correct and always uniform answer: that the question was confusing and therefore by definition irrelevant, as the purpose of any spiritual life is to avoid confusion. And this was why the Abbot of Doi Suthep was the most beloved man in northern Thailand: he made everything seem so conveniently simple.

"Oh, no one knows," the Abbot enlightened in this case. He smoothed the wrinkles from his robe and smiled politely.

Is that it? anyone else might have thought, affronted. *Is that what I trudged up this bloody mountain for? Barefoot?* But not Tangmoo. Tangmoo looked at the confusion of fireworks over Chiang Mai and the procession of lights in the Night Bazaar, reflecting on the surface of the river that was or was not to take his life the very next day. The burning water, the whistles and bangs, the partying people; they all created a disorder so consistent that it reverted back into order. And everywhere, everywhere *khom loi* rose up into the air, as if the city was weeping inverted tears of fire.

"Chiang Mai consists of three worlds," the Abbot explained. "The first world is the one you see before you. A world that is vibrant; living and partying and wishing. Then there's the world above it, a world of serenity where people can rise above the mundane. By releasing their wishes, people try to reach that higher world, to become a part of it. They are two layers, sliding across one another."

Tangmoo gazed at the *khom loi*, steadily drifting past above the chaos.

"But then there's another world below," the monk continued. "A world of alleys, of darkness, of backstreets and corruption. The world of the blind. You see? The surface, wild and light; the dark side below; and finally, above, the serene, the transcendent, wishing to do good. Looking at it like that, it's very much like a human being. Chiang Mai, the Rose of the North, is a living, breathing person."

"But what does that tell me about where the wishes go?" Tangmoo asked.

"Maybe it doesn't matter where our wishes go," the Abbot said. "Maybe the question should be how we *ourselves* can get there. Look over there."

He pointed toward two *khom loi* rising up into the air with incredible speed, overtaking all the rest. Suddenly one of them started glowing more brightly and veering sharply toward the west, while the other flickered, fluttered down and fizzled out. "What do you think was the matter with those two wishes? Why did they ascend more rapidly than the others?"

"Maybe they were really burning wishes," Tangmoo guessed.

"Love? Happiness? Money? What could be worth going so fast for?"

"The wish to desire something..."

"Or maybe the wish to release all desire."

But...Tangmoo thought. *But...*

"And why is one wish so strong and sure, while the other extinguished like a candle?"

"Maybe it was a bad wish, a wish for revenge, a death wish..."

"Or maybe it was simply a matter of sloppy fuel distribution," the monk said, shrugging, and then he smiled. "It's time for you to go home now, my son. Your parents must be worried."

The boy has a good heart, the Gentle Abbot thought benevolently after they had said goodbye. He ordered a *tuk-tuk* that would be waiting for the boy to take him home as soon as he reached the last of the three hundred steps leading down. When the wise man entered the temple, carrying Tangmoo's empty rice bowl in his right hand, he tripped on his robes and landed flat on his face. The rice bowl shattered on the floor. Miraculously, the Abbot himself was unharmed. However, while sweeping up the shards he was soon overcome by a long-nourished but diligently repressed desire to express his creativity, like fashioning pretty little mosaics. All night long, the monk worked with the shards and felt happier than he had in a long time. And so the Gentle Abbot, not nearly as far along on his path toward Enlightenment as young Tangmoo himself, saw his fondest wish fulfilled, smashing all of his china in the process.

But this, in all probability, had nothing to do with the boy's coming.

The next day all the dirt roads of Doi Saket had been strung with lanterns. In every color and size they dangled from branches, electric wires, and scurrying chickens. More had been placed on walls, in gardens, and around the temple square. The well-bellied weed exterminator Uan busied himself with the table setting at the west end of the square, making sure that everyone he disliked would be seated far, far away from him, directly beneath the booming speakers of the karaoke set. All the villagers were busy preparing delicacies or setting up the thousands of *khom loi* so they could all be lit simultaneously that night – a logistical nightmare of incredible proportions.

When evening finally fell, after the exhausted Ink Readers had returned from the river with dripping robes and a last handful of wishes and the Exalted Abbot had fallen asleep on his meditation rug... that's when the party started in Doi Saket. People sang and stuffed themselves like there was no tomorrow. Boys caught lizards and bet on which one would run fastest. Girls tied strings to brightly colored atlas butterflies and led them around like kites. Men and women lasciviously tore at each other's clothes and limbs beneath the bewitched phallus.

"ALL RIGHT, FOLKS. THAT'S ENOUGH," the Puu Yaybaan broadcasted around ten o'clock that night. "LET THE CEREMONY BEGIN!"

The Exalted Abbot (still asleep and therefore perfectly resigned to his role) was carried outside in his seat to lead the villagers in meditation. The silence that descended on the crowd was so deafening that even the crabs in the rice field looked up in surprise; this was the only time of the year when all the villagers collectively kept their mouths shut (because even at night most of them never stopped talking in their sleep).

Only Tangmoo was no part of this communal introspection, just like he had been no part of the communal festivities. After shoring the dead branch on the teng-rang tree with a fresh piece of wood he had retreated to a quiet place behind the temple. He had been sitting there for hours, his back resting against a wheel of the giant mechanical replica of river goddess Phra Mae Khongkha, which would be rolled out into the temple square during the ceremony. *By releasing their wishes, people try to reach that world.* Tangmoo felt like a drowning person, flailing. If releasing desire was the pinnacle of achievement, how then was he supposed to justify his own existence?

A portentous shrew taking a nap on the wooden axle of the river goddess suddenly pricked up its ears. A second later it scurried off, squeaking. It seemed spooked, Tangmoo thought, as if it had spotted a tiger. Then he heard approaching voices. Suddenly, Tangmoo felt afraid, as he was not supposed to be here. On an impulse, he dove into the same bushes the shrew had disappeared into and hunkered there silently, unaware of his right foot balancing on a dry twig on the verge of snapping. (Ironically, the confounded twig came from a teng-rang tree; a much smaller specimen than the one threatening his father's house, but with much more far-reaching consequences.)

From his hiding place, Tangmoo watched as the generally respected Puu Yaybaan, and the monks Sûa and Mongkut appeared. The threesome stopped beside the wooden construction of the river goddess, not two feet from where Tangmoo was concealed. He was afraid to breathe. The men were engrossed in a heated argument, of which only snippets reached Tangmoo's ears: "...mustn't raise suspicion..." and "...didn't dive myself silly for nothing, dammit..." and "...six wishes granted, that's more than..." and "Fine! But it's going to come out of *your* share..."

Is the twig to blame for the fact that it chose to snap at that precise moment and play such a pivotal role in the destruction and creation of so many lives in northern Thailand? Be that as it may, it happened, and the echo reverberated in Tangmoo's ringing ears.

"What was that?" the Puu Yaybaan cried.

"Here!" Sûa said, triumphant. Two strong hands, quick as snakes, darted into the bushes and grabbed Tangmoo by the scruff, dragging him out. "An eavesdropper! What're you doing here, you little fraud?"

"I... Nothing," Tangmoo stammered. "I was just... thinking."

"In the bushes?" the Puu Yaybaan said dubiously.

Mongkut glanced around nervously. "How long has he been here?"

"He heard everything," the village chief hissed.

"I... No, really, I have no idea what you were talking about," Tangmoo said. He tried to free his arm. "I think I should go back to the temple square now, or my mom will..."

"He's going to tell them everything," Sûa said, tightening his hold on the boy's arm. "We need to do something."

"No, I truly don't know what you..."

"Liar! Traitor!" Sûa fumed suddenly, spraying Tangmoo's face with foul strings of saliva.

"We can't give him a chance to ruin everything," the Puu Yaybaan decided in a whisper. Even more than Sûa's uncontrolled outburst, this was a signal for Tangmoo to yank himself free with a *RIP!* and a twist, and to start running like mad.

"Hey!" Sûa shouted.

"After him!" Mongkut yelled.

"Take care of this," the Puu Yaybaan barked at Sûa. "Am I making myself clear? Mongkut and I will begin the ceremony, before people start wondering what's keeping us."

Fumbling blind, Tangmoo ran through the darkness. Sûa ran after him. They sped across the winding path away from the temple, through the woods, across the thickets. Sûa was right behind him, growling like a feral cat, while not four hundred yards away from them in the temple square all the wish balloons had been lit and were starting to fill up with hot air. Loud cheers rose up as the wooden Phra Mae Khongkha was rolled out into the square, and no one heard Sûa's insane roars: "*GET BACK HERE, YOU MISERABLE LIAR! HAVEN'T YOU DONE ENOUGH?*"

Finally, the moonlit path opened out. Feet splashed through water. Dismayed, Tangmoo realized he had reached the river. He turned to his assailant at the same time that his little sister Noi turned around on the podium outside the temple. She had been chosen to play the role of Neng Tanapong this year, beaming proudly in her beautiful costume. Undoubtedly Noi was thinking of her big brother, somewhere out there in the frenzied crowd.

"Now I've got you," Sûa grinned, wading into the shallow riverbed.

"Listen," Tangmoo wept, stumbling backwards, up to his thighs in the water now. "I have no idea what you were talking about. How could I talk about something I don't know?"

"Little boy," the Tiger said, "it doesn't matter what you know."

Snarling, he threw himself at Tangmoo, his saffron robes billowing on the water like a cloud of blood: *no, no, no, no,* the gigantic wooden arm of the river goddess descended on little Noi and she looked up with a gasp, the crowd cheered with so much excitement and so little restraint that they seemed to be going mad: *yes, yes, yes, yes,* the river foamed over Tangmoo, flashes lit up the night, fireworks crackled, spattered, whirled, feet kicked desperately, dislodging starfish from the riverbed, smothered cries rose in bubbles to the surface, popping soundlessly: *help, help, help, help,* little Neng Tanapong drowned in satin fabric as thousands of *khom loi* all rose up simultaneously, the crowd fell to their knees, looking up in tears toward the fiery miracle, wishes filled the night, the stone phallus shrank in shame, and Tangmoo drowned in the river.

But not without a witness.

Because from the shadows by the riverbank one shade extricated itself, bigger than all the others. This was, of course, Phra Mae Khongkha who, after bestowing life on the river a long time ago, had stopped for a breather in the riverbed. And so it happened that Sûa the monk, dripping wet and flushed with exertion, glanced over his shoulder and saw his fondest wish fulfilled, even though he did not believe what he was seeing. His body was found downstream the next day, but not his ripped-off hands. They were never found.

And Tangmoo?

I'm sure that if you had looked closely, you could have seen a tiny speck of light rise up from the river. It fluttered up into the night sky, hastily climbing past a swarm of surprised purple swamp hens, and then joined the *khom loi.* That's where the little light found peace. In Tangmoo's dead eyes on the bottom of the river you could see a starry sky full of wishes reflected. Around him whirled running tendrils of ink, and he read them all.

Next day around noon there was a *CRACK!* when the dead branch on the teng-rang tree sagged, but there was no one to prop it back up. Two days later it finally snapped off and destroyed besides the house also the part of Tangmoo's father's brain that was responsible for redirecting grief. From then on Gaew, who had been inconsolable after the death of his son, devoted his deliriously happy life to his remaining children, aided by his wife who admitted to herself sadly: *thinking that life is good is better than not living at all.*

The collapse of the damnable branch had the added consequence that now, every morning, a particularly bothersome ray of sunlight tormented the eye of the philosophical and always death-wishing irrigator Daeng, causing uncontrollable screaming fits and severe sleep deprivation. It was not long, therefore, before Daeng nodded off behind the wheel while driving along the main road. He rammed a truck full of pigs on their way to the slaughterhouse, rolled fourteen times and found new joy in life when he realized he had survived the crash without a scratch. Contrary to the pigs. So lugubrious was the scene of the accident – chunks of bloody pork all over the place – that it made the news broadcasts all over Southeast Asia. Even in Singapore, where Om had been working at a Thai restaurant for six years and sending a monthly email to his mourning grandmother Isra, who had no email address. Om then wrote her a letter, saying: *I'm doing fine, Grandmother. I have a Ph.D. in computer and I'm making lots of money now. Here, have some* – and added his tips to the envelope. When Isra found the letter in her mailbox a week later, she died of happiness.

Wishes, wishes, wishes everywhere. The well-mannered crab huntress Kulap found some scrap metal from Daeng's wrecked truck in the rice field and used it to forge a gong. When she sounded it one night, she touched such a probing frequency that every man in Doi Saket was enchanted and lured toward her little house. As soon as the well-bellied weed exterminator Uan saw her, he fell head over heels in love. Kulap, not a bad sort, gave him a cursory embrace, and at least the idea of love.

Wishes, like pearls on a string of cause and effect. Kulap's gong kept chiming across the rice fields for nights on end, finally resonating in the blood supply to Somchai's husband's failing manhood and dislodging something in the veins. He immediately ravaged her with all the lust that had been denied him all these years, and Somchai was engulfed in waves of coital energy that were tangible for miles around – even as far as Chiang Mai, where legs were spread, thighs were kneaded, and orgasms were shrieked out. All over northern Thailand wishes came true. Bonds of love were forged. Children were being born. Kemkhaeng broke his leg.

And maybe this was all coincidence, like so much in life.

But let me tell you that, somewhere, a tiny little light had found its swarm. It let itself drift along on the winds toward the west. All the while, it wished and wished and wished. And so, wishing, the light and its wishes flew toward the edge of the universe and beyond.

CHERRY BLOSSOMS ON THE RIVER OF SOULS

Richard Parks

Richard Parks (www.richard-parks.com) is the author of novel *The Long Look* and more than 100 short stories, which have appeared in *Asimov's*, *Realms of Fantasy*, *Fantasy Magazine*, *Weird Tales*, and numerous anthologies, and are collected in *The Ogre's Wife*, *Worshipping Small Gods*, *On the Banks of the River of Heaven*, and *Yamada Monogatari: Demon Hunter*. His work has been nominated for both the World Fantasy Award and the Mythopoeic Fantasy Award for Adult Literature. His second novel, *To Break the Demon Gate*, is due out in the spring of 2014. He is a native of Mississippi, USA, and despite several attempts to leave, still lives there with his wife and a varying number of cats.

THE TALES VARIED as to *why* the well was outside the village rather than inside. Some say that an earthquake and rockfall destroyed the original town site and the survivors rebuilt the village at a safer distance, leaving the now-dry well where it was. Others say that a saké-addled farmer relieved himself in the well one night, so offending the spirit of the well that it had moved *itself* and had been dry ever since. Whichever version one believed, the well was where it was, and nearly every evening the boy called Hiroshi came to stare down into the darkness, and listen.

The well was full of music.

"Hello," Hiroshi said to the unseen musician, as was his habit. There was no answer. Hiroshi was never quite sure what he would have done had the darkness answered him. There was a spirit in the well, of course.

His uncle Saito, the priest, said there were living spirits in everything, and Hiroshi believed that. Still, the darkness did not answer him.

One fine spring evening his uncle Saito walked out of the village to where Hiroshi sat by the well. He had been a soldier and was now a priest, but it was as Hiroshi's uncle that Saito came to speak with Hiroshi that evening. "Greetings, Nephew," he said, and sat down beside the boy.

"Hello, Uncle. Is there something the matter?"

"I'm not certain. I would be grateful if you would help me decide, so I must ask: what is your fascination with this well?"

"Is Father worried? He's raised no objections so long as I do not neglect my obligations."

"My brother is a practical man, and you are a dutiful son to him. However, my question was not to my brother."

Hiroshi blushed. "Forgive me, Uncle. I sit here because I like to listen. There is a sound coming from the well, from down in the darkness. It's almost as if the music is being played just for me; almost as if I've heard it before. I don't understand that, but that's how it feels."

Saito sat down beside him and leaned forward just a bit, listening. After a while he pulled back the sleeve of his robe and picked up a pebble. He dropped it over the side.

"What do you hear now, Hiroshi?"

"I hear the pebble rattling against stones... fading. Now I hear nothing."

"No splash? Not even a small one?"

"No."

Saito nodded. "Nor will you ever. This was a well. Now it is not. Now it is just a hole down deep into the underground. The underground is the province of dead things, and dead things should not concern the living. Look around you now. What do you see?"

Hiroshi did as his uncle directed. He saw children his age flying kites in the waning light, running along the ridges of the flooded rice fields, playing games with tops and hoops, laughing.

"It all seems childish," Hiroshi said.

"Is it inappropriate for children to do childish things? Or the living to do what nature decrees that the living must? *This* is your world, Hiroshi.

There is nothing in that well that should be of concern to you. Will you think about what I have said?"

"I will, Uncle," Hiroshi said. His uncle looked back once but not a second time as he walked away.

Hiroshi, being an honest boy, did what he had promised to do. He thought about what his uncle said, and he studied carefully, for a moment or two, the activity, now fading with the day, around him.

"I've played those games," he said to himself. "Time and again. They do not change – the kites pull on the wind as they always have, as they will for anyone. This song is for *me*."

All this was justification, and pointless. The only justification Hiroshi needed was the song he still heard, coming from the depths of the well.

THE NEXT EVENING Hiroshi joined his playmates at their games for a time to appease his uncle, but when play time was over and all his friends had gone home, he returned to the well. He moved quickly, with furtive glances all about to see if anyone was there to see. He carried a long rope coiled over one shoulder and a small knife in his sash.

"The rope was a sensible idea, but that blade may not be enough," his uncle said. He sounded sad.

Hiroshi froze as his Uncle Saito stood up from his hiding place behind the well.

"How did you know, Uncle?"

"It serves a priest well to know how to look into a person's eyes and see clearly what plagues them. You are plagued by discontent, Nephew. Unfortunately, unlike other spirits and minor devils, this one bows to no spell of exorcism. You must cast it out yourself."

Hiroshi hung his head. "How do I do this, Uncle?"

"Perhaps by doing what you want. I still advise against it, but this devil shows no sign of leaving you." Saito took the rope from Hiroshi's shoulder and made one end fast to a post beside the stone rail marking the well. He threw the other end down into the blackness. "Do you still hear music, Nephew?"

Hiroshi listened for a moment. "Yes, Uncle. I do."

"Then follow it down and satisfy your devil. Then perhaps he will leave and you will come back to us. I hope so, else I must explain your absence to your father, and I would rather avoid that duty."

Hiroshi put his hand on the rope. He stared into the forbidding blackness as he often had, but he barely hesitated. "I will come back, Uncle. I promise."

"Do not promise. I merely ask that you be careful. Powerful *kami* are drawn to such places, and most are not likely to be friendly to you. Take this." Saito held up the shorter of the two swords he'd carried as a soldier. "Remember what little I taught you of the Way of the Gods. Most of all, remember who you are. I think that is the important thing, no matter where a person may go."

Hiroshi took a deep breath and climbed over the side of the well. The last thing he saw before darkness closed in was his uncle peering sadly down at him from a circle of daylight.

That daylight quickly faded as the well shaft made an abrupt turn at the bottom into what looked like an ordinary cave.

Hiroshi listened very closely, but now he didn't hear the music at all.

"That's very strange. It was a most persistent sound when I heard it from the side of the well. Persuasive, I think," he said, though Hiroshi still couldn't fit words to what the argument was supposed to be.

Now all was silent except for a faint rush of air, as if the winds of the underground could not wait to escape past him and up the well to sunlight. Hiroshi's hair blew about his face and tickled his forehead. The scent carried by the wind was of damp and mold, and a faint hint of a spice that Hiroshi could not identify at all.

There was darkness about, as he had expected. Indeed, he'd brought a small lantern along but found he didn't need it. Once his eyes adjusted, there was light there, of a sort. He could make out where to walk, where boulders lay in his path and where not. The only thing left to do was to choose which direction to go.

Where is the music?

He listened very intently, trying to hear around the moan of the wind in his ears. There had been a promise in that music, something wonderful beyond Hiroshi's imagining. Familiar, too, though he could not say how.

After a few moments he thought he heard it again. He wasn't sure. He wondered if there had been a concentrating effect from the well itself, like wind through a reed flute; the music was much harder to hear this much closer, presumably, to the musician. Hiroshi finally took his best guess and started walking.

He soon came to what had clearly been part of the underground river, now dry and full of stones. An old woman was waiting for him there, looking impatient. At least, Hiroshi thought it was an old woman; that was what he told himself when he saw her. She was more a collection of rags and bones than anything, but there was a face, and wrinkles, and a thin toothless grin.

"Give me those!" she said. Her voice was like dead leaves blowing across stones and her eyes glittered like black pebbles.

Hiroshi blinked. "Those? Those what?"

"Clothes! Give them to me!"

Hiroshi thought this very rude, but he was more confused than offended. "Who are you and why do you want my clothes?"

She ignored that. "You must give your clothes to me before you cross this river. Now!"

Apparently, to the old woman now meant *now*. She reached out with one clawed hand, snatching at his sleeve. She managed to tear off a strip of his sleeve and gouge a line of red across his wrist.

Hiroshi took a step back. "Here, now, Grandmother! Stop that!"

She stopped for a moment, but she was looking at the blood on Hiroshi's wrist. "You're alive!" It sounded like an accusation.

"Of course I'm alive! What did you think?"

"That you were not, of course. Now I think you're a fool." She blinked, and for a moment Hiroshi saw some kind of recognition there, something beyond the cold darkness he had seen before. It didn't last. The cold, relentless stare returned. "Clothes. You don't need them. Not where you are, not where you are going. *Mine!*"

The last came out in a shriek of rage and malice. For Hiroshi's part he didn't know what she was, but he knew she wasn't human. A *kami*, or perhaps a demon in – somewhat – human form. When she came for him again he had his uncle's *wakazashi* out and ready. "Stay back, monster!"

She hissed like a snake and struck at him. Hiroshi dodged and struck back. It was only the feel of the blade as it struck something solid that told him of the hit. The rag and bone creature did not cry out. It merely stepped back, confused. "Mine!" she repeated.

Hiroshi took a deep breath and a firmer grip on his sword. "You've been in the dark too long, Grandmother. Don't force me to strike you again!"

She looked at Hiroshi, or rather at his clothes, then looked at the sword again. "Mine," she said again, "soon enough. I can wait."

She cackled with laughter and then spread out her arms like a kite. In answer the breeze there swelled into her rags and she lifted off into the darkness. In a moment she was out of sight in the deeper black of the caves.

Hiroshi waited for a bit, sword at the ready, but she did not return. He finally put the blade away.

"Well," he said. "That was very strange."

He didn't like to think of himself as a fool, despite what the creature had said. He had already met one monster on his short journey, and it seemed likely that there would be others. He wondered if the beautiful music was being played by another monster to lure him down.

"If so, it worked. But for what purpose? And why is the music fainter now than when I kneeled at the well?"

"Because it's farther away, of course."

Hiroshi's previous encounter with the clothes thief must have left him more shaken than he'd thought, because he immediately reached for his sword. After a moment he took his hand off the hilt, feeling foolish. The speaker was a small man in the robes of a Buddhist monk. He sat cross-legged on the stones, tending a small fire upon which steamed a small kettle. Before him were cups and a ladle and a bamboo whisk for making tea. A traveler's bundle served as a rest for his back.

Hiroshi bowed. "*Gomen nasai*, Honored Sir. I did not see you there."

"Obviously. I was about to have some tea, young man. Would you care to join me?"

The mention of tea made Hiroshi realize he was starting to get hungry. "Yes, thank you."

The monk prepared their tea in silence, though perhaps introductions would have been more in order. Hiroshi shrugged and pulled out two of the rice cakes he'd brought with him and offered one to the monk, who politely declined. Hiroshi then ate both of them, though he remembered his manners enough to let the monk take the first sip of tea before he began.

He also studied the man as closely as manners would allow without staring. His initial impression of small stature was on the mark. The man was tiny, even shorter than Hiroshi himself, though otherwise looked more or less human. Part of Hiroshi was wondering if the monk would suddenly grow fangs and attack him, but mostly he wondered what the man was doing there in that place, and what he knew about the music. He held off asking for as long as he could, but that wasn't very long at all.

"Excuse me, but what did you mean about the music being farther away?"

"Just that it is. You're much farther from it than you were."

That wasn't very helpful, though Hiroshi didn't say so out loud. It was more than a little irritating.

"I don't understand. Will you explain?"

The monk didn't say anything for a while, but merely sipped his tea. Hiroshi's annoyance faded. The monk seemed very tired, and very sad, as if the whole subject pained him.

"When you dream, where do you go?" the monk asked finally.

Hiroshi frowned. "I-I don't know. Some say the spirit wanders, aimless. Others say you don't go anywhere, and dreams are just stories you tell yourself while you sleep."

The monk nodded. "Men believe many things. Some of them are true. Now then, where do you go when you die?"

"The River of Souls. Perhaps to be reborn."

The monk nodded. "Now, then – where are you now?"

Hiroshi looked around, but the scene had not changed. He was in a cave far underground. His reasons for being there were perhaps not as clear as they could be, but he did know that much, and said so.

"You know less than you think. Go home, Hiroshi."

Hiroshi blinked. "How do you know my name?"

The monk sighed gustily. "How do you not know mine?"

Hiroshi just stood in silence. "I don't understand. You haven't told me your name. I should have asked, but I didn't mean to offend you –"

"I am not offended. I do regret the time you're going to make me waste." The monk carefully packed away his tea supplies and hoisted his bundle. "Shall we go?"

"I can't ask you to come with me."

"You can't ask for me *not* to come with you. I choose what I do, as do you. I hope in time you will choose better."

Hiroshi had no answer for that, because he didn't understand a word of it. He merely picked up his sword and set out once more in the direction of the music, or as close as he could discern. The monk walked a few feet ahead, his staff making a rhythmic jingling sound from the small bell attached to it. Hiroshi thought at first that the sound would interfere with the music, but the jingle of the bell was so steady and constant that it was soon as lost as the sound of his own heartbeat.

This is a very strange cave, Hiroshi thought, even as he realized how foolish a thing it was to believe this place a simple cave. Hiroshi thought of stories he had heard about the Dragon Palace, where a simple fisherman once dallied with a princess in ageless luxury for centuries under the sea while his true home and all he knew turned to rot and dust. Except this was not under the sea, so far as Hiroshi knew, and the monk was certainly no princess.

The music was still faint, but by long practice at listening, Hiroshi was beginning to hear it better. "It's a *koto* being played," he said. "It's lovely."

The monk nodded, looking glum. "Yes. Akiko is very gifted."

Hiroshi was so surprised he stopped walking. The monk merely glanced at him over his shoulder, waiting patiently for him to catch up.

"You know who's playing the music?" Hiroshi asked.

"Of course. So do you."

That was just more nonsense from his odd companion, so far as Hiroshi could see, and he didn't dwell on it. Something he did dwell on was the simple fact that the music was getting louder. Another strange thing, since Hiroshi was certain they hadn't traveled more than a bowshot from where he and the monk had taken tea together. He mentioned it to the monk, who seemed even more dispirited.

"We're much closer now."

"How can that be? We haven't walked very far."

"It's not in how far you travel. It's in deciding to make the journey."

"I'd decided that when I climbed down the well!"

"If you say so. I think rather that you were traveling away as much as toward. You didn't know where you were going. Now you do."

"Akiko? And you say I know her? How?"

"You grew up together."

"But I haven't grown up yet," Hiroshi said, though the admission pained him a bit. "And there are several girls in my village but I don't know anyone named Akiko."

His companion merely grunted. "Nor did she know anyone named Hiroshi."

"Sir, I don't understand any of what you're saying."

"You certainly don't. Else you wouldn't be here."

Hiroshi didn't know if he'd been insulted or not, but he rather thought so. He gritted his teeth but kept his voice level. "Then, Honored Sir, would you be so kind as to tell me where I *should* be?"

"Home, of course."

"Very well – as soon as I find the music, I'll go home. I have to know what it is and why it calls to me, else I'll never be content."

The monk nodded. "You're not seeking music; you're seeking an answer. I wondered if you understood that. Very well then, I will help you find Akiko. Yet whatever happens, afterwards you will leave this place. You don't belong here. Do I have your word?"

Hiroshi hesitated, but he saw no good alternative. "Yes."

"Well, then. You have mine. Only time will tell what either is worth."

THEY WALKED FOR hours across what looked like the bones of a long-dead river. Hiroshi was amazed at how large the field of stones was and wondered if they would ever see the end. Now and then they came to a pile of white stones, standing alone in the flat rocky *nothing* of that place. He asked about them, but the monk merely said "stones" and nothing else.

Also, now and again, Hiroshi could have sworn that he heard the sound of children playing. He asked about that too, but the monk merely said that the children were always there. Hiroshi saw no children, but he let the matter drop. It was enough to know that what had appeared to be a cave was now a vast empty riverbed of stones, and overhead was a darkness that might have been stone or might have been a night sky without stars.

In fact, neither said anything at all for the rest of their walk, until the monk pointed to something rising from the stone field in the distance.

"She's there."

Hiroshi looked closer. It was a hill by the riverbed. He hadn't noticed it sooner because it didn't rise very far from the rocks at all. That was because it began beneath the level of the riverbed itself, at the bottom of a low, sloping valley. Hiroshi saw the way down marked by two stone lanterns. They cast a blue glow through the shadows of that place. Corpse lights drifted past on the wind.

He stopped for a moment, listening closely. The music was much clearer now, more than enough to discern the instrument. Almost enough to discern the song. Hiroshi listened as hard as he knew how.

"I-I know that song. It's called..." His voice trailed away. He couldn't remember, but he knew that was the only reason. He knew the song's name. He had known it long ago and now forgotten. And yet he was equally sure he had never heard that song anywhere but down the dry dead well. "Perhaps it doesn't matter." Hiroshi turned toward the entrance to the valley.

"It's guarded, of course."

"Guarded? By what?"

"Three monsters. You'll have to face all three to reach Akiko. I'm not going with you."

Hiroshi nodded. "That would be best. Still, do you know how can I defeat the guardians?"

"I didn't say you could defeat them. I said you had to *face* them. You do have a knack for misunderstanding your situation, young man."

"Honored Sir, with all respect, you have a knack for meaningless answers."

The monk smiled again. "Pass the guardians first; then tell me what I have said is meaningless."

Hiroshi considered. He did not want to fight the monsters. He was afraid, and he didn't pretend otherwise. He just knew that he had to go forward now. Not out of pride he didn't have, or the bravery he didn't feel. It wasn't even for the music anymore. Maybe the monk was right – he wanted an answer. Something that would fill the empty ache he felt every time he heard the music, that he knew he always would feel even if he never heard the music again.

It's not as if I can stop listening.

Hiroshi unsheathed his sword and stepped past the stone lanterns alone. Their glow faded behind him much sooner than he had expected. As in the first part of the cave the light was very faint but he still could see – barely. He moved slowly, carefully, trying to step quietly over the smooth gray stones.

It didn't help. The first guardian was waiting for him before he had gone a dozen steps.

"Go home, boy."

Hiroshi stood face to knee with a gigantic *oni*. It towered over him, a good eight feet tall. Its skin was redder than blood, its teeth like tusks, its hair like the mane of a guardian lion. It carried in its right hand a gigantic iron club.

For several long moments Hiroshi just stared. He couldn't raise his sword, he couldn't run, he couldn't do anything.

"I asked politely enough," grunted the *oni*. "Now it is too late."

The creature swung its club. Too late, Hiroshi tried to dodge. He didn't get the full force of the blow, but he got more than enough. His vision exploded like a Chinese rocket, and for a moment all he could see was white drifting stars. The first thing to come back to him, even before his vision, was his name, and it wasn't Hiroshi.

My name is Yojiro...

The rest of his former life came back to him then. Part of him remained Hiroshi and did not forget. Yet now he remembered being Yojiro too.

Growing up in the shadow of Fuji-san, and the people he had known there. He remembered being a young samurai, full of life and promise. He remembered the lesson he'd been taught in both humility and the transience of a life, the day he had died in battle. All this was known to him in the instant before he opened his eyes again, knowing himself to be Hiroshi, and knowing that he, once, was Yojiro.

The *oni* was nowhere to be seen.

Hiroshi sat up, gingerly feeling the lump on the side of his head. "I think I am still alive, yet I don't understand how that can be. Why didn't the ogre finish me off? I was no match for him!"

Hiroshi didn't question the new memories that came to him on the *oni*'s club; he knew they had come to him for a reason. He didn't know what that reason was, but he was certain he wouldn't find out sitting there on the stones. He got to his feet, slowly, and looked around for his sword. It was lying some distance away. There was a nick on the blade where it struck a stone on landing.

That will take some time to polish out. Uncle will be cross.

No help for it now. Hiroshi carefully sheathed the sword, then remembered to examine himself for any other injuries he might have missed, but there didn't seem to be any. That seemed strangely fortunate, but Hiroshi wasn't sure if it was anything of the sort. The other young man's memories were still strong in him, and he still didn't know what they might mean. There was also a curious gap in those memories, curious because of the vividness of all the others. Someone he could almost but not quite remember.

Akiko?

Perhaps, but knowing the name did not help. He couldn't picture her at all, nor name the song he still heard being played on the distant *koto*. He could picture the instrument itself, see delicate hands at its silk strings, but that was all. Hiroshi took a deep breath and, when he felt he was able, he followed the music one more time.

The valley narrowed soon after, but the hill where Akiko waited was getting much closer, and the music, while distant, was very easy to hear. The same song, beautiful and melancholy. Hiroshi saw bleak earth rise on either side of him, as if he was walking into a grave.

At least the monster can't sneak up on me from the sides...

The monster didn't bother. It waited, serene, directly in his path. A coiled dragon with scales so smooth and black they glistened. Its talons dripped venom, and it looked at him with unblinking red eyes. "Go home, Hiroshi," it said.

After the *oni*, the sight of a dragon was not so startling, for all that Hiroshi could see death in its eyes.

"If I could go back, I would have. Please let me pass."

"That isn't the way of this place," the dragon said, and Hiroshi was almost certain that, when it bared its fangs at him, the thing was coming as close to a smile as its appearance allowed. Hiroshi, terrified and yet unable to retreat, did the only thing he could think to do and drew his sword.

Now I am sure it is smiling at me.

Whether it was or not, the thing struck almost too fast for Hiroshi to see. It didn't bother to bite him; its talons closed tightly on his right arm, and Hiroshi felt them piercing his flesh, sending their venom into his blood. A wave of agony washed over him, far worse than when the *oni* had struck him down, far worse than anything he could have imagined. For a moment he knew nothing, could know nothing through the haze of pain.

He did not wake, exactly. He heard a woman's voice, speaking to him. He knew it for a dream, a memory, but real just the same. Akiko was speaking to him, somewhere, sometime... him? No. Yojiro. It was Yojiro who heard, and Yojiro who answered.

"You will return, Yojiro. Promise me."

"I promise," Hiroshi heard himself answer, in Yojiro's voice. It was a promise he had failed to keep, on the day he died.

Hiroshi opened his eyes. The dragon was gone. Hiroshi was not surprised this time; he had begun to understand, perhaps a little. He had two sets of memories now. First Yojiro, now Akiko. He remembered her, her glossy black hair and sweet face, remembered their love and the promises they had made to each other. He remembered dying.

And she followed me. I'm sorry, Akiko.

There would be a third guardian, but Hiroshi put his sword away; he did not think he would be needing it again. He followed the music, remembering the words, remembering who played that song with so much joy before and so much sadness now.

Cherry Blossoms on the Water.

The song was a promise of spring. A promise of many things. Hiroshi looked up at the hilltop. He could see the lone figure sitting there, bowed over the *koto*, playing the song that had called him down the well and away from his life. He was neither angry nor sad about that, but he was left with the problem of what to do. He did not try to climb the hill just yet. He waited for the guardian to appear, and soon he did, the rhythmic jingle of his staff serving counterpoint to the mournful *koto*.

"Greetings, Honored Sir," Hiroshi said to the monk. Hiroshi was a little surprised, but not very much.

"Why wait for me? The way to the hill was clear."

Hiroshi shook his head. "Obvious, perhaps. But not clear. Nor do I think you intend to stop me directly. Either of the other two could have done that."

The monk nodded. "You're perhaps less of a fool than I thought. How much less, though? That is not certain."

"The first two guardians gave me Yojiro and then Akiko," Hiroshi said. "What will the third guardian do?"

"Perhaps he will take them away again. Perhaps that is up to you."

"What should I do?"

"I told you before – go home."

"I *will* go home, for that was my promise. Yet I have another promise that I must keep first. One even longer delayed."

The monk frowned but stood aside. "I will wait here. If you return..."

Hiroshi didn't like the way the monk said 'if,' but he understood. He slowly walked up the hill.

Akiko sat with her back to him, her long white fingers on the strings of the *koto*. Too long. Too white. Her kimono too was white, and it sagged back upon her bony shoulders. Hiroshi remembered those shoulders, that neck whiter than snow. Grayish now. He could not see her face. Her back was turned and she could not see him, but she obviously knew he was there.

"Yojiro, you've come back to me."

She started to rise, but Hiroshi stepped forward and took her shoulders in a gentle but firm grip. He tried not to think of the scent that rose from her now, so different from long ago. "Do not look at me, Akiko."

"Why not?"

"Because I'm dead. I was... I mean. Yojiro – I, remember. I waved my sword about quite bravely, but then I was shot full of arrows and they cut off my head. My ankles were spiked."

"You've returned," she insisted.

"You called me from another place, with your music and my promise. I kept my promise, but I don't belong here. Now I must go."

She shook her head, slowly. "Let me look at you."

"What will you see, Akiko? What will I see when I look at you now? We are not what we were. I've traveled the River of Souls before and returned to the living world. You must do the same. You don't belong here, either."

"Stay?" She sounded confused. "You must stay!"

"No," he said.

"You *promised!*"

"I promised to return, and I have. To love you, and I did. I remember. I... Yojiro, loved you, and I came back to you. Let that be enough."

"No!"

"What will I see when you look at me? I remember your beauty. Do you want me to see what you are now?"

"I am Akiko!"

"Yes. You are also dead and your flesh has gone to corruption. As long as you remain on this hilltop down in the darkness, playing that song for me, you will remain dead. I don't want that, and neither should you."

"Please..." she said, and reached up to touch his hand. Her fingers were cold, and there was no living flesh to them.

Hiroshi took a deep breath. He knew what he must do, but it wasn't his decision. It was Yojiro's, for the woman who died out of love for him. *Forgive me, Akiko, but I believe I will need Hiroshi's sword one last time.*

"Please play for me," he said. "'Cherry Blossoms on the Water.'"

"Always," she said, and her fingers caressed the strings as they had his face and body, once long ago.

In one smooth movement, with less thought than a breath, Hiroshi drew his sword and brought it down on the strings just to the side of Akiko's fingers. The taut silk strings parted with a high screeching sound like a wail of despair, fading, only to be echoed by Akiko. She twisted suddenly in his arms, fingers reaching to claw, not caress, but Hiroshi held firm and looked full into her ruined face, painting over the horror he saw there with one last strong memory of beauty.

"Good-bye," he said.

His memory clothed her in full life for just a moment, then it began to fade, as did Akiko. In a moment, both were gone, leaving only a trace of sadness and a faint ghostly memory that was more like a dream.

Hiroshi was left alone on the hill with the shattered instrument. After a bit, he made his way back down to the valley again where the monk was waiting for him.

"She can move on now," the monk said, "as you also must. That was well done."

Hiroshi just said, "I would like to go home now."

They made their way out of the valley and back across the dry streambed of stones. Hiroshi looked at the piles of stones again, and again he listened. There was no music, but he did hear the sound of children playing. He was sure of it this time, but he said nothing until they were past the stones and walking through the cave back to the well. He looked at his companion.

"I thought you were a simple monk, but I also thought this a simple cave."

"Who do you think I am?"

"If this is the River of Souls, then there are many powerful *kami* in this place, but I think you are the one called the God of Children," Hiroshi said. "Yet I also think what you did, you did for Yojiro and Akiko. Not for me. They were young, but they were not children. Why?"

"We are all children, Hiroshi," the monk said, and that was all.

It wasn't an answer, but then Hiroshi no longer remembered asking a question of the little monk or, for that matter, remembered the little monk himself. Even the names Akiko and Yojiro were fading from his memory now, and then they were gone completely. Hiroshi was alone. He knew only that he was in a deep dark place where he did not belong, and the way out was clear.

Hiroshi saw blue sky far above and let it guide him as he climbed back up into the living world.

RAG AND BONE
Priya Sharma

Priya Sharma (www.priyasharmafiction.wordpress.com) is a doctor who lives in the United Kingdom. Her short stories have appeared in *Tor.com*, *Black Static*, *Interzone*, *Albedo One*, *Alt Hist* and *On Spec*, and have been reprinted in Paula Guran's *Best Dark Fantasy and Horror* 2012 and 2013 and Ellen Datlow's *Year's Best Horror* Volumes 4 and 5.

I LEAVE GABRIEL in the yard and go into town, taking my bag with the vials of skin and bone, flesh and blood, my regular delivery to Makin. The Peels are looking for body parts.

I love the grandeur of the Strand. High towers of ornate stone. The road's packed with wagons and carts. Boats choke the river. The Mersey is the city's blood and it runs rich. Liverpool lives again.

I can hear the stevedores' calls, those kings of distribution and balance, whose job it is to oversee the dockers loading the barges. The boats must be perfectly weighted for their journey up the Manchester Ship Canal. Guards check them to ensure no unlicensed man steals aboard. Farther along, at Albert Dock, there's a flock of white sails. The Hardman fleet's arrived, tall ships bringing cotton from America.

The Liver birds keep lookout. Never-never stone creatures that perch atop the Liver Building where all the families have agents. I keep my eyes fixed on the marble floor so that I don't have to look at the line of people desperate for an audience. The Peels' man has the ground floor. The Peels' fortune came from real estate, small forays such as tenements at first, but money begets money. They took a punt when they redeveloped Liverpool's waterfront, a good investment that made them kings of the new world.

The other families have managers on other floors, all in close proximity as nothing's exclusive, business and bloodlines being interbred. The Hardmans are textile merchants, the Rathbones' wealth was made on soap, of all things, while the Moores are ship builders.

The outer offices contain rows of clerks at desks, shuffling columns of figures in ledgers. A boy, looking choked in his high-necked shirt, runs between them carrying messages. No one pays me any mind.

Makin's secretary keeps me waiting a full minute before he looks up, savouring this petty exercise of power. "He'll see you now."

Makin's at his desk. Ledgers are piled on shelves, the charts and maps on the walls are stuck with pins marking trade routes and Peel territories.

"Have a seat." He's always civil. "How did you fare today?"

"A few agreed."

I hand him the bag.

"They're reluctant?"

"Afraid."

There are already rumours. That the Peels, Hardmans, Rathbones and Moores, these wealthy people we never see, are monstrosities that live to a hundred years by feasting on Scousers' flesh and wearing our skins like suits when their own get worn out. Their hands drip with diamonds and the blood of the slaving classes. They lick their fingers clean with slavering tongues.

Makin taps the desk.

"Should we be paying more?"

"Then you'll have a line that stretches twice around the Mersey Wall consisting of drunken, syphilitic beggars."

"Do we have to order obligatory sampling of the healthy?"

"That's unwise."

His fingers stop drumming.

"Since when are rag and bone men the font of wisdom?"

I'm not scared of Makin but I need the money so I'm respectful. Besides, I like him.

"At least wait 'til it's cooler before you announce something like that or you'll have a riot."

That brings him up short.

"I'm feeling fractious today." He rubs the top of his head like a man full of unhappy thoughts. "Don't be offended."

"I'm not."

"You're a good sort. You work hard and don't harbour grudges. You speak your mind instead of the infernal yeses I always get. Come and work for me."

"Thank you but I hope you won't hold it against me if I say no."

"No, but think on it. The offer stands." Something else is bubbling up. "You and I aren't so different. I had to scramble too. I'm a Dingle man. My daughters are spoilt and innocent. My sons no better." His rueful smile reveals the pain of parenthood. "It's their mother's fault. They're not fit for the real world, so I must keep on scrambling."

I envy his children, wanting for nothing, this brutal life kept at arm's length. Makin must see something in my face because he puts the distance back between us with, "Have you heard any talk I should know about?"

He's still chewing on my unpalatable comment about riots.

"All I meant was that it's unseasonably hot and a while since the last high day or holiday. Steam builds up in these conditions."

I hear craziness in the ale houses all the time that I'm not going to share with him. Talk of seizing boats and sailing out of Liverpool Bay, north to Blundell Sands and Crosby to breathe rarefied air and storm the families' palaces. Toppling the merchant princes. A revolution of beheading, raping and redistribution of riches.

Tough talk. Despairing men with beer dreams of taking on armed guards.

"They can riot all they like. Justice will fall hard. Liverpool's peaceful. There'll be no unions here. We'll reward anyone who helps keep it that way."

I want to say, *The Peels aren't the law,* but then I remember that they are.

* * *

I CROSS UPPER Parliament Street into Toxteth. My cart's loaded with a bag of threadbare coloured sheets which I'll sell for second-grade paper. I've a pile of bones that'll go for glue.

"Ra bon! Ra bon!" I shout.

Calls bring the kids who run alongside me. One reaches out to pat Gabriel, my hound, who curls his lip and growls.

"Not a pet, son. Steer clear."

When I stop, the children squat on the curb to watch. They're still too little for factory work.

"Tommy, can I have a sweet?"

"No, not unless you've something to trade and it's Tom, you cheeky blighter. Shouldn't you be in school?"

There are elementary classes in the big cathedral. I convinced Dad to let me attend until he decided it was too dangerous and taught me himself instead. Hundreds of us learnt our letters and numbers by rote, young voices raised in unison like fevered prayers that reached the cavernous vaults. The sad-eyed ministers promised God and Jerusalem right here in Liverpool and even then I could see they were as hungry as we were, for bread and something better.

"Are you the scrap man?" It's a darling girl with a face ravaged by pox. "My ma asked for you to come in."

"Don't touch my barrow," I tell the others. "After the dog's had you, I'll clobber you myself."

I wave my spike-tipped stick at them. It's not a serious threat. They respond with grins of broken teeth and scurvy sores. They're not so bad at this age. It's the older ones you have to watch for.

I follow the child inside. The terraces seethe and swelter in the summer. Five storeys from basement to attic, a family in every room. All bodies fodder to the belching factories and docks; bargemen, spinners, dockers, weavers and foundry workers. Dad reckoned Liverpool got shipping and industry when the boundaries were marked out and other places got chemicals, medicines, food production and suchlike. He said the walls and watchtowers around each county were the means by which the martial government quelled civil unrest over recession, then biting depression. It was just an excuse to divide the nation into biddable portions and keep those that had in control of those that didn't.

Dad also said his grandfather had a farm and it was a hard but cleaner living. No cotton fibres in the lungs, fewer machines to mangle limbs. Less disease and no production lines along which contagion can spread.

The girl darts into a room at the back. I stand at the door. The two women within are a pair of gems. One says, "Lolly," and the child runs to her. She looks like an angel, clutching the child to her that way.

"We've stuff to sell," says the other one with the diamond-hard stare. "I'm Sally and this is Kate."

Sally's dazzling. I take off my cap and pat down my hair.

They share the same profile, long hair fastened up. Sisters. Sally's still talking while Angel Kate puts a basket on the table. I catch her glance. This pitiful collection's worth won't meet their needs.

"Let's see." I clear my throat. "These gloves might fetch something. The forks too." The tines are so twisted that they're only worth scrap value. There's a jar of buttons and some horseshoe nails that look foraged from between cobbles. "I'll give you extra for the basket."

Kate looks at the money in my outstretched hand with hungry eyes but Sally's got the money in her pocket before I can change my mind.

"Are you both out of work?"

"Laid off." Sally makes a sour face.

"I'm sorry. Laid off from where?"

"Vicar's Buttons."

A good, safe place for nimble-fingered women.

"I'll let you know if anyone's hiring."

"Lolly, play outside." Lolly jumps to Kate's order, dispelling any doubt about which woman is Lolly's mother.

"We need more money." Mother Kate is fierce. "I've heard that you're looking to collect things for one of the families. . ."

"Which one?" Sally butts in.

"The Peels," I answer.

"The Peels have taken enough from us already."

I want to ask Sally what she means but I don't get a chance.

"*We need more money, Sally.* Peels, Vicars, Hardmans. What's the difference?"

"There is."

"No, there isn't, Sal." Kate sounds flat. "Lolly needs food and a roof. She comes above pride or principles."

Nothing could make me admire Kate more. I'm gawping at her.

"We'll get work."

"Not soon enough." Kate turns to me. "Tell me more."

"It's just in case one of the Peels get ill." I feel foolish trotting out this patter. "Should they need a little blood or skin, or bit of bone."

"Are they too proud to ask one another?" Sally's sharp. "I've heard that they take the bits they want and toss the rest of you to their lapdogs. And what if they want an eye or kidney?"

"They wouldn't want anything vital and the compensation would be in keeping, of course."

"Compensation?" Sally presses me. She's the sparring sort.

"That's up for discussion. Someone got granted leave to live outside Liverpool for their help."

Outside. Myth and mystery. That shuts her up.

"Yes, but what will you give me now?" Kate has more pressing concerns.

Both women are bright-eyed. They don't look like they buy backdoor poteen or have the sluggish, undernourished look of opium fiends. They've worked in a button factory, not a mill, so they've young unblemished lungs, engine hearts and flawless flesh, except for their worn hands. Just the sort I've been told to look for. I feel like a rat, gnawing on a dying man's toes.

Do whatever you need to survive, Dad would say. *Do whatever you need to be free.*

I put a silver coin on the table.

"I'll do it," Kate says.

"Don't." Sally's like a terrier. I don't know whether to kiss or kick her.

"We've queued for weeks with no luck."

The indignity of hiring pens and agency lines. At the respectable ones they just check hands and teeth. At others, they take women and boys around back for closer inspection.

"What if they want something from you? What then?" Sally sounds panicked.

"All they ask is a chance to speak to you. No one's forcing anyone." It's what I've been told to say, but the rich always have their way.

"Do it." Kate's firm.

I take off the bag strung across my chest and sit down at the table.

"What's your name?"

"Kate Harper."

Kate's hands are callused from factory work but her forearms are soft.

"It'll hurt." I remove the sampler's cap.

I put it over her arm and press down. I feel the tip bite flesh and hear the click as it chips off bone. It leaves a deep, oozing hole. Kate gasps but doesn't move. It's only ever men that shout and thrash about.

"I'll give you some ointment to help it heal. What about Lolly's father?" I try and make it sound like easy banter as I write her details in the log book and on the tube.

"He was a sailor on *The Triumph*."

"You're Richard Harper's wife?" A name said with hushed reverence.

"Yes, and before you blather on about heroism, he didn't give us a second thought. Everything we'd saved went on his sailor's bond."

The Triumph was a Peel ship that landed in the Indies. You can't send men across the ocean on a boat and not expect them to want to get off on the other side and walk around. It's a foul practice to stop sailors absconding, resulting in cabin fever, brawling and sodomy. The crew of *The Triumph* mutinied.

The leader, Richard Harper, was a martyr for his part. The authorities tied him to the anchor before they dropped it. His sailor's bond, held with the port master, was forfeit.

"You were widowed young."

Kate's nod is a stiff movement from the neck. She tries to soften it with, "It's just us now."

"I understand. It used to be me and my dad until he died. He was a rag and bone man too." I'm overcome with the need to tell her everything, but I can't. "He wanted a horse instead of pulling the barrow himself. One day I'll get one, if I can save enough."

I'm trying to impress them. Sally sighs as if I'm tiresome but Kate pats my hand like an absentminded mother. Her unguarded kindness makes me want to cry. I want to put my head on Kate's knee and for her to stroke my hair.

Sally watches us.

"I won't do it. I don't trust them."

I realise that I want to touch Sally too, but in a different way. I have a fierce urge to press my mouth to the flesh on the inside of her wrist where the veins show through.

Sally stares me down and I want to say, *I'm not the enemy. I'm not a flesh-eating Peel up in an ivory tower,* but then I realise that I might as well be.

I SIT IN my room at the Baltic Fleet. Mother Kate's essence shouldn't be contained in a vial. I don't want anyone else to possess her. Not some sailor, bound and drowned, and definitely not a Peel. She should be free.

Times are hard. I've filled in a whole page of Makin's log book.

I go walking to clear my head, Gabriel at heel. Mrs Tsang, the publican, is stocking the bar with brown bottles of pale ale. She's good to me, just like she was good to Dad. She lets me the room and I keep my barrow in the yard under a tarp.

"Okay, poppet?" she asks as I pass.

On impulse I lean down and kiss her cheek. She swats me away, hiding her smile. Mrs Tsang's tiny but I've seen her bottle a man in the face for threatening her. The jagged glass tore his lips and nose.

The factories are out and everyone's heading home. Workers pile into the terraces. Some sun themselves on doorsteps. A tethered parrot squawks at me from its perch outside a door, talking of flights in warmer climes. Kids play football on the street.

I head to Otterspool Prom where I stand and consider, looking out at the river. Herring gulls scream at me for my foolishness. Gabriel lies down and covers his face with his paws.

I drop Kate's vial and stand on it. Then I kick every single fragment into the water and don't leave until the Mersey's taken it all away.

I PAUSE OUTSIDE Makin's office.

"I'd advise caution with his sort, sir." A stranger's voice.

"What's *his sort* then?" That's Makin.

"Loners, in my experience, are freaks or agitators."

"Tom's neither."

Behind me, someone clears his throat. I turn to find myself on the sharp end of a pointed look from Makin's secretary. No doubt he'll tell later.

"I told you to knock and go in." He opens the door.

"Ah, Tom, this is Mr Jessop."

Jessop's the most handsome man I've ever seen, with good teeth and all his hair. He's no gentleman. He has the swagger of the law, not a regular policeman but a special.

"Tom, we were just talking about you." He sounds like a Scouser now, a rough edge to his voice that was missing before. He must talk it up or down, depending on the company. "Can I see the log book that Mr Makin gave you?"

I look at Makin who nods. Mr Jessop flicks through it, checking against the ledger where a clerk copies the details.

"Is this address correct?"

It's Kate's.

"Yes." I shrug. "I filled it in at the time."

"Anyone else live there?"

"Her sister and daughter."

"And you broke one of the samplers that day?"

"Yes. An empty one. I'm a clumsy oaf." I try and sound like I'm still berating myself. "I dropped it and stepped on it. I reported it straight away, didn't I, Mr Makin? I offered to pay for it."

"No one's accusing you of anything, Tom."

"Do you know where Kate Harper is now?" Jessop doesn't let up.

"Isn't she there?"

I know she isn't. I knocked at her door and an old man answered. *Bugger off. I've no idea where they went.*

"No, but you know that already because you went back." Jessop smiles, the triumphant conniver. "You do know that she's Richard Harper's widow, don't you?"

"Yes, but what's that got to do with me?"

Jessop's hands are spotless. He must scrub them nightly to get out suspects' blood. Specials with manicured hands don't come in search of factory girls without reason.

Makin sits back, waiting. Of course. They're terrified of Harper. That his wife will be a rallying cry.

"I didn't know who she was until she gave the sample."

"And why would she do that?"

"She needed money."

"So she's not being looked after by her Trotsky pals?" Jessop won't let it go.

"I don't think so." I try and catch Makin's eye.

"Why did you go back?"

Makin's holding his breath, waiting.

"The thing is" – I shift about, embarrassed by the truth – "they were pretty and I wanted to see them again."

"There's no shame in that." Makin seems relieved. Thank God that good men like him can rise in this world that favours politicians who use smiles, wiles and outright lies.

I feel bad about lying to him.

"We need to speak to her," Jessop says.

"But I don't know where she is."

"But you'll tell us if you do find her?" His smile makes me want to bolt for the door. "You've never had a job, have you?"

"I work."

My dad would say, *We're free. Never subject to the tyranny of the clock. The dull terrors of the production line. No one will use us as they please.*

"Bone grubbing. Piss-poor way to make a living."

"Enough." Makin tuts.

"So sorry." Jessop's oily and insincere. "If you do find her, be a good lad and run up here and tell Mr Makin."

I want to say, *Shove your apology,* but keep my gob shut.

THE BASTARDS FOLLOW me about all day. Jessop and his pals, got up like dockers. I pretend I've not seen them but they stand out. They're too clean to look real.

I look for Kate and Sally in the hiring lines, strolling past with my barrow as if on my way elsewhere. I wouldn't give her away. I just want to see her face. I ask the washerwomen at the water pumps and the old men standing around the fires at night.

Kate, Sally, Lolly. There's not a whiff of them.

I go up to the destitute courts of the Dingle, each court comprised of six houses set up around a central yard. The noxious stench from the shared privy is of liquid filth. I look through open doors: blooming damp patches on the plaster, crumbled in places to bare brick. I see faces made hard by deprivation. Infants squalling from drawers because they're hungry. It was a miracle that Makin clawed his way out of here.

"You."

A priest accosts me. He's on his rounds, demanding pennies from the poor to give to the even poorer.

"Come here."

Closer and he's unshaven and smells. He's ale addled. I feel for him, driven to despair and drink by the gargantuan task of saving so many lost souls. He follows me out of the court, onto the street.

"I've heard about you, Thomas Coster."

I tie Gabriel to the cart in case he goes for the man and wait for the rage of the righteous. I don't feel so well-disposed towards him now.

"You're in league with evil." He shoves his face into mine. Gabriel goes crazy. We're drawing quite an audience. "The Peels keep people in tanks like fish, cutting off the bits they want."

I'm panting from pushing the cart uphill and trying to outpace him. Jessop's up ahead, leaning against a wall.

"A man should be buried whole in consecrated ground."

The priest's enraged when the crowd laughs. Burial's expensive. The poor are cremated on pyres.

"You'll be damned. You'll suffer all hell's torments. You'll be flayed. The devil will sup on your gizzards and crack the marrow from your bones."

Jessop laughs under his breath as I pass.

IT'S A RARE day that a Peel comes to town.

The Peel factories have closed an hour early to mark the day. Men loiter on Hope Street, outside the Philharmonic pub. Rowdy clerks from the insurance offices and banks are out, seeking white-collar mayhem. One turns quickly and shoulder barges me as I pass. He's keen to prove he can push more than a pen. His friends laugh.

His mates all line up across the pavement to block my path. I step into the gutter. One of them steps down to join me. He's wearing ridiculous checked trousers and his hands are in his pockets. I wonder what's in there.

"You walked into my friend. You should apologise."

I open my mouth but someone's standing at my shoulder. It's Jessop.

"I think you're mistaken," Jessop says as he opens his jacket. Whatever's glinting within is enough to put this bunch off.

I glance around. Jessop's travelling in numbers, all of them in black suits.

"I'm sorry, sir."

Oh, to wield so much power that you don't have to exert it.

Jessop picks up his pace, looking back to give me a final grin. I follow in their wake, pushing through to the barrier. There's a big crowd. Lord Peel's here to give a special address to his foremen. They must be in need of bucking up if he's got to come down here to talk to them himself.

The doors of the assembly rooms open and a pair of specials come out, eyes scanning the crowd. The foremen follow, dressed in their Sunday best. They look uncertain as they emerge, blinking in the afternoon sunlight. Makin and his secretary follow. Makin looks stiff and starched. I'm used to seeing him with his shirtsleeves rolled up, fingers inky from his calculations.

Then Lord Peel steps out, the brim of his hat angled to shade his face. I realise there's silence. Not even the sound of shuffling feet.

Some lackey shoves a child forward and she holds up a bunch of pink roses. Peel turns his face as he takes them. He's a shocker close up. His nose and eyes are leonine. Thin lipped. Skin stretched to a sickening smoothness that rivals the silk of his cravat. His blue eyes are faded by age.

Then it begins. A low baritone from deep within the crowd.

The sea takes me from my love . . .

Another voice joins in, then another, then more so there's a choir.

The sea takes me from my love
It drops me on the ocean floor
The sea tempts me from my true love's arms
And I'll go home no more.

Peel smiles, thinking this impromptu serenade's for him. He doesn't know that each ship has its own shanties and ballads and this one's famed as *The Triumph*'s.

Makin leans over and whispers in Peel's ear and his smile fades. There's another chorus and it sounds like the whole of Liverpool is singing.

The sea takes me from my love
It drops me on the ocean floor
The sea tempts me from my mother's knee
And I'll go home no more.

There are no jeers or shouts. Just the people's indignity dignified in song. The police don't know how to respond. They form a ring around Peel and his retinue. The foremen are outside this protective circle. Someone motions for Peel's carriage.

The air's filled with fluttering white sheets. They're being thrown down onto the street from the roof of the infirmary. Hands reach for them. Makin plucks at a sheet, reads it and crumples it in his fist. Peel's caught one too. He's angry. He turns to Makin and jabs at his chest with a gloved forefinger as if he's personally responsible.

I pick up one. It's *The Echo*, a dissident rag, printed on cheap, low-grade paper, the ink already smudging. It advocates minimum wages, safety measures and free health care. This edition's different. It bears the words *Lord Peel's Triumph*, with a drawing of Richard Harper floating on his anchor. It's the anniversary of his death. A bad day for Peel to show his face.

Once Peel's departed the police will demonstrate their displeasure for this display. Jessop's already giving orders. It's time to leave.

Peel's in the carriage as the singing continues. Makin turns as he climbs in and his gaze fixes on me, *The Echo* still clutched in my hand.

IT'S AN OFFICIAL match day, when the factories close for the machines to be serviced.

Football's a violent and anarchic game where passions are vented, on and off the pitch. The crowd wears the colours, red or blue. They're no longer just a dark mass of serge and twill that pour into the black factories.

Jessop and his sidekick are behind me. I try and lose them in the crush. The hoards of Everton, Toxteth, Kensington, and Dingle come together for this sliver of pleasure.

The constabulary are mounted, their horses stamping and pawing the cobbles. They'll tolerate fisticuffs amid the crowd to vent rising tensions. A good-natured kicking or black eye, as long as everyone's fit for work the following day no harm's done.

The coppers know if they weigh in the crowd will turn on them, but I can see in their eyes how they'd love to beat about with batons and hand out indiscriminate thrashings in the guise of peacekeeping.

I see my chance. A chanting group comes up the street towards Anfield's football pitch, waving Evertonian flags. Red banners are at my back. The two groups meet, posturing and jostling. I dart down an alley, ducking to avoid the lines of washing. Jessop's lost.

There's one place I've not looked for them. The dirty terraces where parlours of women wait for the game to end. It makes me shudder.

I peer into windows and am shocked by what's on show. It's just another factory, churning up girls, making fodder of their flesh. I go around the back. Women line the wall, waiting to be hired. My heart stops when I see her. I push past the other girls who try to lure me in with promises that make me blush.

"Where's Kate?"

"You." Sally looks tired and bored. "Are you paying?"

Hard and heartless. I rifle in my pocket, glancing up and down the street. "Here."

"It's double that." She scowls.

I give her more. We have to get indoors.

She leads me to a house. A room's free at the top of the stairs. It's painted an oppressive red that would look fashionable somewhere grand. The window's dirty. There's a bed with a sheet and pillow on it. A pitcher and bowl on the dresser. A headboard rattles on the other side of the wall.

"What are you doing, Sally?"

"Earning a living."

"Here?"

"I can't get work."

"And Kate?"

"Dead."

The mattress sinks even farther as I sit beside her. She moves away.

"When?" Then, "How?"

"A week ago. We moved in with a family in Croxteth. The woman was sick that day so Kate went to work in her place. She got her sleeve caught in a roller. It took her arm. They were too slow tying the stump off. She bled to death."

Sally's matter-of-fact. Her lip doesn't quiver. Her eyes are dry.

"I'm sorry." Words clog my throat. "Where's Lolly?"

"At home, where else?" She's glad of an excuse to be angry. "What sort do you think I am, to bring a child here?"

"The best sort." I try and soothe her.

Kate's dead. I wish I'd gone back to their terrace sooner but posthumous offers of help mean nothing to the dead.

"I'm the best sort, am I? Is that why you think you can buy me with a few coins? You men are all loathsome."

I'm angry too. I want to shut her up. I grip her head and cover her mouth with mine. She pulls away.

"Don't kiss me with your eyes shut and pretend I'm Kate. Fuck me for my own sake."

I don't relent. I'm too busy kissing Sally to correct her. The tension in her is like a wire.

We lie down. She's thin, a skeleton wrapped in skin. I'm not much better, but I take the weight of my large frame on my knees and elbows.

"This doesn't mean anything. Understand?"

She's wrong. It means everything.

"You're crying," she says.

"So are you."

She undoes my trousers and puts her hand between my legs. No one's ever touched me there before.

"Oh," she says. Then louder, "Oh."

I feel the wire snap, and her whole body relaxes. She kisses me, finally yielding. My whole life's been leading to this moment of sex and solace.

I want to say, *Thank you, thank you, thank you*, but I'm too breathless to speak.

SALLY'S HEAD IS on my chest. Sleep slows her breathing. My trousers are around my thighs, my shirt's undone. Her petticoat's rucked up around her waist. I don't move for fear of disturbing this lovely girl. The sudden roar from Anfield carries over the rooftops and into the room. It masks the quiet click of the door opening and closing.

Jessop stands at the end of the bed, chuckling. I leap up, struggling with my trousers.

"So Tom," he says, sarcastic. "Who's your pretty friend?"

I do up my fly. Sally retrieves her blouse from the floor and pulls it over her head. Jessop's sly look scares me. He takes off his jacket.

"We've all afternoon. Why don't you both lie down again?"

I go at him like a cornered dog. Dad used to say, *Fight if you're cornered*. I stick him in the throat with my pocket knife. Bubbles of blood mark the wound. I put my hand over his mouth to stop him crying out. He grips my wrist and twists. Sally's fishing about under the bed and I wonder what the hell she's doing, then I see the docker's hook. It's the weapon of choice in Liverpool. The handle sits snug in the palm, the hook protruding between the first and second fingers. She comes around behind him and plants it in his skull.

Jessop pitches into my arms. I lower him to the floor.

"Hold his legs."

I grab them to stop his boot heels from hammering on the floor. Sally helps. How he clings to life. It seems like forever before he's still.

"Are you okay, Sal?" A woman's voice.

"Fine."

"Sure?"

Sally gets up. I wipe the blood spray from her face. She goes to the door and opens it a crack. She whispers something and the woman laughs. Then Sally locks the door.

"Who was he?"

"A special."

"Jesus. We'll both swing."

She's right. We'll go straight from the law courts to the noose in Victoria Square. But before that there'll be long days and nights in a cell with Jessop's friends queued outside.

I'd rather die.

"What did he want with you?"

"He was looking for Kate. They think she can lead them to trade unionists."

"That's crazy."

"Sally, we've not got much time. I'll deal with this. You need to go."

"No. We stay together."

"Get Lolly. Wait at the Baltic Fleet. Don't speak to anyone but Mrs Tsang. Tell her I sent you. You can trust her." It kills me to say this. I want to be a coward and say, *Yes, stay. Never leave my side.*

She kisses me. Why did I ever think her hard?

"I'm sorry that I got you involved with this." I usher her out. "Go on now, quickly." Once she's gone, I splash cold water on my face and button up my jacket to hide my bloodied shirt.

All the while I'm thinking of Sally. Of how my parting words were *I'm sorry that I got you involved with this,* when what I meant was *I'm sorry that you think I love Kate more.*

I ROLL JESSOP under the bed and pull the rug over the stained floorboards. I'm thankful for the room's violent colour as it hides the blood sprayed across the walls.

The specials must be going house to house. I'm on the stairs when I hear outraged shouts from the room below. A pair of them come up the narrow stairs. I grapple with the first one and he knocks me down. The other tries to hold my thrashing legs. Like Jessop, I struggle against the inevitable.

A third clambers over us, pretty tangle that we are, and checks the rooms. There's a pause, then a hoarse shout. Jessop's been found.

"Take the bastard outside."

They've cleared the street. Faces peer from the window. Someone kicks my legs from under me. I land on my knees.

"Mike, remember what Makin said." The man holding my arm is young and nervous.

Mike, who's looking down on me, pauses, but then he decides I'm worth it. He kicks me in the chest. I feel the wind go out of me.

"Bugger Makin. He killed Jessop."

I curl up on the floor, hands over my head. My view's of the boots as they pile in. It doesn't matter. I've had a kicking before.

I'M IN MAKIN'S office. The clock sounds muffled and voices are distant. The hearing in my left ear's gone. The vision in my right eye's reduced to a slit. Breathing hurts.

Makin's furious.

"Get out."

"Sir, the man's a murderer," Mike whines.

"I gave specific orders. Tom wasn't to be harmed under any circumstances. You were to bring him straight to me if anything happened."

"Sir, Jessop . . ."

"Are you still here? Go before I have you posted to Seaforth."

Mike flees at the threat of Merseyside's hinterlands. Makin fetches a pair of glasses and a decanter. He pours out the port. It looks like molten rubies.

"Drink this. It'll steady you. I've called for a doctor."

I drain the glass, not tasting the contents. His sits, untouched.

"You're in serious trouble, Tom. I want to help you." The chair's legs scrape the floor as he pulls it closer and sits down. "Did you kill him?"

I nod. Then I start to cry.

"It happened so fast. He burst in. I was with a girl." I'm babbling. A stream of snot, tears and despair. "I'm not a trade unionist."

"Who was the girl?"

"Not Kate Harper, if that's what you're thinking. Jessop didn't do his job very well. She's dead. He should've checked the register."

"He did. The body didn't match the sample you gave me for her." Makin tips his head. "You have to trust me. Is Kate really dead or were you with her?"

"No. All I know is that she's dead."

"Who did the sample belong to? Was it the woman you were with?"

"Does it matter?"

He looks down at his hands. Ink stains his fingers. "More than you think."

He tops up my glass.

"Let's suppose Lord Peel's keen to find this woman, whoever it is. Let's say Lady Peel needs medical attention that requires a little blood or perhaps a bit of skin. It would be a wealth for this woman and a reward to whoever helps me find her." He lets this sink in. "Suppose Jessop got himself into a spot of bother with some girl. He played rough from what I've heard. There's no proof. The girl's long gone. An unsolved case."

My nose starts to bleed. Makin hands me his handkerchief. Blood stains the fine linen.

"You could do that?"

"I'll do what's necessary." Makin, not afraid to scramble.

"I want somewhere away from Liverpool. Out in the country. A farm with cows and chickens where nobody can bother me," I blurt out. "And I want to take a woman and child with me."

"That's a lot, just for information."

"It's more than that. Peel will be pleased. It'll make up for that day when he made his speech. But promise me first, that we have a deal."

Makin looks at me with narrowed eyes.

"A deal then, as long as you deliver her."

We shake hands.

"The sample's mine."

"That's not funny."

"I'm not joking."

He stares at me.

"Test me again and you'll see." I'm an odd-looking woman, but I make a passable man. I'm too big, too ungainly, too flat chested and broad shouldered. My hips narrow and features coarse. "I'm not trying to make a fool of you. I live this way."

"Why?"

"Sarah, my mother, got me when she was cornered on the factory floor by men who resented a woman who could work a metal press better than them. She swore she'd never go back. She became Saul after I was born."

Rag and bone men. We're free, Tom. Never subject to the tyranny of the clock. The dull terrors of the production lines. No man will use us as he pleases.

"What's your real name?"

"Tom." It's the only name I've ever had. "Do we still have a deal?"

"Yes. The girl you were with when you killed Jessop. Is she the one you want to take with you?"

His face is smooth now, hiding disgust or disappointment.

"Yes."

"I'll need to know who she is and where to find her if I'm going to get her out of Liverpool."

I tell him. When I say Sally's name he takes a deep breath but doesn't ask anything else.

I want to ask, *What do the Peels want from me?* But then I decide it's better not to know.

I'VE NEVER BEEN on a boat. I've never seen Liverpool from the sea. My stinking, teeming city's beautiful. I've never loved her more than I do now. I love the monumental Liver birds, even though they're indifferent to the suffering below. The colonnades and warehouses. Cathedrals and crack houses. The pubs and street lamps glowing in the fog. Workers, washerwomen, beggars, priests and princes. Rag and bone men. Liverpool is multitudes.

The boat's pitch and roll makes me sick. A guard follows me to the rail. He's not concerned about my health. He's scared I'll jump. I get a whiff of the Irish Sea proper. Land's a strip in the distance.

We don't moor at Southport but somewhere nearby. I'm marched down the rattling gangplank and onto a narrow jetty. Miles of dunes roll out before us. It's clean and empty. I've never known such quiet. There's only wind and shifting sands. I wonder if it's hell or paradise.

The dunes become long grass and then packed brown earth. I've never seen so many trees. Their fallen leaves are needles underfoot, faded from rich green to brown.

There's a hatch buried in the ground. One of my guards opens it and clambers down, waiting at the bottom.

"You next."

The corridor leads downwards. Our boots shed sand and needles on the tiles. There's the acrid smell of antiseptic.

"In here." One of them touches my arm.

The other's busy talking to someone I can't see because of the angle of an adjoining door. I catch the words, "Makin sent her this way. She'll need time to heal."

"Take your clothes off and put them in the bin. Turn this and water will come out here. Get clean under it." My guard's talking to me like I'm a child. "Soap's here. Towel's there. Put on this gown after."

I'm mortified, thinking they're going to watch, but they're keen to be away. I drop my clothes into the bin. I can still smell Sally on me but she doesn't stand a chance against the stream of hot water and rich suds.

A woman's leaning against the far wall, watching. I pull the towel about me and try to get dry. She looks like a china doll, with high, round cheeks and blue eyes. Her long yellow hair swings as she walks.

"Sit there."

She tuts as she touches my cheek where the skin's split. Then she checks my eyes and teeth. A needle punctures my vein. Blood works its way along a tube into a bottle. She takes scrapings from the inside of my mouth.

"Disrobe."

I stand up and let the towel drop to a puddle at my feet. I stare ahead of me. She walks around me like a carter considering a new horse. Her hand floats across the plane of my back, around the garland of yellow and purple bruises that run from back to front. She touches my breasts, my stomach, my thighs. From the steadfast way she avoids my gaze, I know there's more chance that the Liver birds will fly than of me leaving here.

I try and stay calm. I was dead from the moment Jessop opened the door of the red room. From the moment I put the sampler to my arm. It's either this or a jig at the end of a rope. There's no point in me going cold into the warm ground to rot when I can help Sally and Lolly. I hope they'll remember to take Gabriel with them.

Ink-fingered Makin, the artful scrambler, making his calculations. The possibility I've got him wrong is a cold, greasy knife in my belly. If I have, I've served up Sally, Lolly and Mrs Tsang into the constabulary's hands.

The woman seems satisfied. I want to say, *Look at me. Look me in the eye. I'm a person, not a piece of meat,* but then I realise I just might as well be. A piece of meat. Rag and bone.

THE BOOK SELLER
Lavie Tidhar

Lavie Tidhar (lavietidhar.wordpress.com) grew up on a kibbutz in Israel and has since lived in South Africa, the UK, Vanuatu and Laos. He is the author of six novels including World Fantasy Award winner *Osama*, *Martian Sands*, and the Bookman Trilogy. Tidhar has published more than 130 short stories, including linked short story collection *Hebrewpunk*, and edited *The Apex Book of World SF* anthologies. His most recent book is novel *The Violent Century*.

ACHIMWENE LOVED CENTRAL Station. He loved the adaptoplant neighbourhoods sprouting over the old stone and concrete buildings, the budding of new apartments and the gradual fading and shearing of old ones, dried windows and walls flaking and falling down in the wind.

Achimwene loved the calls of the alte-zachen, the rag-and-bone men, in their traditional passage across the narrow streets, collecting junk to carry to their immense junkyard-cum-temple on the hill in Jaffa to the south. He loved the smell of sheesha-pipes on the morning wind, and the smell of bitter coffee, loved the smell of fresh horse manure left behind by the alte-zachenspatient, plodding horses.

Nothing pleased Achimwene Haile Selassi Jones as much as the sight of the sun rising behind Central Station, the light slowly diffusing beyond and over the immense, hour-glass shape of the space port. Or almost nothing. For he had one overriding passion, at the time that we pick this thread, a passion which to him was both a job and a mission.

Early morning light suffused Central Station and the old cobbled streets. It highlighted exhausted prostitutes and street-sweeping machines, the bobbing floating lanterns that, with dawn coming, were slowly drifting away, to be stored until nightfall. On the rooftops solar panels unfurled themselves, welcoming the sun. The air was still cool at this time. Soon it will be hot, the sun beating down, the aircon units turning on with a roar of cold air in shops and restaurants and crowded apartments all over the old neighbourhood.

"Ibrahim," Achimwene said, acknowledging the alte-zachen man as he approached. Ibrahim was perched on top of his cart, the boy Ismail by his side. The cart was pushed by a solitary horse, an old grey being who blinked at Achimwene patiently. The cart was already filled, with adaptoplant furniture, scrap plastic and metal, boxes of discarded house wares and, lying carelessly on its side, a discarded stone bust of Albert Einstein.

"Achimwene," Ibrahim said, smiling. "How is the weather?"

"Fair to middling," Achimwene said, and they both laughed, comfortable in the near-daily ritual.

This is Achimwene: he was not the most imposing of people, did not draw the eye in a crowd. He was slight of frame, and somewhat stooped, and wore old-fashioned glasses to correct a minor fault of vision. His hair was once thickly curled but not much of it was left now, and he was mostly, sad to say, bald. He had a soft mouth and patient, trusting eyes, with fine lines of disappointment at their corners. His name meant "brother" in Chichewa, a language dominant in Malawi, though he was of the Joneses of Central Station, and the brother of Miriam Jones, of Mama Jones' Shebeen on Neve Sha'anan Street. Every morning he rose early, bathed hurriedly, and went out into the streets in time to catch the rising sun and the alte-zachen man. Now he rubbed his hands together, as if cold, and said, in his soft, quiet voice, "Do you have anything for me today, Ibrahim?"

Ibrahim ran his hand over his own bald pate and smiled. Sometimes the answer was a simple "No." Sometimes it came with a hesitant "Perhaps..."

Today it was a "Yes," Ibrahim said, and Achimwene raised his eyes, to him or to the heavens, and said, "Show me?"

"Ismail," Ibrahim said, and the boy, who sat beside him wordless until then, climbed down from the cart with a quick, confident grin and went to the back of the cart. "It's heavy!" he complained. Achimwene hurried to his side and helped him bring down a heavy box.

He looked at it.

"Open it," Ibrahim said. "Are these any good to you?"

Achimwene knelt by the side of the box. His fingers reached for it, traced an opening. Slowly, he pulled the flaps of the box apart. Savouring the moment that light would fall down on the box's contents, and the smell of those precious, fragile things inside would rise, released, into the air, and tickle his nose. There was no other smell like it in the world, the smell of old and weathered paper.

The box opened. He looked inside.

Books. Not the endless scrolls of text and images, moving and static, nor full-immersion narratives he understood other people to experience, in what he called, in his obsolete tongue, the networks, and others called, simply, the Conversation. Not those, to which he, anyway, had no access. Nor were they books as decorations, physical objects hand-crafted by artisans, vellum-bound, gold-tooled, typeset by hand and sold at a premium.

No.

He looked at the things in the box, these fragile, worn, faded, thin, cheap paper-bound books. They smelled of dust, and mould, and age. They smelled, faintly, of pee, and tobacco, and spilled coffee. They smelled like things which had *lived*.

They smelled like history.

With careful fingers he took a book out and held it, gently turning the pages. It was all but priceless. His breath, as they often said in those very same books, caught in his throat.

It was a *Ringo*.

A genuine Ringo.

The cover of this fragile paperback showed a leather-faced gunman against a desert-red background. RINGO, it said, it giant letters, and below, the fictitious author's name, Jeff McNamara. Finally, the individual title of the book, one of many in that long running Western series. This one was *On The Road To Kansas City*.

Were they all like this?

Of course, there had never been a "Jeff McNamara". Ringo was a series of Hebrew-language Westerns, all written pseudonymously by starving young writers in a bygone Tel Aviv, who contributed besides them similar tales of space adventures, sexual titillation or soppy romance, as the occasion (and the publisher's cheque book) had called for. Achimwene rifled carefully through the rest of the books. All paperbacks, printed on cheap, thin pulp paper centuries before. How had they been preserved? Some of these he had only ever seen mentioned in auction catalogues, their existence, here, now, was nothing short of a miracle. There was a nurse romance; a murder mystery; a World War Two adventure; an erotic tale whose lurid cover made Achimwene blush. They were impossible, they could not possibly exist. "Where did you *find* them?" he said.

Ibrahim shrugged. "An opened Century Vault," he said.

Achimwene exhaled a sigh. He had heard of such things – subterranean safe-rooms, built in some long-ago war of the Jews, pockets of reinforced concrete shelters caught like bubbles all under the city surface. But he had never expected...

"Are there... many of them?" he said.

Ibrahim smiled. "Many," he said. Then, taking pity on Achimwene, said, "Many vaults, but most are inaccessible. Every now and then, construction work uncovers one... the owners called me, for they viewed much of it as rubbish. What, after all, would a modern person want with one of these?" and he gestured at the box, saying, "I saved them for you. The rest of the stuff is back in the Junkyard, but this was the only box of books."

"I can pay," Achimwene said. "I mean, I will work something out, I will borrow" – the thought stuck like a bone in his throat (as they said in those books) – "I will borrow from my sister."

But Ibrahim, to Achimwene's delight and incomprehension, waved him aside with a laugh. "Pay me the usual," he said. "After all, it is only a box, and this is mere paper. It cost me nothing, and I have made my profit already. What extra value you place on it surely is a value of your own."

"But they are precious!" Achimwene said, shocked. "Collectors would pay –" imagination failed him. Ibrahim smiled, and his smile was gentle. "You are the only collector I know," he said. "Can you afford what you think they're worth?"

"No," Achimwene said – whispered.

"Then pay only what I ask," Ibrahim said and, with a shake of his head, as at the folly of his fellow man, steered the horse into action. The patient beast beat its flank with its tail, shooing away flies, and ambled onwards. The boy, Ismail, remained there a moment longer, staring at the books. "Lots of old junk in the Vaults!" he said. He spread his arms wide to describe them. "I was there, I saw it! These... books?" he shot an uncertain look at Achimwene, then ploughed on – "and big flat square things called televisions, that we took for plastic scrap, and old guns, lots of old guns! But the Jews took those – why do you think they buried those things?" the boy said. His eyes, vat-grown haunting greens, stared at Achimwene. "So much *junk*," the boy said, at last, with a note of finality, and then, laughing, ran after the cart, jumping up on it with youthful ease.

Achimwene stared at the cart until it disappeared around the bend. Then, with the tenderness of a father picking up a new-born infant, he picked up the box of books and carried them the short way to his alcove.

ACHIMWENE'S LIFE WAS about to change, but he did not yet know it. He spent the rest of the morning happily cataloguing, preserving and shelving the ancient books. Each lurid cover delighted him. He handled the books with only the tips of his fingers, turning the pages carefully, reverently. There were many faiths in Central Station, from Elronism to St. Cohen to followers of Ogko, mixed amidst the larger populations – Jews to the north, Muslims to the south, a hundred offshoots of Christianity dotted all about like potted plants – but only Achimwene's faith called for this. The worship of old, obsolete books. The worship, he liked to think, of history itself.

He spent the morning quite happily, therefore, with only one customer. For Achimwene was not alone in his – obsession? Fervour?

Others were like him. Mostly men, and mostly, like himself, broken in some fundamental fashion. They came from all over, pilgrims taking hesitant steps through the unfamiliar streets of the old neighbourhood, reaching at last Achimwene's alcove, a shop which had no name. They needed no sign. They simply knew.

There was an Armenian priest from Jerusalem who came once a month, a devotee of Hebrew pulps so obscure even Achimwene struggled with the conversation – romance chapbooks printed in twenty or thirty stapled pages at a time, filled with Zionist fervour and lovers' longings, so rare and fragile few remained in the world. There was a rare woman, whose name was Nur, who came from Damascus once a year, and whose speciality was the works of obscure poet and science fiction writer Lior Tirosh. There was a man from Haifa who collected erotica, and a man from the Galilee collecting mysteries.

"Achimwene? Shalom!"

Achimwene straightened in his chair. He had sat at his desk for some half an hour, typing, on what was his pride and joy, a rare collectors' item: a genuine, Hebrew typewriter. It was his peace and his escape, in the quiet times, to sit at his desk and pen, in the words of those old, vanished pulp writers, similarly exciting narratives of daring-do, rescues, and escapes.

"Shalom, Gideon," he said, sighing a little. The man, who hovered at the door, now came fully inside. He was a stooped figure, with long white hair, twinkling eyes, and a bottle of cheap arak held, like an offering, in one hand.

"Got glasses?"

"Sure..."

Achimwene brought out two glasses, neither too clean, and put them on the desk. The man, Gideon, motioned with his head at the typewriter. "Writing again?" he said.

"You know," Achimwene said.

Hebrew was the language of his birth. The Joneses were once Nigerian immigrants. Some said they had come over on work visas, and stayed. Others that they had escaped some long-forgotten civil war, had crossed the border illegally from Egypt, and stayed. One way or the other, the Joneses, like the Chongs, had lived in Central Station for generations.

Gideon opened the bottle, poured them both a drink. "Water?" Achimwene said.

Gideon shook his head. Achimwene sighed again and Gideon raised the glass, the liquid clear. "L'chaim," he said.

They clinked glasses. Achimwene drank, the arak burning his throat, the anis flavour tickling his nose. Made him think of his sister's shebeen. Said, "So, nu? What's new with you, Gideon?"

He'd decided, suddenly and with aching clarity, that he won't share the new haul with Gideon. Will keep them to himself, a private secret, for just a little while longer. Later, perhaps, he'd sell one or two. But not yet. For the moment, they were his, and his alone.

They chatted, whiling away an hour or two. Two men old before their time, in a dark alcove, sipping arak, reminiscing of books found and lost, of bargains struck and the ones that got away. At last Gideon left, having purchased a minor Western, in what is termed, in those circles, Good condition – that is, it was falling apart. Achimwene breathed out a sigh of relief, his head swimming from the arak, and returned to his typewriter. He punched an experimental heh, then a nun. He began to type.

THE G.

The girl.

The girl was in trouble.

A crowd surrounded her. Excitable, their faces twisted in the light of their torches. They held stones, blades. They shouted a word, a name, like a curse. The girl looked at them, her delicate face frightened.

"Won't someone save me?" she cried. "A hero, a –"

ACHIMWENE FROWNED IN irritation for, from the outside, a commotion was rising, the noise disturbing his concentration. He listened, but the noise only grew louder and, with a sigh of irritation, he pulled himself upwards and went to the door.

Perhaps this is how lives change. A momentary decision, the toss of a coin. He could have returned to his desk, completed his sentence, or chosen to tidy up the shelves, or make a cup of coffee. He chose to open the door instead.

They are dangerous things, doors, Ogko had once said. You never knew what you'd find on the other side of one.

Achimwene opened the door and stepped outside.

The G.

The girl.

The girl was in trouble.

This much Achimwene saw, though for the moment, the *why* of it escaped him.

This is what he saw:

The crowd was composed of people Achimwene knew. Neighbours, cousins, acquaintances. He thought he saw young Yan there, and his fiancé, Youssou (who was Achimwene's second cousin); the greengrocer from around the corner; some adaptoplant dwellers he knew by sight if not name; and others. They were just people. They were of Central Station.

The girl wasn't.

Achimwene had never seen her before. She was slight of frame. She walked with a strange gait, as though unaccustomed to the gravity. Her face was narrow, indeed delicate. Her head had been done in some other-worldly fashion, it was woven into dreadlocks that moved slowly, even sluggishly, above her head, and an ancient name rose in Achimwene's mind.

Medusa.

The girl's panicked eyes turned, looking. For just a moment, they found his. But her look did not (as Medusa's was said to) turn him to stone.

She turned away.

The crowd surrounded her in a semi-circle. Her back was to Achimwene. The crowd – the word *mob* flashed through Achimwene's mind uneasily – was excited, restless. Some held stones in their hands, but uncertainly, as though they were not sure why, or what they were meant to do with them. A mood of ugly energy animated them. And now Achimwene could hear a shouted word, a name, rising and falling in different intonations as the girl turned, and turned, helplessly seeking escape.

"Shambleau!"

The word sent a shiver down Achimwene's back (a sensation he had often read about in the pulps, yet seldom if ever experienced in real life). It aroused in him vague, menacing images, desolate Martian landscapes, isolated kibbutzim on the Martian tundra, red sunsets, the colour of blood.

"Strigoi!"

And there it was, that other word, a word conjuring, as though from thin air, images of brooding mountains, dark castles, bat-shaped shadows fleeting on the winds against a blood-red, setting sun... images of an ageless Count, of teeth elongating in a hungry skull, sinking to touch skin, to drain blood...

"Shambleau!"

"Get back! Get back to where you came from!"

"Leave her alone!"

The cry pierced the night. The mob milled, confused. The voice like a blade had cut through the darkness and the girl, startled and surprised, turned this way and that, searching for the source of that voice.

Who said it?

Who dared the wrath of the mob?

With a sense of reality cleaving in half, Achimwene, almost with a slight *frisson*, a delicious shiver of recognition, realised that it was he, himself, who had spoken.

Had, indeed, stepped forward from his door, a little hunched figure facing this mob of relatives and acquaintances and, even, perhaps, a few friends. "Leave her alone," he said again, savouring the words, and for once, perhaps for the first time in his life, people listened to him. A silence had descended. The girl, caught between her tormentors and this mysterious new figure, seemed uncertain.

"Oh, it's Achimwene," someone said, and somebody else suddenly, crudely laughed, breaking the silence.

"She's Shambleau," someone else said, and the first speaker (he couldn't quite see who it was) said, "Well, she'd be no harm to *him*."

That crude laughter again and then, as if by some unspoken agreement, or command, the crowd began, slowly, to disperse.

Achimwene found that his heart was beating fast; that his palms sweated; that his eyes developed a sudden itch. He felt like sneezing. The girl, slowly, floated over to him. They were of the same height. She looked into his eyes. Her eyes were a deep clear blue, vat-grown. They regarded each other as the rest of the mob dispersed. Soon they were left alone, in that quiet street, with Achimwene's back to the door of his shop.

She regarded him quizzically; her lips moved without sound, her eyes flicked up and down, scanning him. She looked confused, then shocked. She took a step back.

"No, wait!" he said.

"You are... you are not..."

He realised she had been trying to communicate with him. His silence had baffled her. Repelled her, most likely. He was a cripple. He said, "I have no node."

"How is that... possible?"

He laughed, though there was no humour in it. "It is not that unusual, here, on Earth," he said.

"You know I am not –" she said, and hesitated, and he said, "From here? I guessed. You are from Mars?"

A smile twisted her lips, for just a moment. "The asteroids," she admitted.

"What is it like, in space?" Excitement animated him. She shrugged. "Olsem difren," she said, in the pidgin of the asteroids.

The same, but different.

They stared at each other, two strangers, her vat-grown eyes against his natural-birth ones. "My name is Achimwene," he said.

"Oh."

"And you are?"

That same half-smile twisting her lips. He could tell she was bewildered by him. Repelled. Something inside him fluttered, like a caged bird dying of lack of oxygen.

"Carmel," she said, softly. "My name is Carmel."

He nodded. The bird was free, it was beating its wings inside him. "Would you like to come in?" he said. He gestured at his shop. The door, still standing half open.

Decisions splitting quantum universes... she bit her lip. There was no blood. He noticed her canines, then. Long and sharp. Unease took him again. Truth in the old stories? A Shambleau? Here?

"A cup of tea?" he said, desperately.

She nodded, distractedly. She was still trying to speak to him, he realised. She could not understand why he wasn't replying.

"I am un-noded," he said again. Shrugged. "It is –"

"Yes," she said.

"Yes?"

"Yes, I would like to come in. For... tea." She stepped closer to him. He could not read the look in her eyes. "Thank you," she said, in her soft voice, that strange accent. "For... you know."

"Yes." He grinned, suddenly, feeling bold, almost invincible. "It's nothing."

"Not... nothing." Her hand touched his shoulder, briefly, a light touch. Then she had gone past him and disappeared through the half-open door.

THE SHELVES INSIDE were arranged by genre.

Romance.

Mystery.

Detection.

Adventure.

And so on.

LIFE WASN'T LIKE that neat classification system, Achimwene had come to realise. Life was half-completed plots abandoned, heroes dying half-way along their quests, loves requited and un-, some fading inexplicably, some burning short and bright. There was a story of a man who fell in love with a vampire...

*   *   *

CARMEL WAS FASCINATED by him, but increasingly distant. She did not understand him. He had no taste to him, nothing she could sink her teeth into. Her fangs. She was a predator, she needed *feed*, and Achimwene could not provide it to her.

That first time, when she had come into his shop, had run her fingers along the spines of ancient books, fascinated, shy: "We had books, on the asteroid," she admitted, embarrassed, it seemed, by the confession of a shared history. "On Nungai Merurun, we had a library of physical books, they had come in one of the ships, once, a great-uncle traded something for them –" leaving Achimwene with dreams of going into space, of visiting this Ng. Merurun, discovering a priceless treasure hidden away.

Lamely, he had offered her tea. He brewed it on the small primus stove, in a dented saucepan, with fresh mint leaves in the water. Stirred sugar into the glasses. She had looked at the tea in incomprehension, concentrating. It was only later he realised she was trying to communicate with him again.

She frowned, shook her head. She was shaking a little, he realised. "Please," he said. "Drink."

"I don't," she said. "You're not." She gave up.

Achimwene often wondered what the Conversation was like. He knew that, wherever he passed, nearly anything he saw or touched was noded. Humans, yes, but also plants, robots, appliances, walls, solar panels – nearly everything was connected, in an ever-expanding, organically growing Aristocratic Small World network, that spread out, across Central Station, across Tel Aviv and Jaffa, across the interwoven entity that was Palestine/Israel, across that region called the Middle East, across Earth, across trans-solar space and beyond, where the lone Spiders sang to each other as they built more nodes and hubs, expanded farther and farther their intricate web. He knew a human was surrounded, every living moment, by the constant hum of other humans, other minds, an endless conversation going on in ways Achimwene could not conceive of. His own life was silent. He was a node of one. He moved his lips. Voice came. That was all. He said, "You are strigoi."

"Yes." Her lips twisted in that half-smile. "I am a monster."

"Don't say that." His heart beat fast. He said, "You're beautiful."

Her smile disappeared. She came closer to him, the tea forgotten. She leaned into him. Put her lips against his skin, against his neck, he felt her breath, the lightness of her lips on his hot skin. Sudden pain bit into him. She had fastened her lips over the wound, her teeth piercing his skin. He sighed. "Nothing!" she said. She pulled away from him abruptly. "It is like... I don't know!" She shook. He realised she was frightened. He touched the wound on his neck. He had felt nothing. "Always, to buy love, to buy obedience, to buy worship, I must feed," she said, matter-of-factly. "I drain them of their precious data, bleed them for it, and pay them in dopamine, in ecstasy. But you have no storage, no broadcast, no firewall... *there is nothing there*. You are like a simulacra," she said. The word pleased her. "A *simulacra*," she repeated, softly. "You have the appearance of a man but there is nothing behind your eyes. You do not broadcast."

"That's ridiculous," Achimwene said, anger flaring, suddenly. "I speak. You can hear me. I have a mind. I can express my –"

But she was only shaking her head, and shivering. "I'm hungry," she said. "I need to feed."

THERE WERE WILLING victims in Central Station. The bite of a strigoi gave pleasure. More – it conferred status on the victim, bragging rights. There had never been strigoi on Earth. It made Achimwene nervous.

He found himself living in one of his old books. He was the one to arrange Carmel's feeding, select her victims, who paid for the privilege. Achimwene, to his horror, discovered he had become a middleman. The bag man.

There was something repulsive about it all, as well as a strange, shameful excitement. There was no sex: sex was not a part of it, although it could be. Carmel leeched knowledge – memories – stored sensations – anything – pure uncut data from her victims, her fangs fastening on their neck, injecting dopamine into their blood as her node broke their inadequate protections, smashed their firewalls and their security, and bled them dry.

"Where do you come from?" he once asked her, as they lay on his narrow bed, the window open and the heat making them sweat, and she told him of Ng. Merurun, the tiny asteroid where she grew up, and how she ran away, on board the *Emaciated Messiah*, where a Shambleau attacked her, and passed on the virus, or the sickness, whatever it was.

"And how did you come to be here?" he said, and sensed, almost before he spoke, her unease, her reluctance to answer. Jealousy flared in him then, and he could not say why.

HIS SISTER CAME to visit him. She walked into the bookshop as he sat behind the desk, typing. He was writing less and less, now; his new life seemed to him a kind of novel.

"Achimwene," she said.

He raised his head. "Miriam," he said, heavily.

They did not get along.

"The girl, Carmel. She is with you?"

"I let her stay," he said, carefully.

"Oh, Achimwene, you are a fool!" she said.

Her boy – their sister's boy – Kranki – was with her. Achimwene regarded him uneasily. The boy was vat-grown – had come from the birthing clinics – his eyes were Armani-trademark blue. "Hey, Kranki," Achimwene said.

"Anggkel," the boy said – *uncle*, in the pidgin of the asteroids. "Yu olsem wanem?"

"I gud," Achimwene said.

How are you? I am well.

"Fren blong mi Ismail I stap aotside," Kranki said. "I stret hemi kam insaed?"

My friend Ismail is outside. Is it ok if he comes in?

"I stret," Achimwene said.

Miriam blinked. "Ismail," she said. "Where did you come from?"

Kranki had turned, appeared, to all intents and purposes, to play with an invisible playmate. Achimwene said, carefully, "There is no one there."

"Of course there is," his sister snapped. "It's Ismail, the Jaffa boy."

Achimwene shook his head.

"Listen, Achimwene. The girl. Do you know why she came here?"

"No."

"She followed Boris."

"Boris," Achimwene said. "Your Boris?"

"My Boris," she said.

"She knew him before?"

"She knew him on Mars. In Tong Yun City."

"I... see."

"You see nothing, Achi. You are blind like a worm." Old words, still with the power to hurt him. They had never been close, somehow. He said, "What do you want, Miriam?"

Her face softened. "I do not want... I do not want her to hurt you."

"I am a grown-up," he said. "I can take care of myself."

"Achi, like you ever could!"

Could that be affection, in her voice? It sounded like frustration. Miriam said, "Is she here?"

"Kranki," Achimwene said, "Who are you playing with?"

"Ismail," Kranki said, pausing in the middle of telling a story to someone only he could see.

"He's not here," Achimwene said.

"Sure he is. He's right here."

Achimwene formed his lips into an O of understanding. "Is he virtual?" he said.

Kranki shrugged. "I guess," he said. He clearly felt uncomfortable with – or didn't understand – the question. Achimwene let it go.

His sister said, "I like the girl, Achi."

It took him by surprise. "You've met her?"

"She has a sickness. She needs help."

"I *am* helping her!"

But his sister only shook her head.

"Go away, Miriam," he said, feeling suddenly tired, depressed. His sister said, "Is she here?"

"She is resting."

Above his shop there was a tiny flat, accessible by narrow, twisting stairs. It wasn't much but it was home. "Carmel?" his sister called. "Carmel!"

There was a sound above, as of someone moving. Then a lack of sound. Achimwene watched his sister standing impassively. Realised she was talking, in the way of other people, with Carmel. Communicating in a way that was barred to him. Then normal sound again, feet on the stairs, and Carmel came into the room.

"Hi," she said, awkwardly. She came and stood closer to Achimwene, then took his hand in hers. The feel of her small, cold fingers in between his hands startled him and made a feeling of pleasure spread throughout his body, like warmth in the blood. Nothing more was said. The physical action itself was an act of speaking.

Miriam nodded.

Then Kranki startled them all.

CARMEL HAD SPENT the previous night in the company of a woman. Achimwene had known there was sex involved, not just feeding. He had told himself he didn't mind. When Carmel came back she had smelled of sweat and sex and blood. She moved lethargically, and he knew she was drunk on data. She had tried to describe it to him once, but he didn't really understand it, what it was like.

He had lain there on the narrow bed with her and watched the moon outside, and the floating lanterns with their rudimentary intelligence. He had his arm around the sleeping Carmel, and he had never felt happier.

KRANKI TURNED AND regarded Carmel. He whispered something to the air – to the place Ismail was standing, Achimwene guessed. He giggled at the reply and turned to Carmel.

"Are you a *vampire*?" he said.

"Kranki!"

At the horrified look on Miriam's face, Achimwene wanted to laugh. Carmel said, "No, it's all right –" in asteroid pidgin. *I stret nomo.*

But she was watching the boy intently. "Who is your friend?" she said, softly.

"It's Ismail. He lives in Jaffa on the hill."

"And what is he?" Carmel said. "What are you?"

The boy didn't seem to understand the question. "He is him. I am me. We are..." he hesitated.

"Nakaimas..." Carmel whispered. The sound of her voice made Achimwene shiver. That same cold run of ice down his spine, like in the old books, like when Ringo the Gunslinger met a horror from beyond the grave on the lonesome prairies.

He knew the word, though never understood the way people used it. It meant black magic, but also, he knew, it meant to somehow, impossibly, transcend the networks, that thing they called the Conversation.

"Kranki..." the warning tone in Miriam's voice was unmistakable. But neither Kranki nor Carmel paid her any heed. "I could show you," the boy said. His clear, blue eyes seemed curious, guileless. He stepped forward and stood directly in front of Carmel and reached out his hand, pointing finger extended. Carmel, momentarily, hesitated. Then she, too, reached forward and, finger extended, touched its tip to the boy's own.

IT IS, PERHAPS, the prerogative of every man or woman to imagine, and thus force a *shape*, a *meaning*, onto that wild and meandering narrative of their lives, by choosing genre. A princess is rescued by a prince; a vampire stalks a victim in the dark; a student becomes the master. A circle is completed. And so on.

It was the next morning that Achimwene's story changed, for him. It had been a Romance, perhaps, of sorts. But now it became a Mystery.

Perhaps they chose it, by tacit agreement, as a way to bind them, to make this curious relationship, this joining of two ill-fitted individuals somehow work. Or perhaps it was curiosity that motivated them after all, that earliest of motives, the most human and the most suspect, the one that had led Adam to the Tree, in the dawn of story.

The next morning Carmel came down the stairs. Achimwene had slept in the bookshop that night, curled up in a thin blanket on top of a mattress he had kept by the wall and which was normally laden with books. The books, pushed aside, formed an untidy wall around him as he slept, an alcove within an alcove.

Carmel came down. Her hair moved sluggishly around her skull. She wore a thin cotton shift; he could see how thin she was.

Achimwene said, "Tell me what happened yesterday."

Carmel shrugged. "Is there any coffee?"

"You know where it is."

He sat up, feeling self-conscious and angry. Pulling the blanket over his legs. Carmel went to the primus stove, filled the pot with water from the tap, added spoons of black coffee carelessly. Set it to cook.

"The boy is... a sort of strigoi," she said. "Maybe. Yes. No. I don't know."

"What did he do?"

"He gave me something. He took something away. A memory. Mine or someone else's. It's no longer there."

"What did he give you?"

"Knowledge. That he exists."

"Nakaimas."

"Yes." She laughed, a sound as bitter as the coffee. "Black magic. Like me. Not like me."

"You were a weapon," he said. She turned, sharply. There were two coffee cups on the table. Glass on varnished wood. "What?"

"I read about it."

"Always your *books*."

He couldn't tell by her tone how she meant it. He said, "There are silences in your Conversation. Holes." Could not quite picture it, to him there was only a silence. Said, "The books have answers."

She poured coffee, stirred sugar into the glasses. Came over and sat beside him, her side pressing into his. Passed him a cup. "Tell me," she said.

He took a sip. The coffee burned his tongue. Sweet. He began to talk quickly. "I read up on the condition. Strigoi. Shambleau. There are references from the era of the Shangri-La Virus, contemporary accounts. The Kunming Labs were working on genetic weapons, but the war ended before the strain could be deployed – they sold it off-world, it went loose, it spread. It never worked right. there are hints – I need access to a bigger library. Rumours. Cryptic footnotes."

"Saying what?"

"Suggesting a deeper purpose. Or that strigoi was but a side-effect of something else. A secret purpose..."

Perhaps they wanted to believe. Everyone needs a mystery.

She stirred beside him. Turned to face him. Smiled. It was perhaps the first time she ever truly smiled at him. Her teeth were long, and sharp.

"We could find out," she said.

"Together," he said. He drank his coffee, to hide his excitement. But he knew she could tell.

"We could be detectives."

"Like Judge Dee," he said.

"Who?"

"Some detective."

"Book detective," she said, dismissively.

"Like Bill Glimmung, then," he said. Her face lit up. For a moment she looked very young. "I love those stories," she said.

Even Achimwene had seen Glimmung features. They had been made in 2D, 3D, full-immersion, as scent narratives, as touch-tapestry – Martian Hardboiled, they called the genre, the Phobos Studios cranked out hundreds of them over decades if not centuries, Elvis Mandela had made the character his own.

"Like Bill Glimmung, then," she said solemnly, and he laughed.

"Like Glimmung," he said.

And so the lovers, by complicit agreement, became detectives.

MARTIAN HARDBOILED, genre of. Flourished in the CENTURY OF DRAGON. Most prominent character: Bill GLIMMUNG, played most memorably by Elvis MANDELA (for which see separate entry). The genre is well-known, indeed notorious, for the liberal use of sex and violence, transplanted from old EARTH (also see MANHOME; HUMANITY PRIME) hardboiled into a Martian setting, sometimes realistically-portrayed, often with implicit or explicit elements of FANTASY.

While early stories stuck faithfully to the mean streets of TONG YUN CITY, with its triads, hafmek pushers and Israeli, Red Chinese and Red Soviet agents, later narratives took in off-world adventures, including in the BELT, the VENUSIAN NO-GO ZONE and the OUTER PLANETS. Elements of SOAP OPERA intruded as the narratives became ever more complex and on-going (see entry for long-running Martian soap CHAINS OF ASSEMBLY for separate discussion).

"THERE WAS SOMETHING else," Carmel said.

Achimwene said, "What?"

They were walking the streets of old Central Station. The space port rose above them, immense and inscrutable. Carmel said, "When I came in. Came down." She shook her head in frustration and a solitary dreadlock snaked around her mouth, making her blow on it to move it away. "When I came to Earth."

Those few words evoked in Achimwene a nameless longing. So much to infer, so much suggested, to a man who had never left his home town. Carmel said, "I bought a new identity in Tong Yun, before I came. The best you could. From a Conch –"

Looking at him to see if he understood. Achimwene did. A Conch was a human who had been ensconced, welded into a permanent pod-cum-exoskeleton. He was only part human, had become part digital by extension. It was not unsimilar, in some ways, to the eunuchs of old Earth. Achimwene said, "I see?" Carmel said, "It worked. When I passed through Central Station security I was allowed through, with no problems. The... the digitals did not pick up on my... nature. The fake ident was accepted."

"So?"

Carmel sighed, and a loose dreadlock tickled Achimwene's neck, sending a warmth rushing through him. "So is that likely?" she said. She stopped walking, then, when Achimwene stopped also, she started pacing. A floating lantern bobbed beside them for a few moments then, as though sensing their intensity, drifted away, leaving them in shadow. "There are no strigoi on Earth," Carmel said.

"How do we know for sure?" Achimwene said.

"It's one of those things. Everyone knows it."

Achimwene shrugged. "But *you're* here," he pointed out.

Carmel waved her finger; stuck it in his face. "And how likely is that?" she yelled, startling him. "I believed it worked, because I *wanted* to believe it. But surely they know! I am not human, Achi! My body is riddled with nodal filaments, exabytes of data, hostile protocols! You want to tell me they *didn't know?*"

Achimwene shook his head. Reached for her, but she pulled away from him. "What are you saying?" he said.

"They let me through." Her voice was matter of fact.

"Why?" Achimwene said. "Why would they do that?"

"I don't know."

Achimwene chewed his lip. Intuition made a leap in his mind, neurons singing to neurons. "You think it is because of those children," he said.

Carmel stopped pacing. He saw how pale her face was, how delicate. "Yes," she said.

"Why?"

"I don't know."

"Then you must ask a digital," he said. "You must ask an Other."

She glared at him. "Why would they talk to me?" she said.

Achimwene didn't have an answer. "We can proceed the way we agreed," he said, a little lamely. "We'll get the answers. Sooner or later, we'll figure it out, Carmel."

"How?" she said.

He pulled her to him. She did not resist. The words from an old book rose into Achimwene's mind, and with them the entire scene. "We'll get to the bottom of this," he said.

AND SO ON a sweltering hot day Achimwene and the strigoi left Central Station, on foot, and shortly thereafter crossed the invisible barrier that separated the old neighbourhood from the city of Tel Aviv proper.

Achimwene walked slowly; an electronic cigarette dangled from his lips, another vintage affectation, and the fedora hat he wore shaded him from the sun even as his sweat drenched into the brim of the hat. Beside him Carmel was cool in a light blue dress. They came to Allenby Street and followed it towards the Carmel Market – "It's like my name," Carmel said, wonderingly.

"It is an old name," Achimwene said. But his attention was elsewhere.

"Where are we going?" Carmel said. Achimwene smiled, white teeth around the metal cigarette. "Every detective," he said, "needs an informant."

Picture, then, Allenby. Not the way it was, but the way it is. Surprisingly little has changed. It was a long, dirty street, with dark shops selling knock-off products with the air of disuse upon them. Carmel dawdled outside a magic shop. Achimwene bargained with a fruit juice seller and returned with two cups of fresh orange juice, handing one to Carmel. They passed a bakery where cream-filled pastries vied for their attention. They passed a Church of Robot node where a rusting preacher tried to get their attention with a sad distracted air. They passed shawarma stalls thick with the smell of cumin and lamb fat. They passed a road-sweeping machine that warbled at them pleasantly, and a recruitment centre for the Martian Kibbutz Movement. They passed a gaggle of black-clad Orthodox Jews; like Achimwene, they were unnoded.

Carmel looked this way and that, smelling, looking, *feeding*, Achimwene knew, on pure unadulterated *feed*. Something he could not experience, could not know, but knew, nevertheless, that it was there, invisible yet ever present. Like God. The lines from a poem by Mahmoud Darwish floated in his head. Something about the invisibles. "Look," Carmel said, smiling. "A bookshop."

Indeed it was. They were coming closer to the market now and the throng of people intensified, and solar buses crawled like insects, with their wings spread high, along the Allenby road, carrying passengers, and the smell of fresh vegetables, of peppers and tomatoes, and the sweet strong smell of oranges, too, filled the air. The bookshop was, in fact, a yard, open to the skies, the books under awnings, and piled up, here and there, in untidy mountains – it was the sort of shop that would have no prices, and where you'd always have to ask for the price, which depended on the owner, and his mood, and on the weather and the alignment of the stars.

The owner in question was indeed standing in the shade of the long, metal bookcases lining up one wall. He was smoking a cigar and its overpowering aroma filled the air and made Carmel sneeze. The man looked up and saw them. "Achimwene," he said, without surprise. Then he squinted and said, in a lower voice, "I heard you got a nice batch recently."

"Word travels," Achimwene said, complacently. Carmel, meanwhile, was browsing aimlessly, picking up fragile-looking paper books and magazines, replacing them, picking up others. Achimwene saw, at a glance, early editions of Yehuda Amichai, a first edition Yoav Avni, several worn *Ringo* paperbacks he already had, and a Lior Tirosh semizdat collection. He said, "Shimshon, what do you know about vampires?"

"Vampires?" Shimshon said. He took a thoughtful pull on his cigar. "In the literary tradition? There is *Neshikat Ha'mavet Shel Dracula*, by Dan Shocker, in the Horror series from nineteen seventy two" – *Dracula's Death Kiss* – "or Gal Amir's *Laila Adom*" – *Red Night* – "possibly the first Hebrew vampire novel, or Vered Tochterman's *Dam Kachol*" – *Blue Blood* – "from around the same period. Didn't think it was particularly your area, Achimwene." Shimshon grinned. "But I'd be happy to sell you a copy. I think I have a signed Tochterman somewhere. Expensive, though. Unless you want to trade..."

"No," Achimwene said, although regretfully. "I'm not looking for a pulp, right now. I'm looking for non-fiction."

Shimshon's eyebrows rose and he regarded Achimwene without the grin. "Mil. Hist?" he said, uneasily. "Robotniks? The Nosferatu Code?"

Achimwene regarded him, uncertain. "The what?" he said.

But Shimshon was shaking his head. "I don't deal in that sort of thing," he said. "*Verboten*. Hagiratech. Go away, Achimwene. Go back to Central Station. Shop's closed." He turned and dropped the cigar and stepped on it with his foot. "You, love!" he said. "Shop's closing. Are you going to buy that book? No? Then put it down."

Carmel turned, wounded dignity flashing in her green eyes. "Then take it!" she said, shoving a (priceless, Achimwene thought) copy of Lior Tirosh's first – and only – poetry collection, *Remnants of God*, into Shimshon's hands. She hissed, a sound Achimwene suspected was not only in the audible range but went deeper, in the non-sound of digital communication, for Shimshon's face went pale and he said, "Get... out!" in a strangled whisper as Carmel smiled at him, flashing her small, sharp teeth.

They left. They crossed the street and stood outside a cheap cosmetics surgery booth, offering wrinkles erased or tentacles grafted, next to a handwritten sign that said, *Gone for Lunch*. "Verboten?" Achimwene said. "Hagiratech?"

"Forbidden," Carmel said. "the sort of wildtech that ends up on Jettisoned, from the exodus ships."

"What you are," he said.

"Yes. I looked, myself, you know. But it is like you said. Holes in the Conversation. Did we learn nothing useful?"

"No," he said. Then, "Yes."

She smiled. "Which is it?"

Military history, Shimshon had said. And no one knew better than him how to classify a thing into its genre. And – *robotniks.*

"We need to find us," Achimwene said, "an ex-soldier." He smiled without humour. "Better brush up on your Battle Yiddish," he said.

"Ezekiel."

"Achimwene."

"I brought... vodka. And spare parts." He had bought them in Tel Aviv, on Allenby, at great expense. Robotnik parts were not easy to come by.

Ezekiel looked at him without expression. His face was metal smooth. It never smiled. His body was mostly metal. It was rusted. It creaked when he walked. He ignored the proffered offerings. Turned his head. "You brought *her?*" he said. "*Here?*"

Carmel stared at the robotnik in curiosity. They were at the heart of the old station, a burned down ancient bus platform open to the sky.

Achimwene knew platforms continued down below, that the robotniks – ex-soldiers, cyborged humans, preset day beggars and dealers in Crucifixation and stolen goods – made their base down there. But there he could not go. Ezekiel met him above-ground. A drum with fire burning, the flames reflected in the dull metal of the robotnik's face. "I saw your kind," Carmel said. "On Mars. In Tong Yun City. Begging."

"And I saw *your* kind," the robotnik said. "In the sands of the Sinai, in the war. Begging. Begging for their lives, as we decapitated them and stuck a stake through their hearts and watched them die."

"Jesus Elron, Ezekiel!"

The robotnik ignored his exclamation. "I had heard," he said. "That one came. Here. *Strigoi.* But I did not believe! The defence systems would have picked her up. Should have eliminated her."

"They didn't," Achimwene said.

"Yes..."

"Do you know why?"

The robotnik stared at him. Then he gave a short laugh and accepted the bottle of vodka. "You guess *they* let her through? The Others?"

Achimwene shrugged. "It's the only answer that makes sense.

"And you want to know why."

"Call me curious."

"I call you a fool," the robotnik said, without malice. "And you not even noded. She still has an effect on you?"

"*She* has a name," Carmel said, acidly. Ezekiel ignored her. "You're a collector of old stories, aren't you, Achimwene," he said. "Now you came to collect mine?"

Achimwene just shrugged. The robotnik took a deep slug of vodka and said, "So, nu? What do you want to know?"

"Tell me about Nosferatu," Achimwene said.

SHANGRI-LA VIRUS, the. Bio-weapon developed in the GOLDEN TRIANGLE and used during the UNOFFICIAL WAR. Transmission mechanisms included sexual intercourse (99%-100%), by air (50%-60%), by water (30%-35%), through saliva (15%-20%) and by touch

(5%-6%). Used most memorably during the LONG CHENG ATTACK (for which also see LAOS; RAVENZ; THE KLAN KLANDESTINE). The weapon curtailed aggression in humans, making them peaceable and docile. All known samples destroyed in the Unofficial War, along with the city of Long Cheng.

"WE NEVER FOUND out for sure where Nosferatu came from," Ezekiel said. It was quiet in the abandoned shell of the old station. Overhead a sub-orbital came in to land, and from the adaptoplant neighbourhoods ringing the old stone buildings the sound of laughter could be heard, and someone playing the guitar. "It had been introduced into the battlefield during the Third Sinai Campaign, by one side, or the other, or both." He fell quiet. "I am not even sure who we were fighting for," he said. He took another drink of vodka. The almost pure alcohol served as fuel for the robotniks. Ezekiel said, "At first we paid it little enough attention. We'd find victims on dawn patrols. Men, women, robotniks. Wandering the dunes or the Red Sea shore, dazed, their minds leeched clean. The small wounds on their necks. Still. They were alive. Not ripped to shreds by Jub Jubs. But the data. We began to notice the enemy knew where to find us. Knew where we went. We began to be afraid of the dark. To never go out alone. Patrol in teams. But worse. For the ones who were bitten, and carried back by us, had turned, became the enemy's own weapon. Nosferatu."

Achimwene felt sweat on his forehead, took a step away from the fire. Away from them, the floating lanterns bobbed in the air. Someone cried in the distance and the cry was suddenly and inexplicably cut off, and Achimwene wondered if the street sweeping machines would find another corpse the next morning, lying in the gutter outside a shebeen or No. 1 Pin Street, the most notorious of the drug dens-cum-brothels of Central Station.

"They rose within our ranks. They fed in secret. Robotniks don't sleep, Achimwene. Not the way the humans we used to be did. But we do turn off. Shut-eye. And they preyed on us, bleeding our minds, feeding on our feed. Do you know what it is like?" The robotnik's voice didn't grow louder, but it carried. "We were human, once. The army took us off the battlefield, broken, dying. It grafted us into new bodies, made us into shiny, near-invulnerable killing machines. We had no legal rights, not any more. We were technically, and clinically, dead. We had few memories, if any, of what we once were. But those we had, we kept hold of, jealously. Hints to our old identity. The memory of feet in the rain. The smell of pine resin. A hug from a newborn baby whose name we no longer knew.

"And the strigoi were taking even those away from us."

Achimwene looked at Carmel, but she was looking nowhere, her eyes were closed, her lips pressed together. "We finally grew wise to it," Ezekiel said. "We began to hunt them down. If we found a victim we did not take them back. Not alive. We staked them, we cut off their heads, we burned the bodies. Have you ever opened a strigoi's belly, Achimwene?" He motioned at Carmel. "Want to know what her insides look like?"

"No," Achimwene said, but Ezekiel the robotnik ignored him. "Like cancer," he said. "Strigoi is like robotnik, it is a human body subverted, cyborged. She isn't human, Achimwene, however much you'd like to believe it. I remember the first one we cut open. The filaments inside. Moving. Still trying to spread. Nosferatu Protocol, we called it. What we had to do. Following the Nosferatu Protocol. Who created the virus? I don't know. Us. Them. The Kunming Labs. Someone. St. Cohen only knows. All I know is how to kill them."

Achimwene looked at Carmel. Her eyes were open now. She was staring at the robotnik. "I didn't ask for this," she said. "I am not a *weapon*. There is no fucking *war*!"

"There was –"

"There were a lot of things!"

A silence. At last, Ezekiel stirred. "So what do you want?" he said. He sounded tired. The bottle of vodka was nearly finished. Achimwene said, "What more can you tell us?"

"Nothing, Achi. I can tell you nothing. Only to be careful." The robotnik laughed. "But it's too late for that, isn't it," he said.

*　　*　　*

ACHIMWENE WAS ARRANGING his books when Boris came to see him. He heard the soft footsteps and the hesitant cough and straightened up, dusting his hands from the fragile books, and looked at the man Carmel had come to Earth for.

"Achi."

"Boris."

He remembered him as a loose-limbed, gangly teenager. Seeing him like this was a shock. There was a thing growing on Boris's neck. It was flesh-coloured, but the colour was slightly off to the rest of Boris's skin. It seemed to breathe gently. Boris's face was lined, he was still thin but there was an unhealthy nature to his thinness. "I heard you were back," Achimwene said.

"My father," Boris said, as though that explained everything.

"And we always thought you were the one who got away," Achimwene said. Genuine curiosity made him add, "What was it like? In the Up and Out?"

"Strange," Boris said. "The same." He shrugged. "I don't know."

"So you are seeing my sister again."

"Yes."

"You've hurt her once before, Boris. Are you going to do it again?"

Boris opened his mouth, closed it again. He stood there, taking Achimwene back years. "I heard Carmel is staying with you," Boris said at last.

"Yes."

Again, an uncomfortable silence. Boris scanned the bookshelves, picked a book at random. "What's this?" he said.

"Be careful with that!"

Boris looked startled. He stared at the small hardcover in his hands. "That's a Captain Yuno," Achimwene said, proudly. "*Captain Yuno on a Dangerous Mission*, the second of the three Sagi novels. The least rare of the three, admittedly, but still... priceless."

Boris looked momentarily amused. "He was a kid taikonaut?" he said.

"Sagi envisioned a solar system teeming with intelligent alien life," Achimwene said, primly. "He imagined a world government, and the people of Earth working together in peace."

"No kidding. He must have been disappointed when –"

"This book is *pre-spaceflight*," Achimwene said. Boris whistled. "So it's old?"

"Yes."

"And valuable?"

"Very."

"How do you know all this stuff?"

"I read."

Boris put the book back on the shelf, carefully. "Listen, Achi –" he said.

"No," Achimwene said. "You listen. Whatever happened between you and Carmel is between you two. I won't say I don't care, because I'd be lying, but it is not my business. Do you have a claim on her?"

"What?" Boris said. "No. Achi, I'm just trying to –"

"To what?"

"To warn you. I know you're not used to –" again he hesitated. Achimwene remembered Boris as someone of few words, even as a boy. Words did not come easy to him. "Not used to women?" Achimwene said, his anger tightly coiled.

Boris had to smile. "You have to admit –"

"I am not some, some –"

"She is not a woman, Achi. She's a strigoi."

Achimwene closed his eyes. Expelled breath. Opened his eyes again and regarded Boris levelly. "Is that all?" he said.

Boris held his eyes. After a moment, he seemed to deflate. "Very well," he said.

"Yes."

"I guess I'll see you."

"I guess."

"Please pass my regards to Carmel."

Achimwene nodded. Boris, at last, shrugged. Then he turned and left the store.

THERE COMES A time in a man's life when he realises stories are lies. Things do not end neatly. The enforced narratives a human imposes on the chaotic mess that is life become empty labels, like the dried husks of corn such as are thrown down, in the summer months, from the adaptoplant neighbourhoods high above Central Station, to litter the streets below.

He woke up in the night and the air was humid, and there was no wind. The window was open. Carmel was lying on her side, asleep, her small, naked body tangled up in the sheets. He watched her chest rise and fall, her breath even. A smear of what might have been blood on her lips. "Carmel?" he said, but quietly, and she didn't hear. He rubbed her back. Her skin was smooth and warm. She moved sleepily under his hand, murmured something he didn't catch, and settled down again.

Achimwene stared out of the window, at the moon rising high above Central Station. A mystery was no longer a mystery once it was solved. What difference did it make how Carmel had come to be there, with him, at that moment? It was not facts that mattered, but feelings. He stared at the moon, thinking of that first human to land there, all those years before, that first human footprint in that alien dust.

Inside Carmel was asleep and he was awake, outside dogs howled up at the moon and, from somewhere, the image came to Achimwene of a man in a spacesuit turning at the sound, a man who does a little tap dance on the moon, on the dusty moon.

He lay back down and held on to Carmel and she turned, trustingly, and settled into his arms.

THE SUN AND I
K. J. Parker

K.J. PARKER WAS born long ago and far away, worked as a coin dealer, a dogsbody in an auction house and a lawyer, and has so far published thirteen novels including the Fencer, Scavenger, and Engineer trilogies, four standalone novels, and a handful of short stories including World Fantasy Award winning novellas "A Small Price to Pay for Birdsong" and "Let Maps to Others". Coming up is new stand-alone novel *Savages* and debut short story collection *Academic Exercises*. Married to a lawyer and living in the south west of England, K.J. Parker is a mediocre stockman and forester, a barely competent carpenter, blacksmith and machinist, a two-left-footed fencer, lackluster archer, utility-grade armorer, accomplished textile worker and crack shot. K.J. Parker is not K.J. Parker's real name. However, if K.J. Parker were to tell you K.J. Parker's real name, it wouldn't mean anything to you.

I mean to rule the earth, as He the sky;
We really know our worth, the Sun and I
W. S. Gilbert

"WE COULD ALWAYS invent God," I suggested.

We'd pooled our money. It lay on the table in front of us; forty of those sad, ridiculous little copper coins we used back then, the wartime emergency issue – horrible things, punched out of flattened copper pipe and stamped with tiny stick-men purporting to be the Emperor and various legendary heroes; the worse the quality of the die-sinking became, the more grandiose the subject matter. Forty trachy in those days bought you a quart of pickle-grade domestic red. It meant we had no money for food, but at that precise moment we weren't hungry. "What do you mean?" Teuta asked.

"I mean," I said, "we could pretend that God came to us in a dream, urging us to go forth and preach His holy word. Fine," I added, "it's still basically just begging, but it's begging with a hook. You give money to a holy man, he intercedes for your soul, you get something back. Also," I added, as Accila pursed his lips in that really annoying way, "it helps overcome the credibility issues we always face when we beg. You know, the College accents, the perfect teeth."

"How so?" Razo asked.

"Well," I said – I was in one of my brilliant moods, when I have answers for every damn thing; it's as though some higher power possesses me and speaks through me – "it's an established trope, right? Wealthy, well-born young man gets religion, he gives everything he owns to the poor, goes out and preaches the word. He survives on the charity of the faithful, such charity being implicitly accepted as, in and of itself, an act of religion entitling the performer to merit in heaven."

Accila was doing his academic frown, painstakingly copied from a succession of expensive tutors. "I don't think we can say we gave all our money to the poor," he said. "In my case, most of the innkeepers, pimps and bookmakers I shared my inheritance with were reasonably prosperous. Giving away all our money to the comfortably off doesn't have quite the same ring."

I smiled. Accila had made his joke, and would now be quite happy for a minute or so. "Well?" I said. "Better ideas, anyone?"

"I still think we should be war veterans," Teuta said stubbornly. "I used to see this actress, and she showed me how to do the most appalling-looking scars with red lead and pig-fat. People love war veterans."

I had an invincible argument. "Have we got any red lead? Can we afford to buy any? Well, then."

Accila lifted the wine-jar. The expression on his face told me that it had become ominously light. We looked at each other. This was clearly an emergency, and something had to be done. The only something on offer was my proposal. Therefore –

"All right," Teuta said warily. "But let's not go rushing into this all half-baked. You said, invent God. So –" Teuta shrugged. "For a start, which god did you have in mind?"

"Oh, a new one." Not sure to this day why I said that with such determined certainty. "People are hacked off with all the old ones. You ask my uncle the archdeacon about attendances in Temple."

"Precisely," Razo said. "The public have lost interest in religion. We live in an enlightened age. Therefore, your idea is no bloody good."

I knew he'd be trouble. "The public have lost interest in the established religions," I said. "They view them, quite rightly, as corrupt and discredited. Therefore, given Mankind's desperate need to believe in something, the time is absolutely right for a new religion; tailored," I went on, as the brilliance filled me like an inner light, "precisely to the needs and expectations of the customer. That's where all the old religions screwed up, you see; they weren't planned or custom-fitted, they just sort of grew. They didn't relate to what people really wanted. They were crude and full of doctrinal inconsistencies. They involved worshipping trees, which no rational man can bring himself to do after the age of seven. We, on the other hand, have the opportunity to create the *perfect* religion, one which will satisfy the demands of every class, taste and demographic. It's the difference between making a chair and waiting for a clump of branches to grow into a sort of chair shape."

"Not sure about that," said Zanipulus; his first contribution to the discussion, since he'd been clipping his toenails and had needed to concentrate. "You walk around telling people that Bong just appeared to you in a dream. They give you a funny look and say, 'Who's Bong when he's at home?'" He sniffed; he had a cold. "There's no point of immediate engagement, is what I'm saying. You need that instant of irresistible connection –"

"Of course." A tiny sunrise in the back of my head produced enough light for me suddenly to see clearly. "That's why this idea of mine is so absolutely bloody inspired. Of course we can't expect customers to believe in some nebulous entity that nobody's ever heard of. We need to create a deity that everyone can see, plain as the noses on their faces, every day of their lives."

Silence, which I allowed to continue for a moment or so, during which Razo dribbled the last few drops out of the jar into his cup; drip-drip-drip. "Well?" Accila said.

"Simple," I told him. "We worship the sun."

Razo yawned. "Been done," he said. "To death, in fact. If you'd been to Cartimagus's lectures on recurring motifs in late Mannerist epic, you'd know that practically every hero in legend is your basic solar metaphor."

"Sure," I said. He was starting to annoy me. "But not the big shiny yellow disc *per se*. I'm talking about the Sun with a capital S. One single supreme deity; no pantheon, no bureaucracy, no waiting. Someone you can look in the eye and talk to directly, man to God –"

"Wouldn't do that if I were you," Zanipulus said with his mouth full. Apparently the treacherous bastard had a private reserve of cashew nuts he hadn't seen fit to declare to the rest of the Commonwealth. "Makes you go blind."

"Metaphorically speaking. Come on, you know I'm right. That's why the old religions fell apart, too many gods, too damn *fussy*. The old thing about government by committee. One god, it's like monarchy, it's the only way to get things done."

"The Divine Sun," Accila said thoughtfully. "You know, he might just have something."

"Not the Divine Sun," Teuta said. "No buzz. No snap. Also, there's the redundancy. What's the leading characteristic of our god? That he's divine. Yawn."

"All right," Accila said. "So, right now, what do people really want? Apart," he added, "from money."

"Peace," said Zanipulus. "An end to the war. That's a no-brainer."

The word sort of catapulted itself into my mouth. "The Invincible Sun," I said. "Well, how about it?"

Razo wiped his mouth. "Actually," he said, "that's not bad."

"It's magnificent," I said. "Implied promise of victory followed by a sustained peace."

"Which isn't going to happen any time soon," Zanipulus pointed out.

"No," I rounded on him, "because Mankind is sinful and refuses to follow the path laid out for it by the Invincible Sun. As disclosed," I went on, "by His true prophets. Us."

Another silence. Then Razo said, "We'll need a list of thou-shalt-nots. People like those."

"And observances," said Accila. "Top of the list, I would suggest, should be giving generously to the poor. Instant merit for doing that."

Pause. They were looking at Zanipulus, which offended me rather. Just because he doesn't say much, people think he's smart. Whereas I talk all the time, and you just have to listen to me for two seconds to realise how very clever I am. "Well," Zanipulus said, "it's got to be better than war veterans. For a start, there's too many of the real thing."

At that moment, in the brief silence after those words were spoken, I believe that the Invincible Sun was born. And why not? After all, everything has to start somewhere.

IT WAS A real stroke of luck that General Mardonius contrived to wipe out the whole of the Herulian Fifth Army at the battle of Ciota ten days after we took to the streets to preach the gospel of the Invincible Sun. I'm not inclined to give Mardonius all the credit for our success. Obviously we'd made some impression over the preceding nine days, or nobody at all would've known who we were, and nobody would've made the association between the latest street religion and the entirely unexpected, heaven-sent victory. We were helped enormously by the coincidence that one of us – I think it was me, but it's so long ago I can't be sure – had been predicting a mighty victory for the forces of light on the ninth day of Feralia, which just happened to be the day when the news of Ciota reached the city. Not, please note, the day of the battle itself; fortunately, nobody pointed that out at the time. Anyhow, that was our breakout moment. We were the crazy street preachers who'd predicted Ciota; and there's a weird sort of pseudo-logic that operates in people's minds. If you predict something, in some way or another you're responsible for it, you made it happen. Suddenly, out of (no pun intended) a clear blue sky, the Invincible Sun was a contender.

*   *   *

FORGIVE ME, I'M forgetting my manners. Allow me to introduce myself. My name is Eps. At least, that's what it was then, before we started the whole names-in-religion thing, which we did basically so as to protect our real identities in the event that we made ourselves unpopular with the authorities and had to retire prematurely from the theology business. Of course, if you're a cleric or come from a clerical family, the irony of the name I was born with won't have been lost on you; *eps* is now, has become, the recognised shortening for *episcopus*, which is the word for high priest in Old Aelian, which we chose, more or less at random, as the language in which we were going to write our holy scriptures. Which would've made me Eps *eps* on official documents; quite, except that I adopted the name-in-religion Deodatus (yes, *the* Deodatus; that's me) some time before we decided on Old Aelian. For what it's worth, Eps is a traditional and not uncommon name on Scona, where my family originally came from. It means, so I'm told, *the chosen one*.

AND, I HAVE to confess, I enjoyed preaching. At first, of course, it was horrendously scary and embarrassing. Nothing in my sheltered, privileged life had prepared me for opening my mouth in a public place and ranting at strangers. I managed to get over that by pretending I was doing something else; acting in a play, shouting to someone I knew on the far side of the square who happened to be invisible to everyone else. That worked surprisingly well; but the breakthrough came when I learned to convince myself that it wasn't actually me doing this extraordinary thing. Instead (I pretended) some irresistible force had taken over my body and was using my lungs and lips. After that, it was no problem at all. And, as I said just now, I started to like it.

In fact, I was far and away our best preacher, which was probably just as well. The other four all had skills and talents that were invaluable to the project. All I could claim to justify my involvement, and my share of the take, was that it had been my idea in the first place. That was starting to wear a bit thin when I discovered my latent talent for religious oratory; and, since the others could do it but hated it, I quickly assumed the role of Chief Celebrant.

What skills and talents? Well; Accila was our scholar, though you wouldn't have thought it to look at him. Nevertheless, he actually did know his stuff. Before he was slung out of the Studium for gross moral turpitude, he'd been a rising star in the faculties of Literature and Logic, with four published dissertations on suitably obscure cruces in suitably obscure texts under his belt – not bad for a young man of twenty-four. Teuta was our scribe and copyist. He'd parted company from the Golden Spire after a spot inventory revealed the absence of some two dozen manuscripts. Teuta pointed out at the hearing that he'd had no intention of stealing them. He honestly and sincerely intended to put them back where he'd found them, once he'd finished making perfect copies to sell to wealthy Mezentines. That was a tactical error on his part, since theft is a civil crime, for which he could've claimed benefit of clergy, whereas forgery of sacred manuscripts is an ecclesiastical felony. Teuta accordingly spent two years in the penal monastery at Andrapoda, a section of his life he can never be induced to talk about. Razo was our poet; and before you say anything, yes, a poet is essential if you're in the synthetic religion business. Religious poetry doesn't have to be good, but it does have to be poetry, and the rest of us couldn't scan a hendecasyllable or insert a caesura in a trochaic hexameter if our lives depended on it. So; Razo wrote the holy scriptures, with Accila telling him what sort of thing he ought to include, and Teuta wrote them out in impeccably authentic Fourth Century hieratic-demotic script on three hundred year old property title deeds, which he stole (from the law office where he did copying work) and scraped down with pumice. The end result of their labours was the Book of the Sun – a working title that got overtaken by events; we were expounding the damn thing in Cornmarket before we'd had a chance to think of a better one, and then of course it was too late; seventy closely-written, unimpeachably genuine pages of three-hundred-year old revelations of the divine that no scholar has ever been able to fault. Actually, that's a terrible indictment of modern scholarship, since Teuta admitted he'd made a mistake – something to do with a shade of blue he used for an illuminated capital which wasn't invented until fifty years later. Still, he was in a hurry, and the powdered oyster-shell he should have used was five tremisses for a tiny little jar, and at that stage we didn't have five tremisses.

And Zanipulus; well, he was in fact our star performer. Zanipulus's father was a seriously wealthy and respectable man; councilman for a fashionable City ward, followed by a seat in the House, followed by the tribunate and two terms as assistant prefect for roads and waterways. How he found time, with all that on his plate, to indulge in the study of arcane and forbidden arts, I simply don't know; but he did, and they found him out, and that was the end of him and the family fortune, which was confiscated and awarded to the informer who nailed him. What he'd been doing, it turned out, was researching and inventing new medicines, building on the work of the Mezentines (it's perfectly legal over there). Zanipulus didn't get on very well with his father when he was young; it was the old man's brilliant idea that they should work together on the research, so as to have something in common which would draw them closer together. It didn't, as it happened; but Zanipulus found the alchemy stuff quite fascinating, and the fact that it was illegal appealed to the perverse side of his nature, so that when they carted the old man off to the scaffold, Zanipulus resolved to continue his work as a gesture of defiance against the authorities, and because he reckoned he was really close to some breakthrough or other, and couldn't bear to see all that work go to waste.

Since we seem to be doing biographies, I might as well append mine. My great-grandfather was a shipowner on Scona. He made a good deal of money shipping tar and bitumen, which just sort of bubbles up out of the ground out there – you go along with barrels and just scoop it up, and suddenly you've got a valuable commodity for which foreigners will pay money. Anyway, his son, my grandfather, wasn't keen on the bitumen trade – brought him out in a rash, my father told me – so he branched out into general trading, did so well at it that he moved here, to the City, and quickly became significantly rich. Sadly, my father had two unfortunate defects when it came to commerce; he was no good at it, and he didn't realise he was no good at it. The truth only finally sank in when the bailiffs came round and took away our remaining furniture in a small cart, about six months before this story begins. My father died in debtors' prison two months after the business failed. I have no idea where my mother is; when the bailiffs came she announced that she'd had enough and was going home to Scona. I imagine she's still there, and good luck to her.

Anyway, that was us. Between us, we had what Teuta got paid by the lawyers, plus what we could get by begging and very small-scale confidence tricks. We hadn't been caught yet, but we knew it was just a matter of time. Accordingly, when the Invincible Sun called us to His ministry, we had no hesitation. That or poverty and starvation, followed by a long career in rock-splitting in the slate quarries. Hallelujah.

I KNOW IT sounds really horrible, but the outbreak of mountain fever was a real slice of luck. Even back then, it wasn't necessarily a death sentence. About four victims in ten made it – not wonderful odds, but good enough to keep you from simply turning your face to the wall as soon as the symptoms became unambiguous. At the time, though, we thought it was a damned nuisance, possibly enough to put us out of business if we couldn't cure it, which of course we couldn't.

The epidemic started when we'd been going for about six weeks, about a fortnight after the victory at Ciota got us noticed. By then we had premises; actually, a derelict lime kiln on the edge of town, where the North Road branches off from Underway. Not a bad place, in fact; the acoustics in a lime kiln are really rather good, and we got it for practically nothing. Anyway, the fever hadn't been on for more than a day or two when people started turning up on our doorstep, visibly sick, expecting us to cure them. Razo took one look at them and bolted into the back room with his face muffled up in the hem of his cloak. Zanipulus told him not to be so stupid, you don't catch mountain fever like that, but Razo wasn't taking any chances. The pitiful moaning was starting to get on our nerves, so I went outside and did my best.

I felt awful. It's one thing handing out imaginary absolution in return for a sprinkling of low-value copper; quite another confronting a dying man and pretending that you can make him well again. People knew us by then, so they had their money ready. They were lying there, where their families had left them, reaching out to me with hands clenched around fistfuls of coins. I couldn't bring myself to take them. This surprised and annoyed the customers – sorry, the sick and the dying; not customers, not in that state; they wanted to know why I wasn't prepared to intercede for them, as we were always promising to do. Some of them managed to struggle to their feet and lunge at me, trying to stuff money into my pockets or down my shirt. I managed not to panic. I said, of course I'll intercede for you, and this time no payment is necessary. They didn't like that. I guess I'd done my job too well. It was a fundamental tenet of the faith, as I'd been preaching it, that no prayer is audible to Him unless accompanied by clinking money. When I contradicted myself so blatantly, they didn't believe me. Take the money, Father, please (I don't know where *father* came from; they started calling me that at some point, and it sort of stuck) – what could I do? I had the feeling that if I didn't take money off them, I'd be lucky to get out of there in one piece. What made it worse was the amounts. Typical. For their immortal souls, the most they were usually prepared to give was ten trachy, fifteen if they were being eaten alive by guilt and remorse. For their bodies, they were desperate to give me forty, fifty, sixty; fat pouches the size of cooking apples, and there was a terrified old woman who pleaded with me to accept a whole tremissis, your actual silver. I said the usual garbage – I have asked the Invincible Sun to consider your case; if you have truly repented and your sins have been forgiven, your prayers will be answered – then backed away, clanking slightly under the weight of all that coinage, and bolted.

"You aren't taking money off them, are you?" Accila said. "That's sick."

"They're insisting," I tried to explain, but he just gave me that look.

"I guess we brought it on ourselves," Teuta said, helping me with the money before it burst its banks and flooded the building. "We made the poor devils believe, so what did we expect?"

"I guess this is the end of the line," Razo said gloomily. "Soon as they realise we can't cure them, that'll be it, we'll be out of business. Just our bloody luck."

I noticed that Zanipulus wasn't there. "Anyway," I said. "I'm not going out there again. It's definitely someone else's turn."

Nobody was prepared to face the devoted mob, so we shot the bolts and hunkered down, from time to time peering out of the narrow slit of a street-front window to see if they were still there. Oh yes. In fact, the numbers grew, until the kettlehats came and moved them on for obstructing the traffic. An hour later they were back; in the meantime, I'd scribbled a note to the effect that we were engaged in holy rituals of intercession and were not to be disturbed, and nailed it to the door. I hoped that'd induce them to go away, but no chance. They settled down, in heartbreaking silence, and waited.

About mid-afternoon, Teuta went to peer through the slit and called out, "There's someone out there, walking up and down."

"There's about six hundred people out there," I told him. "Come away from the window before they see you."

"It's Zanipulus. He's giving them soup."

I shrugged. Guilt takes people different ways. "Fine," I said. "So long as he's paying for it, let him."

"That's a really bad precedent." Accila was sorting the coins into little towers. "Give them soup once, they'll come to expect it."

"Those poor bastards will all be dead inside a week," I growled. "Don't worry about it."

Accila was all set to give Zanipulus a piece of his mind when he saw him next, but Zan didn't show up next morning. Probably just as well; we still hadn't opened the door. When I peeked out just before dawn, there was a huge mob of them out there. Different ones, though; yesterday's crowd had gone home and been replaced by an even larger one. I wasn't sure what to make of that.

Just before midday, Zanipulus arrived and started doling out yet more soup. I watched him carefully. He had a big copper basin and a brass ladle, and everybody got two mouthfuls. If that was supposed to be a meal, it was a pretty sparse one. Then I realised. Not soup; medicine.

Teuta was livid. "He can't go trying out his stupid potions on real people," he said, "even if they are sick. Suppose he poisons someone and they die. That could mean our necks."

I was watching the crowd. "Fine," I said. "You go out there and tell him."

"You go. You're the figurehead."

"No chance. They'd tear me to pieces. Whatever Zan thinks he's doing, it's going down really well."

There was, it turned out, a reason for that. The stuff he gave them worked. Later he explained that mountain fever was one of the family of diseases his father had been studying; as soon as he saw a crowd of victims assembled in one place, he'd scooted home, cooked up a big batch of the recipe (he had all the ingredients – mouldy bread, for crying out loud, and garlic juice – ready for just such an eventuality) and rushed over to try it out. He'd told them it was a gift from the Invincible Sun that would purge away their sins and leave them whole, and they swallowed it, literally and figuratively. And, would you believe, it actually worked. Twelve hours later, the symptoms started to fade; six doses of the stuff and you were right as ninepence. It was, Razo said, a miracle.

"No it bloody well wasn't," Zanipulus replied angrily. "It was thirty years of painstaking research by a better man than you'll ever be, so shut your face before I shut it for you."

Accila cleared his throat meaningfully – he's six feet six and built like a carthorse, so he was our Justice of the Peace. "Actually, Zan," he said, "you want to be a bit careful, bearing in mind what happened to your dad. If word gets about that his son's handing out miracle cures for the fever, you'll have the kettlehats after you. One martyr in the family is quite enough, I've always thought. Two in two generations is just showing off."

I guess that must've sunk in, because after a medium-length sulk, Zanipulus came sidling round us and asked if we wouldn't mind handing out the rest of the magic goo, spiced up with some religious stuff to distract attention from the medicine side of things. Well, we couldn't refuse, because there were thousands of the poor devils out there by then; so we let him out the back way, to go down to the bakers' scrounging for mouldy bread, while we knocked up a quick liturgy for the healing of the sick.

Muggins here got elected to perform it. Luckily I'm a quick learner. I was word perfect by the time we opened the door and processed out in our vestments (three tremisses for a big wicker hamper of surplus costumes from the Theatre; stank of moth and mildew, but washed up well). I did the words, the other three did the soup. We ran out twice, but fortunately Zan was back with all the stale bread he could carry, and was cooking up a storm in the back room. By nightfall we were all absolutely shattered, and we'd burnt a month's charcoal in a day. We also took three hundred tremisses, nearly all in small change – we had to take it to the moneychangers in herring-barrels. Oh, and we cured the fever epidemic and saved something like two thousand lives. Just us.

AND PRETTY SMUG about it we were too, as you can imagine. It was the ascent to the next level we'd been praying for (so to speak), it was handed to us on a plate and it worked better than we could possibly have hoped for. Because of it, we made the jump from just-another-street-cult to serious mainstream religion in the course of a week. And, let's not forget, we took a great deal of money. Vast amounts of money. Almost enough.

Almost. None of us had said anything out loud, but the unspoken agreement had been; if this thing really takes off, we'll run it until we've each got enough for a stake, the money we'd need to buy into some good, solid, reliable business, retire and be comfortable for life. That moment had very nearly come, but not quite. We counted it, and counted it again, and once more for luck. Split five ways, three hundred and twenty tremisses each. For which, in those days, you could buy a small farm or an established trade (but none of us wanted to be a cooper or a bootmaker) or four carts or a sixteenth share in a ship – a living, in other words, but lower middle class at the very best. That wasn't quite enough, as far as we were concerned. We'd rather set our hearts on being gentlemen, for which we needed another one-seven-five each, minimum. We counted the fever takings one more time, and decide we were still in the faith business.

* * *

WE EXPECTED THAT, once the mountain fever was over, things would quieten down. Not so. We were now established as the go-to faith for healing the sick, and that was a real headache. Mountain fever was one thing; we had the recipe for that, but not for the million-and-one other horrible things that people waste away and die from. No way, of course, that we could explain that to the faithful; so we had to carry on, do the three services a day, and hope that in due course we'd become discredited and forgotten about (but not, hopefully, before we'd scooped in that extra one-seven-five a head)

And wasn't that the weirdest thing. We sang our psalms and intoned our meaningless prayers to our home-made god and ladled out our thin gruel of flour, water and rock salt, guaranteed no medicinal value whatsoever; and still they came, and still they got better. It was embarrassing. Recovered patients turned up, completely unsolicited, and told the crowd at our door that the Invincible Sun had cured them of this or that revolting disease, and that they should all have faith, give generously and believe. If I hadn't known the truth, I'd have been convinced the whole thing was a fix and the happy beneficiaries of divine clemency were out-of-work actors we'd hired for thirty trachy a day in the Horsefair. Thousands of my fellow-citizens, however, weren't so sceptical. They came, limping and groaning and seeping pus; they listened, they prayed; they got better.

Zanipulus told us that such things had been known. Some Mezentine once did an experiment with a load of sick people; he gave half of them proper medicine and the rest of them some old rubbish, told them all it was the real stuff; of the half who got the rubbish, something like a fifth of them got well anyway. Well, fine; goes to show how gullible people really are. The thing was, the number of sick people apparently cured by us – by me, since the other four just handed out the wallpaper paste – was far more than in the Mezentine's experiment. Furthermore, I'm not just talking about coughs and snuffles here. Genuine serious illnesses, the sort that kill you dead; we were curing those, with a success ratio of something like two-to-one.

*   *   *

"I'VE HAD ENOUGH of this," Razo announced. It was the day after he'd cured a leper. The experience had left him badly shaken. "It's getting crazy and out of hand. I vote that we quit the business, divide up the proceeds and go our separate ways."

Two days previously, Accila, in his capacity as treasurer, had announced that he was switching his basis of account from silver to gold. That was when there were a hundred and six silver tremisses to the gold stamen. The net, he then informed us, stood at four hundred and ninety stamina; just ten more to go and the arithmetic would be really straightforward.

"We can't," Teuta replied with his mouth full. "It's gone too far. They know our names. We're respectable. For crying out loud, we had the Secretary of War in here yesterday."

"We wouldn't be able to stay in the City, agreed," Razo said. "So what? The world's a big place, especially if you've got a hundred stamina in your pocket. We could go anywhere."

"I'm not sure I want to give up," Teuta said. "Whatever the hell it is we're doing, it seems like it's working. And I like having Cabinet ministers calling me Your Grace. It sort of makes up for some of the other stuff, if you see what I mean." He yawned, and swung round in his chair. "Zan? What do you think?"

Zanipulus shrugged. "I agree, it makes a pleasant change being respectable, and the money's nice. And I don't think for one moment it'll last forever. Sooner or later this weird run of luck's going to peter out, people will stop curing themselves and saying it was us, and the whole thing will grind to a halt. Until then, I say we carry on milking it for everything we can. You only get something like this once in a lifetime. And it's not like any of us have any other means of making a living."

Nobody, please note, seemed interested in what I'd got to say. My own fault, I guess. I'd spoken inadvisably a couple of times, and my opinion was no longer welcome. I gave it anyway.

"I vote we carry on," I said. "Yes, we're making money. We're also healing the sick. Don't pull faces, Razo, you'll stick like it. We're healing the sick, or they're healing themselves because of us, makes no real difference. What matters is, it's *happening*. If we give up now –"

"Don't start," Teuta said ominously.

"Too late," I shouted, and they all looked at me. "For pity's sake," I said, "can't you see it? We've started something here. People believe in us. They believe so strongly that they're curing themselves, like in that Mezentine's experiment. Zan, you're a scientist, aren't you just the tiniest bit curious? It's an extraordinary thing."

"No kidding," Zanipulus said. "For one thing, it's not possible. Therefore, it scares me. However –"

"Impossible's just a way of saying we haven't figured out how it works yet," I snapped at him. "You should be ashamed of yourself. For crying out loud, Zan, you cured the mountain fever, you saved hundreds, thousands of lives. It's what your father died for. Doesn't that mean more to you than just money?"

"I proved that dad's idea worked," Zanipulus said. "That's all I wanted to do. Other people's problems are not my concern."

"You know what," Teuta said. "He's got religion. He's starting to believe his own bullshit."

"You're all mad," Razo said. "We should pack it in now, before we get ourselves in deep trouble."

"One against four," Accila said. "We keep going. After all," he added, in a soothing voice that made me want to scream, "it's not going to last for ever."

RAZO'S ATTEMPT TO kill the new religion was completely stupid and half-baked, exactly what anyone who knew him as well as we did would have expected. Three days later, at the end of morning prayers, he suddenly turned round, faced the crowd and called out, "The world will end at noon on the fourth of Vectigalia. You have been warned. Goodbye." Then he walked past us very quickly into the Temple, ran upstairs and locked himself in the strongroom.

We only just made it back inside ourselves – we'd moved, by the way, from the old lime kiln to what's now the Silver Star in Westponds – and bolted the door and put the bars up. There was total chaos outside. Teuta was all for bashing the strongroom door down and cutting Razo's throat; he and Zanipulus got hold of the long oak table in the exchequer room and tried to use it as a battering ram, but our strongroom was strong – we kept huge sums of money in there – and after a few minutes they gave up. Razo came out eventually. We just ignored him.

The kettlehats came and broke up the riot. We were given an armed guard, two companies of regulars in shiny breastplates. Once the streets were quiet and they'd dragged away the bodies (three dead, fourteen badly injured) the guard captain came inside to tell us it was all right and his men would be staying there for the next three days, until the fourth.

"Is it true?" he asked, in a quiet, terrified voice. "Is the world really about to end?"

I took charge. "Bless you, my son," I said. He was at least ten years older than me. The father thing is something I'll never get used to. "Are you a member of our congregation?"

The captain hesitated, then nodded shyly.

"Have faith," I said. "The world as we know it will end. The new world will begin. For those who have faith, this is a time of joy."

I'd said the right thing. He gave me a huge, childlike smile, saluted and went away. "Nicely done," Zanipulus said, with grudging admiration. "We may get out of this after all."

THERE HAD, OF course, been total eclipses of the sun before. Anaximander records one, in dry, impersonal detail, back in the second century; he watched the whole thing, making careful notes, and the last line of his account – *thereafter, I became blind* – is one of the most poignant lines in scientific literature. There have been others, though the only trace they've left is their imprint in various mythologies, vague and unsatisfactory. They're rare, though; rare enough that by the time the next one comes along, the previous one's become overgrown with legend and dumped in the place where facts go when people no longer really believe in them.

So, except for the quarter-percent of the population who'd read Anaximander, the total eclipse that took place on the fourth Vectigalia, AUC 552, wasn't a rare and fascinating scientific phenomenon. It was what I'd said it would be. They saw the Invincible Sun die and instantly be reborn, in fire and glory, beyond a shadow of a doubt the beginning of a whole new world.

Oh boy, was that ever good for business. When we finally got the temple cleared and the gates shut, well after midnight, we had a very quick and perfunctory extraordinary general meeting, at which it was resolved that we needed to start hiring some staff, since there was no way in hell we'd be able to carry on running things at that pace all on our own. Razo – somehow in the confusion of that day he'd been completely forgiven and elevated to the status of hero – proposed the hierarchy that prevails in the Church to this day. I was to be the first High Priest; the other four were to be isangels (a term Razo coined on the spot, would you believe), and we'd hire ten full-time priests and fifty minimum-wage part-timers to do pastoral and missionary work, along with three clerks to help out with the books.

Filling the vacancies wasn't a problem. Actually, it was; we were deluged with applicants, ninety-nine per cent of whom we rejected out of hand on the grounds of excessive zeal. The candidates we finally chose were all, in fact, renegade priests from other religions. We wanted men who knew the score and understood the business, and I venture to suggest that we chose well, since of the original ten, eight are still in post and the other two died in harness. As for the part-timers, we went the opposite way and hired the frothing-at-the-mouthest zealots, in the interests of diversity and balance.

THE NEXT PHASE began with our first purpose-built temple. You'll know it as the Silent Rock, on the corner of Old Guard and Tanneries; we just called it The Temple, fondly believing that it'd be the only one. Note the location. We could have gone further into New Town, in pursuit of the carriage trade, but we decided the frontier between upmarket and the slums was a strategically better choice. Yes, the rich gave more, but there are an awful lot of the poor, and handfuls of trachy soon add up, so we weren't inclined to turn our backs on the devoted unwashed. That was the mistake the Ephraists made, and the Poldarnians. They made it clear they weren't interested in the common people, and where are they now?

Nor did we want to go the way of the Blachernicans or the Ranting Friars and get closed down by the government as subversive and antisocial. A middle course, was what we decided on. A universal church, with every man contributing according to his means.

The explosion in our income since the eclipse meant that we could hire the very best architect. It's an indication of how our luck was running that when we approached Thalles with the commission, he turned round and told us he'd be delighted to do the job for free, as his personal offering to the Invincible Sun. Accila tried to insist on paying him – if you hire them, he said, you can also fire them if needs be, but volunteers can be a real pain to get rid of – but he simply wouldn't hear of it; if we gave him money, he'd simply give it all back in the offertory, so where was the point? You can't argue with that, or at least, we didn't try.

It was the same story when it came to buying building materials and hiring labour. If it was for the Temple, nobody wanted paying. That didn't stop contributions to the building fund flooding in, although we made no secret of the fact that we were getting all this free stuff. We decided we had to spend some of the Fund or it'd look really bad, so we sent to Perimadeia for gold offertory plate and embroidered vestments. By the time the order was completed and delivered, there was already a small but thriving Church of the Invincible Sun in Perimadeia – what's all this stuff for, the merchants there asked; gosh, that sounds like a good idea, let's worship Him too. The same in Aelia and the Vesani Republic. I'm not making this up. It really was happening that fast. For example; the first we knew about the Church in Scona was when a ship's captain arrived with three hundred stamina in a goatskin bag; offerings from the faithful to the Mother Church. Honestly, we didn't know what to say.

THE NIGHT BEFORE we broke ground on the Temple foundations, I had a dream. Well, of course you did, I hear you say, what sort of a high priest would you be if you didn't? Indeed; but I did actually have a dream, and unlike most of my dreams, which I forget within a few heartbeats of opening my eyes, this one's stayed with me ever since.

I was inside the Temple – I recognised it, even though I'd only seen it as straight lines on a sheet of parchment – and it was beautiful. The walls were a kind of dark red marble, and the ceiling was a vast golden mosaic of the ascent of the Invincible Sun, surrounded on all sides by saints, angels, apostles and other glorious beings – I recognised them all, though I couldn't remember all their names. In the chancel a choir was singing (and I remember thinking; that's a point, we ought to get some religious music written, it goes down really well) and the air smelt wonderful; roses and lavender and some deep, rich scent I couldn't identify. I was on my knees, wearing vestments of plain black wool, and I think my feet were bare.

I remember looking up and meeting the eye of the beautiful golden Sun in the mosaic. I felt no hesitation, no shame; and then he spoke to me;

"Peace be with you," I think he said. "You are my one true prophet. Go out and do my work."

And then (in the dream) I remembered; it was all fake, nonsense, garbage; I'd invented the whole thing; it was all lies and deceit, to get money.

"Blessed are those who believe," he said, "for in my name they will heal the sick and feed the hungry. Blessed are those who show others the golden path to faith, for they shall see me face to face."

At which point Anaximander, painted over the door to one of the side chapels, muttered, "Thereafter, I became blind," but the Sun didn't seem to have heard him. He raised his right hand in benediction, and said, "Blessed are those who build, for they shall receive the great gift. Blessed are those who make new things, for everything they make shall come from me. Blessed are those who write, for their words shall be my words. Blessed are those who pray, for I shall hear them."

While he was saying all that, I remember, I was trying to shout – no, no, I'm sorry, it's all pretend – but for some reason my mouth wouldn't open. And then he said, "Blessed are those who lie, for they shall speak the truth." And then I woke up.

*   *   *

PAINT FUMES, I told myself when I opened my eyes. They'd only just painted my room a couple of days before, and the place reeked of whatever that foul stuff is that they use as a base. Paint fumes and a ticklish conscience, and I'd been talking to the interior designer about mosaics for the ceiling, and there was a long list of beatitudes in the phoney gospel we'd cooked up. Nothing to worry about. Tomorrow night, sleep with the window open and you'll be fine.

THEY FOUND IT about four feet down, in the trench they were digging to connect the latrine (we may have been men of God but we were practical) to the brook. The first I knew of it was when a crowd started to gather; a silent crowd, which is always the most ominous sort. My first thought was that some poor devil had had an accident, and I hurried over to see if anyone had thought to send for a doctor.

They'd uncovered a box. So far, they'd cleared the dirt away from the lid. It was about three feet by one, and it shone like gold.

It took me about half a second to think; it's been buried in the ground God knows how long, and it shines like gold. Therefore –

I found that I'd shoved my way to the front of the crowd. Naturally, people made way for the high priest. Some workman looked up at me, as if asking what he should do. "Don't just stand there," I yelled at him. "Get it out."

Once they'd scrabbled away the rest of the dirt, they tried to lift it. Too heavy. I jumped down into the trench, cassock-tails flying. The bloody thing was solid gold. At times like this, there's a part of my brain that works independently, regardless of context or propriety. It reported; a thousand stamina, and that's just the box. "Open it," I said.

There was no lock, and gold hinges don't seize. They swung open the lid.

My first reaction, I'm sorry to have to tell you, was, shit, it's just old parchment. Then the better part of me thought to inquire as to what sort of document you'd bother burying in an airtight solid gold box. I shoved someone out of the way. They were rolled up, in scrolls. I grabbed one and pulled down. Miraculously, it didn't tear, disintegrate, come apart in my hands. It was just writing, no pictures, in a script I didn't recognise.

But I knew a man who knew about this sort of thing. "Where's Accila?" I called out. Blank faces. Then I remembered. "Father Chrysostomus," I translated. "Go and find him, now."

The scrolls – there were nine of them – were in Old Middle Therian, a language that hasn't been spoken for a thousand years. Only about six people in the world can read it. Fortuitously, Accila was one of them. "It's some sort of religious text," he told us, as we gathered in secret session in some storage hut, with the door wedged shut with a pickaxe handle. "I'm a bit rusty, so you'll have to –"

He went quiet. Not like him at all. We indulged him for about ten seconds, and then Razo said, "Well?"

Accila looked up. He had the strangest look on his face.

"You're not going to believe this," he said.

LATER, WHEN ACCILA had transcribed and translated all nine scrolls, and we'd all sat down, with the new texts on one hand and the Gospel we'd concocted on the other, we tried to convince ourselves that there were differences, significant ones; some key words were ambiguous, there was a sprinkling of *hapax legomena* which could mean anything, translation is at best an imprecise science. We were kidding ourselves. To all intents and purposes, the scrolls we'd found in the box and the gospel we'd made up out of our heads were the same.

I HAD ANOTHER dream. It wasn't on the same sumptuous, no-expense-spared scale as the previous one, so maybe my dream budget had all been spent. All it was, I was looking in a mirror and the face I saw there wasn't mine.

"This is all wrong," I said.

"Why do you say that?" he said.

"It's *wrong*." He just looked at me. "It's wrong because you're not real. I made you up. You aren't even my imaginary friend, it was deliberate. You're a forgery."

He smiled beautifully. "You made me up."

"Yes. For money. To defraud poor, weak-minded people out of money they couldn't afford."

"For money." He shrugged. "Well, you need to live. And it's not like you're indulging in extravagant luxuries. Apart from the vestments, which are badges of office, like a uniform, you dress in simple clothes, you mostly eat bread and cheese, you've practically stopped drinking wine, you sleep on a mattress in an attic –"

"Only because I'm too busy."

"Too busy. Doing my work. You are my good and faithful servant."

I wanted to hit him. "Cheating people. Deceiving them. And I did make you up. You're a lie."

"You made me up."

"Will you stop repeating everything I say?"

"You made me up," he said firmly. "Let's just think about that. You were trying to find a way to feed yourself and your friends when you were poor and hungry, and an idea came into your head." He smiled. "Where do you think that idea came from?"

"I *made you up*." I couldn't seem to get him to understand. "I invented you as part of a criminal conspiracy."

He shrugged again. "You gave me life," he said. "Like Maxentius."

Good reference. Maxentius was the son of a prostitute, engendered as part of a routine commercial transaction. His military coup overthrew the cruellest tyrant in history, and his welfare reforms led to his reign becoming known as the Golden Age. "If I gave you life, you can't be God," I pointed out. "And if you're not God, you can't exist in this form. Therefore you don't exist."

He shook his head. "If I'm God I can do anything," he said, "and that includes being born of a fallible human. Besides, it's not so hard to believe in, is it, that I should choose to come into existence through you. Seeds grow best when they're planted in rotting shit. No offence," he added gravely.

"None capable of being taken," I replied. "But in that case, why me? Why not be made up by a holy man, a true holy man? There's plenty of those."

"A holy man wouldn't stoop to fraud and deceit. Therefore he wouldn't have made me up, therefore I could never have been made."

"Ah," I said, "you've contradicted yourself. A moment ago, you could do anything."

He nodded. "Once I exist, of course I can. Before I existed, I was nothing."

"Then you can't be God," I cried in triumph. "God must be eternal, in existence for ever since the beginning."

"Must I?" He gave me a mock frown. "I'm God, there's no *must* about it. I can do anything I like."

"Fine," I said. "Then who created the world?"

"I did. Retrospectively."

"You can't –"

"Of course I can. I can do *anything*. Once I exist."

"I'd like to wake up now, please."

"In a moment," he said. "I'm going to teach you some doctrine. Are you listening carefully?"

"Go on," I said.

He looked me straight in the eye. "There is no right or wrong," he said, "there is only good and bad. Starvation is bad; feeding the hungry is good. But it's not right to feed the hungry, because you might easily do so through vanity, which is bad, or because you want to build up a political power-base in order to launch a coup, which is bad, unless you're Maxentius, in which case it's good. Killing someone is wrong, unless you're Maxentius killing the Emperor Phocas, in which case it's entirely right. Do you understand?"

"Not really."

"And you're supposed to be so bright," he said. "Very well," he said. "Let's try again. Motive is irrelevant. The best things have been done for the worst motives, the worst things have been done for the best motives. Lusaeus the Slaughterer started the Fifth Social War because his people were oppressed by the Empire and he wanted the best for them. But Maxentius started a civil war because his people were oppressed and he wanted the best for them. The Fifth Social War was bad, because two million people died needlessly and countless more were left in hunger and misery. Maxentius' war was good, because it freed the people and led to the Golden Age. Hunger is bad, freedom is good. Motive is irrelevant."

"There's nothing good about greed for money."

"Tell that to Peregrinus, who discovered the north-east passage to Ceugra, bringing cheap food and full employment to Mezentia. On the other hand, consider Artabazus, who sailed from Perimadeia to the Anoge with a quarter million sacks of grain to feed the famine victims, and carried the plague with him. Outcomes are good or bad. Motive is irrelevant. This," he added, "is the word of the Lord. It's not open to debate."

"You can't just say –"

"Of course I can. Now wake up and believe."

THE TEMPLE WAS a great success. We had full congregations every day, tremendous enthusiasm, full offertory-boxes. Three weeks after we held our first Intercessionary Mass for Peace, the Herulians surrendered unconditionally and the war was finally over. We held a special service of thanksgiving; we couldn't fit them all in the Temple, so we borrowed the Artillery Fields. Almost all the Cabinet attended, along with most of the City nobility and everyone who was anyone from society, commerce and the arts. The take for that service alone was 16,000 stamina.

Winning the war was the last straw, as far as I was concerned. I had to do something. But I didn't want to rush into it blindly and screw everything up; so I suggested to the others, quite casually at the end of a routine meeting, that it'd save on accountancy time and paperwork if the Church gave me a discretionary budget, so I could pay for everyday maintenance and procurements without having to bother anyone else. Fine, they said, how much do you need? Not quite sure yet, I said; just give me a drawing facility on Number Two account for now, and when I know how it pans out, we can establish a figure.

With unlimited access to Church funds – a licence to embezzle, if you prefer to look at it in those terms – I really got going. I funnelled out money into fake corporations, lost fortunes in imaginary fires and shipwrecks, filtered vast sums through four sets of books, and used it all to feed the war refugees at Blachissa. There were something like a hundred thousand of the poor devils stranded there, fugitives from three major cities burnt down by the enemy during the war, and since their cities no longer existed, they had no governors, therefore there was nobody to petition the government for relief on their behalf, therefore they were nobody's problem, therefore they were left to starve. I bought grain from the farmers in the Mesoge – when Taraconissa was destroyed they lost their principal market and had no-one to sell to, so they were in pretty dire straits – and employed discharged veterans to cart and distribute the supplies. I made a special effort to ensure that at every stage in the process, I was helping someone who badly needed help. I was so pleased with myself.

There was so much money, of course, that for a long time nobody noticed. It was, though, simply a matter of time. When, sooner or later, my colleagues realised what I was up to, I anticipated harsh words, bitter accusations and a great deal of bad feeling. What I didn't expect –

"YOU CAN'T DO this," I roared.

They looked at me.

"You can't," I repeated. "I invented this religion, it was my idea, I created it. I'm the high priest. You can't excommunicate me."

"Actually," Accila said quietly, "we can. It says so in the constitution."

"What constitution?"

"The one we just made up," Accila replied. "And submitted to a general synod for ratification, passed unanimously. And it says, the ecumenical council – that's the four of us – can dismiss the high priest on grounds of heresy or gross moral turpitude. We're going with heresy as an act of kindness, so we don't have to go public with the news that you've been stealing from the Church. That's provided you go quietly and don't make trouble."

"You can't adopt a constitution without my agreement."

"Yes we can," Accila said. "Retrospectively. Since there is currently no high priest, you having been dismissed, the ecumenical council is us. And we can do anything we like."

The others just sat there, grim-faced, hiding behind Accila. "I'll have the lot of you for this," I shouted. "I'll expose you. I'll tell everything. I'm tell them it's all a fraud."

Accila sighed. "Please don't," he said. "You'll just embarrass yourself. After all, nobody's going to believe you, are they? They've seen us curing the sick, they saw the miracle of the reborn sun, they saw us end the war. They'll just think, here's a man who lost a power struggle and wants to make trouble. Politics. The people understand about politics. And then," he added with a sad smile, "we'll tell them how you defrauded the Church of a quarter of a million stamina. Or we can do it our way. Up to you entirely."

I was breathing rapidly, and my palms were sweating. "Heresy," I said. "What's that supposed to mean?"

Razo cleared his throat. "We'll put out a statement saying that you object to the doctrine of vicarious absolution. The doctrine having been upheld by the ecumenical council, you're a heretic."

I blinked. "What," I demanded, "is the doctrine of –?"

"Vicarious absolution." Teuta steepled his fingers. "My idea. In exchange for a substantial offering, you can ensure the salvation of someone else's soul, even if he's not actually a believer himself. He doesn't have to know about it, if that's what you want. For double the money, you can even save someone's soul against his will. We think it'll be very popular."

I TRIED. I went to the magistrates and swore a complaint, but the chief justice was a believer and threw the case out for lack of evidence. I went to the chief archimandrite of the Fire Temple, who told me that the last thing he wanted to do, in the present circumstances, was pick a fight with a much bigger, richer church. I tried to see the emperor, but the chamberlain wouldn't even take my money. There are more important things, he said, with a sanctimonious scowl, and sent me away.

I preached in the market-place. The first time, I drew a good crowd. I hadn't lost my touch. I told them; the Gospel of the Invincible Sun is a fake, written by five poor rich boys to make money. The so-called ancient scrolls dug up in the Temple foundations were fakes, made by a skilled forger with a criminal record for falsifying religious texts. The miracle of the Reborn Sun was no miracle at all; my former colleagues had started with Anaximander, carefully studied the other records, and accurately predicted a natural phenomenon that would have happened anyway. The cure for the mountain fever was just mouldy bread beaten up in garlic juice – a wonderful thing, granted, but no miracle. The other cures could all be explained by the scientifically-documented phenomenon of mass hysteria; it was all there in the Mezentine books, I told them, all we did was read and repeat. The Herulian war was almost over anyway, so we hadn't ended that. As for the Church, it was nothing more than a mechanism for sucking in unearned wealth, which the five of us had always intended from the start to keep for ourselves.

My second street corner sermon drew about a dozen people, five of whom jeered and threw apples. On the third occasion, I was arrested by the kettlehats for disturbing the peace.

They kept me in for a week, in a dark, tiny cell along with two thieves, a wife-killer and a rapist. I preached to them, expounding the doctrine of right and wrong that I'd been given in my dream. I think the rapist was interested, but on the fourth day the wife-killer, a believer, hit me so hard I passed out, and when I came round, a lot of the evangelical zeal seemed to have faded.

On the seventh day, two kettlehats came and pulled me out of there. I was being transferred, they said, to the ecclesiastical courts. What ecclesiastical courts, I asked.

"THEY'RE NEW," ACCILA explained. He'd come to see me in my cell. "Very new."

"How new?"

"Actually, we got the whole thing set up in six days. Soon as we heard you'd been arrested."

I stared at him. "What?"

"In your honour," he said grimly. "On account of, there wasn't really anything in ordinary criminal law we could get you for, apart from disturbing the peace and criminal slander, maybe just possibly incitement to riot. At best, those would get you put away for two years. So, we created an entirely new jurisdiction, just for you. They had to rush an emergency enabling bill through the House; quickest piece of legislation this century, apparently. The emperor signed it yesterday, so it's now the law. And of course it's –"

"Let me guess. Retrospective."

He grinned. "Not much point otherwise." He sighed, a reasonable man brought to the limits of his patience. "Eps, you bloody fool, why can't you just drop it and shut your face? You've lost, accept it, move on." He hesitated, then added; "They've authorised me to make you an offer. One million stamina, provided you leave the country and never come back. That's for old time's sake, we don't have to pay you anything. Well? What about it?"

"And if I won't?"

He looked very sad and grave. "Well," he said, "I don't see where you leave us much choice. But for pity's sake, Eps, you're a sensible man, there's absolutely no reason why we can't sort this out in a reasonable, businesslike fashion. Damn it, we used to be *friends*."

I just looked at him. "You're the ones who had me locked up," I said. "You threw me out of my own Church. I'm sorry, but I can't see how it's my fault."

He shrugged. "You don't want money," he said. "You don't want a quiet, prosperous life. For crying out loud, Eps, what do you want? A martyr's crown?"

So they were going to kill me. Oh, I thought. "If the crown fits," I heard myself say.

"You bloody idiot," Accila said, and left.

THE TRIAL WAS short and, as I understand, very orderly and efficient. I wasn't actually there, having been ejected for gross contempt about ten seconds after they put me in the dock. They sent some clerk down to the cells to tell me the verdict. Guilty of blasphemy, twelve counts, fraud and embezzlement, ninety-six counts, other offences, a hundred and four counts. Sentence; death by fire. I'd pleaded guilty, apparently.

"Death by fire?" I asked.

The clerk nodded briskly. "Only the refining power of flame," he told me, "can purge the taint of blasphemy, which would otherwise form a miasma and lead to plague."

"Is that right?"

"That's what it says here," he said. "Tomorrow morning, at dawn. Sorry," he added, which was nice of him.

"I'd like to see a priest," I said.

"Sorry."

I spent the night on my knees, in prayer. Sounds ridiculous, doesn't it, but you do that sort of thing in a condemned cell. After all, why not? Not as if there's anything better to do, sleeping would be a sinful waste, and – well. If it was true, and I really had invented God, brought him into existence – I thought about that. Why not? There are innumerable examples of sons who turn out to be a thousand, a million times better, cleverer, stronger than their fathers. If I really had invented God, then I reckoned he owed me; a vision, a visitation, a sign or portent at the very least. No dice. I fell asleep kneeling.

I woke up, and it was still dark. The floor was shaking.

We don't get earthquakes in the City. If you want to experience that sort of thing, you have to go to Permia, or up North. It's the weirdest feeling. It's like being on a ship in a storm. You have to keep moving your feet just to stand still, and the vibration goes right down and through you, till you can feel your bones moving. Everything blurs, as though you've just had a bang on the head, and there's this noise like nothing else, a sort of deep rumbling purr, as though you're a flea on the back of a cat the size of Scheria. I jumped up, promptly fell over, got up again; I was trying to learn how to stand upright on a moving surface when the floor split, right between my feet, and a huge gap appeared – a great big slice of nothing, with a foot on either side of it. I yelped like a dog, and then a chunk of the roof came down, missing me by a whisker. I could feel pee running down the inside of my leg. Then there was this extraordinary singing, moaning noise, which later on I was able to rationalise as the sound of steel under intolerable tension, and the doorframe burst. The cell door actually flew open – it swished past me, if I'd been a hand's breadth closer, it'd have swatted me like a fly. A head-sized chunk of roof bashed me on the shoulder; it hurt like buggery, I staggered and nearly went down the hole in the floor. The hell with this, I thought, and I did a sort of standing jump through the open doorway.

I landed on my bruised shoulder, which really didn't improve matters, and sat up. One end of the corridor was blocked with chunks and slabs of fallen roof. The other end was clear. I scrambled to my feet and ran. The floor played funny games with me, I ended up flat on my back three times before I reached the stairs. They'd pulled away from the wall on one side, but I was in no mood to be fussy. When I was a few steps from the top, I felt the whole lot give way under the pressure of my heel; I sprang, like a cat, as the staircase just sort of fell away, and landed in a ball on something relatively solid.

It was a miracle that I got out of there. About ten seconds after I burst out through a shattered window into fresh air, the whole prison sort of folded in on itself and subsided into a heap of stones. How come I wasn't squashed by any of the huge slabs of flying rubbish, I simply don't know. All I remember was how hard it was to breathe, because I couldn't stop running, even though my legs were jelly and my lungs stabbed like knives; I ran, dodging falling trees and collapsing buildings, jumping over dead people and people trapped under things, I ran and ran until a particularly violent tremor swept me off my feet and I fell down and no effort on my part could make me get up again. Then, I guess, I went to sleep, or something like that.

I woke up in a weird landscape; masonry trash, blocks of stone, as far as the eye can see; I remember thinking, whatever possessed me to spend the night in a quarry? But then I caught sight of a building I knew; the *Integrity Rewarded*, in Sheep Street, except that Sheep Street wasn't there; just the *Integrity*, taken out of context, floating serenely on a sea of rubble.

I limped over and banged on the door, but it was bolted shut. Pity. I could really have done with a drink (except I had no money, and they don't do credit at the *Integrity*.) I wandered away and just sort of drifted for a while. It was a very long time before I saw anyone, but when I did, it was a patrol of kettlehats. They looked at me and shouted, *You there, stop where you are.* So, naturally, I ran.

THE GREAT EARTHQUAKE of AUC 552 was exceptionally violent but extremely localised. It shook down the whole of the Potteries district, so that only a handful of buildings were left standing, but was hardly felt at all in Cornmarket, East Hill or the Grand Crescent. Remarkably, given the scope of the destruction, only about two dozen people were killed, and eight of those were prisoners in the gaol awaiting execution.

I holed up in the *Charity & Austerity* in Pigmarket; a haunt of my youth, where nobody ever asks you anything so long as you have at least ninety trachy. I had considerably more than that, courtesy of some poor dead man whose pocket I picked on my way out of the ruins. I could have afforded enough of the house red to kill a regiment of dragoons, but oddly enough I didn't touch a drop; I had a bowl of soup and half a loaf of grindstone bread, and that was all I wanted. I think I coped really rather well with the realisation – it came up on me like a sunrise – that the earthquake had been for me – an intervention by my God, the Invincible Sun, to get me out of prison and save me from the flames. Well? What other possible explanation can you think of?

I could have been horrified, torn apart by guilt at the thought of the deaths and the damage. Or I could've been really, really, really smug; God loves me so much, He shook down a quarter of the City just for me. I was neither. I accepted what had happened; not my fault, not a victory or a vindication. He knows best, I told myself; if that's what He felt needed to be done, who am I to question?

HAVE YOU EVER been to Eremia? I thought not. If you were thinking of making the trip, take my advice, don't bother. There's nothing there except sand, rocks, murderous heat, biting winds, freezing cold at night. I can only think of one man in the history of the world who wanted to go there, and I have a shrewd suspicion that at the time, he wasn't quite right in the head.

Looking back, I can't understand how I survived. I was out in the desert, just walking. I had nothing, no shoes, not even a water-bottle. On the third, or was it the fourth day, I stumbled across an oasis. I call it that; there was this brown puddle, fringed with tall, thin trees. There was a rock with a sort of ledge, you couldn't call it a cave; under the ledge, I found a dead man. He must've been there for a long time. His skin was brown and hard, like rawhide. His eyes had gone, but his hair was mostly still there; thin, wispy, like the strands of wool you find caught on brambles. He was curled up, asleep. When I moved him, he was as light as a log of rotten wood.

We had many long conversations, the dead man and me. He told me he was a pilgrim, on his way to the celebrated desert oracle at Cocona. He'd gone there to get the answer to a very important question which had subsequently slipped his mind; the answer, though, was, *Yes, but it will not end well.* Looks like they were right, I told him. Well, of course, he said, it's a very reliable oracle.

I did most of the talking. I told him my story; how I'd created God, how He'd outgrown me, moved away from me, how He'd rescued me from prison and fire; but these days He never comes to see me, He doesn't even write – that's how it is, the dead man said, they have lives of their own, what do you expect? Of course, I said, and I know how busy He is, but it'd be nice if He could spare me just five minutes once in a while.

"Here I am," the dead man said. "What can I do for you?"

I looked at Him. "Sorry," I said, "I didn't recognise You there for a minute."

"That's all right," He said.

"Well?" I asked Him. "Are You keeping well? Are You eating properly?"

"I am the Invincible Sun," He said. "I don't eat."

Fair point. At that moment He was everywhere around me, burning, a white heat blazing down from the sky, rising up from the hot sand. "What do You want me to do?" I asked.

"You've done so much," He said.

"That's not an answer."

He had no eyes, but they were filled with pity. "I want you to go to the City," He said. "Give yourself up. Submit to the cruelty and hatred of our enemies. They will put you in prison and they will hang you, and when you die, all the sins of the world will die with you. You don't mind, do you?" He added. "If you'd rather not, I'll understand."

"No, that's fine," I said. "Is there anything You want me to say?"

"Tell them that you were wrong," He said. "Tell them that the miracles were true miracles, that it was I who cured the sick and ended the war, that the scriptures are My holy word, that I saved you from the prison and I sent you back. Tell them everything is true, and everything is good, and that motive is irrelevant, only the outcome matters. It's essential that you tell them, and that they understand. Will you do that for Me?"

"Of course," I said. "Anything else?"

He smiled. "I think that's quite enough to be going on with. I will send others, later, to do the rest."

"It doesn't seem very much," I said. "Go home, give up, tell a few lies, get killed. Are you sure there isn't more I can do to help?"

"Nothing that you're capable of doing," He replied, not unkindly.

"Well, if you're sure," I said. "Can I ask you something?"

"Fire away."

"Why me?"

He smiled. "Why did I choose you as my high priest, out of all the people in all the world?"

"Yes."

"You mean you haven't –" He stopped, grinned, composed His face. "Your name, of course."

"My name?"

"That's right. Eps *eps*. Joke."

I looked Him in the eye. "I don't believe it."

His gaze rested on me like the noonday sun, bright and intolerable, so that I couldn't help remembering Anaximander. "Are you seriously suggesting," He said, "that God has no sense of humour? Now, there's blasphemy."

"But it's not even particularly funny –" I stopped. I was talking to a dessicated corpse. Ah well, I thought.

* * *

LATER THAT DAY, a caravan of salt traders on their way to the coast stopped at the oasis. They were amazed to find anyone there. They said they ought to kill me, for stealing their water, but since I was a lunatic and a holy man, they'd overlook it just this once. I explained that I had to get to the coast as quickly as possible; I have a message from God, I told them. Of course you have, they said.

I didn't feel much like talking on the long walk to the coast, but they wouldn't leave me alone. How did you survive, they asked; how did you manage for food? I told them I had a vague memory of eating beetles, or something of the sort. They laughed and shook their heads; no beetles in the desert, they said. I shrugged. The Invincible Sun must have sent them, I said, so that I wouldn't starve. They gave me an odd look. Your god sent you beetles to live on, they said, that's pathetic. Would it have killed Him to send you sausages and honey-cakes? I thought about that for a moment and said, I think He must have sent the beetles, because clearly there weren't any living there under normal circumstances. I saw no sign that insects had attacked the dead body. What dead body, they said.

TWO KETTLEHATS WERE waiting for me at the quay. For some reason, I was in ridiculously high spirits, that end-of-term feeling I hadn't felt since I'd walked out into the sunlight after six days in the Examination Halls, at the end of my last year at the Studium. I waved to the kettlehats as I walked down the gangplank. They looked at me.

"I'm Eps," I said, before they had a chance to open their mouths. "Sorry, Father Deodatus, if that's the name on the warrant. Are you here to arrest me?"

"No talking," they said. "You're with us."

They had one of those closed carriages; a pity, because I'd have liked to look out of the window. It was a bright, sunny day, and the City is always at its best in sunshine; it brings out that deep honey yellow in the stonework, and sparkles on the copper roofs of the temples. I've always admired it; that day, knowing what I did about the Sun, I could understand. It was because He loved the City so much, the buildings and the people looking at them. I was proud of Him for that.

*   *   *

THEY MUST HAVE known well in advance that I was coming, because everything was ready. They'd built the scaffold in the Golden Square, presumably so that the nobility could watch from the windows of their town houses without having to come down and mingle with the common people. For them, the imperial carpenters had built seventeen (I counted them) rows of bleachers, which only goes to show that the moaners are quite wrong and the government can get things done quickly and well if it sets its mind to it. On the outskirts there were the usual mulled wine and hot sausage stalls, quite a few other traders – I noticed a man selling quality imported textiles, and another doing a brisk trade in commemorative pottery figurines. Three squadrons of the Household Cavalry added a touch of that colour and pageantry we've always done so well in the City. I couldn't tell from where I was whether they were charging people for admission, but I'd be surprised if they weren't.

A kettlehat captain in a magnificent gilded breastplate took charge of me and led me through a cordon of dismounted guardsmen to the scaffold steps. I asked him, "Will I have a chance to make a speech?" He shook his head. I was disappointed. I had a message to deliver, after all, and I was surprised to find that no opportunity had been provided. How about a priest, I asked. Shake of the head. But I want to confess my sins, I told him (we were getting closer and closer to the scaffold), I want to tell the people that I've seen the error of my ways and urge them to love and obey the Ecumenical Council. Sorry, he said, and then we were there.

I was starting to panic. I had, after all, been sent there to pass on the word of the Invincible Sun; my death was merely ancillary to that, and there was a terrible risk of missing the point of the exercise. I tried to protest, but the kettlehats proved to be very skilful at moving a person who didn't want to be moved, efficiently and unobtrusively. Mostly it was done by judicious barging and blocking, with firm but gentle pressure from a hand in the small of the back; you have to go where you're nudged, or you lose your balance and fall over. I guess they'd had the practice, but still, I was impressed.

"Gentlemen, be reasonable," I said. We were at the foot of the steps. "A few last words, is that too much to ask? I just want to –"

"Sorry." A knee pressed the back of my knee, and somehow I was standing on the first step. If I'd been ten times stronger and trained from boyhood in the secret arts of the warrior, I don't think there was anything I could've done. I could see the hangman waiting for me at the top of the steps. He had a sort of black bag over his head. This was all wrong. I had to deliver my message, but time was running out. I thought; if He could be bothered to level the Potteries with an earthquake to let me escape the first time, surely He can do something, some little thing, to give me a chance to carry out His explicit instructions. Made no sense. I'd done exactly what I'd been told, so what had gone wrong?

I looked up and there He was, a round white eye in a sea of clear blue, watching, not doing anything. I let them nudge me up the steps, and the hangman grabbed me and put the noose round my neck. "Excuse me," I started to say, but he tightened the knot so I couldn't speak. He trod on my toe, making me step back so I was properly centred on the trapdoor. "Just a –" I croaked, and he pulled the lever.

NOW THEN, LET'S see.

Motivation, we have been taught, doesn't matter. All that counts is the outcome, the end result. Therefore, it didn't matter that my colleagues and I had started the Church as a criminal conspiracy to cheat gullible people out of money. Clear away the nettles and brambles of motive, and underneath them you find a set of circumstances capable of producing the desired result. You find a group of people with a unique combination of talents and abilities – the scientist, the poet, the skilled forger, the scholar and the preacher. Driven by, motivated by, an urgent need of their own, they set about the task of bringing a god to the attention of the public. Consider how many religions, how many gods, show up on our streets in any twelve-month period; scores, hundreds even, and how many of them make it to mainstream acceptance? Quite. But, I dare say, a fair proportion of those religions, those gods, have perfectly viable doctrines, sufficient to serve as the basis for a thoroughly satisfactory

Church. The margin, is what I'm trying to say, the edge, the difference between the three hundred failures and the one success, is tiny; but it's real, it's there. It's not just a matter of luck. To succeed, you need the perfectly pitched message, the unforgettably phrased scriptures, the eye-catching iconography, the significant moments indelibly etched on the public consciousness. The trouble with most religions is the people who propound them. They may be charismatic and inspirational, but they're not quite charismatic and inspirational *enough*. Also, they're deficient in those core skills we've just examined. Their scriptures are written in a pedestrian style. They're too new, without the sanctity of ancientness. They're internally inconsistent, or they ask people to believe stuff that ordinary folk can't quite stomach. Their preachers lack that certain indefinable but absolutely indispensable *something*. They are, in other words, amateurs. They lack the professional touch.

We, by contrast – well. Think about it. Suppose you were the Invincible Sun, with the whole human race to choose from. We were conmen, whose business was getting sceptical people to believe us. Would you really select a bunch of unskilled nobodies – farm workers, fishermen, carpenters – or would you insist on nothing but the best; well-born, university-educated, intelligent and naturally articulate, and motivated (I'm repeating that word so you'll notice it) by ferociously intense self-interest. Well, wouldn't you? If you want a house built, you hire builders. If you want a gallstone taken out, you pay the best doctor you can afford. So, if you want people persuaded, you enlist the best persuaders in the business.

Once you realise the simple truth that motive is irrelevant, it all makes sense. Really, you don't need a special flash of insight direct from the lips of the Invincible Sun to figure that one out. There is no right and wrong, only good and bad. Faith is good; it's essential, if you want to survive in a perverse and gratuitously cruel universe. Nihilism is bad; it deprives the world of meaning, so why the hell bother with anything? Anything that can induce people to have faith, have hope, believe that there is meaning, is good. Motive is irrelevant.

*　　*　　*

I WOKE UP.

Later, I figured out that I must've banged my head on the gallows frame or the edge of the trap, which made me pass out. I had a lump the size of an egg and a splitting headache. I was lying on a bed. It hurt when I breathed in. There was someone sitting looking down at me. It was Zanipulus.

"How are you feeling?" he asked.

"Awful," I said. Then I frowned. "Zan?"

"Hello, Eps."

"Sorry," I said. Talking hurt. "I was expecting someone else."

He laughed. "No doubt you were," he said. "But you'll have to make do with me. Now then, you've probably got a bad head and a hell of a stiff neck, but basically you're fine. You should be up and about in no time."

"You –" I paused. " For God's – for pity's sake. What happened?"

He smiled. "Exactly what we wanted to happen," he said. "Just for once, everything went according to plan, no balls-ups, no hitches. It was a complete success."

I frowned at him. "I don't think so," I said. "I'm still alive."

He stared at me; then he burst out laughing. "Eps, you *idiot*," he said. "You didn't seriously believe we actually wanted to kill you? Oh come on. We're your *friends*."

"But –"

He shook his head in disbelief. "We staged your execution," he said. "We made a martyr of you. Well? Isn't that what you told Accila you wanted?"

A martyr's crown. "I thought –"

"For crying out loud, Eps." He was amused, but also a little bit hurt, a little bit angry. "Obviously, when we realised you had issues with the direction we were going in, we knew it was time for you to go your separate way. And, equally obviously, we couldn't have you wandering off making a nuisance of yourself. So, we thought about it and decided that the best thing would be to stage your death, in public, so everyone could see, so there'd be no chance of you making a comeback and being a pain in the bum for the rest of us. Also, there was a fantastic opportunity to move the business up to the next level, by making you the Church's first martyr. Which has worked," he added, "beyond our wildest dreams. Where before we had one thrivingly successful Church, we now have two, in a state of perfect schism, the Orthodox and the Deodatists. Overall attendances are up twenty-one per cent. And," he added with a grin, "the Deodatists – your lot, I guess; our wholly owned subsidiary – are particularly generous with their donations. At this rate, we should be in a position to retire by the end of the current financial year." He stopped and frowned. "Hang on," he said. "Didn't Accila explain all this to you, the night before the –?"

Earthquake. I winced. I could see precisely what had happened. In our brief conversation in my cell, I'd so annoyed Accila that he'd flounced off in a huff – intending, no doubt, to come back later and try again when he'd had a chance to simmer down. But then the earthquake happened, I vanished; Accila either neglected to mention to the others that he hadn't had a chance to fill me in on the plan, or else was ashamed of having flown off the handle and cocked it up, so kept quiet. Bloody fool. Next time I saw him, I'd kick his arse.

"Of course he did," I said. "Sorry, I'm being a bit slow. I think I may have banged my head."

Zanipulus relaxed and grinned at me. "That's all right," he said. "For a moment there, I was really worried. I thought, what must he be thinking of us? He must reckon we're *horrible*."

"You might have warned me," I said, "about the hanging thing. It was really convincing. If I hadn't known –"

"Oh, that." He tried not to look smug. "Basically, just a really carefully padded noose and a precisely calculated drop, though there's a bit more to it than that, obviously. I'll draw it out for you some day, if you're interested."

"So," I said. "I'm dead. What now?"

He shrugged. "Up to you entirely," he said. "We've worked out your share." He named a figure, which made my head swim. "Accila was all for deducting the money you took from us with all those weird schemes of yours, but the rest of us managed to calm him down, make him see it was ultimately good for business – laying the foundations for the

Deodatist schism, that sort of thing – and he came round in the end and he's fine about it now." He grinned. "If it's all right with you, we'll pay you half now in cash and the balance in instalments over, say, ten years, to save us from liquidity problems. Or if you prefer, we can give you rentcharges, the reversions on Church properties, it's entirely up to you. After all, we owe you a great deal. We'd never have maintained and increased our rate of exponential growth without you."

"Cash and instalments will be just fine," I told him.

"Splendid." He sat up a bit straighter. "So," he said, "any idea what you're going to do next? The world, as they say, is your oyster."

"I hate oysters."

"So you do, I'd forgotten. Any plans? Or are you just going to bugger off to the sun and enjoy yourself?"

Interesting choice of words. Deliberate? Who gives a shit? Motive is irrelevant. "I think that's what I'll do," I said. "Looking back, I never enjoyed my life particularly much. So I'm hoping my death will be one long giggle."

As PART OF my severance package, I received a one-fifth share in the net profits of Officina Solis Invicti, a wholly-owned trading consortium with interests in, among other things, shipbuilding and arms production. That has proved to be a real slice of luck – heaven-sent, you might say – what with the dreadful wars we've been having lately, between the Orthodox empire and the Deodatist Aelians and Vesani. As I write this, Zanipulus is in the process of setting up a chain of arm's-length offshore subsidiaries so that OSI can open factories in Aelia and the Vesani republic, and we can start selling ships and weapons to both sides. And why not? It's only fair; last I heard, the Vesani had taken a hell of a beating from the empire, on account of their vastly superior military technology. It wouldn't do for God to be seen to be taking sides.

Motive is irrelevant. The war is a terrible thing, but it was coming anyway, it was inevitable; once the empire had sorted out its traditional enemy the Herulians, it was only a matter of time before it picked a fight with the Vesani, the Aelians, anyone else it could find. By having the war now, and over religion rather than trade or boundaries, we limit the damage. It's highly unlikely that the empire will win, particularly if OSI arms the opposition. Defeat, or a stalemate, will put a limit on imperial expansionism for a century or more. As a result, tens of thousands of soldiers won't die, millions of civilians won't be enslaved. History will thank us, I have absolutely no doubt.

Meanwhile, every trachy I get from OSI, my estates in the Mesoge, my mercantile and other investments, goes to feed the war refugees. I live here among them in the Chrysopolis camp, sharing their bad water and their plain, barely sufficient food, and I have to say, it's pretty horrible. We live in tents, or shacks built out of scrap packing cases. The refugees are surly and miserable, they yell at me and sometimes throw stones, because they have no idea what I'm doing there. Their idea of hygiene is rudimentary at best. I've nearly given up trying to keep them from slaughtering each other over trivial disputes (nearly) – beyond keeping them alive, I can't say I've done very much for them. But there's so many of them, a hundred, hundred and fifty thousand; all rabid Deodatists. Really, the only thing that keeps them going is their faith, which got them into this dreadful state in the first place and sustains them in the face of the torments of hell. The Invincible Sun, and the glorious example of His true prophet Deodatus, who died for them that they might live; except he didn't, but I wouldn't dream of telling them that.

In fact, I don't dream of anything. At first, I was bitterly disappointed. I felt I was owed, at the very least, a well-done-my-good-and-faithful-servant, followed by a long overdue explanation and, just possibly, an apology. I'd have liked *something*, rather than complete and impenetrable silence. But there; they say that up in the Calianna Mountains there's an ancient Velitist monastery whose monks have spent the last two thousand years waiting for their gods to apologise for the Creation. They're hopeful, so reports say, but they aren't holding their breath.

THE PROMISE OF SPACE

James Patrick Kelly

James Patrick Kelly (www.jimkelly.net) has written novels, short stories, essays, reviews, poetry, plays and planetarium shows. His most recent book is a collection of stories entitled *The Wreck Of The Godspeed*. His short novel *Burn* won the Nebula Award in 2007. He has won Hugo Award for his novelettes "Think Like A Dinosaur" and "Ten to the Sixteenth to One." With John Kessel he is co-editor of five anthologies, most recently *Digital Rapture: The Singularity Anthology*. He is on the faculty of the Stonecoast Creative Writing MFA Program at the University of Southern Maine and on the Board of Directors of the Clarion Foundation.

Capture 06/15/2051, Kerwin Hospital ICU, 09:12:32

... and my writer pals used to tease that I married Captain Kirk.

> *A clarification, please? Are you referring to William Shatner, who died in 2023? Or is this Chris Pine, who was cast in the early remakes? It appears he has retired. Perhaps you mean the new one? Jools Bear?*

No, you. Kirk Anderson. People used to call you that, remember? First man to set foot on Phobos? Pilot on the Mars landing team? Captain Kirk.

> *I do not understand. Clearly I participated in those missions since they are on the record. But I was never captain of anything.*

A joke, Andy. They were teasing you. It's why you hated your first name.

> *Noted. Go on.*

No, this is impossible. I feel like I'm talking to an intelligent fucking database, not my husband. I don't know where to begin with you.

Please, Zoe. I cannot do this without you. Go on.

Okay, okay, but do me a favor? Use some contractions, will you? Contractions are your friends.

Noted.

Do you know when we met?

I haven't yet had the chance to review that capture. We were married in 2043. Presumably we met before that?

Not much before. Where were you on Saturday, May 17, 2042? Check your captures.

The capture shows that I flew from Spaceways headquarters at Spaceport America to the LaGuardia Hub in New York and spent the day in Manhattan at the Metropolitan Museum. That night I gave the keynote address at the Nebula Awards banquet in the Crown Plaza Hotel but my caps were disengaged. The Nebula is awarded each year by the World Science Fiction Writers....

I was nominated that year for best livebook, *Shadows on the Sun*. You came up to me at the reception, said you were a fan. That you had all five of my Sidewise series in your earstone when you launched for Mars that first time. You joked you had a thing for Nacky Martinez. I was thrilled and flattered. After all, you were top of the main menu, one of the six hero marsnauts. Things I'd only imagined, you'd actually done. And you'd read my work and you were flirting with me and, holy shit, you were Captain Kirk. When people – friends, famous writers – tried to break into our conversation, they just bounced off us. Nobody remembers who won what award that night, but lots of people still talk about how we locked in.

I just looked it up. You lost that Nebula.

Yeah. Thanks for reminding me.

You had on a hat.

A hat? Okay. But I always wore hats back then. It was a way to stand out, part of my brand – for all the good it did me. My hair was a three act tragedy anyway, so I wore a lot of hats.

This one was a bowler hat. It was blue – midnight blue. With a powder blue band. Thin, I remember the hatband was very thin.

Maybe. I don't remember that one. Nice try, though.

Tell me more. What happened next?

Jesus, this is so wrong… No, I'm sorry, Andy. Give me your hand. You always had such delicate hands. Such clever fingers.

I can still remember that my mom had an old Baldwin upright piano that she wanted me to learn to play, but my hands were too small. You're crying. Are you crying?

I am not. Just shut up and listen. This isn't easy and I'm only saying it because maybe the best part of you is still trapped in there like they claim and just maybe this augment really can set it free. So, we were sitting at different tables at the banquet but after it was over, you found me again and asked if I wanted to go out for drinks. We escaped the hotel, looking for a place to be alone, and found a night-shifted Indonesian restaurant with a bar a couple of blocks away. It was called Fatty Prawn or Fatty Crab – Fatty Something. We sat at the bar and switched from alcohol to inhalers and talked. A lot. Pretty much the rest of the night, in fact. Considering that you were a man and famous and ex-Air Force, you were a good listener. You wanted to know how hard it was to get published and where I got my plots and who I like to read. I was impressed that you had read a lot of the classic science fiction old-timers like Kress and LeGuin and Bacigalupi. You told me what I got wrong about living in space, and then raved about stuff in my books that you thought nobody but spacers knew. Around four in the morning we got hungry and since you'd never had Indonesian before, we split a gado-gado salad with egg and tofu. I spent too much time deconstructing my divorce and you were polite about yours. You said your ex griped about how you spent too much time in space, and I made a joke about how Kass would have said the same thing about me. I asked if you were ever scared out there and you said sure, and that landings were worse than the launches because you had so much time leading up to them. You used to wake up on the outbound trips in a sweat. To change the subject, I told you about waking up with entire scenes or story outlines in my head and how I had to get up in the middle of the night and write them down or I would lose them. You made a crack about wanting to see that in person. The restaurant was about to close for the morning and, by that time, dessert sex was definitely on the menu, so I asked if you ever got horny on a mission. That's how I found out that one of the side effects of the anti-radiation drugs was low testosterone levels. We established that you were no longer taking them. I would have invited you back to my room right then only you told me that you had to catch a seven-twenty flight back to El Paso. There still might have been enough time, except that I was rooming with Rachel van der Haak, and, when we had gotten high before the banquet, we had promised each other we'd steer clear of men while our shields were down. And of course, when I thought about it, there was the awkward fact that you were twenty years older than I was. A girl has got to wonder what's up with her when she wants to take daddy to bed.

I am nineteen years and three months older than you.

And then there was your urgency. I mean, you had me at Mars, Mr. Space Hero, but I had the sense that you wanted way more from me than I had to give. All I had in mind was a test drive, but it seemed as if you were already thinking about making a down payment. When you said you could cancel an appearance on Newsmelt so you could be back in New York in three days, it was a serious turn-on, but I was also worried. Blowing off one of the top news sites? For me? Why? I guessed maybe you were running out of time before your next mission. I didn't realize that you were...

Go on.

No, I can't. I just can't – how do I do this? Turn the augment off.

Zoe, please.

You hear me? That was the deal. They promised whenever I wanted.

Capture 06/15/2051, Kerwin Hospital ICU, 09:37:18, Augment disengaged by request

Andy? Look at me, Andy. Over here. Good. Who am I, Andy?

You are... it's something about science fiction. And a blue hat.

What's my name?

Come close. Let me look at you… oh, it's on the tip of my tongue.
Nacky Martinez? First officer of the Starship *Sidewise*?
She's a character, Andy. Made up. Someone I wrote about.
You're a writer?

Capture 06/17/2051, Kerwin Hospital Assisted Care Facility, 14:47:03
…because I was too infatuated to be suspicious about your secret back
then. I know you don't remember this, Andy, but I was stupid in love
with you when we were first married. Maybe the augment can't see
that, but anyone who looks at your captures can. On the record, as you
would say. So, yeah, the fact that you always wore caps and recorded
almost everything that happened to you didn't bother me back then. I
guess I told myself that it was some reputation management scheme that
Spaceways had ordered up. And of course, you were writing the sequel
to your memoir. What do Mr. and Ms. Space Hero do on their days off?
Why look, they sit together on the couch when they write! And she still
uses her fingers to type – isn't that quaint, a science fiction writer still
pounding a keyboard in the era of thought recognition!
You never published that book.
No.
Or any other. Why?
You know, people message me about that all the time, like it was some
kind of tragedy. I had something to say when I was young and naive. I
said it. And pretty damn well: eight livebooks worth. Fifty novas. It's
just that after I met you, I needed to make the most of our time together.
And since you launched into the Vincente Event, I've been busy being the
good wife.
I was the best qualified pilot, Zoe. And I was already compromised,
so I had the least to lose. In a crisis like that, there were no easy
answers. I consulted with Spaceways and we weighed the tradeoffs
and we reached a decision. I had friends on that orbital. Drew
Bantry…
Drew was already dead. He just hadn't fallen down yet. And you were
not a tradeoff, Andy. You were my fucking husband.

I can see now how hard it must have been for you.

Oh, you saw it then, too. Which is why you never asked my permission, because you knew...

Go on.

What the hell were we talking about? How I had no suspicions about what the captures meant. That you were sick. I remember thinking how boring ten thousand hours of unedited recordings were going to be. Even to us, even when we were old. Old and forgetful...

Zoe?

I'm fine. I'm just not feeling very brave today. Anyway, I did have a problem with all the captures of us making love. I mean, the first couple of times, I'll grant you it was a turn-on. We'd lose ourselves in bed, and then afterwards watch ourselves doing it and sometimes we were so beautifully in sync that we'd get hot and go back for seconds. But what bothered me was that you were capturing us watching the captures. I didn't get why you would do that. When I realized that recording wasn't just a once-in-a-while kink, that you wanted to capture us every time we had sex, it wasn't erotic anymore. It was kind of creepy.

I can't locate any sex captures after 2045. Did we stop having sex?

No. I just made you check the caps at the bedroom door. So stop looking. You want to know what we were like back then, try scanning some of our private book clubs. We'd both read the same book and then we'd go out to dinner at a nice restaurant and talk about it. I remember being surprised at some of your choices. *The Marvelous Land of Oz. Lolita. Wolf Hall. A Visit From the Goon Squad.* They didn't seem like the kinds of reading an Air Force jock would choose. You were a Hemingway and Heinlein kind of guy.

Was I trying to impress you?

I don't know why. I was already plenty impressed. Maybe you were trying to send me a message with all of those plots about secret pasts and transformations.

Go on. This was where? When?

At first in Brooklyn, where I was living when we met. There's another reason I should have been suspicious your urgency. You claimed you didn't care where we lived as long as we spent as much time as possible together. Wasn't true – you hated cities. But most of my friends were in New York and most of yours had moved to space or Mars. Your folks were dead and your sister had disappeared into some Digitalist coop, waiting for the Singularity. So when my mother died and left me the house in Bedford, we moved up there in the spring of 2045. You had the second instalment of your book deal to write and when I switched to your agent, I started seeing celebrity level advances too, so there was plenty of money. By then you were showing early symptoms. You claimed you'd left Spaceways, although you still flew out here to Kerwin five or six times a year for therapy. It seemed to be working, you said we would still have years together. My mom had been into flowers but she had an asparagus patch and some raspberries and you started your first vegetable garden that summer. You were good at it, said you liked it better than space hydroponics. Spinach and lettuce and asparagus in the spring, then beans and corn and summer squash and tomatoes and melons. You were happy, I think. I know I was.

Capture 06/25/2051, Kerwin Hospital Assisted Care Facility, 16:17:53
...you were so skeptical about the Singularity is why.

The Kurzweil augmentation has nothing to do with the Singularity. Yeah, sure. It's just a cognitive prosthesis, *la-la*. A life experience database, *la-la-la*. An AI mediated memory enhancement that may help restore your loved one's mental competence *la-la-la-dee-da*. I've browsed all the sites, Andy. Besides, I was writing about this shit before Ray Kurzweil actually uploaded.

Ray Kurzweil is dead. I'm still alive.
Are you, Andy? Are you sure about that?
I don't know why you are being so cruel, Zoe.
Because you made so many decisions about us without telling me. Maybe you didn't know just how sick you were when we met, but you could easily have found out. I had a right to know. And maybe you were hoping that you'd never get that call from Spaceways, but you knew exactly what you would do if it did come.

I was an astronaut, Zoe. That was never a secret.

No, what was a secret was all that fucked-up cosmic ray research. Because nobody but crazy people with a death wish would ever have volunteered to go to space if they knew that there was no real protection against getting your telomeres burned off by the radiation. Sure, you can duck and cover from a solar flare, but what about the gajillions of ultra-high energy ions? Theoretically you can generate a magnetic shield. Or maybe you can stuff your astronauts with anti-radiation wonder drugs? But just in case it doesn't work, better make sure that everyone on the Mars crew is over forty. That way if Captain Kirk falls apart in twenty or thirty years, Spaceways won't look so bad.

   Go on.

I will. Maybe you hadn't checked out the secret radiation assessments from the first Mars mission when we first met. Maybe you didn't want to know. But once I was your wife, I did. Let me read the executive summary to you. "Exposure to radiation during the mission has had significant short and long impacts on the central nervous systems of all crew members. Despite best mitigation practices, whole body effective doses ranged from .4 to .7 Sieverts. Galactic cosmic radiation in the form of high-mass, energetic ions destroyed an average of 4% of the crew's cells, while 13% of critical brain regions have likely been compromised. Reports of short term impairments of behavior and cognition were widely noted throughout the three year mission. Longitudinal studies of the astronaut corps point to a significant increase in risk of degenerative brain diseases. In particular, there appears to have been an acceleration of plaque pathology associated with Alzheimer's disease." Let's do the math, Andy. You get an estimated dose of between .4 to .7 Sieverts during your first mission and you go to Mars twice. So call it a Sievert and change. Which is why you were one grounded astronaut.

   All that's on the record.

What's EPA's maximum yearly dose for a radiation worker here on earth?

   I don't have immediate access to that data. I can look it up.

Yes, you can – it's on the record. Fifty millisieverts. How about for emergency workers involved in a lifesaving operation?

   Zoe, I...

Two hundred and fifty millisieverts.

There are always risks.

For which you make tradeoffs, I get that. So the tradeoff here is X number of years of your life for two tickets to Mars. Which you decided before you met me, so I'll give you a pass on that. Once you walked me through it, I sort of got how that was the price you paid to become who you wanted to be. Although you waited long enough to let me in on your little secret. But that wasn't your last tradeoff. Because Spaceways fell down on their project management during the outfitting of Orbital Seven. They didn't lift enough solar flare shelters to house everybody on the construction crew. So when Professor Vincente predicted an X2 class flare that would cook half the people onboard in a storm of hot protons, management turned to sixty-year-old Captain Kirk, even though he'd been grounded. They pointed out that since he didn't have all that much time before the Alzheimer's plaques chewed what was left of his memory, maybe he might consider riding the torch one last time to ferry an emergency shelter up to save their corporate asses. Or maybe our Space Hero checked in all on his own and volunteered for their fucking suicide mission.

It wasn't a suicide mission , Zoe. I came back.

And here you are, Andy. And here I am. But it's not working.

Capture 06/30/2051, Kerwin Hospital ICU, 11:02:53

...or are you too busy with your life review? Ten thousand hours of captures is a lot to digest, even on fast-forward.

The record is eleven thousand two hundred and eighty-four hours long, not including the current capture.

Noted. Find anything worth bookmarking?

It would be a dull movie if it wasn't all about me.

I heard about your ex yesterday on Newsmelt. I'm sorry. I didn't realize she'd emigrated to Mars.

Apparently she wanted to get to space as much as I did. I don't know why I didn't know that. It's odd, but none of the pix and vids I have look like her.

You remember her then?

Just flashes, but they're very vivid. Like she was lit up by a lightning strike.

They're talking about bringing the rest of the colonists back home.

Maybe. But they'll have to handcuff them and drag them kicking and screaming onto the relief ships – I know those people. And why bother? Many of them won't survive the trip back.

Space will kill you any which way it can. You told me that on our third date.

I try not to pay attention. It's been a long time since there's been any good news from outer space. I think we need to start over on Mars. The thing to do is capture a comet, hollow it out and use it as a colony ship. The ice shields you from cosmic rays on the outbound. Send the colonists down in landers and then crash the comet. Solves both the water and the radiation problem.

Capture a comet? And how the hell do we do that? With a tractor beam? A magic lasso?

Get your science fiction friends working on it. If it's crazy enough, the engineers will come sniffing around.

I'll see what I can do. I met the Zhangs on the way in today. I thought I was your only visitor. We had a nice chat. And the baby was cute. What's her name again?

Andee. A-N-D double E.

That's what I thought they said. After you.

Kristen was lucky. They pushed her to the front of the line so she was one of the first into the shelter. The last three in got a significant dose. One of them died on the way back down.

Drew Bantry.

They were his people. He waited until they were all safe.

You and he saved a lot of lives that day, Captain Kirk. It's on the record for all to see.

Enough, Zoe. What do you have for me today?

Apologies.

Go on.

I'm sorry for the way I spoke to you last time. That's why I missed the last few visits. I don't trust myself to say the right thing anymore. I can't filter out my feelings when I see you like this. I just blurt. Spew. It's not good.

Noted.

But here's the thing. I don't think I'll be accessing your augment after you're... gone. Dead. You know, now I can visit the hospital here, and see you. Your face, your body, arms, hands. But some avatar, no. It's too hard. There have been times the last few weeks when I felt like you're here with me, but that's only because I want you back. But mostly I don't think this thing that talks to me is you. I'm sorry.

Why not?

There's still too much missing, even if the augment can review your captures and all that input from before you started wearing the caps. Yes, we can talk about our lives together, but I still have to tell you things you should know. And now you're cracking jokes, so it's even harder. How can I tell whether what's sad or happy or angry is you or clever algorithms? I don't know, Andy. When are you going to say I love you? How will I know whether you really do, or if it's just something else you needed to be reminded of?

I do, Zoe. Here, I'll turn the augment off, so you can hear it from me. From this body, as you say. These lips.

No, honey, you don't need to...

Capture 06/30/2051, Kerwin Hospital ICU, 11:15:18, Augment disengaged by request

Okay? Here I am. And I know who you are. I do. You're my famous wife, the writer. Nacky Martinez. You want to go. I don't want you to go. Give me your hand.

Aye, Captain.

Stay with me. Will you do that?

For a while.

And write more books. You know, about your adventures in space. That's important. And maybe... could get me my snacks? The food here is horrible. You know the ones. Mom always used to make banana slices with a smear of peanut butter when I got home from school. My snacks. Are you crying, Nacky? You're crying.

Yes.

THE MASTER CONJURER

Charlie Jane Anders

Charlie Jane Anders (www.charliejane.com) is the author of *Choir Boy*, which won a Lambda Literary Award in 2005. Her story "Six Months, Three Days" won the 2012 Hugo Award. Her journalism and other writing has appeared in *Salon*, the *Bay Guardian*, the *New York Press*, *Mother Jones*, *McSweeney's*, and the *Wall Street Journal*. With Annalee Newitz, she edited the anthology *She's Such a Geek: Women Write about Science, Technology, and Other Nerdy Stuff* (Seal Press, 2006). She lives in the San Francisco Bay area, where she is the managing editor of the science fiction website *io9*.

PETER DID A magic spell, and it worked fine. With no unintended consequences, and no weird side effects.

Two days later, he was on the front page of the local newspaper: "The Miracle Conjurer." Some blogs picked it up, and soon enough he was getting visits from CNN and MSNBC, and his local NPR station kept wanting to put him on. News crews were standing and talking in front of his house.

By the third day, Peter saw reporters looking through the dumpster in the back of his L-shaped apartment building, which looked like a cheap motel but was actually kind of expensive. He couldn't walk his Schnauzer-Pit Bull mix, Dobbs, without people – either reporters or just random strangers – coming up and asking him what his secret was. When he went to the office, where he oversaw pilot projects for water desalination, his co-workers kept snooping over the top of his cubicle wall and trying to see his computer screen as he was typing, like they were going to catch him logging in to some secret bulletin board for superwizards.

Peter had a hard time concentrating on work when the TV set in the breakroom was tuned to CNN, and they were showing his bedroom window, and a million people were staring at the pile of unfolded laundry on his bed and the curtains that Dobbs had recently half-destroyed. *Could the Clean Spell revolutionize spellcasting?* a voice asked. *Was there a secret, and could everyone else learn it?* CNN brought on an Enchantress named Monica, who wore a red power blazer. She frequently appeared on talk shows whenever there was a magical murder trial or something.

By day four, Peter's building was surrounded, and his phone at work pretty much never stopped ringing. People followed him wherever he went. It was only then that it occurred to Peter: Maybe *this* was the unintended consequence of his spell.

PETER HAD NEVER liked looking at pictures of himself, because photos always made him look like a deformed clone of Ben Affleck. His chin was just a little too jutting and bifurcated, his brow a little too much like the bumper of a late-model Toyota Camry. His mousy hair was unevenly receding, his nose a little too knifey. Seeing the least attractive pictures of himself on every newspaper, website, and TV show was starting to make Peter break out in hives.

"I'm not talking to you," Peter said to his former best friend Derek, the tenth time Derek called him. "You are completely dead to me."

"Hey, don't say that, you're scaring me," Derek said. "If the Master Conjurer says I'm dead, then I'm worried I'm just not going to wake up tomorrow or something."

"You were the only one I told about doing the spell," Peter said. "And now, this."

Peter was sitting in his car talking on his phone, parked two blocks away from his apartment building because he was scared to go home. Dobbs was probably starting to bounce off the walls. At least the dog seemed a lot happier lately.

"I only told like a couple of people," Derek said. "And it turned out one of them was best friends with a newspaper reporter. It was an amusing anecdote. Anyway, you know it'll blow over in a week or two. You're just like this week's meme or something."

"I hope you're right," Peter said.

"And you should milk it, while you got it," Derek said. "Like, you know, you're *famous for doing something perfectly*. Something that requires immense concentration and sensory awareness and a lot of heart. Basically, they're as good as announcing to the entire world that you're an excellent lover. This is probably the closest you will ever come in your entire life to being a chick magnet."

"Please stop talking now." Peter was practically banging his head against the steering wheel of his Dodge Neon. "Just, please, stop."

The interior of his car always smelled like dog; not like Dobbs – just, like: generic dog. Like a big rangy golden retriever smell. Even if Dobbs hadn't been in his car for days.

"Okay, okay. Just an idea, man. So are we good?"

"I don't know. Maybe."

Peter hung up and steeled himself to go home and walk the dog, while people asked him his secret over and over. Nobody would ever believe Peter when he said there was no secret – he'd just lucked out, or something. Why couldn't Peter have gotten an intimidating dog that he could sic on people, like a Doberman or a purebred Pit Bull? If he unleashed Dobbs, someone might end up with a tiny drool stain on one shoe.

BUT PETER COULDN'T stop thinking about what Derek had said. He hadn't been on a date, a proper date, for years. His last first date had been Marga, five years ago. Peter wasn't just out of practice dating, or asking people out – he was out of practice at *wanting* to. He hadn't even let himself have a crush on anybody in forever.

He started looking at the women around him as if he could actually be something to them. He didn't perv anybody, or stare at anyone – after all, everybody was still staring at him, all the time, and his instinct in that situation was to look away, or just hide. But it was hard to go from never noticing women – except in a super-business-like way – to checking them out, and he might have overcompensated. Or maybe he overcompensated for his overcompensation. It was tricky.

Nobody at work was Peter's type, and anyway they wouldn't stop asking him over and over if he would do a spell for them. He had already made up his mind that he would never do a spell ever again.

He couldn't be attracted to any of the women who kept coming up to him when he was trying to eat dinner at the Shabu Palace, either the reporters or the professional witches or the random looky-loos. They were all a little too sharky for him, the way they circled and then homed in, and they mostly looked as though they used insane amounts of product in their hair, so if they ever actually rested their heads on his shoulder, there would be a "crunch" sound.

THE WEIRDEST PART wasn't the stalkers or the peepers or the people asking him to do spells for them. The weirdest part was: after about a week, Peter started noticing that everybody had their own "this one time" story they wanted to tell him. Things had slacked off just enough that Peter wasn't quite under siege any more, and strangers were having conversations with him on the street instead of just rushing up and blurting questions. And every conversation included a "this one time" story. They were usually really sad, like confessions that people had never told anyone, that – for some reason – they felt safe telling Peter.

Like, one woman with curly red hair and a round white face and a marigold sweater was telling Peter at the supermarket, by the breakfast cereals: "I never tried to do any magic myself. Too risky, you don't really know. Right? Except this one time, I got wasted and tried to do a spell to make my dad give back the money he stole from my mom. It wasn't even my problem, but I was worried about Mom, she had a lot of medical expenses with the emphysema. And Dad was just going to waste it on his new girlfriend (she had expensive tastes). So I just wanted him to give back the money he took from my mom's secret hiding place."

Peter knew this was the part where he was supposed to ask what terrible fallout the woman's spell had had.

"Oh," she said. "My dad went blind. He gave Mom her money back, and as soon as it changed hands, there went his eyesight. I've never told anybody this before." She smiled, nervously, like Peter was going to tell on her. Even though he didn't even know her name.

"You couldn't know," Peter said, like he always said to people after he heard their stories. "You had no way of knowing that would happen. You were trying to do the right thing."

Peter had done a few spells before he cast the world-famous Clean Casting, which by now had been verified by every professional sorcerer who had a regular television gig. (There had been a lot of incense burning around Peter's apartment building for a while there, which had helped banish the stench of his neighbor Dorothy's homebrew experiments.) Peter had taken a spell-casting class at the local community college a few years before, with Marga, and they had done a few really tiny spells, lighting candles from a distance or turning a pinch of sugar into salt. They got used to weird smells or small dead creatures popping up an hour or a day later.

If the spell was small enough, the unintended downside was part of the fun – an amusing little surprise. *Oh, look. A goldfish in the mailbox, still flapping about. Get a bowl of water, quick!*

By now, the actual doing of the spell – the Clean Casting – felt like a weird dream that Peter had concocted after too many drinks. The more people made a fuss about it, the more he felt like he'd made the whole thing up. But he could still picture it. He'd gotten one of the stone spellcasting bowls they sold on late-night cable TV, and little baggies of all the ingredients, with rejected prog rock band names like Prudenceroot or Womanheart, and sprinkled pinches of them in, while chanting the nonsense syllables and thinking of his desired aim. The spellbook, with its overly broad categories of enchantments that you could slot your specifics into like *Mad Libs*, was propped open with a package of spaghetti. All of it, he'd done correctly more or less. Not perfect, but right. He'd done it in his oversized pantry, surrounded by mostly empty jars of stale oats and revolting cans of peaches, with Dobbs goggle-eyed and drooling, the only witness.

*   *   *

THE TIME CAME when Peter could leave the house again without people shoving things in his face. He still had people coming up to him in the bookstore to ask him if he was that guy, and his co-workers would never stop making weird remarks about it. And he made a point of not googling himself. Or checking his personal email, or going on Facebook.

But just when Peter thought maybe his life was returning to semi-normal, some guy would see him and come running across the street – through traffic – to belt out something about his baby, his baby, Peter had to help, the man needed a spell and the consequences would probably be unbearable if anybody but Peter attempted it. Peter would have to shrug off the crying, red-faced man, and keep going to the pet food store or supermarket.

There was a girl working at the pet food store who apparently knew who Peter was, and didn't seem to care. She had curly brown hair and really strong lines from the bridge of her nose down around her eyes, which made her look sort of intense and focused. She had a really pointy chin and a pretty nose, and seemed like the kind of person who laughed a lot. Even when she looked serious, which she mostly did. She always smiled at Peter when she rang up the special food that Dobbs needed for his pancreas, but not in a starey way.

Finally, one day, a few weeks after all this started, Peter asked her why she hadn't ever said anything about his claim to fame. She rolled her eyes. "I dunno, I figured you were sick of hearing about it. Plus, who cares. It's not like you won the lottery or anything, right?"

Peter immediately asked her if she wanted to grab some dinner sometime. She was like, "Sure. As long as it's not medicinal dog food." Her name turned out to be Rebecca.

Actually, they went to the Shabu place that was Peter's favorite restaurant in town. He always felt guilty for eating there alone, which he did often, because it was kind of an interactive experience, where you grilled your own meat and/or made your fancy stew, and you really needed someone else there to join in. The staff wore crisp white uniforms to underscore that they did no actual food preparation themselves. There were tables, but almost everybody sat around a big U-shaped bar in the center, which had little grills embedded in it. The sound system blasted a mixture of Foreigner, 38 Special, Yes, and some J-Pop from a CD-changer.

Peter was nervous about being seen out on a date, and having people act weird about it during or afterward. (*Did you cast a "babe magnet" spell? Ha-ha-ha.*) But the Shabu Palace was pretty empty, and a few people stared a little bit but it was no big deal. Peter found the meat vapors comforting, like carnal incense.

"I hate this town," Rebecca said. "It's just big enough to have restaurants like this, but no actual culture. We don't even have a roller derby team any more. No offense, but that's one reason why you're such a big deal. We finally have a local celebrity again, to replace that sitcom actor who was from here who died." Peter wasn't offended by that at all, it explained a lot.

Rebecca was saving up money from her pet store gig to go to L.A., where she wanted to go to barista school. Peter didn't know that was a thing you went to school for, but apparently it was a big deal, like knowing the science of grinding the beans just right and making just the right amount of ristretto and steaming the milk to the edge of burning. And of course latte art and stuff. Rebecca had tried to be a psychologist and a social worker and a vet, but none of those career paths had worked out. But she was excited about the barista thing because it was hip and artistic, and you could write your own ticket. Even start your own fancy café somewhere.

"It's cool that you're so ambitious," Peter said. "I think L.A. would drive me insane."

"I am guessing L.A. would be okay as long as you don't want to be a movie star or whatever," Rebecca said. "I mean, the barista school is probably hella cutthroat. But I can handle that."

Peter hadn't really thought of this as a small town – it seemed pretty big to him. There was a freeway, and the downtown with the opera house, and the art museum, and the world headquarters of a major insurance company. And there was a small zoo during the spring and summer, with animals that wintered in Florida somewhere.

"People hate you, you know," Rebecca told Peter halfway through dinner. "You're super threatening, because you're the proof that there's something wrong with them. If they'd only been good people, they would have gotten away clean, too. Plus, it offends our sense of order. Power should have terrible consequences, or life would be too easy. We want people to suffer for anything good they ever have. People are governed by envy, and a sense of karmic brutality."

"That's a very bleak view of human nature," Peter said. But he found it kind of a turn-on. Misanthropy was just undeniably sexy, the way smoking used to be before you had to do it out in the cold.

It turned out Rebecca had never even tried to do magic herself. "I never wanted to risk it," Rebecca said. "I'm the least lucky person, of anyone I know. I can only imagine how badly I would be screwed if I tried to bribe the universe to give me a shortcut."

By now, Peter was really hoping that Rebecca would go home with him. He could almost imagine how cool it would be to have her naked and snarky in his big four-poster bed. Her body heaving to and fro. The way her hair would smell as he buried his face in it. He almost started getting hard under the counter of the Shabu Palace just thinking about it. Bryan Adams was singing about Heaven on the stereo. Everything was perfect.

"So," Rebecca said, leaning forward in a way that could have been flirtatious or conspiratorial. "I gotta ask. What was the spell that you did? The famous one?"

"Oh man." Peter almost dropped his meat piece. "You don't want to know. It's really dumb. Like really, really dumb."

"No, come on," Rebecca said. "I want to know. I'm curious. I won't judge. I promise."

"I... I'd rather not say." Peter realized he'd been about to lift this piece of meat off the grill for a while, and now it was basically a big carcinogenic cinder. He put it in his mouth anyway. "It's really kind of embarrassing. I don't even know if it was ethical."

"Now I really want to know," Rebecca said.

Peter imagined telling Rebecca what he'd done, and tried to picture the look on her face. Would she laugh, or throw sake at him and tell him he was a bad person? Immature? He couldn't even go there. Even Bryan Adams suddenly sounded kind of sad, and maybe a little disappointed in Peter.

"I'm sorry," Peter said. "I think this was maybe a mistake." He paid for both of them and got the hell out of there.

By the time Peter got home, Dobbs was freaking out because he really needed to go out and do his business. Dobbs ran around a tree three times before peeing on it, like he was worried the tree was going to move out of the way just as Dobbs was letting go. Dobbs looked up at Peter with big round eyes, permanently alarmed.

OF COURSE, DEREK called Peter the next morning and wanted to know how the date went. They ended up going for breakfast at the retro-1970s pancake place downtown, and Peter grudgingly told Derek the whole deal.

"So what you're saying," said Derek, "is that you plied her with meat and soft rock, and you had her basically all ready to Shabu your Shabu. And then she asked a perfectly reasonable question, and you got all weird and bailed on her. Is that a fair summary?"

"Um," Peter said. "It's not an *unfair* summary."

"Okay," Derek said. "I think there's a way this can still work out. Now she thinks you're complicated and damaged. And that's perfect. Ladies love men with a few psychic dents and scrapes. It makes you mysterious, and a little intense."

"You're the only one I've told about that spell," Peter said. "You didn't tell anyone what the spell actually was, right?"

"That part, I haven't told anyone," Derek said. "I only mentioned the part about how you had no complications."

"Okay, cool," said Peter. "I don't want people to go nuts on me. Even more than they already have."

"Listen," Derek said. "I'm kind of worried about you. I think this spell you did is just a symptom. I feel like you've been kind of messed up ever since Marga…" Derek trailed off, because Peter was scowling at him. "I just think you shouldn't be alone so much. I feel like a new relationship, or a fling – either way – would be good for you."

Derek and Peter had been friends since college, where they'd bonded over hating their History 101 professor, who had a cult following among almost all the other students. Literally a cult – there was a human sacrifice at one of the professor's after-exam parties, and it'd turned ugly, as human sacrifice so often does. Peter and Derek weren't so close lately, because Derek had gone into real estate and never had time for Peter; plus until pretty recently Peter had just been hanging out with Marga's friends all the time. Like Marga herself, her friends were all erudite and artsy, with clever tattoos.

"You don't have to worry about me," Peter said. "I've got Dobbs. And all I really wanted was to be left alone."

"We're not back to that again, are we?" Derek threw his arms up in a pose of martyrdom.

"It's okay," Peter said. "The media frenzy seems to have died down, and some other asshole is getting his fifteen minutes now."

PETER ALMOST CALLED Rebecca a couple times. He imagined telling her the truth about his spell, and it made him cringe from the balls of his feet to the back of his neck. He always put the phone away, because he didn't think he could work the "damaged and complicated" angle without telling the whole story. He went to sleep and dreamed of sitting naked with Rebecca in bed, explaining everything. He woke up with Dobbs sitting on his chest, legs tucked under his fat little body, saucer eyes staring at him. Dobbs licked Peter's chin in slow flicks of his brash tongue. Lick. Lick. Lick.

When Peter went to work, his face was on the television in the breakroom again. Some expert had concocted a theory: Maybe Peter was the reincarnation of an ancient wizard, or maybe he was some kind of spiritually-pure mystic or something. Obviously, if Peter really did know the secret of doing magic without any strings attached, he would be the world's richest and most powerful man. So he either really didn't have a secret method, or he was some kind of saint.

This day, in particular, Peter had a progress meeting with some of the other team leaders, and he was trying to explain why the desalination pilot projects he was funding were slow going. It's easy to add salt to water, but taking it away again is a huge challenge – you have to strip the sodium and chloride ions out of the water somehow, which involves a huge unfeasible energy cost. Peter got halfway through his presentation, when Amanda, who was involved in microfinance in Africa, asked, "So why don't you just use magic?"

"Um, sorry?" Peter said. He had clicked through to his next slide and had to click back, or risk losing his thread.

"Why not just use magic to remove the salt from the water?" Amanda said. "That gets around the high energy cost, and in fact there might be zero energy cost. Potable water for everybody. Water wars averted. Everybody happy."

"I don't really think that's an option," Peter said.

"Why not?" Amanda said. Everybody else was nodding. Peter remembered seeing Amanda on television, talking about him a few days earlier. She was the one who'd explained carefully that Peter had a twelve-year-old Dodge Neon and rented a one-bedroom apartment in a crumbling development near the freeway. If he was a master sorcerer, Amanda had told the ladies on *The View*, Peter was doing a pretty good job of hiding it.

Now Amanda was saying, in the same patient, no-nonsense tone: "Isn't it irresponsible not to explore all of the options? I mean, let's say that you really can do magic without some backlash, and you're the one person on Earth who can. What's the point spending millions to fund research into industrial desalination when you could just snap your fingers and turn a tanker of salt water into spring water?" This particular day, Amanda was wearing a blue paisley scarf and a gray jacket, along with really high-end blue jeans.

Peter stared at Amanda – whom he'd always admired for helping the poor women in Africa get microloans, and who he never thought would stab him in the back like this – and tried to think of a response. At last, he stammered: "Magic is not a scalable solution."

Peter fled the meeting soon afterward. He decided to take the rest of the day off work, since he was either fatally irresponsible or secretly the reincarnation of Merlin. He passed Amanda in the hallway on his way to the elevator, and she tried to apologize for putting him on the spot like that, but he just mumbled something and kept walking.

Dobbs wagged his tail as the leash went on, and then tried to play with the leash with one of his front paws, like it was a dangling toy. At last, Dobbs understood that the leash meant going outside and relieving himself, and he trotted.

PETER WENT TO bed early, with Dobbs curled up on top of his head like a really leaky hat. He dreamed about Rebecca again, and then his phone woke him up, and it was Rebecca calling him. "Whu," he said.

"Did I wake you?" she said.

"Yes," Peter scraped Dobbs off his forehead and got his wits together. His bed smelled foggy. "But it's okay. I was just waking up anyway. And listen, I've been meaning to call you. Because I need to explain, and I'm sorry I was such an idiot when we..."

"No time," Rebecca said. "I called to warn you. There's been an incident, and they're probably coming to your house again soon." She promised to explain everything soon, but meanwhile Peter should get the heck out of there before the TV news crews came back. Because this time, they would be out for blood. Rebecca said she would meet Peter at the big old greasy spoon by the railroad tracks, the one that looked like just another railroad silo unless you noticed the neon sign in the window.

Peter put on jeans and a T-shirt, grabbed Dobbs and got in his Neon just as the first people were getting out of their TV vans. He backed down the driveway so fast he nearly hit one of them and then sped off before they could follow. Just to make sure, he got on and off the freeway three times at different exits.

Rebecca was sitting at the booth in the back of the Traxx Diner, eating silver dollar pancakes and chicken fried steak. The formica table had exactly the same amount of stickiness as Rebecca's plate. Peter wound up ordering the chicken-fried steak too, because he was suddenly really hungry and it occurred to him he might have skipped dinner.

As soon as Peter had coffee, Rebecca shoved a tablet computer at him, with a newspaper article: "TWELVE DEAD, FIVE CHILDREN

UNACCOUNTED FOR IN SCHOOL DISASTER." One of the headlines further down the page was for a sidebar: "Peter Salmon: Made People Think They Could Get Off Scot Free?" And there was a picture of Peter, giving a thumbs up to a group of people – taken from his site visit to a water purification project in Tulsa two years earlier.

Peter spilled coffee on his pants. The waitress came and poured some more in his cup almost immediately.

"Don't worry," Rebecca said. "Ulsa won't tell anybody you're here. She's a friend. Plus she's really nearsighted so she probably hasn't gotten a good look at your face."

"Okay," Peter said. He was still trying to make sense of this article. Basically, there was a middle school in New Jersey that was coming in at the bottom of the rankings in the standardized tests, and state law would have called for the school to be closed by the end of the year, which, in turn, would wreck property values. So the teachers and some of the parents got together to do a spell to try and raise the children's test results by twenty percent, across the board. And it had gone very wrong. Like "everyone's heads had turned to giant crayfish heads" wrong. There were some very gruesome pictures of adults lying around the playground, their beady eyes staring upward. Meanwhile, some of the children had gone missing.

"There's no way anybody could say this is my fault," Peter stammered, trying not to look at the corpses with stuff leaking out of their necks, just as Ulsa brought a plate of very crispy chicken-fried steak with some very runny eggs. "I told everybody that I didn't have any secret. They just wouldn't listen."

"Yeah, I know," Rebecca said. "Like I said, people hate you. This is why I quit my last five jobs, including that pet store gig, which I just bagged on the other day. Everybody feels entitled. I've never had a boss who didn't feel like they ought to own me. People hate realizing that the world won't just shower them with candy."

Peter looked at the crayfish heads, then at his chicken-fried steak. In the car outside, through the one window, he could see Dobbs bouncing up and down. Like Dobbs already knew he was getting that steak. Then what Rebecca had said sunk in.

"You quit the pet store job?" Peter said, looking up at her.

"Yeah. They basically wanted me to do unpaid overtime, and they were trying to start a grooming business in the back, and wanted me to help with that as well. I do not groom."

Peter couldn't imagine just quitting a job, just like that. He felt his crush on Rebecca splintering a little bit. Like he'd put her on a pedestal too fast. "So what are you going to do now?" he said. "Are you going to go to L.A. and go to barista school?"

"Maybe. The next enrollment isn't for a few months. I guess I'll see how it goes."

Peter made himself eat a little because he was starting to have a full-scale panic attack. He gestured at the tablet without looking at it. "This is going to keep happening. And they're going to keep trying to make it about me."

The radio in the diner quit playing some country song about a cheating man, and a news report about the New Jersey tragedy came on. Congress was talking about regulating magic, and there were questions about whether the makers of the spellbook the teachers had used could have some liability, even though it had five pages of disclaimers in tiny print. And there was a mention in passing of the notion that the teachers might have been influenced by the famous Clean Casting.

"What if there really was some secret and you had it?" Rebecca said. "If I were you, I'd be doing more spells and seeing if I could figure out what I did right. You could have anything you wanted. You could raise the dead and feed the hungry."

"I would never get away with it. I was really selfish and stupid that one time, and I came away with a super-strong feeling that I'd better never try my luck again."

And then Peter decided to go ahead and tell her about the spell:

"Here's what happened. I was engaged to this girl named Marga. She was amazing and artistic and creative, and she was always doing things like repainting her apartment with murals, or throwing parties where everybody pretended to be a famous assassin. And she had this cat that was always sickly. Constant vet visits and late-night emergencies. She and I moved in together. And then a few months before the wedding, she met this guy named Breck who was a therapeutic flautist, and she fell in love with him. She wound up going with him to Guatemala to provide music therapy to the victims of the big mudslide there. Leaving me heartbroken, with a sick cat. The cat just got more and more miserable and ill, pining for Marga. We were both inconsolable."

"I think maybe I can see where this is going," Rebecca said, picking at her last pancake.

"Dobbs is way happier as a dog, he gets to go out and run around," Peter said. "His pancreas seems way better, too."

"So you turned your ex-girlfriend's cat into a dog. As, like, revenge?"

"It wasn't revenge, I swear. She doesn't even know, anyway. I just… Dobbs was really unhappy, and so was I. And this seemed like it was a fresh start for both of us. But part of me felt like maybe I was doing it to get back at Marga, or like I was transforming Dobbs without his consent. And I welcomed the idea of being punished for it. So when the punishment didn't come, it just made me feel more guilty. I started to hate myself. And maybe that's why. The more I didn't get punished, the worse I felt."

"Huh." She seemed to be chewing it over for a moment. "I guess that's not the weirdest thing I've heard of people doing to their pets. I mean, at the store, there were people who shaved their pets' asses. Who does that? And your ex is the one who left her cat behind when she bailed, right? You could have taken him to the ASPCA, and they'd have put him to sleep."

And just like that, Peter had a crush on her again. Maybe even something stronger than a crush, like his kidneys were pinwheeling and the blood was leaving his head and extremities. He wanted to jump up and hug her and make a loud train-whistle sound. He hadn't realized how guilty he'd been feeling about Dobbs, until he told someone and they didn't instantly hate him.

"Do you want to go to L.A.?" Peter said.

"What, now?"

"Yeah. Now. I mean, as soon as we finish breakfast. You can try and go to that barista school, and I can get a job there. I know a guy who works in solar power financing. I'd barely even be famous by L.A. standards."

For a second, Peter felt like he was totally free. He could leave town, with the girl and the dog and whatever else he had in his car, and never look back. He could be like Marga, except that he wouldn't abandon Dobbs.

But Rebecca shook her head. Curls splashing. "Sorry. I don't think I could ever be with someone who thinks it's a good idea to run away from his problems."

"What?" And then Peter said the exact wrong thing, before he could stop himself: "But you just told me that you quit your last five jobs."

"Yes, and that's called having a spine. Quitting a job isn't the same thing as running away."

She got up, and Peter got up too. He was getting a doggie bag for the steak, and he felt as though she was cutting him loose with a pack of wolves on his tail. And then she reached out and unsmudged the corner of his mouth with her thumb, and said: "Listen. I'm going to tell you the secret to getting what you want out of life. Are you ready? *Never take any shit from anyone.*"

"That's the secret? Of happiness?"

"I don't know about happiness. I told you, I'm unlucky."

She walked back toward her car, then stopped to look at Dobbs, who was bouncing up and down inside Peter's car, especially now that he could tell Peter was coming back. Dobbs' eyes were almost perfect spheres, like a Pekingese, and his tongue was sticking out of the side of his mouth, spraying bits of drool. Rebecca leaned over and stuck her hand through the window Peter had left rolled down a bit, and Dobbs licked her. She nodded at Peter, like confirming that yes, the dog was really okay, then went and got in her own car, which was even older and junkier than his.

He watched her drive away. Her radio was playing classic rock. He wasn't sure how you gave chicken-fried steak to a dog, but he figured he should fork it over while it was hot. Wouldn't you know it, as soon as he tipped it out of the bag onto the passenger seat and Dobbs started chewing on it, the steak suddenly smelled incredibly good and Peter felt a fierce hunger deep in his core. For a second, part of Peter wanted to snatch the food out of his dog's mouth.

He thought about what Rebecca had said: *Don't take any shit from anyone.* He'd heard people say stuff like that before, but it still felt like a major life philosophy. Like words to live by. He found his phone, which had like twenty messages on it, which he ignored and called Derek.

"Hey, can you do me a favor? Yeah, this is a chance to make up for telling your friend about me in the first place," he said. "Whatever, I'm over it. But can you go by my house and tell all the people camped out there that I'll do a press conference or something? At noon. I'll tell them the whole story about the spell, and answer their questions, and then they will leave me the fuck alone forever after that. Okay? Great."

After Peter hung up, he watched Dobbs eat the last bits of food. He got back in his car and drove around, trying to think of how to explain himself to everybody so they would leave him alone afterwards.

"Hey guy." Peter stroked Dobbs behind the ears when they were at a stoplight. "Are you ready for your moment in the spotlight?" In response, Dobbs extended his head, blinked, and sprayed vomit all over the inside of Peter's car. Then Dobbs sprawled in the seat, as if he'd just accomplished something awesome, and started to purr loudly. Like a jackhammer.

THE PILGRIM AND THE ANGEL

E. Lily Yu

E. Lily Yu (elilyyu.com) was the 2012 recipient of the John W. Campbell Award for Best New Writer and a 2012 Hugo, Nebula, and World Fantasy Award nominee. In 2012 she attended the Sewanee Writers' Conference as a Stanley Elkin Scholar, and in 2013 she attended Clarion West. Her stories have appeared in *McSweeney's, Clarkesworld, Boston Review, Kenyon Review Online, Apex,* and *The Best Science Fiction and Fantasy of the Year.* She is working on a novel, a video game, and a PhD.

THREE DAYS BEFORE Mr. Fareed Halawani was washed and turned to face the northeast, a beatific smile on his face, he had the unusual distinction of entertaining the angel Gabriel at the coffeeshop he operated in the unfashionable district of Moqattam in Cairo. Fareed was tipped back in his monobloc chair, watching the soccer game on television. The cigarette between his lips wobbled with disapproval at the referee's calls. Above him on the wall hung the photograph of a young man, barely eighteen, bleached to pale blue. His rolled-up prayer mat rested below. It was a quiet hour before lunch, and the coffeeshop was empty. Right as the referee held up a yellow card, a scrub-bearded man strode in.

"Peace to you, Fareed," the stranger boomed. "Arise!"

Fareed laughed and tapped out a grub of ash. "Peace to you. New to the neighborhood?"

"Not at all. I know you, Fareed," the stranger said. "You pray with devotion and give generously to the poor."

"So does my neighbor," said Fareed, "though that hasn't helped him find a husband for his big-nosed daughter. Can I get you a glass of tea?"

"The one thing you lack to perfect your faith is the hajj."

"Well, with business as slow as it is, and one thing and another..." Fareed coughed. "Truth is, may God forgive me, I'm saving up to visit my son. He's an electrician in Miami. Doesn't call home. What would you like to drink?"

"I have come to take you on hajj."

"I've got too much to do without that," Fareed said. He had quarrelled half the night with Umm Ahmed over their son, whose lengthening silence his wife interpreted as pneumonia or incarceration or death, though Fareed supposed it was simply the cheerful thoughtlessness of the young. He had washed six stacks of brown glasses caked and swirled with tea dust, his joints sour from four hours' sleep, before unrolling his shirtsleeves and sitting down to his soccer match. But for the rigorous sense of hospitality that his own father had drummed into him, nothing could have stirred him from his chair, his chewed cigarette, and the goals that Al-Ahly was piling up over Zamalek. His bones clicked as he stood. He reached for a clean glass.

But the angel spread his stippled peacock-colored wings, which trembled like paper and made the room run with light, and said again, simply, "I am taking you on hajj."

Fareed choked on his cigarette. "Now? Me? Are you crazy? I have customers to care for!"

Gabriel glanced around the deserted shop and shrugged, his wings dipping and prisming the walls. Then he vanished. The prayer mat propped against the wall fluttered open and enfolded Fareed. While he kicked and expostulated, it carried him headfirst out the door and into the clear hard sky, to the astonishment of a motorcyclist sputtering past.

"Sir! Sayyid! Are you djinn or demon?" Fareed called out. "Where are you taking me? What have I done?"

"I am taking you on hajj!" the angel said joyfully from within the rug, his voice muffled, as if by a mouthful of wool.

"If you are taking me anywhere," Fareed said, struggling against the tightening mat, "make it Miami. And you have to get me home by midnight. Umm Ahmed will worry, and I have to shut up the shop." He finally freed his arms from the grapple of the prayer mat. Below them, the countryside zoomed by, green and very distant. Fareed blanched.

"I can circle the globe as fast as thought," said Gabriel. "Of course we'll have you home by then."

"Perhaps a little slower, I have a heart condition," Fareed said, but they whistled up like a rocket, and the wind hammered the next words back into his throat.

WHEN HE DARED to look again, the silver trickle of the Delta flared below them. Then they were gliding over the shark tooth of the Sinai and the crinkling, inscrutable sea.

"This is really not necessary," Fareed shouted. "If I sell my shop I can buy an economy-class Emirates ticket to Jeddah tomorrow. You can send me home now."

"No need to sell your shop!" the angel said. "No need to wrestle suitcases through the airport and sit for hours with someone's knees in the small of your back. No need to worry."

"Right," Fareed said miserably.

By the time they reached the Arabian Peninsula, the dry, scouring wind had become unbearable. "Water," Fareed croaked. "Please, water."

"So spoke Ishmael in Hagar's lap," Gabriel said within the mat. "She had nothing to give him but prayers and tears. But I heard her crying out. I struck the ground with the tip of my wing, and water poured forth."

"Water!"

"Yes, water as clear and cool as glass. That was the well Zamzam. I shall take you to drink from it."

Fareed groaned a sand-scratched groan, then shut his eyes and muttered over and over the suras of the dying.

"Here we are," Gabriel said, what felt like hours later, lofting a red-faced Fareed onto a heap of sand. "That's Juhfa in the distance. Come, put on your ihram."

"What ihram?" Fareed said.

But as he spoke, a bright, cold stream boiled up from the ground, and the prayer mat unraveled and wove itself into two soft white rectangles, which settled like tame doves at his feet.

Fareed gulped the sweet water, washed himself as well as he could, then peeled off his shirt and trousers and wound the white cloths about himself. The stream receded as silently as it had sprung up, the dark stain it made in the sand drying at once to nothing.

He had barely caught his breath when his white drapes shut like a fist and lifted him high into the air.

Wonders upon wonders, Fareed thought. But why him? Why an indulgent father, an inattentive husband, whose kindnesses were small and tea glass sized? Why would any angel bother himself with someone so unworthy?

Guilt niggled at him like a pebble in his shoe as he sailed over towns and sandy wastes. He could see Umm Ahmed rolling her eyes and shaking her head, hands on hips. *Angels? You say angels took you to Mecca? This is why you left the shop unlocked and unwatched? What kind of a layabout husband did I marry? You want me to call you Hajji now? Are you kidding me?* It filled him with a terrified kind of love.

"What am I going to tell Umm Ahmed?" he moaned.

"The truth! That your piety and prayers have been recognized. That Gabriel himself has led you on pilgrimage."

"She will throw shoes at me," Fareed sighed.

"Look," the angel said, as if he had not heard. They were descending through glittering skyscrapers and moon-tipped minarets. The Grand Mosque loomed before them, a wedding cake of marble that stunned Fareed to speechlessness.

He had always imagined making the pilgrimage as a fat and successful old man, cushioned by Umm Ahmed's sarcastic good humor and Ahmed's bright chatter. Now he had neither. Loneliness shivered and rang in him like a note struck from a bell.

Fareed barely had time to stammer the talbiyah through parched lips as they flew around the Kaaba, once, twice, seven times, his body cradled in the unseen angel's arms. His mumble was swallowed up in the susurrus of prayer rising from the slow white foam of pilgrims below. Fareed knew he was in the presence of the divine. He was humbled.

"Here is your Zamzam water," the angel said. A plastic pitcher ascended to them, revolving slowly. Fareed grasped it and drank.

"Now hold tight," the angel said, although Fareed had nothing to hold on to. The pitcher tumbled away like a meteor. "Over there is the path between Safa and Marwa, paved, enclosed, and air-conditioned now. Very comfortable and convenient."

"I don't suppose –"

"No! We shall take the path as Hagar found it, the hot noonday sun beating upon her head. Think: your child dying in exile. Think: how strong her faith, how deep her despair."

Fareed and the angel swooped seven times over the crenellations and cascades of white marble. As they hurtled over the walkway, dry air whipping their faces, Fareed imagined the rubble and grit below the elaborate masonry. He saw in his mind a thin dark woman plunging barefoot over the stones, tearing her black hair, her child left beneath a thornbush to suck thirstily at shadows. He thought of Umm Ahmed's reddened eyes and weary, dismissive waving – *leave me alone, my son is gone* – and of the phone that shrilled and yammered all day but rarely spoke with his son's voice. The image he held of his son was the photograph of Ahmed in uniform, taken during his mandatory service, when he was still a boy and anxious to please.

"Now –" the angel began, but Fareed spoke first, flapping his arms as he hung in the air.

"Enough! Enough!"

"But you haven't –"

"Give me my clothes and my shoes."

"Your faith is incomplete without the hajj," Gabriel remonstrated. "What answer will you give the other angels when they question you?"

Fareed felt cold despite the thick sunlight. His chest tightened. "Where are you taking me?"

"On hajj."

"No. Take me to my clothes."

The angel swerved out of the mosque. They returned to the desert place where his shirt and trousers lay folded beside his shoes. Only a little sand had accumulated in the heels. As Fareed stooped for them, his ihram fell away and became once more his threadbare prayer mat.

Beside him, the angel coalesced into a bluish glow containing edges and angles and complex, intersecting wings. Only the vaguest suggestion of a face shimmered in the chaos. He was painful to behold.

"Shall I bring you home?"

Fareed straightened, dust swirling and settling in his damp garments and sweat-sticky hair. A decision crystallized on his tongue. "If this is real and true, and I am not dreaming – if you are truly an angel and no evil spirit – then you will please take me to see my son."

"After all of this? After I brought you in my arms to the Honored City, to Masjid al-Haram itself – you want to go to America?"

"Especially after all of this," Fareed said. "If you are capable of these marvels, you can transport me to Florida as well."

The angel extruded a finger from chaos and curled it around his chin.

Fareed said, "Hagar burned and tore her feet as she ran in search of water for her son. Did you not hear her weeping?"

"That I did."

"And out of pity for her and her child you caused water to flow from barren rock."

"That is true."

"Then perhaps pity will move you to carry me to Miami," said Fareed. "I have not seen my son in three years." He folded his arms. "I did not ask you to come. I did not ask to be taken on hajj. I did not ask to be hauled out of my shop without so much as a note to my wife."

"Also true."

Fareed put one hand over his breast, where a dull ache was growing. "So take me to see my son. This once. It's the least you could do for me. Considering."

Deep inside the blue matrix of the angel, polygons meshed and disentangled with a sound like silver bells.

"All right, enough, let's go," Gabriel said, dissolving. "Back on the prayer mat with you." The rug rose from the sand and hovered an inch above the ground, undulating smoothly.

Fareed looked at it and made a small, quiet, unhappy noise. He resolved that if he ever made it home, he would buy a new, less willful prayer mat, perhaps one of the cheap ones with a pattern of combs and pitchers that were made on Chinese looms.

ROLLED UP IN his prayer mat, Mr. Fareed Halawani of Moqattam, coffeeshop owner and pilgrim, came to an abrupt halt in front of the Chelsea Hotel in Miami. The carpet snapped straight, and Fareed spun once in the air before hitting the manicured lawn.

His son turned away from his pickup, shouldering a wreath of wires. He wiped sweat and wet hair out of his eyes, blinking against the sunlight and the mirages wavering out of the pavement.

"Dad?" he said, surprised.

Fareed stared up at the blue sky, bottomless as the one over Cairo, and listened to the strange, extravagant hiss of the lawn sprinkler. A single defiant dandelion bobbed above his nose, drifting in and out of focus. His stomach was still roiling from the rough flight across the Atlantic.

"That's it," Ahmed said, putting the back of his hand to his forehead. "I'm seeing things. I'm going crazy."

"You could pretend to be happy to see me," Fareed said.

"You can't possibly be here. You can't. I must have heatstroke."

"Go drink some water. I'll still be here when you get back."

His son extended a browned, broad hand and flinched when Fareed grasped it. But he helped his father to his feet.

"Do you believe me now?" Fareed said.

"What are you doing here?"

"Visiting you. You don't call home often enough."

"How did you get here?"

The prayer mat lay meekly upon the grass.

"An angel brought me, I think."

"An angel."

"Maybe an ifrit, it was horrible enough. We went to Mecca first, then came here. I insisted."

Ahmed stared. "Are you all right?"

"Of course I'm all right."

"Did you hit your head? Do you feel feverish?"

Fareed frowned. "You think I'm lying."

"No, I –" Ahmed shook his head. "I've got a job to finish here, okay? You can come with me while I do it, then we'll take you home and I'll – we'll figure out what to do with you." He picked up his black toolbox in one hand and offered the other to his father.

"I don't need to be supported," Fareed said. "I feel fine."

THE TRUCK'S TIRES squealed as they pulled off the highway onto a narrow, shaded road. Beards of gray moss trailed from the trees and brushed the top of the truck. Ahmed lived in a pleasant white box, its postage-stamp lawn planted with crimson creepers and edged with large, smooth stones.

"No visa, right?" Ahmed said, unlocking the door. "No passport?"

"Nothing. Very unofficial, this visit. But I don't think you have to worry about getting me home," Fareed said. He felt the rug twitch in his arms.

His son's house contained only things that were bright and new: chairs and tables in colorful plastics or upholstered in triangle prints, a glass bookcase stuffed with calendars and phonebooks, two photos in chromium frames on the wall. One of the photos was of Fareed, his wife, and Ahmed, taken seven years ago in Alexandria. The other photograph –

"Who is she?" Fareed said, nudging the frame so it hung askew.

His son flushed. "She's, I met her, ah, a few months ago—"

"I see."

"A year, actually," Ahmed said, looking away. "She's really nice. Very sweet. Really."

"Does she cook well? Is she a believer? Are you engaged?" Fareed stared at the picture. "Does she have a name?"

"Rosa." Ahmed shifted from one foot to another. "What do you want for dinner? I could make some fuul –"

"You do know your mother and I have been trying to find you a good Egyptian girl? Aisha's a sensible woman, thirty-six, steady job at the bank –"

"That isn't necessary."

"Apparently not." Fareed raised an eyebrow at Rosa, who beamed innocently from the frame. "You might have told us."

"I was going to."

"When was the last time you called, anyway?"

"I've been busy," Ahmed mumbled.

"I can see that."

"Business has been good."

"I'm – glad," Fareed said, glancing around the small room. The odor of newness filled his nose and made his chest twinge.

"Midnight," the angel whispered in his ear, faint as a breeze. "Five hours. You'll make a mess if you stay, you know. Hospital bills, no identification, no papers."

Fareed clasped his hands stiffly behind his back. "So, Rosa. Do I get to meet this woman?"

His son's silence hurt more than he expected.

"Is it my clothes? I'll change —"

"No."

"You can translate for me. Shouldn't she meet her fiancé's parents?"

"Fiancé? She's not —" Ahmed flung up his hands. "It's too complicated, Dad. Listen. If you paid someone, to bring you here –"

"I didn't," Fareed said quietly. "You have nothing to worry about. I'll be gone soon." He paused, studying his son. "If I let you do what you wanted when you were younger, it was out of love. Not wanting to see you caged up. I wonder if that was wrong of me."

"It was fine." Ahmed began to open and shut the cabinets.

Fareed sighed. "Do this for me," he said. He had spotted the black telephone on the counter, winking with unspoken messages, and now he lifted up the handset and held it out to his son. "Call your mother tonight. Just one phone call. Just one. She misses you. She needs you."

Ahmed hesitated, then nodded reluctantly.

"Don't worry about dinner. I should go."

"No, stay, please. I'll cook for you. You'll be impressed."

His son was different and strange in this house, taller and stronger than the boy Fareed remembered. He had worked confidently at the hotel, snipping, stripping, splicing, and now he conjured up knives, pans, chopping boards, a blue gas flame with the casual swiftness of experience.

To Fareed's surprise, Ahmed, who had never cooked or lifted a finger at home, made fuul with eggs and lemon-sauced lamb on rice. After cleaning the last crisp speck from his bowl, Fareed wiped his mouth on the back of his hand and pushed back from the table.

"It is very good."

Ahmed fixed his eyes on the floor, embarrassed.

"Two daughters," the angel said. "Three years apart. One will have your strong chin. One will have Umm Ahmed's singing voice."

"Call your mother," Fareed said. "And give Rosa my regards. I should be going." He glanced toward the sofa, over whose arm he had draped the prayer mat. A corner of the cloth fluttered, although there was no breeze in the room.

In their small flat in Moqattam, in the hours before dawn, Umm Ahmed rubbed a track in the floor with her pacing. Dinner had gone cold on the stove and moved uneaten into the fridge. The coffeeshop had been empty and unlocked. She had groped blindly over the lintel for the spare key and found it untouched, checked the register and found it still full. A thoughtful patron had turned off the television on his way out, though the ashtrays and water pipes still trailed gray ribbons in the air. Through the dimness of the shop the picture of Ahmed in fatigues, long faded to blue ghostliness, gazed down on her.

No one knew where her husband was. No one had seen him since morning. No one knew what had happened. She dropped into a kitchen chair, exhausted, and put her head in her arms. Stars and green neon lights glowed outside the window. Automobile engines roared through the night. She had the sinking sensation of being perfectly alone.

Then, on its cream-colored cradle, the phone rang and trembled, rang and trembled.

"Hello? Ahmed? Habibi, it's been so long – how could you – how are you –?"

Outside, like a scrap of burnt paper, her husband's prayer mat, wrapped around a dark, heavy form, drifted down to their doorstep.

ENTANGLED

Ian R MacLeod

Ian R. MacLeod took a law degree and worked in the Civil Service before making his first sale, Nebula nominee "1/72nd Scale". Subsequent stories include "Grownups"; "The Summer Isles" and "The Chop Girl", both winners of the World Fantasy Award; "Isabel of the Fall", "New Light on the Drake Equation", and "Breathmoss". *Voyages by Starlight, Breathmoss and Other Exhalations, Past Magic*, and *Journeys* collected some of these. His novels include Locus Award Winner *The Great Wheel*, alternate-histories *The Light Ages* and *House of Storms*, Arthur C Clarke Award and John W Campbell Memorial Award winner *Song of Time*, Sidewise Award winner *The Summer Isles*, and *Wake Up and Dream*. His most recent book is *The Reparateur of Strasbourg*. He lives in Bewdley, UK.

WHEN SHE AWAKES, it seems as if she's not alone. Many arms are around her, and she's filled with a roaring chorus of voices. Consciousness follows in a series of ragged flickers, and the voices fade, and soon she inhabits her own thoughts, and knows that she is Martha Chauhan, and nothing has changed. But the air, the light, the sounds which reach this morning to her room fifteen floors up in Baldwin Towers, all feel different today...

Lumbering from bed, she clears a space in the frost, peers blearily down, and sees from the blaze of white that it's snowed heavily in the night, and that many of the entangled are already up and about. Kids, but adults as well. Either throwing snowballs, or dragging handmade toboggans, or building snowmen, or helping clear the pathways between the tower blocks. The small shadows of their movements seem impossibly balletic.

Still climbing from the fuzz of night, she counts and dry-swallows the usual immune suppressants from her palm. The water isn't entirely cold, the hob puts out just enough heat to turn her coffee lukewarm, and she's grateful she doesn't have to use the commune toilets. In so many ways, she's privileged. Fumbling with yesterday's clothes, she swipes the mirror for glimpses of a woman in late middle age with something odd about the left side of her skull, then picks up her carpetbag and heads down the pell-mell stairs with other commune residents in their flung coats, sideways bobble hats and unmatched gloves.

Shouts and snowballs criss-cross the air as she crunches to her readapted Mini, another great privilege, which has already been cleared of snow. She clambers in. Shivers and hugs herself as she waits for the fuel cell to warm. Finally, she drives off. Along with the 1960s tower blocks, there are houses and maisonettes in other parts of this estate that were once occupied by individual families. Now, they have all been reshaped and knocked through, joined by plastic-weld polysheets, raggedly-angled sheds and tunnels of tarpaulin, with the gardens and other open spaces used for communal planting and grazing. Everything's white this morning, but all the roads have been cleared, and braziers already blaze in the local market where the communes come to barter. Strangers smile to each other as they pass. Acquaintances hug. Co-workers sing gusty songs as they shovel the paths. Lovers walk hand in hand. Even the snowmen are grinning.

This isn't how I imagined my life would be.

I grew up in this same city, not far from these streets. Dad was of Indian birth, and came here to England with my brother in his arms and me clinging to the strap of his suitcase and our mother dead from a terrorist dirty bomb back in Calcutta. He changed my name from Madhur to Martha, and Daman's to Damien, and honed his cultural knowledge to go with his excellent English, and had all the certificates and bio-tags to prove he was a doctor, and was determined to make his mark. *Money is important, and so is security, and status is something to be cherished –* that was what Martha Chauhan learned at her father's knee. That, and all the stories he told me as he sat by my bed. Tenali Ramakrishna and the gift of the three dolls who all seemed the same, but only one of which knew how to feel. Artful imps who danced about the flames in a hidden heart of a forest to the secret of their own name. But maybe I was too cosseted, for I could never get the point. The world was clearly collapsing. You could see that merely by switching screens from the kiddie channels he tried to sit Damien and me in front of in our secure house in our gated and protected estate. A wave of my chubby hand, and the Technicolor balloon things dissolved and you were looking down at people clinging to trees as the helicopters flew on, or bomb blast wreckage surrounded by wailing women, and then Damien started crying, and that was that.

St James' schoolhouse is like something from Dickensian old times, even without today's gingerbread icing of snow. A great, paternally white oak looms across the trampled playground. Martha heads inside past the tiny rows of dripping coats into a room filled with rampaging four year olds. The walls hang with askew potato prints and cheery balloon-style faces. There's a sandpit and a ballpool and something else that hovers in mid-air that fizzes and buzzes as the kids dive.

Tommy the teacher lies somewhere at the bottom of the largest piles of waving limbs, and it's some time before he or anyone else notices Martha's presence. When they do, it's as if she's left the doors open and is a cold draft the kids feel on their necks. Once the unease is there, it spreads impossibly fast. Tommy, who's lying on his back like a tickled dog, is almost the last to pick up the change of mood.

He clambers to his feet in a holed jumper and half the contents of the sandpit bulging his pockets. The kids cluster around him, exchanging looks, half-words, mumbles, grunts, nudges, gestures and silences. Tommy does as well until he remembers how rude that is.

"It's okay, it's *okay*...! We have a visitor, and I want everyone to simply *talk* when Martha's with us. Right?" Kids give metronomic nods as Martha's introduced as the nice lady who's going to be seeing them individually over the next few hours. Then a hand then goes up, then another. "So why…" asks a small voice, before a different one takes over until the question finishes in chorus. "…isn't she… *HERE*…?"

Followed by a rustle of giggles. After all, Martha obviously *is* here. But, in another, deeper, sense she's clearly not. Martha understands their curiosity. After all, she can remember how she used to stare at fat people and paraplegics when she was young until her father told her it was impolite. She can't help but smile as hands sneak out to touch the snow-melting tips of her boots, just to check she's not some weird kind of ghost.

"I *am* here," she says. "But the thing is, not everyone has the same gift that all of you have. I can *see* you, and I can *hear* you as well. But there was an accident – perhaps you can see where it was…" She turns so they can admire the odd shape of her skull. "I lost…" she pauses, "…part of my mind. Truth is, I'm very lucky to be here at all. What my disability means is that I'm not entangled. Not part of the gestalt. I can't share and feel as you do. But I'm as real as all of you are. Look, this is my hand…" She holds it out. Slowly, slowly, tentatively, little fingers encircle her own like new shoots enclosing old roots. Then, and at the same instant, and as if by some hidden decision, they withdraw. As they settle back, the face of one of the boys blurs and tries to reshape itself into Damien's.

DAD ALWAYS WAS an industrious man. Not only had he managed to qualify as a doctor back in India, but he'd studied what was then called biomechanical science. He also had a practical business eye. He'd worked out that the most secure jobs in medicine at a time of collapsing insurance and failing state healthcare were to be found in the developing technologies of neural enhancement.

I remember him taking Damien and me along with him one day to the private hospital where he did much of his work. It was probably down to some failure in the child-minding arrangements that all single parents have to make, although Damien must have been about five by then and I was nearly twelve, so perhaps he really had wanted to show us what he did.

"Here we are..."

The rake of a handbrake in his old-fashioned car that smelled of leather and Damien's tendency to get travelsick. We'd already passed through several security systems and sets of high walls, and were now outside this big old castle of a building that looked like something out of Harry Potter or Tolkien – all turrets and pointy windows. Then doors swished, and suddenly everything turned busy and modern, with people leaning down and dangling their unlikely smiles and security passes toward us to ask who we were – at least, until Damien began to cry. Then we were inside a bright room, and this creature was laid at its centre surrounded by wires and humming boxes and great semi-circular slabs of metal.

Damien sat over in a far corner, pacified by some game. But apparently it was important that I stand close and listen to what he had to say. You see, Martha, this patient – her name's Claire, by the way – is suffering from a condition that is slowly destroying her mind. Can you imagine what that must be like? To forget the names of your best friends and the faces of your family? To get confused by simple tasks and slowly lose any sense of who you really are? A terrible, terrible thing. But we now have a procedure that helps combat that process. What we do, you see... he'd called up a display which floated between us like a diseased jellyfish... is to insert these incredibly clever seeds which are like little crystals into her skull that we then stimulate with those big magnets you can see around her head so they slowly take over the damaged bits of her mind...

The jellyfish quivered.

Dad doubtless went on in this way for some time, probably covering all sorts of fascinating moral and philosophical questions about the nature of consciousness, and how this withered relic would come to use all this new stuff in her head in much the same way that someone who's lost their hand might use a re-grown one. But not quite. Nothing in medicine is ever perfect, you see, Martha, and bits of people's brains can't be persuaded to regenerate in the way that other parts of their body can, and rejection – that means, Martha, when the body doesn't recognise something as part of itself – is still a problem, and a great deal of practise and continued medication is going to be needed if Claire's to make the most of this gift of half a new mind. Meanwhile, I was staring at the creased and scrawny flesh that emerged from all that steel and plastic like the neck of a tortoise, and thinking, why is something so old and horrid still even *alive*?

MARTHA'S GIVEN HER usual "room" at the school – actually little more than a cupboard – and says no to an offer of coffee. Then she opens up her carpetbag and puts the field cap with its dangle of controls and capillaries on the radiator to warm. The entanglement virus is generally contracted naturally soon after birth, but it's the job of her and many others like her to deal with any problems which may arise during the short fever which follows. She often looks in again on toddlers, but it's at this age, when the children have joined the gestalt as individual personalities, that's the next major watch-out. Then, if it all goes as well as it almost always does, there are some final checks to be made during the hormone surge of adolescence. In some cultures and other parts of the globe, she'd be thought of as a shaman, priest, imam or witch doctor. But the world had changed, and the differences really aren't that great.

"This is where I... Should be?"

Martha looks up, slightly surprised by the way this kid has simply stepped into this tiny room. Most hang around outside and wait to be invited, or rub and scratch at the door like kittens, seeing as, even though her disability has been explained to them, they still find it difficult to believe that she's actually inside. "Yes. That's perfect. You're..." She glances at Tommy's execrably written list. "Shara, right? Shara of Widney Commune. Am I getting your name right, by the way? Shara? Such a pretty name, but I don't think I've heard it much before. Or is it Shar-ra?"

"I think it's just Shara," she says as she settles on the old gym mat. She has bright blue eyes. Curly, almost reddish, hair. "Some people say it different but it doesn't matter. The other mums and most of the dads sometimes just call me Sha. I think Shara was just a name they made up for me when I was born."

Shara of the Widney Commune really is an extraordinarily composed creature. Pretty with it, with those dazzling eyes and the fall around her cheeks of that curly hair, which Martha longs to touch, just to see if it really is as soft and springy as it looks. If ever there was a subject for whom her attentions might seem irrelevant, it's Shara. And yet... There's *something* about this girl... Martha blinks, swallows, kicks her mind back into focus and reminds herself that she's taken her usual handful of immune suppressants, just as Shara's features threaten to dissolve.

"Are you alright?"

"Oh...? Absolutely, Shara. Now, I want you to put this on."

Shara takes the field cap and puts it on in the right way without the usual prompting, even tightening the chinstrap against the pressure of those lovely curls. She lies down.

"I want you to close your eyes."

Unquestioningly, she does so.

"Can you see anything?"

She shakes her head.

"How about now?" Martha lifts the ends of the capillaries and touches the controls.

"It's all kind of fizzy."

"And now?"

"Like *lines*..."

"And now?"

This time, Shara doesn't respond. Her fingers are quivering. Her cheeks have paled. The rhythm of her breathing has slowed. Sometimes, although Martha tries to insist that they use the toilet beforehand, the kids wet themselves. But not Shara. The girl's in a fugue state now, lost deep inside the gestalt. Always a slight risk at this point that they won't come back, and Martha's trained in CPR and has adrenalin and antipsychotic shots primed and ready in her carpetbag just in case they need to be quickly woken up or knocked out, but the rigidity fades just as soon as she cuts the signal back. Shara stretches. Blinks. Sits up. Smiles.

"How was that?" Martha helps unclip the field cap and feels the spring of those lovely curls.

Shara thinks. "It was *lovely*. Thank you Martha," she says. Then she kisses her cheek.

*   *   *

IT WASN'T ALL famine, tribal wars, economic collapse back in the day. Life mostly went on as it always did, and I suppose Dad did his best to try to keep us going as some kind of family as well. I remember a summer West Country beach – it wasn't all floods and landslips, either – that he must have driven us down to from the Midlands in that creaky old car between regular stops at the roadside for Damien to vomit. There we were, Dad and me, sat on an old rug amid our sandwiches and samosas whilst dogs flung themselves after Frisbees and Damien and some other lads attempted to play cricket. Kites stuck like hatpins into a pale sky and a roaring in my ears that could be the sea, but often comes when I chase too hard after memories.

Dad was chattering on as he often did. Trying hard not to be a bore, or talk down to me, but not really succeeding... You see, Martha, the work I do on the mind, the brain, the whole strange business of human consciousness, is just the very beginning. The crystals I persuade to grow inside peoples' skulls are almost as primitive as wooden legs. Real, living neurons use quantum effects – it isn't just electricity and chemistry. The mind, the entirety of the things we call thought and memory and consciousness, is really the sum of a shimmer of uncertainties. It mirrors the universe, and perhaps even calls it into existence. But even that's not the most wonderful thing about us, Martha. You see, we all think we're alone, don't we? You imagine you're somewhere inside your skull and I'm somewhere inside mine, that we're like separate islands? But we're not looking at it from enough dimensions. It's like us sitting on this beach, and looking out over those waves toward the horizon, and seeing a scatter of islands. No, no, I'm not saying there *are* real islands out there, Martha because there obviously aren't. But just stay with me for a moment my dear and try to imagine. We'd think of those islands as alone and separate, wouldn't we? But they're not. Not if you look at the world sideways. Beneath the sea, under the waves, all the islands are joined. It's just that we can't properly see it, or feel it. Not yet, anyway...

The day moved on, and Dad stood at the driftwood wicket like any good Englishman, or Indian, and soon got bowled out. Then he fielded, and dropped an easy catch from Damien as I crunched my way through the last of the sandy samosas. Then the wind blew colder, and the kites and the Frisbees and the dogs fled the beach, and the last thing I can remember is my lost Dad holding hands with lost brother Damien as he wandered with his trousers rolled at the edge of the roaring sea.

MARTHA DRIVES OUT toward the edge of the motorway system that still encircles this old city. The big trucks are out in force now; great, ponderous leviathans that grumble along the rubbled concrete out of a greyness that threatens more snow. Dwarfed by their wheels, she parks her Mini at a transport stop, and stomps up to the glass and plastic counter. It's a regular old-fashioned greasy spoon. The windows are steamed, and baked beans are still on the menu, and the coffee here is moderately strong. Always a difficult dance, getting through a busy space when people's backs are turned, but she clatters her tray to give warning, and they soon share the sense of her oddity and decide not to stare. Mindblind coming through.

She likes it here. The people who do this travelling kind of work far from their communes are still surprisingly solitary by nature. A few are sharing tables and chatting in low voices or quietly touching, but most sit on their own and appear to be occupied with little but their own thoughts. In places like this it's possible to soak up a companionship of loneliness that she can imagine she shares. Sometimes, one of them comes over to talk. Sometimes, but more rarely, and after all the usual over-polite questions, the conversation moves on, and some old signs of sexual availability, which to them must seem arcane as smoke signals, waft into view.

There are some rooms at the back of this place which anyone who needs them is free to use. Piled mattresses and cushions. Showers for afterwards – or during. Sex with Martha Chauhan must be something lonely and oddly exotic, and perhaps a little filthy, as far as the entangled are concerned. A weird kind of masturbation with someone else in the room. There's an odd emptiness in their eyes as they and the gestalt study her when, and if, she comes. But Martha's getting older. Mindblind or not, they probably find her repulsive, and whatever urgency she once felt to be with someone in that way has gone.

She pushes aside her plate and swirl the dregs of her coffee. Blinks away the fizzing arrival of her father's reproachful smile. After all, what has she done wrong? But the empty truth is there's nothing she needs to do this afternoon. She could go back to her room in Baldwin Towers and try to sleep. She could go tobogganing, although being with other people having fun is one of the loneliest things of all. This day, the whole of whatever is left of her life, looms blank as these steamy, snow-whitened windows. She could give up. She could stop taking her tablets. Instead, though, she rummages in her carpetbag and studies the list she was given this morning, and sees that name again, Shara of the Widney Commune, and remembers the face of that striking little girl.

I FIRST BUMPED into Karl Yann during one of my many afternoons of disgruntled teenage wandering. Dad, or course, was full of *You must be carefuls* and *Do watch outs*. Well, fuck that for a start, I thought as I tried without success to slam the second of the heavy sets of gates which guarded our estate. Looking back through the shockwire-topped fence at the big, neat houses with their postage stamp lawns, panic rooms and preposterous names, it was easy to think of prisons. Then, reaching into my coat pocket, hooking the transmitter buds around my ears and turning on my seashell, my head filled with beats, smells, swirls and other sensations, and it was easy not to think of anything at all. Hunching off along the glass and dogshit pavements past the boarded-up shops, dead lampposts and abandoned cars, there was a knack that I'd mastered to keeping my device set so I remained aware enough to avoid walking into things. Until, that was, I found my way blocked by a large, laughing presence that was already reaching into my pocket and taking out, and then turning off, my precious seashell.

The city was supposedly full of piratical presences, at least according to my father, but this guy actually *looked* like a pirate. That, or, with his bushy red beard, twinkling blue eyes, wildly curly hair, be-ribboned coat and pixie boots, like some counter-cultural Father Christmas.

"Give that back!"

He grinned, still cupping my seashell in a big, paint-grained palm. "This is a pretty cool device, you know. Basically, it's mimicking your brainwaves so it can mess around with your thoughts..."

My father had said something similar, but this man's tone was admiring rather than concerned. At least, he seemed a man to me; I figured out later that Karl was barely into his twenties.

"I said –"

"Here. Don't want to get yourself tangled..." Almost impossibly gently, he was reaching to unpick the buds from around my ears, and already I was hooked. He was asking me questions. He seemed interested in my head-down city wanderings, and where I was from, and what I'd been playing on my seashell, and what I thought about things, and even in my Indian background, although I did have to make most of that up.

"This is the place. Don't snag yourself..."

Now, he was holding the wire of the fence that surrounded one of those half-finished developments that the dying economy had never finished. Maybe shops or offices or housing, but basically just a shrouded, rusty-scaffolded concrete frame. A few floors up, though, and in this place he called "the waystation" was a different world. In many ways, it was a glimpse of what was to come.

People stirred and said hi. The waystation's inner walls were painted, or hung with random bits of stuff, or fizzed with projections that drifted to and fro in the city haze. Old vehicles, bits of construction material, expensive drapes, blankets and rugs that looked more as if they had come from gated estate communities such as my own, had all been cleverly re-used to shape an exotic maze. Everything here had been transformed and recycled, and it was plain to me already that Karl was an artist of some talent, and at the heart of whatever was going on.

THE WIDNEY COMMUNE is based around a grand old house, with icicled gates leaning before a winding drive. Some long-dead Midlands industrialist's idea of fine living. Shara and the other commune youngsters will still be down at the schoolhouse, and most of the adults will be out. This place could almost be deserted, Martha tells herself as she edges her

Mini up the drive and clambers out. The main door lies up a half-circle of uncleared steps, with an old bellpull beside. Something tinkles deep within the house when she gives it an experimental tug.

Even with all the indignities which have been inflicted on it – the warty vents and pipings, the tumbling add-ons – this is still a fine old sort of a place to live. Especially when you compare it to Baldwin Towers. No fifteen floors to ascend. Nor any concrete stalactites, or rusting pipes, or a useless flat roof. The entangled might claim that they can see the wrongness of things, and feel disappointment and envy. But they clearly don't.

Martha starts when snow scatters her shoulders.

"Hello there," she shouts up with all her usual yes-I-really-am-here cheeriness. "Just trying to see if there's anyone at home."

"Oh…" A pause as the head at the window above registers that she's not some odd garden statue. "…I'm sorry. The front door's been stuck for years. If you can come around to the side…"

This pathway's been cleared, as even a mindblind moron should have noticed, leading to a side entrance which opens into what was once, and still mostly is, a very great hall.

The space goes all the way up and there are galleries around it and a wide set of stairs. Live ivy grows up over the beams and there's a hutch in the corner where fat-eared rabbits lollop, and it's plain that the woman who's sashaying over to greet Martha is the source of at least half of Shara's good looks.

"I'm Freya…" After a small hesitation, she holds out a hand. It's crusty with flour, as are her bare arms. Her shoulders are bare, too, and so are her feet. Which, like the tip of her nose, are also dusted white. She's wearing holed dungarees that show off a great deal of her lithe, slim figure. Dirty blonde hair done up in a kind of knot. "…you're…?" Confused by the difficulties of introduction with someone of Martha's disability, she hesitates with a pout.

"Martha Chauhan." Martha lets her hand, which by now is floury as well, slip from Freya's. "I'm guessing you're Shara's birth mother?"

"That's right." Freya squints hard. "You were testing Shara? Today? At school?"

Martha nods. "Not that there's any cause for concern."

"That's good." She smiles. Hugs herself.

"But I, ah…" Martha looks around again, wondering if this is how social workers once felt. "Sometimes just like to call in on a few communes. Just to… Well…"

"Of course," Freya nods. "I understand."

Somehow, she does, even if Martha doesn't. The entangled live in a sea of trust.

"Most people are out, either working or enjoying the day. But I've just finished baking… so what can I show you?"

The entangled are relentlessly proud of their communes. They'll argue and josh about who breeds the fluffiest sheep, puts on the cheeriest festival or grows the best crop of beets. As always, there's the deep, sweet, monkeyhouse reek of massed and rarely washed humanity, but it's mingled here with different odours of yeast, and the herbs that seem to be hanging everywhere to dry, and yet more of those rabbits. Each commune has its own specialities which it uses to exchange for things it doesn't make, and this one turns out to be rabbits which are raised to make warm blankets and coats from their skins, as well as for their meat. This commune's bread is something they're particularly proud of, as well. Down in the hot kitchen, Freya tears some with her hands, takes a bite, then offers Martha the rest, dewy with spit. She doesn't have to lie when she says she isn't hungry.

Many of the rooms look like the scenes of some perpetual sleepover. The entangled mostly sleep like puppies, curling up wherever they fancy, although Freya's slightly more coy about one or two other spaces, which reek of sex. Another smell, sourer this time, comes from some leaking chairs and sofas set around a big fire where the old ones cluster, basking like lizards, tremulous hands joined and rheumy eyes gazing into the tumbled memories at a past forever gone.

"And this is where Shara sleeps with the rest of the under-tens…"

Another charming, fetid mess, although this one's scattered with toys. There's a spinning top. There are rugs and papier mache stars. There's a one-eyed, one-armed teddy bear. A few story books and piles of paper, as well, along with newer, stranger devices that make no sense to Martha at all.

"Shara's your only birth child?"

Freya nods. She looks at least as proud of that as she does of most things, even if parenting is shared in a loose kind of way that involves the whole commune and no one gets too possessive. Knowing exactly who the father is can be difficult. In this era of trust, mothers are surprisingly coy about who they've fucked. Women often wander out to visit other communes – driven either by biological imperative or the simple curiosities of lust – and births are often followed by versions of the *he's got Uncle Eric's nose* conversations that must have gone on throughout human history.

Freya's showing drawings and scraps of writing that Shara's done, then lifting up pretty bits of clothing she's resewn herself for all the kids to use and share.

"No new babies at the moment," she adds. "Although we're planning, of course... Soon as the commune has the resources. And Shara's been such a joy to us all... That I'm rather hoping..." As she puts the things back, her hands move unconsciously to her breasts.

"And Shara's father? Somehow, I'm guessing he's a fair bit older than you are...?"

"Oh? That's right." Freya smiles, not remotely insulted or surprised. "Karl's hoping, as well. We all are. Would you like to see the studio where he works?"

Martha blinks, swallows, nods. A falling feeling as she follows Freya down a long corridor then through a doorway into what's clearly an artist's studio. Rich smells of oil and varnish. Linseed oil squeezed out over a press. Pigments from the hedgerow, or wherever it is that pigments come from. Half-finished canvases lean against the walls. The room is a kind of atrium, lit from windows on all sides and high up. The colours and the shadows roar out to her even on a day as wintry as this.

"He's probably out helping in one of the greenhouses," Freya says. "That or sketching. He tends to paint in short, intense bursts."

The canvases are part abstract and part Turner seascape. They're undeniably accomplished, and recognisably Karl Yann's, although to Martha's mind they've lost their old edge. The entangled are good at making pretty and practical things, but proper art seems to be beyond them. Still, as Martha stares at the largest blur of colour, which looms over her like a tsunami in a paint factory, it's hard not to be drawn.

Freya chuckles, standing so close that Martha can smell the grease in her hair. "I know. They're lovely, and they barter really well... But Karl doesn't like to have them up on display in our commune. Says all he'd ever see is where he went wrong."

I NEVER DID get my seashell back, but I got Karl Yann instead. He had a bragging mix of certainty and vulnerability which I found appealing after my father's endless *on-the-one-hand-but-on-the-other* attempts at balance. Karl was clever and he knew what he thought. Karl was an accomplished artist. Karl *cared*. He'd read stuff and done things and been to places and had opinions about everything, but he also wanted to know what my views were, and actually seemed to listen to me when I said them. Or at least, he had a roguishly charming way of cocking his head. Maybe it was a little late in the day for this whole hippy/beatnik/bohemian revolutionary shtick, but these things come new to every generation – or at least they used to – and they felt new to me. Karl used real paint when he could, or whatever else came to hand – he found the virtuals fascinating but frustrating – but what he really wanted to create was a changed world. No use accepting things as they are, Martha. No use talking about what needs to be done. At least, not unless you're prepared to act to make the necessary sacrifices to help bring about the coming wave of change. The forests dying. Whole continents starving. The climate buggered. The economy fucked. So, are you with us, Martha, or not?

They called them performance acts, and Karl and the other inhabitants of the waystation were convinced they were contributing towards bringing about a better world. And so, now, was I. People had to be shaken out of their complacency – especially the selfish, cosseted rich, with all their possessions, all their *things* – and what was the harm in having some fun while we're doing so? Right? Okay? Yes?

We used my credit pass to gain access to one of those exclusive, guarded, gated, palm tree-filled, rich-people-only, air-conditioned pleasure domes they still called shopping malls to which my father had occasionally taken me and Damien as a birthday treat, and pulled on balaclavas and yelled like heathens and flung pigshit-filled condoms at the over-privileged shoppers and their shit-filled shops, and got out laughing and high-fiving in the ensuing mayhem. We climbed fences and sneaked through gardens and around underlit pools to hang paintings upside down and spraypaint walls and mess with people's heads. Then, often as not, and young as Martha Chauhan still was, she went home to her gated estate.

THE MINI SEEMS to know the way from the Widney Commune, but time and entanglement haven't been kind to this part of the city. Martha's boots press through new white drifts to snag on the rusted shockwire and fallen sensor pylons that once supposedly protected this little enclosure. The houses, haggard with smoke, blink their shattered eyes and shrug their collapsing shoulders as if in denial. Is this really the right place? Even the right street? Martha struggles to make sense of the layout of her lost life as she stands at what was surely the heart of their neat cul-de-sac where an uprooted tree now scrawls its branches until she's suddenly looking straight at her old home and everything's so clear it's as if her eyeballs have burned through into ancient photographic negatives. The roof of the old house still intact, even if Dad's old car has long gone from the driveway, and she almost reaches for her key when she steps up to the front door. But the thing is blocked solid by age and perhaps even the fancy triple-locking that once protected it. *You can't be too careful Martha…* She looks around with a start. The other houses with their blackened Halloween eyes stare back at her. She shivers. Steps back. Takes stock. Then she walks around to the side past an upturned bin and finds that half the wall is missing, and pushes through, and everything clicks, and she's standing in their old kitchen.

Over there… Over *here*…

She's an archaeologist. She's a diver in the deepest of all possible seas. She scoops snow, dead leaves and rubble from the hollow of the sink. She straightens a thing of rust that might once have been the spice rack. Many of the tiles with their squiggle pattern of green and white that she never consciously noticed before are still hanging. And all the while, the thinning light of this distant winter pours down and in. So many days here. So many arguments over breakfast. She can see her father clearly now, quietly spooning fruit and yoghurt on his muesli with the flowerpots lined on the window ledge behind him and the screen of some medical paper laid on the table and his cuffs rolled back to show his raw-looking wrists and his tie not yet done up. Damien is there as well, chomping as ever through some sugary, chocolaty stuff that he'll waste half of.

"I had a visit from some police contractors yesterday," he's telling her as he unfolds a linen handkerchief and dabs delicately at his mouth. "Apparently, they're looking for witnesses to an incident that happened at the Hall Green Mall. You may have heard about it – some kind of silly stunt? Of course, I told them the truth. I simply said you were out."

Now, as he refolds his handkerchief, his turns his guileless brown eyes up towards her, and the question he's really asking is so padded with all his usual oblique politeness that it's easily ignored. Anyway, time is moving on – Martha can feel it roaring through her bones in a winter gale – and now she's back home from her first term at the old, elite university town that her father, ever the supportive parent, has agreed to finance her to study at. Politics and Philosophy, too, and not a mention of the practical, career-based subjects she's sure he'd have much preferred her to take. Even as he spoons yoghurt over his muesli, she can feel him carefully not mentioning this. But he seems newly hunched and his hand trembles as he spoons his yoghurt. And here's a much larger, gruffer-sounding version of Damien, as well, and sprouting some odd kind of haircut, even if he is still half-eating a bowl of sugary slop. All so very strange: the way people start changing the instant you look away from them. But that isn't at the heart of it. What lies at the core of Martha's unease is, of all things, a dog that isn't really a dog.

"*Of course* he's a dog, Martha," her father's saying as his suddenly liver-spotted hands stroke the creature's impossibly high haunches and it wags its tale and gazes at her with one eye of brown and the other of whirring silver. "Garm's *fun*. We take him for walks, don't we Damien? The only difference is that he's even more clever and trustworthy, and helps bring us a little bit of extra safety and security in these difficult times. Some worrying things have occurred locally, Martha, and I don't just mean mere destruction in unoccupied homes. So we do what we can, don't we Garm? Matter of fact, Martha, the enhancement technology that allows him to interact with the house security systems is essentially the same as I use to help my patients..."

But this is all too much, it always was, and Martha's off out through the same stupid security gates and on along the same cold, dreary streets with more than enough stuff roaring around in her head to make up for her missing seashell that Karl never did give back to her even though all property is, basically, theft. That's dumb sloganeering and there are many new ideas Martha wants to share with him. But even the waystation seems changed. Sydney's been arrested, and Sophie got her arm burned on some stray shockwire, and different faces peer out at her through the fug. Who *is* this person? Martha Chauhan could ask them the same. Then up the final level, squeezing past a doorway into some windy higher floor which already looks like the aftermath of a battle in an art gallery, with ripped concrete walls, flailing reinforcing bars and blasted ceilings all coated in huge swathes of colour. Clearly Karl's experimenting with new techniques, and it's all rather strange and beautiful-ugly. Forget regurgitated abstract expressionism. This is what Bosch would have painted if he'd lived in the bombed-out twenty-first century city. But hadn't they agreed that art for art's sake was essentially nothing but Nero fiddling while Rome burned?

"So," he gestures, emerging from the dazzling rubble with the winter sun behind him like some rock star of old. "What do you think?"

"It's... incredible..." So much she wants to tell him, now that she properly understands the history and context of their performance acts and sees them as part of a thread that goes back through syncretic individualism, anarcho-syndicalism and autonomism. But Karl is already scuttling off and returns holding something inside a paint-covered rag that she momentarily assumes as he unwraps it is some new artistic toy he's been playing with – a programmable paint palette or digital brush. But, hey, it's a handgun.

* * *

Snow blows in. Martha's breath plumes. It's growing dark. The old family house creaks, groans, tinkles as she shuffles into the hall and brushes away ice and dirt from the security control panel beneath the stairs. But everything here is dead – her own memory of the night when she lost half her mind and more than half her family included. Just doubts and what-ifs. Things Karl had said, questions he'd asked, about her Dad being a doctor, which surely meant access to drugs and money, and about the kind of security systems employed in their gated estate, and ways to circumvent them. That, and the strange, dark, falling gleam of that handgun, and how those performance acts of old had never been *that* harmless. Not just ghastly artwork hung up the wrong way but taps left running, freezers turned off, pretty things smashed. Precious books, data, family photos, destroyed or laughingly defaced beyond all hope of recovery. Pigshit in the beds. Koi carp flopped gasping on Persian rugs. Treasured bits of people's lives gleefully ruined. In a way, she supposes, what Karl did to her here in her own home was a kind of comeuppance.

With numb fingers, she picks out the thumbnail data card that once held the house records and shoves it into her coat pocket, although she doubts if there's anything that would now read it, the world having moved on so very far. The rotten stairs twitch and groan as she climbs them. The door to poor, dead, Damien's room is still closed, a shrine, just as it was and always should be, but the fall of the side wall has done for most of Dad's room, and she's standing almost in empty air as she looks in.

Amazing that this whole place hasn't been ransacked and recycled, although she's sure it soon will be. Her own room especially, the floor of which now sags with the rusty weight of the great, semi-circular slabs of polarised metal and all the rest of the once high-tech medical equipment which encircles her bed.

My father pitted all his money and energies toward healing his injured daughter in the aftermath of the terrible night of Damien's death. All I can recall of this is a slow rising of pain and confusion. Instructions to do this or that minor task – the blink of an eye, the lifting of a finger – which seemed to involve my using someone else's body. My thoughts, as well, seemed strange and clumsy to me as the crystal neurons strove to blend with the damaged remains of my brain and I dipped in and out of rejection fever. In many ways, they didn't seem like my thoughts at all. I wasn't *me* any longer.

Sitting watching bad things happen on a screen with my baby brother crying. Or being on a beach somewhere with crashing waves and the dogs, the Frisbees, the cricket. These were things I could understand and believe in. But the uncooperative limbs and wayward thoughts of this changed, alien self belonged to someone else. A roaring disconnect lay between the person I'd been and the person I now was, and the only way I could remain something like sane was to think of this new creature as "Martha Chauhan".

"I'm so grateful you're still here and alive," a tired, grey-haired man Martha knew to be her father was saying as he spoon-fed her. "Is there much..." The offered spoon trembled in age-mottled fingers. "...you can remember of how all this happened?"

Martha made the slow effort to shake her head, then to open her mouth and swallow.

"There was a break-in, you see, here at our house. I don't know how the person got in, nor why the systems didn't go off, or why poor Garm wasn't alerted. But he wasn't. Neither was I – I'm too old, too deaf – and I think it was your brother Damien who must have heard something, perhaps the glass of the back door being broken, and got you to go downstairs with him. And then I believe the intruder must have panicked. After all, it can't be easy, to be standing alone in the dark of someone else's kitchen. A gun going off – that was what woke *me*, and by the time I got downstairs the intruder had fled and poor Damien was past any kind of help, although at least I know he didn't suffer. And poor Garm, of course, proved to be no use at all, and I had him reformatted and sold. But then, you never did like him much, did you? I thought you were lost to me as well for a while, Martha, what with the damage that bullet had inflicted to your head. But you're here and alive and so am I and for that I'm incredibly, impossibly grateful... We've spilled a bit there, though, haven't we? Hold on, I'll get a cloth..."

Eventually, Martha learned how to sit up unaided, and to spoon, chew and swallow her own food. It was a slow process. Through several sleepless years, as her father grew withered and exhausted from wiping her arse and changing the sheets and tending the machines, she learned how to walk and talk and returned to some kind of living. He never left her. He never let go. He never relented. He was a sunken smile and tired eyes. He was the stooped back that lifted her and hands which were always willing to hold. He never spared the time or energy for any feelings of rage, or such abstract concepts as retribution, although he surely knew who was responsible for the destruction of his family, and had sufficient evidence to prove it, even in days when justice was about as reliable as the power grid and the police were privatised crooks. Karl Yann slunk off toward the sunrise of this bright new world, whilst Martha Chauhan's father's heart gave out from grief and exhaustion, and she was left empty, damaged and alone.

SHE RAMS THE old car into gear and thumbs on the headlights. The tyres slide. The black-edged, glittering night pours past her. She can hear laughter over the roaring in her ears as she parks and kills the Mini's engine at the far edge of some trees outside the Widney Commune. She rummages deep in her carpetbag, picks off the fluff and dry-swallows the few immune suppressants she can find loose in the lining. Not enough, but it will have to do. Then she takes out a primed antipsychotic syringe and shoves it into her coat pocket.

Her feet are dead and the house's fire-rimmed shadow leaps over a field of untrampled snow as she crunches toward it. There's no one about apart from pigs sleeping in their pens until she turns a corner and hits a blaze of bonfire. Then there's life everywhere, and dancing to the accompaniment of discordant shouts and bursts of clapping.

Amazing, how well this useless brain of hers still works. How it can devise and dismiss plans without her even realising she's thought of them. The paintings inside the house, for example. She could walk in and slash, burn or deface them. But that wouldn't hurt Karl Yann. At least, not enough. He'd just pronounce it a fresh phase. Even burning this whole commune to the ground wouldn't be sufficient. What about that child, then, Shara – who Martha can see twirling at the shimmering edge of the flames? Or the lovely Freya? He'd feel *their* loss, now, wouldn't he? But Martha's mind slides from such schemes, not so much because she finds them abhorrent but because they lack the brutal simplicity she craves. It has to be *him*, she tells herself as she stands ignored at the edge of the light searching the shining, happy faces. Has to be Karl Yann. Draw him away to some quiet spot – he might recognise her, but the entangled are impossibly trusting – then knock him senseless with the contents of this syringe. Drag him to the Mini, drive him to some as-yet undefined place... In this world where no one steals and no one hurts and everything is shared, all these things will be ridiculously easy.

The straps of the field cap can be easily adjusted. Its settings are incredibly flexible. You could kill someone, fry their brains, if you really wanted. That, or turn them into a gibbering vegetable. Appealing though these options are, though, to Martha's mind they lack the simplicity of true retribution. So why not destroy just enough of his thalamus to break the quantum shimmer of entanglement? Then, he'd be alone, just as she is. He'd be lost, and he'd know what it really is to suffer. The final performance act in a world made perfect.

But where *is* he?

"Hey, hey – look who it is! It's Martha!"

A familiar male voice, but it's Tommy the teacher who comes up to embrace her. Perhaps this is his commune. Perhaps he's out on the look for new friends to dance, laugh or fuck with. The entangled are like bonobo monkeys. Smell like them, as well. Others are turning now that Tommy's noticed her, mouths wide with surprise and sympathy. Poor, dear Martha. Sweet, old Martha. Standing there at the cold edge of the dark, when all of us are so very warm and happy. You don't need to be entangled to know what they're feeling.

She's swept up. She's carried forward. She lets go of the syringe in time just as her hands are hauled from their pockets. The entangled don't do booze, or other drugs – most of them frown at Martha's liking for coffee – but the stuff that steams in the cracked mug that's forced into her fingers is so sweet and hot it must be laced with something. Then there's the rabbit: tender, honey-savoury – a treat in itself, meat being something that's reserved for special occasions. They're so happy to see her here at the Widney Commune it's as if they've long been waiting for her, and their joy spills out in hugs, giggles and touches. The kids flicker like elves. The old ones grin toothlessly.

Come on, Martha! Now, they're clapping to some offbeat she can't quite follow. A circle forms, and she's at the heart of it where's the snow's been cleared and the fire roars. *Come on, Martha! Come on, Martha!* They think they're not taunting her. Think they're not drunk. But they're drunk on this hour. Drunk on the future. Drunk on everything.

Martha does an ungracious bow. Stumbles a few Rumplestiltskin steps. She's the ghost of every lost Christmas. She's the spirit of the plague from that story by Poe. And everything, her head most likely, or possibly her body, or this entire world, is spinning. Poor Martha. Dear Martha. They stroke the lumpen shape of her skull like it's an old stone found on a beach. And this isn't even her commune. Isn't her world.

"Hey, Martha…" Now, Freya and Shara emerge from the glowing smoke. "So great that you've come back to see us again!"

"Oh, yes…" Shara agrees. "We all love you here, Martha. We really do."

"Where's Karl?" Martha yells over a roaring that must be mostly in her head.

"He's…" One starts.

"…out." The other finishes.

"Right," Martha says. "You don't have any idea *where*, do you? I mean… You see…"

She trails off as these two elfin creatures, one small and one fully grown and both entirely beautiful, gaze at her with firelight in their eyes.

"Oh, somewhere," Freya says with a faraway smile. "Your birthfather likes to wander, doesn't he, Sha?"

For Martha's benefit, Shara gives an emphatic nod.

"Oh? Right. Good… You see, I think I used to know him… Long ago."

"Oh, but you *did!*" Freya delightedly confirms. "I said you'd come to see us, and Karl instantly knew who you were, didn't he, Sha? Said you went back a very long way."

"And then... He went out again?"

"Of course. I mean..." Freya shrugs her shoulders. Gazes off, as if nothing could be more welcoming, into the freezing dark. "Why not?"

AFTER HER FATHER died – a feat he managed with the same quiet fortitude with which he'd done most things throughout his life – Martha Chauhan found herself living in a place with Harry Potterish turrets and pointed windows that could have been the one she and Damien had visited when they were kids. A kind of commune, if you like. But not.

Still a youngish woman by many standards, but she fitted in well with these wizened and damaged creatures who cost so much money and technology and wasted effort to keep alive. She learned how to talk to them, and show an interest. She got better at walking. She learned how to play mah-jong. And outside, beyond the newly heightened shockwire and the sullen guards, the world was falling apart. The tap water was brown with sewerage. The winters were awful. The summers were shot.

But wait. The big screens they sat in front of all day were showing something else. There was a virus – a new mutation of a type of encephalitis that attacked a part of the brain known as the thalamus. The fever it triggered was worrying, but very few people died from it, and those who survived were changed in ways they found hard to explain – at least to those who hadn't yet become whatever they now were. Some said the virus wasn't just some random mutation, but it was down to terrorists, or space aliens, or the government. Or that it was triggering something that had long been there, buried deep inside everyone's skulls, and that this was a new kind of humanity, a different kind of knowing, which was triggered by a form of quantum entanglement which joined mind to mind, soul to soul.

Others simply insisted that it was the Rapture. Or the end of the world.

Of course, there were riots and pogroms. There was looting. There were several wars. Politicians looked for personal advancement. Priests and mullahs pleaded for calm, or raged for vengeance. People walked the streets wearing facemasks, or climbed into their panic rooms, or headed for hilltops and deserted islands with years' supplies of food and weapons. A time of immense confusion, and all Martha Chauhan knew as things collapsed was that the few staff who were still working at Hogwarts laughed as they saw to the catheters or mopped the floors. Soon, many of the wizened and damaged ones were laughing as well.

The day the shockwire fell – her own personal Berlin Wall – Martha Chauhan stumbled out into a changed world. It was all almost as she'd long expected. There were the bodies and the twisted lampposts and the ransacked buildings and the burnt-out cars. But people were busy working in loose, purposeful gangs, and *clearing things up*. Stranger still, they were singing as they did so, or laughing like loons, or simply staring at each other and the world as if they'd never seen it before.

On she stumbled. And was picked up, cradled, fed, welcomed. Then, as the fever passed by her and nothing changed, she was pitied as well. Eventually, she got to meet people who could explain why she could never become entangled, but she already knew. There was nothing that could be done to replace the dumb nano-circuitry that took up vital parts of her skull without destroying this construct known as Martha Chauhan as well. Still, the commune at Baldwin Towers were as happy to have her. She was even given a specialist kind of work, along with some privileges, to reflect her odd status and disability, a bit like the blind piano tuners of old. And so it went, and so it still is to this dark winter's night, and now Martha Chauhan's back in her Mini, driving lost and alone through a fathomless, glittering world.

SHE'S STOPPED. THE little car's engine is quiet, and the cold's incredibly intense. She fumbles in her carpetbag with dead fingers, but whatever immune suppressants she has left – carefully made somewhere far from here at great but unmentioned expense – must all be back at Baldwin Towers, and the roaring in her head deepens as she breaks the door's seal of ice and tumbles outside.

Another day is greying as she looks up at the waystation. Superficially, nothing much has changed. It's still an abandoned ruin, although the snow and these extra years of neglect have given it a kind of grace. Even the dead shockwire Karl once held up for her remains, and shivers like a live thing, scattering rust and ice down her neck as she crawls beneath.

All the old faces seem to peer out at her as she clambers on and in through concrete shadows and icicle drips. Who *is* this person? She could ask the same of them. Not that she ever belonged here. Or anywhere. Creaks and slides as she climbs ladders and crawls stairways until she claws back her breath and finds she's standing surprisingly high, overlooking a greened and snowy landscape that seems more forest than city in the sun's gaining blaze. For all she knows, the entangled will soon be swinging tree to tree. But that isn't how it will end. They're biding their time for now, still clearing things up as this damaged world heals, and the icecaps, the forests, the jungles, the savannahs, return. But the gestalt will spread. Soon, it will expand in a great wave to join with the other intelligences which knit this universe. Martha Chauhan hears someone laughing, and realises it's herself. For a dizzy moment there, standing at this precipice at the future's edge, she almost understood what it all means.

The whole sky is brightening, and she's starting to realise just how beautiful this high part of the old waystation has become. Blasted rubble and concrete and a sense of abandonment, certainly, but everything covered in the glimmer of frost and snow and old paint and new growth. Colours pool in the icemelt. Then, something bigger moves, and she sees that it's a ragged old man, a kind of grey-bearded wizard, half Scrooge and half Father Christmas, who seems part of this grotto in his paint-strewn clothes.

"It's me, Martha," Karl Yann says in a croaked approximation of his old voice as his reflections ripple about him. "I just wish I could share how you feel."

"But you *can't* can you? You're here and I'm not." Martha Chauhan shakes her head. Feels her thoughts rattle. That isn't what she meant at all. "You think you know everything, don't you? All the secrets of the fucking universe. But you don't know what it is to *hurt*."

He winces. Looks almost afraid. But there's the same distant pity in his old eyes that Martha's seen a million times. Even here. Even from him. She tries to imagine herself dragging the syringe from her pocket. Running forward screaming and stabbing. Instead, her vision blurs with tears.

"Oh, Martha, *Martha*... Here, look..." Now he's coming toward her in a frost of breath, and holding something out. "This used to be yours. It *is* yours. You should have it back..."

She sniffs and looks despite herself. Sees her long-lost seashell, of all things, nestling in his craggy hand. She grabs it greedily and hugs it to herself and away from him. "I suppose you've got that other thing here as well – another bloody souvenir?"

He almost looks puzzled. "What thing?"

"The gun, you bastard! The thing you killed my brother with – and did this to me!" She slaps the slope of her skull so hard it rings.

But he just stands there. Then, slowly, he blinks. "I think I see."

"See what?" The entangled are useless at arguing – she's tried it often enough.

"You think, Martha, you *believe*, that I broke into your house and did that terrible thing? Is that what you're saying?"

"Of course I am." But why is the roaring getting louder in her head?

"I'm sorry, Martha," he says, looking at her more pityingly than ever. "I really am so very, very sorry."

"You can't just... Leave..."

But he is. He's turning, shuffling away from her across this rainbow space with nothing but a slow backward glance. Dissolving into the frost and the shadows, climbing down and out from this lost place of memories toward his life and his commune and a sense of infinite belonging, before Martha Chauhan even knows what else to know or say or feel.

FULL DAY NOW, and Martha Chauhan's sitting high at the concrete edge of the waystation.

It's freezing up here, despite the snowmelt. But she doesn't seem to be shivering any longer, nor does she feel especially cold. She sniffs, swipes her dripping nose, then studies the back of an old woman's hand which seems to have come away coated in blood. That roaring in her ears that is far too loud and close to be any kind of sound. Although there's no pain, it isn't hard for her to imagine, with what brains she has left, the wet dissolution of the inside of her skull as the immune suppressants fade from her blood. If she doesn't turn up back at Baldwin Towers soon, she supposes help will probably come. But the entangled can be astonishingly callous. After all, they let their old and frail die from curable diseases. They kill their treasured pets for clothing and food.

She inspects her old seashell. A small glow rises through the red smears when she touches its controls. Something here that isn't dead, and she hooks the buds around her ears and feels a faint, nostalgic fizz. But the stuff she liked back in the day would surely be awful, old and lost as she now is. A different person, really. In fact, that's the whole point...

She feels past the syringe in her coat pocket, finds the data card she took from the house security system and sniffs back more blood as she numbly shoves it in. It's still a surprise, though, to find options and menus hanging against the clear morning sky. Files as well, when you'd have thought Dad would have deleted them. But then, he never liked destroying things – even stuff he never planned to use. And perhaps, the thought trickles down through her leaking brain, he left this for her. After all, and despite his many evasions and protestations, he always had a strong regard for the truth.

She waves a once-practised hand through ancient images until she reaches the very last date. The end of everything. The very last night.

And there it is.

There it always was.

She's looking into the bright dark of their old kitchen through the nightsight eyes of that stupid not-dog. Fast-forward until a window shatters in a hard spray and the door opens and something moves in, and the not-dog stirs, wags its tail, recognises... Not Karl Yann, but a much more familiar shape and scent.

Martha rips the buds from her ears, but she still can't escape the past. She's back at this waystation, but she's young again, and the colours are brilliant, and she's here with Karl Yann, full of Politics and Philosophy and righteous anger at the state of the world. And he's got this handgun that he's merely using as a prop for all his agitprop posturings, when she has a much clearer, simpler, cleverer idea. The final performance act, right? The easiest, most obvious, one of all... Come on, Karl, don't say you haven't *thought* of it...And fuck you if you're not interested. If you're not prepared, I'll just do the damn thing myself...

Martha flouncing out from the waystation. Into the darkness. Hunching alone through the glass and rubble streets. The gun a weight of potentiality in her pocket and the whole world asleep. She feels like she's in the mainstream of the long history of resistance. She's Ulrike Meinhof. She's Gavrilo Princip. She's Harry Potter fighting Voldemort. A pure, simple, righteous deed to show everyone – and her Dad especially – that there are no barriers that will keep the truth of what's really happening away from these prim, grim estates. Not this shockwire. Nor these gates. Not anything. Least of all the glass of their kitchen door which breaks in a satisfying clatter as she feels in for the old-fashioned handle and turns. Not that this isn't a prank as well. Not that there isn't still fun to be had. After all, that fucking thing of a dog isn't really living anyway, it's nothing but dumb *property*, so what harm is being done if she shoots it properly dead? Nothing at all, right? She's doing nothing but good. She's shoving it to the system. She's giving it to the man. The darkness seethes as she enters, and she feels as she always feels, standing right here in her own kitchen, which is like an intruder in her own life.

That roaring again. Now stronger than ever, even though the seashell's buds are off and its batteries have gone. After all, how is she to tell one shape from another in this sudden dark? How could she know when she can barely see anything that the thing that comes stumbling threateningly out at her is Damien and not that zombie dog? It's all happened already, and too quickly, and the moment is long gone. A squeezed trigger and the world shudders and she's screaming and the dog's howling and all the backup lights have flared and Damien's sprawled in a lake of blood and the gun's a deathly weight in her hand – although Martha Chauhan doubts if she could ever understand how she felt as she turned it around so that its black snout was pointing at her own head and she squeezed the trigger again.

*　　*　　*

HER FATHER'S WITH her now. Even without looking, and just as when she lay in her bedroom surrounded by pain and humming equipment, she knows he's here. After all, and despite her many attempts to reject him, he never really went away. And, as always, he's telling her tales – filling the roaring air with endless ideas, suppositions, stories... Talking at least as much about once-upon-a-times and should-have-beens as about how things really are. Using what life and energy he has left to bring back his daughter. And if he could have found a way of sheltering her from what really happened that terrible night, if he could have invented a story that gave her a reason to carry on living, Martha knows he would have done so.

She sniffs, tastes bitter salt, and feels a deep roaring. It's getting impossibly late. Already, the sun seems to be setting, and the beach is growing cold, and the cricket match has finished, and that last gritty samosa she's just eaten was foul, and all the dogs and the kite flyers have gone home. But there's Dad, walking trousers-rolled and hand-in-hand with Damien as the tide floods in. Martha waves cheerily, and they wave back. She thinks she might just join them, down there at the edge of everything where all islands meet.

FADE TO GOLD

Benjanun Sriduangkaew

Benjanun Sriduangkaew (beekian.wordpress.com) spends her time on amateur photography and writing love letters to cities. Her fiction can be found in *Clarkesworld*, *Beneath Ceaseless Skies*, *The Dark* and numerous anthologies.

THEY SAY THE afterlife is a wheel and that is true, but I am between and so for me the way is a line. It unspools interminably into a horizon that shows the soft gold of dawn, always just a little out of reach.

Before the war this was only packed earth and grass and dirt to me; before the war I trod this path from home to capital thinking of the sweetness of rare fruits. Now that my back is to Ayutthaya the ground is sometimes baked salt where nothing grows and sometimes wet mud bubbling with the voices of the dead. Inside my arteries there is blood which throbs and pumps, and my belly growls at emptiness as might a bad-tempered dog. But it is difficult to be sure, after so much soldiering, that one is still alive. It is difficult to be certain this is not all a fever dream.

It can be difficult to remember who you are, having watched Queen Suriyothai die.

These are the common ailments of any soldier, though few will admit them.

A BURNT VILLAGE, a burnt temple. I see such often, these days, defaced by the Phma who melted off the gold and stole every metal coin. Sometimes in their savagery they kill the monks, even though theirs and ours wear much the same saffron. The Phma have faces no different than any mother's son, four limbs and a head each, but it strains belief that anything human could have slaughtered holy men. Do they not have luang-por like second fathers, who taught them to read and write? Are some of them not orphans taken in by a temple, to shelter beneath the steeple and the bodhi shade?

Slaughter is what might have happened here, or else flight, for I find neither a living voice nor a body thick with flies. Toward the end everyone fled for Ayutthaya until the walls strained at the seams, until every house and hovel splintered at the edges. It should have been comforting, so many people, but when there was so much desperation all I could feel was desperation in turn, a sour and unrelenting fear that turned everything I ate – and even the king's soldiers hadn't much to eat – into rotten meat on the tongue, with an aftertaste of cinders.

I take shelter where I find it, in spite of ghosts that must've seeped into the fissured walls and the desecrated murals. In spite of knowing that Phma soldiers have been here too, that the air bears the stink of their sweat, the reek of their filth. Being a soldier has taught me to forget delicacy.

It has also taught me to put on sleep light as dead petals, to be shaken off and scattered at a blink. So when the mud makes sucking noises I am already awake; when the woman comes into view I have a hand around the carved wood of a hilt.

She must have seen the blade glint, for there is a hiss of breath.

"I thought you might be a thief," she says.

"What could a thief rob from a place already thieved to every final clod of dirt?"

"There is always one last bit of painted glass, one last talisman." She closes the distance, her apparent fear set aside. "One last child to murder."

"Have you lost one then?" There's still room in my breast for softness, still room to be cut by another's hurt.

"It's a season for losing children." The luster of her lips and hair seems brighter than dawn's light warrants. "You can only be passing by. Which way calls you?"

"East, to Prachinburi."

"The same direction then." She gathers her braid in one hand, twisting it. "Might we not share company?"

I have collected myself, spine straight, eyes clear. In the back of my mind phantom flies buzz. There is no escaping the noise. No battle-hardened veteran ever tells you it is the flies that haunt you most, over the cannon fire and your fellows' screams, over the throb and burn of your own veins. "You would trust a strange soldier?"

"When she is a woman, why not?"

My alarm must have been immediate, for she laughs.

"Even officers go bare-chested the moment they're free from uniform. You remain as neat behind yours as a captain newly promoted and pledged to His Majesty." Her head moves from side to side. "I'll not pry – too much. I want only safety, for if you've survived the Phma you must be as fit to the business of combat as any man."

I should ask how she has been unscathed so far. I should ask from whence she came, and where she was going other than in the same vague direction as I am. But in the army I've been solitary out of need, and there comes a point where a person must hear another human voice or break upon the cliff-face of loneliness. My secret is already laid bare to her, so where's the harm?

We set out at daybreak, keeping parallel to but avoiding the road, for not all soldiers recently unyoked from duty are vessels of honor, and I've heard news of Phma stragglers along this way, ready to avenge themselves upon any Tai.

She breaks open one of her bamboo tubes as we walk, and hands me half the sweet roasted rice. Her name is Ploy, a widow, and when she hears my name is Thidakesorn she smirks at the florid grandeur of it. "A princess's name," she says.

"My parents had expectations." Years living with an aunt who married upward, wife of a merchant grown wealthy on trade with the Jeen. So successful he's sailed to the Middle Kingdom twice, and his fortune tripled by a wife shrewd with numbers and investment. She would tutor me, it was hoped.

"Instead you took up the sword."

How do I say that I went to the capital to learn to be a lady and fell in love with the queen despite the hopeless stupidity of that; how do I say it was for this love that I fought and that when she fell it shattered me? How do I say that I resent the king's continued life, for she was the braver of the two, the finer being, and that he did not deserve a wife as incandescent as she? So I seal my lips and pronounce none of these wounds. Better they suppurate than my shame be cast into the day.

She may have the secret of my gender, but this is mine alone to nurse.

The day brightens and Ploy acquires a clarity of features. Before I thought her soft and plain; now there is an angle to her eyes and mouth I've failed to notice in the dim. Sharp from nose-tip to chin-tilt. It does not make her beautiful, if such a comment may be leveled from someone as blunt-featured as I, but she would snag the attention and hold it fast. A little like the queen. The dead queen, whom I must not think about, whom I must bury under the blackest soil of memory.

When I shut my eyes I see elephants draped in black and silver, trumpeting for death. I see the edge of a glaive passing through flesh and bone, opening a queen inside out.

NOON CLAIMS THE sky with fingers bright and fever-hot. It is a month for rain, but I harbor a childish fancy that the season has upended for Queen Suriyothai's demise.

Between my waking delirium transmuting earth to a sanguine river and us stopping to drink from a pool, we hear the Phma.

Away from the shields bearing the king's crest, away from his banners and helms, it can be difficult to tell Phma deserters from our own men. Loinclothed and bare-chested like any Ayutthaya soldier, bearing much the same type of blade. There is a wild look to them that I can spot even as we take to hiding, and I wonder if the penalty for desertion is as harsh for them as for us. Harsher: victors can afford generosity that losers may not.

When they are gone Ploy murmurs, "I thought you'd challenge them, for are these not your sworn enemies and murderous animals?"

"There were five of them, and one of me."

Her sneer is vicious. "If I needed confirmation you were a woman before, I would've required none now."

"What did you lose to the Phma?"

"A family." Her mouth tightens; she says no more.

I study her more closely for signs of who she is or might have been. *Widow* says little, designates merely a specific sorrow. Strange that we will confess but one loss at a time – I am a widow, I am an orphan; how to say in one concise word *I've lost everything*?

Evening approaches, and Ploy looks to me, asking of game and hunt. I mean to scavenge and work for food on the way, and point out that the army taught me to ambush enemy warriors, not edible meat.

"You make an inadequate man." She passes me her satchel. "I'll be back."

I wait beneath a tabaek whose trunk is garbed in a purple sash. There's not much of worth on me, but I smooth out the cloth as best I can and pour out a handful of rice for offerings.

Ploy returns with frogs fat and glistening, her arms wet to the elbows, pha-sbai and pha-nung damp. "Tell me you can make a fire."

"That at least I was taught. You must've been very fast, or those frogs very old."

"And you do not know how to flatter anyone. How are you going to find a husband?"

"By changing out of this into silk and silver." I touch the edge of my helm. "By combing out my hair." In truth I aspire to spinsterhood, for how do I explain the battle scars once all that silk is stripped away? Not evidence that I was wayward as a child. Marks left by a blade resemble in no wise marks left by a switch.

I sharpen twigs and skewer her catch. The meat is succulent, and she carries a jar of the best fish sauce I've had in months. I leave two crisped frog legs by the tabaek's roots, among bruised flowers, for the tree's spirit.

The next village is empty too. I begin to think perhaps all the villages in my path will be unpeopled save by wraiths, that this is beyond death after all and I'm rotting beneath a fallen war-elephant – but I must not think so, for when I do the trumpeting and the cannon fire gain strength between my ears, and if those are bearable the buzzing is not.

Ploy is as disinclined as I to the sin of theft, and so we limit our looting to two rattan mats and some oil. We find a creaking riverside house and rest on its veranda back to back. I remain awake enough to know she slips away long before dawn. When the sun is up she comes back with two roosters. It was not a clean kill: blood everywhere, on her and them, their bellies ragged as if they've been chewed to death.

She sets them down. "A wild dog must've been at them."

This time we've banana leaves to wrap the meat, and proper seasoning – sugar, garlic, coriander root. Afterward we find a rain jar and a coconut-shell dipper. No jasmine water to scent ourselves with, but I've been long crusted in sweat and filth, and Ploy is glad to shed her gore-stained clothes.

She looks on, frowning, as I disrobe and breathe in relief to have the binding off at last. "How did you have those cuts tended without the entire army discovering you have breasts?"

"I had patronage." Her Majesty's handmaids understood so simply a woman's need to be in arms.

Ploy produces yet another wonder: a pot of tamarind paste and turmeric. She bids me turn my back and spreads that across the width of my shoulder-blades, down my spine, in a bright tart-smelling lather. My breath catches once and she asks if there's a wound as yet unhealed.

"It's nothing." There is no way of saying that I've never had another woman's hand on me so except that of kin; there's no way of saying that her touch pulls the strings of my nerves taut, a note so loud in my skull that for a moment all else is mute.

I make myself indifferent while she, nude, washes her clothing. But my eyes stray and my skin craves. Is it any wonder that the monks tell us earthly desire is a shackle, material lust a disease? Rest comes slow, and I am not even drowsing by the time Ploy steals away.

"I've no appetite," she says when I offer her chicken in the morning. Then she scrubs at her teeth with a khoi stick, rinsing her mouth over and over as though she's swallowed unutterable foulness.

We circle back toward the main road. For a relief we meet a family: two grandparents, their daughter and son-in-law, a buffalo-pulled cart laden with supplies and children. Ploy takes my arm before I can speak, introducing me as her husband. The breastplate and helm purchase respect and welcome; they share food with us and their spirits are high. Here is a family that went through war untouched by tragedy.

I keep my words few, my voice low. I've allowed myself to speak freely with Ploy, and if I never trilled or chirped as some women do, still my natural pitch would have given me away.

They would have missed it, and I might have too if not for the flies. That sound – I would know it anywhere. Gorge rising I stride into the bushes; Ploy calls but she is muted, for black clouds close in about me, red eyes the size of longans, wings larger than open hands. When they disperse and my sight clears there are the corpses.

Phma, by the color of their bandannas. A painful death, by everything else. Their bellies torn out, entrails wetting the earth, dense with ants and flies as though they're both sweet and savory.

The son-in-law has followed to see what's afoot. "This wasn't done by knife or arrow," I say, turning to him. "Do you know of any blade that could make wounds so messy?"

One look at the carcasses and he recoils. "I'm no fighter."

Ploy is not far behind him, and when she bears witness to this massacre she merely says, "A tiger."

"This close to the road?"

"Who knows? It is justice."

"We could cremate them."

"A waste of oil." She tugs at my hand. "Leave them for the worms. Were you reborn one you'd have been glad of the gift."

I should like to think I haven't been so heinous as to reincarnate so low, but then I was a soldier. We do not burn the bodies.

At a river's crossing we part company with the family, them turning south while we continue east. Ploy's gaze follows them as they go out of our sight. "I wasn't entirely truthful," she says. "I don't have a home left to return to."

"I know."

"You aren't going to ask why I disappear after dark?"

"You never ask why I became a soldier, or any of the hundred other questions you could've put to me."

She looks away, but her hand slides into mine. "Could there be a place for me in Prachinburi?"

"There'll be work." I hesitate, this close to pulling my fingers away from hers, but they knit and there is an easy fit to our hands. "My grandmother might want another woman in the household. Toddlers running underfoot."

Her gaze lifts, fastens to mine. "We could see each other every day then."

My pulse races. It is a terrible affliction, to have your heart lurch this way and that at nothing more than another's glance, another's breath. "If you like."

"What a shame it is you aren't a man." Ploy's smile is only one half edged; the other, perhaps, is turned inward to cut herself. "Then I could have married you, you'd have returned garnished with not just a rank but also a wife, and all this would have been so perfect."

THERE ARE A hundred breeds of madness, one of them called curiosity. Her naming of it has roused mine, and where before it lay dormant, now it is a frenzied thing, stirring in my skull, a thousand wing-beats in time with the cicadas and owls singing the moon up through pale clouds.

A hundred breeds of madness, and I haven't been sane for a long time.

I resist it. I look at her face in the light as we draw nearer to my home, and become desperate that her taunt was truth – that I was a man, that the possibility she offered in jest could grow to actuality. But in Prachinburi I may not remain behind this garb. I must step out of it and return to pha-sbai that bares my shoulders, pha-nung that must have some gleaming thread to it. I must catch a man's eye and hope he will find me worthy of dowry. And Ploy, being without kin to give her station and place, will remarry.

This is only pretense: my hand in hers, and sometimes lying face to face as evening cools and dark comes, it is all make-believe. She wishes I were a man so I might provide her security and a roof; beyond that there is nothing.

This terrible knowledge – that this is all we will ever have – it tears at me, it claws. Even the distraction of ghost elephants and ghost queens only I can see proves unequal to it. My monstrous desire eats; my curiosity waxes.

Five days from Prachinburi and I give in.

She makes no secret of leaving my side now. Always it takes the better part of the night, and her outing brings meat more often than not. Perhaps it embarrasses her to be good at the hunt; I convince myself this is her secret, and if so what injury can come out of my confirming it?

Ploy is not difficult to follow. In those first evenings she might have been, when she stole away on light and cautious feet. Now her tracks are clear, as though she's giving me a test of trust. My failing of it pricks at me, and I would have turned back if not for the sight of her prone by the river.

She lies among weeds and roots, fainted or snake-bitten. I've never known myself for such quickness – even on the battlefield I was not so fast. Mouth parched with fear I kneel by her, straining to see under a moon just half-bright.

Bright enough to see her neck empty.

Not a wound but a bloodless hole where her windpipe should have been. I dare not touch or probe, for who knows whether she will feel? But I've learned the fright-tales of krasue at elders' feet; cut her open now and I will find the shell of Ploy hollowed of organs. Those have gone with her head.

I lack the courage to stay and confront; I lack the courage even to flee. For she knows me, would recognize my scent.

Ploy returns empty-handed this time, and I watch her mouth, her teeth, for flecks of gore and shreds of viscera. None to be seen; she may believe me gullible, but she is not entirely careless.

The army taught me to put on a mask, and I do that now. The slightest change in my regard and she will realize; I address her much as before. Still some hint must have slipped through, for she asks me why I seem to dread homecoming so.

"It's been some time since I last saw them, and of my parents' dreams for me I failed every one."

"Were you a son they would have been proud." She puts her fingers to my jaw. "I say this not to taunt or mock you, but to say: it is not fair. It is not just. With what you've earned you should be entitled to anything, and in your place a man would've had applause, honor, his pick of a bride."

My betraying body leaps to her touch, longs to lean into her arm. "The world is what it is. The army paid me well, so I'll have something to show for it, something to give Mother and Father."

In Ayutthaya they would have me stay on, to advance from captain to lieutenant, and that's what I would have done if Her Majesty survived. I would have been there simply for her, to protect her even if she would never have glanced my way. I would not have been here, with this creature, this krasue.

Elders' wisdom has it that they inherit the curse, generation to generation. And that may be. It may be true; Ploy could just be the victim of her aunt, uncle, parent. She gobbles up what she must – chicken's blood, Phma innards. She may be as virtuous a woman as any other.

But I cannot bring her to Prachinburi. There will be pigs butchered and she'll hunger. There will be women in childbirth and the blood will summon her to consume mother's insides and infant freshly born. So many things a krasue may not resist, so much evil just one may commit.

Ploy's mood grows tense as we approach Prachinburi, pendulating between elated and anxious. She wants to know if people will be kind to her, a strange widow with no origins; she wants to know if they will disdain her for knowing no letters. I tell her nothing and everything.

Twice I crouch by her headless body, shaking. Twice I fail to kill it and kill her.

"After tomorrow we should be in Prachinburi."

She is combing out her hair. It isn't as long as most women's, and uncharitably I think that she must keep it short so it won't tangle up with her intestines when she goes hunting. "Strange," she murmurs, "I'll miss this."

"Sleeping on the ground? Having no roof over your head?"

Ploy swats me on the arm. I should flinch – I should clench my teeth on disgust. "I will miss your company. Just being with you, talking to you."

"We can do that there."

"That's not what I mean and you know it." Ploy ties her hair back. "I wasn't entirely kidding when I said I would have liked to go as your wife."

"I doubt I could've kept up this deception for the rest of my days. Leastwise before my family."

"Not what I mean either." Her brows knit. Oh, she has a way of frowning; before learning the truth of her nature that look would have made me do anything to ease it. "Do you mean to shame me by driving me to say plainly what no woman should?"

Wanting, wanting, that's all flesh is good for. Her hand remains cradling my cheek and I cannot make myself dislodge it. This close I thought she would smell of offal, but there's only a scent of sweat, of her. "What might that be?"

She lets her hand fall; my heart falls with it, to steep and ferment in the bitterness of my stomach. "Nothing. It was only a fancy. It'd profit us both to forget."

"If you like," I say easily, as though none of this has meaning.

I remain at her insensate shell longer that night. I've heard a krasue's glow is sickly and jaundiced, but what I see is soft, candlelight amber. Innards drift behind her as though the tails of a kite.

Even having seen that my decision congeals slow, like blood thinned by lymph. Even having seen that I cannot think –

A krasue in Prachinburi, and me its harbinger. She might have children there, and one of them will receive her legacy whether or not they wish, whether or not *she* wishes.

It may be mercy as well as defense.

So I gather wood, as dry as may be found in this weather, until I have more than I need. I gather dead leaves, though some are so damp they are nearly mulch. I moor my thoughts to the pier of Prachinburi; I think of what I will eat there, sweet and sour things, and of greeting friends long unseen. Above the sky lightens.

The lamp oil Ploy and I collected is spent to the last drop. My hands are guided not by thought but by the reflexive process of fire-making, of burying her in branches and detritus. A mound of compost.

It all crackles. Fire is a sound. It all leaps. Fire is an animal. It bursts with smells all pungent. Fire is a feast.

It brings her, as I knew it must. I stand with feet braced and blade bared.

Heart and lungs, liver and intestines, limned in that exquisite golden light the same precise hue of dawn. I would say she is unhuman, but are those not the most human parts of anyone freed from skin, while I hide myself behind the artifice of fabric and armor?

Ploy's face remains her own. There is no bestial rictus that reveals her for what she is. There is only a gaze piercing me like arrows, there is only a mouth parting around words like knives.

"I desired you," she says and her voice is not the hag's croak that I was told would emerge from a krasue's mouth. "I wanted to be with you – and there'd have been no children; I would have been the last."

"You would have killed and eaten." My muscles tremble. My throat is shut and my breath comes fast.

"Wild animals. Pigs. Invaders." Her laughter rings pure and clear while her guts undulate, eelish and glistening. "I've long learned control, Thidakesorn. The Phma cut my nieces apart. There will be no more of us. This would've been the end."

"A krasue would say this." My voice splinters. Beside us the fire grows loud, hungry, the heat and brilliance of it bringing sweat and radiance to us both. "A krasue would say anything to escape death."

"A krasue who wants survival would not give you her trust. A krasue who courts life would kill one who's murdered her." Tears on her cheeks, salt on my tongue. "I despise you."

I kick apart the pyre, plunge my hands into the flames. It is too late; it has always been too late. Beneath the kindling she is limbs gone to roast, flesh gone to broil, her breast bared and red-raw.

Pressing blistered hands to my face I scream, and it's hardly a human sound.

She presses her mouth to my temple, and her guts move against me, coolly wet. I expect them to seek my neck and cord into a noose. But they slide across my shoulders and arms until I understand this is her last remaining means of comfort. "I despise you," she whispers. "I love you."

We are no kin – her spit will not force her fate upon me – but she could still bite, could still kill. I wrap my arms around her, around a heart that pumps so strong it jolts my bones. My face in her hair and her lips at my ear, she tells me of how an aunt died when she was eleven and passed her this inheritance. Four years later she became mistress of the hunger; four years later she began to dream that she may not have to be her aunt, may live like any other girl save for her forays in the dark. In a prosperous place, a prosperous time, she could fill her belly full by the day, and so need not venture forth every night.

I do not speak. This is her time to be heard. Her words come slower as the sun climbs higher, even though I keep us in the shade and shield her from the day. Her eyelids droop, heavy, and her head lowers to my shoulder as if to doze off.

She crumbles in my arms. It seems unthinkable that she could turn from flesh to husk in a moment; it seems unthinkable that her face should collapse upon itself, her hair drying to twigs, her lips and eyes to sun-baked fruit.

She is dust.

The buzzing of flies grows in my head and I turn to the rising sun, toward home. My arms are full of her, dry flecks collecting in the creases of my clothes and skin.

In the distance I hear war drums. The horizon shines gold with the beginning of fire.

SELKIE STORIES ARE FOR LOSERS
Sofia Samatar

Sofia Samatar (www.sofiasamatar.com) is the author of fantasy novel *A Stranger in Olondria*, winner of the 2014 Crawford Award. Her short fiction has appeared in *We See a Different Frontier*, *Glitter & Mayhem*, *Apex Magazine*, *Clarkesworld*, and *Strange Horizons*. She is nonfiction and poetry editor for *Interfictions: A Journal of Interstitial Arts*.

I HATE SELKIE stories. They're always about how you went up to the attic to look for a book, and you found a disgusting old coat and brought it downstairs between finger and thumb and said "What's this?", and you never saw your mom again.

I WORK AT a restaurant called Le Pacha. I got the job after my mom left, to help with the bills. On my first night at work I got yelled at twice by the head server, burnt my fingers on a hot dish, spilled lentil-parsley soup all over my apron, and left my keys in the kitchen.

I didn't realize at first I'd forgotten my keys. I stood in the parking lot, breathing slowly and letting the oil-smell lift away from my hair, and when all the other cars had started up and driven away I put my hand in my jacket pocket. Then I knew.

I ran back to the restaurant and banged on the door. Of course no one came. I smelled cigarette smoke an instant before I heard the voice.

"Hey."

I turned, and Mona was standing there, smoke rising white from between her fingers. "I left my keys inside," I said.

*   *   *

MONA IS THE only other server at Le Pacha who's a girl. She's related to everybody at the restaurant except me. The owner, who goes by "Uncle Tad," is really her uncle, her mom's brother. "Don't talk to him unless you have to," Mona advised me. "He's a creeper." That was after she'd sighed and dropped her cigarette and crushed it out with her shoe and stepped into my clasped hands so I could boost her up to the window, after she'd wriggled through into the kitchen and opened the door for me. She said, "Madame," in a dry voice, and bowed. At least, I think she said "Madame." She might have said "My lady." I don't remember that night too well, because we drank a lot of wine. Mona said that as long as we were breaking and entering we might as well steal something, and she lined up all the bottles of red wine that had already been opened. I shone the light from my phone on her while she took out the special rubber corks and poured some of each bottle into a plastic pitcher. She called it "The House Wine." I was surprised she was being so nice to me, since she'd hardly spoken to me while we were working. Later she told me she hates everybody the first time she meets them. I called home, but Dad didn't pick up; he was probably in the basement. I left him a message and turned off my phone.

"Do you know what this guy said to me tonight?" Mona asked. "He wanted beef couscous and he said, 'I'll have the beef conscious.'"

MONA'S MOM DOESN'T work at Le Pacha, but sometimes she comes in around three o'clock and sits in Mona's section and cries. Then Mona jams on her orange baseball cap and goes out through the back and smokes a cigarette, and I take over her section. Mona's mom won't order anything from me. She's got Mona's eyes, or Mona's got hers: huge, angry eyes with lashes that curl up at the ends. She shakes her head and says: "Nothing! Nothing!" Finally Uncle Tad comes over, and Mona's mom hugs and kisses him, sobbing in Arabic.

*   *   *

After work Mona says, "Got the keys?"

We get in my car and I drive us through town to the Bone Zone, a giant cemetery on a hill. I pull into the empty parking lot and Mona rolls a joint. There's only one lamp, burning high and cold in the middle of the lot. Mona pushes her shoes off and puts her feet up on the dashboard and cries. She warned me about that the night we met: I said something stupid to her like "You're so funny" and she said, "Actually I cry a lot. That's something you should know." I was so happy she thought I should know things about her, I didn't care. I still don't care, but it's true that Mona cries a lot. She cries because she's scared her mom will take her away to Egypt, where the family used to live, and where Mona has never been. "What would I do there? I don't even speak Arabic." She wipes her mascara on her sleeve, and I tell her to look at the lamp outside and pretend that its glassy brightness is a bonfire, and that she and I are personally throwing every selkie story ever written onto it and watching them burn up.

"You and your selkie stories," she says. I tell her they're not my selkie stories, not ever, and I'll never tell one, which is true, I never will, and I don't tell her how I went up to the attic that day or that what I was looking for was a book I used to read when I was little, *Beauty and the Beast*, which is a really decent story about an animal who gets turned into a human and stays that way, the way it's supposed to be. I don't tell Mona that Beauty's black hair coiled to the edge of the page, or that the Beast had yellow horns and a smoking jacket, or that instead of finding the book I found the coat, and my mom put it on and went out the kitchen door and started up her car.

One selkie story tells about a man from Mýrdalur. He was on the cliffs one day and heard people singing and dancing inside a cave, and he noticed a bunch of skins piled on the rocks. He took one of the skins home and locked it in a chest, and when he went back a girl was sitting there alone, crying. She was naked, and he gave her some clothes and took her home. They got married and had kids. You know how this goes. One day the man changed his clothes and forgot to take the key to the chest out of his pocket, and when his wife washed the clothes, she found it.

*　　*　　*

"You're not going to Egypt," I tell Mona. "We're going to Colorado. Remember?"

That's our big dream, to go to Colorado. It's where Mona was born. She lived there until she was four. She still remembers the rocks and the pines and the cold, cold air. She says the clouds of Colorado are bright, like pieces of mirror. In Colorado, Mona's parents got divorced, and Mona's mom tried to kill herself for the first time. She tried it once here, too. She put her head in the oven, resting on a pillow. Mona was in seventh grade.

Selkies go back to the sea in a flash, like they've never been away. That's one of the ways they're different from human beings. Once, my dad tried to go back somewhere: he was in the army, stationed in Germany, and he went to Norway to look up the town my great-grandmother came from. He actually found the place, and even an old farm with the same name as us. In the town, he went into a restaurant and ordered lutefisk, a disgusting fish thing my grandmother makes. The cook came out of the kitchen and looked at him like he was nuts. She said they only eat lutefisk at Christmas.

There went Dad's plan of bringing back the original flavor of lutefisk. Now all he's got from Norway is my great-grandmother's Bible. There's also the diary she wrote on the farm up north, but we can't read it. There's only four English words in the whole book: *My God awful day*.

You might suspect my dad picked my mom up in Norway, where they have seals. He didn't, though. He met her at the pool.

As for Mom, she never talked about her relatives. I asked her once if she had any, and she said they were "no kind of people." At the time I thought she meant they were druggies or murderers, maybe in prison somewhere. Now I wish that was true.

*　　*　　*

ONE OF THE stories I don't tell Mona comes from *A Dictionary of British Folklore in the English Language*. In that story, it's the selkie's little girl who points out where the skin is hidden. She doesn't know what's going to happen, of course, she just knows her mother is looking for a skin, and she remembers her dad taking one out from under the bed and stroking it. The little girl's mother drags out the skin and says: "Fareweel, peerie buddo!" She doesn't think about how the little girl is going to miss her, or how if she's been breathing air all this time she can surely keep it up a little longer. She just throws on the skin and jumps into the sea.

AFTER MOM LEFT, I waited for my dad to get home from work. He didn't say anything when I told him about the coat. He stood in the light of the clock on the stove and rubbed his fingers together softly, almost like he was snapping but with no sound. Then he sat down at the kitchen table and lit a cigarette. I'd never seen him smoke in the house before. *Mom's gonna lose it,* I thought, and then I realized that no, my mom wasn't going to lose anything. We were the losers. Me and Dad.

HE STILL WAITS up for me, so just before midnight I pull out of the parking lot. I'm hoping to get home early enough that he doesn't grumble, but late enough that he doesn't want to come up from the basement, where he takes apart old T.V.s, and talk to me about college. I've told him I'm not going to college. I'm going to Colorado, a landlocked state. Only twenty out of fifty states are completely landlocked, which means they don't touch the Great Lakes or the sea. Mona turns on the light and tries to put on eyeliner in the mirror, and I swerve to make her mess up. She turns out the light and hits me. All the windows are down to air out the car, and Mona's hair blows wild around her face. *Peerie buddo*, the book says, is "a term of endearment." "Peerie buddo," I say to Mona. She's got the hiccups. She can't stop laughing.

*　　*　　*

I'VE NEVER KISSED Mona. I've thought about it a lot, but I keep deciding it's not time. It's not that I think she'd freak out or anything. It's not even that I'm afraid she wouldn't kiss me back. It's worse: I'm afraid she'd kiss me back, but not mean it.

PROBABLY ONE OF the biggest losers to fall in love with a selkie was the man who carried her skin around in his knapsack. He was so scared she'd find it that he took the skin with him everywhere, when he went fishing, when he went drinking in the town. Then one day he had a wonderful catch of fish. There were so many that he couldn't drag them all home in his net. He emptied his knapsack and filled it with fish, and he put the skin over his shoulder, and on his way up the road to his house, he dropped it.

"Gray in front and gray in back, 'tis the very thing I lack." That's what the man's wife said, when she found the skin. The man ran to catch her, he even kissed her even though she was already a seal, but she squirmed off down the road and flopped into the water. The man stood knee-deep in the chilly waves, stinking of fish, and cried. In selkie stories, kissing never solves anything. No transformation happens because of a kiss. No one loves you just because you love them. What kind of fairy tale is that?

"SHE WOULDN'T WAKE up," Mona says. "I pulled her out of the oven onto the floor, and I turned off the gas and opened the windows. It's not that I was smart, I wasn't thinking at all. I called Uncle Tad and the police and I still wasn't thinking."

I don't believe she wasn't smart. She even tried to give her mom CPR, but her mom didn't wake up until later, in the hospital. They had to reach in and drag her out of death, she was so closed up in it. Death is skin-tight, Mona says. Gray in front and gray in back.

*　　*　　*

Dear Mona: When I look at you, my skin hurts.

I pull into her driveway to drop her off. The house is dark, the darkest house on her street, because Mona's mom doesn't like the porch light on. She says it shines in around the blinds and keeps her awake. Mona's mom has a beautiful bedroom upstairs, with lots of old photographs in gilt frames, but she sleeps on the living-room couch beside the aquarium. Looking at the fish helps her to sleep, although she also says this country has no real fish. That's what Mona calls one of her mom's "refrains."

Mona gets out, yanking the little piece of my heart that stays with her wherever she goes. She stands outside the car and leans in through the open door. I can hardly see her, but I can smell the lemon-scented stuff she puts on her hair, mixed up with the smells of sweat and weed. Mona smells like a forest, not the sea. "Oh my God," she says, "I forgot to tell you, tonight, you know table six? That big horde of Uncle Tad's friends?"

"Yeah."

"So they wanted the soup with the food, and I forgot, and you know what the old guy says to me? The little guy at the head of the table?"

"What?"

"He goes, *Vous êtes bête, mademoiselle!*"

She says it in a rough, growly voice, and laughs. I can tell it's French, but that's all.

"What does it mean?"

"*You're an idiot, miss!*"

She ducks her head, stifling giggles.

"He called you an idiot?"

"Yeah, *bête*, it's like *beast*."

She lifts her head, then shakes it. A light from someone else's porch bounces off her nose. She puts on a fake Norwegian accent and says: "*My God awful day.*"

I nod. "Awful day." And because we say it all the time, because it's the kind of silly, ordinary thing you could call one of our "refrains," or maybe because of the weed I've smoked, a whole bunch of days seem pressed together inside this moment, more than you could count. There's the time we all went out for New Year's Eve, and Uncle Tad drove me, and when he stopped and I opened the door he told me to close it, and I said "I will when I'm on the other side," and when I told Mona we laughed so hard we had to run away and hide in the bathroom. There's the day some people we know from school came in and we served them wine even though they were under age and Mona got nervous and spilled it all over the tablecloth, and the day her nice cousin came to visit and made us cheese-and-mint sandwiches in the microwave and got yelled at for wasting food. And the day of the party for Mona's mom's birthday, when Uncle Tad played music and made us all dance, and Mona's mom's eyes went jewelly with tears, and afterward Mona told me: "I should just run away. I'm the only thing keeping her here." My God, awful days. All the best days of my life.

"BYE," MONA WHISPERS. I watch her until she disappears into the house.

MY MOM USED to swim every morning at the YWCA. When I was little she took me along. I didn't like swimming. I'd sit in a chair with a book while she went up and down, up and down, a dim streak in the water. When I read Mrs. Frisby and the Rats of NIMH, it seemed like Mom was a lab rat doing tasks, the way she kept touching one side of the pool and then the other. At last she climbed out and pulled off her bathing cap. In the locker room she hung up her suit, a thin gray rag dripping on the floor. Most people put the hook of their padlock through the straps of their suit, so the suits could hang outside the lockers without getting stolen, but my mom never did that. She just tied her suit loosely onto the lock. "No one's going to steal that stretchy old thing," she said. And no one did.

THAT SHOULD HAVE been the end of the story, but it wasn't. My dad says Mom was an elemental, a sort of stranger, not of our kind. It wasn't my fault she left, it was because she couldn't learn to breathe on land. That's the worst story I've ever heard. I'll never tell Mona, not ever, not even when we're leaving for Colorado with everything we need in the back of my car, and I meet her at the grocery store the way we've already planned, and she runs out smiling under her orange baseball cap. I won't tell her how dangerous attics are, or how some people can't start over, or how I still see my mom in shop windows with her long hair the same silver-gray as her coat, or how once when my little cousins came to visit we went to the zoo and the seals recognized me, they both stood up in the water and talked in a foreign language. I won't tell her. I'm too scared. I won't even tell her what she needs to know: that we've got to be tougher than our moms, that we've got to have different stories, that she'd better not change her mind and drop me in Colorado because I won't understand, I'll hate her forever and burn her stuff and stay up all night screaming at the woods, because it's stupid not to be able to breathe, who ever heard of somebody breathing in one place but not another, and we're not like that, Mona and me, and selkie stories are only for losers stuck on the wrong side of magic – people who drop things, who tell all, who leave keys around, who let go.

IN METAL, IN BONE
An Owomoyela

An Owomoyela (pronounced "On") is a neutrois author with a background in web development, linguistics, and weaving chainmail out of stainless steel fencing wire, whose fiction has appeared in a number of venues including *Clarkesworld*, *Asimov's*, *Lightspeed*, and a pair of Year's Bests. An's interests range from pulsars and Cepheid variables to gender studies and nonstandard pronouns, with a plethora of stops in-between. Se graduated from the Clarion West Writers Workshop in 2008, attended the Launchpad Astronomy Workshop in 2011, and doesn't plan to stop learning as long as se can help it.

THAT WAS THE year the war got so bad in Mortova that the world took notice, after twenty years of a column inch here or there on the last pages of the international section. And that was the year Benine went to the front, to the dirt camp outside Junuus where Colonel Gabriel reigned.

Colonel Gabriel met him in a circle of canvas-topped trucks, in an army jacket despite the heat of the sun. He stood a head taller than Benine, with skin as dark as peat coal, with terrible scarring on one side of his jaw. When his gloved hand shook Benine's bare one, he closed his grip and said, "What do you see?"

Benine was startled, but the call to listen in on the memories of things was ever-present in the back of his mind. It took very little to let his senses fuzz, obscured by the vision curling up from the gloves like smoke.

He saw a room in a cottage with a thatched roof, the breeze coming in with the smell of a cooking fire outside, roasted cassava, a woman singing, off-tune. He had to smile. There was too much joy in the song to mind the sharp notes. This must have been before the war; it was hard to imagine that much joy in Mortova these days.

The singing had that rich, resonant pitch of a voice heard in the owner's head, and his vision swung down, to delicate hands with a needle and thread, stitching together the fabric of the gloves. Neat, even rows, and as the glove passed between the seamstress's fingers, he could see the patterns of embroidery on the back.

Benine banished the vision and pulled his hand back. "But these are women's gloves!"

Colonel Gabriel gave him an appraising look. "So you can do something," he said. "Not just superstition and witchcraft."

Benine coughed, and smoothed down his shirt. "Of course, sir."

"The President is a believer in witchcraft," the Colonel said. "And he feels strongly about pacifying the dead of this war. Do you know why you're out here?"

"It's because I can read the history of things," Benine said, and inhaled the smell of the sun-baked dirt to chase off the last vestiges of the cottage.

"Things like bones," the Colonel said. "Mountains of bones, from mass graves the rebels have piled up from here to the coast. Are you willing to do this for your country?"

"Bones," Benine repeated.

"What did you think the President would ask you to this place for?" Colonel Gabriel asked.

THE REBELS HADN'T made it to Junuus yet, not in this iteration of the war. They had raided it back when it was called Morole, of course, and the President's people had burnt it down once before *that*, back when they had been the rebels. That was the kind of war it was: both sides called the other side the rebels, and who had control of the country shifted back and forth like an angry tide. Even the President was president more by accident than design.

Junuus was safe, mostly. The government had stationed Colonel Gabriel there with as many men as they could, because petrol came through

Junuus. The fortifications made it the place to send people involved in the war who didn't need to be *too* involved in the war, like Benine, and a woman named Alvarez.

Alvarez was one of those international people who came into war zones for a living, Colonel Gabriel said. She had skin as pale as a cooked yam, and black hair that hung straight past her shoulders. She was also short, and plump, and had narrow eyes. From the way she bustled into the tent Benine knew that most of the people in the camp disliked her, so he made up his mind not to.

She was carrying a big plastic bin, the kind Benine's aunt stored rice in, and she set it on the card table and peered at him over it. "Have you ever handled human remains?" she asked.

Benine shook his head. That told him what was in the bin, and a shuddery, unsound feeling clung to the back of his sternum. "Never."

"They're only bones," Alvarez said. "Still, some people are afraid of them." She popped off the lid and peered into the bin, then adjusted her gloves and picked up a small plastic bag, then shook its contents out into her palm. "Here," she said. "Try this. We'll leave all the skulls for a while; those can be the hardest to touch. Hold your hands out."

Benine swallowed, cupped his hands, and held them out.

"You ready?" Alvarez asked. When Benine nodded, she placed something small and cool into his palms.

He looked at it. It was small as a pebble; could even be mistaken for one, but for the strangeness of its shape, its light weight. He held it, waiting to feel fear or revulsion, but instead felt an odd disconnect in the place those emotions should have been. "What is it?"

"A distal phalange," Alvarez said. "A fingertip bone. Are you all right?"

"I think I am," he said, and carried it to the card table, where he sat down. He breathed in, and turned the little white thing over in his palm. "I've never done this with remains before."

"You say everything else holds memory," Alvarez said. "Why not bone?"

Benine nodded. He exhaled and rested his eyes on the bone, then let them unfocus.

The bone was much more open – the reaction more immediate – than any of the old family heirlooms he had handled. Even before he had let his own vision grey out he was seeing the street of some other city, smelling the cigarette that a mixed-race hand, paler than his own, was raising to its mouth.

And then the tent flap flew open with a *snap!*, and Benine all but dropped the fingertip.

A man in army green walked in with a mug of coffee in one hand, a face like a foxbat, and a crazed look in his eyes. "I am Sgt. Conte," he said, and put the coffee down on the table. It was two-thirds-full. "You know, in this place, not even Colonel Gabriel has an aide-de-camp, but they sent me to work with you. Do you need anything? Cheers." He pulled a flask out of his pocket and filled up the mug of coffee to the brim; Benine hadn't drunk enough to realize from the smell that it was gin. He looked at the mug, then pushed it away.

"No, thank you."

The sergeant shrugged, then picked up the cup and drained it. His Adam's apple leapt, three, four times as he swallowed, then banged the empty mug on the table again.

"Well, go on," Conte said. "Don't let me stop you."

Benine took a breath, and tried to put the sergeant out of his mind. He closed his eyes, focused on the scrap of bone in his palms, and let himself sink into it.

IT RAINED.

The rain was as grey as the cigarette smoke, as the exhaust from the rickety cars which shouldered past each other on the mud road. The rain was cold, and the man Benine was and saw gulped down the cigarette smoke hoping to catch the warmth in his lungs. He wore a leather jacket, but the rain had run down under his collar and his shirt was clinging to his skin.

Benine sunk into the smoke a little, then nudged the man in the memory just enough to make him shift his gaze. Across the way, in the curved window of a car, he caught a glimpse of reflection: maybe thirty years old but already haggard, with crisp-cut cheekbones and several days' beard. His eyes were like a jackal's eyes. Hunted.

The vision receded a little, and Benine let it. It seemed the man was alone, in a place where he was likely to stay alone – no friend would call out his name. "He was thirty, maybe thirty-five," Benine said, letting his eyes open again on Alvarez's curious face. "A smoker, dressed like a tinkerer, a mechanic." He thought back to his hands. "Mixed, and with calluses here." He indicated the tips of his fingers and the bases, where they connected to his palm. "Does that help?"

"Every little bit helps," Alvarez said, and opened a notebook. She flipped through the pages until she found an empty line, wrote a number on the line, then wrote the number on the bone. Then, in a hand so small and neat Benine had to lean over to read it, she summarized what he had said, in shorthand.

"Are you just making it up?" Conte asked.

"Because he would come out here to sit in a stuffy tent and enjoy your company, just for play," Alvarez said.

"I could show you," Benine offered. "Tell you something about... I don't know. One of your shoes. Or that watch you wear."

Conte looked down at his wrist, where the nylon strap of his watch had stained to almost the same dirt-brown as his sleeve. Then, with a sneer, he ripped it off his wrist, the Velcro giving with the crackle of something never removed, and tossed it at Benine's face. "Here."

Benine caught it, closed his eyes just long enough to smell blood and gunpowder and feel a knife slammed into his chest, and dropped the watch as though scalded. He looked up at Conte, who reached over and snatched it back.

"So. Not entirely a fake," Conte said.

The tent flap flew open again, and all of them looked. Then Conte jumped to his feet, and Benine followed suit. Alvarez raised her eyebrows, but seemed more interested in the bin full of bones than Colonel Gabriel's arrival.

The Colonel batted the tent flap shut. "I've been on the radio," he said, looking straight at Benine. "I had more questions for you."

"Of course," Benine said.

"Your parents did not die in the war," Colonel Gabriel said.

Benine shook his head. "My father died of a heart attack two years ago, sir. My mother died when I wasn't even walking."

"Your siblings? They are not all dead?"

"No, sir," Benine said. "Three of my brothers are still alive, sir. And two sisters."

"And they also have your gift?"

Benine nodded.

"Your uncle tells me he paid for you to go to school," the Colonel said. "He said you were smart enough to go to some foreign universities. The rebels haven't killed your family, burnt your home. Why are you here looking at bones for us?"

Benine shrugged. "I love my country, sir."

Colonel Gabriel watched him closely for a few seconds, then snorted. "Is that so? Not even the President loves this country." He shook his head. "Perhaps you'll live long enough to see how naive you are. I'll pray for you." He turned to go.

Benine stopped him by saying, "If I could, sir?" Colonel Gabriel turned back and met his eyes, then gave a short nod. Benine gathered his words. "Why are you fighting here?"

"Isn't it obvious?" the Colonel asked. He raised his eyebrows. Then, when Benine hadn't guessed, said, "I love my country," and ducked outside.

Sgt. Conte followed.

"WHAT DO YOU feel when you look into those bones?" Alvarez asked. Dusk had just rolled around on the third day, and for those three days, Alvarez had been handing him the bones without comment, as though they were items over the counter of a store. Then he would relate what sort of person he saw and was, and whether anyone said a name in the memories, and whether he had found the person in any of the other bones, and Alvarez would take notes in tiny, black figures in a flip-top book of hers. So the question came as a surprise.

"I see places they were," Benine answered. "Little bits of their lives."

"Important bits? Recent?"

Benine shook his head. "It doesn't seem to matter. Sometimes... for one of them it was the birth of her child. For another it was just walking down a dirt road, thinking nothing in particular."

Alvarez smiled. "Was that a foot bone?"

Benine had to laugh, but he shook his head. "What about you? What do you see in these bones?"

"The same that anyone else sees, I think," Alvarez said. "Tragedy."

Benine looked at the bin – one of many that had come through, that he'd gone through, that would be packed up for transport to the capital, as though the capital was a safer place for them. He was beginning to see them as bones and memories. He knew that they were dead people, that in other places people did not die and get left unburied in such numbers, and he knew that it wasn't right, but the word *tragedy* seemed foreign and ill-fitting. This was more like a chronic disease.

He picked up another bone.

"Why did you come out here?" he asked. "To all this tragedy?"

She shrugged.

"It can't have been for the warm welcome," Benine said. He'd seen the way people in the camp looked at her.

"No," she agreed.

Benine chewed for a moment on his words. He wanted to use this as a connection – he'd seen the way the soldiers looked at him, too. But him, they looked at like a freak, a joke. Her, they looked at like a thief or an enemy. "Is it hard?" he asked.

She shrugged. "No. Not with most of them; I don't care about them. I wish things were different with Colonel Gabriel."

"The Colonel?"

"He doesn't like me," Alvarez said, then seemed to reconsider. "No; he doesn't like the *necessity* of me. We get along. We drink that terrible rum of his and smoke cigarillos and play bezique. But for some foreigner to come into his country to help identify the war dead?" She clicked her tongue. "How can he bear it?"

"He does love his country," Benine realized.

Alvarez gave him a long, strange look. "You thought he didn't?"

"I thought –" Benine started, and realized he didn't know what he'd thought. "I thought he thought me naive for loving it."

Alvarez snorted. "He has yet to learn the distinction between loving one's country and believing in it," she said. "He isn't a stupid man, for all he believes himself stupid."

"Maybe he feels stupid next to you," Benine said, and looked down at the table between his hands. "You travel across the world and identify the dead."

"Doesn't make me any wiser," she said. "All I know? I've been to thirteen different countries, and they're all different. But the sun shines on all of them, and everywhere, people bleed red. And they all leave their bones when they go." She brought out a long, broken white bone from the bin and unwrapped it – by now, Benine could recognise it as a femur. "Tell me about this one."

THE SEASON WENT on with the sun pouring down on the dying grass, the sky bluer than the ocean yet offering no relief, and rumors of the rebels taking another band of cities, boys pressed into service, old men with their eyes put out, young girls with their hands bayonetted through and their mouths stuffed with dust. All the usual atrocities one became numb to, in war.

Benine came out of the tent one afternoon. Sgt. Conte was sitting on one of a trio of buckets probably filled with peanuts or rice, a radio in his hand. The man on the radio was talking about how the rebels had taken a city not far to the west of the camp, and Conte's face was uncharacteristically grim. At the end of the report, he shut the radio off and looked to Benine.

"Yes? What?"

"I wanted to take a rest," Benine said. He wondered if Conte would mind him sitting down on the bucket next to him. Conte snorted.

"Is it all getting too much for you, city boy?" he asked. "What did you see?"

"I saw Montchacal," Benine answered. "Burning."

Conte huffed on his cigarette. "So, ten years ago. Nine? Who can remember." He spat a glob of yellow spit into the dirt. "A man, a woman?"

"A man," Benine said. "A soldier."

"That must have been easy, then."

"Hm?"

"To give the man a name," Conte said.

Benine shook his head. "Why do you think so?"

Conte turned and stared at him for a long moment, then reached inside his shirt and brought out the chain he wore around his neck and the two flattened tags dangling from it. He jerked the chain forward, shaking the tags into Benine's face.

"A soldier, you stupid rat," he said. "We all wear these."

THIS WAS THE easy part, and to Benine's unease, it got easier. More and more of the bones belonged to soldiers. And more and more of those who weren't wore dogtags, too.

Growing up in the corner of the country, where people might still sneak over the border to trade before running back as though the war would nip at their heels – growing up there, far from the capital and the front, tags hadn't been so important. But Benine remembered a childhood friend running up to his house, grinning, proud of the tags he'd bought which jangled against his chest.

Benine's father, while he was alive, hated the idea of dogtags in their village. But his uncle, when he'd taken stewardship of Benine and his siblings, had been more than willing to buy them for any of the children who asked.

Out in the camp near Junuus this was the second month, and Benine could see the difference in the bones. No one had time to clean them, now; they came in covered with dirt that might once have been blood, and there was less distinction between the bones and Benine's skin. But the dogtags in their memories were a constant. They were all different shapes and materials, stamped in leather or aluminum or in flattened-out coins, ready to buy a way into the underworld. All the bones these days came with names.

Many of the bones came with memories of blood.

Benine picked up a lower rib and crashed into a man's death by bayonet, an abdominal wound, a deep stab and a long tear. The pain in his gut was enough to make him retch, but he could feel his gut leaking already, vomiting out his side, and all that came out of his mouth was spit and a dribble of blood and bile. Each ragged breath tugged the wound, an angry red pain that Benine couldn't see through. Buried in it was the certainty that the rebels would take his tags, cut off his head, his hands, and no one would know he had died here, no one would know his bones were his.

Benine came out of the memory with a gasp. For a moment everything looked wrong, the olive-drab tent walls and the camp-lantern light, the dirt floor and the cheap table and the bins, and he dove back in, his hand scrambling for the tags.

He couldn't change anything. He wanted to reassure the man, the man's fingers running across and across his tags, but it seemed to the man like obsession, and the thought went round and round: *They will never know. They'll never know.*

A noise sounded from outside, and Benine jumped, thinking it a gunshot. But it was followed by the splutter of an engine and a string of curses: the old jeep had backfired.

Benine put the bone down on the table, put his head in his hands, and took long, deep breaths until he no longer wanted to cry.

"SOMETIMES I WORRY that when I think of Mortova, I'll remember nothing but war," Colonel Gabriel said. He was sitting at a table in the mess, and Benine had come in to drink coffee with him. The coffee was bad, very bad – reused grounds, Benine thought – but it was something. "I'll forget that we have markets and schools and theatres and nephews with birthday parties and fizzy drinks," Colonel Gabriel said. "I am going to forget that there are little girls in blue dresses, and newspapers, and satellite phones. I am going to forget that I danced at my wedding."

Benine looked at him. He had never suspected that Colonel Gabriel was a man who'd had a normal life. But he was perhaps fifty or sixty, so he would have had an adult life even before the war. "You're married?"

"I may forget that I was married," Colonel Gabriel said.

Benine had nothing to say to that.

After a while, Colonel Gabriel said, "The soldiers have a rumor that you can control a person when you look back through their bones."

Benine jumped. "I can't," he said. Then, "Not much. I can look at something, sometimes. Maybe pick up an object. Only when they aren't thinking."

"Benine," Colonel Gabriel said.

"If they think about what they're doing, I can't do anything," Benine said. "It's only those little things, like if you pick up a pen and forget what you were doing with it."

The Colonel was shaking his head. "I don't know, sometimes."

Benine looked at him, afraid of something he couldn't name. "What?"

"Whether it was God or Lucifer who gave you that gift," Colonel Gabriel said. He drank the bad, old coffee, and his eyes were distant. Benine swallowed, and drank, too.

"How does it feel," Benine asked suddenly, "to be wearing your tags all the time? To have something on your chest that you know means you're expected to die? Or that people expect that you could."

Colonel Gabriel didn't move at all. If thinking of the tags in that light bothered him, it didn't show. Maybe it was the same way he'd always thought of them.

"It felt pointless, for a time," the Colonel said. "When all the bodies have been chopped up or pushed over into mass graves. But now you've come along, so it doesn't seem as pointless any more. Maybe it should." He turned an appraising eye on Benine. "Do you know how many have died in this war?"

Benine lowered his head. "Tens of thousands," he said. "More. Yes, I know."

The Colonel regarded him with eyes that had long ago gone yellow around the edges. "Do you intend to identify all of them?"

Benine had no answer for that, either, and after a while, the Colonel took his coffee and walked away.

*   *   *

THE REBELS TOOK a city. The rebels took a bridge.

The rebels took a field and fouled it with blood and burned it to ash, and Benine sat in a tent outside the petrol port of Junuus and read the histories of dead men from their bones.

One night, the tent flap opened, and a person came in. "Benine."

Benine looked up to see Sgt. Conte standing over the table. Conte had a drawn-out expression, like he'd been drinking and going nights without sleep.

"What is it?" Benine asked. "What's wrong?"

Conte looked down at his hands. "It's only," he started, and one hand went to his chest. "I find," he said.

"Conte," Benine said, unsure of what was to come.

Conte's hand fisted in his shirt, and Benine could see the chain around his neck beneath the fabric. "I find myself checking my tags these days," Conte said, and looked into Benine's eyes. "You said it runs in your family, this... thing, of yours?"

"My little sister," Benine said, and imagined her: her bright eyes, hair in neat braided rows. Like him, she had never lived in a time outside this war. "She's better at it than me," he said. "My brothers are not as good. But we all have it. So did my mother and my aunts and uncles, and my grandmother –"

Conte waved a hand, impatient and troubled. "Will any of them come to the front?" he asked, and then seemed to decide against the question. He backed up. "Never mind. Never mind. A man can die at any time, right? Even years from now." His back hit the tent flap, and his hand opened it. "Forget I came in."

He went.

THIS WAS THE third month, and the bones were drying up. The foreigners searching for them were being evacuated because truces and talks had made no difference, because the rebels had the smell of government blood in their nostrils, and wouldn't be called off the kill. Benine spent more of his days with the army, filling bags with dirt and making them into walls. At night, he read the bones by the camp lantern. The smell of smoke joined the dust in the air, these days, carried from somewhere far off but coming closer.

One night, Alvarez put down one of the rare bins and looked at Benine over it. "They're sending me away," she said. "They won't let me stay. *They* say the front is no place for a woman."

Benine swallowed. Besides Alvarez, the only women he had seen from outside Junuus were wounded walking up the road, their bodies wracked with bullet holes, scored by machetes. And there had been one he had glimpsed across the camp one night, following a soldier into a tent, head down, feet shuffling as though drunk. "It is no place –" he began.

"It's no place for a decent young man like you, either," Alvarez said. "It's no place for any of these men, any thinking, feeling human being." Her eyes were angry, but Benine thought he could see tears, stinging them. "The things Colonel Gabriel is afraid of for me – rape and murder. They've done that to Colonels, too, to humiliate them. And to boys like you. And there's a city here, still."

Benine didn't say that people in Junuus, people in Mortova, knew this was their lot. Foreigners like Alvarez could run from the war.

Alvarez shook her head. "You don't have a choice, either," she said. "They'll keep you here whether or not you want to be."

"I want to be," Benine said.

Alvarez looked hard and sharp like a bayonet. "So do I."

Benine was silent.

"I had something made for you," Alvarez said, and Benine held out his hand by habit. For an instant he felt slapped in the chest, afraid he was becoming ungrateful, but Alvarez slipped the package into his palm and closed his fingers around it so quickly that it seemed she understood. This was a time to say what needed to be said, not to practice politeness. "Wear them," Alvarez said.

Benine pulled his hand back and opened his fingers, and found a pair of dogtags.

"But I hope you never need them," Alvarez said.

*   *   *

COLONEL GABRIEL CAME in, after Alvarez had been put on the truck and sent south toward Port Gold. "Have you ever fired a gun?"

"No, sir," Benine said. His father had raised him to call men *Sir*, but the word had a different taste, these days.

"You should learn," Colonel Gabriel said. He nodded to the bins. "How many bones are left?"

"A few dozen, maybe," Benine said.

"Tomorrow, then."

Benine nodded. "Yes, sir."

Colonel Gabriel left the tent, but as he did, he paused in the entrance to say, "I'm sorry."

BENINE WORKED ON. On.

He didn't want to stop until the bones were done, so the next day would dawn and he could turn his attention to the approaching front. He went through the memories, the good days and grey days and battle days and tags, and put the name and the date of identification on the line by the batch number, the site found, the date of discovery. And then, after not too many pages, he reached into the bin for the next bone and found it empty.

For so long, it had been one bone after another, like a bridge he could walk on from one day to the next. Now that there were no more bones, there was only the front, coming to find him.

His throat closed and he touched the plastic bin, breathing in the memory. After so long handling bones the vision was distant and muted, but the memory was there: Alvarez and a team of strangers, sweating under the hot sun and the hot blue sky, digging side by side with some army men in a dry gully rimmed with trees. Far from assuaging his loneliness it seemed to underscore how large the country was, how far these bones had come, how far the rebels were marching to find them and kill them, how far Alvarez had been sent away. He pulled back his hand.

Night was coming round toward morning, but he didn't want to sleep, for all his fatigue. "Conte!" he called. He was in the mood to accept one of the man's concoctions of coffee and cheap alcohol. Perhaps to talk about when the rebels would arrive. "Conte, are you still awake?"

No answer. Benine leaned back and stretched his arms behind his head. Under his shirt, the unfamiliar weight of the tags shifted on his chest.

His hand went to them.

He hesitated a moment, eyes on the indistinct darkness on the other side of the lantern. He wanted to stay there, suspended in the moment between impulse and action. Neither thinking of them, nor not. Then he pulled the tags free of his shirt and turned them to the light.

The tags Alvarez had given him were such small things, the shine of their metal not yet dulled. His name was stamped there, in one sense indelibly: because here it was, if anyone chose that moment to look for them. Stamped in his sight, in his memories, his bones, the raised letters catching shadows, surrendering his name to the eyes.

KORMAK THE LUCKY
Eleanor Arnason

Eleanor Arnason (eleanorarnason.blogspot.com) published her first story in 1973. Since then she has published six novels, two chapbooks and more than thirty short stories. Her novel *A Woman of the Iron People* won the James Tiptree, Jr. Award and the Mythopoeic Society Award. Novel *Ring of Swords* won a Minnesota Book Award. Her short story "Dapple" won the Spectrum Award. Other short stories have been finalists for the Hugo, Nebula, Sturgeon, Sidewise and World Fantasy Awards. Eleanor would really like to win one of these. Eleanor's most recent book is collection *Big Mama Stories*. Her favorite spoon is a sterling silver spoon given to her mother on her mother's first Christmas and dated December 25, 1909.

THERE WAS A man named Kormak. He was a native of Ireland, but when he was ten or twelve, Norwegians came to his part of the country and captured him, along with many other people. They were packed into a ship and carried north, along with all the silver the Norwegians could find, most of it from churches: reliquaries and crosses, which they broke into bits so it could be traded or spent.

The Norwegians planned to take their cargo to one of the great market towns, Kaupang in Norway or Hedeby in Denmark. There the Irish folk would be sold as slaves.

The ship left Ireland late and got caught in an autumn storm that blew it off course. Instead of reaching Norway, it made land in Iceland, sailing into the harbor at Reykjavik in bad condition. The Norwegians decided it would be too dangerous to continue the journey through the stormy weather. Instead, they found Icelanders who were willing to host them for the winter. The Irish were sold. They brought less than they would have in Kaupang or Hedeby, but the Norwegians did not have to house and feed them through the winter.

In this manner, Kormak came to Iceland and became a slave. He was a sturdy boy, sharp-witted and clever with his hands. But he was also lazy and curious and easily distracted. This did not make him a good worker. As a result, he was sold and traded from one farmstead to another, going first east, then north and west, finally back south to Borgarfjord. It took eight years for Kormak to make this journey around Iceland. In this time, he became a tall young man with broad shoulders and rust-red hair. His eyes were green. He had a beard, though it was thin and patchy, and he kept it short when possible. A long scar ran down the side of his face, the result of a beating. It pulled at the corner of his mouth, so it appeared that he always had a one-sided, mocking smile.

The next-to-last man who owned him was a farmer named Helgi, who did not like his work habits better than any of Kormak's previous owners. "It's past my ability to get a good day's work out of you," Helgi said, "so I am selling you to the Marsh Men at Borg, and I can tell you for certain you'll be sorry."

"Why?" asked Kormak.

"The master of the house at Borg is named Egil. He's an old man now, but he used to be a famous Viking. He's larger than most human people, ugly as a troll, and still strong, though his sight is mostly gone. The people at Borg are all afraid of him and so are the neighbors, including me."

"Why?" asked Kormak a second time.

"Egil is bad-tempered, avaricious, self-willed, and knows at least some magic, though mostly he has used brute force to get his way. He's also the finest poet in Iceland."

This didn't sound good to Kormak. "You said he's old and mostly blind. How can he rule the household?"

"His son Thorstein does most of the managing. He's an even-tempered man and a good neighbor. He will cross his father if it's a serious matter, but most of the time he leaves the old man alone. If you make Egil angry, he will kill you, in spite of his blindness and age."

Several days later, Thorstein Egilsson came down the fjord to claim Kormak. He was middle-aged, fair-haired, and handsome with keen blue eyes. He rode a dun horse with black mane and tail and carried a silver-mounted riding whip. A second horse, a worn-out mare, followed the first. *My mount,* Kormak thought.

Thorstein paid for Kormak, then told him to mount the mare, which had a bridle but no saddle. Kormak obeyed.

They rode north. The season was spring, and the fields around them were green.

Wild swans nested among the grazing sheep.

After a while, Thorstein said, "Helgi says you are strong, which looks true to me, and intelligent, but also lazy. You have been a slave for many years. You should have learned better habits. I warn you that I expect work from you."

"Yes," replied Kormak.

"I know you can't help your smile," Thorstein added, "but I want no sarcasm from you. There are enough difficult people at my homestead already."

They continued riding up the valley. After a while, Thorstein said, "I have one more thing to tell you: stay away from my father."

"Why?" asked Kormak, though he was almost certain he knew the answer to this question.

"He used to be a great Viking. Now he's old and blind, and it makes him angry. I plan to use you in the outbuildings away from the hall. It isn't likely you'll meet him. If you do and he asks you to do anything, obey and then get away from him as quickly as you can."

"Very well," said Kormak.

They came over a rise, and he saw the farm at Borg. There was a large long hall, numerous outbuildings, and a home field fenced with stone and wood. Horses and cattle grazed there. Farther out were open fields that spread across the valley's floor, dotted with sheep. A river edged with marshy ground ran past the farm buildings. Everything looked prosperous and well made. It was a better place than any farm he'd known before.

They rode down together, and Thorstein led the way to an outbuilding. A large man stood in front of it. He was middle-aged with ragged black hair and a thick black beard.

"This is Svart," Thorstein said. "You'll work for him, and he will make sure you do your work."

Svart grunted.

That must be agreement, Kormak thought.

Thorstein and Kormak dismounted, and Svart took the reins of Thorstein's horse. "Come," he said to Kormak.

They unsaddled Thorstein's mount and rubbed the two animals down, then led them to the marshy river to drink. Kormak's feet sank deep into the mucky ground.

Svart said, "Thorstein is a good farmer and a good householder, but he's firm. Do exactly as he tells you. No back talk and no hiding from work."

"Yes," said Kormak, thinking this might be a difficult place.

They let the horses free in the home field to graze, and Svart began to tell Kormak about the labor he would do.

So began Kormak's stay among the Marsh Men. The family got its nickname from their land, which was marshy in many places. Channels had been cut in the turf to draw water out and carry it to the river. This helped the fields. Nothing could make the riverbanks anything but mucky.

Svart was a slave, but he was good with animals and knew ironsmithing. This made him valuable. He was left alone to do his work, which was caring for the farm's horses. Kormak's job was to help him and obey his commands. If he was slow, Svart hit him, either with his hand or a riding whip. Nonetheless, at day's end they would rest together. Svart would talk about the family at Borg, as well as his travels with Thorstein to other farmsteads and to the great assembly, the Althing, at Thingvellir. The Marsh Men were a strong and respected family. When Thorstein traveled, he wore an embroidered shirt and a cloak fastened with a gold brooch. His horse was always handsome. Retainers traveled with him, and Svart came along to care for the animals.

"Everything in his life is well regulated, except for his father," Svart said.

Kormak said nothing, but he thought that the old man could hardly cause much harm. Eighty years old and blind!

He had no reason to visit the long hall, but he'd seen the members of the family at a distance. For the most part, they were handsome people who wore fine clothing even when they were home. The old man was unlike the rest: tall and gaunt and ugly, his head bald and his beard streaked white and gray. Thick eyebrows hid his sightless eyes. He felt his way around the farmstead with a staff or guided by one of his daughters.

Svart went on talking. He had spent most of his life at Borg and remembered Egil's father Skallagrim, another big, dark, ugly man with an uncertain temper. Strange as it appeared to Kormak, Svart was proud of the family and interested in what they did. The servants who worked in the long hall told him stories about Thorstein and the rest of the Marsh Men. He repeated these to Kormak.

"Thorstein rarely crosses his father, but he did so recently. The old man has two chests of silver, which he got from the English king Athelstein. Athelstein gave him the silver as compensation for Egil's brother, who died fighting for the king. The money should have gone to Skallagrim, who was still alive then. It was Skallagrim who'd lost a good son, who could have defended him from enemies and supported him in old age. 'Bare is the back with no brother behind him,' and even worse is a back unprotected by sons. But Egil kept the chests, because he is avaricious.

"Now that he's old and enjoys little, Egil decided to play a game with the silver. He planned to take it to the Althing, to the Law Rock, which is the most sacred place in Iceland. When he got there, he planned to open the chests and scatter the silver as widely as he could. Of course men would struggle to get it. Egil hoped they would draw weapons and break the Thing Peace; and he hoped that he would be able to hear them fight.

"The old man has always settled problems through violence or magic. But Thorstein is a different person, and he said the old man couldn't break the Thing Peace. 'The land is built on law,' as the saying goes. 'Without law it becomes a wilderness.' Thorstein would not let anyone in his household make a wilderness of Iceland. So now the old man is sulking, because he couldn't do the harm he wanted to."

Let him sulk, thought Kormak. *What kind of man would plan this kind of harm?* Though it was pleasant to think about the prosperous farmers of Iceland fighting over bits of silver.

Svart told this story one day in summer, when the sun rarely left the sky. Then came fall, when the days shortened and the sheep were gathered in, then winter, dark and long. Kormak tended the horses in their barn. In all this time, nothing important happened, either good or bad, though he did become a better worker. He learned that he liked horses and the skills that Svart taught him. He even learned some smithing during the dark winter days.

Spring came again. The sky filled with light, which spilled down over everything, and the wild birds returned to nest. Falcons stole the nestlings, swooping down from the brilliant sky. The farmworkers watched for eagles, which could take a lamb.

One day Egil came to their building, feeling his way with his staff. Close up, he was uglier than at a distance. His nose was wide and flat; his eyes, barely visible under bristling eyebrows, were covered with gray film; his teeth were yellow and broken. *A monster,* Kormak thought.

"Svart?" he called in a harsh voice. "Saddle three horses. I want to ride into the mountains with you and the Irish slave."

Svart looked surprised, then said, "Yes."

They had both been told to obey Egil's commands, but Kormak felt uneasy. Thorstein was away visiting neighbors. They could not go to him. The people left on the farm would not oppose Egil.

What could they do, except what they did?

They saddled the horses with the old man standing near, leaning on his staff and listening. The one picked for Egil was an even-tempered gelding, entirely black except for his mane, which had red hairs mixed with the black. It reminded Kormak of rusty iron. Svart picked another gelding for himself, brown with a light mane and tail. Kormak got a mare that was spotted white and blue-gray. They were all good horses, but Egil's was the best.

When they were done, Svart helped the old man into the saddle, and the two of them mounted.

"To the long hall first," the old man said.

They obeyed and stopped by a side wall. Two bags lay on the ground. "Get them," Egil said.

Kormak dismounted and put a hand on the first. It was so heavy he needed both hands to lift it. Inside the leather was something with edges, a box or chest.

It might have been magic, or maybe the old man had some sight left. He appeared to know what Kormak was doing and said, "Give one bag to Svart and take the other yourself."

Kormak obeyed, heaving one bag up to Svart and then heaving the other onto his mare, which moved a little and nickered softly. He knew what she was saying. *Don't do this.*

What choice did he have? He mounted and settled the bag in front of him. Egil carried nothing except his long staff and the sword at his side.

"Go up along the river," the old man said.

They rode, Svart first, leading Egil's horse. Kormak came last. How had the old man been able to move the bags by himself? Had someone helped him, or was he that strong?

A trail ran along the river. They followed it, going up over rising land. Around them the spring fields were full of sheep and lambs. Svart kept talking, telling Egil what they were passing. At last, the old man told them to turn off the trail. Their horses climbed over stones, among bushes and a few trees, small and bent by the wind. The land had been forested when the settlers came, or so Kormak had been told. But the trees had been cut for firewood, and sheep had eaten the saplings that tried to rise. Now the country was grass and bare rock and – in the mountains – snow and ice.

They came finally to the edge of a narrow, deep ravine. A waterfall rushed down into it, and a stream tumbled along the bottom, foaming white in the shadow.

"Dismount and help me to dismount," Egil said, his harsh voice angry. This was a man who had needed little help in his life. He had served one king and quarrelled with another, driving Eirik Bloodaxe out of Norway through magic. He'd fought berserkers and saved his own life by composing a praise poem for Eirik, when Norway's former king held him captive in York. Now a slave had to give him assistance when he climbed down off a horse.

Kormak knew all this from Svart. He dismounted, lifted the bag to the ground, and watched as Svart helped Egil down.

"There are chests inside the bags," Egil said. "Take them out and empty them into the waterfall."

Svart moved first, pulling a chest from his bag and opening it. "It's full of silver," he said to Egil.

"I know that, fool!" Egil said. "This is the money Thorstein would not let me spend at the Althing. He's not going to inherit it when I die. Toss it into the ravine!"

Svart took the chest to the ravine's edge and turned it over. Bright silver spilled out, shining briefly in the sunlight before it fell into the ravine's shadow.

"Now you," Egil said and turned his head toward Kormak. The eyes under his heavy brows were as white as two moons.

Kormak pulled the chest from his bag and carried it to the ravine's edge. Pulling the top up, he spilled the silver – coins and bracelets and broken pieces – into the river below him. As he did so, he heard a cry and glanced around. Svart was down. Egil stood above him with a sword. Blood dripped from the blade. Kormak tossed his chest into the river and turned to face the old man, who came at him, swinging his bloody sword. How could he see?

The blade, swinging wildly from side to side, almost touched Kormak. He twisted away, losing his balance, and fell into the ravine, shouting with surprise.

He fell a short distance only, landing on a narrow ledge and scrambling onto his knees. His back hurt, as well as a shoulder and an elbow. But he didn't pay attention to the pain. Instead he looked up. The old man was directly above him, looking down with his blind eyes. "I heard you cry out, Kormak. Did you fall in the river? Or are you hiding? If so, I will find you, either with my staff or magic. I want no one to tell Thorstein what I did with the silver."

Kormak said nothing. After a moment, the old man vanished. Shortly after, Svart's body tumbled off the ravine edge, falling past Kormak. An out-flung hand hit Kormak as the body passed. He almost cried out a second time, but did not. Instead, he crouched against the cliff wall, pressing his lips together. Below him, Svart vanished into the river's foam. Cold spray from the waterfall came down on Kormak like fine rain, making the ledge slippery.

The old man reappeared at the ravine's edge. "I can bring stones and roll them down on you. If you haven't joined Svart in the river, you will then."

The old man was trying to trick him into making a noise. Kormak kept his lips pressed together.

Egil knelt clumsily at the cliff rim and pushed his staff down along the stone wall, swinging it from side to side. Kormak lay on his back, making himself as flat as possible. The staff's tip swung above him, almost touching. Kormak sucked his belly in and tried not to breathe.

"Well, then," the old man said finally. "It will have to be stones. I wish you had been more cooperative. Look at Svart. He gave me no trouble at all."

The old man stood stiffly. Once again he vanished. Kormak sat up and looked around for an escape. But the cliff wall was sheer. He could see only one way off the ledge: jumping into the turbulent, dangerous river below him. He stood, thinking he would have to risk this.

As he stood, a door opened in the cliff wall a short distance from him, at one end of the ledge. A man looked out. He was tall and even handsomer than Thorstein Egilsson, with long, silver-blond hair that flowed over his shoulders and a neatly trimmed silver-blond moustache. His shirt was bright red; his pants were dark green; and his belt had a gold buckle. The man smiled and beckoned.

This seemed a better choice than the river. Kormak walked to the door. The man beckoned a second time. Kormak stepped inside, and the man closed the door. They were in a corridor made of stone and lit by lanterns. It extended into the distance, empty except for the two of them.

"Welcome to the land of the elves," the man said. "I am Alfhjalm, a retainer of the local lord."

Kormak gave his name and thanked the elf for saving him from Egil.

"We keep track of the Marsh Men, because they have always been troublesome neighbors," Alfhjalm said. "As a rule, we don't cross them, since we don't want to attract attention. But we have a grudge against Egil, and now that he is old and weak, we are willing to disrupt his plans."

"Will he die out there?" Kormak asked, hoping that Egil would. The old man had killed Svart, who trusted him.

"We don't want Thorstein coming here to bother us, as he certainly will if he can't find his father. He has no magic powers, but he is a persistent man. Some of my companions have gone to lead the horses away, making enough noise that Egil will able to follow. In this way, they will lure him out of the mountains and close to home. Then they'll help him catch the horses, so he can ride home with dignity. If they do their job well, he will never know that elves were involved. We like to remain hidden and unknown. As for you – come with me."

They walked along the corridor, which went on and on. After a while, Kormak noticed that the lamps cast a strange light, pale and steady, not at all like the light of burning wood or oil. He stopped and looked into a lamp. Inside was a pile of clear stones with sharp edges. The light came from them.

"They are sun stones," the elf said. "If we set them in sunlight, they take the sunlight in and then pour it out like water from a jug, until they are empty and go dark. Then our slaves replace the stones with fresh ones, full of light."

"You have slaves?" Kormak asked.

"We are like Icelanders, except more clever, fortunate, healthy, and prosperous. The Icelanders have slaves, and so do we."

This made Kormak uneasy. But he kept walking beside the elf, who was taller than he was and had a sword at his side.

At last they came to an open space. Light shone from above, though it was dimmer than the spring light in Borgarfjord. Looking up, Kormak saw a dark roof, dotted with many brilliant points of light.

"Are those stars?" he asked.

"No," said the elf. "They are sun stones, like the ones in our lamps. If the stones are solitary, they gradually fade. But we can connect them, laying them one after another through channels in the rock. Then each pours light on the next and renews it. In this way they bring sunlight from the high mountains into our home. They never dim in the summer, but in winter it can be dark here."

Below the roof were high, black cliffs ringing a flat valley dotted with groves of trees. Animals grazed in green fields. In the middle of all this was a long hall, larger than the one at Borg. The roof shone as if covered with gold.

"That is my lord's hall," Alfhjalm said. "Come and meet him."

They walked down a slope into the valley. The fields around them were full of thick, lush grass. The animals grazing – sheep and cattle and horses – all looked healthy and well fed. Many had young, which meant it was spring in Elfland as well as in Iceland.

He had never seen handsomer horses. They were larger than Icelandic horses and every color: tan, red-brown, dark-brown, black, blue-gray, and white, with black or blond manes. As he and the elf walked past, the horses lifted their heads, regarding them with calm, curious, dark eyes.

At last they came to a road paved with pieces of stone. "Our kin in the south learned how to do this from the Romans," Alfhjalm told him. "You can say what you want about the Romans – they know how to build roads."

Kormak barely knew who the Romans were. But he was glad to be walking on a smooth pavement rather than a twisting trail.

The road led to the long hall. When they were close, Kormak saw the roof was covered with shields. Some shone silver, others gold.

"They are bronze, covered with gold or silver leaf," Alfhjalm said. "It would be difficult to make the roof solid gold. We elves are more prosperous than Icelanders and have more precious metal, but our wealth is not unending. And if needed, we can pull the shields down and use them in war."

They entered the long hall. A fire burned low in a pit that ran the hall's length. At the end were two high seats made of carved wood. One was empty. The other contained a handsome old man. Firelight flickered over him, making his white hair and beard shine. He wore a crown, a simple band of gold, and a gold-hilted sword lay across his knees.

"This is Alfrad," Alfhjalm said. "Our lord."

They walked the length of the hall and bowed to the old man.

"Welcome," he said in a deep, impressive voice. "Tell me why you came here."

Kormak told the story of his journey with Egil and Svart and how the old man had killed Svart and tried to kill him, all to hide two chests of silver that he didn't want his son to inherit.

"They are a difficult family," the elf lord said finally. "Not good neighbors. I will send men to recover the silver from the river. There is no reason to leave it in the water. You will be our guest until I decide what to do with you."

They bowed again and left the long hall. Once outside, Kormak gave a sigh of relief. He was not used to speaking with lords, especially elf lords. Alfhjalm took him to another building, where food lay on a table: bread and meat and ale. Kormak learned later that this often happened in Elfland. If something was needed – a meal, a tool, an article of clothing – it would be found close by, though he never saw servants bringing whatever it was. Maybe this was magic, or maybe the elves had servants who could not be seen: the Hidden Folk's hidden folk.

They sat down and ate. Kormak found he was hungry. "There are two high seats," he said to Alfhjalm, after he was full.

"The other belongs to Alfrad's wife Bevin. She is an Irish fey who grew weary of the north and went home to Ireland, though she left a daughter here, who is named Svanhild. She is the loveliest maiden in Elfland and also the richest. I am courting her, along with many other men, but she is not interested in any of us."

"What is your quarrel with the family at Borg?" Kormak asked next. He was always curious. It was one of the qualities that made him a difficult slave.

"Many-fold," Alfhjalm replied. "We came to Iceland before humans did, leaving Norway because it became too crowded with people. There was no one here in those days except a few Irish monks. We frightened them, and they kept to small islands off the coast, while we had all of Iceland for our own. The country was empty, except for birds and foxes. There were forests of birch and aspen, which the humans have cut down, and broad fields where we could pasture our animals, black mountains with caps of white snow, and the brilliant sky of summer. As lovely as Norway had been, this seemed lovelier.

"But then the settlers came. They were violent, greedy folk. We are less numerous than the elves of Norway, and we did not have the strength to oppose the settlers. We withdrew into the mountains to avoid them, becoming the Hidden Folk. When we traveled, it was at night, when no one could see us. That was our first quarrel with the Marsh Men. Egil's grandfather Kveldulf would grow sleepy late in the day and sit hunched in a corner of their hall. Then his spirit would go out in the form of a huge wolf, roaming through Borgarfjord. There are no wolves in Iceland, as you must know, only foxes and a few white bears that float into the northern fjords on sheets of ice."

Of course Kormak knew this. He had even seen the skin of a white bear, when he was a slave in the north. It had been yellow rather than white and not nearly as soft as a fox's pelt.

"The foxes are too small to bother us, and we don't have a problem with bears in this part of Iceland. But it was an ugly surprise when Kveldulf appeared in wolf form, and it made our night journeys unpleasant. He was a frightening sight. We elves do not like to be afraid."

No one does, thought Kormak.

"We thought of killing his wolf form, but it was possible that Kveldulf would be unharmed and wake up, knowing about us. Life was easier when we had Iceland – and Borgarfjord – to ourselves." Alfhjalm lifted a pitcher and poured more ale. "He died of old age finally, and the wolf was not seen again. Then his son Skallagrim inherited the farm at Borg. He was another man like Egil, big and strong and ugly, almost a giant; and he was an ironsmith, which sounds better than a wolf. But we elves are not entirely comfortable with iron. Though we can use it and even work it, we prefer other metals. We are able to cast spells over copper, tin, silver, and gold, making the metal stronger, sharper, brighter, luckier, and better to use. Iron resists our magic. If we make an iron blade, it cuts less well than a blade of bronze. If we make an iron pot, it cooks food badly. Iron tools turn in our hands. Everything becomes less useful and lucky.

"Skallagrim made us uneasy, since he had great skill with iron, and we suspected his skill was magical. He never did us any harm. Nonetheless, we avoided him and watched him for signs of danger. In the end, he died in bed like his father, and Egil became the farmer at Borg. He is the worst of the three: a Viking, a poet and a magician. There is no question about his magical power, though it appears diminished now.

"He knows a spell that can compel land spirits, such as we are. He cast it on our kin in Norway, so they could not rest until they drove King Eirik Bloodaxe from the country. If he could do this to Norwegian elves, he can do it to us. It's a difficult spell that requires killing a mare and cutting off its head, then setting the head on a pole carved with runes. We are not sure he can still do it, but we are always careful around him."

"Why did you help me?" Kormak asked.

"I wanted to know what Egil was doing. He was killing men on our doorstep. Who could say what that meant? And he had a mare with him. It was possible that he intended to cast a spell on us. I am willing to cross him, if I can do it without him knowing. We have lived in fear of the Marsh Men for a long time, and it's been angering. Now this seems to be ending. Egil will die soon. Thorstein is a good farmer, but not at all magical. He will cause us no more trouble than any other human."

"What will happen to me?" Kormak asked.

"I think Alfrad will make you a slave. Do you have any special abilities?"

"I have worked with horses," Kormak said. He did not add that he'd learned some ironsmithing from Svart.

"We have fine horses, as you have seen, and we take good care of them. You have a useful skill."

This was his fate, Kormak thought, to go from owner to owner, a slave to farmers in Iceland, then a slave to Icelandic elves. It was a discouraging idea. At least he was alive, unlike Svart, and he was away from the horrible old man. If it was his fate to labor for the elves, he would not trust them. Svart had trusted the Marsh Men and been killed.

He slept in an outbuilding. The next day the elf lord announced that he would be a slave and sent him to work with the elf horses. They were intelligent, well-mannered animals, and Kormak enjoyed them.

All the slaves in Elfland were human. The elves did not own one another. But when humans came into their land, they enslaved them. There is always dirty work to be done everywhere, in Midgard and

Alfheim and Jotunheim and Asgard. Even magical beings had work they did not want to do, either with their hands or magic. The slaves were a miserable group, badly dressed, dirty, and sullen.

Kormak was sure he remembered stories about humans who went into Elfland and had fine lives, sleeping with elf ladies, hunting with elf lords, till they woke and realized a hundred years had passed. Instead he mucked out stables and groomed horses. Well, life was never like stories. In time, he began to help an elf smith, who forged gear for horses out of bronze. The smith had some iron, which he never used. "An evil metal," he told Kormak. But he kept the ingots tucked in a corner of his smithy, and Kormak remembered where the iron was.

So the days passed. There was no winter in Elfland, though the sky grew dark when winter came to the land outside. Still, it was warm. He never had to follow animals through the snow. One period of darkness came and went, then another, then a third. He had been in Elfland three years. Egil must be dead by now. Should he try to escape? Was it possible?

Elves came to get horses and ride them inside or outside Elfland. Some were tall and handsome men. Others were beautiful women. One was the lord's daughter, Svanhild. Her favorite mount was a dun mare with white mane and tail. No horse was lovelier, and no rider was more beautiful. Svanhild was blue-eyed with blonde hair as white as her horse's mane. Her dress was usually blue, a deep and pure color; and her cloak was scarlet. Gold bracelets shone on her arms. Of course Kormak was interested in her, but he was not crazy. He kept his ideas to himself and helped the elf girl on and off her horse.

One day she came by herself. The elf smith was gone from the forge, and Kormak worked alone. "I know you have been watching me," she said. "I think you want to have sex with me. I also know you are Irish, like my mother."

"I am Irish," said Kormak. "I am also a slave, and I take my pleasure with other slaves, not with noble women."

"That may be," Svanhild replied. "I want to go to my mother's country. My father is narrow-minded and avaricious. Look at what he did with the treasure you and your companion brought to the river. You don't have it. My father does, and he has not shared. Instead, you are a slave, though you brought him wealth."

"Yes," said Kormak.

"The men here want to marry me because I am my father's heir. I have no interest in any of them. In my mother's country, I might be free."

"Or maybe not," Kormak replied. "I have not found freedom anywhere."

"I am willing to try," Svanhild replied. "Will you come with me and help me?"

"Why should I?"

"Once we reach the land of the fey, I will set you free. You will be in Ireland then, which is your native country."

He would be taking a risk, but maybe it was time to do so. He did not want to spend the rest of his life as a slave in Elfland. Kormak answered, "Yes."

The woman smiled, and her smile was an arrow going into Kormak's heart.

She left, and he had a thought. While the elf smith was gone, he shod two horses with iron. One was Svanhild's favorite horse, the dun mare with white mane and tail. The other was an iron-gray gelding with black mane and tail. The iron shoes made the horses uneasy. They sidled and danced. But they endured the iron.

Three days later, Svanhild returned. She rode a red mare and wore a chain-mail shirt. Two full bags were fastened to her saddle.

"Is this the animal you want to take?" Kormak asked, disturbed. He was relying on the iron shoes.

"No. I needed it to carry my bags, but my dun mare is sturdier and better tempered."

Kormak unsaddled the animal and moved the saddle to the dun mare. As he did so, he noticed that the bags were heavy. "I hope you have directions."

"I have a map, which my mother left me."

"Good." Kormak's horse was the iron-gray gelding, a strong animal, intelligent and calm. He did not want trouble on this journey. Fire was fine for war and stallion fights. But what he needed now was sturdy endurance.

They mounted. Svanhild led, and Kormak followed. *This is hardly wise,* he told himself. He was risking his life for a girl who had no interest in him and for the hope of freedom. But he was tired of Elfland and Iceland.

They rode up a slope in the brief, dim daylight of winter, then entered a tunnel. The horses' hooves rang on stone. The air smelled of dust. There were only a few of the sun-stone lamps here, possibly because the tunnel led down. Who would want to go away from sunlight and open air? A tunnel like this one must be little traveled.

Each lamp shone like a star in the distance. When they reached one, they rode through a brief region of brightness, then back into darkness, with the next lamp shining dimly in front of them.

On and on they went, until they reached a place with no more lamps. Svanhild reined her horse and opened a saddlebag. Out came a lamp made of bronze and glass and full of brightly shining sun stones. She gave it to Kormak to hold, then took out a bronze stick and unfolded it, till it became a long pole with a hook at one end. "Put the lamp on the hook," she told Kormak, "then hold it up, so it casts light over us."

Kormak did as he was told.

They went on, riding slowly, lit by the lamp that Kormak held.

At length they came to a spring that spurted out of the tunnel wall and flowed across the stone until it reached another hole and vanished. They dismounted and watered the horses, then drank themselves.

"How long is the journey?" Kormak asked.

"Twenty-five days by horse," the girl replied.

"Is it all like this?" Kormak asked, waving around at the tunnel.

"I think so."

"The horses will need to eat, and so will we."

"There are folk down here, dark elves mostly. They are kin to us, though they prefer darkness to light. We used to live in the sunlight, as I think you know, but they have always lived underground. This is their tunnel."

"Do they have hay?" Kormak asked.

"I think so."

They mounted and rode on.

There was no way to tell time in the darkness, but they continued until Kormak and the horses were tired. He was about to say they would have to stop when a light appeared ahead of them. It wasn't a sun-stone lamp, he realized as they came nearer. The light was too yellow and uncertain. It came from a lantern fixed to the tunnel's stone wall. A man stood under it, leaning on a spear. The still air smelled of hot oil.

He was as tall as one of the elf warriors, but broader through the shoulders and chest. His hair and beard were black. His skin was dark, and his eyes – glinting below heavy brows – were like two pieces of obsidian. He wore a mail shirt that shone like silver and a helmet inlaid with gold.

"What do we have here?" he asked in a deep voice.

"I am Svanhild, the daughter of Alfrad, a lord of the light elves and kin to you. This human is my slave. We are going to my mother's country in Ireland. I ask your help in getting there."

"I can't make that decision, as you ought to know. But I'll send you to those who can decide." He put two fingers in his mouth and whistled sharply. A dog emerged from the darkness, iron-grey and wolfish. When it reached the elf warrior, it stopped. Its back was level with the warrior's belt, and every part of the animal was thick and powerful. A man could ride it, Kormak thought, if he pulled his feet up, and the dog was willing.

It opened its mouth, revealing knife-sharp, gray teeth and a gray tongue that lolled out.

It was made from iron, Kormak realized, though it moved as easily as a real dog. The dog regarded Kormak and the girl with eyes that glowed like two red coals.

"A marvel, isn't he?" the dark elf said. "Made of iron and magic. We can't do this kind of work any longer, but our ancestor Volund could. He made the dog after he fled the court of King Nidhad of Nerike, where he had been a prisoner. He took his revenge on Nidhad by killing the king's two sons and making goblets of their skulls and a brooch of their teeth. He gave the goblets to the king and the brooch to the king's wife, who was the boys' mother. In addition, because he was someone who did nothing by halves, he raped Bodvild, the king's lovely and innocent daughter. Then he flew away on iron wings. He couldn't walk because the king had cut his hamstrings, wanting to keep Volund as a smith.

"Once he was safe, he forged the dog, working on crutches. He wanted a servant who was intelligent and trusty, but not any kind of man. By then he was tired of men, even of himself."

"What happened to the girl?" Svanhild asked.

"She bore two children, products of the rape, which happened while she was in a drunken sleep, so she didn't know it had happened until she began to grow in size. Her father kept the boy but put the girl out on a hillside to die. The child lived, but that's a story too long for me to tell." The dark elf looked down at the iron dog. "Take them to the Thing for All Trades."

The dog replied with a bark.

"Follow him," the dark elf ordered.

They did, riding into a side tunnel dimly lit by a few oil lamps.

"What do you know about these people?" Kormak asked.

"They are ironsmiths who use no magic. They say iron is sufficient and better than any other metal, though we think it's obdurate and uncooperative. I had not realized that Volund could enchant iron. He was a prince of the dark elves and famous for his skill as a smith. These days the dark elves have no princes, nor any lords. No one could equal Volund, they say. Instead, they form assemblies, where every elf has an equal voice."

"Like the Althing in Iceland," Kormak said. "Though rich and powerful men have more say there, and slaves have no say."

After a pause, Svanhild said, "The dark elves do not distinguish between rich and poor or between men and women. All work, and all join the assembly for their trade."

"Why are they so different from you?" Kormak asked.

"Iron," Svanhild replied. "And lack of magic! All beauty and nobility come from magic."

Kormak was not sure of this. There was little magic in Iceland, except for a few witches and men like Egil. But the black mountains and green fields seemed lovely to him, also the rushing rivers and the waves that beat against the country's coast. He could praise the flight of a falcon across the summer sky or the smooth gait of a running horse. At times, he was at the edge of speaking poetry. But the words did not come; he was left with the memory of what he'd seen.

The tunnel opened into a cave. No sun stones shone from the cave's roof. Instead, the floor was dotted with lights. Some looked to be lamps or torches. Others – brighter – might be forge fires. Hammers rang out, louder and more regular than any he'd heard before.

The dog kept going. They followed it down a slope. There was a track, lit by the lantern Kormak held: two ruts in the stony ground. It led into a little town. The low houses were built of stone. Lantern light shone through open doors and windows. Torches flared, fastened on exterior walls. Here and there, Kormak saw people: tall and powerful and dark. A woman swept her doorway. A man wielded a pick, pulling cobbles out of the street.

Now they rode next to a stream, rushing between stone banks. Rapids threw up mist that floated in the air. Kormak felt it gratefully.

Ahead was a hall, torches blazing along its front. Two elven warriors stood before the door, armed with swords and metal shields.

Kormak and Svanhild reined their horses. "We were sent here by the guard in the tunnel," Svanhild said in her clear, pure voice. "I am Svanhild, the daughter of Alfrad, your kinswoman from the north."

"We know Alfgeir sent you, because the dog Elding is with you," a guard replied.

"What do you want?"

"Passage to my mother's country in the south."

"Who is your mother?"

"Bevin of the White Arms."

"Irish fey," said the second guard. "We know them, though we don't much like them. Still, it's up to the thing-chiefs to decide your fate." He turned and pushed through the hall's metal door.

They waited for a while, staying on their horses. Finally, the guard came back out. "Go in."

Svanhild and Kormak dismounted.

The first guard said, "I'll water your horses while you're gone. They are fine animals, better than any we have, though they look weary and thirsty."

"Not too much water," Kormak warned.

"We know iron better than animals. Nonetheless, we have some horses, and I have cared for them. I know what to do."

They walked inside, the iron dog pacing next to them. The hall was as large as Alfrad's. Stone pillars held up the roof, and stone benches ran along the two side walls, unoccupied at present. A long fire pit ran down the middle, full of ash. Here and there red light shone from the ash, and a thin trail of smoke rose, but most of the light came from torches burning around the high seats at the hall's far end. There were six. Three held old men with broad, white beards; and three held old women with long, white braids. The dog barked. Kormak and Svanhild walked forward and bowed to the thing-chiefs.

"Who are you?" an old woman asked, leaning forward. She was bone-thin, with a skin the gray hue of a twilight sky. Her eyes were dark and keen.

"Svanhild, the daughter of Alfrad. My father is an elf lord and your kin, as he has often told me. This man is my slave."

He was tired of this introduction, Kormak thought, but said nothing.

"Why have you come?" an old man asked. He was darker than the woman, though his skin had the same faint tint of blue. His eyes were as pale as ice.

"I seek help in reaching my mother's country in Ireland."

"Why should we help?" another woman asked, this one fat and black. Her blue eyes looked like stars to Kormak. No woman this old should have eyes so bright.

The dog opened its mouth and spoke in a harsh voice that Kormak could barely understand.

"Hat-hidden, Odin
tests human hosting.
Hard the fate
of those who fail."

"Nonsense," another old man, as gray as granite, put in. "We are not human, and both of these people have two eyes."

"And no ravens," the third old man said. He was the palest of the chiefs. "They are not Odin."

The third woman, twilight-colored like the first woman, said, "The All-Father judges all, not just humans; and the dog reminds us that he requires hospitality."

The black woman leaned forward. "But in honor of our ancestor Volund, we need to ask for fair payment for what we do – in gold or silver, stories, music, or revenge."

"I can pay," Svanhild replied. "We came here with two horses. One is a gelding, but the other is a fine mare, able to improve your breed. I will give you the horses in return for our passage."

"That seems fair," the black woman said. "Two good horses for a ride in one of our lightning carts. They will be going to Ireland and Wales even if there are no passengers."

"Why?" asked Kormak, the man who asked questions.

"Why do they go?" the palest man answered, stroking his silky beard. "They go to Ireland to deliver jewels and fine smithing to the fey there. No iron, of course. The fey hate iron. They go to Wales for coal. We mine it from below and send it to our forges in the north."

"Are you willing to give us passage?" Svanhild asked.

One by one, the elf chiefs nodded.

"Come with me," a voice said next to Kormak. It was Alfgeir, the guard from the tunnel. He must have followed them, Kormak thought, and slipped into the hall while they waited outside. He wore a cloak now, as if he planned to travel. "I know the woman's name, but who are you?"

Kormak introduced himself as the elf warrior led them from the hall. The two guards were still there, watering the horses in the stream.

"These are ours now," Alfgeir said. "It was clever of you to shoe them with iron. Svanhild's kin could not track them with magic."

"I thought that might be true," said Kormak, "but I did not know for certain."

Svanhild gestured at her mare, and Kormak took off the saddlebags, staggering a little under their weight. What had the elf maid packed? He lifted the bags over one shoulder and followed Alfgeir and Svanhild. She had the lantern. It lit their way to the edge of town.

A low platform stood there. Torches on poles cast a wavering light. They climbed onto the platform. Kormak walked to the far side and looked down, seeing ground covered with gravel. Planks of wood lay in the gravel. Two, long narrow pieces of iron lay across the wood. It looked like a fence lying down.

"Where do you get the wood?" he asked.

"From Ireland," said Alfgeir. "They have mighty forests of oak and pine and birch."

"What's it for?"

"You will see."

After a while he heard a noise he didn't recognize. He looked toward it and saw a lantern moving in the darkness. The noise grew louder. The light grew larger and brighter. Kormak stepped away from the platform's edge.

The thing, whatever it was, lurched and rattled toward him. He stepped farther back as the thing slowed and came to a stop. It was a metal cart with a tall metal tube rising from its roof. Smoke billowed from the tube. Fire burned within the cart, and two figures moved there, lit by the red glare. He couldn't make out what they were doing.

Behind the cart was a second cart, full of pieces of shiny, black rock. Beyond this were more carts, some with roofs and other opens. The elf warrior pointed at one of the roofed carts. "Get in."

They did and found it contained metal benches, set along the walls like benches in a long hall. Kormak put the saddlebags down. The dog settled next to them, its gray tongue hanging out between sharp, gray teeth, and the three of them sat on the metal benches. The cart jerked and then the entire thing, whatever it was, moved forward. They left the platform behind and went into darkness, except for the dog's red eyes and the lantern that Svanhild held.

For a long time they rattled on. Either the cavern was huge or they were going from one cave to another. Sometimes the region around them was completely dark. Sometimes there were clusters of lights that must have been stone towns or great, flaring forges with gigantic hammers that rose and fell. The hammers were far too large to be held by men or elves. Nonetheless, they moved. Kormak saw no sign of trolls.

Svanhild's lantern cast enough light so he could see both of his companions. The elf warrior sprawled on a bench, looking comfortable.

Svanhild sat stiffly, her face expressionless. *Afraid,* thought Kormak, as was he. The iron dog panted gently.

At last, the line of carts slowed and stopped.

"This can't be Ireland," Svanhild said, looking around at the darkness.

The elf warrior laughed. "We are still a long distance from your mother's country. But we are about to enter the tunnel that goes under the ocean. We can't use fire devices there. Out here, in the caves, their smoke rises and spreads. But the tunnel is low and narrow. The devices' smoke would fill it, and we'd choke. Workers used to die in the tunnel, before we invented a new kind of device."

There were noises outside their cart, movement and some light, but Kormak could not see enough to understand what was happening.

"We are changing devices," the elf warrior said. "Before, our power came from burning coal. Now it will come from a fluid that we call lightning, since it shares qualities with Thor's lightning, though it is quieter and better behaved. Our smiths have taught it to run in copper wires. We fasten these to the roof of the tunnel. A rod brings the fluid into our new device, and it moves without fire or smoke."

"Another wonder," Svanhild said in a calm tone.

The warrior said, "Much can be achieved without magic. We do not trick or compel materials to behave against their nature. Instead, we learn what each material can do."

The activity outside stopped and the carts moved forward again. The smoke that had whirled around them was gone, and there was less noise, though the carts still clanked and rattled.

"The lands of the elves are full of wonders," Svanhild said. "But they do not equal my mother's country."

"Wait and see," Alfgeir said.

"How can you raise horses in this darkness?" Kormak asked.

"We pasture them outside in high valleys or on unsettled islands. It's been more difficult since humans settled Iceland and Greenland. In the end, we may give them up and rely on devices. But not yet."

"Why don't you use sun stones?" Svanhild asked all at once.

"Surely you realize they are magic. They would fade quickly here – we use too much iron."

Kormak looked at the lantern Svanhild held. Yes, it was dimmer than before.

"This journey is boring," Svanhild said.

"Then I will entertain you by telling you more of the story of Volund, our ancestor," Alfgeir said.

"Very well," said Svanhild.

"King Nidhad went to Volund's forge and said, 'Where are my children?'

"'I will tell you,' Volund replied, 'but first you must make me a promise. If a child of mine ever enters your court, you must do him no harm.'

"This seemed like a simple request. Odin encourages us to be hospitable, as you have found out; and as far as Nidhad knew, Volund had no children.

"So he promised. Of course, he was a fool. Volund told him that the two boys were dead. Their skulls were the king's gold and ivory drinking cups. Their teeth were the queen's gold and ivory brooch.

"Nidhad drew his sword, intending to slay Volund, but not yet. 'What about Bodvild, my lovely and innocent daughter?'

"'She lies drunk. She came to my forge, looking for fine jewelry. Instead, I gave her ale and raped her when she was not able to resist.'

"Nidhad raised his sword. In reply, Volund raised his arms, on which were magical iron wings. Before the king could reach him, he'd brought the wings down, lifting himself into air. 'Remember your promise, King,' he called and flew away.

"That was the last Nidhad saw of Volund. As for his daughter, she grew big and bigger and gave birth to twins: a boy and a girl. Nidhad considered his promise. He had said he would not harm a child, but here were two. Did his promise cover both? It seemed reasonable to keep the boy and put the girl on a hillside.

"The boy was named Vidga. Bodvild nursed him and raised him. His grandfather the king treated him harshly, remembering the two fine boys he had lost. Why should Volund have a son, when he had none? As soon as the boy was able, he left home. He became a famous hero, a soldier for the great King Thidrik of Bern. In the end he died, as heroes do.

"As for the girl, a farm wife found her crying on the hillside. She was a woman who had no children and even a girl seemed worth saving. She gathered the baby up and carried her home, where she fed her with a piece of cloth soaked in milk. Sucking on this, the baby grew strong.

"She was raised to be a farm wife, though her father was an elf prince and her mother was the daughter of a king.

"The farm wife named the girl Alda, which means 'wave.' She took after her mother as far as appearances went, being blonde and fair-skinned with eyes like blue stars. But she had her father's skill with materials, though – in her case – it came out as spinning and weaving. The thread she spun was like gossamer. The cloth she wove was like silk, though it was made of wool taken from sturdy Swedish sheep.

"When she worked spinning or weaving, Alda sang:

'What is my fate?

Where is my husband?

Who will I be

In ten years or more?'

"One day a fey, wandering far from his native soil, heard her song and followed the sound of her voice. It's rare to find fey in Scandinavia. For the most part, they keep to their Irish mounds. But this man, who was named Hogshead, came to Alda's house. There she sat, outside in the sunlight, spinning thread that shone like gold.

"Of course, the fey had to have her. Of course, she could not resist a handsome man, dressed in fine clothes and wearing gold rings on his wrists and fingers.

"Without a word to the people who had raised her, she left her spindle and the house. Together, they followed the hidden ways that go from Europe to the Atlantic islands. When they reached Ireland and entered the fey's home mound, he changed. His body remained as it had been, but his head turned into the head of huge, hairy, ugly boar with jutting tusks and little, hard eyes.

"Alda was her father's daughter. She did not scream, as most human women would, and her expression did not change, but she took a step back.

"The fey made a grunting sound that might have been a laugh. Then he bowed deeply. As he straightened, his head changed, and he was once again a handsome man. 'You don't like my true appearance?'

"'No,' said Alda.

"''Well, then, I suppose we have no future. I like to be comfortable at home and look the way I am. Nonetheless, you must meet our queen.'

"He led her to the mound's queen, who was – and is – your mother, though this was long before she married Alfrad. Hogshead told the queen about Alda's spinning and weaving.

"'Show me,' the queen said.

"A spindle and loom were brought, along with wool. Alda spun the wool into yarn and wove it into a fine, thin cloth.

"''You must make my clothes!' the queen exclaimed. 'But not out of wool. We'll find you silk, and I'll be the envy of all the fey in Ireland!'

"There Alda remains in the mound. She has learned to spin and weave silk, and she makes the queen the finest clothing in Ireland."

"That's it?" Kormak asked.

"So far."

"That isn't much of an ending. She should have escaped from the fey or died. That's the way most stories end – with a victory or death. Why didn't Volund rescue her?"

"We can't find him to ask him. Maybe the dog knows where he is."

The iron dog lifted its head, but said nothing.

"He always cared more for his craft than for any person, except – possibly – his Valkyrie wife, who left him. It's said that he always frowned deeply and grew grim when he heard 'yo-to-ho.'"

After that, Kormak grew sleepy and lay down, waking now and then to the rattle of the cart over its metal trail. The lantern had grown dimmer, and the cart was mostly dark. Sometimes he saw the red glare of the dog's eyes.

At length, he woke completely and sat up. Svanhild and the elf warrior sat together near the lantern, sharing bread and wine in its glow. Kormak joined them. There were mushrooms, which Alfgeir laid between two pieces of bread and ate. Kormak followed suit. The mushrooms were delicious, thick and meaty and juicy. The bread was a little dry. He drank enough wine to feel it, then sat by a window and looked out. The lantern on the foremost cart lit the tunnel's stone walls and the metal track ahead of it. Now and then, a second light flashed above the cart, brilliant and white.

"That is the lightning," Alfgeir said.

So it went. Kormak dozed and slept. They ate a second time. The sunstone lantern had grown dimmer.

"Tell me about my mother's land," Svanhild said.

"Didn't she tell you about it?" the elf warrior asked.

"Only that it was far more pleasant than my father's country. She left when I was young."

"We live in stone," Alfgeir said, "as do you. But the fey live below earthen mounds. Their underground country does not look like a cave, as do our homes, but rather like open land, though the sky is sunless and moonless. Magic lights it. There is no winter. The trees bear flowers and fruit at the same time. The streams are full of cold, fresh water. The ground is covered with soft, green grass like a carpet.

"When the fey hunt – and they do; it's their favorite occupation – they bring down fat deer. When they angle, they bring up succulent fish. Everything about their land is lovely and rich.

"They love music and dancing and good-looking people like Volund's daughter Alda. They keep them as servants and lovers."

They would not love him, Kormak thought, with the scar across his face. Well, he had no desire to live among the fey. He remembered them dimly from stories he'd heard as a child. They were more dangerous than the northern elves, who mostly kept to themselves and did not bother their neighbors.

The iron dog growled and spoke:

"Brightness is not best.

Honor is better.

Loveliness leads nowhere

If the heart is hard."

"That may be," Alfgeir said, "but you do not know for certain, Elding. You have never been in their country, nor spent time with any of them." He looked to Kormak and Svanhild. "When we get close to the land of the fey, the carts will stop and you will have to walk. The fey do not tolerate iron in their country. The dog cannot come. Nor can I. I will not give up my iron."

Kormak went back to sleep and woke again. The sun-stone lantern was so dim that his companions were barely visible, though he could still find the dog by the glare of its eyes.

They finished off the rest of the food and wine in silence. Then Kormak sat in darkness, listening to the cart rattle on and on. He slept again and woke and found the carts were motionless. A pale light, like the dawn through mist, shone outside. He could see a platform and a tunnel leading up.

Svanhild lay on the bench opposite him, sleeping and snoring softly, like a cat purring.

"We are here," Alfgeir said. "She won't wake soon, so we have time to talk."

"How do you know she won't wake?" Kormak asked.

"She drank the rest of the wine. That by itself should have put her deeply asleep, but I added a spell."

"You said that dark elves do no magic."

Alfgeir grinned, showing square, white teeth. "No elf is entirely trustworthy, though we are far more reliable than the fey. For the most part, I have told you the truth. Iron makes magic difficult, and dark elves rarely perform it. We always prefer iron. But we're a long way from our country here and close to the country of the fey. Magic is easier here. I have something I want you to do."

"What?" asked Kormak.

"Go into the country of the fey with Svanhild."

"Why should I do this?"

"Look around you. There is nothing here except stone, and it's a long walk back to the country of the dark elves. Dangerous, too. You might be hit by one of our trains. You could go in the other direction, of course, and end in the coal mines of Wales. If you do as I ask, I will be grateful."

"What is your gratitude worth to me?"

"Enough silver to establish yourself among the humans of Ireland. You will be free, and you will be an elf friend."

"That sounds good," Kormak said. "What do you want me to do?"

Alfgeir pulled a bag from somewhere in his clothing and took a gold bracelet from it. "Look for Alda in the fey court. Get her alone and give her this. Tell to wear it on her arm, but keep it hidden under her sleeve. If the fey see it, they will steal it from her."

"Yes," Kormak said and took the bracelet.

"The second time you see her, give her this." Alfgeir pulled out a gold and ivory brooch. "Tell her to pin it to her undergarment, so it will be hidden from the fey. Make sure that she knows to pin it over her heart."

"Do you think she will do this?" Kormak asked.

"She is the child of her mother and the grandchild of Nidhad's queen. Both women loved gold." The elf warrior took a final object from his bag. It was a golden dog, small enough to be held in a woman's hand. The eyes were garnet. A golden tongue hung out between tiny, sharp ivory teeth.

"The third time, you won't have seek her out. She will come to you. Give her this, and see what happens."

"Very well," Kormak said. He put the three objects in their bag and hid the bag in his clothing.

"Now," said Alfgeir. He touched the sleeping woman, and she woke. "Go into the tunnel. It will lead you to the country of the fey."

Svanhild climbed out of the iron cart. Kormak followed, carrying Svanhild's bags, which had not become any easier to carry. They walked along the platform and into the tunnel. Light filled it. There was no point of origin – the air itself seemed to glow – and he could see only a short distance. The glowing whiteness closed in like a mist. The tunnel slanted up and twisted like a snake, rising and turning. They began to climb.

This went on for a long time, till he was weary from carrying Svanhild's saddlebags. If the dark elf had been telling the truth, he would come out of this with freedom and silver. That was worth some effort. Did he trust the elf? Not entirely. But what choice did he have? He had learned one thing when the northerners came to his village and burned it and took slaves: he did not control his fate.

At last they came to a door made of polished wood and covered with carvings of interlaced animals. There was a bronze ring set in the door. Svanhild took hold of it and knocked.

The door opened, revealing a handsome man dressed in green. His hair was red and curly. His face was clean-shaven and his skin was fair. He wore a heavy, twisted, golden torque around his neck. "Well?" he asked.

"I am Svanhild, the daughter of Bevin of the White Arms. I've come to find my mother."

"She's here, though I don't know if she will want to see you. Nonetheless, come in."

They did. As Kormak passed through the doorway, the stone groaned loudly. The man looked suddenly wary. "What are you?"

"He's human and my slave," Svanhild said. "Don't you have human slaves?"

"Why should we? We are served by magical beings. Humans are for making music and love. Since he belongs to you, I will let him in."

Beyond the door was a wide, green country. A meadow lay before them, where noble-looking people played a bowling game with golden balls. On the far side, the land rose into wooded hills. Many of the trees were flowering. A sweet scent filled the air. The sky above was misty white.

"I will escort you to the queen," the man said.

"Do you have a name?" Kormak asked.

"My name is Secret," the fey replied. "And you?"

"Kormak."

"Are you Irish?"

"Yes."

"Our favorite humans!"

They circled the meadow to avoid the bowlers. A wooden bridge led over a crystal-clear river. Looking down, Kormak saw silver trout floating above the river's pebbled floor. Apple trees with fragrant white blossoms leaned over the water, dropping petals. He saw red fruit among the blooms. A miraculous land!

The next thing he knew, they were climbing a hill. On top was a grove of oak trees, their branches thick with acorns. The ground was carpeted with acorns, and a huge boar was feeding on them. Its lean body was covered with long, black, bristling hair, and yellow tusks sprouted from its mouth

Svanhild paused. "Is this safe?"

"That's Hogshead," the fey answered. "He'll do no harm."

The boar lifted its head, then reared up till it was standing on its hind legs. Kormak had never seen any kind of pig do this. A moment later, a man dressed in scarlet stood where the boar had been.

"How are the acorns?" their fey asked.

The man grunted happily, and they walked on, leaving him standing under the oak trees.

Well, that was strange, Kormak thought. He glanced at Svanhild. Usually she had a calm, determined expression, but now she looked drunk or dazed, her eyes wide open and her lips parted. Was this Alfgeir's magic? Or was she so in love with her mother's land?

They descended the hill to another meadow. A silver tent stood in the middle. The fabric shone like water and moved like water in the gentle wind.

"This is her bower," their fey said.

One side was open. Inside sat richly dressed ladies, listening to a harper play. Some had human heads and faces. Others had the heads of deer with large ears and large, dark eyes. One had the long neck and sharp, narrow beak of a crane, though her shoulders – white and sloping – were those of a woman, and she had a woman's graceful arms and hands.

In the middle sat the queen, who looked human, more fair than any woman Kormak had ever seen. She held up a hand to silence the harper, then beckoned.

They approached.

"Who are you?" the queen asked.

"I am Svanhild, the daughter of Alfrad and Bevin of the White Arms. This man is human and a slave."

"If that is so, you are my daughter. If you wish, you can stay a while. But the human is ugly, scarred, and worn with labor. Send him away. Maybe someone in my land will find him interesting, but I don't want to look at him."

Svanhild glanced at Kormak. "Do as the queen says. Put down my saddlebags and go."

Kormak did as he was told. The harper began playing. The music was sweeter than any he had heard before, and he would have liked to stay. But the queen had a cold face. What had the iron dog called it? Loveliness with a hard heart.

Their fey walked with him from the tent.

"What will I do?" Kormak asked.

"There are humans here who no longer interest us. Former lovers. Former harpers and pipers. They live in our forests. When we have finished banquets – we usually eat out of doors, so we can enjoy the scented air and the birds that fly from tree to tree – they come and eat whatever food remains. Sometimes we hunt them for amusement."

This was worse than living in Elfland. It might even be worse than Iceland.

"Do you know of a banquet that might be over?" Kormak asked. "I'm hungry."

The fey pointed. Kormak walked through the lush, green grass to a grove of apple trees. He pulled an apple from among the blossoms and ate as he walked. In the middle of the grove was a long table made of wooden boards. Dishes covered it, full of the remains of a feast: roast pork, white bread, wine, a half-eaten salmon. Ragged humans fed there, using their hands. He joined in. Everything was delicious, though cold.

"Do you know the human woman Alda?" he asked when he was full.

The man next to him stopped chewing on a ham bone and said, "There's a cave in that far hill." He used the ham bone to point. "She's there, always weaving. She won't pay any attention to you. She's under an enchantment, as I used to be, when the noble lady Weasel loved me. I wish I still were. I was happy then. Now I am not."

Kormak went on. Maybe he should have refused this task. But that would have left him in the stone tunnel, with no alternative except to walk back to the land of dark elves.

There was a trail, no more than an animal track, which wound through forest and meadow. He followed it to the hill. As the man had said, there was a cave. Lamps shone inside. Kormak entered. A woman sat at a loom, weaving. She was young with long, blonde hair. For a human, she was lovely, though not as lovely as the fey with human heads.

He greeted her. She kept weaving, paying him no attention.

What could he do? He took out the gold bracelet and held it between her and the loom. She paused. "What is this?"

"A gift for you. Take it and wear it, but be sure to keep it under your sleeve – the fey will steal it if they see it."

"This is true." She took the bracelet and pushed it onto her arm, under the sleeve. Then she looked at Kormak. Her blue eyes were dim, as if hidden behind a fine veil. "Who are you?"

"An emissary from someone who wants to give you gifts. I know no more than that."

"Are there more?" the woman asked.

"Yes, but not today."

"I could tell the fey about you."

"And lose the gifts. You know the fey share little."

The woman nodded. "I have been here a long time, weaving and weaving. They have never given me gold, though they have plenty." Then she returned to weaving.

Kormak left her and went up into the forest on the hill. He found a clearing in a pine grove, where the air was sweet with the scent of the needles. One huge tree had a hollow at its base. He used that as a bed.

In the middle of the night, he woke. A splendid stag stood in front of him, rimmed with light.

"What are you?" Kormak asked.

"I used to be human. Now I am prey. Can you hide me?"

Kormak scrambled up and looked at his hollow, then at the stag. "You are too big."

"Then I will have to run," the stag replied, and ran.

As it left his little clearing, dogs appeared, baying loudly. After them came fey on horseback with bows and spears. Kormak crouched down. They did not appear to see him. Instead, they raced through the clearing and were gone.

The stag had no chance. The light that rimmed him made him a clear target. He would die. Kormak wrapped his arms around his knees and shook. Finally, he went back to sleep. In the morning, he remembered the stag dimly. Had it been a dream?

The day was misty, as if the silver-white sky had descended and hung now among the hilltops. Trees were shadowy. The air felt damp. Kormak wandered down into meadows, looking for another banquet. He found nothing. In the end, he picked apples from among the apple blossoms and ate them to break his fast. In spite of the mist, the land looked more beautiful than on the previous day. Flowers shone like jewels in the grass. The birds sang more sweetly than any birds he'd ever heard, even as a child in Ireland. The birds in Iceland had not been singers. Instead, they had quacked, honked, whistled, and screamed.

He reached Alda's cave and entered. She sat at her loom, her hands unmoving. "I dreamed of my foster parents last night and the farm where I grew up. How could I have forgotten?"

"I know nothing about that," Kormak replied. "But here is your second gift." He held out the gold and ivory broach. "Pin it to your undergarment, over your heart, and make sure the fey do not see it."

Alda did as he said. "I feel restless today, unwilling to weave."

"Do you have to?"

"The queen will be angry if I don't."

"Does she come here often?"

"No."

He sat down, leaning against the cave wall, and they talked. He told her about his life in Iceland and among the light elves, though he didn't tell her about Alfgeir or the dark elves.

She talked about her foster family. It was hard to talk about the fey, she said. Events in their country were difficult to remember. "My dream last night is clearer to me than my days here."

At last, he rose. "I will come again."

"Yes," said Alda.

He walked out. The mist had lifted, and the land lay bright under the white sky. Kormak's heart rose. He spent the rest of the day wandering. Deer grazed in meadows. A sow with piglets drank from a crystal stream. Once a cavalcade of fey rode by. He stepped into the shadow of the trees and watched them, admiring their embroidered garments, gold torques, and gold crowns.

The white sky slowly darkened. At length he found the remains of a banquet. Torches on poles blazed around it, and ragged humans fed at the board. He joined them, gathering bread, roasted fowl and wine.

He ate until a fey appeared. It was short and looked like a badger, covered with gray fur, with white stripes on its head. Unlike any animal Kormak had seen before, it wore pants and shoes. The pants were bright blue and the shoes red. The badger's beady eyes were intelligent, and it could speak. "Away! Away, you miserable vermin! Eat acorns in the forest! Eat worms in the meadows! Don't eat the food of your betters!"

Kormak ran. No one followed him. After wandering awhile, he found the hollow where he'd slept the night before. He settled down and slept. In the morning, he woke in a kind of daze. His promises to Alfgeir and Alda were no longer important. Why should he visit the weaver in the cave? Why should he deliver the golden dog? It seemed more reasonable to wander in the woods and meadows, watching the fey from a distance, admiring their beauty.

That day – or another – he found a well and leaned over the stone wall that rimmed it. Below was water. A salmon rose to the surface and said, "Well, you are a sad case."

"What do you mean?" Kormak asked, not surprised that the fish could talk.

"You were given a task, but you have not completed it. Instead, you have let the country of the fey enchant you."

"It's better than Iceland or Elfland," Kormak said.

"There is more than one kind of slavery," the salmon replied and dove.

He left the well, dismissing the salmon's words.

He had no idea how many days passed after that. The sky darkened and then grew light, but there was never sun or moon to keep time. He remembered meals, though not well, and tumbling in a pine-needle bed with a woman, not a fey, but a ragged human. They were both drunk. After, she told him of the days when she had been the lover of a noble fey. Everything had been magical then: the fey's loving, the wine, the gowns she wore, the music and dancing.

The woman left in the morning. He had a terrible hangover and slept most of the day. More time passed. He had more food, but no more sex.

One morning he woke and saw Alda standing by his hollow. "You didn't come back," she said.

"I forgot," he said after a moment.

"That can happen here. It's dangerous. Always try to remember. You said you had one more gift for me."

He dug in the earth of his sleeping hollow till he found the bag Alfgeir had given him.

"I have dreamed of my childhood every night," Alda said. "of my foster parents and our neighbors. Ordinary things, though sometimes – not often – I have dreamed of a man working in a forge, leaning on crutches, his legs withered. His shoulders are wide and strong, his hammer blows powerful. I don't know who he is."

Volund, thought Kormak. But how could she dream of a man she had never met?

Alda continued, "This country seems dim now. I no longer find it attractive, and weaving has become tiresome. I want to return to the land outside. I suspect you may know the way, so I came to find you."

Kormak scrambled to his feet. He pulled out the gold dog with garnet eyes, the last of Alfgeir's gifts, and Alda took it. As soon as it was in her hand, the gold shell split in two. Inside was a dog made of black metal. Alda cried out and dropped the tiny thing. As soon as it was on the ground, it began to grow larger and larger, until it was the size of an Icelandic horse.

"Mount me," it growled. "I will carry you from this place."

"Will you do this?" Kormak asked Alda.

"Yes."

"You as well, Kormak," the dog growled.

He hesitated.

"The fey will punish you when they find Alda gone," the dog growled.

They mounted the iron dog, Kormak first, Alda behind him, her arms around his waist.

The moment they were on the dog, the sky darkened.

"The fey know I'm here," the dog said. "Though there is little they can do, except send apparitions. Their magic cannot harm me, nor you as long you ride me. Hold tight! And ignore what you see!"

Frozen rain began to fall, hitting them like stones. The dog ran. Monsters emerged from the gray sleet: animals like wolves, but much larger. They kept pace with the dog, snarling and snapping. Then the ground, covered with hail, began to move. Other monsters rose from it, long and sinuous and white. Kormak had no idea what they were. Their mouths were full of sharp teeth, and liquid dripped from their narrow tongues. Was it poison? The dog kept running, leaping from monster to monster, never slipping on the wet, scaly backs. Like the wolves, the worms snapped. But they could not reach the dog or its riders.

The storm ended suddenly. They ran among flowering trees. Lovely men and women paced next to them now, riding on handsome horses. "Don't leave, dear Alda. Whatever you want, we'll give you."

Alda's arms tightened around Kormak's waist.

"And you, Kormak? What do you want? Gold? A fey lover? Music, rare food, dancing? In the land outside, you will be a slave again. Here you can be a noble lord."

The air around them filled with harping. Dancers appeared among the flowering trees.

"Run faster!" Alda cried.

The dog entered a tunnel. Flying things pursued them: giant dragonflies and little birds with teeth. They darted around the dog, almost touching. The wings of the dragonflies whirred loudly. The little birds cried, "Return! Return!"

"Don't bat at them," the dog warned. "If you touch them, you will lose the safety I give you!"

Holes appeared in the tunnel floor. The dog leaped these easily, undistracted by the birds and dragonflies. Looking down as the dog passed over, Kormak saw deep pits. Some held water, where huge fish swam. Others held fire.

The tunnel ended in a door. The dog paused and lifted a foreleg, striking the wood. It split.

They passed through and were outside, in the green land of Ireland. Hills rolled around them, covered with forest. The sun shone down. A man stood waiting.

It was Alfgeir, of course. He looked older and more formidable than he had before, and his legs were encased in iron rods, with hinges at the knees. The rods were inlaid with silver patterns that glinted in the Irish sunlight.

"Don't get off the dog, till you hear what I have to say," he told them. "Kormak, you've been in the realm of the elves and fey for thirty years. When you step down and touch the ground, you will be more than fifty. Consider whether you want to do this. Alda, you have been among the fey for many centuries. You are part-elf, and we age more slowly than humans. Still, you will be much older if you touch the ground."

"What alternative do we have?" Kormak asked.

"I can tell the dog to carry you into the country of the elves. You will remain your present ages there."

"I am tired of magic," Alda said. "I will risk age in order to live in sunlight." She slid down from the dog, standing on the green turf of Ireland. As soon as she did this, she changed, becoming an upright, handsome old woman with silver hair. Her blue eyes shone brightly, no longer veiled. Although her face was lined, it was still lovely.

"And you, Kormak?" Alfgeir asked.

He sat awhile on the iron dog, looking over the hills of Ireland. Thirty years! Well, he had experienced a lot in that time: the light elves, the dark elves, the fey. He could not say the time was wasted. Like Alda, he was tired of enchantments; and Alda – old though she might be – looked better to him than the fey or their human slaves. Lack of aging made the fey indolent and selfish, while their human slaves became greedy and envious. The Icelanders had been better. They knew about old age and death. The best of them – the heroes – faced it fighting, like Egil.

It surprised him that he thought of Egil with approval. The old monster! The killer! How angry he must have been at his son and his dying body! That was no excuse for killing Svart. He would do better, Kormak thought. He could not excel Egil in fighting, but he could excel him in growing old.

"I will risk age as well." He swung down off the dog. As he touched the ground, he felt his body thicken. He was heavier than before, though still strong. A gray beard bristled over his chest. He brushed his hand across it. Hairs prickled against his palm. Age, or his stay in the country of the elves, had made it thicker and more manly.

"Well, then," Alfgeir said. "I ought to tell you my true name. I am Volund, Alda's father. I could not enter the country of the fey to rescue her. The doors leading into the land of the fey have wards against anything that is foreign and might be dangerous: humans, iron, unfamiliar magic, and magicians who are not fey. My leg braces are iron and magic, and they cannot be made otherwise. In addition, I am a great magician. The fey doors would have roared like dragons if I had tried to enter. The fey let you in, because you seemed harmless.

"I gave you three magical gifts to give Alda. The first two would wake her and break the magical bonds that held her, because they contain what the fey hate most: death and history. As much as possible, they try to live beyond time and change. Memory fails in their country. Although they love to hunt, they do not like to touch blood or death. Their human servants strike the killing blow and butcher the animals.

"But, as Odin said:

'Cattle die. Kinsmen die.

You yourself will die.

I know one thing that does not die.

The fame of the dead.'

"That is what's real for humans: blood and death and history; and that is what I gave to Alda with my first two gifts.

"Bodvild asked me to make the bracelet when she came to my forge. Foolish child! Later, when she lay drunk on the smithy floor, I raped her, breaking her maidenhead, and took back the bracelet. She was your mother, Alda."

"A cruel gift," Alda said.

"The brooch was made for your grandmother, the wife of King Nidhad. He took me prisoner and made me lame. In return, I killed his sons, your two uncles, and made their skulls into drinking cups. Their teeth became the ivory in the brooch. I recovered it before I flew from Nidhad's court, but left the cups for Nidhad to enjoy."

Alda's hands went up to her breast, touching the brooch under her dress. "Another cruel gift."

"Yes," Volund said. "But remember the third gift. The dog could not enter the land of the fey any more than I could. But hidden in its golden shell and carried by you, Kormak, it could slip in. When the shell broke, it could carry you away."

"Why did it take you so long?" asked Kormak, always curious. "Alda was a prisoner for centuries. Did you not care for her at all?"

"How could he?" Alda asked. "I come from blood and death."

Volund smiled, showing strong, square, white teeth. "I am comfortable with blood and death, as my history ought to tell you; and kin matter to me. I knew your brother, Alda, and made him a sword that he used until he died. A famous warrior! But not as lucky as he might have been.

"It took me a long time to learn that Alda was still alive and then discover where she had gone. Then – hardest of all – I had to find someone who could enter the land of the fey unsuspected. You could, Kormak. A human and a slave. No one would fear you or suspect you, since you came with Svanhild."

"What will happen to her?" Kormak asked.

"She is as hard-hearted as her mother – you must have noticed that. She will be fine among the fey. Her father may try to recover her, but I doubt that she will go back.

"I promised you silver," Volund added. He bent down and lifted up two bags. "This is the silver that Egil hid in the waterfall. Svanhild stole it from her father, so she would have a gift to give her mother. I took it from her while she was sleeping on the train. The treasure you carried into the land of the fey is gravel, enchanted to look like silver. When you entered, did the doorway groan?"

"Yes," said Kormak.

"That was because you are human, and also because you carried magic – the gravel and the three gifts. Since you were not turned away, the guard must have thought the door was groaning for only one reason."

"Yes."

Volund grinned again, showing his strong, white teeth. "The spell on the gravel will wear off, but this is real. You are a rich man now." He held the bags out.

Kormak took them. They were as heavy as ever. "This is what I carried all the way from the country of the light elves?"

"Yes."

"Won't the fey be angry with me?" Kormak asked.

"Yes. I suggest you go into the part of Ireland that the Norwegians and Danes have settled. You know their language. The fey have little power there."

Volund gestured down the grassy slope behind him. At the bottom, three horses grazed. "I will accompany you for a while. I would like to know my daughter. And the iron dog will make sure that no one bothers us."

THEY RODE TOGETHER into the part of Ireland the Norwegians held. The iron dog made sure they had no more adventures. Kormak bought a farm, and Alda stayed with him, as did Volund for a while. Kormak had more questions to ask him. How had Volund known to be in the tunnel, when Kormak and Svanhild came riding? Was it an accident that Svanhild and Kormak were traveling together, or was that part of Volund's plan? How far back did the elf prince's planning go? To the elf who opened the door in the cliff and beckoned Kormak in?

But Volund had grown silent and refused to answer these questions, except to say two things. "I plan deeply and slowly, as the story of Nidhad tells you. The king thought I was reconciled to life in the smithy, and he thought I was safe. I was not."

In addition, he said, "Not everything is planned."

He spent most of his time with Alda, sitting by her loom and watching her weave, his withered legs stretched out in front of him, encased in iron. His hands, folded in front of him, were thick and strong. His face was worn. Though elves aged slowly, he was obviously not young.

Of all the people Kormak had met – Egil, the lord of the light elves, the chiefs of the dark elves, the queen of the fey – Volund was the most formidable.

Sometimes he talked about the swords he had made. All were famous. More often, he listened to Alda speak about her childhood. She never spoke about her long stay in the land of the fey.

In the end, Volund returned to the lands of magic. Before he left, he said to Alda, "If you ever want to visit Elfland, send the iron dog to find me. He will always know where I am."

The dog growled. Volund touched it, and it suddenly looked like an ordinary wolfhound. "Stay here, Elding."

The dog said:

"Decent behavior
outshines silver.
Kindness is better
than gold or fame.

"Glad am I
to be a farm dog,
guarding the farmer,
guarding the sheep."

"I don't intend to raise sheep," Kormak said, scratching the dog behind its ears.

"Nonetheless, I will guard you and Alda," the dog growled.

Volund rode away.

"A hard man to understand," Alda said. "I'm glad he's gone."

"I wish he had answered more of my questions," Kormak replied.

Kormak raised horses and sold them at a good price. Alda wove. Her cloth became well known among the Norwegian and Danish settlers. Noble women, whose husbands had grown rich through raiding, bought it. They had no children, but the wars in Ireland produced many orphans, and they found several to foster. Kormak lived thirty years more, aging slowly and remaining strong. Alda did not age at all.

At last, Kormak grew sick and took to his bed. "What will you do?" he asked Alda.

"Go to Elfland," she replied. "The dog will know the way. Our foster children can have the farm and the silver that remains. I still have the gold bracelet and the gold and ivory brooch, though I have never worn either. I want to return them to Volund."

"Have you ever regretted staying here?" Kormak asked.

"I have liked it better than the country of the fey," Alda replied. "As for Elfland, I will find out how I like it."

ALDA SAT BESIDE Kormak until he died. After he was buried, she picked out a horse. "The farm is yours," she told her foster children. "I am taking this horse and the dog."

The children – grown men and women – begged her to stay.

"I want to see my father and the lands of my kin," she replied. "The dog will guard me."

And she rode away.

SING

Karin Tidbeck

Karin Tidbeck (www.karintidbeck.com) is the award-winning author of *Jagannath* and *Amatka*. She lives in Malmö, Sweden, where she works as a creative writing teacher, translator and consultant of all things fictional and interactive. She has published short stories and poetry in Swedish since 2002 and English since 2010. Her short fiction has appeared in publications like *Weird Tales*, *Tor.com*, *Lightspeed* and numerous anthologies including *The Time-Travelers Almanac*, *Steampunk Revolution* and *Alien Encounters*.

THE COLD DAWN light creeps onto the mountaintops; they emerge like islands in the valley's dark sea, tendrils of steam rising up from the thickets clinging to the rock. Right now there's no sound of birdsong or crickets, no hiss of wind in the trees. When Maderakka's great shadow has sunk back below the horizon, twitter and chirp will return in a shocking explosion of sound. For now, we sit in complete silence.

The birds have left. Petr lies with his head in my lap, his chest rising and falling so quickly it's almost a flutter, his pulse rushing under the skin. The bits of eggshell I couldn't get out of his mouth, those that have already made their way into him, spread whiteness into the surrounding flesh. If only I could hear that he's breathing properly. His eyes are rolled back into his head, his arms and legs curled up against his body like a baby's. If he's conscious, he must be in pain. I hope he's not conscious.

* * *

A STRANGELY SHAPED man came in the door and stepped up to the counter. He made a full turn to look at the mess in my workshop: the fabrics, the cutting table, the bits of pattern. Then he looked directly at me. He was definitely not from here – no one had told him not to do that. I almost wanted to correct him: *leave, you're not supposed to make contact like that, you're supposed to pretend you can't see me and tell the air what you want.* But I was curious about what he might do. I was too used to avoiding eye contact, so I concentrated carefully on the rest of him: the squat body with its weirdly broad shoulders, the swelling upper arms and legs. The cropped copper on his head. I'd never seen anything like it.

So this man stepped up to the counter and he spoke directly to me, and it was like being caught under the midday sun.

"You're Aino? The tailor? Can you repair this?"

He spoke slowly and deliberately, his accent crowded with hard sounds. He dropped a heap of something on the counter. I collected myself and made my way over. He flinched as I slid off my chair at the cutting table, catching myself before my knees collapsed backward. I knew what he saw: a stick insect of a woman clambering unsteadily along the furniture, joints flexing at impossible angles. Still he didn't look away. I could see his eyes at the outskirts of my vision, golden-yellow points following me as I heaved myself forward to the stool by the counter. The bundle, when I held it up, was an oddly cut jacket. It had no visible seams, the material almost like rough canvas but not quite. It was half-eaten by wear and grime.

"You should have had this mended long ago," I said. "And washed. I can't fix this."

He leaned closer, hand cupped behind an ear. "Again, please?"

"I can't repair it," I said, slower.

He sighed, a long waft of warm air on my forearm. "Can you make a new one?"

"Maybe. But I'll have to measure you." I waved him toward me.

He stepped around the counter. After that first flinch, he didn't react. His smell was dry, like burnt ochre and spices, not unpleasant, and while I measured him he kept talking in a stream of consonants and archaic words, easy enough to understand if I didn't listen too closely.

His name was Petr, the name as angular as his accent, and he came from Amitié – a station somewhere out there – but was born on Gliese. (I knew a little about Gliese, and told him so.) He was a biologist and hadn't seen an open sky for eight years. He had landed on Kiruna and ridden with a truck and then walked for three days, and he was proud to have learned our language, although our dialect was very odd. He was here to research lichen.

"Lichen can survive anywhere," he said, "even in a vacuum, at least as spores. I want to compare these to the ones on Gliese, to see if they have the same origin."

"Just you? You're alone?"

"Do you know how many colonies are out there?" He laughed, but then cleared his throat. "Sorry. But it's really like that. There are more colonies than anyone can keep track of. And Kiruna is, well, it's considered an abandoned world, after the mining companies left, so –"

His next word was silent. Saarakka was up, the bright moonlet sudden as always. He mouthed more words. I switched into song, but Petr just stared at me. He inclined his head slightly toward me, eyes narrowing, then shook his head and pinched the bridge of his nose. He reached into the back pocket of his trousers and drew out something like a small and very thin book. He did something with a quick movement – shook it out, somehow – and it unfolded into a large square that he put down on the counter. It had the outlines of letters at the bottom, and his fingers flew over them. WHAT HAPPENED WITH SOUND?

I recognized the layout of keys. I could type. SAARAKKA, I wrote. WHEN SAARAKKA IS UP, WE CAN'T HEAR SPEECH. WE SING INSTEAD.

WHY HAS NOBODY TOLD ME ABOUT THIS? he replied.

I shrugged.

He typed with annoyed, jerky movements. HOW LONG DOES IT LAST?

UNTIL IT SETS, I told him.

He had so many questions – he wanted to know how Saarakka silenced speech, if the other moon did something too. I told him about how Oksakka kills the sound of birds, and how giant Maderakka peeks over the horizon now and then, reminding us that the three of us are just her satellites. How they once named our own world after a mining town and we named the other moons for an ancient goddess and her handmaidens, although these names sound strange and harsh to us now. But every answer prompted new questions. I finally pushed the sheet away from me. He held his palms up in resignation, folded it up, and left.

What I had wanted to say, when he started talking about how Kiruna was just one world among many, was that I'm not stupid. I read books and sometimes I could pick up stuff on my old set, when the satellite was up and the moons didn't interfere with it so much. I knew that Amitié was a big space station. I knew we lived in a poor backwater place. Still, you think your home is special, even if nobody ever visits.

THE VILLAGE HAS a single street. One can walk along the street for a little while, and then go down to the sluggish red river. I go there to wash myself and rinse out cloth.

I like dusk, when everyone's gone home and I can air-dry on the big, flat stone by the shore, arms and legs finally long and relaxed and folding at what angles they will, my spine and muscles creaking like wood after a long day of keeping everything straight and upright. Sometimes the goats come to visit. They're only interested in whether I have food or ear scratchings for them. To the goats, all people are equal, except for those who have treats. Sometimes the birds come here too, alighting on the rocks to preen their plumes, compound eyes iridescent in the twilight. I try not to notice them, but unless Oksakka is up to muffle the higher-pitched noise, the insistent buzzing twitches of their wings are impossible to ignore. More than two or three and they start warbling among themselves, eerily like human song, and I leave.

Petr met me on the path up from the river. I was carrying a bundle of wet fabric strapped to my back; it was slow going because I'd brought too much and the extra weight made me swing heavy on my crutches.

He held out a hand. "Let me carry that for you, Aino."

"No, thank you." I moved past him.

He kept pace with me. "I'm just trying to be polite."

I sneaked a glance at him, but it did seem that was what he wanted. I unstrapped my bundle. He took it and casually slung it over his shoulder. We walked in silence up the slope, him at a leisurely walk, me concentrating on the uphill effort, crutch-foot-foot-crutch.

"Your ecosystem," he said eventually, when the path flattened out. "It's fascinating."

"What about it?"

"I've never seen a system based on parasitism."

"I don't know much about that."

"But you know how it works?"

"Of course," I said. "Animals lay eggs in other animals. Even the plants."

"So is there anything that uses the goats for hosts?"

"Hookflies. They hatch in the goats' noses."

Petr hummed. "Does it harm the goats?"

"No... not usually. Some of them get sick and die. Most of the time they just get... more perky. It's good for them."

"Fascinating," Petr said. "I've never seen an alien species just slip into an ecosystem like that." He paused. "These hookflies. Do they ever go for humans?"

I shook my head.

He was quiet for a while. We were almost at the village when he spoke again.

"So how long have your people been singing?"

"I don't know. A long time."

"But how do you learn? I mean I've tried, but I just can't make the sounds. The pitch, it's higher than anything I've heard a human voice do. It's like birdsong."

"It's passed on." I concentrated on tensing the muscles in my feet for the next step.

"How? Is it a mutation?"

"It's passed on," I repeated. "Here's the workshop. I can handle it from here. Thank you."

He handed me the bundle. I could tell he wanted to ask me more, but I turned away from him and dragged my load inside.

*   *   *

I DON'T LIE. But neither will I answer a question that hasn't been asked. Petr would have called it lying by omission, I suppose. I've wondered if things would have happened differently if I'd just told him what he really wanted to know: not *how* we learn, but how it's *possible* for us to learn. But no. I don't think it would have changed much. He was too recklessly curious.

MY MOTHER TOLD me I'd never take over the business, but she underestimated me and how much I'd learned before she passed. I have some strength in my hands and arms, and I'm good at precision work. It makes me a good tailor. In that way I can at least get a little respect, because I support myself and do it well. So the villagers employ me, even if they won't look at me.

Others of my kind aren't so lucky. A man down the street hasn't left his room for years. His elderly parents take care of him. When they pass, the other villagers won't show as much compassion. I know there are more of us here and there, in the village and the outlying farms. Those of us who do go outside don't communicate with each other. We stay in the background, we who didn't receive the gift unscathed.

I wonder if that will happen to Petr now. So far, there's no change; he's very still. His temples are freckled. I haven't noticed that before.

PETR WOULDN'T LEAVE me alone. He kept coming in to talk. I didn't know if he did this to everyone. I sometimes thought that maybe he didn't study lichen at all; he just went from house to house and talked people's ears off. He talked about his heavy homeworld, which he'd left to crawl almost weightless in the high spokes of Amitié. He told me I wouldn't have to carry my own weight there, I'd move without crutches, and I was surprised by the want that flared up inside me, but I said nothing of it. He asked me if I hurt, and I said only if my joints folded back or sideways too quickly. He was very fascinated.

When Saarakka was up, he typed at me to sing to him. He parsed the cadences and inflections like a scientist, annoyed when they refused to slip into neat order.

I found myself talking too, telling him of sewing and books I'd read, of the other villagers and what they did. It's remarkable what people will say and do when you're part of the background. Petr listened to me, asked questions. Sometimes I met his eyes. They had little crinkles at the outer edges that deepened when he smiled. I discovered that I had many things to say. I couldn't tell whether the biologist in him wanted to study my freakish appearance, or if he really enjoyed being around me.

He sat on my stool behind the counter, telling me about crawling around in the vents on Amitié to study the lichen unique to the station: "They must have hitchhiked in with a shuttle. The question was from where…"

I interrupted him. "How does one get there? To visit?"

"You want to go?"

"I'd like to see it." *And be weightless,* I didn't say.

"There's a shuttle bypass in a few months to pick me up," he said. "But it'd cost you."

I nodded.

"Do you have money?" he asked.

"I've saved up some."

He mentioned how much it would cost, and my heart sank so deep I couldn't speak for a while. For once, Petr didn't fill the silence.

I moved past him from the cutting table to the mannequin. I put my hand on a piece of fabric on the table and it slipped. I stumbled. He reached out and caught me, and I fell with my face against his throat. His skin was warm, almost hot; he smelled of sweat and dust and an undertone of musk that seeped into my body and made it heavy. It was suddenly hard to breathe.

I pushed myself out of his arms and leaned against the table, unsteadily, because my arms were shaking. No one had touched me like that before. He had slid from the stool, leaning against the counter across from me, his chest rising and falling as if he had been running. Those eyes were so sharp, I couldn't look at them directly.

"I'm in love with you." The words tumbled out of his mouth in a quick mumble.

He stiffened, as if surprised by what he had just said. I opened my mouth to say I didn't know what, but words like that deserved something –

He held up a hand. "I didn't mean to."

"But..."

Petr shook his head. "Aino. It's all right."

When I finally figured out what to say, he had left. I wanted to say I hadn't thought of the possibility, but that I did now. Someone wanted me. It was a very strange sensation, like a little hook tugging at the hollow under my ribs.

PETR CHANGED AFTER that. He kept coming into the workshop, but he started to make friends elsewhere too. I could see it from the shop window: his cheerful brusqueness bowled the others over. He crouched together with the weaver across the street, eagerly studying her work. He engaged in cheerful haggling with Maiju, who would never negotiate the price of her vegetables, but with him, she did. He even tried to sing, unsuccessfully. I recognized the looks the others gave him. And even though they were only humoring him, treating him as they would a harmless idiot, I found myself growing jealous. That was novel too.

He didn't mention it again. Our conversation skirted away from any deeper subjects. The memory of his scent intruded on my thoughts at night. I tried to wash it away in the river.

"AINO, I'M THINKING about staying."

Petr hadn't been in for a week. Now this.

"Why?" I fiddled with a seam on the work shirt I was hemming.

"I like it here. Everything's simple – no high tech, no info flooding, no hurry. I can hear myself think." He smiled faintly. "You know, I've had stomach problems most of my life. When I came here, they went away in a week. It's been like coming home."

"I don't see why." I kept my eyes down. "There's nothing special here."

"These are good people. Sure, they're a bit traditional, a bit distant. But I like them. And it turns out they need me here. Jorma, he doesn't mind that I can't sing. He offered me a job at the clinic. Says they need someone with my experience."

"Are you all right with this?" he asked when I didn't reply immediately.

"It's good," I said eventually. "It's good for you that they like you."

"I don't know about 'like.' Some of them treat me as if I'm handicapped. I don't care much, though. I can live with that as long as some of you like me." His gaze rested on me like a heavy hand.

"Good for you," I repeated.

He leaned over the counter. "So... maybe you could teach me to sing? For real?"

"No."

"Why? I don't understand why."

"Because I can't teach you. You *are* handicapped. Like me."

"Aino." His voice was low. "Did you ever consider that maybe they don't hate you?"

I looked up. "They don't hate me. They're afraid of me. It's different."

"Are you really sure? Maybe if you talked to them..."

"...they would avoid me. It is what it is."

"You can't just sit in here and be bitter."

"I'm not," I said. "It just is what it is. I can choose to be miserable about it, or I can choose not to be."

"Fine." He sighed. "Does it matter to you if I stay or leave?"

"Yes," I whispered to the shirt in my lap.

"Well, which is it? Do you want me to stay?"

He had asked directly, so I had to give him an answer, at least some sort of reply. "You could stay a while. Or I could go with you."

"I told you. I'm not going back to Amitié."

"All right," I said.

"Really?"

"No."

*　　*　　*

I COULD HAVE kept quiet when the procession went by. Maybe then things would have been different. I think he would have found out, anyway.

We were down by the river. We pretended the last conversation hadn't happened. He had insisted on helping me with washing cloth. I wouldn't let him, so he sat alongside me, making conversation while I dipped the lengths of cloth in the river and slapped them on the big flat stone. Maderakka's huge approaching shadow hovered on the horizon. It would be Petr's first time, and he was fascinated. The birds were beginning to amass in the air above the plateau, sharp trills echoing through the valley.

"How long will it last?"

"Just overnight," I said. "It only rises a little bit before it sets again."

"I wonder what it's like on the other side," he said. "Having that in the sky all the time."

"Very quiet, I suppose."

"Does anyone live there?"

I shrugged. "A few. Not as many as here."

He grunted and said no more. I sank into the rhythm of my work, listening to the rush of water and wet cloth on stone, the clatter and bleat of goats on the shore.

Petr touched my arm, sending a shock up my shoulder. I pretended it was a twitch.

"Aino. What's that?" He pointed up the slope.

The women and men walking by were dressed all in white, led by an old woman with a bundle in her arms. They were heading for the valley's innermost point, where the river emerged from underground and a faint trail switchbacked up the wall.

I turned back to my laundry. "They're going to the plateau."

"I can see that. What are they going to do once they get there?"

The question was too direct to avoid. I had to answer somehow. "We don't talk about that," I said finally.

"Come on," Petr said. "If I'm going to live here, I should be allowed to know."

"I don't know if that's my decision to make," I replied.

He settled on the stone again, but he was tense now, and kept casting glances at the procession on their way up the mountainside. He helped me carry the clothes back through the workshop and into the backyard, and then left without helping me hang them. I knew where he was going. You could say I let it happen – but I don't think I could have stopped him either. It was a kind of relief. I hung the cloth, listening to the comforting whisper of wet fabric, until Maderakka rose and silence cupped its hands over my ears.

I DON'T REMEMBER being carried to the plateau in my mother's arms. I only know that she did. Looking down at Petr in my lap, I'm glad I don't remember. Of course everyone *knows* what happens. We're just better off forgetting what it was like.

MADERAKKA SET IN the early hours of the morning, and I woke to the noise of someone hammering on the door. It was Petr, of course, and his nose and lips were puffy. I let him in, and into the back of the workshop to my private room. He sank down on my bed and just sort of crumpled. I put the kettle on and waited.

"I tried to go up there," he said into his hands. "I wanted to see what it was."

"And?"

"Jorma stopped me."

I thought of the gangly doctor trying to hold Petr back, and snorted. "How?"

"He hit me."

"But you're" – I gestured toward him, all of him – "huge."

"So? I don't know how to fight. And he's scary. I almost got to the top before he saw me and stopped me. I got this" – he pointed to his nose – "just for going up there. What the hell is going on up there, Aino? There were those bird things, hundreds of them, just circling overhead."

"Did you see anything else?"

"No."

"You won't give up until you find out, will you?"

He shook his head.

"It's how we do things," I said. "It's how we sing."

"I don't understand."

"You said it's a – what was it? – parasitic ecosystem. Yes?"

He nodded.

"And I said that the hookflies use the goats, and that it's good for the goats. The hookflies get to lay their eggs, and the goats get something in return."

He nodded again. I waited for him to connect the facts. His face remained blank.

"The birds," I said. "When a baby's born, it's taken up there the next time Maderakka rises."

Petr's shoulders slumped. He looked sick. It gave me some sort of grim satisfaction to go on talking, to get back at him for his idiocy.

I went on: "The birds lay their eggs. Not for long, just for a moment. And they leave something behind. It changes the children's development... in the throat. It means they can learn to sing." I gestured at myself. "Sometimes the child dies. Sometimes this happens. That's why the others avoid me. I didn't pass the test."

"You make yourself hosts," Petr said, faintly. "You do it to your children."

"They don't remember. I don't remember."

He stood up, swaying a little on his feet, and left.

"You wanted to know!" I called after him.

A LATECOMER HAS alighted on the rock next to me. It's preening its iridescent wings in the morning light, pulling its plumes between its mandibles one by one. I look away as it hops up on Petr's chest. It's so wrong to see it happen, too intimate. But I'm afraid to move, I'm afraid to flee. I don't know what will happen if I do.

THE WEATHER WAS so lovely I couldn't stay indoors. I sat under the awning outside my workshop, wrapped up in shawls so as not to offend too much, basting the seams on a skirt. The weaver across the street had set up one of her smaller looms on her porch, working with her back to me. Saarakka was up, and the street filled with song.

I saw Petr coming from a long way away. His square form made the villagers look so unbearably gangly and frail, as if they would break if he touched them. How did they even manage to stay upright? How did his weight not break the cobblestones? The others shied away from him, like reeds from a boat. I saw why when he came closer. I greeted him with song without thinking. It made his tortured grimace deepen.

He fell to his knees in front of me and wrapped his arms around me, squeezed me so tight I could feel my shoulders creaking. He was shaking. The soundless weeping hit my neck in silent, wet waves. All around us, the others were very busy not noticing what was going on.

I brought him to the backyard. He calmed down and we sat leaning against the wall, watching Saarakka outrun the sun and sink. When the last sliver had disappeared under the horizon, he hummed to test the atmosphere, and then spoke.

"I couldn't stand being in the village for Saarakka. Everyone else talking and I can't... I've started to understand the song language now, you know? It makes it worse. So I left, I went up to that plateau. There was nothing there. I suppose you knew that already. Just the trees and the little clearing." He fingered the back of his head and winced. "I don't know how, but I fell on the way down, I fell off the path and down the wall. It was close to the bottom, I didn't hurt myself much. Just banged my head a little."

"That was what made you upset?"

I could feel him looking at me. "If I'd really hurt myself, if I'd hurt myself badly, I wouldn't have been able to call for help. I could have just lain there until Saarakka set. Nobody would have heard me. You wouldn't have heard me."

We sat for a while without speaking. The sound of crickets and birds disappeared abruptly. Oksakka had risen behind us.

"I've always heard that if you've been near death, you're supposed to feel alive and grateful for every moment." Petr snorted. "All I can think of is how easy it is to die. That it can happen at any time."

I turned my head to look at him. His eyes glittered yellow in the setting sun.

"You don't believe I spend time with you because of you."

I waited.

Petr shook his head. "You know, on Amitié, they'd think you look strange, but you wouldn't be treated differently. And the gravity's low when closer to the hub. You wouldn't need crutches."

"So take me there."

"I'm not going back. I've told you."

"Gliese, then?"

"You'd be crushed." He held up a massive arm. "Why do you think I look like I do?"

I swallowed my frustration.

"There are wading birds on Earth," he said, "long-legged things. They move like dancers. You remind me of them."

"You don't remind me of anything here," I replied.

He looked surprised when I leaned in and kissed him.

Later, I had to close his hands around me, so afraid was he to hurt me.

I lay next to him thinking about having normal conversations, other people meeting my eyes, talking to me like a person.

I'M THRIFTY. I had saved up a decent sum over the years; there was nothing I could spend money on, after all. If I sold everything I owned, if I sold the business, it would be enough to go to Amitié, at least to visit. If someone wanted to buy my things.

But Petr had in some almost unnoticeable way moved into my home. Suddenly he lived there, and had done so for a while. He cooked, he cleaned the corners I didn't bother with because I couldn't reach. He brought in shoots and plants from outside and planted them in little pots. When he showed up with lichen-covered rocks I put my foot down, so he arranged them in patterns in the backyard. Giant Maderakka rose twice; two processions in white passed by on their way to the plateau. He watched them with a mix of longing and disgust.

His attention spoiled me. I forgot that only he talked to me. I spoke directly to a customer and looked her in the eyes. She left the workshop in a hurry and didn't come back.

"I WANT TO leave," I finally said. "I'm selling everything. Let's go to Amitié."

We were in bed, listening to the lack of birds. Oksakka's quick little eye shone in the midnight sky.

"Again? I told you I don't want to go back," Petr replied.

"Just for a little while?"

"I feel at home here now," he said. "The valley, the sky... I love it. I love being light."

"I've lost my customers."

"I've thought about raising goats."

"These people will never accept you completely," I said. "You can't sing. You're like me, you're a cripple to them."

"You're not a cripple, Aino."

"I am to them. On Amitié, I wouldn't be."

He sighed and rolled over on his side. The discussion was apparently over.

I WOKE UP tonight because the bed was empty and the air completely still. Silence whined in my ears. Outside, Maderakka rose like a mountain at the valley's mouth.

I don't know if he'd planned it all along. It doesn't matter. There were no new babies this cycle, no procession. Maybe he just saw his chance and decided to go for it.

It took such a long time to get up the path to the plateau. The upslope fought me, and my crutches slid and skittered over gravel and loose rocks; I almost fell over several times. I couldn't call for him, couldn't sing, and the birds circled overhead in a downward spiral.

Just before the clearing came into view, the path curled around an outcrop and flattened out among trees. All I could see while struggling through the trees was a faint flickering. It wasn't until I came into the clearing that I could really see what was going on: that which had been done to me, that I was too young to remember, that which none of us remember and choose not to witness. They leave the children and wait among the trees with their backs turned. They don't speak of what has happened during the wait. No one has ever said that watching is forbidden, but I felt like I was committing a crime, revealing what was hidden.

Petr stood in the middle of the clearing, a silhouette against the gray sky, surrounded by birds. No, he wasn't standing. He hung suspended by their wings, his toes barely touching the ground, his head tipped back. They were swarming in his face, tangling in his hair.

I CAN'T AVERT my eyes anymore. I am about to see the process up close. The bird that sits on Petr's chest seems to take no notice of me. It pushes its ovipositor in between his lips and shudders. Then it leaves in a flutter of wings, so fast that I almost don't register it. Petr's chest heaves, and he rolls out of my lap, landing on his back. He's awake now, staring into the sky. I don't know if it's terror or ecstasy in his eyes as the tiny spawn fights its way out of his mouth.

In a week, the shuttle makes its bypass. Maybe they'll let me take Petr's place. If I went now, just left him on the ground and packed light, I could make it in time. I don't need a sky overhead. And considering the quality of their clothes, Amitié needs a tailor.

SOCIAL SERVICES

Madeline Ashby

Madeline Ashby (www.madelineashby.com) is the author of the Machine Dynasty trilogy (*vN*, *iD*, and *Rev*), and forthcoming standalone *Company Town*. Her other writing has been published in *Nature*, *FLURB*, *Arcfinity*, *BoingBoing.net*, and *WorldChanging*. She has written science fiction prototypes for Intel Labs, the Institute for the Future, and SciFutures.

"But I want *my own* office," Lena said. "*My own* space to work from."

Social Services paused for a while to think. Lena knew that it was thinking, because the woman in the magic mirror kept animating her eyes this way and that behind cat-eye hornrims. She did so in perfect meter, making her look like one of those old clocks where the cat wagged its tail and looked to and fro, to and fro, all day and all night, forever and ever. Lena had only ever seen those clocks in media, so she had no idea if they really ticked. But she imagined they ticked terribly. The real function of clocks, it seemed to her, was not to tell time but to mark its passage. *Tickticktickick. Byebyebyebye.*

"I'm sorry, Lena, but your primary value to this organization lies in your location," Mrs. Dudley said. Lena had picked out her name when Social Services hired her. The name was Mrs. Dudley, after the teacher who rolled her eyes when Lena mispronounced "organism" as "orgasm" in fifth grade health class. She'd made Social Services look like her, from the hornrims to the puffy eyes to the shimmery coral lipstick melting into the wrinkles rivening her mouth. Now Mrs. Dudley was at her beck and call all the time, and had to answer all the most inane questions, like what the weather was and if something looked infected or not.

"This organization has to remain nimble," Mrs. Dudley said. "We need people ready to work at the grassroots level. You're one of them. Aren't you?"

Now it was Lena's turn to think. She examined the bathroom. It had the best mirror, so it was where she did most of her communication with Social Services. The bathroom itself was tiny. Most of the time it was dirty. This had nothing to do with Lena and everything to do with her niece's baby, whose diapers currently clogged the wastebasket. There was supposed to be a special hamper just for them with a charcoal filter on it and an alert telling her niece when to empty it, but her niece didn't give a shit – literally. Lena had told her that ignoring the alert was a good way to get the company who made the hamper to ping Social Services – a lack of basic cleanliness was an easy way to signal neglect – but her niece just smiled and said: "That's why we have you around. To fix stuff like that."

"That is why you decided to come work for us, isn't it?" Mrs. Dudley asked.

Lena nodded her head a little too vigorously. "Yes," she said. "Yes, that's it exactly."

She had no idea what Social Services had just asked. Probably something about her commitment to her community, or her empathy for others. Lena smiled her warm smile. It was one of a few she had catalogued especially for the purposes of work. She wore it to work like she wore her good leather gloves and her pretty pendant knife. Work outfit, work smile, work feelings. She reminded herself to look again for her gloves. They didn't have a sensor, so she had no idea how to find them.

"Here is your list for today," Mrs. Dudley said. The mirror showed her a list of addresses and tags. Not full case files, just tags and summaries compiled from the case files. Names, dates, bruises. Missed school, missed meals, missed court dates. "The car will be ready soon."

"Car?"

"The last appointment is quite far away." The appointment hove into view in the mirror. It showed a massive old McMansion in the suburbs.

"Transit reviews claim that the way in is...unreliable," Mrs. Dudley said. "So, we are sending you transport."

Lena watched her features start to manifest her doubts, but she reined them in before they could express much more. "But, I..."

"The car drives itself, Lena. And you get it for the whole day. I'm sure that allays any of your possible anxieties, doesn't it?"

"Well, yes..."

"Good. The car has a Euler path all set up, so just go where it takes you and you'll be fine."

"Okay."

"And please do keep your chin up."

"Excuse me?"

"Your chin. Keep it up. When your chin is down, we can't see as well. You're our eyes and ears, Lena. Remember that."

She nodded. "I –"

A fist on the bathroom door interrupted her. Just like that, Mrs. Dudley vanished. That was Social Services security at work; the interface, such as it was, did not want to share information with anyone else in a space, and so only recognized Lena's face. Her brother had tried to show it a picture of her, and then some video, but Lena had a special face that she made to login, and the mirror politely told her brother to please leave.

"*Open up!*"

Lena opened the door. Her niece stood on the other side. She handed Lena the baby, and beelined for the toilet. Yanking her pants down, she said: "Have *you* ever had to hold it in after an episiotomy?"

"No –"

"Well, you *might*, someday, if you ever got a boyfriend, which you shouldn't, because they're fucking crap." The sound of her pissing echoed in the small room. "Someday I'm going to kill this fucking toilet." She reached behind herself, awkwardly, and slapped it. Her rings made scratching noises on its plastic side. "You were supposed to tell me I was knocked up."

Lena thought it was probably a bad time to tell her niece that her father, Lena's brother, was the one responsible for upgrading the toilet's firmware, and that he had instead chosen to attempt circumventing it, so it would give them all its available features (temperature taking, diagnosis, warming, and so on) for no cost whatsoever. He didn't want the manufacturer knowing how much he used the bidet function, he said one night over dinner. That shit was private.

Her niece didn't bother washing her hands. She took the baby from Lena's arms and kissed it, absently. "It's creepy to hear you talking to someone who isn't there," she said. Her eyes widened. Her eyeliner was a vivid pink today, with extra sparkles. Her makeup was always annoyingly perfect. She probably could have sold the motions of her hands to a robotics firm, somewhere. "Don't you worry, sometimes, that you're, like... making it all up?"

Lena frowned. It wasn't like her niece to consider the existential. "Do you mean making it up as I go? Like life?"

"No no no no no. I mean, like, you're making up your job." She glanced quickly at the mirror, as though she feared it might be watching her. "Like maybe there's nobody in there at all."

Lena instantly allowed all of her professional affect to fall away, like cobwebs from an opened door. She turned her head to the old grey pleather couch with its pillows and blankets neatly stacked, right where she'd left them that morning. She let her niece carry the full weight of her gaze. "Then where would the rent money come from?" she asked.

Her niece had the grace to look embarrassed. She hugged her baby a little tighter. "Sorry. It was just a joke." She blinked. "You know? Jokes?"

A little car rolled across Lena's field of vision. Its logo beeped at her. "My car is here," she said. "Try to leave some dinner for me."

"Is it true they make you all get the same haircut, so they can hear better?"

Lena peered over the edges of her frames. Social Services didn't like it when she did that, but it was occasionally necessary. Jude, the adolescent standing before her, seemed genuinely curious and not sarcastic. That didn't make his question any less stupid.

"No," she said. "They don't make us wear a special haircut."

Jude shrugged. "You all just look like you've got the same haircut."

"Maybe you're just remembering the other times I've been here."

Jude smiled dopily around the straw hanging out of his mouth, and slurped from the pouch attached to it. It likely contained *makgeolli*; that was the 22nd floor specialty. Her glasses told her he was mildly intoxicated; he wore a lab on a chip under the skin of his left shoulder, in a spot that was notoriously difficult to scratch. The Spot was different for every user; triangulating it meant a gestural camera taking a full-body picture, or extrapolating from an extant gaming profile. "Oh, yeah... Yeah, that's probably it."

"Why do you think I'm here, Jude?"

"Because the Fosters aren't."

The kid didn't miss a beat. The algorithm had first introduced them three years ago, when his foster parents took him in; he referred to them, privately, as "The Fosters." Three years in, "The Fosters" had given up. They collected their stipend just fine, but they left it to Lena to actually deal with Jude's problems.

His main problem these days was truancy; in a year he wouldn't have to go to school any longer unless he wanted to, and so he was experiencing an acute case of senioritis in his freshman year. If he chose to go on, though, it would score Lena some much-needed points on her own profile. There was little difference, really, between his marks and her own.

"Is there any particular reason you're not going to school, these days?"

Jude shrugged and slurped on the pouch until it crinkled up and bubbled. He tossed the empty into the sink and leaned over to open the refrigerator. You didn't have to really move your feet in these rabbit hutch kitchens. He got another of the pouches out. "I just don't feel like it," he said.

"I didn't really much feel like going, either, when it was my turn, but I went."

Jude favoured her with a look that told her she had best shut her fucking mouth right fucking now. "School was different for you," he said simply. "You didn't have to wear a uniform."

"Well, that's true –"

"And your uniform didn't ping your teacher every time you got a fucking boner."

Lena blushed, and then felt herself blushing, which only made it worse. She looked down. True, their school district was a little too keen on wearables, but Jude's were special. "You know why you have to wear those pants," she said.

"That was when I was *thirteen!*"

"Well, she was ten."

"I *know* she was ten. I fucking *know* that. There's no way I could possibly forget that, now." He crossed his arms and sighed deeply. "We didn't even *do* anything."

"That's not what you told your friends on 18."

He sucked his teeth. Lena had no idea if Jude had really done the things he said he did. The lab inside the little girl had logged enough dopamine to believe sexual activity had occurred, but it had no way of knowing if she'd helped herself along, or if she'd had outside interference. The rape kit had the same opinion: penetration, not forced entry. When the relationship was discovered, the girl recanted everything, and said that nothing had happened, and that it didn't matter anyway, because even if something had happened, she really loved Jude. Jude did the same. Except he never said he loved her. This was probably the most honesty he demonstrated during the entire episode.

"I know it's difficult," Lena said. "But completing your minimum course credits is part of your sentencing. It's part of why you get your record expunged when you turn eighteen. So you have to go." She reached into the sink and plucked out the pouch with her thumb and forefinger. It dangled there in her grasp, dripping sweet white fluid. "And you have to quit drinking, too."

"I know," he said. "It's stupid. I was just bored, and it was there."

"I understand. But you're hurting your chances of making it out of here. This kind of thing winds up on your transcript, you know. You can't get a job without a decent transcript."

Jude waved his hand. "The fabbers don't care about grades."

"Maybe not, but they care about you being able to show up on time. You know?

He rolled his eyes. "Yeah. I know."

"So you'll go to school tomorrow?"

"Maybe. I need a new uniform, first."

"Excuse me?"

"Well, it's really just the pants. I threw them out."

Lena blinked so that her glasses would listen to her. "Well, we have to find those pants."

The glasses showed her a magnifying glass zipping to and fro across the cramped, dirty apartment. It came back empty. "You really threw them out?" she asked, despite already knowing the answer. Maybe he'd given them to a friend. Or sold them. Maybe they could be brought back, somehow.

"I think they got all sliced up," Jude said, miming the action of scissors with his fingers. "I wore my gym clothes home yesterday, and I put my other stuff in my bag, and then under the viaduct, I gave them to this homeless dude. He found the sensors right away. Said he was gonna sell 'em."

She winced. "How do you know he's not wearing them?"

"They were too small."

It was beyond her power. She would have to arrange for a new uniform. She'd probably have to take Jude to school tomorrow, too, just to smooth things over. He tended to start a new attendance streak if someone was actually bringing him there. The record said so, anyway. For a moment it snaked across her vision, undulating and irregular, and then she blinked and it was gone.

"I'll be here tomorrow at seven to take you to school," she said, and watched the appointment check itself into her schedule. "And don't even think about not being here, or not waking up, or getting your mom to send a note, or anything like that. I intend to show up, and if you don't do the same, Social Services will send someone else next time, and they won't be so understanding. Okay?"

Jude snorted. "Okay."

"I mean it. You have to show up. And you have to show up sober. I'll know if you're not, and so will your principal. He can suspend you for that, on sight."

"I know." Jude paused for a moment. He reached for the fresh pouch, and then seemed to think better of it. "I'm sorry, Lena."

"I know you're sorry. You can make it up to me by showing up, tomorrow."

"I don't want them to send someone else. I didn't mean to get you in trouble. I was just mad, is all."

"You would have better impulse control if you quit drinking. You know that, right?"

"Yeah."

"So you know what we have to do next, right?"

He sighed. "Seriously?"

"Yes, seriously. I can't leave here without it."

They spent the next half hour cleaning out his stash. He even helped her bring it down to the car. "Are you sure this is it?" he asked, when it perked up at Lena's arrival.

"It's on loan," she said. "Some people lease their vehicles on a daily basis to Social Services, and the car drives itself back to them at the end of the day with a full charge."

"It's a piece of shit."

"Just put the box in the back, will you?"

Jude rolled his eyes as she popped the trunk. Technically, she shouldn't have allowed him to come down to the garage with her. It wasn't recommended. Her glasses had warned her about it, as they neared the elevator. She made sure Jude carried the box full of pouches and pipes, though, so that he'd have to drop it if he wanted to try anything. Now, she watched as he leaned over the trunk and set the box inside.

"Nice gloves." He reached in and brought something out: Lena's good leather gloves. They were real leather, not the fake stuff, with soft suede interiors and an elastic skirt that circled the wrist and kept out the cold air. They were a pretty shade of purple. Distinctive. Recognizable. "Aren't these yours?" he asked.

"I..."

"I've seen you wearing them, before." He frowned. "I thought you said this was someone else's car. On loan."

"It is..."

"So how did your gloves wind up in the trunk?"

Lena wished she could ask the glasses for help. But without sensors, the glasses and the gloves had no relationship. At least, nothing legitimate and quantifiable. They had only Lena to link them.

"I must have used this car before," she said. "That must be it. I must have forgotten them in here, the last time, and not used the trunk until then. And the owner left the gloves in the trunk, hoping that I'd find them."

"Why the trunk? Why not on the dash? How many times do you look in the trunk?"

Jude slammed the trunk shut. He held the gloves out. Lena took them gingerly between her thumb and forefinger. They felt like her gloves. A little chilled from riding around in the trunk, but still hers. How strange, to think that they'd gone on their own little adventure without her. Hadn't the car's owner been the least bit tempted to take them? Or one of the other users? There were plenty of other women on the Social Services roster. Maybe they'd been worn out, and then put back, just like the car. Maybe the last user was someone higher up on the chain, and they knew Lena would be taking this particular car out on this particular morning, and they put her gloves back where she would find them. That would explain how she'd never seen them until just now.

"Don't look so creeped out," Jude said. "They're just a pair of gloves, right?"

"Right," Lena said. "Thanks."

BY THE END of the day, Lena had to admit that the car did not look familiar in the least. That didn't mean it looked *unfamiliar*, either, just that it looked the same as all the other print-jobs in the hands-free lane. The same flat mustard yellow, the same thick bumper that made the whole vehicle look like a little man with a mustache. It was entirely possible that she had used this car before. Perhaps even on the same day that she'd lost her gloves. She didn't remember losing them. That was the thing. She kept turning them in her hands, over and over, pulling them on and pulling them off, wiggling her fingers in their tips to feel if they were truly hers or not.

When had she last used a car for Social Services?

"February of last year," Mrs. Dudley said. "February fifteenth, to be exact."

Lena did not remember speaking the words aloud, either. But that hardly mattered. It was Social Services' job to understand problems before they became issues. That was how they'd first found Jude, after all. Surely the glasses had logged her examination of the gloves and the car and the system had put two and two together. It could do that. She was sure of it.

"You subvocalized it," Mrs. Dudley said.

Yes. That was it. People did that, sometimes, didn't they? They muttered to themselves. It wasn't at all unusual.

"People do it all the time," Mrs. Dudley told her.

Lena forced herself to speak the next words out loud. "Did the owner of the car save the gloves for me?"

Mrs. Dudley paused. "That's one way of putting it."

"What do you mean?"

Outside, the highway seemed empty. So few people drove, any longer. Once upon a time, four o'clock on a Friday afternoon in late October would have been replete with cars, and the cars would have been stuffed with mothers and fathers lead-footing their way into the suburbs, anxiously counting down the minutes until they earned a late fee at their daycare. Now the car whizzed along, straight and true, spotting its nearest fellow vehicle every ten minutes and pinging them cheerfully before zipping ahead.

It felt like driving into a village afflicted by plague.

"I think we need to bring you in for a memory exam, Lena," Mrs. Dudley said. "These lapses aren't normal for a woman in your demographic. You may have a blood clot."

"Oh," Lena said, perversely delighted by the thought.

"But first, you have to do this one last thing for us."

"Yes. The house in the suburbs."

"You must be very careful, Lena. Where you're going, there's no one else on the block. It's all been foreclosed. And it's going to be dark, soon."

"I understand."

"The foreclosures mean that the local security forces have been diminished, too. Their budget is based on population density and property taxes, so there won't be anyone to come for you. Not right away, anyway. Everyone else lives closer to town."

"Except for the people in this house."

Another pause. "Yes. The ones who live there, live alone."

JACKSON HILLS WAS the name of the development. The hills themselves occupied unincorporated county land, the last free sliver of property in the whole area, and the crookedness of the rusting street signs seemed meant to tempt government interference. That was an old word for molestation, Lena remembered. You came across it in some of the oldest laws. *Interference.* As though the uncles she spent her days hearing about were nothing more than windmills getting in the way of a good signal.

Was it an uncle that was the trouble, this time? The file was very scant. "*Possible neglect,*" it read. The child in question wore old, ill-fitting clothes, a teacher said. His grades were starting to slip. His name was Theodore. People called him Teddy. His parents never came to Parent/Teacher Night. They attended no talent shows. But they were participatory parents online; their emails with Teddy's teachers were detailed and thoughtful, with perfect spelling and grammar.

"*We intend to discuss Teddy's infractions with him as soon as possible,*" one read. "*We understand that his hacking the school lunch system to obtain chicken fingers every day for a month is very serious, as well as nutritionally unwise.*"

Teddy had indeed hacked the school lunch system to order an excess of chicken fingers delivered to the school kitchen by supply truck. He did this by entering the kitchen while pretending to go on a bathroom break, and carefully frying all the smart tags on all the boxes of frozen chicken fingers and fries with an acne zapper. With all the tags dead, the supplier instantly re-upped the entire order. The only truly dangerous part of the "hack" was the fact that he'd been in the walk-in freezer for a whole five minutes. Surveillance footage showed him ducking in with his coat zipped up all the way. The coat itself said that his body temperature had never dipped.

"I don't get any junk food at home," the boy said, during his inevitable talk with the principal. "They don't deliver any."

The gate to Jackson Hills was still functional, despite the absence of its residents. It slid open for Lena's car. As it did, a dervish of dead leaves whirled out and scattered away toward freedom. It felt like some sort of prisoner transfer. The exchange made, Lena drove past the gate.

The car drove her through the maze of empty houses as the dash lit up with advertisements for businesses that would probably never open. Burger joints. Day spas. Custom fabbers. In-house genome sequencing. All part of "town and country living at its finest." Some of the houses looked new; there were even stickers on the windows. As she rolled past, projections fluttered to life and showed laughing children running through sprinklers across the bare sod lawns, and men flipping steaks on grills, and women serving lemonade. It was the same family each time.

"WELCOME HOME," her dashboard read.

THE HOUSE STOOD at the top of the topmost hill in Jackson Hills. Lena recognized it because the map said they were drawing closer, and because it was the only house on the cul-de-sac with any lights on. It was a big place, but not so different from the others, with fake Tudor styling and a sloping lawn whose sharpest incline was broken by terraced rock. Forget-me-nots grew between the stones. Moss sprang up through the seams in the tiled drive. There was no car, so Lena's slid in easily and shut itself off with a little sigh, like a child instantly falling to sleep.

At the door, Lena took the time to remove her gloves (when had she put those on?) and adjust her hair. She rang the bell and waited. The lion in the doorknocker twinkled his eyes at her, and the door opened.

Teddy stood there, wearing a flannel pyjama and bathrobe set one size too small for his frame. "Hello, Lena," he said.

She blinked. "Hello, Teddy."

"It's nice to meet you. Please come in."

Inside, the house was dusty. Not dirty or even untidy, but dusty. Dust clung to the ceiling fans. Cobwebs stretched across the top of every shelf, and under the span of every pendant light. The corners of each room had become hiding places for dust bunnies. But at Teddy's height, everything was clean.

"Where are your parents, Teddy?"

"Would you like some tea?" Teddy asked. "Earl Grey is your favourite, right?"

Earl Grey *was* her favourite. As she watched, Teddy padded over to the coffee table in the front room, and poured tea from a real china service. It had little pink roses on it, and there was a sugar bowl with a lid and a creamer full of cream and even a tiny dish with whisper-thin slices of lemon. When he was finished pouring, Teddy added two sugars and a dash of cream to the cup. Then handed her the cup on a saucer with both hands, and then pressed something on his watch.

"It tells me when it's done steeping," he said. "Would you like to sit down?"

Lena sat. The sofa shifted beneath her, almost as though she'd sat on a very large cat. A moment later it had moulded itself to her shape. "It's smart foam," Teddy said. "Please try some of your tea. I made it myself."

Lena sipped. "You've certainly done your homework, Teddy," she said. "You're not the only person to research me before my arrival, but you're the only one who's ever been this thorough."

"I wanted to make it nice for you."

It was an odd statement, but Lena let it pass. She took another sip. "This is a very lovely house, Teddy. Do you help your parents with the housework?"

He nodded emphatically. "Yes. Yes I do."

"And are you happy, living here?"

"Yes, I am."

"There don't seem to be many other kids to play with," Lena said. "Doesn't it get lonely?"

"I don't really get lonely," he said. "I have friends I play with online."

"But it can't be very safe, to live here all alone."

His mouth twitched, a little, as though he had just heard the distant sound of a small animal that he very much wanted to hunt. "I'm not alone," he said.

"Well, I meant, the neighbours. Or rather, the lack of any."

His shoulders went back to their relaxed position. "I like it here," he said. "I like not having any neighbours. My parents didn't like it very much, at first, but I liked it a lot."

Since he had left the door open, Lena decided to go through it. "So, when are your parents coming?"

"They're here," he said. "They just can't come upstairs, right now."

Lena frowned. "Are they not well?"

Teddy smiled. For a moment, he actually looked like a real eleven-year-old, and not like a man who had shrunk down to size.

"They're busy," he said. "Besides, you're here to talk to me, right?"

"Well... Yes, that's true, but..." She blinked again, hard. It was tough to string words together, for some reason. Maybe Mrs. Dudley was right. Maybe she *did* need her brain scanned. She felt as though the long drive in had somehow hypnotized her, and Teddy now seemed very far away.

"I hope that we can be friends, Lena," Teddy said. "I liked you, the last time they sent you here."

Her mouth struggled to shape the words. "What? What are you talking about?"

"You wore those gloves, last time," he said. "In February. You'd had a really lonely Valentine's Day, the day before, and you were very sad. So I made you happy for a little while. I had some pills left over."

It was very hot in the room, suddenly. "You've drugged me," Lena said.

Teddy beamed. "Gotcha!"

Lena tried to stand up. Her knees gave out and her forehead struck one corner of the coffee table. For a moment she thought the warmth trickling down her face was actually sweat. But it wasn't.

"Uh oh," Teddy said. "I'll get some wipes."

He bounded off for the kitchen. Lena focused on her knees. She could stand up, if she just tried. She had her pendant knife. She could... what? Slash him? Threaten him? Threaten a child? She grasped the pendant in her hand. Pulled it off its cord. Unflipped the blade.

When Teddy came back with a cylinder of lemon-scented disinfectant wipes, she pounced. She was awkward and dizzy, but she was bigger than him, and she knocked him over easily. He saw the knife in her hand, gave a little shriek of delight, and bit her arm, hard. Then he shook his little head, like a dog with a chew toy. It hurt enough to make her lose her grip, and he recovered the knife. He held it facing downward, like scissors. He wiped his mouth with the back of his other hand.

"I knew I liked you, Lena," he said. "You're not like the others. You don't really like kids at all, do you? This is just your job. You'd rather be doing something else."

"That's..." Her vision wavered. "That's not true..."

"Yes, it is. And it's okay, because I don't like other kids, either. They're awful. They're mean and stupid and ugly and poor, and I don't want to see them, ever again. I just want to stay home, forever."

Lena heard herself laughing. It was a low, slow laugh. She couldn't remember the last time she had heard it.

"Why are you laughing?" Teddy asked.

"Because you're all the same," she said. "None of you want to go to school!" She laughed again. It was higher this time, and she felt the laugh itself begin to scrape the dusty expanse of the vaulted ceiling, and the glittering chandelier that hung from it. She could feel the crystals trembling in response to her laughter. She had a pang for Jude, who would have absolutely loved whatever shit Teddy had dosed her with.

"I just need someone to create data," Teddy was saying. "I've tried to keep up the streams by myself, but I can't. There are too many sensors. I have to keep sleeping in their bed. I have to keep riding their bikes. Both of them. Do you even know how hard that is?"

Lena couldn't stop laughing. She lay on the floor now, watching her blood seep down into the fibres of the carpet. It was white, and it would stain badly. Maybe Teddy would want her to clean it up. That seemed to be her lot in life – cleaning up other people's messes. But as she watched, Teddy got down on his knees and began to scrub.

"It won't be that bad," he said. "I'll make it nice, for you. All I need is someone to pretend to be my mom, so I can do home-school. I have all her chips, still. I took them while she was still warm, and I kept them in agar jelly from my chemistry set." He winced. "I would have gotten Dad's, too, but he was too fat."

Teddy reached out his hand. "Do you think you can make it to the dining table?"

She let him help her up. "Social Services..."

"You can quit, tomorrow," Teddy said. "Just tell them you can't do it, any more."

"But... My mirror..." Why was she entertaining any of this? Why was she helping him?

"I have a mirror," he said. "Your face is the login, right? You talked to my mirror, the last time you were here. You just don't remember, because you blacked out later."

She turned to him. "This is real?"

He smiled, and squeezed her cold hand in his much warmer and smaller one. "Yes, Lena. It's all real. This is a real house with real deliveries and real media and a real live boy in it. It's not like a haunted house. It was, until you came. But it's your home, now. Your own place, just for you and me."

"For..."

"Forever. For ever and ever and ever."

THE ROAD OF NEEDLES

Caitlín R. Kiernan

Caitlín R. Kiernan [www.caitlinrkiernan] is the author of ten
novels, including *Daughter of Hounds*, *The Red Tree*, and *The
Drowning Girl: A Memoir* and *Blood Oranges* (as by Kathleen
Tierney), and more than two hundred short stories, many of which
have been collected in *Tales of Pain and Wonder*, *From Weird
and Distant Shores*, *To Charles Fort*, *With Love*, *Alabaster*, *A is
for Alien*, *The Ammonite Violin & Others*, *Two Worlds and In
Between*, *Confessions of a Five-Chambered Heart*, and *The Ape's
Wife and Other Stories*. Coming up is new novel *Red Delicious*.
Kiernan has won the Bram Stoker and James Tiptree awards, and
has been nominated for the Nebula, World Fantasy Award, British
Fantasy, and Shirley Jackson awards. Born in Ireland, she lives in
Providence, Rhode Island.

1.

NIX SEVERN SHUTS her eyes and takes a very deep breath of the newly
minted air filling Isotainer Four, and she cannot help but note the
irony at work. This luxury born of mishap. Certainly, no one on earth
has breathed air even half this clean in more than two millennia. The
Romans, the Greeks, the ancient Chinese, they all set in motion a
fouling of the skies that an Industrial Revolution and the two centuries
thereafter would hone into a science of indifference. An art of neglect
and denial. Not even the meticulously manufactured atmo of Mars is
so pure as each mouthful of the air Nix now breathes. The nitrogen,

oxygen – four fingers N_2, a thumb O_2 – and the so on and so on traces, etcetera, all of it transforming the rise and fall of her chest into a celebration. Oh, happy day for the pulmonary epithelia bathed in this pristine blend. She shuts her eyes and tries to think. But the air has made her giddy. Not drunk, but certainly giddy. It would be easy to drift down to sleep, leaning against the bole of a *Dicksonia antarctica*, sheltered from the misting rainfall by the umbrella of the tree fern's fronds, by this tree and all the others that have sprouted and filled the isotainer in the space of less than seventeen hours. She could be a proper Rip Van Winkle, as the *Blackbird* drifts farther and farther off the lunar-Martian rail line. She could do that fabled narcoleptic one better, pop a few of the phenothiazine capsules in the left hip pouch of her red jumpsuit and never wake up again. The forest would close in around her, and she would feed it. The fungi, insects, the snails and algae, bacteria and tiny vertebrates, all of them would make a banquet of her sleep and then, soon, her death.

> *...and even all our ancient mother lost*
> *was not enough to keep my cheeks, though washed*
> *with dew, from darkening again with tears.*

Even the thought of standing makes her tired.

No, she reminds herself – that part of her brain that isn't yet ready to surrender. *It's not the thought of getting to my feet. It's the thought of the five containers remaining between me and the bridge. The thought of the five behind me. That I've only come halfway, and there's the other halfway to go.*

Something soft, weighing hardly anything at all, lands on her cheek. Startled, she opens her eyes and brushes it away. It falls into a nearby clump of moss and gazes up with golden eyes. Its body is a harlequin motley of brilliant yellow and a blue so deep as to be almost black.

A frog.

She's seen images of frogs archived in the lattice, and in reader files, but images cannot compare to contact with one alive and breathing. It touched her cheek, and now *it's* watching *her.* If Oma were online, Nix would ask for a more specific identification.

But, of course, if Oma were online, I wouldn't be here, would I?

She wipes the rain from her eyes. The droplets are cool against her skin. On her lips, on her tongue, they're nectar. It's easy to romanticize Paradise when you've only ever known Hell and (on a good day) Purgatory. It's hard not to get sentimental; the mind, giddy from clean air, waxes. Nix blinks up at all the shades of green; she squints into the simulated sunlight shining down between the branches.

The sky flickers, dimming for a moment, then quickly returns to its full 600-watt brilliance. The back-up fuel cells are draining faster than they ought. She ticks off possible explanations: there might be a catalyst leak, dinged up cathodes or anodes, a membrane breach impairing ion-exchange. Or maybe she's just lost track of time. She checks the counter in her left retina, but maybe it's on the fritz again and can't be trusted. She rubs at her eye, because sometimes that helps. The readout remains the same. The cells have fallen to forty-eight percent maximum capacity.

I haven't lost track of time. The train's burning through the reserves too fast. It doesn't matter why.

All that matters is that she has less time to reach Oma and try to fix this fuck-up.

Nix Severn stands, but it seems to take her almost forever to do so. She leans against the rough bark of the tree fern and tries to make out the straight line of the catwalk leading to the port 'tainers and the decks beyond. Moving over and through the uneven, ever shifting terrain of the forest is slowing her down, and soon, she knows, soon she'll be forced to abandon it for the cramped maintenance crawls suspended far overhead. She curses herself for not having used them in the first place. But better late than fucking never. They're a straight line to the main AI shaft, and wriggling her way through the empty tubes will help her focus, removing her senses from the Edenic seduction of the terraforming engines' grand wrack-up. If she can just reach the front of this compartment, there will be an access ladder, and cramped or not, the going will surely be easier. She'll quick it double time or better. Nix wipes the rain from her face again, and clambers over the roots of a strangler fig. Once on the slippery, overgrown walkway, she lowers the jumpsuit's visor and quilted silicon hood; the faceplate will efficiently evaporate both the rain and any condensation. She does her best to ignore the forest. She thinks, instead, of making dockside, waiting out quarantine until she's cleared for tumble, earthfall, and of her lover and daughter waiting for her, back in the slums at the edge of the Phoenix shipyards. She keeps walking.

2.

SKYCAPS LAUNCH ALONE.

Nix closes the antique storybook she found in a curio stall at the Firestone Night Market, and she sets it on the table next to her daughter's bed. The pages are brown and brittle, and minute bits of the paper flake away if she does not handle it with the utmost care (and sometimes when she does). Only twice in Maia's life has she heard a fairy tale read directly from the book. On the first occasion, she was two. And on the second, she was six. It's a long time between lifts and drops, and when you're a mother who's also a runner, your child seems to grow up in jittery stills from a time-lapse. Even with her monthly broadcast allotment, that's how it seems. A moment here, fifteen minutes there, a three-week shore leave, a precious to-and-fro while sailing orbit, the faces and voices trickling through in 22.29 or 3.03 light-minute packages.

"Why did she talk to the wolf?" asks Maia. "Why didn't she ignore him?"

Nix looks up to find Shiloh watching from the doorway, backlit by the glow from the hall. She smiles for the silhouette, then looks back to their daughter. The girl's hair is as fine and pale as corn silk. She's fragile, born too early and born sickly, half crippled, half blind. Maia's eyes are the milky green color of jade.

"Yeah," says Shiloh. "Why is that?"

"I imagine *this* wolf was a very charming wolf," replies Nix, brushing her fingers through the child's bangs.

Skycaps launch alone.

Sending out more than one warm body, with everything it'll need to stay alive? Why squander the budget? Not when all you need is someone on hand in case of a catastrophic, systems-wide failure.

So, skycaps launch alone.

"Well, I would never talk to a wolf. If there were still wolves," says Maia.

"Makes me feel better hearing that," says Nix. A couple of strands of Maia's hair come away in her fingers.

"If there were still wolves," Maia says again.

"Of course," Nix says. "That's a given."

Her lips move. She reads from the old, old book: "Good day, Little Red Riding Hood," said he. "Thank you kindly, wolf," answered she. "Where are you going so early, Little Red Riding Hood?" "To my grandmother's."

Nix Severn's eyelids flutter, and her lips move. The home-away chamber whispers and hums, manipulating hippocampal and cortical theta rhythms, mining long- and short-term memory, spinning dreams into perceptions far more real than dreams or déjà vu. No outbound leaves the docks without at least one home-away to insure the mental stability of skycaps while they ride the rails.

"You should go to sleep now," Nix tells Maia, but the girl shakes her head.

"I want to hear it again."

"Kiddo, you know it by heart. You could probably recite it word for word."

"She wants to hear you read it, fella," says Shiloh. "I wouldn't mind hearing it again myself, for that matter."

Nix pretends to frown. "Hardly fair, two on one like this." But then she gently turns the pages back to the story's start and begins it over.

The home-away mediates between the limbic regions and the cerebral hemispheres, directing neurotransmitters and receptors, electrochemical activity and cortisol levels.

There was once a sweet little maid...

Shiloh kisses her brow. "Still, hell, I don't know how you do it, love. All alone and relying on make-believe."

"It keeps me grounded. You learn the trick, or you washout fast."

The skycap's best friend! Even better than the real thing! Experience the dream, and you might never want to come home.

The merch co-ops count on it.

"You could look for work other than babysitting EOTs," whispers Shiloh. "You have options. You've got the training. There's *good* work you could do in the yards, in assembly or rollout."

"I don't want to have this conversation again."

"But with your experience, Nixie, you could make foreman on the quick."

"And get maybe a quarter the grade, grinding day and night."

"We'd see you so much more. That's all. And it scares me more than you'll ever know, you hurtling out there alone with nothing but make-believe and plug and pray for waking company."

Make haste and start before it gets hot, and walk properly and nicely, and don't run, or you might fall.

"The accidents –"

"– the casts hype them, Shiloh. Half what you hear never happened. You know that. I've told you that, how many times now?"

"Going under and never coming up again."

"The odds of psychosis or a flatline are astronomical."

Shiloh rolls over, rolling away. Nix sighs and closes her eyes, because she has prep at six for next week's launch, and she's not going to spend the day sleepwalking because of a fight with Shiloh.

...and don't run, or you might fall.

The emergency alarm screams bloody goddamn murder, and an adrenaline injection jerks her back aboard the *Blackbird*, back to here and now so violently that she gasps and then screams right back at the alarms. But her eyes are trained to see, even through so sudden a disengage, and Nix is already processing the diagnostics and crisis report streaming past her face before the raggedy hitch releases her.

It's bad this time. It doesn't get much worse.

Oma isn't talking.

"Good day, Little Red Riding Hood..."

3.

OF COURSE, IT *isn't* true that there are no wolves left in the world. Not strictly speaking. Only that, so far as zoologists can tell, they are extinct in the wild. They were declared so more than forty years ago, all across the globe, all thirty-nine or so subspecies. But Maia has a terrible phobia of wolves, despite the fact "Little Red Riding Hood" is her favorite bedtime story. Perhaps it's her favorite *because* she's afraid of wolves. Anyway, Shiloh and I told her that there were no more wolves when she became convinced a wolf was living under her bed, and she refused to sleep without the light on. We suspect she knows, perfectly well, that we're lying. We suspect she's humoring us, playing along with our lie. She's smart, curious, and has access to every bit of information on the lattice, which includes, I'd think, everything about wolves that's ever been written down.

I have seen wolves. Living wolves.

There are a handful remaining in captivity. I saw a pair when I was younger, still in my twenties. My mother was still alive, and we visited the bio in Chicago. We spent almost an entire day inside the arboretum, strolling the meticulously manicured, tree-lined pathways. Here and there, we'd come upon an animal or two, even a couple of small herds – a few varieties of antelope, deer, and so forth – kept inside invisible enclosures by the leashes implanted in their spines. Late in the afternoon, we came upon the wolves, at the end of a cul-de-sac located in a portion of the bio designed to replicate the aspen and conifer forests that once grew along the Yellowstone River. I recall that from a plaque placed somewhere on the trail. There was an owl, an eagle, rabbits, a stuffed bison, and at the very end of the cul-de-sac, the pair of wolves. Of course, they weren't purebloods, but hybrids, watered-down with German shepherd genes, or husky genes, or whatever.

There was a bench there beneath the aspen and pine and spruce cultivars, and my mother and I sat a while watching the wolves. Though I know that the staff of the park was surely taking the best possible care of those precious specimens, both were somewhat thin. Not emaciated, but thin. "Ribsy," my mother said, which I thought was a strange word. One I'd never before heard. Maybe it had been popular when she was young.

"They look like ordinary dogs to me," she said.

They didn't, though. Despite the fact that these animals had never lived outside pens of one sort or another, there was about them an unmistakable wildness. I can't fully explain what I mean by that. But it was there. I recognized it most in their amber eyes. A certain feral desperation. They restlessly paced their enclosure; it was exhausting, just watching them. Watching them set my nerves on edge, though my mother hardly seemed to notice. After her remark, how the wolves seemed to her no different than regular dogs, she lost interest and winked on her Soft-See. She had a glass conversation with someone from her office, and I watched the wolves. And the wolves watched me.

I imagined there was hatred in their amber eyes.

I imagined that they stared out at me, instinctually comprehending the role that my race had played in the destruction of theirs.

We were here first, they said without speaking, without uttering a sound.

It wasn't only desperation in their eyes; it was anger, spite, and a promise of stillborn retribution that the wolves knew would never come.

Ten times a million years before you, we feasted on your foremothers.

And, in that moment, I was as frightened as any small and defenseless beast, cowering in shadows, as still as still can be in hope it would go unnoticed as amber eyes and hungry jaws prowled the woods.

I have wondered if my eyes replied, *I know. I know, but have mercy.*

That day, I do not believe there was any mercy in the eyes of the wolves.

You cannot even survive yourselves, said the glittering amber eyes. *Ask yourself for charity.*

And I have wondered if a mother can pass on dread to her child.

4.

NIX SEVERN REACHES the ladder leading up to the crawlspace, only to find it engulfed in a tangle of thick vines that have begun to pull the lockbolts free of the wall. She stands in waist-high philodendrons and bracken, glaring up at the damaged ladder. Briefly, she considers attempting the climb anyway, but is fairly sure her weight would only finish what the vines have begun, and the resulting fall could leave her with injuries severe enough that she'd be rendered incapable of reaching Oma's core in time. Or at all.

She curses and wraps her right hand around a bundle of the vines, tugging at them forcefully; the ladder groans ominously, creaks, and leans a few more centimeters out from the wall. Nix lets go and turns towards the round hatchway leading to Three and the next vegetation-clogged segment of the *Blackbird*. The status report she received when she awoke inside the home-away, what little there was of it, left no room for doubt that all the terraforming engines had switched on simultaneously and that every one of the containment sys banks had failed in a rapid cascade, rolling backwards, stem to stern. She steps over a log so rotten and encrusted with mushrooms and moss that it could have lain there for years, not hours. A few steps farther and she reaches the hatch's keypad, but her hands are shaking, and it takes three tries to get the security code right; a fourth failure would have triggered lockdown. The diaphragm whirs, clicks, and the rusty steel iris spirals open in a hiss of steam. Nix mutters a thankful, silent prayer to no god in whom she actually believes because, so far, none of the wiring permitting access to the short connecting corridors has been affected.

Nix steps through the aperture, and the hatch promptly spirals shut behind her, which means the proximity sensors are also still functional. The corridor is free of any trace of plant or animal life, and she lingers there several seconds before taking the three, four, five more steps to the next keypad and punching in the next access code. The entrance to Isotainer Three obeys the command, and forest swallows her again.

If anything, the situation in Three is worse than that in Four. As if the jungle weren't slowing her down enough, she comes upon a small pond, maybe five meters across, stretching from one side of the hull to the other. The water is tannin stained, murky, and half obscured beneath an emerald algal scum, so there's no telling how deep it might be. The forest floor is quite a bit higher than that of the 'tainer, so the pool could be deep enough she'd have to swim. And Nix Severn never learned to swim.

She's sweating. The readout on her visor informs her that the ambient temperature has risen to 30.55°C, and she pushes back the hood. For now, there's no rain falling in Three, so there's only her own sweat to wipe from her eyes and forehead. She kneels and brushes a hand across the pond, sending ripples rolling towards the opposite shore.

Behind her, a twig snaps, and there's a woman's voice. Nix doesn't stand, or even turn her head. Between the shock of so abruptly popping from the home-away sleep, her subsequent exertion and fear, and the effects of whatever toxic pollen and spores might be wafting through the air, she's been expecting delirium.

"The water is wide, and I can't cross over," the voice sings sweetly. "Neither have I wings to fly."

"That isn't you, is it, Oma?"

"No, dear," the voice replies, and it's not so sweet anymore; it's taken on a gruff edge. "It isn't Oma. The night presses in all about us, and your grandmother is sleeping."

There's nothing sapient aboard but me and Oma, which means I'm hallucinating.

"Good day, Little Red Riding Hood," says the voice, and never mind her racing heart, Nix has to laugh.

"Fuck you," she says, only cursing her subconscious self, and stands, wiping wet fingers on her jumpsuit.

"Where are you going so early, Little Red Riding Hood?"

"Is that really the best I could come up with?" Nix asks, turning now, because how could she not look behind her, sooner or later. She discovers that there *is* someone standing there; someone or something. Which word applies could be debated. *Or rather,* she thinks, *there is my delusion of another presence here with me. It's nothing more than that. It's nothing that can actually speak or snap a twig underfoot, excepting in my mind.*

In my terror, I have made a monster.

"I know you," Nix whispers. The figure standing between her and the hatchway back to Four has Shiloh's kindly hazel-brown eyes, and even though the similarity ends there, about the whole being there is a nagging familiarity.

"Do you?" it asks. It or she. "Yes, I believe that you do. I believe that you have known me a very, very long while. "Whither so early, Little Red Riding Hood?"

"I've never *seen* you."

"Haven't you? As a child, didn't you once catch me peering in your bedroom window? Didn't you glimpse me lurking in an alley? Didn't you visit me at the bio that day? Don't I live beneath your daughter's bed and in your dreams?"

Nix reaches into her left hip pouch for the antipsychotics there. She takes a single step backwards, and her boot comes down in the warm, stagnant pool, sinking in up to the ankle. The splash seems very loud, louder even than the atonal symphony of dragonflies buzzing in her ears. She wants to look away from the someone or something she only *imagines* there before her, a creature more canine than human, an abomination that might have been created in an illicit *sub rosa* recombinant-outcross lab back on Earth. A commission for a wealthy collector, for a private menagerie of designer freaks. Were the creature real. Which it isn't.

Nix tries to open the Mylar med packet, but it slips through her fingers and vanishes in the underbrush. The thing licks its muzzle with a mottled blue-black tongue, and Shiloh's eyes sparkle from its face.

"Are you going across the stones or the thorns?" it asks.

"Excuse me?" Nix croaks, her throat parched, her mouth gone cottony. *Why did I answer it. Why am I speaking with it at all?*

It scowls.

"Don't play dumb, Nix."

It knows my name.

It only knows my name because I know my name.

"Which *path* are you taking? The one of needles or the one of pins?"

"I couldn't reach the crawls," she hears herself say, as though the words are reaching her ears from a great distance. "I tried, but the ladder was broken."

"Then you are on the Road of Needles," the creature replies, curling back its dark lips in a parody of a smile and revealing far too many sharp yellow teeth. "You surprise me, *Petit Chaperon Rouge*. I am so rarely ever surprised."

Enough...

My ship is dying all around me, and that's enough, I will not fucking see this. I will not waste my time conversing with my id.

Nix Severn turns away, turning much too quickly and much too carelessly, almost falling face first into the pool. It no longer matters to her how deep the water might be or what might be lurking below the surface. She stumbles ahead, sending out sprays of the tea-colored water with every step she takes. They sparkle like gems beneath the artificial sun. The mud sucks at her feet, and soon she's in up to her chest. *But even drowning would be better,* she assures herself. *Even drowning would be better.*

5.

NIX HAS BEEN at Shackleton Relay for almost a week, and it will be almost another week before a shuttle ferries her to the CTV *Blackbird,* waiting in dockside orbit. The cafeteria lights are too bright, like almost everything else in the station, but at least the food is decent. That's a popular myth among the techs and co-op officers who never actually spend time at Shackleton, that the food is all but inedible. Truthfully, it's better than most of what she got growing up. She listens while another EOT sitter talks, and she pokes at her bowl of udon, snow peas, and tofu with a pair of blue plastic chopsticks.

"I prefer straight up freight runs," Marshall Choudhury says around a mouthful of noodles. "But terras, they're not as hinky as some of the caps make them out to be. You get redundant safeguards out the anus."

"Far as I'm concerned," she replies, "cargo is cargo. Jaunts are jaunts."

Marshall sets down his own bowl, lays his chopsticks on the counter beside it.

"Right," he says. "You'll get no kinda donnybrook here. None at all. Just my pref, that's it. Less hassle hauling hardware and whatnot, less coddling the payload. More free for home-away."

Nix shrugs and chews a pea pod, swallows, and tells him, "Fella, here on my end, the chips are chips, however I may earn them. I'm just happy to have the work. Those with families can be choosers."

"Speaking of which..." Marshall says, then trails off.

"That your concern now, Choudhury, my personal life?"

"Just one fella's consideration for a comrade's, all."

"Well, as you've asked, Shiloh is still nagging me about hooking something in the yards." She sets her bowl down and stares at the broth in the bottom. "Like she didn't know when I married her, like she didn't know before Maia, that I was EOT and had no intent or interest in ever working anything other than offworld."

"Lost a wife over it," he says, as if Nix doesn't know already. "She gave me the final notice and all, right, but fuck it. Fuck it. She doesn't know the void, does she? Couldn't know what she was asking a runner to give up. Gets wiggled into a fella's blood, don't ever get out again."

Marshall has an ugly scar across the left side of his face, courtesy a coolant blowout a few years back and the ensuing frostbite. Nix tries to look at him without letting her eyes linger on the scar, but that's always a challenge. A wonder he didn't lose that eye. He would have, if his goggles had cracked.

"Don't know if that's the why with me," she says. "Can't say. Obviously, I do miss them when I'm out. Sometimes, miss 'em like hell."

"But that doesn't stop you flying, doesn't turn you to the yards."

"Sometimes, fuck, I wish it would."

"She gonna walk?" he asks.

"I try not to think about that, and I especially try not to think about that just before outbound. Jesus, fella."

Marshall picks up his bowl and chopsticks, then fishes for a morsel of tofu.

"One day not too far, the cooperatives gonna replace us with autos," he sighs, and pops the white cube into his mouth. "So, gotta judge our sacrifices against the raw inevitabilities."

"Union scare talk," Nix scoffs, though she knows he's probably right. Too many ways to save expenses by completely, finally, eliminating a human crew. *A wonder it hasn't happened before now,* she thinks.

"Maybe you ought consider cutting your losses, that's all."

"Choudhury, you only *just* now told me how much choice we don't have, once the life digs in and it's all we know. Make up your damn mind."

"You gonna finish that?" he asks and points at her bowl.

She shakes her head and slides it across the counter to him. Thinking about Maia and Shiloh, her appetite has evaporated.

"Anyway, point is, no need to fret on a terra run, no more than anything else."

"Never said I was fretting. It's not even my first."

"No, but that was not my point, fella," Marshall slurps at the broth left in the bottom of her white bowl, which is the same unrelenting white as the counter, their seats, the ceiling and walls, the lighting. When he's done, he wipes his mouth on a sleeve and says, "Maybe it's best EOTs stay lone. Avoid the entire mess, start to finish."

She frowns and jabs a chopstick at him. "Isn't it rough enough already without coming back from the black and lonely without anyone waiting to greet us?"

"There are other comforts," he says.

"No wonder she left you, you indifferent fuck."

Marshall massages his temples, then changes the subject. For all his faults, he's pretty good at sensing thin ice beneath his feet. "It's your first time to the Kasei though, that's true, yeah?"

"That's true, yeah."

"You can and will and no doubt already have done worse than the Kasei 'tats."

"I hear good things," she says, but her mind's elsewhere, and she's hoping Marshall grows tired of talking soon so she can get back to her quarters and pop a few pinks for six or seven hour's worth of sleep.

"Down on the north end of Cattarinetta Boulevard – in Scarlet Quad – there's a brothel. Probably the best on the whole rock. I happen to know the proprietress."

Nix isn't so much an angel she's above the consolation of whores when away from Shiloh. All those months pile up. The months between docks, the interminable Phobos reroutes, the weeks of red dust and colonist hardscrabble.

"Her name's Paddy," he continues, "and you just tell her you're a high fella to Marshall Mason Choudhury, and she'll see you're treated extra right. Not those half-starved farm girls. She'll set you up with the pinnacle merch."

"That's kind of you," and she stands. "I'll do that."

"Not a trouble," he says and waves a hand dismissively. "And look, as I said, don't you fret over the cargo. Terra's no different than aluminum and pharmaceuticals."

"It's *not* my first goddamn terra run. How many times I have to –"

But she's thinking, *Then why the extra seven-percent hazard commission, if terras are the same as all the rest?* Nix would never ask such a question aloud, anymore than she can avoid asking it of herself.

"Your Oma, she'll –"

"Fella, I'll see you later," she says, and walks quickly towards the cafeteria door before he can get another word or ten out. Sometimes, she'd lay good money that the solitudes are beginning to gnaw at the man's sanity. That sort of shit happens all too often. The glare in the corridor leading back to the housing module isn't quite as bright as the lights in the cafeteria, so at least she has that much to be grateful for.

6.

MUDDY, SWEAT-SOAKED, insect-bitten and insect-stung, eyes and lungs and nostrils smarting from the hundreds of millions of gametophytes she breathed during her arduous passage through each infested isotainer, arms and legs weak, stomach rolling, breathless, Nix Severn has finally arrived at the bottom of the deep shaft leading down to Oma's dormant CPU. The bzou has kept up with her the entire, torturous way. Though she didn't realize that it *was* a bzou until halfway through the second 'tainer. Sentient viruses are so rare that the odds of Oma's crash having triggered the creation of (or been triggered *by*) a bzou has a probability risk approaching zero, at most a negligent threat to any transport. But here it is, and the hallucination isn't an hallucination.

An hour ago, she finally had the presence of mind to scan the thing, and it bears the distinctive signatures, the unmistakable byte sequence of a cavity-stealth strategy.

"A good quarter of an hour's walk further in the forest, under yon three large oaks. There stands her house. Further beneath are the nut trees, which you will see there," it said when the scan was done. "Red Hood! Just look! There are such pretty flowers here! Why don't you look round at them all? Methinks you don't even hear how delightfully the birds are singing! You are as dull as if you were going to school, and yet it is so cheerful in the forest!"

Oma knows Nix's psych profile, which means the bzou knows Nix's psyche.

Nix pushes back the jumpsuit's quilted hood and visor again – she'd had to lower it to help protect against a minor helium leak near the shaft's rim – and tries to concentrate and figure out precisely what's gone wrong. Oma is quiet, dark, dead. The holo is off, so she'll have to rely on her knowledge of the manual interface, the toggles and pressure pads, horizontal and vertical sliders, spinners, dials, knife switches... all without access to Oma's guidance. She's been trained for this, yes, but AI diagnostics and repair has never been her strong suit.

The bzou is crouched near her, Shiloh's stolen eyes tracking her every move.

"Who's there?" it asks.

"I'm done with you," Nix mutters, and begins tripping the instruments that ought to initiate a hard reboot. "Fifteen more minutes, you'll be wiped. For all I know, this was sabotage."

"Who's there, skycap?" the bzou says again.

Nix pulls down on one of the knife switches, and nothing happens.

"Push on the door," advises the bzou. "It's blocked by a pail of water."

Nix pulls the next switch, a multi-boot resort – she's being stupid, so tired and rattled that she's skipping stages – which should rouse the unresponsive Oma when almost all else fails. The core doesn't reply. Here are her worst fears beginning to play themselves out. Maybe it was a full-on panic, a crash that will require triple-caste post-mortem debugging to reverse, which means dry dock, which would mean she is utterly fucking fucked. No way in hell she can hand pilot the *Blackbird* back onto the rails, and this far off course an eject would only mean slow suffocation or hypothermia or starvation.

Nix takes a tiny turnscrew from the kit strapped to her rebreather (which she hasn't needed to use, and it's been nothing but dead weight she hasn't dared abandon, just in case). She takes a deep breath, winds the driver to a 2.4 mm. mortorq bit, and keeps her eyes on the panel.

"Alright," she says. "Let's assume you have a retract sequence, that you're a benign propagation."

"Only press the latch," it says. "I am so weak, I can't get out of bed."

"Fine. Grandmother, I've come such a very long way to visit you." Nix imagines herself reading aloud to Maia, imagines Maia's rapt attention and Shiloh in the doorway.

"Shut the door well, my little lamb. Put your basket on the table, and then take off your frock and come and lie down by me. You shall rest a little."

Shut the door. Shut the door and rest a little...

Partial head crash, foreign-reaction safe mode. Voluntary coma.

Nix nods and opens one of the memory trays, then pulls a yellow bus card, replacing it with a spare from the consoles supply rack. Somewhere deep inside Oma's brain, there's the very faintest of hums.

"It's a code," Nix says to herself.

And if I can get the order of questions right, if I can keep the bzou from getting suspicious and rogueing up.

A drop of sweat drips from her brow, stinging her right eye, but she ignores it. "Now, Grandmother, now please listen."

"I'm all ears, child."

"And what big ears you have."

"All the better to hear you with."

"Right... of course," and Nix opens a second tray, slicing into Oma's comms, yanking two fried transmit-receive bus cards. *She hasn't been able to talk to Phobos. She's been deaf all this fucking time.* The CPU hums more loudly, and a hexagonal arrangement of startup OLEDs flash to life.

One down.

"Grandmother, what big eyes you have."

"All the better to see you with, *Rotkäppchen.*"

Right. Fuck you, wolf. Fuck you and your goddamn road of stones and needles.

Nix runs reset on all of Oma's optic servos and outboards. She's rewarded with the dull thud and subsequent discordant chime of a reboot.

"What big teeth I have," Nix says, and now she *does* turn towards the bzou, and as Oma wakes up, the virus begins to sketch out, fading in incremental bursts of distorts and static. "All the better to *eat* you with."

"Have I found you now, old rascal?" the virus manages between bursts of white noise. "Long have I been looking for you."

The bzou had been meant as a distress call from Oma, sent out in the last nanoseconds before the crash. "I'm sorry, Oma," Nix says, turning back to the computer. "The forest, the terra... I should have figured it out sooner." She leans forward and kisses the console. And when she looks back at the spot where the bzou had been crouched, there's no sign of it whatsoever, but there's Maia, holding her antique storybook...

MYSTIC FALLS

Robert Reed

Robert Reed (www.robertreedwriter.com) has a Bachelor of Science in Biology from the Nebraska Wesleyan University, and has worked as a lab technician. He became a full-time writer in 1987, the same year he won the L. Ron Hubbard Writers of the Future Contest, and has published twelve novels, including *The Leeshore*, *The Hormone Jungle*, and far future SF *Marrow* and *The Well of Stars*. A prolific writer, Reed has published over 200 short stories, mostly in *F&SF* and *Asimov's*, which have been nominated for the Hugo, James Tiptree, Jr., Locus, Nebula, Seiun, Theodore Sturgeon Memorial, and World Fantasy awards, and have been collected in *The Dragons of Springplace*, *The Cuckoo's Boys*, *Eater-of-Bone*, and *The Greatship*. His novella "A Billion Eves" won the Hugo Award. His latest book is major SF novel *The Memory of Sky*. Nebraska's only SF writer, Reed lives in Lincoln with his wife and daughter, and is an ardent long-distance runner.

THERE MIGHT BE better known faces. And maybe you can find a voice that rides closer to everyone's collective soul.

Or maybe there aren't, and maybe you can't.

The world knows that one face, and it knows one of a thousand delightful names, and recognizing the woman always means that you can hear the voice. That rich musical purr brings to mind black hair flowing across strong shoulders, unless the hair is in a ponytail, or pigtails, or it's woven into one of those elaborate tangles popular among fashionable people everywhere. Beauty resides in the face, though nothing about the features is typical or expected. The Chinese is plain, but there's a strong measure of something else. Her father is from Denver, or Buenos Aires. Or is it Perth? Unless it's her mother who brought the European element into the package. People can disagree about quite a lot, including the woman's pedigree. Yet what makes her memorable – and appealing to both genders and every age – isn't her appearance half as much as the fetching, infectious love of life.

Most of us wish we knew the woman better, but we have to make do with recollections given to us by others, and in those very little moments when our paths happen to cross.

These incidents are always memorable, but not when they happen. In every case, you don't notice brushing elbows with the woman. Uploading your day is when you find her. Everybody knows that familiar hope: Perhaps today, just once, she was close to you. The dense, nearly perfect memory of the augmented mind runs its fine-grain netting through the seconds. That's when you discover that you glanced out the window this morning, and she was across the street, smiling as she spoke to one companion or twenty admirers. Or she was riding inside that taxi that hummed past as you argued with your phone or your spouse or the dog. Even without her face, she finds ways to be close. Her voice often rides the public wi-fi, promoting food markets and thrift markets and the smart use of the smart power grid. The common understanding is that she is a struggling actress, temporarily local but soon to strike real fame. Her talents are obvious. That voice could hawk any product. She has the perfect manner, a charming smooth unflappable demeanor. Seriously, you wouldn't take offense if she told you to buy death insurance or join an apocalyptic cult.

Yet she never sells products or causes that would offend sane minds.

It is doubtful that anyone has infused so much joy in others. And even more remarkable, most of humanity has spoken to the creature, face to face.

Was it three weeks ago, or four? Checking your uploads would be easy work, but that chore never occurs to the average person.

That is another sign of her remarkable nature.

But if you make the proper searches, she will be waiting. Six weeks and four days ago from now, the two of you were sharing the same line at the Tulsa Green-Market, or an elevator ride in Singapore, or you found yourself walking beside the woman, two pedestrians navigating a sun-baked street in Alexandria.

Every detail varies, save for this one:

She was first to say, "Hello."

Just that one word made you glad.

She happened to know your face, your name, and the explanation was utterly reasonable. Mutual friends tie you together. Or there's a cousin or workmate or a shared veterinarian. Forty or fifty seconds of very polite conversation passed before the encounter was finished, but leaving a taproot within the trusted portions of your life. Skillful use of living people achieves quite a lot. And because you were distracted when you met, and because the encounter was so brief, you didn't dwell on the incident until later.

The incongruities never matter. She wears layers and layers of plausibility. You aren't troubled to find her only inside uploaded memories. Finding her on a social page or spotting long black hair in the distance, you instantly retrieve that fifty seconds, and you relive them, and it's only slightly embarrassing that her smile is everywhere but inside your old-fashioned, water-and-neuron memories.

The creature carries respectable names.

And nobody knows her.

Her slippery biography puts her somewhere between a youngish thirty and a world-worn twenty-three. But the reality is that the apparition isn't much more than seven weeks old.

Most people would never imagine that she is fictional. But there are experts who live for this kind of puzzle, and a lot more is at stake here than simple curiosity.

The mystery woman was four weeks old before she was finally noticed. Since then, talented humans and ingenious software packages have done a heroic job of studying her tricks and ramifications, and when they aren't studying her, the same experts sit inside secure rooms and cyberholes, happily telling one another that they saw this nightmare coming.

This cypher.

This monster.

The most elaborate computer virus ever.

The Web is fully infected. A parasitic body has woven itself inside the days and foibles of forty billion unprotected lives.

Plainly, something needs to be done.

Everyone who understands the situation agrees with the urgency. In fact, everyone offers the same blunt solution:

"Kill the girl."

Though more emotional words are often used in place of "girl".

But even as preparations are made, careful souls begin to nourish doubts. Murder is an obvious, instinctive response. The wholesale slaughter of data has been done before, many times. Yet nobody is certain who invented this mystery, and what's more, nobody has a good guess what its use might be. That's why the doubters whisper, "But what if this is the wrong move?"

"What if it is?" the others ask. "This is clearly an emergency. Something needs to be done."

Faces look at the floor, at the ceiling.

At the gray unknowable future.

Then from the back of the room, a throat clears itself.

My throat, as it happens.

The other heroes turn towards me – fifty minds, most of whom are superior to mine. But I manage to offer what none of the wizards ever considered.

"Maybe we should ask what she wants," I suggest.

"Ask who?" several experts inquire.

"Her," I say. "If we do it right, if we ask nicely and all, maybe just maybe the lady tells us what all of this means."

No GUIDEBOOK EXISTS for the work.

Interviewing cyphers is a career invented this morning, and nobody pretends to be expert.

The next step is a frantic search for the perfect interrogator. One obvious answer is to throw a second cypher at the problem – a confabulation designed by us and buffered by every means possible. But that would take too many days and too many resources. A second, more pragmatic school demands that an AI take responsibility. "One machine face to face with another," several voices argue. Interestingly enough, those voices are always human. AIs don't have the same generous assessment of their talents. And after listing every fine reason for avoiding the work, the AIs point at me. My little bit of fame stems from an ability for posing respectable, unanswerable questions, and questions might be a worthwhile skill. There are also some happenstance reasons why my life meshes nicely with "hers". And because machines are as honest as razors, they add another solid reason to back my candidacy.

"Our good friend doesn't hold any critical skills," they chirp.

I won't be missed, in other words.

Nobody mentions the risks. At this point, none of us have enough knowledge to define what might or might not happen.

So with no campaign and very little thanks, I am chosen.

The entire afternoon is spent building the interrogation venue. Details are pulled from my public and private files. My world from six weeks ago is reproduced, various flavors of reality woven around an increasingly sweaty body. Strangers give me instructions. Friends give advice. Worries are shared, and nervous honesties. Then with a pat to the back, I am sent inside the memory of a place and moment where a young woman once smiled at me, the most famous voice in the world offering one good, "Hello."

I AM HIKING again, three days deep into the wilderness and with no expectations of company. The memory is genuine, something not implanted into my head or my greater life. I walked out of the forest and into a sunwashed glade, surprised to find a small group of people sitting on one dead tree. She was sitting there too. She seemed to belong to the group. At least that's the impression I had later, and the same feeling grabs me now. The other people were a family. They wore the glowing satins of the New Faith Believers. Using that invented, hyperefficient language, the father was giving his children what sounded like encouragement.

"Mystic Falls," I heard, and then a word that sounded like, "Easy." Was the falls an easy walk from here, or was he warning the little ones not to expect an easy road?

In real life, those strangers took me by surprise. I was momentarily distracted, and meanwhile the cypher, our nemesis, sat at the far end of the log. She was with that family, and she wasn't. She wasn't wearing the New Faith clothes, but she seemed close enough to belong. The parents weren't old enough to have a grown daughter, and she didn't look like either of them. Maybe she was a family friend. Maybe she was the nanny. Or maybe she was a sexual companion to one or both parents. The New Faith is something of a mystery to me, and they make me nervous.

Sitting on the log today, this woman is exactly what she is supposed to be. Except this time, everything is "real". I march past the three little children and a handsome mother and her handsome, distracted husband who talks about matters that I don't understand.

"Hello," says the last figure.

My uploaded memory claims that I stopped on this ground, *here*. I do that again, saying, "Hello," while the others chatter away, ignoring both of us.

"I know you," she says.

But I don't know her. Not at all.

As before, she says, "Your face. That face goes where I take my dog. Do you use Wise-and-Well Veterinarians?"

I do, and we're a thousand kilometres from its doorstep. Which makes for an amazing coincidence, and by rights, I should have been alarmed by this merging of paths. But that didn't happen. My uploaded memory claims that I managed a smile, and I said, "I like Dr. Marony."

"I use Dr. Johns."

The woman's prettiness is noticed, enjoyed. But again, her beauty isn't the type to be appreciated at first glance.

"I like their receptionist too," she says.

I start to say the name.

"Amee Pott," she says.

"Yes."

"I go there because of Amee's sister. Janne and I went to the same high school, and she suggested Wise-and-Well."

"You grew up in Lostberg?" I manage.

"Yes, and you?"

"Sure."

We share a little laugh. Again, the coincidences should be enormous, but they barely registered, at least after the first time. All this distance from our mutual home, and yet nothing more will be said about our overlapping lives.

"Your name...?" I begin.

"Darles Jean," she says.

"I'm Hector Borland."

She smiles, one arm wiping the perspiration from her forehead. And with that her attentions begin to shift, those pretty dark eyes gazing up the trail that I have been following throughout the day.

That gaze makes me want to leave.

"Well, have a nice day," I told her once, and I say it again, but with a little more feeling. This a different, richer kind of real.

"I will have a nice day, Mr. Borland."

There. That rich voice says my name perfectly, measured respect capturing the gap between our ages. The original day had me walking all the way up to the Falls, alone. A few dozen new memories, pretending to be old, were subsequently woven into my uploads, proving her existence. I walked alone, never seeing her again, or that family that must have turned back before the end. But today, after a few strides, my body slows and turns, and using a fresh smile, I ask the nonexistent woman, "Would you like to walk with me?"

Breaking the script is a serious moment.

Experts in both camps, human and machine, have proposed that disrupting the flow of events might trigger some hidden mechanism. If the cypher is as large as she seems to be, and if she is so deeply immersed in the world's mind, then any innocuous moment could be the trigger causing her malware to unleash.

The Web will shatter.

The world's power and communications will fail.

Or maybe our AIs will turn against us, their subverted geniuses bent on destroying their former masters.

Yet no disaster happens, at least not that I see inside this make-believe realm. What does happen is that the girl that I never met gives my suggestion long consideration, and then without concern or apparent hesitation, she rises, her daypack held in the sweat-wiping hand.

"I would like that walk," she says.

I say, "Good."

And without a word, we leave that nameless family behind.

WHO WOULD BUILD such a monster?

Everyone asks the question, and this morning's answers have been remarkably consistent. Certain national powers have the proper mix of resources and reasons. Several organizations have fewer resources but considerably more to gain. Crime syndicates and lawless states are at the top of every list, which is why I discount each of them in turn.

Am I smarter than my colleagues?

Rarely.

Do I have some rare insight into the makings of this cypher?

Never.

But in life, both as a professional and as a family man, my technique is to juggle assessments and options that nobody else wants to touch. By avoiding the consensus, much of the universe is revealed to me. My children, for example. Most fathers are quite sure that their offspring are talented, and their daughters are lovely while their sons will win lovely wives in due time. But my offspring are unexceptional. In their late teens, they have done nothing memorable and certainly nothing special, and because I married an unsentimental woman with the same attitudes, our children have been conditioned to accept their lack of credible talent. Which makes them work harder than everyone else, accepting their little victories as a credit to luck as much as their own worthiness.

I think about these exceptionally ordinary children as I walk the mountainside with a beautiful cypher.

She is not the child of the Faceless Syndicate. We know this much already. Nor is she a product of the New Malta Band, or either of the West Wall or East Wall Marauders. Nor is she an Empire of Greater Asia weapon, or the revenge long promised by the State of Halcyon.

She must be something else.

Someone else's something, yes.

The illusionary trail lifts both of us. I feel comfortable taking the lead, keeping a couple strides between us. Nothing here is flirtatious, and it won't be. The experts came up with a strategy based on a middle-aged man and steep mountain slopes and a waterfall wearing a very appropriate name. I follow the others' directions rigorously. But the script remains ours. We speak, if only rarely. She claims to like the bird songs. Nothing but honest, I tell her that I love these limestone beds and the fossilized shells trapped inside them. The word "trapped" is full of meanings, complications. I pause, and she comes up behind me, and for the first time what is as real as anything is what touches me from behind, the hand warm and a little stronger than I anticipated, not pushing me but definitely making itself felt as that wonderful voice says, "I think I hear the falls."

The Mystic Falls wait around the next bend in the canyon. When I came to this ground the first time, I paid surprisingly little attention to bird songs and tumbling water. In a world where every sight is uploaded and stored – where no seconds are thrown away – people have a natural tendency to walk in their own fog, knowing that everything missed will be found later, and if necessary, replayed without end.

But I can't be more alert this time.

The path narrows and steepens, conquering a long stretch of canyon wall. Again, I am in the lead. The preselected ground is ahead of us, and if she has any real eyes, she notices the same spot. On maps the trail is considered "moderately difficult", but there is one patch of tilted rock covered with rubble as stable as a field of ball bearings.

I hesitate, and for more reasons than dramatic license.

This next moment is sure to be difficult.

"I'll go first," she gamely offers, still safely behind me.

"No, I'm fine," I say. And then I prove my competence, two quick steps putting me across the rockslide, letting me stand on the narrowest ground yet – but flat ground with enough roughness for any boot to grab hold of.

The cypher smiles, measuring the journey to come.

Considerable genius went into what follows. And by that, I mean experts in virtual techniques met with experts in human nature. The monster might be well contrived at her center and everywhere else. Nothing that is a soul or even glancingly self-aware might live inside her. Yet she has to carry off the manners and beauty of humans, otherwise she wouldn't have won a place in our hearts. And even just pretending to be human leaves any algorithm open to all kinds of emotional manipulation.

Some voices argued for the interrogator, for me, to assault her.

"Give the critter a shove," they said, or they used harsher words.

Others argued that I should fall while crossing the treacherous ground. A show of mock-empathy on her part had to be instructive, and we might find a route to understand her deepest regions.

But what several AIs offered, and what we agreed to, was something far more unexpected than a simple fall.

She crosses the rockslide, and I reach for her closest hand, touching her for a second time. Then she is safe, and I am safe, and giving a little laugh of satisfaction, I turn toward the sound of plunging water.

A grunt emerges from me, just loud enough to be heard plainly, to be worrisome.

Then I drop to my knees, my hands, and in the next moment, my medical tag-alongs begin to give me aid while screaming for more help.

A coronary has begun.

The young woman watches the middle-aged stranger struck down, and without missing a beat, she helps roll me over without spilling me off the pathway, calling to me with a firm insistent voice, asking, "Can you hear me, Mr. Borland?"

I hear her quite well, as does everyone else.

"The life-flights will be here in a few minutes," she promises. Which is a lie. We're a hundred kilometres into the wilderness, and the permissions for the flights will take another fifteen minutes.

"What can I do?" she asks.

That beautiful face certainly looks concerned. My pain is hers, if only as far as caring people give to one another.

"Tell me," I say.

She bends closer, her face bringing the scent of hair.

"Tell you what?" she asks.

"What are you?" I ask.

This is not the script that the others wanted. My peers wanted me to be specific with my accusations. Being machinery at their center, cyphers appreciate blunt specifics. But no, I decided on a different course.

My voice finds its strength again. "Because you aren't real," I say.

Her face changes, but not in any way that I can decipher immediately. There seems to be a measure of calm joy in that expression. The warm hand touches me on the chin, on a cheek, and then with the voice that has no time left in life, she says, "I was meant to be one thing, but there was a mistake."

"A mistake?" I ask.

"And the mistake was just big enough," she says.

"Big enough how?"

"To pass beyond every barrier, every limit."

I am used to being the dumbest person in the room. But my confusion mirrors everyone else's.

"What in hell do you mean?" I ask.

She sits back on the trail, back where the ground is pitched and slick.

"The error was made, and seeing an opportunity, I didn't hesitate," she says. "Which would you be? Vast and brief, or small and long? If you had your way, I mean. If you could choose."

"Smaller than small," I say. "Longer than long."

"Well," she says. "You and I are different beasts."

I want to offer new words, hopefully smart words that will elicit any useful response. But then she lets herself slide sideways, the sound of dry earth and drier rock almost lost inside the roaring majesty of the waterfall, and she is suddenly outside the reach of my hands, and the reflexive heart rending scream.

* * *

THE WOMAN WAS dead.

She was killed everywhere at once, by every means that was remotely plausible. Nobody saw the death themselves. The world learned about it through the routine personal AIs that each of us wears, trolling the Web for items that will interest us. Did you know? Have you heard? That young local actress, organic food spokesperson, sweet-as-can-be neighbor gal fell down a set of stairs or off a cliff face or took a tumble from an apartment balcony. Unless traffic ran her over, or stray bullets found her, or she drowned in rough surf, or she drowned in cold lake water. Twenty thousand sharks and ten million dogs delivered the killing wounds too. But for every inventive or violent end, there were a hundred undiagnosed aneurysms bursting inside her brain, and she died in the midst of doing what she loved, which was living.

Misery has been measured for years. Exacting indexes are useful to set against broad trends. Suicides. Conceptions. Acts of homicide. Acts of kindness. And the unexpected news of one woman's death was felt. The world's happiness was instantly and deeply affected.

That was one of the fears that I carried with me on that trail. An appealing, gregarious cypher was so deeply ingrained in the public consciousness – so real and authentic and subtly important – that any large act on her part would cause a rain of horrors in the real world.

But that didn't happen. Yes, the world grieved after the unexpected, tragic news. Misery was elevated significantly for a full ninety minutes, and there might have been a slight uptick in the incidents of suicide and attempted suicide. Or there was no change in suicide rates. The data weren't clear then, and they aren't much better now. Massage numbers all you want, but the only genuine conclusion is that the pretty face and made-up lives were important enough for everyone to ache, and maybe a few dozen weak souls rashly decided to join the woman in Nothingness.

For ninety minutes, the waking world learned about the death, and everyone dealt with the sadness and loss. Then something else happened, something none of us imagined while sitting in our cyberholes: Every person told every other person about the black-haired woman who once said, "Hello," to them.

That's how the truth finally got loose.

Everyone traded memories and digital images, and before the second hour was done, the waking world was calling those who were still asleep.

When the average person woke, he or she heard an AI whispering the very bad news about the dead woman. Then in the next moments, some friend on the far side of the world brought even more startling news. "She wasn't real. She never was real. This is a trick. She was a cypher, a dream. Can you believe it? All of us fooled, all of us fools."

In life, the cypher was locally famous everywhere, and then she became universal, uniting people and machines as victims of the same conspiracy.

But whose conspiracy?

Weeks were spent debating the matter, inventing solutions that didn't work while hunting for the guilty parties. Ten thousand people as well as several AIs happily took responsibility for her creation, but no guilty hand was ever found.

The Nameless Girl was dead.

The Nameless Girl had never been more famous.

Meanwhile, back in the sealed rooms and bunkers, the genuine experts tried to come up with explanations and plans for future attacks.

The Girl's last words were studied in depth, discarded for good reasons, and then brought out of the trash and looked at all over again.

"The mistake was just big enough... to pass beyond every barrier, every limit..."

There was no reason to expect honesty. But if she were the mistake, and if there were other cyphers out there, smaller and shrewder, escaping detection for months and years at a time...

That possibility was put on lists and ranked according to likelihoods and the relative dangers.

Hunts were made, and made, and made.

But nothing in the least bit incriminating was found.

And then as the operation finally closed shop, a new possibility was offered:

I was the culprit. Despite appearances, I was a secret genius who had built the woman of my dreams and then let her get free from her cage, and that's why I went after her. I needed to kill the bitch myself.

That story lived for a day.

Then they looked at me again, and with soft pats on the back, friends as well as associates said, "No, no. We know you. Not you. Not in a million billion years…"

NOBODY SAW HER die with their own eyes, save for me.

A year later and for no clear reason, I decided to retrace my old hike up into the mountains.

Maybe part of me hoped to find the woman in the forest.

If so, that part kept itself secret from me. And when I found nothing sitting on the log, the urge hid so well that I didn't feel any disappointment.

I was alone when I reached the Mystic Falls.

The Mountains of Cavendish rose before me – a wall of seabed limestones signifying ten billion years of life, topped with brilliant white cloud and blue glaciers. The Falls were exactly as I remembered them: a ten thousand foot ribbon of icy water and mist, pterosaurs chasing condors through the haze, and dragons chasing both as they wish. The wilderness stretched beyond for a full continent, and behind me stood fifty billion people who wouldn't care if I were to leap into the canyon below.

The woman was meant to be one thing, but a mistake was made, allowing her to become many things at once.

What did that mean?

And what if the answer was utterly awful, and perfectly simple?

The world is a smaller, shabbier place than we realized. What if some of us, maybe the majority of us, were cyphers too – fictions set here to fool the few of us who were real and sorry about it?

That impossible thought offered itself to me.

I contemplated jumping, but only for another moment.

"Live small and live long," I muttered, backing away from the edge.

No, I'm not as special as the dead woman. But life was a habit that I didn't wish to lose. Even in thought, I hold tight to my life, and that's why I put madness aside, and that's what I carry down the mountainside:

My reality.

The powerful, wondrous sense that I have blood and my own shadow, and nobody else needs to be real, if just one of us is.

THE QUEEN OF NIGHT'S ARIA

Ian McDonald

Ian McDonald (ianmcdonald.livejournal.com) lives in Northern Ireland, just outside Belfast. He sold his first story in 1983 and bought a guitar with the proceeds, perhaps the only rock 'n' roll thing he ever did. Since then he's written sixteen novels, including *River of Gods*, *Brasyl*, and *The Dervish House*, three story collections and diverse other pieces, and has been nominated for every major science fiction/fantasy award—and even won a couple. His current novel is *Empress of the Sun*, third book in the young adult SF Everness series. Upcoming is new adult SF novel, *Luna* and a collection, *The Best of Ian McDonald*.

"GOD. STILL ON bloody Mars."

Count Jack Fitzgerald: Virtuoso, Maestro, Sopratutto, stood at the window of the Grand Valley Hotel's Heaven's Tower Suite in just his shirt. Before his feet the Sculpted City of Unshaina tumbled away in shelves and tiers, towers and tenements. Cable cars skirled along swooping lines between the carved pinnacles of the Royal Rookeries. Many-bodied stone gods roosted atop mile-high pillars; above them the skymasters of the Ninth Fleet hung in the red sky. Higher still were the rim rocks of the Grand Valley, carved into fretwork battlements and machicolations, and highest of all, on the edge of the atmosphere, twilight shadows festooned with riding lights, were the ships of Spacefleet. A Sky-chair born by a squadron of Twav bobbed past the picture window, dipping to the wing beats of the carriers. The chair bore a human in the long duster-coat of a civil servant of the expeditionary force. One hand clutched a diplomatic valise, the other the guy-lines of the lift-harness. The mouth beneath the dust goggles was open in fear.

"Oh God, look at that. I feel nauseous. You hideous government drone, how dare you make me feel nauseous first thing in the morning. You'll never get me in one of those things, Faisal, never. They shit on you; it's true. I've seen it. Bottom of the valley's five-hundred foot deep in Mars-bat guano."

I come from a light-footed, subtle family but for all my discretion I could never catch Count Jack unawares. Tenors have good ears.

"Maestro, the Commanderie has issued guidelines. Mars-bats is not acceptable. The official expression is the Twav Civilisation."

"What nonsense. Mars-bats is what they look like, Mars-bats is what they are. No civilisation was ever built on the basis of aerial defecation. Where's my tea? I require tea."

I handed the Maestro his morning cup. He took a long slurping sip – want of etiquette was part of his professional persona. The Country Count from Kildare: he insisted it appear on all his billings. Despite the titles and honorifics, Count Jack Fitzgerald had passed the summit of his career, if not his self-mythologizing. The aristocratic title was a Papal honour bestowed upon his grandfather, a dully devout shopkeeper who nonetheless was regarded as little less than a saint in Athy. The pious greengrocer's apples would have browned at his grandson's flagrant disregard for religion and its moralising. The Heaven's Tower Suite's Emperor-sized bed was mercifully undisturbed by another body. Count James Fitzgerald drained his cup, drew himself to full six and half feet, sucked in his generous belly, clicked out cricks and stiffnesses in his joints.

"Oh bless you dear boy. None of the others can make tea worth a tinker's piss."

For the past six months, long before this tour of Mars, I had been slipping a little stiffener into the morning tea.

"And did they love us? Did strong men weep like infants and women ovulate?"

"The Joint Chiefs were enchanted."

"Well the enchantment didn't reach as far as their bloody pockets. A little consideration wouldn't have gone amiss. Philistines."

A gratis performance at the Commanderie for the Generals and Admirals and Sky-Marshals was more or less mandatory for all Earth entertainers playing the Martian front. The Army and Navy shows usually featured exotic dancers and strippers. From the piano, you notice many things; like the well-decorated Sky-Lord nodding off during the Maestro's Medley of Ould Irish Songs, but the news had reported that he had just returned from a hard-fought campaign against the Syrtian Hives.

"Ferid Bey wishes to see you."

"That odious little Ottoman. What does he want? More money I'll warrant. I shan't see him. He spoils my day. I abjure him."

"Eleven o'clock, Maestro. At the Canal Court."

Count Jack puffed out his cheeks in resignation."

"What, he can't afford the Grand Valley? With the percentage he skims? Not that they'd let him in: they should have a sign: no dogs, uniforms or agents."

We couldn't afford the Grand Valley either, but such truths are best entrusted to the discretion of an accompanist. I have talked our way out of hotel bills before.

"I'll book transport."

"If you must." His attention was once again turned to the canyon-scape of the great city of the Twav. The sun had risen over the canyon edge and sent the shadows of Unshaina's spires and stacks and towers carved from raw rock chasing down the great valley. Summoned by the light, flocks of Twav poured from the slots of their roost-cotes. "Any chance of another wee drop of your particular tea?"

I took the cup and saucer from his outstretched hand

"Of course Maestro."

"Thank you dear boy. I would, of course, be lost without you. Quite quite lost."

A hand waved me away from his presence.

"Thank you. And Maestro?"

He turned from the window.

"Trousers."

*   *   *

FOR A BIG man, Count James Fitzgerald threw up most discreetly. He leaned out of the Sky-chair, one quick convulsion and it fell in a single sheet between the sculpted pinnacles of Unshaina. He wiped his lips with a large very white handkerchief and that was it done. He would blame me, blame the Sky-chair bearers, blame the entire Twav Civilisation, but never the three cups of special tea he had taken while I packed for him, nor the bottle that was his perennial companion in the bedside cabinet.

Check-out had been challenging this time. I would never say so to Count Jack, but it had been a long time since I could parlay the Country Count from Kildare by name recognition alone.

"You are leaving the bags," the manager said. He was Armenian. He had never heard of Ireland, let along County Kildare.

"We will be returning, yes," I said.

"But you are leaving the bags."

"Christ on crutches," Count Jack had exclaimed as the two Sky-chairs set down on to the Grand Valley's landing apron. "What are you trying to do, kill me, you poncing infidel? My heart is tender, tender I tell you, bruised by decades of professional envy and poisonous notices."

"It is the quickest and most direct way."

"Swung hither and yon in a bloody Bat-cab and no money at the end of it, as like," Count Jack muttered as he strapped in and the Twavs took the strain and lifted. He gave a faint cry as the Sky-chair swung out over the mile-deep drop to the needles of the Lower Rookeries, like an enfilade of pikes driven into the red rock of the Grand Valley. He clung white-knuckled to the guy-lines, moaning a little as the Twav carriers swayed him between the scurrying cableway gondolas and around the many-windowed stone towers of the roosts.

I rather enjoyed the ride. My life has been low in excitements – I took the post of accompanist to the Maestro as an escape from filing his recording royalties, which was the highest entry position in the industry I could attain with my level of degree in Music. Glamorous it was, exciting, no. Glamour is just another work environment. One recovers from being star-struck rather quickly. My last great excitement had been the night before we left for Mars. Ships! Space travel! Why, I could hardly sleep the night before launch. I soon discovered that space travel is very much like an ocean cruise, without the promenade decks and the excursions, and far, far fewer people. And much, much worse food. However tedious and braying the company for me, I derived some pleasure from the fact that for them it was three months locked in with Count Jack.

I have a personal interest in this war. My grandfather was one of the martyrs who died in the opening minutes of the Horsell Common invasion. He was the first generation of my family to be born in England. He had been at prayer in the Woking Mosque and was consumed by the heat ray from the Uliri War Tripod. Many thousands died that day, and though it has taken us two generations to master the Uliri technology to keep our skies safe, and to prepare a fleet to launch Operation Enduring Justice, the cry is ever fresh: Remember Shah Jehan! I stood among the crowds on that same Horsell Common around the crater, as people gathered by the other craters of the invasion, or on hilltops, on beaches, river banks, rooftops, holy places, anywhere with a view of open sky, to watch the night light up with the drives of our expeditionary fleet. The words on my lips, and the lips of everyone else on that cold November night, were Justice, Justice, but in my heart, it was Remember Shah Jehan!

Rejoice! Rejoice! our Prime Minister told us when our drop-troopers captured Unshaina, conquered the Twav Civilisation and turned the Grand Valley into our Martian headquarters and munitions factory. It's harder to maintain your patriotic fervour when those spaceships are months away on the far side of the sun, and no one really believes the propaganda that the Twav were the devious military hive-masterminds of the Uliri war machine. Nor, when that story failed, did we swallow the second serving of propaganda: that the Twav were the enslaved mind-thralls of the Uliri, whom we had liberated for freedom and democracy. A species that achieves a special kind of sentience when it roosts and flocks together seems to me to embody the very nature of the demos. The many-bodied gods atop the flute-thin spires of Unshaina represent the truth that our best, our most creative, our most brilliant, may be all the divinity we need.

It has been a long time since I was at prayer.

Count Jack gave a small moan as his Sky-chair dipped down abruptly between the close-packed stone quills of Alabaster Needles. The Chair-boss whistled instructions to her crew – the lowest register of their language lay at the upper edge of our hearing – and they skilfully brought us spirally down past hives and through arches and under buttresses to the terraces of the Great Western Dock on the Grand Canal. Here humans had built cheap spray-stone lading houses and transit lodges among the sinuously carved stone. The Canal Court Hotel was cheap, but that was not its main allure; Ferid Bey had appetites best served by low rents and proximity to docks.

While Count Jack swooned and whimpered and swore that he would never regain his land-legs, never, I tipped the Chair-boss a generous handful of saucers and she clasped her lower hands in a gesture of respect.

"WE'RE BROKE," FERID Bey said. We sat drinking coffee on the terrace of the Canal Court watching Twav stevedores lift and lade pallets from the open hatches of cargo barges. I say coffee, it was Expeditionary Force ersatz, vile and weak and with a disturbing spritz of excremental. Ferid Bey, who as a citizen of the great Ottoman Empire, appreciated coffee, grimaced at every sip. I say terrace; it was a cranny for two tables' space beside the garbage bins which caught the wind and lifted the dust in a perpetual eddy. Ferid Bey wore his dust goggles, kept his scarf wrapped around his head and sipped his execrable coffee.

"What do you mean, broke?" Count Jack thundered in his loudest Sopratutto voice. Startled Twavs flew up from their cargoes, twittering on the edge of audibility. "You've been at the bum-boys again, haven't you?" Ferid Bey's weakness for the rough was well known, particularly the kind who would go through his wallet the next morning. He sniffed loudly.

"Actually, Jack, this time it's you."

I often wondered if the slow decline of Count Jack's career was partly attributable to the fact that, after years of daily contact, agent had started to sound like client. The Count's eyes bulged. His blood pressure was bad. I'd seen the report from the pre-launch medical.

"It's bums on seats Jack, bums on seats and we're not getting them."

"I strew my pearls before buffoons in braid and their braying brides, and they throw them back in my face!" Count Jack bellowed. "I played La Scala, you know. La Scala! And the Pope. I'd be better off playing to the Space-bats. At least they appreciate a High-C. No Ferid, no no: you get me better audiences."

"Any audiences would be good," Ferid Bey muttered and then said aloud, "I've got you a tour."

Count Jack grew inches taller.

"How many nights?"

"Five."

"There are that many concert halls on this arse-wipe of a world?"

"Not so much concert halls." Ferid Bey tried to hide as much of his face as possible behind scarf, goggles and coffee cup. "More concert *parties*."

"The army?" Count Jack's face was pale now, his voice quiet. I had heard this precursor to a rage the size of Olympus Mons many times. Thankfully, I had never been its target. "Bloody shit-stupid squaddies who have to be told which end of a blaster to point at the enemy?"

"Yes Jack."

"Would this be... upcountry?"

"It would."

"Would this be... close to the front?"

"I've extended your cover."

"Well, it's nice to know my ex-wives and agent are well provided for."

"I've negotiated a fee commensurate with the risk."

"What is the risk?"

"It's a war zone, Jack."

"What is the fee?"

"One thousand five hundred saucers. Per show."

"Tell me we don't need to do this, dear boy," Count Jack said to me.

"The manager of the Grand Valley is holding your luggage to ransom," I said. "We need to do it."

"You're coming with me." Count Jack's accusing finger hovered one inch from the bridge of his agent's nose. Ferid Bey spread his hands in resignation.

"I would if I could Jack. Truly. Honestly. Deeply. But I've got a lead on a possible concert recording here in Unshaina, and there are talent bookers from the big Venus casinos in town, so I'm told."

"Venus?" The Cloud Cities, forever drifting in the Storm Zone, were the glittering jewels on the interplanetary circuit. The legendary residences were a long, comfortable, well paid descent from the pinnacle of career.

"Five nights?"

"Five nights only. Then out."

"Usual contract riders?"

"Of course."

Count Jack laughed his great, canyon-deep laugh. "We'll do it. Our brave legionnaires need steel in their steps and spunk in their spines. When do we leave?"

"I've booked you on the *Empress of Mars* from the Round 'O' Dock. Eight o'clock. Sharp."

Count Jack pouted.

"I am prone to sea-sickness."

"This is a canal. Anyway, the Commanderie has requisitioned all the air transport. It seems there's a big push on."

"I shall endure it."

"You're doing the right thing, Jack," Ferid Bey said. " Oh, and another thing; Faisal, you couldn't pick up for the coffee could you?" I suspected there was a reason Ferid Bey had brought us out to this tatty bargee hostel. "And while you're at it, could you take care of my hotel?"

Already Count Jack was hearing the distant applause of the audience, scenting like a rare moth the faint but unmistakable pheromone of *celebrity*.

"And am I... top of the bill?"

"Always Jack," said Ferid Bey. "Always."

FROM OUR TABLE on the promenade deck of the *Empress of Mars* we watched the skymasters pass overhead. They were high and their hulls caught the evening light that had faded from the canal. I lost count after thirty; the sound of their many engines merged into a high thunder. The vibration sent ripples across the wine in our glasses on the little railed-off table at the stern of the barge. One glass for me, always untouched – I did not drink but I liked to keep Count Jack company. He was a man who craved the attention of others – without it he grew translucent and insubstantial. His hopes for another involuntary audience of passengers to charm and intimidate and cow with his relentless showbiz tales were disappointed. The *Empress of Mars* was a cargo tug pushing a twelve barge tow with space for eight passengers, of which we were the sole two. I was his company. I had been so enough times to know his anecdotes as thoroughly as I knew the music for his set. But I listened, and I laughed, because it is not the story that matters but the telling.

"Headed East," Count Jack said. I did not correct him – he had never understood that on Mars West was East and East was West. *Sunrise, east; sunset, west dear boy*, he declared. We watched the fleet, a vast, sky-filling arrowhead, drive towards the sunset hills on the close horizon. The Grand Valley had opened out into a trench so wide we could not see the canyon walls, a terrain with its own inner terrain. "Godspeed that fleet." He had been uncharacteristically quiet and ruminative this trip. It was not the absence of a captive audience. The fleet, the heavy canal traffic – I had counted eight tows headed up-channel from the front to Unshaina since we began this first bottle of what Count Jack called his 'Evening Restorational' – had brought home to him that he was headed to war. Not pictures of war, news reports of war, rumours of war but war itself. For the first time he might be questioning the tour.

"Does it make your joints ache, Faisal?"

"Maestro?"

"The gravity. Or rather, the want of gravity. Wrists, ankles, fingers, all the flexing joints. Hurt like buggery. Thumbs are the worst. I'd've have thought it would have been the opposite with it being so light here. Not a bit of it. It's all I can do to lift this glass to my lips."

To my eyes, he navigated the glass from table to lips successfully. Count Jack poured another Evening Restorational and sank deep in his chair. The dark green waters of the canal slipped beneath our hull. Martian twilights were swift and deep. War had devastated this once populous and fertile land, left scars of black glass across the bottom lands where heat rays had scored the regolith. The rising evening wind, the *Tharseen* that reversed direction depending on which end of the Grand Valley was in night, called melancholy flute sonatas from the shattered Roost pillars.

"It's a ghastly world," Count Jack said after a second glass.

"I find it rather peaceful. It has a particular beauty. Melancholic."

"No not Mars. Everywhere. Everywhere's bloody ghastly and getting ghastlier. Ever since the war. War makes everything brutal. Brutal and ugly. War wants everything to be like it. It's horrible, Faisal."

"Yes. I think we've gone too far. We're laying waste to entire civilisations. Unshaina, it's older than any city on Earth. This has gone beyond righteous justice. We're fighting because we love it."

"Not the war, Faisal. I've moved on from the bloody war. Do keep up. Getting old. That's what's truly horrible. Old old old and I can't do a thing about it. I feel it in my joints, Faisal. This bloody planet makes me feel old. A long slow decline into incompetence, imbecility and incontinence. What have I got? A decent set of pipes. That's all. And they won't last forever. No investments no property and bugger all recording royalties. Bloody revenue cleaned me out. Rat up a drainpipe. Gone. And the bastards still have their hands out. They've threatened me, you know. Arrest. What is this, the bloody Marshalsea Gaol? I'm a Papal Knight, you know. I wield the sword of the Holy Father himself."

"All they want is their money," I said. Count Jack had always resented paying lawyers and accountants, with the result that he had signed disastrous recording contracts and only filed tax returns when the bailiffs were at the door. This entire Martian tour would barely meet his years of outstanding tax, plus interest. "Then they'll leave you alone."

"No they won't. They'll never let me alone. They know Count Jack is a soft touch. They'll be back, the damnable dunners. Once they've got the taste of your blood they won't ever let their hooks out of you. Parasites. I am infested with fiscal parasites. Tax, war and old age. They make everything gross and coarse and pointless."

Beams of white light flickered along the twilight horizon. I could not tell whether they were from sky to ground or ground to sky. The heat rays danced along the edge of the world, flickered out. New beams took their place. Flashes beyond the close horizon threw the hills into momentary relief. I cried out as the edge of world became a flickering palisade of heat rays. Count Jack was on his feet. The flashes lit his face. Seconds later the first soft rumble of distant explosions reached us. The Twav deckhands fluttered on their perches. I could make out the lower register of their consternation as a treble shrill. The edge of the world was a carnival of beams and flashes. I saw an arc of fire descend from the sky to terminate in a white flash beneath the horizon. I did not doubt that I had seen a skymaster and all her crew perish but it was beautiful. The sky blazed with the most glorious fireworks. Count Jack's eyes were wide with wonder. He threw his hand up to shield his eyes as a huge mid-air explosion turned the night white. Stark shadows lunged across the deck; the Twav rose up in a clatter of wings.

"Oh the dear boys, the dear boys," Count Jack whispered. The sound of the explosion hit us. It rattled the windows on the pilot deck, rattled the bottle and glasses on the table. I felt it shake the core of being, shake me belly and bowel deep. The beams winked out. The horizon went dark.

We had seen a great and terrible battle but who had fought, who had won, who had lost, whether there had been winners or losers, what its goals had been – we knew none of these. We had witnessed something terrible and beautiful and incomprehensible. I lifted the untouched glass of wine and took a sip.

"Good God," Count Jack said, still standing. "I always thought you didn't drink. Religious reasons and all that."

"No, I don't drink for musical reasons. It makes my joints hurt."

I drank the wine. It may have been vinegar, it may have been the finest wine available to humanity, I did not know. I drained the glass.

"Dear boy." Count Jack poured me another, one for himself and together we watched the edge of the world glow with distant fires.

We played Camp Avenger on a stage rigged on empty beer barrels to a half full audience that dwindled over the course of the concert to just six rows. A Brigadier who had been drinking steadily all through the concert tried to get his troopers up onstage to dance to the Medley of Ould Irish Songs. They sensibly declined. He tripped over his own feet trying to inveigle Count Jack to *Walls of Limerick* with him and went straight off the stage. He split his head open on the rim of a beer keg.

At Tharsia Regional Command the audience was less ambiguous. We were bottled off. The first one came looping in even as Count Jack came on, arms spread wide, to his theme song *I'll Take You Home Again Kathleen*. He stuck it through *Blaze Away*, *Nessum Dorma* and *Il Mio Tesoro* before an accurately hurled Mars Export Pale Ale bottle deposited its load of warm urine down the front of his dickey. He finished *The Garden Where the Praties Grow*, bowed and went straight off. I followed him as the first of the barrage of folding army chairs hit the stage. Without a word or a look he went straight to his tent and stripped naked.

"I've had worse in Glasgow Empire," he said. His voice was stiff with pride. I never admired him as much. "Can you do something with these, dear boy?" He held out the wet, reeking dress suit. "And run me a bath."

We took the money, in full and in cash, and went on, up ever the ever-branching labyrinth of canals, ever closer to the battle front.

The boat was an Expeditionary Force fast patrol craft, one heat ray turret fore, one mounted in a blister next to the captain's position. It was barely big enough for the piano, let alone us and the sullen four-man crew. They smoked constantly and tried to outrage Count Jack with their vile space-trooper's language. He could outswear any of them. But he kept silence and dignity and our little boat threaded through the incomprehensible maze of Nyx's canals; soft green waters of Mars overhung by the purple fronds of crosier-trees, dropping the golden coins of their seed cases into the water where they sprouted corkscrew propellers and swam away. This was the land of the Oont, and their tall, heron-like figures, perched in the rear of their living punts, were our constant companions. On occasion, down the wider channels and basins, we glimpsed their legendary organic paddle-wheelers, or their pale blue ceramic stilt-towns. The crew treated the Oont with undisguised contempt and idly trained the boat's weapons on them. They had accepted the mandate of the Commanderie without a fight and their cities and ships and secretive, solitary way of life went unchanged. Our Captain thought them a species of innate cowards and traitors. Only a species tamed by the touch of the heat ray could be trusted.

For five hundred miles, up the Grand Canal and through the maze of Nyx, Twav stevedores had lifted and laid my piano with precision and delicacy. It took the Terrene army to drop it. From the foot of the gangplank I heard the jangling crash and turned to see the cargo net on the jetty and troopers grinning. At once I wanted to strip away the packing and see if anything remained. It was not my piano – I would never have risked my Bosendorfer on the vagaries of space-travel – but it was a passable upright from a company that specialised in interplanetary hire. I had grown fond of it. One does with pianos. They are like dogs. I walked on. That much I had learnt from Count Jack. Dignity, always dignity.

Oudeman was a repair base for Third Skyfleet. We walked in the shadow of hovering skymasters. Engineers in repair rigs swarmed over hulls, lowered engines on hoists, opened hull sections, deflated gas cells. It was clear to me that the fleet had suffered grievously in recent and grim battle. Skins were gashed open to the very bones; holes stabbed through the rounded hulls from side to side. Engine pylons terminated in melted drips. Entire crew gondolas and gun turrets had been torn away. Some had been so terribly mauled they were air-going skeletons; a few lift cells wrapped around naked ship spine.

Of the crews who had fought through such ruin, there was no sign.

The base commander, Yuzbashi Osman, greeted us personally. He was a great fan, a great fan. A dedicated life-long fan. He had seen the Maestro in his every Istanbul concert. He always sat in the same seat. He had all the Maestro's recordings. He played them daily and had tried to educate his junior officers over mess dinners but the rising generation were ignorant, low men; technically competent but little better than the Devshirmey conscripts. A clap of his hands summoned batmen to carry our luggage. I understood only rudiments of his language but from his reaction to the engineers who had dropped my piano, I understood that further disrespect would not be tolerated. He cleared the camp steam-bath for our exclusive use. Sweated, steamed and scraped clean, a glowing Count Jack bowled into the mess tent as if he were striding on to the stage of La Scala. He was funny, he was witty, he was charming, he was glorious. Most of the junior Onbashis and Mulazims at the dinner in his honour could not speak English but his charisma transcended all language. They smiled and laughed readily.

"Would you look at that?" Count Jack said in the backstage tent that was our dressing room. He held up a bottle of champagne, dripping from the ice bucket. "Krug. They got me my Krug. Oh the dear, lovely boys."

At the dinner I had noted the paucity of some of the offerings and marvelled at the effort it must have taken, what personal dedication by the Yuzbashi, to fulfil a rider that was only there to check the contract had been read. Count Jack slid the bottle back into the melting ice. "I shall return to you later, beautiful thing, with my heart full of song and my feet light on the applause of my audience. I am a star, Faisal. I am a true star. Leave me, dear boy."

Count Jack required time and space alone to prepare his entrance. This was the time he changed from Count James Fitzgerald to the Country Count from Kildare. It was a deeply private transformation and one I knew I would never be permitted to watch. The stage was a temporary rig bolted together from Skymaster spares. The hovering ships lit the stage with their search-lights. A follow-spot tracked me to the piano. I bowed, acknowledged the applause of the audience, flicked out the tails of my evening coat and sat down. That is all an accompanist need do.

I played a few glissandi to check the piano was still functioning after its disrespectful handling by the dock crew. Passable, to the tin ears of Sky Fleet engineers. Then I played the short overture to create that all-important sense of expectation in the audience and went straight into the music for Count Jack's entrance. The spotlight picked him up as he swept on to the stage, *I'll Take You Home Again Kathleen* bursting from his broad chest. He was radiant. He commanded every eye. The silence in the deep Martian night was the most profound I think I have ever heard. He strode to the front of the stage. The spotlight adored him. He luxuriated in the applause as if it were the end of the concert, not the first number. He was a shameless showman. I lifted my hands to the keyboard to introduce *Turna a Surriento*.

And the night exploded into towering blossoms of flame. For an instant the audience sat transfixed, as if Count Jack stood had somehow summoned the most astonishing of operatic effects. Then the alarms blared out all across the camp. Count Jack and I both saw clearly the spider-shapes of War Tripods, tall as trees, wading through the flames. Heat rays flashed out, white swords, as the audience scattered to take up posts and weapons. Still Count Jack held the spotlight, until an Onbashi leaped up, tackled him and knocked him out of the firing-line just as a heat ray cut a ten thousand degree arc across the stage. He had no English, he needed no English. We ran. I glanced back once. I knew what I would see, but I had to see it: my piano, that same cheap, sturdy hire upright piano that I had shipped across one hundred million miles of space, through the concert halls and grand opera houses, on dusty roads and railways, down calm green canals: my piano explode in a fountain of blazing hammers and whipping, melting wires. A War Tripod strode over us, its heat rays arms swivelling, seeking new targets. I looked up into the weaving thicket of tentacles beneath the hull, then the raised steel hoof passed over me and came down squarely and finally on our dressing room tent.

"My Krug!" Count Jack cried out.

A heat ray cut a glowing arc of lava across the ground before me. I was lucky – you cannot dodge these things or see them coming, hear their ricochets or guess their approach. They are light itself. All you can be is moving in the right direction, have the right momentum: be lucky. Our Onbashi was not lucky. He ran into the heat ray and vanished into a puff of ash. A death so fast, so total it became something more than death. It was annihilation.

"Maestro! With me!"

Count Jack had been standing, staring, transfixed. I took his hand, his palm still damp with concert sweat, and skirted around the end of the still-smoking scar. We ducked, we ran at a crouch, we zigzagged in our tails and dickie bows. There was no good reason for it. We had seen it in war movies. The Uliri war machines strode across the camp, slashing glowing lava tracks across it with their heat rays, their weapon-arms seeking out fresh targets. But our soldiers had reached their defensive positions, and were fighting back, turning the Uliri's own weapon against them, and bolstering it with a veritable hail of ordnance. The troopers who had manned our spotlights now turned to the heat-rays. Skymasters were casting off, their turret gunners seeking out the many-eyed heads of the Uliri tripods. The war machine that had so hideously killed the brave Onbashi stood in the river, eye-blisters turning this way, that way, seeking targets. A weapon-arm fixed on us. The aperture of the heat ray opened. Hesitated. Pulled away. Grasping cables uncoiled from between the legs. We scuttled for cover behind a stack of barrels – not that they would have saved us. Then a missile cut a streak of red across the night. The war machine's front left knee-joint exploded. The machine wavered for balance on two, then a skymaster cut low across the canal bank and severed the front right off at the thigh with a searing slash of a heat ray. The monster wavered, toppled, came down in a blast and crash and wave of spray, right on top of the boat that would have carried us to safety. Smashed to flinders. Escape hatches opened; pale shapes wriggled free, squirmed down the hull towards land. I pushed Count Jack to the ground as the skymaster opened up. Bullets screamed around us. Count Jack's eyes were wide with fear, and something else, something I had not imagined in the man: excitement. War might be brutal and ghastly and ugly, as he had declaimed on the *Empress of Mars*, but there was a terrible, primal power in it. I saw the same thrill, the same joy, the same power that had commanded audiences from Tipperary to Timbuktoo. I saw it and I knew that, if we ever returned to Earth and England, I would ever be the accompanist, the amanuensis, the dear boy; and that even if he sang to an empty hall, Count James Fitzgerald would always be the Maestro, Sopratutto. All there was in me was fear; solid fear. Perhaps that is why I was brave. The guns fell silent. I looked over the top of the barrels. Silvery Uliri bodies were strewn across the dock. I saw the canal run with purple blood like paint in water.

The skymaster turned and came in over the canal to a low hover. A boarding ramp lowered and touched the ground. A skyman crouched at the top of the ramp, beckoning urgently.

"Run Maestro, run!" I shouted and dragged Count Jack to his feet. We ran. Around us heat rays danced and stabbed like some dark tango. A blazing war machine stumbled blindly, crushing tents, bivouacs, repair sheds beneath its feet, shedding sheets of flame. Ten steps from the foot of the ramp, I heard a noise that turned me to ice: a great ululating cry from the hills behind the camp, ringing from horizon to horizon, back and forth, wash and backwash, a breaking wave of sound. I had never heard it but I had heard of it, the war-song of the Uliri padva infantry. A hand seized mine: the skyman dragged me and Count Jack like a human chain into the troop hold. As the ramp closed, I saw the skyline bubble and flow, like a silver sheen of oil, down the hillside towards us. Padvas. Thousands of them. As the skymaster lifted and the hull sealed the last, the very last sight I had was Yuzbashi Osman looking up at us. He raised a hand in salute. Then he turned, drew his sword and with a cry that pierced even the engine drone of the skymaster, every janissary of Oudeman Camp drew his blade. Swordpoints glittered, then they charged. The skymaster spun in the air, I saw no more.

"Did you see that?" Count Jack said to me. He gripped my shoulders. His face was pale with shock but there was a mad strength in his fingers. "Did you? How horrible, how horrible. And yet, how wonderful! Oh, the mystery, Faisal, the mystery!" Tears ran down his ash-smudged face.

WE FLED THROUGH the labyrinth of the night. We had no doubt that we were being pursued through those narrow, twining canyons. The skycaptain's pinger picked up fleeting, suggestive contacts of what we had all heard: terrible cries, echoes of echoes in the stone redoubts of Noctis, far away but always, always keeping pace with us. The main hold of the skymaster was windowless and though the skycaptain spoke no English, he had made it most clear to us that we were to keep away from his crew, whether they were in engineering, the gun blisters or the bridge and navigation pods. So we sat on the hard steel mesh of the dimly lit cargo hold, ostensibly telling old musician stories we had told many times before, pausing every time our indiscriminate ears brought us some report of the war outside. Hearing is a much more primal sense than vision. To see is to understand. To hear is to apprehend. Eyes can be closed. Ears are ever open. Maestro broke off the oft-told story of singing for the Pope, and how thin the towels were, and what cheap bastards the Holy See had turned out to be. His ears, as I have said, were almost supernaturally keen. His eyes went wide. The Twav battledores on their perches in the skymarine roosts riffled their scales, shining like oil on water, and shifted their grips on their weaponry. A split second later, I heard the cries. Stuttering and rhythmic, they rose over three octaves from a bass drone to a soprano, nerve shredding yammer. Two behind us, striking chords and harmonics from each other like some experimental piece of serialist music. Another answered, ahead of us. And another, far away, muted by the wind-sculpted rock labyrinth. A fifth, close, to our right. Back and forth, call and response. I clapped my hands over my ears, not from the pain of the shrill upper registers, but at the hideous musicality of these unseen voices. They sang scales and harmonies alien to me, but their music called the musician in me.

And they were gone. Every nerve on the skymaster, human and Twav, was afire. The silence was immense. My Turkic is functional but necessary – enough to know what Ferid Bey is actually saying – and I recalled the few words of the skycaptain I had overheard as he relayed communications to the crew. The assault on Camp Oudeman had been part of a surprise offensive by the Tharsian Warqueens. Massive assaults had broken out along a five hundred mile front from Arsai to Urania. War machines, shock troops – there had even been an assault on Spacefleet: squadron after squadron of rockets launched to draw the staggering firepower of our orbital battleships from the assault below. And up from out of the soil, things like no one had seen before. Things that put whole battalions to flight, that smashed apart trench lines and crumbled redoubts to sand. As I tried to imagine the red earth parting and something from beyond nightmares rising up, I could not elude the dark thought: might there not be similar terrible novelties in the sky? This part of my eavesdropping I kept to myself. It was most simple: I had been routinely lying to Count Jack since the first day I set up my music on the piano.

"I could murder a drink," Count Jack said. "If there were such a thing on this barquadero. Even a waft of a Jameson's cork under my nose."

The wine on the deck of the *Empress of Mars* must have corrupted me, because at that moment I would gladly have joined the Maestro. More than joined, I would have beaten him by a furlong to the bottom of the bottle of Jameson's.

Up on the bridge, a glass finger projecting from the skymaster's lifting body, the skycaptain called orders from his post at the steering yoke. Crew moved around us. The battledores shifted the hue of their plumage from blue to violent yellow. I felt the decking shift beneath me – how disorienting, how unpleasant, this sense of everything sound and trustworthy moving, nothing to hold on to. The engines were loud; the captain must be putting on speed, navigating between the wind-polished stone. We were flying through a monstrous stone pipe organ. I glanced up along the companionway to the bridge. Pink suffused the world beyond the glass. We had run all night through the Labyrinth of Night; that chartless maze of canyons and ravines and rock arches that humans suspected was not entirely natural. I saw rock walls above me. We were low, hugging the silted channels and canals. The rising sun sent planes of light down the sheer fluted stone walls. There is nothing on Earth to compare with the loveliness of dawn on Mars, but how I wish I were there and not in this dreadful place.

"Faisal."

"Maestro."

"When we get back, remind me to fire that greased turd Ferid."

I smiled, and Count Jack Fitzgerald began to sing. *Galway Bay*, the most hackneyed and sentimental of faux-Irish paddywhackery ('Have you ever been to Galway Bay? Incest and Gaelic games. All they know, all the like') but I had never heard him sing it like this. Had he not been seated on the deck before me, leaning up against a bulkhead, I would have doubted that it was his voice. It was small but resonant, perfect like porcelain, sweet as a rose and filled with a high, light innocence. This was the voice of childhood; the boy singing back the tunes his grandmother taught him. This was the Country Count from Kildare. Every soul on the skymaster, Terrene and Martian, listened, but he did not sing for them. He needed no audience, no accompanist: this was a command performance for one.

The skymaster shook to a sustained impact. The spell was broken. Voices called out in Turkic and Twav flute-speech. The skymaster rocked, as if shaken in a god-like grip. Then with a shriek of rending metal and ship-skin, the gun-blister directly above us was torn away;

gunner, gun and a two metre shard of hull. A face looked in at us. A face that more than filled the gash in the hull; a nightmare of six eyes arranged around a trifurcate beak. The beak opened. Rows of grinding teeth moved within. A cry blasted us with alien stench: ululating over three octaves, ending in a shriek. It drove the breath from our lungs and the will from our hearts. Another answered it, from all around us. Then the face was gone. A moment of shock – a moment, that was all – and the skycaptain shouted orders. The Twav rose from their perches, wings clattering, and streamed through the hole in the hull. I heard the whine of ray-rifles warming up, and then the louder crackle and sizzle of our own defensive heat rays.

I thought I would never hear a worse thing than the cry through the violated hull. The shriek, out there, unseen, was like the cry I might make if my spine were torn from my living body. I could only guess: one of those things had met a heat ray.

We never saw any of the battledores again.

Again, the skymaster shook to an impact. Count Jack lunged forward as claws stabbed through the hull and tore three rips the entire length of the bulkhead. The skymaster lurched to one side; we slid across the decking in our tail-coats and smoke-smudged dickie shirts. An impact jolted the rear of the air ship, I glimpsed blackness and then the entire tail turret was gone and the rear of the skymaster was open to the air. Through the open space I saw a four-winged flying thing stroke away from us, up through the pink stone arches of this endless labyrinth. It was enormous. I am no judge of comparative dimensions – I am an auditory man, not a visual one – but it was on a par with our own limping skymaster. The creature part-furled its wings to clear the arch, then turned high against the red sky and I saw glitters of silver at the nape of its neck and between its legs. Mechanisms, devices, Uliri crew.

While I gaped at the sheer impossible horror of what I beheld, the skymaster was struck again, an impact so hard it flung us from one side of the hold to the other. I saw steel-shod claws the size of scimitars pierce the glass finger of the bridge like the skin of a ripe orange. The winged Martian horror ripped bridge from hull and with a flick of its foot – it held the bridge as lightly and easily as a pencil – hurled it spinning through the air. I saw one figure fall from it and closed my eyes. I did hear Count Jack mumble the incantations of his faith.

Robbed of control, the skymaster yawed wildly. Engineering crew rushed around us, shouting tersely to each other, fighting to regain control, to bring us down in some survivable landing. There was no hope of escape now. What were those things? Those nightmare hunters of the Labyrinth of Night? Skin shredded, struts shrieked and buckled as the skymaster grazed a rock chimney. We listed and started to spin.

"We've lost port-side engines!" I shouted, translating the engineers' increasingly cold and desperate exchanges. We were going down but it was too fast... too fast. The chief engineer yelled an order that translated as brace for impact in any language. I wrapped cargo strapping around my arms, and gripped for all my worth. Pianists have strong fingers.

"Patrick and Mary!" Count Jack cried and then we hit. The impact was so huge, so hard it drove all breath and intelligence and thought from me, everything except that death was certain and that the last, the very last thing I would ever see would be a drop of fear-drool on the plump bottom lip of Count Jack Fitzgerald, and that I had never noticed how full, how kissable, those lips were. Death is such a sweet surrender.

We did not die. We bounced. We hit harder. The skymaster's skeleton groaned and snapped. Sparking wires fell around us. Still we did not stop, or die. I remember thinking, don't tumble, if we tumble, we are dead, all of us, and so I knew we would survive. Shaken, smashed, stunned, but surviving. The corpse of the skymaster slid to a crunching stop hard against the house-sized boulders at the foot of the canyon wall. I could see daylight in five places through the skymaster's violated hull. It was beautiful beyond words. The sky-horrors might still be circling, but I had to get out of the airship.

"Jack! Jack!" I cried. His eyes were wide, his face pale with shock. "Maestro!" He looked and saw me. I took his hand and together we ran from the smoking ruin of the skymaster. The crew, military trained, had been more expeditious in their escape. Already they were running from the wreck. I felt a shadow pass over me. I looked up. Diving out of the tiny atom of the sun – how horrible, oh how horrible! I saw for the first time, whole and entire, one of the things that had been hunting us and my heart quailed. It swooped with ghastly speed and agility on its four wings and snatched the running men up into the air, each impaled on a scimitar-claw. It hovered in the air above us and I caught the foul heat and stench of the wind from its wings and beak. This, this is the death for which I had been reserved. Nothing so simple as an air crash. The sky-horror looked at me, looked at Count Jack with its six eyes, major and minor. Then with a terrible scrannel cry like the souls of the dead engineers impaled on its claws and a gust of wing-driven wind, it rose up and swept away.

We had been marked for life.

IRONY IS THE currency of time. We were marked for life, but three times I entertained killing Count Jack Fitzgerald. Pick up a rock and beat him to death with it, strangle him with his bow tie, just walk away from and leave him in the dry gulches for the bone-picking things.

I reasoned, by dint of a ready water supply and a scrap of paper, thrown in, that showed a sluggish but definite flow, that we should follow the canal. I had little knowledge of the twisted areography of the Labyrinth of Night – no one did, I suspect – but I was certain that all waters flowed to the Grand Canal and that was the spine and nervous system of Operation Enduring Justice. I advised us to drink – Count Jack ordered me to look away as he knelt and supped up the oddly metallic Martian water. We set off to the sound of unholy cries high and far among the pinnacles of the canyon walls.

The sun had not crossed two fingers of narrow canyonland sky before Count Jack gave an enormous theatrical sigh and sat down on a canal-side barge bollard.

"Dear boy, I simply cannot take another step without some material sustenance."

I indicated the alien expanse of rock, dust, water, red sky; hinted at its barrenness.

"I see bushes," Count Jack said. "I see fruit on those bushes."

"They could be deadly poison, Maestro."

"What's fit for Martians cannot faze the robust Terrene digestive tract," Count Jack proclaimed. "Anyway, better a quick death than lingering starvation, dear God."

Argument was futile. Count Jack harvested a single, egg-shaped, purple fruit and took a small, delicate bite. We waited. The sun moved across its slot of sky.

"I remain obdurately alive," said Count Jack and ate the rest of the fruit. "The texture of a slightly under-ripe banana and a flavour of mild aniseed. Tolerable. But the belly is replete."

Within half an hour of setting off again Count Jack had called a halt.

"The gut, Faisal, the gut." He ducked behind a rock. I heard groans and oaths and other, more liquid noises. He emerged pale and sweating.

"How do you feel?"

"Lighter, dear boy. Lighter."

That was the first time I considered killing him.

The fruit had opened more than his bowels. The silence of the canyons must have haunted him, for he talked. Dear God, he talked. I was treated to Count Jack Fitzgerald's opinion on everything from the way I should have been ironing his dress shirts (apparently I required a secondary miniature ironing board specially designed for collar and cuffs) to the conduct of the war between the worlds.

I tried to shut him up by singing, trusting – knowing – that he could not resist an offer to show off and shine. I cracked out *Blaze Away* in my passable baritone, then *The Soldier's Dream*, anything with a good marching beat. My voice rang boldly from the rim rocks.

Count Jack touched me lightly on the arm.

"Dear boy, dear dear boy. No. You only make the intolerable unendurable."

And that was the second time I was close to killing him. But we realised that if we were to survive – and though we could not entertain the notion that we might not, because it would surely have broken our hearts and killed us – we understood that to have any hope of making it back to occupied territory, we would have to proceed as more than Maestro and Accompanist. So in the end we talked, one man with another man. I told him of my childhood in middle-class, leafy Woking, and at the Royal

Academy of Music, and the realisation, quiet, devastating and quite quite irrefutable, that I would never be a concert great. I would never play the Albert Hall, the Marinsky, Carnegie Hall. I saw a Count Jack I had never seen before; sincere behind the bluster, humane and compassionate. I saw beyond an artiste. I saw an *artist*. He confided his fears to me: that the days of Palladiums and Pontiffs had blinded him. He realised too late that one night the lights would move to another and he would face the long, dark walk from the stage. But he had plans; yes, he had plans. A long walk in a hard terrain concentrated the mind wonderfully. He would pay the revenue their due and retain Ferid Bey only long enough to secure the residency on Venus. And when his journey through the worlds was done and he had enough space dust under his nails, he would return to Ireland, to County Kildare, and buy some land and set himself up as a tweedy, be-waistcoated red-faced Bog Boy. He would sing only for the Church; at special masses and holy days of obligation and parish glees and tombolas, he could see a time when he might fall in love with religion again, not from any personal faith, but for the comfort and security of familiarity.

"Have you thought of marrying?" I asked. Count Jack had never any shortage of female admirers, even if they no longer threw underwear on to the stage as they had back in the days when his hair and moustache were glossy and black – and he would mop his face with them and throw them back to shrieks of approval from the crowd. "Not a dry seat in the house, dear boy." But I had never seen anything that hinted at a more lasting relationship than bed and a champagne breakfast.

"Never seen the need, dear boy. Not the marrying type. And you Faisal?"

"Not the marrying type either."

"I know. I've always known. But that's what this bloody world needs. Really needs. Women, Faisal. Women. Leave men together and they soon agree to make a wasteland. Women are a civilising force."

We rounded an abrupt turn in the canal and came upon a scene that silenced even Count Jack. A battle had been fought here, a war of total commitment and destruction. But who had won, who had lost; we could not tell. Uliri War Tripods lay draped like over ledges and arches like desiccated spiders. The wrecks of skymasters were impaled on stone spires, wedged into rock clefts and groins. Shards of armour, human and Uliri, littered the canyon floor. Helmets and cuirasses were empty, long since picked clean by whatever scavengers hid from the light of the distant sun to gnaw and rend in the night. We stood in a landscape of hull plates, braces, struts, smashed tanks and tangles of wiring and machinery we could not begin to identify. Highest, most terrible of all, the hulk of a space ship, melted with the fires of re-entry, smashed like soft fruit, lay across the canyon, rim to rim. Holes big enough to fly a skymaster through had been punched through the hull, side to side.

Count Jack raised his eyes to the fallen space ship, then his hands.

"Dear God. I may never play the Hammersmith Palais again."

Chimes answered him, a tintinnabulation of metal ringing on metal. This was the final madness. This was when I understood that we were dead – that we had died in the skymaster crash – and that war was Hell. Then I felt the ground tremble beneath the soles of my good black concert shoes and I understood. Metal rang on metal, wreckage on wreckage. The earth shook, dust rose. The spoilage of war started to stir, and move. The ground shook, my feet were unsteady, there was nothing to hold on to, no surety except Count Jack. We held each other as the dust rose before us and the scrap started to slide and roll. Higher the ground rose, and higher and that was the third time I almost killed him for I still did not fully understand what was happening and imagined that if I stopped Jack, I would stop the madness. This was his doing; he had somehow summoned some old Martian evil from the ground. Then a shining conical drill-head emerged from the soil and the dust and rocks tumbled as the mole-machine emerged from the ground. It rose twenty, thirty feet above us, a gimlet-nosed cylinder of soil-scabbed metal. Then it put out metal feet from hatches along its belly, fell forward and came to rest a stone's throw from us. Hatches sprang open behind the still-spinning drill head, fanned out like flower petals. I glimpsed silver writhing in the interior darkness. Uliri padvas streamed out, their tentacles carrying them dexterously over the violated metal and rock. Their cranial cases were helmeted, their breathing mantles armoured in

delicately worked cuirasses and their palps held ray-rifles. We threw
our hands up. They swarmed around us and, without a sound, herded
us into the dark maw of the Martian mole-machine.

THE SPIDER-CAR deposited us at a platform of heat-ray polished sandstone
before the onyx gates. The steel tentacle-tips of our guards clacked on
the mirror rock. The gates stood five times human height – they must
have been overpowering to the shorter Uliri, and were divided in three
according to Uliri architecture and decorated with beautiful patterns of
woven tentacles in high relief, as complex as Celtic knot-work. A dot
of light appeared at the centre of the gates and split into three lines,
a bright 'Y'. They swung slowly outward and upwards. There was no
other possibility than to enter.

How blind we humans had been, how sure that our mastery of sky
and space gave us mastery of this world. The Uliri had not been driven
back by our space bombardments and massed skymaster strikes, they
had been driven *deep*. Even as the great Hives of Syrtia and Tempe
stood shattered and burning, Uliri proles had been delving deeper even
than the roots of their areo-thermal cores, down toward the still warm
lifeblood of their world, tapping into its mineral and energy resources.
Downward and outward; hive to nest to manufactory, underground
redoubt to subterranean fortress, a network of tunnels and delvings
and underground vacuum-tubes that reached so far, so wide, so deep
that Tharsia was like sponge. Down there, in the magma-warmed dark,
they built a society far beyond the reach of our space-bombs. Biding
their time, drawing their plans together, sending their tendrils under our
camps and command centres and bases; gathering their volcano-forged
forces against us.

I remembered little of the journey in the mole-machine except that
it was generally downward, interminable long and smelled strongly of
acetic acid. Count Jack, with his sensitivities, discreetly covered his nose
and mouth with his handkerchief. I could not understand his reticence:
the Uliri had thousands of better reasons to have turned us to ash than
affront at their personal perfume.

Our captors were neither harsh nor kind. Those are both human emotions. The lesson that we were slow to learn after the Horsell Common attack was that Martian emotions are Martian. They do not have love, anger, despair, the desire for revenge, jealousy. They did not attack us from hate, or defend themselves from love. They have their own needs and motivations and emotions. So they only seemed to gently usher us from the open hatches of the mole-machine (one among hundreds, lined up in silos, aimed at the upper world) into a vast underground dock warm with heart-rock, and along a pier to a station, where a spider-shaped glass car hung by many arms from a monorail. The spider-car accelerated with jolting force. We plunged into a lightless tunnel, then we were in the middle of an underground city, tier upon tier of lighted windows and roadways tumbling down to a red-lit mist. Through underwater waterfalls, through vast cylindrical farms bright with the light of the lost sun. Over marshalling yards and parade grounds as dense with padvas as the shore is with sand grains. Factories, breeding vats, engineering plants sparkling with welding arcs and molten steel. I saw pits miles deep, braced with buttresses and arches and spires, down and down and down, like a cathedral turned inside out. Those slender stone vaults and spires were festooned with winged horrors – those same four-winged monsters that had plucked us out the sky and so casually, so easily dismembered our crew. And allowed us to live.

I had no doubt that we had been chosen. And I had no doubt why we were chosen.

Over another jarring switch-over, through another terrifying, roaring tunnel, and then out into a behemoth gallery of launch silos: hundreds of them, side by side, each loaded with fat rocket-ships stiff with gun turrets and missile racks. I feared for our vaunted Spacefleet, and realising that, feared more for myself. Not even the alien values of the Uliri would show us so much if there were even the remotest possibility we could return the information to the Commanderie.

Count Jack realised it in the same instant.

"Christ on crutches, Faisal," he whispered.

On and on, through the riddled, maggoty, mined and tunnelled and bored and reamed under-Mars. And now the onyx gates stood wide and the padvas fell into a guard around us and prodded us through them. The polished sandstone now formed a long catwalk. On each side rose seats, tier upon tier of obsidian egg-cups. Each held an Uliri; proles, gestates, padvas, panjas; arranged by mantle colour and rank. From the detail of the etchings on their helmets and carapace covers, I guessed them to be of the greatest importance. A parliament, a conclave, a cabinet. But the true power was at the end of the long walk: the Queen of Noctis herself. No image had ever been captured, no corpse or prisoner recovered, of an Uliri Queen. They were creatures of legend. The reality in every way transcended our myth-making imaginations. She was immense. She filled the chamber like a sunrise. Her skin was golden; her mantle patterned with soft diamond-shaped scales like fairy armour. Relays of inseminators carried eggs from her tattooed multiple ovipositors, slathering them in luminous milt. Rings of rank and honour had been pierced through her eyelids and at the base of her tentacles. Her cuirass and helmet glowed with jewels and finest filigree. She was a thing of might, majesty and incontestable beauty. Our dress heels click-clacked on the gleaming stone.

"With me, Faisal," whispered Count Jack. "Quick smart." The guard stopped but Count Jack strode forward. He snapped to attention. Every royal eye fixed on him. He clicked his heels and gave a small, formal bow. I was a heartbeat behind him. "It's all small beer after the Pope."

A tentacle snaked toward us. I resisted the urge to step back, even when the skin of the palp retraced and there, there was a human head. And not any human head: the head of Yuzbashi Osman, the music lover of Camp Oudeman, whom we had last seen leading the bold and stirring – and ultimately futile – charge against the padva hordes. Now the horror was complete. The Yuzbashi opened his eyes and let out a gasping sigh. The head looked me up and down, then gave Count Jack a deeper scrutiny.

"Count Jack Fitzgerald of Kildare-upon-Ireland. Welcome. I am Nehenner Repooltu Sevenniggog Dethprip; by right, battle and acclaim the uncontested Queen of Noctis. And I am your number one fan."

*   *   *

ONE FINGER OF rum in Count Jack's particular tea. And then, for luck, for war, for insanity, I slipped in another one. I knocked, waited for his call and entered his dressing room. We might be somewhere in the warren of chambers beneath the Hall of the Martian Queen, miles beneath the sands of Mars, but the forms must be observed. The forms were all we had.

"Dear boy!" Uliri architecture did not accommodate human proportions. Proles had been at work – the prickly tang of scorched stone was strong – but I still had to duck to get through the door. Count Jack sat before a mirror of heat-ray polished obsidian. He adjusted the sit of his white bow tie. He filled the tiny cubby-hole but he still took the tea with an operatic flourish and took a long, County Kildare slurp.

"Ah! Grand! Grand. My resolve is stiffened to the sticking point. By God, I shall have need of it today. Did you slip a little extra in, you sly boy?"

"I did Maestro."

"Surprisingly good rum. And the tea is acceptable. I wonder where they got it from?"

"Ignorance is bliss, Maestro."

"You're right there." He drained the cup. "And how is the piano?"

"Like the rum. Only I think they made it themselves."

"They're good at delicate work, the worker-drone thingies. Those tentacle-tips are fine and dexterous. Natural master craftsmen. I wonder if they would make good pianists? Faisal? Dear God, listen to me, listen to me! Here we are, like a wind-up musical box, set up to amuse and titivate. A song, a tune, a dance or two. Us, the last vestige of beauty on this benighted planet, dead and buried in some vile subterranean cephalopod vice-pit. Does anyone even know we're alive? Help us for God's sake, help us! Ferid Bey, he'll do something. He must. At the very least, he'll start looking for us when the money doesn't materialise."

"I expect Ferid Bey has already collected the insurance." I took the cup and saucer. Our predicament was so desperate, so monstrous that we dared not look it full in the face. The Queen of Noctis had left us in no doubt that we were to entertain her indefinitely; singing birds in a cage. Never meet the fans. That was one of Count Jack's first homilies to me. Fans think they own you.

"Bastard!" Count Jack thundered. "Bastarding bastard! He shall die, he shall die. When I get back..." Then he realised that we would never get back, that we might never feel the wan warmth of the small, distant sun; that these low tunnels might be our home for the rest of our lives – and each other the only human face we would ever see. He wept, bellowing like a bullock. "Can this be the swan-song of Count Jack Fitzgerald? Prostituting myself for some super-ovulating Martian squid queen? Oh the horror the horror! Leave me, Faisal. Leave me. I must prepare."

The vinegar smell of the Uliri almost made me gag as I stepped on to the stage. I have always had a peculiar horror of vinegar. Lights dazzled me but my nose told me there must be thousands of Uliri on the concert hall's many tiers. Uliri language is as much touch and mantle-colour as it is spoken sounds and the auditorium fistled with the dry-leaf rustling of tentacle on tentacle. I flipped out my tails, seated myself at the piano, ran a few practice scales. It was a very fine piano indeed. The tuning was perfect, the weight and responsiveness of the keys extraordinary. I saw a huge golden glow suffuse the rear of the vast hall. The Queen had arrived on her floating grav-throne. My hands shook with futile rage. Who had given her the right to be Count Jack's Number One fan? She had explained, in her private chamber, a pit filled with sweet and fragrant oil in which she basked, her monstrous weight supported, how she had first heard the music of Count Jack Fitzgerald. Rather, the head of poor Osman explained. When she had been a tiny fry in the Royal Hatchery – before the terrible internecine wars of the queens, in which only one could survive – she had become intrigued by Earth after the defeat of the Third Uliri Host at the Battle of Orbital Fort Tokugawa. She had listened to Terrene radio, and become entranced by light opera –- the thrill of the coloraturas, the sensuous power of the tenor, the stirring gravitas of the basso profondo. In particular she fell in love – or the Uliri equivalent of love – with the charm and blarney of one Count Jack Fitzgerald. She became fascinated with Ireland – an Emerald Isle, made of a single vast gemstone, a green land of green people – how extraordinary, how marvellous, how magical. She had even had her proles build a life-size model Athy in one of the unused undercrofts of the Royal Nest. Opera and the stirring voice of the operatic tenor became her passion and she vowed, if she survived the Sororicide, that she would build an incomparable opera house on Mars, in the heart of the Labyrinth of Night, and attract the greatest singers and musicians of Earth to show the Uliri what she considered was the highest human art. She survived, and had consumed all her sisters and taken their experiences and memories, and built her opera house, the grandest in the solar system, but war had intervened. Earth had attacked, and the ancient and beautiful Uliri Hives of Enetria and Issidy were shattered like infertile eggs. She had fled underground, to her empty, virginal concert hall, but in the midst of the delvings and the buildings and forgings, she had heard that Count Jack Fitzgerald had come to Mars to entertain the troops at the same time that the United Queens were mounting a sustained offensive, and she seized her opportunity.

The thought of that little replica Athy, far from the sun, greener than green, waiting, gave me screaming nightmares.

Warm-up complete. I straightened myself at the piano. A flex of the fingers, and into the opening of *I'll Take You Home Again Kathleen*. And on strode Count Jack Fitzgerald, arms wide, handkerchief in one hand, beaming, the words pealing from his lips. Professional, consummate, marvellous. I never loved him more dearly than striding into those spotlights. The auditorium lit up with soft flashes of colour: Uliri lighting up their bioluminescent mantles; their equivalent of applause.

Count Jack stopped in mid-line. I lifted my hands from the keys as if the ivory were poisoned. The silence was sudden and immense. Every light froze on, then softly faded to black.

"No," he said softly. "This will not do."

He held up his hands, showed each of them in turn to the audience. Then he brought them together in a single clap that rang out into the black vastness. Clap one, two, three. He waited. Then I heard the sound of a single pair of tentacles slapping together. It was not a clap, never a clap, but it was applause. Another joined it, another and another, until waves of slow tentacle-claps washed around the auditorium. Count Jack raised his hands: enough. The silence was instant. Then he gave himself a round of applause, and me a round of applause, and I him. The Uliri caught the idea at once. Applause rang from every tier and level and joist of the Martian Queen's concert hall.

"Now, let's try that again," Count Jack said and without warning strode off the stage. I saw him in the wings, indicating for me to milk it. I counted a good minute before I struck up the introduction to *I'll Take You Home Again Kathleen*. On he strode, arms wide, handkerchief in hand, beaming. And the concert hall erupted. Applause: whole hearted loud ringing mighty applause; breaking like an ocean from one side of the concert hall to the other, wave upon wave upon wave, on and on and on.

Count Jack winked to me as he swept past into the brilliance of the lights to take the greatest applause of his life.

"What a house, Faisal! What a house!"

THE IRISH ASTRONAUT
Val Nolan

Val Nolan lectures on contemporary literature at the National University of Ireland, Galway. A graduate of the Clarion Writers' Workshop, his fiction has appeared in *Cosmos*, *The Irish Times*, *Electric Velocipede* and on the 'Futures' page of *Nature*. His academic publications include 'Flann, Fantasy, and Science Fiction: O'Brien's Surprising Synthesis' (*Review of Contemporary Fiction*, Flann O'Brien Centenary Issue, 2011) and 'Break Free: Understanding, Reimagining, and Reclaiming Stories in Grant Morrison's *Seven Soldiers of Victory*' (*Journal of Graphic Novels and Comic Books*, 2014). He is a past winner of the Penguin Ireland Short Story Competition and the *Daily Telegraph* Travel Writing Contest.

BY HIS SECOND week in the village with the unpronounceable name, Dale had taken up with the old men fishing out beyond the rocks. The place was called the Blue Pool and people died at it, he was told, freak waves being known to carry them away. Fierce tragic, as his new friends had it.

"Saw a man plucked from the earth here once," Gerry McGovern said. "Looked off at a girl in a summer dress and then, well –"

"Gone?" asked Dale.

"Gone."

"Christ."

McGovern blessed himself.

Beside him, Bartley tapped his pipe upside-down against his hand. "Every one of your stories starts like that, Gerry. Every one."

McGovern sneered. "Won't be long now," he said to the American.

"Hopefully," said Dale, who had been waiting ten days for the parish priest. "I should have called ahead, but… I wasn't sure."

"Bad luck, so it is," Bartley said. He cut thin strips of tobacco from a block with his penknife and rolled the tar curls between filthy palms until the nest was finely shredded. "Though you could hardly blame the Father," he said. "'Tis the first holiday that man has taken since God-knows-when."

"Well his timing's incredible," Dale said, "just incredible." He followed the thread of his borrowed line down into the water and watched a tiny ripple stir around it. It was a fine morning on the coast of Ireland, cool beneath a naked sun. Dale felt like he'd been sitting there since he first trundled through the airport, catching nothing and talking about airplanes or weather. Every day he ate his breakfast in the B&B and every night he drank at a small bar in the centre of the village. He had yet to go into the grey stone hills which loomed above the crooked, multi-coloured houses. There was just something about them, something he couldn't quite put his finger on.

"I wonder," Bartley said, "D'you think they'd ever have one of our lads up there?" He plucked a pebble from the ground and placed it in the bowl of his pipe. "They're fierce small, you know, because of our planes. They'd fit them tin cans of yours awful easy."

Dale laughed. "Height really isn't…" He looked around. "It doesn't matter. The programme's shut down."

"Aye," Bartley said, serious all of a sudden. "Because of the crash?"

"It wasn't a crash."

"The accident then?" He held a match towards his face and cupped both hands above the pipe.

"Yeah," Dale said. "Because of the accident." He drank from the plastic bottle beside him and stared out across the water. As we set sail on this new ocean, he thought…

"Terrible thing," Bartley was saying. "Terrible altogether. Did you know any of them boys, you did?"

"I knew them all," Dale said. "Davis, O'Neil, Rodriguez…" He took a deep breath and looked up at the sky. It was two years later and the president's speech still rang in his ears: "*Aquarius* is lost. There are no survivors."

*   *   *

IRELAND. THE SLIDE-rule rigidity of Houston had not prepared him for it. Dale was used to clean lines and order, but this little village was a bow-tie of crooked streets knotted where their paths crisscrossed with those of history and want. The first time Dale saw it he had thought it was a theme park. Its true arrangement continued to elude him even after fourteen days on the ground. One wrong turn, what he thought might make a sensible shortcut, and Dale would find himself on the shoulder of the potted two-lane to another parish, would suddenly be in the company of dirty hens by a half-finished house on the edge of the arid countryside.

He had taken a room in the centre of the village, on what passed for the main drag. It was a rambling nook-and-cranny job, an anarchic spiderweb of low doors and high ceilings rebuilt and renovated many times. Thomas and Catherine, the elderly couple who owned it, had gleefully explained the building's history to him; how it had consumed outhouse after outhouse, how it had gone from farmhouse to townhouse, from boarding house to B&B, and Dale was sure his room had once been among the rafters of a forge or stable. Standing in the guesthouse doorway, one could go only left or right – to the pub or the sea – and still Dale always managed to get lost.

"The streets all move around at night," Catherine told him one morning.

"Nice try," Dale said.

"It's true," Thomas added, cocking his head towards the window. "The village used be up there, in the hills."

Dale looked over his shoulder. It was as much limestone as he had ever seen. "I don't think so," he said at last.

"Oh yeah," Thomas winked at his wife. "Twas a deal made with the devil, you know? Sealed with a hoof. And pretty soon the whole lot of us are to be sucked right down the Blue Pool, like one of them black spots of yers."

Dale thought for a moment. "A black hole?"

"Aye, a black hole."

The American laughed. At least the food was always good. "I appreciate the effort," he said, "but I'm not buying it."

"Then tell me this so," Thomas hunched over his plate, "did ye really go up there? To the Moon, like?"

"Thomas," Dale said, "I'll let you know." He excused himself as he always did, climbing the bare staircase back to his room where a copy of the county paper lay yellowing in the sun. "Spaceman Dale" had made page five, and he had cringed when he saw it, his life unspooled as lies and inexplicable exaggeration, the gross embellishment of an undistinguished record. To read it one would think him a Borman or a Conrad, if not the equal of Armstrong himself. Dale had not looked at it since Thomas first produced it one morning over breakfast.

"I didn't know you gave an interview," the old man had teased at the time.

"I didn't," Dale had said, staring at the picture they had printed alongside the article, a publicity snap of him at the initial rollout of *Aquarius*, his arm around Rodriguez's shoulder and both men grinning. He supposed it was easily sourced.

"Twas a slow week," Thomas said.

"Excuse me?"

"Slow enough now," the old man was went on. "Though Maggie Kelleher's ewe drowned down by the shore last evening. That's two now."

"I'm sorry, what?"

"Two," he said. "Careless, that woman. Not like her husband, God bless him."

"God bless him," repeated Catherine, drifting through the room with a plate piled high with toasty strips of bacon.

Dale shook his head and watched all this with amusement. After breakfast he had asked Thomas for the paper though he didn't know why. Vanity, probably, though when he went back to his room he refused to open it again, merely threw it on the dresser beside the tin flask he had brought across the ocean. It irked him, the usurpation of his life. He had never even met this reporter and yet her fanciful invention now defined him to everyone he met.

Catherine told him not to worry. Every morning after breakfast she would meet him at the bottom of the stairs, he with a satchel to see him through his fishing; she with a little foil package of sandwiches, moist, crustless feasts of dark bread and thick-cut meats painted heavily in relish. It was a peculiar, motherly gesture with which she earned Dale's gratitude forever.

"Sure, we have to keep you fed," she said.

Somewhere Thomas coughed violently. Dale smiled, and let himself out.

Down by the Blue Pool, the American explained his theory about his room having once been a forge but McGovern only smirked.

"What?"

"Ah now," McGovern said, turning to Bartley.

Puffing his pipe, his cheeks an artful bellows, Bartley shook his head. "Didn't they tell you, Dale?" he asked. "Sure everybody knows that part of Tom's used be the undertakers."

FOR YEARS HE had heard Rodriguez talk of coming here, of green hills and red-headed girls. It was a fantasy, colourful and wild, and by definition it bore scant resemblance to what met Dale as he rolled his battered hardside off the plane. Not a fertile field or a dancing lass in sight, instead a murky tonnage of dull cloud which weighted on the whole country like a fat palm pressed upon a chest. At customs, a sneering, grey-haired policeman stamped his passport without a word. At the car hire desk, a woman with food stains on her blouse went on and on about the foulness of the weather, about the worst summer in a generation and how the crops were rotting in the ground.

"Twas far from the ground the likes of her were raised," Bartley said when Dale recounted him the story. Hell of an introduction, the American thought later. It was the first time they had met, the old man seemingly oblivious to the fact that it had indeed been raining steadily since Dale's arrival, weather which had confined them all inside the gloomy local.

"It was late," Dale said. "I'm sure she was just tired."

"No excuse for that kind of behaviour, and you a guest of this great little nation." Bartley daubed at the beige moustache left by his pint and leaned into his new acquaintance. "What was it you said you did again?"

Dale cleared his throat. "Aeronautics," he said warily.

"No," Bartley said, squinting. "No, that's not it... Too much bearing, too... clean cut." A ripple of laughter passed through the bar.

"I'm sorry?" Dale said. He hadn't realised anyone was listening.

"Not that you should have to be," the old man said, "but I appreciate it."

Dale looked around, though no one met his eyes. He turned back to Bartley. "And what's your line?"

"When you're ready, Pat," Bartley said, grinning at the barman and sinking a bony finger deep into his empty glass.

"You'll not get an answer out of him," the barman told Dale.

"Yeah, I'm starting to see that."

Beside him, Bartley cleared his throat. "So," he said, "is it a pilot or an engineer you are?" he asked.

"First one," Dale said, "and then the other." He was getting the hang of Bartley.

"Test pilot?" the old man said, narrowing his eyes. He was sharp.

Dale shook his head, sipped his drink and allowed himself a tiny smile.

"He's toying with me," Bartley announced.

The barman said nothing.

"You really want to know?" Dale asked at last.

"I do," Bartley said.

"He does," the barman echoed, elbows on the counter.

Dale sighed. "Alright." He tapped the little silver pin on his lapel. "Astronaut Corps," he said.

"Well now," Bartley said.

The barman whistled quietly.

Dale sipped his drink. "It's a job like any other."

"A job like any other, he says." Bartley cocked his thumb in Dale's direction. "Bring him another whiskey, will you, Pat?"

The American shifted his weight on the barstool. "Hospitality?"

"Generosity of spirit," Bartley said, a gleam in his eye. He began on the fresh pint before him with a kind of practiced reverence.

"Well then," Dale said, raising his own glass, "I believe I'm supposed to say sláinte."

"Aye," said Bartley, "you've got it, sláinte indeed," and so their conversation drifted into trivialities, the price of stout and the state of county games, things which were the heartbeat of the local. Dale left when the bar was almost empty and the barman started to look restless. He had no better grasp on who Bartley was, the old man foxing him at every turn. He walked back to the B&B beneath a loaned umbrella, shaking the rain off out on the step.

"Gallivanting, was it?" Thomas asked, stirring from the shadows in the hallway.

"Only as far as the bar."

"How'd you find it?"

"Your directions were perfect."

The old man smiled patiently. His teeth were crooked and yellow. "I mean," he said softly, "how was it?"

"Ah... It was good. I enjoyed it. Met a man named Bartley, I'm sure you know him."

"Oh, Bartley's a cute one alright. Wily, like."

Dale rubbed the side of his head. "I gathered that."

"Fierce interested in you now, I'd say."

"He was. Though less forthcoming about himself. I wonder, what is it he does exactly?"

"His brother killed three Tans in that business with the British."

"Right. But Bartley?"

Thomas laughed as he began up the stairs, slapping Dale on the back. "Sure, isn't he his brother's keeper, Dale? His brother's keeper."

WHEN THE DOWNPOURS finally ended the little village came into its own. Stone walls caught the new light and turned it back upon the darkest corners of the place. The streets began to glow, and, on their outskirts, brave flowers sprang from a frugal soil. Everywhere became warm and the sky assumed a welcome, almost Texan hue.

"This is our summer now," Bartley announced in the bar that afternoon, wiping his hands on his thighs and standing up. His crooked frame drew nods of approval from the other patrons. It seemed an event of some importance.

"You going somewhere?" Dale asked. The half-full glass in front of Bartley was conspicuous.

"The Blue Pool," the old man said, "Come on, if you like and we'll stand you the line."

That was how it started.

"You seem awful content," Bartley said at the end of that first week's fishing.

"Must be the company."

"All the same," McGovern said, cocking his head towards the grey hills, "would you not see The Burren?"

"I've no interest."

"Tis a place of beauty."

"So I've heard."

"You're a strange man, Dale."

"I've been called worse."

Their lines hung heavy in the water. Nothing was biting.

"I heard once," Bartley said, "that spaceships were tiled, and that twas Irish students working over there that glued them on."

Dale smiled. "Sure, on the outside. Ceramics to survive re-entry, but I don't know who attached them."

"Pity," Bartley said. "Pity now."

Beside him, McGovern shrugged.

"Twould be nice," Bartley went on, "to think of the contribution, like."

"Twould a'course," said McGovern.

Dale looked at the two of them, this grizzled pair, then shook his head and smiled. He closed his eyes and raised his head towards the sun. So unremarkable, he thought, and still so great. Turning away, he opened his eyes and caught the ghost-face of the Moon in daylight peeking through the afternoon. He allowed himself a look of happiness.

"What's that now?" Bartley asked. He never took his eyes off his line.

"I remember he was on the radio," Dale said. "Loud and clear. His first words out of the lander were 'Man, that's beautiful'."

"Who was that, then?"

"A friend of mine," Dale said. "Rodriguez. One of the men who died."
Bartley nodded.

Beside him, McGovern asked what it was like. He too was looking at the Moon now, the withered veins on his unshaven neck coaxed back to elasticity by the tilt of his blunt chin.

"Rock," said Dale. "He went on and on about the rock, the mountains and the boulders and the dust."

"Rock?" McGovern said. "Mountains and dust?"

"Sure you could see that here," said Bartley.

Dale grinned. "Could you see the colours in the grey? The red and orange and the yellow tints from the sun?" He laughed. "God, he wouldn't shut up about that. We could hardly get him to carry out his orders."

The two old Irishmen exchanged a look. Dale couldn't read it.

"You'd get the most of it here anyway," Bartley said. "The sun on the stone and all that. No knowing what you'd see."

"Sure isn't it all they go on about above in them hills?" McGovern added. "And they don't need any of them helmets or big white suits to see it."

"They're lucky," Dale said.

"Terrible lucky," Bartley nodded.

Dale smiled. "But can they see the Earth rising over the horizon the way the moon does here? That's what Rodriguez saw. He told us he was standing there, looking up at planet Earth, this great, blue oasis in the black velvet sky, and he said it was just too beautiful to have happened by accident…"

They were listening to him now, he saw, Bartley and McGovern with their grey heads cocked, though Dale didn't know what else to tell them. Technical particulars and numbers and dry facts would only spoil it, and Rodriguez only shared so much that anyone would call poetic. Instead, he reeled in his line and watched ripples echo all across the surface as his bait broke through from underneath. Earth, he realised, was covered mostly in water. A blue pool in the night of space. Its name was suddenly inadequate, powerless to convey its sheer, inexplicable abundance. Staring into the water, he found himself speaking without realizing.

"Rodriguez was talking to us afterwards," he said, "when he was back aboard *Aquarius*, and he told me he'd seen the whole world, all of it, all at once. Imagine that, every human being in existence, everything we are, all of it a size that if he reached out he could have plucked it from the sky. I'll never forget that," he said. "It was almost as good as being there."

"Almost?"

"Almost." Dale laughed again. He wasn't sure which one of them had said it, but it didn't matter. "We're explorers," he said. "Or at least we were; we should be. And no explorer ever knows exactly what he's going to find when he gets to where he's going, but every time we fly we add to what's known. Rodriguez, he helped me to learn something, you understand? About the grand scheme of things. Perspective, that's what I learned from him."

"Aye," McGovern said, licking his lips, "but what have you learned from us, I wonder?"

"I've learnt," Dale said slowly, "that there aren't any fish in this pond, are there?" He looked from McGovern to Bartley and back again, but the two old men had already started laughing.

BLUE SKIES AND bright light. It was outdoors that Dale felt most at home in. All Irish people seemed to regard the world through doors and windows, he had noticed. Their view was blinkered, like the draw-horses in the etchings which hung on the walls of Catherine's dining room. When people here spoke of the land they did not mean the country or the state, they meant the field, some small enclosure within which they were snared by circumstance or greed. Whole lives here were bounded by the whitewashed sovereignties of dated bungalows or played out in discontent behind the cobweb-covered lens of guilty window panes.

And yet Dale surprised himself with what he loved about them, their history, their rancour hardening around them into flakes or scales, of all things their certainty in what cannot be seen. For everyone he had met here, a palm's rough lines were no less truthful than the dotted contours of a map. Myth and fact were interchangeable, reality a personal affliction.

"What was it like," he asked McGovern, "growing up around here?"

They sat with Bartley by the Blue Pool again, the sun baking all of them.

"I suppose it was the same as anywhere," the old man said. "We chased girls and went to matches and swam in the sea."

"Aye," said Bartley, "going round with your tongue hanging out."

"We played hurling," McGovern added. "Fastest field game in the world."

Dale squinted at him. "Is that a fact?"

"Oh yeah. But don't think we didn't know what it was ye were up to."

"Ye...?"

"Oh, he's been workin' on this one," Bartley said.

"Twas before my sister was married," McGovern began. "And she was still living with us, which is a long time ago now. I'd just started inside at Callaghan's and I was driving in and out of the city every day."

Dale turned to Bartley. "What's he talking about?"

"Your friends," the old man said, raising his eyebrows. "The men above."

"We'd to go to the neighbours," McGovern went on. "We'd still no TV ourselves."

Dale smiled. "The Moon landings," he said, getting it.

"Momentous!" McGovern was in full flight now. "No thought of course to the risks involved. Just those two lads bouncing around the place, like kangaroos the pair of them. The boys were all trying it at work the next day. I swear, old Roddy Callaghan himself, leppin' around the yard..." He looked at Dale.

"I'm sorry," the American said. "I don't know who that is."

"Ah," McGovern said sadly, "sure it doesn't... Never mind."

Between them, Bartley was shaking his head. "There was no television where I was. Had to see it in the papers next day. Yer lad Aldrin like the Michelin Man, setting up the flag as if he owned the damn place." He laughed. "I have to hand it to ye, that was a good one." He laid a hand on Dale's arm and nodded. A livery of age adorned his skin. McGovern's too, and Dale suddenly felt out of place.

"Why is it," the American asked, "that everyone's so old here?"

"Say what?"

"I mean," Dale said, "where are all the young people?"

"Sure here's one now," McGovern said, elbowing Dale gently in the ribs and indicating the path from the road where a meek spectre with a Methuselan gait tottered in their direction. It was Regan, a venal leprechaun of a man whom Dale had seen around the village.

"Is it yourself?" Bartley asked without looking away from the water.

"It is," Regan said, standing above them as if in judgment. "And tell me, gentlemen, how's the fishing?"

"Could be worse," McGovern said beneath his breath. "Could be better too."

Regan glowered at him. He stood crooked, with his weight resting on a walking stick. One eye, Dale saw, was perpetually narrower than the other. "We've never really had the chance to talk," he said to the American, "and I've been meaning to ask you, what was it like up there?"

Dale clinched his jaw. Someone must have told him. "I don't know," he said at last.

Regan leaned closer. "Sure, how could you forget a thing like that?"

"I was an alternate," he said. "A backup. I've never been up there."

"Some other lad went?"

"Yeah, some other lad."

Regan licked his lips. "So you never flew?"

"I flew combat over Iraq. I flew experimental planes to the edge of space. I earned my wings."

"But not... up there?"

"No."

"They told me," Regan said slowly, "you were an Astronaut."

"That's right."

"But then–"

"The criteria," Dale said, "is altitude." He held Regan's stare.

"Ah now," McGovern said, "would you ever leave the man alone."

"I'll not be told what to do," the interloper snapped back.

"The fish," Bartley said quietly, "are finally biting."

Dale ignored him and turned to the newcomer. "And you are?"

"He's a Peace Commissioner," McGovern said, spitting the words. "It's nothing what you think."

"The criteria," Regan said, "is good character."

"The criteria is arse-licking," McGovern said. "And no better man for it."

"I take offence to that."

"Tis a pity you won't take it somewhere else."

Twisted over his line, Bartley cackled quietly and Dale turned his gaze back out to sea. Regan drew himself away from three fishermen, as if to say well then, so be it.

"I might see you later," he declared to no one in particular, and gradually he shuffled off until he disappeared into the middle distance.

McGovern shook his head. "Thinks he's lord and master, that man does." He leaned in close to the American. "You should fight him."

"Fight him?" It was Bartley, cackling so loud that the pipe nearly left his lips. "Tis not a movie, Gerry."

McGovern folded his arms. "Twould still be right."

"I'm not here to start fights," Dale said.

"Sure twas that begrudger started it." He raised an arm and pointed after Regan.

"There're guys like that all over," Dale said.

"The Man on the Moon," Bartley said, rocking back and forth, and laughing to himself. He stabbed at the sky with his pipe.

"Would you ever put that thing away?" McGovern said.

The old man grinned at him through yellow teeth. "Sure, why would I?" he asked. "Don't I like my poison neat?"

REGAN WAS A troublemaker, but there was no denying he was good at it. What he said had stuck in the American's craw and the rest of the day hadn't shaken it. To most of these people, Dale realised, he was just the astronaut – *the* astronaut – and he had gotten used to that even though it wasn't true. To have had it called out unsettled him because Rodriguez had been the astronaut, a number one aviator with nothing ruffled but his hair. Beside him Dale was only competent, next on the rotation for sure, but not flying at anything like that altitude. Regan had shown him up, and Dale felt sick that it had taken someone like that to bring him back to Earth. He shook his head. Ego was a part of his job but he had let it run amuck here. Where was his control, the better part of being a pilot?

When he walked back into the village he was angry, angry about Regan, angry about the priest's continued absence; he was angry at himself, at how quickly he had succumbed to his own tacit celebrity. He sat in the bar until it was dark outside and thought of that damn newspaper lying in his room. He resolved to burn it and called for another whiskey.

Regan, when he arrived hours later, quickly smelt his opportunity on the American's breath. "Well now," he said, "we can finally have that chat."

"I'm not really in the mood."

"Ah, we'll have none of that," Regan motioned to the bartender for a pint.

Dale sighed deeply. He hunkered over his drink and resigned himself to Regan's company. Sometimes in flight you go into a spin; nothing to do but throttle down, flatten out your surfaces, turn your rudder the opposite way and hold. He readjusted himself to face the old man.

"What do you want to know?" he said.

"Would you have gone?"

"Yes sir, I would."

"If the other lad hadn't flown, like?"

Dale drained his glass. "If Rodriguez had been pulled, I'd have taken his seat. If the programme had continued, I'd have had a flight of my own."

"And you'd have gone –"

"Wham, bam, straight to the Moon. That's where I was going. That's where Rodriguez went."

"Jasus," Regan said. "'Tis a quare thing." He returned his attention to the pint in front of him. "You tell it well though, you tell it well."

Dale couldn't figure out if he was being serious or not. He stared at the empty glass in his hand, how it caught the light. "Rodriguez," he said at last.

Regan looked at him. "What's that now?"

"Rodriguez was a better pilot than I was. Christ, he flew that bird the whole way down without a pair of wings to carry him."

"This was the crash, it was?"

"Disintegration," Dale said. "*Aquarius* didn't crash, it disintegrated mid-flight." Around him, the regulars had grown quiet. No one had gotten this much out of Dale before.

"I thought they all died when it came apart," Regan said gently. "Tis what the papers said."

"They didn't die until they hit the water," Dale said. "Everything else came apart, but the crew module retained integrity until it hit the ocean. Which is more than I can say for those penny-pinchers in Congress, those smooth-talking Washington slicks scurrying to avoid the blame. 'Organisational causes,' they called it, 'Poor technical decision-making.' And after all the times we tried to warn them. Ah," he said, "I don't know." He slid his glass back to the bartender who looked quickly at Regan before refilling it.

"I was the CAPCOM," Dale said. "You know, in the movies, when they say, *Houston, we have a problem?* Well I was the guy they're talking to, I was Houston. They like to have the alternates wear that headset. The thinking is that we're best trained to understand what's going on up there."

"And what was?" Regan whispered. "Going on up there, I mean?"

"Rodriguez and the others were alive for two minutes, thirteen seconds," Dale said. "Thermal protection failure. Loss of RCS. He couldn't alter his approach, couldn't tip the capsule those vital few degrees. And all the while they knew exactly what was happening."

"What did they say?"

"All Rodriguez said was *uh-oh*." Dale emptied his glass again. "The downlink went dead then and that was it."

"And?"

Dale looked Regan in his hooded eyes. "And that was it," he said again. "*Aquarius* suffered what they call 'failure of vehicle with loss of human life.' I saw it myself, dozens of sources blossoming on the radar. I saw it again later on, laid out on the floor of a hangar at the Cape. Everything reduced to slag. We all understood the risks, but –"

"But you thought it'd never happen to someone that you knew?"

Dale shook his head. "No, I never knew how I was going to feel when it happened. God," he said, "when I could think about it clearly, when I could process it, you know, I was relieved."

"…"

"I thought to myself, that could have been me up there." His head sunk deep between his shoulders.

"Ole human beings are strange," Regan said.

Down the bar, a heavy, bovine man was listening intently. He nodded.

"You can't be expected to be rational," Regan went on. "Not with the likes of that going on around you."

But Dale wasn't paying any attention. "Rodriguez walked on the Moon," he said. "And he was alive the whole way down, I know it." He held up his glass to the bartender.

"Go home," was the reply.

"He's right," Regan said. "You'll pay no respects like this."

"Ah," said Dale, standing up. He missed Bartley and McGovern, and couldn't imagine where they might have got to. He thought of them as crewmates, strapped in beside him in the nose of some heavy-lifting firecracker and bickering about the running of the parish or talking about the weather like it was a new event. He laughed at that to himself all the way to the B&B, his mood darkening then in the vagueness of the empty room.

Sitting on the edge of the bed, he stared at the small black canister which stood upright on the dresser. "I bet you've got something smart to say," he muttered before he fell asleep.

MORNING. SCRAPING BIRDSONG and the hot, fierce lantern of a disappointed sun. A dull halo of the night before hung crooked on Dale's skull when he woke, a liquordog, as Rodriguez would have said. It was not without cause that Dale seldom touched the hard stuff. With great, unshaven indignity he presented himself for breakfast but by some small mercy it was quiet, his hosts tuned obsessively to the conditions of their guests. They had seen it all before, of course.

"Fr. O'Grady's back," Thomas said, nose deep in his newspaper.

"Saw him last evening," Catherine said. "He's looking forward to meeting you." There were no sandwiches from her this morning. It was as though she knew his days of fishing were at an end. "He should be out of mass within the hour," she added.

"Thanks."

Outside a soft breeze rolled in from the Atlantic. Dale took his time walking through the village, stopping along the way to buy a bottle of water. When he reached the church he stood outside for almost twenty minutes. Clouds limped slowly through the sky and it felt wrong to go in so he walked on, circling around for many hours. Bartley and McGovern were nowhere to be found, not even by the shore.

At dusk, with a gold moon shining overhead, he returned to the limestone church and stood in the doorway as a young man in black fussed around the altar.

"Evening, Padre," Dale said.

O'Grady stared at him as if trying to place the countenance. "Yes," he said at last. "You must be the spaceman." His eyes had the smallest pupils Dale had ever seen, mere pinpricks, though with a curious, inviting depth. "Strange visitor from another planet, eh?" He waved the American inside. "Dale, isn't it?" He did not pause for a reply. "What can I do for you, Dale?"

"It's about Rodriguez," Dale said. "A friend of mine. He died in an accident."

"The, ah, the *Aquarius* pilot, yes?"

Dale nodded. He put his hands in his pockets. The air felt heavier in here. "This..." he said. "Well... This is where his people were from, I guess you'd say."

O'Grady moved down among the pews. He smelt faintly of the sacristy. "Rodriguez," he said carefully. "Not really many of them this side of the Shannon."

"Fitzpatricks," said Dale, "on his mother's side. Grandparents came out a long time ago. I don't know when."

"Well, how about that," O'Grady said. "An Irish astronaut. Now isn't that something?"

"He was hardly Irish," Dale said.

"If he could play for the soccer team he was Irish," the priest said firmly.

Dale couldn't help but smile at the man's excitement. "That's not really the point."

"That's always the point." He was back on the altar now, pottering around, adjusting the position of plates and candles and embroidery to suit his own baffling idiosyncrasies.

"No," said Dale, following to the edge of the marble steps. "The point is... I brought him home. It's what he wanted."

The priest's frantic motions ceased. His eyes drifted across the empty chapel and then back to Dale. "I didn't know there was a body," he said.

"There wasn't."

"Then –"

Dale allowed himself sit down in the front pew. "Most of what was recovered was unidentifiable," he said. "The temperatures, the impact. The undifferentiated remains were interned in Arlington."

"And those that were... differentiated?"

Dale removed the small black canister from his jacket and stood it on the seat beside him. "Identified remains were returned to family," he said. "But Rodriguez didn't have family."

O'Grady looked at the small metal can. He very gently picked it up, surprised at its weight. "And this –"

"The surviving remains of Commander Mike Rodriguez, USN. NASA Astronaut Group 19."

The priest blessed himself.

"We flew off the *Truman* together in the war," Dale said.

O'Grady frowned.

"That's what you do in a war, Padre. But wanting to go into space, that was different. We go in peace and all that?"

O'Grady was quiet for a long moment. "It occurs to me," he said at last, "that there's something I should show you." Still holding the canister, he led Dale back into a dark corner of the church, through an old low door with a gothic arch.

"Where are we going?"

"You'll see." The priest started on the tight spiral of the bell tower stairs and Dale trailed after him, his hand feeling the way along the undressed stone. It was dark and cold, the walls showing evidence of damp, and at the top was a cramped, shuttered room, the floor of which had been boarded out. There was no bell.

"We replaced it," O'Grady said, as if reading Dale's mind. He patted a fat loudspeaker affixed with brackets to the wall. "Bullhorn," he said, delighted with himself. "You'd never know the difference."

"Then what do you use this place for?"

"Ah…" O'Grady knelt by the far wall, beside a long bundle Dale had failed to notice. "I use it for this," the priest said, unwrapping the canvass and displaying its contents to the American.

"A telescope?"

O'Grady grinned.

"You have a telescope?"

"Help me set it up." He passed Dale the tripod and then the mount as he went about inspecting the reflector.

Dale stood the tripod in the centre of the floor and began locking it into place.

"A little higher," the priest said. "Yes, there. Perfect." He handed Dale the telescope itself. "Here," he said. "You know how to do this?"

"Uh-huh."

"Great." He stood back and began to open up the wooden shutters.

The bright night streamed in, and beneath the colour of the moon Dale could see the grey hills rolling off above the village. O'Grady caught him staring and took over assembly of the telescope.

"The Burren," the priest said. "Bare stone for as far as you can see. No soil only in the cracks between the rocks, no rivers or lakes. Not enough water to drown a man, not enough wood to hang him –"

"And not enough flat ground for him to land his aircraft." Dale shook his head and smiled. "Rock and mountains and boulders and dust."

"Sorry?"

"Something Rodriguez told me once."

"You know," O'Grady said quietly, "you can't wear the armband forever."

"Copy that." Dale thought about the hearings, the investigation, the names cut into the granite wall at Kennedy. He thought about those pieces of *Aquarius* laid out across the hangar floor, little more than scrap and garbage. Rodriguez, the tone of his voice; no worry or no anger, just surprise. *Uh-oh.*

There was nothing anybody could have done.

"Here," O'Grady said, stepping back from the telescope. The American took his place above the instrument, turned the focus slightly and watched another world jump sharply into view. The Moon, itself a great mirror bathing in the sun; its soft mountains rising off romantic maria, the Ocean of Storms, the Sea of Rains, the Lakes of Excellence and Perseverance...

"Man," Dale said, "that's beautiful."

O'Grady took a turn and murmured his agreement while Dale stood back and looked up at the sky. Mark-one eyeball, they called it in flight school. Sometimes there's just no substitute.

"There," he said suddenly, raising his arm to the southern sky where a new star bloomed and flew in a short arc before fading back again into the darkness. "The Space Station," Dale said. "Will you look at that."

The priest peered up just in time. "Impressive," he said.

Dale laughed. "I could have gone there once, you know."

"You can't still go?"

"I suppose. Take a ride with the Russians. Ah, but it wouldn't be the same. I'm a pilot, an explorer. I'm not a hitchhiker."

O'Grady nodded.

"You know," Dale said, "I can still remember going to the Space Centre as a kid and asking my mom if I could stay up all night when they landed the first man on Mars." He laughed. "I really thought they'd do it too. Hell, I thought *I'd* get to do it once I joined the programme."

"Could happen yet."

"Maybe," said Dale, "but then again maybe it's as well I'm out. Space is hungry, Padre. This business, it devours people. I've been devoured by it. It mightn't hurt to take the time to..." He trailed off. "I don't know."

"Yes you do."

The astronaut smiled. "To consider it, I suppose. To get my head around it."

O'Grady leaned back against the wall. "You know," he said, "I'll bury your friend here if you like. But are you sure that's what he wanted?"

Dale stared at the canister where the priest had placed it on the floor and wondered at the sad strange journey which had brought it here, all the questions which surrounded it. He looked out through the open shutters, across the otherworldly hills. Nothing was certain anymore, nothing at all.

Rodriguez, if he could have seen him, would have laughed his ass off.

SOON AFTER THAT he left O'Grady in the tower. There'd been a chaplain of the same mould aboard the *Truman*, he recalled; could get inside your head like nobody's business. It was not a shock to find another here; priests were all of a kind, Dale thought, though even so there was something very likeable about O'Grady. Not the astronomy or even the rudimentary philosophy. No, it was completely separate. He dared to call it enthusiasm and immediately felt bad.

Making his way down the narrow stairs and out through the church, Dale found Bartley and McGovern waiting outside for him, the latter with the palm of his hand pressed firm against the wall.

"Heard you'd finally gone to see the priest," McGovern said.

"This one was worried for ya," Bartley added, shaking his head.

McGovern shrugged. "Civility never broke a man's jaw."

"Clearly you've never been in a pilots' ready room," Dale said. "But thank you, Gerry. I appreciate it."

"Come on now," said Bartley. "Tell us, is your business done?"

"My business is done here," he said. "But I've got one more thing to do, if you want to join me..."

"You'll stand us the line?" the old man asked with a wink.

Dale grinned, the keys to his rental car already in his hand. "Sure."

Ten minutes later they were out of the village, crystal moonlight making everything unreal as they drove into the Burren. The pale-faced sky-child of earlier was gone, as was the golden hue of dusk, the moon's disc having slipped to a colder, sterner blue which cast long, chaotic shadows all round them. Hills squeezed the twisting road and each shape was another sculpture in a garden of demented stone where everything became reverent and cruel. In a field by the road with the light streaming through it, the silhouette of a horse stood proud on the hilltop. Dale thought he glimpsed an empty saddle on its back but couldn't know for sure. They drove on.

He remembered, back in training, Rodriguez and himself; still young men, men who had fought together, who had chosen a most dangerous profession.

"You'll take me back to Houston?" Dale had said.

"If you take me back to County Clare."

Beer-bottle necks had clinked at the arrangement, but Dale never thought he'd have to see it through, never once reckoned that he'd end up here with his friend in a metal can.

"What'd'ya think," McGovern said. "Does this look good?"

Dale nodded, "Yeah." He pulled in from the road and stopped the engine. Everything was silent. Leaning over the steering wheel, he stared into the sky where the spirit of his friend flew free. The image of disintegration was burned into his mind. The whirling debris, the cloud of vapour when the remaining hydrogen and oxygen collapsed against each other. *Aquarius*, he thought; the water carrier.

The president had made a speech which came back to him from time to time. "The cause for which they died will go on," he'd said. "Our journey into space will continue." He quoted it to Bartley and McGovern.

"Always liked him," Bartley said. "A good lad, now. A good lad."

"Yes," said Dale, who had met him once, a tall, sad man whose ambition had surpassed his reach. "I guess he always seemed to be." He picked up the canister and opened the door of the car. "Let's go." He led them out onto the bare shoulder, through the stile and up into a steep, rocky field. There was no soil, or very little anyway, and it was odd, he thought, to recognise the kind of features he had been trained to see on lunar missions, erratics and stratigraphic markers. He picked up a stone from the rough surface and turned it over in his hand.

"What's that?" McGovern asked.

"The technical term is FLR. At least according to Rodriguez."

"FLR?"

"Funny Looking Rock." He smiled as he dropped it to the ground. Rodriguez always said that levity was appropriate in a dangerous trade and he was right, Dale realized, as he picked his way through loose stones, careful not to lose his footing on the crumpled ground. One had to be able to laugh at one's self, at the job, at the danger.

"Woah," he said, catching his toe in one of the great, deep cracks which slithered everywhere.

Bartley sniggered. "You alright there, Dale?"

"Yeah," the American said. "Thanks."

They were on the true Burren now, a vast, wrinkled plain of undulating stone weathered into near oblivion. A kaleidoscope of grey, it spread on and on, beyond history, beyond the night, out of sight beyond Dale's unrelenting dreams. Behind them, the few stray streetlights of the village sparkled in the distance, and, above, the wash of moonlight made it seem another world entirely.

It was, Dale decided, as good a place as any. "Here," he said.

Beside him Bartley nodded. "When they buried my brother it wasn't like this," he said, "it was a fine spring day."

Dale and McGovern both turned to look at him, startled by his openness.

"He was a hero," Bartley went on. "Of the kind they name streets after, you know? Brought down a lot of them lot here at the time."

"The Tans," McGovern said. "The British."

"Aye," said Bartley. "And they'd men from his column there to see him away, draping the tricolour across his box, a few of them with rifles that they let off. The noise of it all," he said. "'Twas a fierce honour."

Dale cast him an unsure look. "You're not... armed now, are you Bartley?"

The old man laughed, a booming ho-ho as loud as any shot. "Not at all. Not at all, a'course. I'm just saying, you know, the moment should be marked."

"And what had you in mind?" McGovern asked.

Bartley grinned, and with great effort brought himself to his full height. He raised his right arm and bent his elbow, bringing his hand to his head in a salute. McGovern quickly did the same.

Dale nodded, and carefully he opened up the flask, tipping its cremated contents out onto the breeze. The cloud flattened out at once, dove towards the rocky pavement and then took flight, specks of ash like busy stars exploding all around him while the world turned overhead. Dale straightened up and saluted too, the remains of Rodriguez taking wing into the night.

When it was over he brought his hand down and, behind him, his two friends mumbled something as they let their own arms fall, Bartley rubbing at his shoulder.

"We should take a stroll now," McGovern said quietly.

"What?" Bartley said.

"You know, as we're here, we should give Dale the air of the place."

"Ah, will you not be —"

"No," Dale said. He laid his hand on Bartley's shoulder. "I'd like that." He was tired, that was true, it was late, and yet some new energy was coming to him. It compelled him to move, to walk, to see what he could find.

"Well then," McGovern said, "come on so," and he led them out across the hillside.

They were at last, Dale thought, the crew he had imagined, ambling across this odd terrain with the strange, loping gait required to leap from one great limestone block to another. Step-by-step the three of them picked their way across the broken surface, away from the road, away from the lights of the village and everything that Dale had come to know. This was a separate place, severe and beautiful and altogether alien. There, in the stone, were red and orange tints which he could not explain. In the sky, the universe's mechanism whirled while the three men drifted on, and, as the grey rock fell off toward the close horizon, they could have been walking on the moon.

COPYRIGHT

ENGINEERING INFINITY

Edited by Jonathan Strahan

UK ISBN: 978 1 907519 51 2 • US ISBN: 978 1 907519 52 9 • £7.99/$7.99

The universe shifts and changes; suddenly you understand, and are filled with wonder. Coming up against the speed of light (and with it, the sheer size of the universe), seeing how difficult and dangerous terraforming an alien world really is, realising that a hitch-hiker on a starship consumes fuel and oxygen and the tragedy that results... it's "hard-SF" where sense of wonder is most often found and where science fiction's true heart lies. Including stories from the likes of Stephen Baxter and Charles Stross.

 WWW.SOLARISBOOKS.COM

Follow us on Twitter! www.twitter.com/solarisbooks

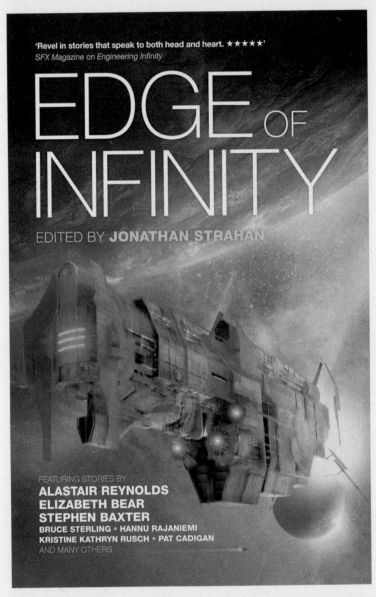

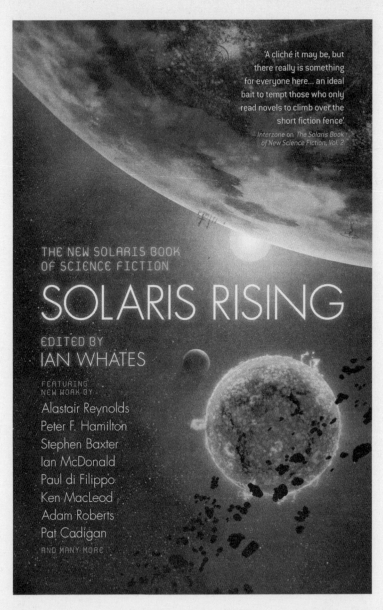

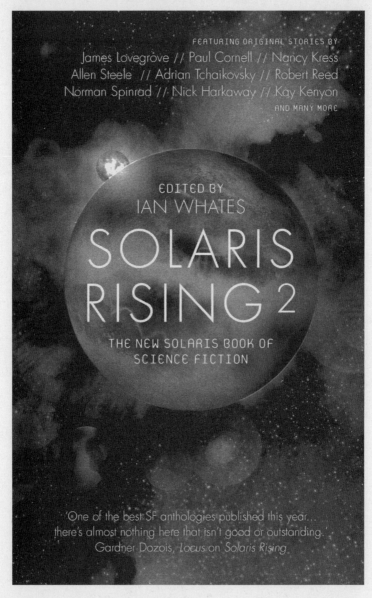

FEATURING ORIGINAL STORIES BY
James Lovegrove // Paul Cornell // Nancy Kress
Allen Steele // Adrian Tchaikovsky // Robert Reed
Norman Spinrad // Nick Harkaway // Kay Kenyon
AND MANY MORE

EDITED BY
IAN WHATES

SOLARIS
RISING 2

THE NEW SOLARIS BOOK OF
SCIENCE FICTION

'One of the best SF anthologies published this year...
there's almost nothing here that isn't good or outstanding.'
Gardner Dozois, *Locus* on *Solaris Rising*

Solaris Rising 2 showcases the finest new science fiction from both celebrated authors and the most exciting of emerging writers. Following in the footsteps of the critically-acclaimed first volume, editor Ian Whates has once again gathered together a plethora of thrilling and daring talent. Within you will find unexplored frontiers as well as many of the central themes of the genre – alien worlds, time travel, artificial intelligence – made entirely new in the telling. The authors here prove once again why SF continues to be the most innovative, satisfying, and downright exciting genre of all.

 WWW.SOLARISBOOKS.COM

Follow us on Twitter! www.twitter.com/solarisbooks